CRITICAL ACCLAIM
FOR THE NOVELS OF GREG ILES

MORTAL FEAR

"An exuberant, relentlessly readable thriller with a high degree of stay-up-all-night-suspense; up-to-the-minute technology will delight Net surfers and Anne Rice fans."

—*Kirkus Reviews*

"The talented Iles uses rich first-person narration and clever plotting to tell a sizzler of a thriller."

—*Publishers Weekly*

"A brilliant serial killer thriller with a lead protagonist who is an antihero turned hero. Pass on all the other novels in this subgenre and go straight to this one. A winner." —Harriet Klausner for *Amazon.com*

"I couldn't stop reading." —Nancy Wartik, *Mademoiselle*

continued . . .

SPANDAU PHOENIX

"A scorching read. . . an irresistible plot . . . suspense in every paragraph."
—John Grisham

"An incredible web of intrigue and suspense, an avalanche of action."
—Clive Cussler

"A terrific thriller. . . a remarkable, impressive novel."
—Nelson DeMille

"Masterful action and suspense . . . a sizzling hot read."
—Stephen Coonts

"Amazing . . . a masterwork . . . a towering novel . . . a thriller whose depth and scope are sweeping."
—*The Tampa Tribune*

"Filled with action, interesting characters, and a compelling plot, *Spandau Phoenix* is a fascinating mixture of political critique and technothriller."
—*New York Daily News*

BLACK CROSS

"A thriller that really thrills . . . on fire with suspense!"
—Stephen King

"Totally absorbing . . . a well-written, fast-paced what-if novel . . . that will be treasured and admired by and for generations."
—Nelson DeMille

"Good enough to be read twice. Iles delivers a swift historical thriller of such brutal accomplishment that it vaporizes almost every cliché about the limits of the genre."
—*Kirkus Reviews*

"This book will keep your heart thumping."
—*St. Louis Post-Dispatch*

Books by Greg Iles

Featuring Penn Cage

MISSISSIPPI BLOOD

THE BONE TREE

NATCHEZ BURNING

THE DEATH FACTORY
(a novella)

THE DEVIL'S PUNCHBOWL

TURNING ANGEL

THE QUIET GAME

Stand-alones

THIRD DEGREE

TRUE EVIL

BLOOD MEMORY

THE FOOTPRINTS OF GOD

SLEEP NO MORE

DEAD SLEEP

24 HOURS

MORTAL FEAR

BLACK CROSS

SPANDAU PHOENIX

GREG ILES

MORTAL FEAR

BERKLEY
New York

BERKLEY
An imprint of Penguin Random House LLC
375 Hudson Street, New York, New York 10014

See page 705 for author copyrights and permissions.

ISBN: 9780451180414

Dutton hardcover edition / February 1997
Signet mass-market edition / February 1998
Berkley premium edition / September 2017

Printed in the United States of America
42 44 46 48 50 51 49 47 45 43

For my wife, Dr. Carrie McGee Iles,
the light at both ends of the tunnel.

ACKNOWLEDGMENTS

As always, to Natasha Kern, my literary agent.

To Ed Stackler, a young editor of the old school, one of the last in a business that doesn't have time for it anymore.

Many thanks to Elaine Koster for wise guidance.

Special thanks to Stephen King.

To Michaela Hamilton for pinch-hitting, Peter Schneider for creative thinking, Hank Doliner on general principles, and the team at Dutton/Signet for their expertise and commitment.

Special thanks to Oriana Green, for contributions too numerous to list here, thank God.

Special thanks to Robert and Frances Royal.

Special thanks to "woodyq."

I owe a great debt to Lou Jacobs, D.O., for generously sharing his insights and experience in neurological surgery.

For general medical assistance: Jerry Iles, M.D., Michael Bourland, M.D., Tom Carey, M.D., John White, M.D., Tom Weed, M.D.

Forensics: Natalie (Raven), the published works of John Douglas, Robert Ressler, Ann Burgess, and Allen Burgess.

For miscellaneous assistance: Robert Savant, D.V.M., John McGee, D.D.S., Keith Rayburn, Jim Easterling, Beverly Halpern, Geoff Iles, John Lanzon, Robert Hag, Mary Lou England, Noah Archer, M.D., Trish Archer, Finley Hootsell, John, George, and Win.

Thanks to the members of CompuServe and America Online, who helped in myriad ways, especially Pat Reinken and Emery Werberg.

I am especially indebted to the works of Joseph Campbell, Camille Paglia, Steven Levy, Jeffrey Burton Russell, Carl Jung, Neil Finn, Toad the Wet Sprocket, and Sting.

Readers: Courtney Aldridge, Betty Iles.

As always, thanks to Madeline for patience, and to her grandmothers for keeping her off my lap long enough to get it done.

All mistakes are mine.

Prologue

Dear Father,

We landed in New Orleans yesterday evening.

A humid city.

Flat, low, dispersed. A single grouping of tall buildings in the distance.

The taxi driver was a Cajun, surprisingly. A thin brown wrinkled man. Rather like getting a Chinese cabbie in Chinatown. I expected an Eastern European, as I see everywhere else.

He kept glancing into the rearview mirror as we passed through a town he called "Metry"—a place where the whites once fled to escape "da niggas." Now they flee across Lake Pontchartrain. I worked at the computer in my lap but kept an ear open to his words.

Night descended over a rising moon as we swept onto an elevated section of freeway and passed the Superdome. Kali must have been a black shadow to him, beside me in the backseat, a shadow with bright black eyes.

She wanted to kill the driver.

I could feel it.

In her handbag, the scarf—sacred weapon. I see an image in her mind: he stops at a traffic light as we descend the ramp to the lower world of surface streets. She slips the noose around his throat and silently steals his life. . . .

I lay a hand lightly on her wrist and feel a twitch that verifies my sense. She is ready.

I know that if I slide my hand beneath her sari I will find her moist. She lives for these nights.

I hope the security is no tighter than I expect.

I slide my hand beneath her sari.

She is wet. Burning.

Time is fire.

So opposite we are, so perfectly opposite. I understand restraint. Control. The defiance of it.

Kali understands only being.

She lets her head loll back on the car seat, black eyes glittering beneath half-closed lids. I move my hand as we descend the ramp onto Poydras, possibly saving the driver's life.

We move toward Canal and the French Quarter.

Kali climaxes soundlessly.

The driver smells her. Pungent, fierce. I see alertness in the back of his neck, the angle of his head. His eyes dart to the rearview mirror. A whore? he wonders.

Kali smiles at him in the mirror. There is death in her smile. Death that a man might walk willingly into. She is startlingly beautiful. And so she should be.

You paid her father good money for her.

We exited the taxi at Galatoire's, entered the restaurant, then left and changed cabs twice again. Tiresome but effective.

Security was heavy at the mansion, but no worse than I had expected. A small army, as befits an American cult figure. Bodyguards hired from God-knows-what agency—probably some outfit run by an ex-policeman who swilled Jax on the job for twenty years.

The ironwork of the fence was exquisite. The French influence. I let my right hand graze the points as we moved along it. They would bruise me, I knew, but I felt fit. Almost reckless. The grillwork matched that on the second-story balconies. Quaint.

The street was crowded with all manner of tourists. Gawkers, most of them. I inclined my head as we passed the gate guards. One nodded slightly, glanced at my briefcase. The other followed Kali with his eyes. Even the billowing sari could not hide the hard contours of her body.

"After we turn the corner?" she asked.

"If the crowd thins."

When we turned the corner, the crowd melted away as though scattered by a stage manager. Kali bunched up her sari and was over the ironwork in seconds, into the palm fronds and banana trees. I was more careful. I passed the briefcase through the bars, then worked my way over.

We stood together in the dripping trees, looking at the floodlit face of the mansion. Solid stonework, like an outbuilding of Versailles. Kali's hand dropped to my distended zipper. She lightly squeezed me, a nurse checking a pulse.

I shivered. "We must wait."

A short intake of breath. "How long?"

I crouched in the tenebrous foliage, booted up the computer, and logged back on to EROS. "She's still at her computer. She's searching for me."

"Then let her find you."

I shut off the computer and put it back into the case. "The rightmost upper window," I said, recalling the photocopied blueprints that the archives so dutifully sent me. "Now."

Crossing the open ground between fence and mansion was daunting for me. For Kali nothing. She believes we are invisible in such moments. Less than shadows. We are our intent.

I opened my briefcase beneath the side balcony. Kali took out the rope and hurled the rubberized hook over the ironwork of the balcony rail. She climbs like a thief.

I tossed up the briefcase.

A rape kit, police would call it.

But it is so much more.

I came prepared for resistance, but the French doors on the balcony were open. So often it happens that way. Evil is an invited guest.

Kali pulled the rope up after us.

We moved up the hallway together. Thick carpeting. Conditioned air whispering out of the ceiling. Somewhere the regular groan of a ceiling fan slowly turning.

I followed the groan.

It led us to the master bedroom. Kali took up her post beside the door. I see it again and again, fate unraveling into chaos:

I open the door as softly as possible.

The patient is seated before her computer, her back to me. She wears a long, flowing garment, like something from one of her early novels. You should tape a penny to one of the blades to stop that noise, I want to say. But I don't. Instead I say:

"I have come, Karin."

The chair tips onto the carpet as she bounds out of it in voiceless terror. Her eyes mostly white behind her glasses. She is heavier than her publicity pictures. The eyes dart to my exposed hand, searching for a knife or a gun. But it is empty.

"How did you get in?" she whispers.

I do not dignify this.

"Wh-who are you?"

"Prometheus."

Her eyes widen beyond the point I believe possible. "But I was just—" She looks back at her computer. "How . . . ?"

"It is not important. I have come for you at last. To give you what you most desire."

She stares, her brain obviously thrumming behind the glassy eyes. "How— Do you have a car for us?" she asks finally.

"I thought you might call for one of yours."

"Yes," she says much too quickly. "If you'll just let me get some things—"

"No."

She freezes near her bedside table. Her eyes dart downward, then back to my face. It is breaking down. Kali was right: fantasy and reality are alternate universes. I come to save, but who can grasp great purpose with vision clouded by terror? My hopes crash around me like shattered icons. I slip my right hand behind my back and grip the butt of the pistol.

"Karin?" I plead, offering one last chance.

Then her mask cracks, revealing her panic as she stabs a hand at the bedside table. I see a button there. An alarm.

I have no choice but to fire.

The feathers of the dart bloom in the midline, just above where her navel must be. The patient looks down with animal incomprehension and pulls out the dart, but it is much too late for that. Then she runs. The brave ones usually do.

She runs right at me. Not actually at me, but toward me, because I stand between her and the door.

I let her run past me.

She gasps.

I turn.

Kali stands in the doorway. Faithful Kali. Saffron sari, nut-brown skin, jet hair, blacker eyes. She holds a dagger, wickedly curved. A fearsome instrument. Simple. Effective in two dimensions, the physical and the psychological.

The patient turns to me for some explanation. How powerfully her heart must be beating!

"Kali," I say, regretting every moment.

The patient starts at the sound of Kali closing the door, watches the young woman move lithely across the floor with my briefcase, like a dark angel.

Kali sets the case on the floor, then stands and unfastens her sari. It falls to the carpet, leaving her utterly naked. I watch the patient trying to work out what is happening as the Ketamine cocktail courses through her system. Why is the Indian woman undressing? Just before she loses consciousness, she might work it out. That Kali is undressing to keep her clothes free of blood.

I must disrobe as well, but first I walk to the computer, log off, type a few commands, and shut off the machine. Then I return to the patient, kneel, and open my briefcase.

"What's in there?" she asks dully, sitting down on the floor.

"My instruments." I lift a stainless steel rongeur from the case and try to smile, but my heart is a black hole.

The patient has done enough research for her

novels to recognize the rongeur. In blind panic she breaks once more for the door, scrambling on all fours like an infant, but Kali channels her flat onto her stomach. I watch silently until I see the dagger flash and press against the patient's throat.

"Don't dare," I say, alarmed by the bloodlust in her eyes. Command rises into my throat. "Strip her."

We took our time with the patient. We could afford to, as Karin allowed no guards inside the mansion. But our options were limited. How I longed to spend myself within that still body. But of course it was impossible.

This time I forced Kali to be careful to get no blood on her feet. After she finished and I had collected my specimen, we retired to the shower. Genuine marble. We wear rubber caps to keep as many hairs as possible out of the drain trap. The blood slipped off our shaved skin and swirled on the white stone. At last I could allow myself release.

Self-control is so important.

Kali knelt before me in the hot spray. I had held back so long that neither her expertise nor her diligence were required. She swallowed every drop of evidence, as she must. She may have left traces of her own arousal, but what will the police make of that? They will be confused enough as it is.

As we stole out of the estate, carrying not only the briefcase but also the rubber bag, now filled, I recalled the patient. So much potential there. For my work. For public relations. All lost, and for what? More homogenate? But I must not dwell on failure. Great souls rejoice in adversity.

Tomorrow is another day.

Chapter 1

Life is simple.

The more complicated you believe yours is, the less you know of your true condition.

For a long time I did not understand this.

Now I do.

You are hungry or you are full. You are healthy or you are sick. You are faithful to your wife or you are not. You are alive or you are dead.

I am alive.

We complain about complexity, about moral shades of gray, but we take refuge in these things. Complexity offers refuge from choice, and thus from action. In most situations, most of us would prefer to do nothing.

Sic transit gloria mundi.

Something is wrong.

I stare at the phone number of the New Orleans police department, which I have just taken down from directory assistance.

I have known something is wrong for some time, at some level, but it took what happened today to make me face it squarely. To override the opposition.

"I have information about the Karin Wheat murder," I say when the call goes through.

"I'll connect you to Homicide," says a female voice.

I glance up from my desk to the small color television

I keep tuned to CNN sixteen hours a day. They're into the International Hour. It was CNN that brought me news of the murder.

"Detective Mozingo," says a male voice.

"I have information relevant to the Karin Wheat case."

"What's your name?"

"Harper Cole."

"Address?"

"I'm calling from Rain, Mississippi."

A pause. "Where?"

"It's a farming area in the Delta."

"How do you know anything about the Wheat case? The body was just discovered six hours ago."

"I saw it on CNN. They cut into a regular newscast to show Wheat's estate. I guess she was more famous than I thought."

I hear the detective sigh and mutter something that sounds like *". . . freakin' high profile . . ."* away from the phone.

"Are you working on that case?" I ask him.

"No, thank God. Mayeux's got it. But I'll take the information. What do you think you know?"

"I think I know how she was killed."

"We know how she was killed, sir."

Nowadays I don't trust anyone who calls me sir. "I'm sorry. I mean how the killer got to her. How he *chose* her."

Another silence. A suspicious one.

"It's sort of complicated," I tell him. "I work as a sysop—I'm sorry, a system operator—for an online computer service. Are you familiar with what that is?"

"Not really," the detective says warily.

"You've heard of America Online? CompuServe?"

"Yeah. The Internet, right?"

"Close enough. The online service I work for is called EROS. It deals exclusively with sex."

"You mean like phone sex?"

Jesus. "Maybe I should wait and talk to Detective—Mayeux, was it?

"Yeah. He's still at the scene, though. Just give me what you've got and . . ."

Mozingo is still talking, but I am no longer listening. I am staring astonished into the face of a man that the CNN caption line identifies as NOPD detective Michael Mayeux. His shirt drenched with sweat, he stands beside the tall black wrought-iron gate of the mansion that belonged to Karin Wheat. I recognize it from the earlier broadcast. The sidewalk before the gate is cordoned off with bright yellow police tapes, but against the tapes stand at least a hundred people ranging in age from fifteen to fifty. More women than men.

Fans.

Detective Mayeux looks irritably at a black female reporter and says, "I can't comment on that at this time." He is a tanned man of medium height, in his early forties, maybe ten pounds overweight. The reporter thrusts the mike into his face.

"What about the reports that Ms. Wheat's body was sexually mutilated?"

Mayeux looks pained. "I can categorically deny that, Charvel," he says, seeming to brighten as disappointment flickers in her eyes.

"Are you *there*?" barks a voice in my ear.

"I'm here," I murmur, watching Mayeux motion for a patrolwoman to keep the crowd back. "I'm watching the guy right now."

"What guy?"

"Your guy. Mayeux. They're showing him live on CNN. Right this second."

"Christ, he gets all the face time."

"Listen," I say, deciding I like Mayeux's look better

than Mozingo's voice. "Does Detective Mayeux have voice mail?"

The detective covers the phone with his palm and then shouts something. "I'll transfer you."

A digital female voice tells me I can leave a message as long as ten minutes.

"My name is Harper Cole," I say slowly. "I'm calling from Mississippi." Then I stop. I can't just leave my name and number. With a murder like this one on his hands, Mayeux might not get around to calling me for days. I say my phone number twice, then pause and gather my thoughts.

"I'm calling because I think this murder—the Karin Wheat murder—may be connected to some other . . . not murders, but . . . possible murders, I guess. I work as a system operator for an online computer service—a national service—called EROS. Over the past few months I've noticed that some women have left the network abruptly for unexplained reasons. They could have simply terminated service, but I don't think they did. The company wouldn't want me to call you like this, but I felt I had to. It's too complicated to explain to a machine, but I'm afraid something may have happened to those other women as well. Something like what happened to Karin Wheat. I think maybe the same person could be involved. You see, Karin Wheat was a client of EROS. That's confidential information, by the way. You won't understand until you talk to me. I'd appreciate a call as soon as possible. I'm always home. I work from here, and I stay up pretty late. Thanks."

On TV, Mayeux has disappeared from the wrought-iron gate. The crowd is larger than before. The camera pans across several male faces painted with eye shadow and eyeliner. Disciples of Karin Wheat's esoteric prose. A black-and-white photo of the author appears, filling one-fourth of the screen. It's the publicity shot from her latest book. I recognize it because I have that novel—*Isis*—on one of my bookshelves. I bought it after I began having online conversations with Karin. Very interesting conversations.

Karin Wheat was a twisted lady.

I get up from the desk and go to my minifridge for an ice-cold Tab. I use them to break the monotony of Diet Coke. Not only do they pack a more powerful fizz rush, but I actually like the stuff. I've drunk half the can by the time I sit down at my Gateway 2000.

Price quotes from the Chicago Mercantile Exchange scroll slowly down the screen. This is my real job. Trading futures. Bonds, indexes, even agriculturals. I do it from my house with only my own money. Keeps it simple. No suicidal clients to deal with. I'm holding a ten lot of S&P contracts right now, but nothing's in crisis mode.

I swig some more Tab and glance across at the postmodern black table that supports the EROS computer and satellite video link. It's late afternoon, and online traffic is light. Mostly housewives right now. Bodice-ripper stuff. The real freaks are on their way home from work.

My wife should be as well. Today she's working in Jackson, the state capital, eighty minutes away from our farmhouse in the flat Delta cotton fields. Drewe is a doctor, three blessed years out of her residency, and the same age I am—thirty-three. I'm thinking I should start cooking us some supper when the phone rings.

"Hello?"

"This is Detective Michael Mayeux, NOPD."

His voice has the radio tinniness that cell phones aren't supposed to have but usually do. "Thanks for calling back so fast."

"Just checked my voice mail," he explains. "I've got twenty-eight nutcase calls already. Vampires killed her.

Mummies. One guy claims he's an incubus and that he killed her."

"So why did you call me?"

"You sounded slightly less nutty than the rest. You said you were calling from Mississippi?"

"That's right. EROS—the company I sysop for—is based in New York City, but I do my job from right here."

"I'm listening, Mr. Cole."

"You know what online services are?"

"Sure. AOL, CompuServe, Delphi. But your message didn't give me the feeling we're talking about people using MUDs or booking vacations by modem."

"No, you're right," I tell him, relieved to have found someone who doesn't need spoon-feeding.

"So what's this EROS? Live chat, e-mail, role-playing, all that stuff?"

"Exactly."

"My kid's a computer fiend. I log on to CompuServe every now and then. I'm no expert, though. Keep it at the idiot level."

"That's my natural level, Detective. I told your machine that Karin Wheat was a member of EROS."

"And you said it was confidential information."

"It is. I mean, according to the rules of the membership agreement. Legally, we're forbidden to give out any client's true identity. There are a lot of married people online with us who don't want their spouses to know. Quite a few celebrities, too."

"But you gave me Wheat's name."

"I wanted you to know how serious I am."

"Hang on—cut over to Chartres, Harry. I'm back, Mr. Cole. You said you thought Wheat's death might be connected to some other women? Disappearances or something?"

"Right. What I'd like to do—for now, at least—is give

you the names of those women and see if you can check them out. On the sly, sort of. You can do that, right?"

Mayeux doesn't answer for a moment. "You mean check and see if they're alive?"

"Right."

"Yeah, we can do that. But why haven't *you* done that, if you're so concerned? You have their phone numbers, don't you?"

"Yes. And I thought about doing it. But frankly . . . I was told not to."

"By who?"

"Someone in the company. Look, can you just take the names? Maybe I'm nuts, but I'd feel better, okay?"

"Shoot."

I read the names and numbers from a notepad. Mayeux repeats them as I give them; I assume he is speaking into a pocket recorder. "That's five different states," he notes. "Six women, five states. Spread across the country."

"Information superhighway," I remind him.

"No shit. Well, I'll get back to you if anything comes of this. Gotta go, Mr. Cole. Time to talk to the fairies and the vampires."

The conversation leaves me strangely excited.

After weeks of suspicion, I have finally *done* something. I am tempted to call Miles in Manhattan and tell him exactly what I've done, but I don't. If Miles Turner turns out to be right—if all those women have slipped contentedly back into the roles of happy housewives or fulfilled career women—then I don't want to give him the satisfaction. But if I turn out to be right—if those women are less than healthy right now . . .

I'm not sure I want Miles to know I know that.

This realization shocks me a little. I have known Miles Turner for more than twenty years. Since grade school.

He was eccentric then. And during the last fifteen years—since he left Mississippi for MIT in 1978—I have seen very little of him. It was Miles who got me working for EROS in the first place. But I can't blame him.

I was a willing Faust.

Hearing the solid door-chunk of Drewe's Acura outside, I hunch low over the keyboard of the Gateway, assuming the posture that announces to my wife that I have been manically trading commodities contracts for the last eight hours.

"Who were you talking to on the phone?" she calls from the hallway.

Busted. During her commute, she must have tried me on her cellular. She often does, as the sight of summer cotton fields lazing by the car windows gets monotonous after the first ten seconds or so.

Drewe leans into my office, pointedly refusing—as she has done for the last few weeks—to enter the domain of the EROS computer. My wife, like many wives, is jealous of my time. But there is more to this conflict than a wife and a computer. EROS is not merely a computer but the nexus of a network of five thousand people (half of them women) who spend quite a bit of their waking hours thinking about sex.

"I picked up some chicken breasts," Drewe says, arching her eyebrows like a comic French chef.

"Great," I say. "Give me a minute and I'll get them going."

It's not that Drewe doesn't think about sex. She does. And it's not that she doesn't enjoy sex. She does that too. It's just that lately she has begun thinking about sex in a whole new way. As a means to an end. By that I mean its natural end.

Children.

She smiles. Childless at thirty-three, Drewe still possesses the tightness of skin and muscle of a woman in her twenties. Her breasts are still high, her face free of wrinkles save laugh lines. I love this about her. I know how selfish it is, wanting to preserve her physical youth. But part of me wants that. Her hair is auburn, her skin fair, her eyes green. Her beauty is not that of a fashion model (her younger sister, Erin, was the model) nor the pampered, aerobicized, overly made-up elegance of a young Junior Leaguer. Drewe's distinctive allure emanates from her eyes. Not only the eyes themselves, which are deep set and clear, but from her brows, which are finely curved yet strong, like the ribs of a ship. What emanates from her eyes is pure intelligence. Cool, quantitative, uncommon *sense*.

Drewe Cole is smart.

Her smile widens to a pixie grin—something I haven't seen much lately—and then she heads off for the kitchen. I take a last look at the Chicago figures and follow.

Our house would be something of a curiosity to anyone not born into a farm family. It began seventy-five years ago as a square, one-story structure just large enough to shelter my maternal grandfather and grandmother (who married at the ages of nineteen and sixteen, respectively) and the first children they expected. But as the farm prospered and more children arrived, my grandfather began adding on rooms—first with a doggedly logical symmetry; later, apparently, anywhere he could most easily tack them on. The result is something like a wooden house of cards built by an eight-year-old. Moving from room to room often involves a sudden stepping up or down to a slightly different elevation, though since I grew up in this house, I no longer sense these changes consciously.

The heart of the house is the kitchen. It is a long room, and too narrow. I once thought of tearing out a wall and expanding it, but a black carpenter friend told me that since the entire house seemed held to this core by some form of redneck magic, I'd do better to enjoy rubbing asses with my wife whenever we passed between the stove and the opposite counter at the same time. That turned out to be good advice.

"Are we richer or poorer today?" Drewe asks from the sink. She is already rinsing off the chicken.

"About even," I say, taking a heavy cast-iron skillet out of the oven and laying it on a hot gas burner.

Her question is perfunctory. The truth is that with ten contracts in play, which is about average for me these days, I could only—in the absolute worst contingency—lose about fifty thousand dollars. This would not seriously affect us.

I am good at my real job.

"Save any lives today?" I ask. My question is not perfunctory. Drewe is an OB-GYN. She delivers the babies that my father (a family practitioner) would have delivered thirty years ago. She doesn't usually deal with car accidents or shootings, but she often handles traumatic births.

She answers my question with a quick shake of her head and plops the chicken breasts into the sizzling skillet. I am peppering them liberally when she asks, "What about EROX?"

She has purposefully botched the acronym, pronouncing it as a disc jockey would: E-Rocks. EROS stands for Erotic Realtime Online Stimulation. Drewe substitutes the X to emphasize the prurient nature of the network. Nine months ago she did not do this. She was as fascinated by the forum as I was, and our sex life had blossomed with her fascination. Nine months ago she spoke of EROS in a tone befitting the Greek god of love and desire.

Now it ranks just above phone sex. Barely.

"Something really bad happened," I tell her.

Drewe looks up from a can of LeSueur peas with apprehension in her eyes. *Family,* she is thinking. *Who died?*

"Karin Wheat was murdered last night."

Her eyes widen. "The author? New Orleans Karin Wheat?"

I nod. "It was on CNN. You believe that?"

"Sure. Anybody who's had movies made of their books—and has fans as weird as she does—is bound to rate some national airtime. I bet it'll be on *Hard Copy* in an hour."

She's probably right. Should I watch? I know from experience that facts will be sparse and titillation rampant. On the other hand, Drewe can't stand more than ten minutes of *Crossfire*.

"You sound really upset," she says, eyeing me with genuine concern.

I look away for a moment, disguising my mental stock-taking with an appraising glance at the chicken. How much to tell? "She was on EROS," I say, not wanting to sound guilty but knowing I do.

"What? Why didn't you tell me?"

I look up, some defiance in my eyes. "You haven't wanted to hear anything about EROS for months, Drewe. Karin only joined a few weeks ago."

She lifts her chin and studies me. "So it's *Karin*," she says finally. "You've talked to her online?"

"Sure. The usual sysop guidance."

"Please." She fits the pea can into the opener and drowns any reply with a grinding flourish. I go back to the chicken.

"Have you had sex with her online?" she asks, not looking at me.

I sigh angrily. "The woman is *dead*, Drewe."

"Jesus," she says, and dumps the peas into a pot. "I should be on *Hard Copy*. 'My Husband Fucks Famous Females Electronically.' "

I surrender. Drewe is even angrier about EROS than I thought.

"Do they know who did it?" she asks in a deadpan voice.

"No." I flip the chicken breasts. "But I think I might."

Chapter 2

Drewe and I watch *Hard Copy* with a mixture of fascination and disgust. Dramatic camera angles, sexual innuendo, and spooky black-and-white video of Karin Wheat's New Orleans mansion (complete with artificially generated fog) give the broadcast a Victorian, Jack-the-Ripper feel. Drewe does not comment as the segment runs, and I find myself rehashing my dinner-table interrogation.

I answered her incisive questions between bites of chicken and dirty rice, taking care not to set her off by revealing more than necessary. She wanted to know why I would even notice six women terminating service among five thousand subscribers. I focused on the technical side of it, explaining that these six women had been active users who suddenly disappeared from the forums yet continued paying their EROS fees, which are expensive by anyone's standard. I mentioned nothing about blind-draft accounts or my close relationships with some of the women.

Thankfully Drewe focused on Miles Turner and his successful attempt to prevent me from initiating an internal investigation by EROS itself. She too has known Miles since our childhood. He based his objections to an investigation on the issue of privacy—"client confidentiality" in his words—and his argument holds water. The female CEO of EROS is serious enough about privacy to insure the secrecy of each subscriber's identity to one million dollars. This unique step in the world of online services went a long way to ensure the exponential growth of her small and costly corner of the digital world. I can only guess what kind of explosion my decision to involve the police will cause at EROS headquarters in New York.

When *Hard Copy* cuts to commercial, Drewe commandeers the kitchen table and telephone to remotely dictate the past few days' accumulation of medical charts. For some reason, patient charts are the one duty my super-organized spouse cannot or will not deal with in a timely manner. The color-coded stacks she brings home from her office are often covered with threatening Post-it notes penned by the hospital records administrator, warning in Draconian tones that Drewe's staff privileges are about to be revoked.

As her monotonic dictation voice drifts through the house, I retreat to my office and pick up one of the five guitars hanging on the wall above the twin bed I crash on when I'm in manic trading mode. I choose a Martin D-28S, with a classical-width neck but steel strings. I slip through some chord changes without thought, letting my mind and fingers run where they will. The music would surprise a casual listener. I am a good guitar player. Not quite a natural, but smooth enough to make a living at it. This is my old job.

I am a failed musician.

The memories of that career still sting. I pick up the instrument more often now, but three years ago I did not touch a guitar or sing for twelve straight months. Even now, I never play my own songs. I just do what I'm doing now, letting whatever part of my brain that controls this function have free rein, and set my mood on automatic pilot.

Sometimes I surprise myself.

Like now. I have somehow wound a soft jazz thing full

of arpeggios and chord extensions into the intro of "Still Crazy After All These Years." I realize I love the sneaky seventh at the end of that line: "I met my o-old lover on the street last night"—*whang*. What the hell, I think, singing on through the song and ending up quite unintentionally with potential murder. "Now I sit by my window and I watch the cars. And I fear I'll do some damage one fine day. But I would not be convicted by a jury of my peers . . ." As I finish to a nonexistent ovation, I realize Drewe is standing inside the door of my office. It's her first time in six weeks.

"Sounds good," she says. "Really good."

"It feels good."

"Thinking about an old lover?"

"No. A jury of my peers. Where do you think they all went?"

She smiles ruefully. "They grew up, got married, and had kids."

Like most men, I have blindly blundered back into our running argument. Having a baby. I suppose a lot of couples our age are in the midst of this debate. Up north and out west anyway. Down South most couples still tend to have their kids in their twenties.

Not us.

Our careers are partly to blame. Itinerant musicians and exhausted medical students are rarely in an ideal position to start a family, even if they are married, which Drewe and I weren't until I gave up music. But that's not all of it. For the past three years—our total married life—we have led a fairly settled existence, and our combined incomes are almost embarrassingly large. My parents are dead, but Drewe's recently crossed the line from gentle jibes to outright questioning of my reproductive capabilities.

If only my sperm count were the problem. Like a lot of people, I have my secrets. Some are small, born in moments when I could have been painfully frank but chose not to be. Others are more serious and invariably involve women other than my wife.

Don't jump to conclusions. From the moment Drewe and I took our marriage vows, I have not touched another woman's naked flesh. But somehow that is small comfort. For the secret that haunts me now is more dangerous than adultery, more shameful. If I were Catholic, I suppose I would call it a mortal sin.

No, I'm not gay.

But I am afraid.

When the telephone finally rings, Drewe and I have been asleep for hours. I spring awake in a sitting position like one of my Scottish ancestors groping for his sword but find a cordless phone in my hand instead.

"Hello?"

"Mr. Cole?"

I blink, trying to clear my eyes and brain simultaneously. "Um . . . what?"

"This is Detective Michael Mayeux. NOPD. We spoke this afternoon?"

Drewe's sleeping body blocks my line of sight to the clock radio. "What time is it?"

"Three-twenty in the morning. Sorry, but I just got around to checking those names you gave me. Those six women?"

"Sure." I sense a strange gravity in Mayeux's voice.

"Harper?" Drewe sits up in bed and points at the window. "There's someone outside. Look."

Prickly flesh rises on my shoulders as I realize that our curtains are being backlit by what must be car headlights. We never have visitors at this hour. We rarely have visitors at all.

"Stay here," I tell her. "I'll get a gun."

"Please don't do that, Mr. Cole." Mayeux's voice startles me. "If you'll look out your window, I think you'll see a patrol car."

"Cairo County doesn't have a police department," I say, moving warily toward the window.

"Part of your farm is in Yazoo County," Mayeux replies. "That should be Sheriff Buckner from Yazoo City. Know him?"

"I know who he is." Parting the curtains slightly, I see a white Chevrolet Caprice cruiser sitting in the gravel drive before our house. "What the hell is he doing in my driveway at three in the morning?"

"Calm down, Mr. Cole. Sheriff Buckner is there to ensure your safety."

Right. "Why don't I believe that, Detective?"

He is silent too long. I signal Drewe not to speak. "What the hell is going on, Mayeux?"

"Those women you told me about. They're all dead."

There is sweat on my face. An instant ago it was not there. I feel it in my hair, on my forearms, behind my knees. That small intuitive part of me that always suspected the worst has taken possession of my body. I was right. I was right, and I should have acted sooner. "All six of them?" I ask, my voice barely audible.

"Every one was murdered in the last nine months, Mr. Cole. And I've got to tell you, there are a lot of people around the country right now—police officers—who want to talk to you about those women."

I do not even try to convert the chemical cyclone in my brain into coherent words.

"Only two of those murders had been connected before tonight, Mr. Cole. They were both in California."

I close my eyes. *Juliet Nicholson. Tara Morgan.*

"What we'd like you to do," Mayeux says in a friendly voice, "if you're not busy tomorrow, that is—is drive down to the main station here in New Orleans and talk to us. What do you say to that?"

I look back through the window. Sheriff Buckner's cruiser is still there, idling low and catlike in the humid darkness.

"You think I killed them," I say in a monotone.

Again Mayeux pauses too long. "To tell you the truth, Mr. Cole, we don't know what to think. I've been telling people that you called me with this information, and that if you're the one who murdered them, you'd be the last one to do that."

"Damn right."

"On the other hand, some people tell me that things like that have happened before. A lot more than you'd think. Is this one of those strange cases, Mr. Cole?"

"I was stupid to call you," I say, meaning it. "Miles was right."

"Miles who?" Mayeux's tone telegraphs an image of him holding a pen over a notebook.

"Do I need a lawyer, Detective?"

"What?" Drewe gets out of bed and hurries to the closet for a housecoat.

"Take it easy," Mayeux says. "My gut tells me you're just Joe Citizen in this thing, trying to do what's right and getting tangled up in the process. That happens more often than it should, I'll tell you right now. If you want a lawyer, you bring one along with you." He pauses a beat. "But if you want my advice, I'd save the money. We just want to know what you know, Mr. Cole. If you've got nothing to hide, you don't need a lawyer." Mayeux's voice drops in volume. "Besides, first impressions are important. You'll look a lot more innocent to certain people if you don't have a lawyer from the get-go."

One thing's for sure. Detective Michael Mayeux didn't just float into New Orleans on a shrimp boat. He is very good at getting people to do what he wants them to do.

This is a talent that I share, and I note the fact like a fighter noting the strength of a potential opponent.

"I suppose you expect me to ride down with Sheriff Buckner?"

"No, sir. Bring your own car, fly a crop duster, whatever you want. Just try to make it before noon. You've got a very anxious audience down here."

I make a rapid decision. "Listen, Detective, no way am I going to fall back asleep after this call. I'm going to talk to my wife, then get dressed and drive straight down there. The sooner I'm out of all this, the better I'll feel."

"Good answer, Mr. Cole."

"See you in about five hours."

"I'll be waiting for you."

By the time I finish explaining the situation to Drewe, Sheriff Buckner's cruiser has quietly disappeared. My wife wants to accompany me to New Orleans, but I talk her out of it. For one thing, she has patients scheduled. For another, I am not sure how deeply the questions of the police will probe. I doubt any man would want his life examined microscopically in the presence of his wife, but lately one of my secrets, like the old shotgun pellet in my calf, has worked its way nearer and nearer the surface. One question with the right edge could slice right through.

I consider calling Miles in New York to tell him what is afoot, then discard the idea. On this point Drewe and I agree. By revealing the name of an EROS client to the police, I have almost certainly exposed myself to a lawsuit. I reassure myself that my perception of lethal danger to other EROS clients justified this breach, but in 1990s America, who is to say? Jan Krislov, the fifty-six-year-old widow who owns EROS, is a nationally known advocate for the right to privacy. She also has more money than God. Better lawyers, anyway.

Yet beneath this anxiety flows a deeper sense of reservation. Drewe feels it as well. Early in our lives, Miles Turner and I were almost like brothers. Then for many years we hardly saw each other. Not quite a year ago he came back into my life, brought me into EROS. Expand your horizons, said my own personal Mephistopheles. Aren't you tired of making money yet? Challenge yourself. It's more fun than you've had since we talked our babysitter into taking off her bra.

I am not having fun now.

Chapter 3

Dear Father,

We landed in Michigan in the afternoon. So gray after the decadent green of New Orleans. As gray as our fatigue. My joints ached constantly; we had to fly through the black heart of a storm.

I varied the transport this time, and the technique. I learned from my mistake with Karin. How disconcerting to recognize naïveté in oneself, even after years of cynicism.

I was drunk with anticipation. Our seduction had been a long and baroque one, a progression from the sacred to the profane. I sat on the patient's patio with the notebook and the cell phone, knowing she believed she was interacting with a man thousands of miles distant, a faceless lover, and me sitting less than twenty feet away.

I crept to her window and watched her typing her responses. Kali stroked me as I watched, spilling my seed in the flower bed. Will the FBI look there, I wonder? For footprints, yes. For semen, no. They will find that where they expect to find it, but of course it will not be mine.

I could not resist telling Rosalind I was there. There was no risk; she could not call the police while linked to EROS, and Kali was already inside.

Terror was absolute. Paralyzing. Kali demonstrated exemplary control, reassuring after the bloodlust of New Orleans. And this time I left a note, a passage you read me long ago:

> I have reached the limits of endurance. My back is to the wall; I can retreat no further. I have found God but he is insufficient. I am only spiritually dead. Physically I am alive. Morally I am free. The world which I have departed is a menagerie. The dawn is breaking on a new world, a jungle world in which the lean spirits roam with sharp claws. If I am a hyena I am a lean and hungry one: I go forth to fatten myself.

I know, I know. But I'm tired of leaving biological refuse. Why not mislead with a little flair? You of all people should appreciate that. This is just the kind of rot they salivate over at Quantico. It will be the only file written in French, but nevertheless I signed it "Henri." Subtlety is wasted on the police. By the time they translate it, the procedure will be complete. The lab work tonight. A day to collect the next patient. Another to rest my joints, to steady my fingers.

Then I cut my way into Valhalla.

Chapter 4

Three hours of hard driving put me over the Louisiana state line with dawn breaking over my left shoulder and New Orleans seventy miles ahead. The last two hundred miles were a slow-motion strobe of darkness and glaring truck-stop light. On any other night I would have taken Highway 61. Not many people do these days. They choose speed over scenery, as I was forced to do tonight.

I-55 runs straight as a pipeline, and most travelers on it never give a thought to the older, more indirect arteries that lie just to the west: Highway 61, a blacktop track of history lined with scorched chimneys like sentinels guarding unquiet land; and beyond the levee, the aorta of the continent, the mile-wide tide of river that ran before man set foot here and will run long after he is gone.

But in this breaking dawn I can afford only the straightest distance between two points. On the passenger seat beside me sits a briefcase full of laser-printed paper—transcripts of the killer seducing his victims—and my best hope of absolution in the matter of the six dead women.

Seven, I think, remembering Karin Wheat.

At La Place I jump down onto I-10 for the final twenty-minute run into New Orleans. The August sun is fully up now, past eight o'clock, and the shallow soupy water of the Bonnet Carre spillway simmers under its lidless gaze. Cranking down the Explorer's windows, I catch an airborne wave of decaying water plants and fish from Lake Pontchartrain.

During the past four hours, I have recalled every step on the mental path that led me to this physical journey. What the police hope to learn from me I am not sure. But the most sensitive question for me is this: why didn't I report my suspicions sooner? I am not quite sure myself. I can only hope that what I have to say will shock the police sufficiently to divert them from that question, at least for a while.

Locating the main New Orleans police station is easy. It's near Drewe's alma mater, the Tulane Medical School, just behind the Orleans Parish criminal court building. Locating Detective Michael Mayeux is easier still. Homicide is on the third floor. The moment I mention my name to the desk sergeant—who sits behind a window of armored glass—I am whisked through a heavy door, through a squad room, down a corridor, and into a small office. Mayeux is seated at a scarred and cluttered metal desk, speaking urgently into a wire telephone. The office has no windows. It does have a computer, an overcrowded bookshelf, and, enshrined in the single clearing amid the chaos, a coffeemaker. A torn red sack of Community dark roast with chicory sits on top of it.

"Help you?" Mayeux asks, hanging up the phone and taking a bite from a sugar-dusted beignet I hadn't noticed.

"I'm Harper Cole."

He freezes in midbite, then sets down the beignet, stands, and begins chewing quickly as he ushers me back into the hall and to another door. He is five eight or so, with good shoulders, noticeable love handles, and a bald spot on the back of his head. At the door he stops and turns back to me, his dark brown eyes reassuring like those of a coach before an important game.

"Just tell these people what you know, Mr. Cole. Take

your time and don't leave anything out. If you get hungry or you need to take a leak, nod your head at me and we'll break. It might get pretty intense. All of a sudden there's a lot riding on what you have to say about these women."

"Hold on," I say, raising my hands. "I thought I was coming down to talk to *you*. Who's in there?"

He gives me a crooked smile. "Don't worry. I'll be beside you the whole time. So will my partner, so will the chief."

Mayeux meant to reassure me, but he's accomplished the opposite. "And . . . ?"

His eyes move off my face. "The other guys will be feds. FBI."

"FBI? What for?"

"These guys are from the Investigative Support Unit. What used to be called Behavioral Science. One special agent and a shrink. Plus two Fibbies from the local office. Remember what I told you. Two of the dead women were killed in California—one in L.A., one in San Francisco. Because their bodies were mutilated in a specific way, and for other reasons, the police out there decided they might be looking at some type of cult murders. They called in the Investigative Support Unit to assist them in coming up with a profile of their UNSUB."

"Their what?"

"UNSUB. Unknown subject. Anyway, soon as I queried the names of those two dead California women, the Unit was on us like you know what. When they heard about you and the other women, they started foaming at the mouth. They think we're looking at a serial murderer here. Maybe a whole new kind of killer. We got detectives flying in from all over the country right now. This is major-league stuff."

"So much for our friendly little chat."

Mayeux starts to turn the doorknob, then hesitates. A

spark of Cajun mischief twinkles in his eyes. "Don't take the shitty vibes personally. Chief Tobin officially requested the Unit's assistance—he knows their chief—but NOPD and the local Bureau office have bad blood from way back. Not your problem. Just tell your story." Mayeux winks. "Show time, *cher.*"

Chapter 5

Detective Mayeux's warning understated the tension level. The bare police conference room reminds me of nothing so much as a room full of lead vocalists. Egos bumping against each other like tethered balloons as their owners strike practiced poses, unaware of any agenda but their own. Four men in business suits sit in a protective phalanx at the far end of a rectangular table. They might as well be wearing lapel tags that read "FBI." The New Orleans police chief, an enormous black man, sports a starched white duty shirt that strains under his bulk. Four stars adorn the blue boards on each hamlike shoulder.

To the right of the chief sits a rail of a guy who has to be Mayeux's partner. He looks like lukewarm hell. Eyes like quarter slots on a Coke machine, hands quivering with the irregular tremor that signals serious sleep deprivation. I know the symptoms well. There is a busty Hispanic secretary beside him. Her left ear is cocked toward the chief, but her eyes stay on the young FBI agents.

"Gentlemen," says Detective Mayeux, "Mr. Harper Cole."

Mayeux is telling me names, but they don't find a permanent memory address. Three of the FBI agents wear blue suits, the fourth charcoal gray. Does this mean he's in charge? He's clearly the oldest, yet he wears his graying hair longer than the others. Mayeux speaks his name softly, giving it unintended emphasis.

Arthur Lenz. *Doctor* Arthur Lenz.

Of course. Lenz is the shrink.

Whenever I meet interesting strangers, I find myself casting them as stand-ins for the stars of my memory. Sometimes I meet an Edmond O'Brien or a George Sanders, maybe a Robert Ryan. I remember those guys from when I was a kid staying up late with my dad, watching Channel 4 out of New Orleans. So it's a habit, trying to slot strangers into the celluloid templates in my head. Some people are just extras, like Mayeux's partner and the secretary. But every once in a while I meet the genuine article. Someone who doesn't just remind me of, say, Fredric March, he could *be* the man.

Doctor Lenz might be the genuine article. He is physically tall—this is obvious even though he is seated—and yet . . . he is limited. Like an actor who never made the jump to the big screen. Perpetually middle-aged, WASP or WASP wannabe, expensive suit, heavy on control. His charisma is undeniable, but somehow he finishes out more TV than film.

In the uncomfortable silence that follows the introductions, one of the blue-suited FBI men—Baxter, I think—gives the police chief an annoyed glance. Then he looks me in the eye and says, "Good morning, Mr. Cole," giving the "mister" that special and contemptuous stress that military men reserve for civilians. "I'm Special Agent Daniel Baxter."

I didn't notice Baxter at first because sizewise he blends with the other two blue-suits. But I see him now. And I get the feeling he's hiding. In the Biblical sense, as in hiding his light under a bushel. He's got weight behind his dark eyes, but he's not a leading man. He's a tough-as-nails sergeant from a black-and-white war movie, thrust into command by the death of his lieutenant.

As if summoned to life by Agent Baxter's words, the police chief greets me in a startling James Earl Jones basso. "Mr. Cole, I'm Chief Sidney Tobin. I thank you for coming down so early today. Needless to say, we're all very interested in whatever you might have to say about these murders. You have our undivided attention."

Detective Mayeux sits, offering me the chair at the head of the table as he does, but I remain standing. I am six feet and one inch tall, 195 pounds, and I know my size gives me a psychological edge when I choose to use it. Today I figure I need any edge I can get.

"Before I say anything," I begin, "there is one very important thing I didn't tell Detective Mayeux on the phone."

"What's that?" rumbles the chief.

"I'm pretty sure I know who killed those women."

Astonished silence blankets the room. Dr. Lenz breaks the impasse. "You have a *name*, Mr. Cole?"

"And an address."

"Christ!" cries Mayeux. "Give it to me."

I open my briefcase and remove a single sheet of paper. From it I read: "David M. Strobekker. That's S-T-R-O-B-E-K-K-E-R. Fourteen-oh-two Moorland Avenue, Edina, Minnesota. It's a suburb of Minneapolis."

"What else you know about this guy?" barks Mayeux's partner.

"He has a checking account at the Norwest Bank in Minneapolis. That's all I know for sure."

"Run it through the computer, Mike," commands the chief. "Right now."

"I can access the Bureau computers by phone," one of the younger FBI men tells Mayeux, who shoots me a furious glance on his way out.

"I could be sued for giving you that name," I tell them.

"Let us worry about that," says Baxter.

"The FBI will provide lawyers to defend me in a civil case?"

Arthur Lenz's face shows a trace of bemusement.

"Let's stick to these murders," says the police chief. "Tell us how you came to know those six names and why you suspected the women might be in trouble."

The door opens and closes behind me. Mayeux reclaims his chair on the right side of the table. "Kiesha's checking on Strobekker, Chief."

"Stop me if I say something you don't understand," I tell them.

The two younger FBI agents smirk at this, but I'm fairly certain they'll soon be strafing me with stupid questions.

"I work for a company called EROS," I say slowly. "That's an acronym—E-R-O-S—which stands for Erotic Realtime Online Stimulation." Seeing a couple of leers, I ignore the mythological connection and push on. "We're an online service that caters to a wide range of clients interested in human sexuality. EROS is a New York–based corporation legally chartered in the State of Delaware—"

"Who owns it?" interrupts Baxter.

"A widow named Jan Krislov."

"What?"

From the sick look on Daniel Baxter's face, I can see that he's familiar with Jan Krislov in some capacity. A flash of instinct tells me it's her fierce championship of electronic privacy rights.

"Please continue, Mr. Cole," instructs Chief Tobin.

"Anyone in the continental U.S. can have full online access to EROS twenty-four hours a day. We also have European subscribers who reach us through the Internet. There are three levels of forum traffic, which people access under aliases—code names—that ensure complete anonymity. Level One is the most diverse. Clients use it to discuss all sorts of sexual topics, from psychology to medical problems to privacy issues."

"Jan fucking Krislov," mutters Baxter.

I take a breath. Hearing no questions, I focus on Mayeux and continue. "Level Two is the first of the two fantasy forums. In Level Two clients write about their fantasies, correspond with each other through forum messages and e-mail, or sometimes just eavesdrop on the fantasies of other subscribers. The exchanges can be group or, if a client prefers, he or she can switch down to one-on-one contact, completely private. We call that a private room. There are also files available at all times from the online library. Popular exchanges from past sessions, stuff like that."

"Stroke files," says Mayeux's partner, opening his red eyes in a glare of challenge. "Right? They're not talking to anybody real-time, so their hands are free. Jack-off time, right?"

The man is crude, but not far off the mark. "That's probably a fair assessment."

"What about Level Three?" asks Doctor Lenz, his eyes alight with fascination.

"Level Three . . ." I often stumble here when explaining EROS to anyone outside the company. I never know quite how to describe Level Three. To be honest, I don't monitor it that much. At least I didn't until I began to have my suspicions about the "missing" women. Most Level Three traffic is nocturnal, and thus Miles's gig. That's another reason I allowed him to persuade me to put off acting for as long as I did.

"Level Three," I say again, "is what you might call the major league of sexual forums. The dialogues are pretty heavy, basically no-holds-barred. Don't get the wrong idea—it's not kiddy porn or anything, but—"

"It's hot," Dr. Lenz finishes.

"Pretty hot, yeah. Until three weeks ago we didn't

even allow transmission of graphic images, but believe me, words alone are powerful enough. We're talking bondage, S and M, homoerotic sex, you name it. Straight sex too, of course."

"How much does it cost to join EROS?" asks Baxter.

"A thousand dollars to join—"

Mayeux whistles long and low.

"—plus five hundred a month flat fee after that, with various payment arrangements. For women it's three hundred a month. EROS has one–eight hundred access numbers, so nobody has any long-distance charges to worry about."

"All the women but Wheat were in their twenties," says Baxter. "Where did they get that kind of money?"

"Inherited it," I reply. "A lot of rich girls on EROS. We get a lot of trophy wives too. They marry money—old money—fake orgasms at night, and log on to EROS during the day. It's safer than adultery, especially in the age of AIDS."

"Karin Wheat was a member of this EROS thing?" Chief Tobin interrupts.

"Yes. For about three months now."

"And those other women? All of them were members?"

"Right. Most of them had been subscribing for more than a year at the time they dropped off the net."

"What exactly do you mean by 'dropped off'?" Lenz asks.

"Just a minute, Doctor," says Chief Tobin, reasserting the temporary supremacy he enjoys in his headquarters. "Mr. Cole, you mean to tell me all these murder victims were members of this super-expensive computer club or whatever it is, and no homicide cop in L.A. or San Francisco or Houston or Portland or the other places managed to link these crimes with billing receipts from your company?"

"I can explain that." I pause, realizing I'm more interested in asking questions than answering them. "Honestly, I'm more surprised by the fact that the murders weren't linked before now by physical evidence. No offense, but isn't that what you guys do?"

"Goddamn," growls Mayeux's partner.

"Plenty of reasons for that," injects one of the FBI agents.

"Different weapon in every case," says his blue-suited cousin. "Forensic evidence indicating multiple perps."

"Multiple perps at the *same scene*," adds the first agent.

"Which is rare," says Baxter, glaring at the younger men. "Highly unusual."

"We're still getting in evidence reports, Chief," says Mayeux, "but the M.O. does seem to have varied a great deal in almost every case."

"As did the signature," says Baxter.

"The killer left notes?" I ask.

Baxter shakes his head. " 'Signature' is the offender's behavior at the crime scene." He looks at me closely, as if judging whether to continue. "Behavior beyond that strictly necessary to commit the crime. Individualized behavior."

"Oh."

"There *is* no signature in these cases," Dr. Lenz says imperiously. "It's all staging. But the trophies in California varied not an iota."

"Trophies?" I echo. "What kind of trophies?"

"Why don't you tell us?" Mayeux's partner asks, pointing an index finger at my chest.

The room goes silent, and in that instant I feel the first ripple of real fear in my chest. "Am I a suspect in this case?"

Several looks are exchanged, none directed at me.

"Do I need to call an attorney?"

Finally Baxter breaks the silence. "Mr. Cole, I'm going

to go out on a limb here. I am not merely a special agent. I'm the chief of the FBI's Investigative Support Unit. We profile and help the police hunt violent serial offenders, whether they're killers, rapists, arsonists, bombers, or kidnappers. When crimes of this nature are committed, the individual who reports any of them is always considered a suspect. Serial offenders frequently report their own crimes as part of an attempt to avoid being found out, or to gain enjoyment by assisting in an investigation of themselves. In this case you've reported *all* the crimes. When I was apprised of this situation last night, the Unit began an exhaustive check of your background, including all your movements during the past two years. It sounds drastic, but it's standard procedure."

Baxter glances at his watch, which he wears with the face inside the wrist, military style. "Dr. Lenz and I have spent the past few hours putting together a preliminary profile of the offender in these murders. And frankly, it's one of the most difficult jobs we've ever undertaken. At this point I won't say why, but Dr. Lenz believes that you are probably not the killer in this case. I concur. I'm not saying you couldn't be involved in some way—it would be irresponsible of me to rule you out—but I'm willing to proceed today on the assumption that you are what you claim to be—a Good Samaritan coming forward in an attempt to see justice done. Obviously, other women's lives are at risk as we speak. An atmosphere of cooperation is the best thing for all of us at this point. If you wish to consult an attorney, that is your right, but at this time no one here"—Baxter fires a sharp glance at the New Orleans police officers—"intends to charge you with any crime."

When he finishes, no one speaks. Everyone but Baxter and Lenz seems to be looking at his shoes. I may be making the worst mistake of my life, but I decide to trust Baxter, at least to the extent of not calling an attorney.

"What kind of trophies?" I ask again.

"An unusual one," Baxter says thoughtfully.

"Maybe he's a taxidermist," cracks Mayeux's partner, winking at Mayeux.

"Make a note of that, Maria," says Chief Tobin, and watches the brunette pounce on her notepad.

"Taxidermists do not mount *glands*," Dr. Lenz says scornfully.

"Houston P.D. says he took the whole goddamn head," snaps Mayeux, unwilling to tolerate the psychiatrist's superior tone. "And that's what he did here."

I am looking for a place to sit down, but no one notices. I whisper, "Someone cut off Karin Wheat's *head*?"

"That's classified information," says Baxter.

Mayeux snorts at the spook-speak.

"That is not accurate, Mr. Cole," corrects Chief Tobin. "Someone did cut off Ms. Wheat's head, but that information is not classified. Still, I would strongly suggest that you keep the knowledge to yourself." The chief shoots me a very clear look: *If you fuck up my investigation in any way, I will hound you to a pauper's grave.* "Now," he says, his gentle bass voice filling the conference room like soft light. "What about my question? Credit card receipts from EROS, canceled checks, phone bills, and suchlike? Why didn't this link the crimes?"

"Chief," says Baxter, "despite our best efforts to familiarize city police departments with our VICAP program, we still have a pretty poor compliance rate. Not nearly enough officers take the time to fill out their violent offender profiles and send them in. This EROS connection is exactly the kind of thing that slips through the cracks. I wouldn't be surprised if homicide detectives in one or more of the involved departments have just such a receipt in an evidence drawer somewhere, but have no idea that detectives in any other cities have the same thing."

"All our fault, as usual," grumbles Mayeux's partner.

"Five of these six cases *were* sent in to VICAP," says Mayeux, giving his partner covering fire. "But they weren't linked. No EROS connection showed up. All had computers in their homes, but nothing related to EROS on their drives. Why not?"

"Well," I say, finally regaining sufficient composure to rejoin the conversation. "As long as the killer wasn't rushed, he could erase the EROS software from the victims' computers and take away any manuals they had. Although it would take a real wizard to wipe every trace from the hard disks. You might have one of your people look into that."

Baxter gives me a wry smile. "No traces so far."

"Karin Wheat paid EROS with her Visa card," says Mayeux. "I checked as soon as you told me she was a member."

"She'll be the only one that did," I tell him.

"How do you know that?" asks Dr. Lenz, his heavy-lidded eyes probing mine.

"Because every other woman—victim, I mean—had set up her account on the blind-draft account system."

"What's that?" asks the chief. "A direct bank draft?"

"Yes, but not the kind you imagine. A lot of EROS subscribers—particularly women—are married, and don't want their spouses to know they're online with us. Some log on only from their workplace. Others from home, but only when their husbands are away. Ms. Krislov makes every effort to ensure that any woman who wants to connect with us has the ability to do so without stigma. To facilitate this, she came up with the 'blind-draft' policy. If a woman doesn't want her husband to know she's online—or vice versa—we advise the user to set up a checking account at a bank not used by the spouse—an out-of-town bank, if possible—and use a P.O. box as her address. We then arrange to draft this secret account directly for payment of the monthly fee."

"Son of a bitch," says Mayeux's partner.

"Every one of the murdered women was on a secret account?" Mayeux asks.

"Except Karin Wheat."

"But three of them weren't married," Mayeux points out. "Who were they hiding from? Boyfriends?"

"Or girlfriends," says Dr. Lenz.

"What about phone bills?" asks Mayeux. "Wouldn't connect-time show up on the phone bills of all the victims?"

"It's an eight hundred number, remember?"

"Shit. So after they were killed, their secret accounts eventually dropped to zero?"

"*Eventually* is exactly why I got suspicious. EROS isn't like CompuServe or America Online, where you might lose interest but keep paying the nine ninety-five per month, thinking you'll get back into it. We're talking three to five hundred bucks a month. EROS users may be wealthy, but when they get bored they close those direct-draft accounts."

"And the murdered women didn't," says Mayeux.

"Right. And two particular women—the third and fourth victims—were very active online. Then *poof*, one day they were gone. But their bank drafts kept coming in. That didn't fit the pattern. I'm not saying it had never happened before—it had. That's why I didn't call the police immediately. But the longer the accounts stayed active without the women showing up online, the more uncomfortable I got. I started probing the accounting program to see how many blind-draft clients were paying regularly but not logging on to the system. There were about fifty, enough to make me think I might be paranoid. And enough for the company to decide not to investigate. But then I remembered that victims three and four had talked to this Strobekker guy a lot. So I started watching for him. Then I started printing out his exchanges. I also asked about him in private e-mail. That's how I came up with the names of the first and second victims. And while I was doing that, he was setting up and killing five and six. He was also talking to at least twenty other women during this period as well."

"Doesn't the company try to contact people when their accounts drop to zero?" Mayeux asks. "In case it was just an oversight?"

"No. It's understood by both parties that if a blind-draft account has insufficient funds for even a single payment, the company assumes the client no longer desires its services, and access is immediately terminated."

"I don't buy that," says Mayeux's partner. "I don't believe any company would kiss off that kind of bread without making sure the client wanted to quit."

How can I explain this to them? "Jan Krislov is the sole owner of EROS. And whether you believe it or not, she's not in it for the money."

"Oh, I believe it," mutters Baxter.

"Then why does she charge so damn much for the service?" Mayeux's partner asks doggedly.

A faint smile crosses Arthur Lenz's patrician face. This alone draws all eyes to him. "The high fee functions as a crude screening system," he says softly. "Correct, Mr. Cole?"

"What kind of screening system?" asks Mayeux's partner.

Lenz answers for me. "By charging an exorbitant rate, Ms. Krislov ensures that her online environment is accessible only to those who have attained a certain position in life."

"Flawed system," says Mayeux. "It assumes rich people aren't assholes."

"I said it was crude," Lenz admits. "But I imagine it works fairly well."

"It works perfectly," I say, unable to keep the admiration out of my voice. "Because there are other constraints on membership."

Curiosity flares in Lenz's eyes. "Such as?"

"EROS is open to any woman who can pay the fee, but any man who wants to join has to submit a writing sample for evaluation."

"Who evaluates the sample?"

"Jan Krislov."

"What are the criteria?"

Unable to resist, I point at Mayeux's partner. "He wouldn't make the cut."

Mayeux lays an arm across his partner's chest and asks, "How many people belong to this thing?"

"Five thousand. Half of them male, half female. The numerical relation is strictly maintained."

"Gays allowed?" Lenz asks.

"Encouraged. And contained within that ratio."

Mayeux shakes his head. "You're telling us this Krislov woman has personally evaluated twenty-five hundred writing samples from men writing about sex?"

"Personally *approved* twenty-five hundred samples. She's evaluated a lot more than that. There's a waiting list of twenty-eight hundred men at this moment."

"So Jan Krislov sits up at night reading her own personal *Penthouse* letters," Baxter says in a gloating voice. "I know some senators who'll eat that up."

"Probably beats watching Leno," pipes up the local FBI agent. "For a woman, I mean," he adds hastily.

Dr. Lenz leans forward in his chair. "I doubt these samples are as crude as you assume. Are they, Mr. Cole?"

"No. There are some gifted people on EROS."

Mayeux's partner snorts.

"To wit, Karin Wheat," says Lenz.

"One more thing," I add. "Not all the men on EROS are wealthy. Certain men have submitted writing samples that impressed Ms. Krislov so much that she gives them access free of charge. Sort of a scholarship program. She says it improves the overall experience for the women."

The secretary nods her head in a gesture I read as, *Right on, girl.*

"I'd be very interested in studying some of these online exchanges," Lenz says. "You have some in that briefcase?"

"Yes."

Baxter asks, "Does anything stand out in your mind that these women had in common?"

I pause for a moment. "Most of them spent a lot of time in Level Two—my level. Their fantasies were fairly conventional, by which I mean they involved more romance than sex. They could get kinky, but they weren't sickos. No torture or revolting bodily substances. The truth is, I don't know anything about these women in real life. Only their fantasies."

"Their fantasies may be the most important thing about them," says Lenz.

"Maybe," I allow, "but that's not the sense I got. I'm not sure why. What did they have in common in real life?"

"None of your goddamn business," snaps Mayeux's partner.

"I see. Well, I guess that's my position too."

Dr. Lenz inclines his head toward Baxter, who says, "All the victims were under twenty-six years old except Karin Wheat, who was forty-seven. All were college educated, all Caucasian except one, who was Indian."

"Native American?" asks Chief Tobin.

"Indian Indian," says Mayeux's partner, tapping a file on the table. "Dot on the fucking forehead."

"I don't recall an Indian name," I say, almost to myself.

"Pinky Millstein," says Baxter. "Maiden name Jathar. Married to a litigation attorney who traveled a lot. There was also an Indian hair found at one of the other crime scenes. Does that mean anything to you?"

"Well . . . one of Strobekker's aliases is Shiva. That's Indian, isn't it?"

"Yes, it is," Dr. Lenz says softly. "Shiva the Destroyer. What are his other aliases?"

"Prometheus. Hermes."

The psychiatrist remains impassive. "What about the victims? Does anything come to mind that links their on-line code names?"

"Not that I could see."

"What else stands out in your mind?" asks Baxter.

"Strobekker himself. No matter what alias he uses, his style is unmistakable."

"How so?"

"He's very literate, for one thing. Intuitive, as well. One minute he's writing extemporaneous poetry, the next he cuts right to the bone with some insight into a woman's character, almost as though he can answer whatever question is in her mind before she asks it. But the strangest thing is this: he must be the best damned typist in the world. Lightning fast, and he never makes a mistake."

"Never?" Lenz asks, leaning forward.

"Not in the first eighty-five percent of contact."

"What do you mean?"

"With the sixth victim, and with Karin Wheat, I realized that Strobekker began making typographic errors—just like anyone else—a few days before each woman dropped off-line. When I went back and studied my printouts of the killer-victim exchanges, I saw that the typos began at about the eighty-five percent point in each relationship. Of course, I didn't know anyone was being killed."

"You sound like you've distilled this thing down to a science," says Baxter.

"I work with numbers."

"Running this sex thing?" asks Mayeux.

I chuckle bitterly. "No, I got into EROS for fun. You believe that? I earn my living trading futures."

My audience stares as if I've announced that I am an alchemist.

"In a dink farmhouse in the Mississippi Delta?" asks one of the young FBI agents. "Who are your clients? Farmers hedging their crops?"

"I only have one client."

"Who?" Mayeux asks suspiciously.

"Himself," says Arthur Lenz.

Dr. Lenz is obviously the alchemist here. "That's right. I only trade my own account."

"You some kind of millionaire?" asks Mayeux's partner. "A goddamn gentleman farmer or something?"

"Keep a civil tongue, Poché," snaps the chief.

"I do all right."

"What about the final fifteen percent of contact?" Lenz asks, plainly irritated by the squabbling.

"He makes mistakes. About as many as anyone else. And his typing gets slower. A lot slower."

"Maybe he starts jacking off with one hand as he gets closer to the time of the hit," suggests Poché.

The chief frowns but lets that pass.

Dr. Lenz strikes a pose of intense meditation as the door behind me opens swiftly. I turn and see a black woman in her twenties holding a computer printout in her hand. There is handwriting scrawled across it in blue ink.

"What is it, Kiesha?" asks the chief.

"We traced Strobekker, David M."

A cumulative catching of breath in the conference room. "Rap sheet?" Mayeux asks tentatively.

"No."

"Minnesota DMV?"

"No citations. Had one car—a Mercedes—but the plate expired last year."

"So who is the guy?"

"An accountant for a glitzy firm in Minneapolis, Minnesota."

I realize that Kiesha is trying to communicate something to Chief Tobin through eye contact alone. Despite her telepathic urgency, she is unsuccessful.

"What is it, dear?" asks Arthur Lenz, as though he has known the woman since childhood.

"He's dead," she says, almost as if against her will. "David M. Strobekker was beaten to death in an alley in Minneapolis eleven months ago."

A hot tingle races across my forearms.

"Holy shit," says Mayeux. "What are we dealing with here?"

Daniel Baxter points a finger as thick as a Colt Python barrel at Kiesha. "Details?"

"Minneapolis homicide says it looked like a mugging gone bad. Strobekker was single, probably homosexual. He was slumming on a bad stretch of Hennepin Avenue. His skull was so pulped his boss couldn't recognize his face."

Dr. Lenz emits a small sound of what I can only interpret as pleasure.

"Positive ID?" asks Mayeux.

"Dental records and a thumbprint," Kiesha replies. "His company kept thumbprint files; don't ask me why. But it was Strobekker for sure."

"Not for sure," I say, surprised to hear my own voice.

"Why not?" Baxter asks sharply.

"Well . . . say Strobekker is the killer. Say he decided to fake his own death so that he'd never be suspected in later crimes. He takes a thumbprint from a wino, puts that in his own personnel file, then kills the wino and pulps his face."

"What about the dental records?" asks Baxter.

I shrug. "I'm just thinking out loud."

"You watch too many movies."

"I must see the body immediately," Lenz says to Baxter, his eyes still on me.

"Jeff, call the Minneapolis field office," orders Baxter. "We want a judge who'll give us an exhumation order ASAP. Then call the airport and book the first flight up there."

"What are you looking for?" I ask.

"A pineal gland, among other things," says Lenz, watching me closely. "Ever heard of it?"

I shake my head while I memorize the term. My knowledge of anatomy is limited, but my wife's is encyclopedic.

"The two women who died in California were linked because a pathologist from San Fransisco happened to mention an unsolved homicide case to a colleague at a convention. A woman had been murdered by strangulation, then had both eyes removed and wooden stakes driven through the sockets. When the pathologist sectioned the brain, he found that the points of both stakes terminated in the third ventricle of the brain—a little too perfectly for him. Stranger still, he found that part of the pineal gland was missing, which the stakes would not account for. The colleague who heard this—a pathologist from Los Angeles—had an unsolved homicide that was completely different in almost every respect. A woman had been beaten to death with a claw hammer, probably by someone she knew. Her brain sustained horrific damage. But this did not explain why much of her pineal gland was gone. This chance conversation ultimately linked the crimes. Then the police promptly charged down the wrong track and decided they were dealing with cult murders."

Lenz's tone of voice when he says "police" earns him

few friends in this room. He points his index finger at me.

"You tied those two victims to four others, through EROS. All four of those women also died from severe head wounds, or sustained postmortem head trauma. Pistol shot, shotgun blast, lethal fall. One was decapitated, as was Karin Wheat. We're exhuming the first three and conducting repeat autopsies on the heads. If the condition of the brains permits it, I strongly suspect we will find that these women are missing all or part of their pineal glands."

The psychiatrist is staring at me as though he expects me to start filling in gaps for him.

"What the hell does the pineal gland do?" I ask.

As Lenz and Baxter stare silently at me, my survival instinct tells me it's time to test the bars on this cage. "Look," I say, directing my words to Chief Tobin, "I think you guys have definitely stepped out of my area of expertise. Can I go home now?"

"Not just yet," Tobin says. "Do people ever use their real names on this sex network?"

I try to suppress the feeling that I'm going to be spending the night in a New Orleans hotel, if not jail. "Almost never. The code names are what allow them the freedom to say and be whatever they wish. They might exchange phone numbers to facilitate an f2f meeting, but—"

"What's f2f?" asks the chief.

"Face-to-face."

"Oh. So did the victims give him their numbers?"

"Not in the conversations I've printed out."

"So how do you think he's learning their names?"

"I think he's somehow gained access to our accounting files. There's a master client list in the company's administrative computer, with account numbers, addresses, everything. That's where I got Strobekker's name."

"Who has access to that list?" asks Baxter.

"Myself, Miles Turner, Jan Krislov. Maybe a few techs. That's it. The computer handles the billing automatically. It's a pretty sophisticated system."

"Who is Miles Turner?" asks Lenz.

"He's the primary sysop. We grew up together in Mississippi, but he lives in New York now. He's the one who got me into this job."

"So you think the killer is hacking into the accounting database," says Baxter.

"I don't know. Miles tells me it's impossible, that the list is protected like nuclear launch codes, but as far as I can see it's the only way the killer could get the names. He must have seen that master list at least once. Maybe printed it out."

"Not the only way," interrupts Mayeux's partner. "You or this Miles character could have given the list to someone. Or *sold* it to them."

I'm on the verge of telling this guy to fuck himself when Baxter asks, "Who does security for EROS?"

"Miles," I reply, still watching Mayeux's scowling partner.

"This Miles Turner is highly proficient with computers?" asks Baxter.

" 'Highly' doesn't come close."

"He has a degree?"

"MIT."

"Serious program," says one of the younger FBI agents.

"Graduate degree?" Baxter presses.

"Degrees, plural. I don't know the exact names, but his specialty is computational physics."

"If he's so damned smart," asks Mayeux's partner, "how did Strobekker break through his security?"

It's clear that everyone detests this little rat as much as

I do, but his question is a good one. "I don't know. And he refuses to believe anyone has."

"How many techs are there?" asks Baxter.

"Four, five. I'm not positive they have access to the master list, but I think if they wanted to see it, they could figure a way. They're good. Miles handpicked every one."

The two younger FBI agents are murmuring between themselves. From the lips of one with whippet eyes I catch, ". . . nail that fuck with a phone trace . . . subcontract some NSA geeks . . . next log-on . . . no time—" before Baxter silences them with a glare.

"Mr. Cole," he says gently, "if you don't mind, we'd like you to draw us a floor plan of the EROS offices before you go."

This startles me. "I can't do that."

"Why not?"

"I've never been there."

"Never?"

"They're obsessively private about the place. Why do you need that anyway?"

No one answers.

"You're not gearing up for some kind of Waco thing, are you? This is nothing like that. There's a reason for all the secrecy. We have very famous clients."

"Relax," Baxter says. "We're not the ATF."

"You're all initials to me, Mr. Baxter."

"We can arrest your ass right now!" yells Mayeux's partner, finally losing control. "I don't know why the hell we haven't already!"

"Go ahead!" I shout back, my anger boiling over. "You want to arrest me for linking these homicides for you? The press might be real interested to hear a story like that. In fact, my wife knows one of the TV news anchors here from her school days. Maybe I should give her a call."

"*Let's* everybody just calm down," Chief Tobin booms.

With his department under fire from all quarters for corruption, the last thing he needs is more press scrutiny.

"Now can I go home?" I ask again.

The chief looks hard at Baxter, who in turn looks to Lenz. Lenz finally gives a reserved nod. Baxter reaches into his inside jacket pocket and passes me a card. "This is the number of our headquarters in Quantico, Virginia. I want you to check in once a day for the next few days. Obviously we'll need to speak with you again. Possibly at some length."

Mayeux's partner looks like he just swallowed a cigarette butt with his coffee, but Chief Tobin's hard gaze keeps him muzzled.

"I'd like to study your EROS printouts on the plane," says Lenz. "You are going to leave them with me?"

I open my case, lift out the thick stack of pages, and drop it at the center of the table. "They're all yours. But when Jan Krislov lands on me with both feet and a dozen lawyers, I'm going to expect some payback from you guys."

"Leave Krislov to us," says Baxter.

Measuring Daniel Baxter against my mental image of EROS's cold-blooded CEO, I stifle a retort and turn to go. One foot is outside the doorway when Lenz says, "Mr. Cole?"

I turn back, expecting some *Columbo* trick just as I taste freedom. Lenz smiles oddly. "What instrument do you play?"

The question throws me off balance. Is this some bullshit Barbara Walters question? What kind of tree would I like to be? But of course it's not. I do play an instrument, and somehow Lenz knows that. "Guitar," I answer blankly.

The psychiatrist nods, a trace of disappointment in his eyes. "Do you sing?"

"Some people think so. I never did."

The rest of the group looks from me to Lenz, then back again, trying to understand this odd coda to our meeting. My bewilderment holds me in place until the psychiatrist says, "Calluses, Mr. Cole. You have well-developed calluses on the fingertips of your left hand."

The hand closes involuntarily. I squint at Lenz, imprinting his face in my memory, then turn and step into the hall.

On my way out of the station, I pass a knot of middle-aged men in sweat-stained suits. They are obviously waiting for something. Their angry voices mark them as anything but Southerners, and before I am out of earshot I realize they are waiting for me.

I quicken my steps.

Once outside, I reflect on Dr. Lenz's little performance. He's an observant man. But is he smart? A smart man would simply have noted the calluses and bade me farewell. Unless he felt that quickly discovering what instrument I play was important. But even then, a smart man would have remained silent after I answered his question, leaving me mystified by his deductive skills. Yet Arthur Lenz insisted on doing a Sherlock Holmes impression for his captive audience of Lestrades. Why?

The doctor was showing off. I don't know why, but this is somehow important. I cannot escape the feeling that the entire low-key meeting was a carefully orchestrated interrogation designed to look and feel like anything but that. Baxter and Lenz playing good cop while the NOPD played the heavy. Or maybe it's more complicated than that. But if they really suspect me, why not arrest me and give me the third degree? Or throw me to the out-of-state wolves who were waiting for me?

One thing is certain. The FBI controlled that meeting. I am free because they want me free. Why do they want that? Could the FBI—like Chief Tobin—be afraid of the media? It's possible. After seven murders—eight including Strobekker—the Bureau's elite serial killer unit has managed to link exactly none of the crimes. Wrongly accusing the good citizen who connected the murders for them might make their precious Unit an object of ridicule on *Nightline*, not to mention *Hard Copy*, which is already feeding on the case.

I have only intuition to go on, but the voiceless voice in my head has rarely failed me. As I pull the inevitable parking ticket off the windshield of my Explorer and drop the crumpled ball into the gutter, that voice is saying one thing loud and clear: *You have more problems today than you had yesterday.*

Chapter 6

One of my office telephones is ringing when I turn the key in the front door of the farmhouse. Thinking it's Drewe, I race to catch it.

"Hello, snitch."

This is not Drewe. The voice in the earpiece is at once strange and familiar. It belongs to Miles Turner.

"You've really shaken things up, haven't you," he says.

"What have you heard?" I ask, shocked at the sauna-level heat that has accumulated inside the house during the day.

"Jan is very upset with you."

"I figured. Did the FBI call her?"

I hear a faint *tsk*. "Did they *phone* her? No, Harper. That would be much too easy for the Federal Bureau of Incompetence. They showed up at the door of our offices with a search warrant."

"What? At EROS? When?"

"Two hours ago. Special agents from the New York office."

"What did they see?"

"Not much. Jan locked the master client list in the file room the minute Reception buzzed her and said the FBI was in the building. She refused to give them a key, and that room is like a vault. Actually, it *is* a vault. It reminds me of your grandfather's bomb shelter—Eisenhower chic. It's got a time lock. Seventy-two hours before that monster opens. I guess the FBI could blow it open or cut it with a blowtorch, but they haven't tried. They just posted two men outside it. They didn't even confiscate our servers. Jan thinks the raid was pure intimidation."

"I don't think so, Miles. All six of those women I told you about were murdered this year. Karin Wheat makes seven. And David Strobekker, the man I thought was the killer, makes eight."

"So says the FBI."

"Come *on*, man. Wake up and smell the fucking coffee! I overheard one guy whispering about phone traces, bringing in the NSA, George Orwell stuff."

"As a matter of fact, Jan is about to give the FBI permission to set up tracing equipment right here in the office."

This stops me. "But you just said she hid the master client list from them."

"She did. But Jan's no fool. She knows she's walking a fine legal line. There is apparently some question of a duty to warn. Warn the subscribers, I mean. She feels that by cooperating with the FBI in tracing Strobekker—or whoever he is—she demonstrates that she's not obstructing the FBI merely for the sake of doing it."

"At least somebody up there is thinking straight. How long do they think it will take to trace Strobekker if he does log on again?"

"If he's stupid, no time at all. Personally, I don't believe they have a chance in hell."

"You sound glad about it, damn it!"

Miles laughs softly. "I haven't heard you this excited in a while. Did Karin's death affect you so deeply?"

I swallow. "You knew her?"

"Of course. We exchanged quite a few messages during the wee hours. Karin was one of the pillars of Level Three. A thoroughly interesting woman."

I think quickly. "I . . . I know that. But—"

"But you never saw any of my aliases in exchanges with her, right? That's what you're thinking?"

"Yes."

"I have many names, Harper. Even you don't know them all." He pauses. "You don't always tell women you're a sysop, do you? That you know who they really are? That would spoil the fun, wouldn't it? It's amazing how the perceived anonymity of a code name lets them open up, isn't it? Especially the actresses. There's nothing quite like boffing a three-million-dollar thespian online while she thinks you think she's someone else, is there? You can play them like your guitar then, can't you?"

I say nothing.

"And how is Drewe Welby, M.D. taking all of this? Did she finally break the camel's back and send you running to the FBI?"

"I didn't go to the FBI," I snap. "I called the New Orleans police. The FBI was already on the case. Damn it, Miles, we're talking about murder."

"So?"

"So?"

"EROS is like an organic system, Harper. Constantly evolving. Powerful emotions flow through it every day. Sexual emotions. We're accustomed to monitoring massive levels of input, or throughput, if you will. But *output* has always been a possibility. And sex has always been integrally bound up with death. Why anyone should be surprised by all this is beyond me."

"Miles, put aside your bullshit philosophizing for a minute. Don't you realize that EROS's primary obligation is to protect the security of its clients?"

"You're the one who trivialized that obligation by revealing the names of subscribers to the police."

I shake my head. "You've finally flipped out, man."

"You realize," he says coolly, "that you've exposed yourself to litigation by your action. Your employment contract is quite specific about that. I would feel derelict as a friend if I didn't warn you that you will almost certainly be hearing from Elaine Abrams in the next few days. I would speak to my attorney."

It suddenly strikes me that Miles Turner—who grew up in Rain, Mississippi—is speaking without a trace of Southern accent. He has finally succeeded in his lifelong goal of erasing his roots.

"Listen to me, Miles," I implore, reaching for some vestige of the boy I once knew so well. "Innocent women are being killed and mutilated. I'm trying to stop that. If you and Krislov don't understand that, you're going to get steamrollered by the FBI. I've met the guys running this investigation. They're from the Investigative Support Unit—the serial killer guys—and they are serious people."

"I gather they are," he says, finally showing a touch of pique. "And you and I are their prime targets."

I am silent.

"Surely you see that, Harper? You and I are the only two men—apart from my technical staff—who have access to the real names of the subscribers. Obviously the master client list is the map the killer is using to choose his victims."

Obviously. "So how did he get access to it?"

"I'm looking into that."

"You told me those files were protected like nuclear launch codes."

"My system architecture is ironclad," he snaps. "Still, even the best operating systems sometimes have flaws no one knows about. They come that way from the factory."

"How many technicians are there, Miles?"

"Six."

More than I'd thought. "If the killer isn't hacking his way through your security, and you or I didn't do the killings, that means one of those six guys did."

"No."

"How do you know?"

"I just do."

This stops me. When Miles Turner sounds this certain, he is always right. The police would never accept that, of course, but I do. But how can he know? Trying not to slide too far down that neural pathway, I say, "Look, am I fired or what?"

"Fired?" he echoes as if the notion has never crossed his mind.

"You just said Krislov was pissed at me. It's not like I'm essential to the running of the network."

"Of course you are. You and I are the only two full-duty sysops."

"What about Raquel Hirsch?"

"She's licking her lesbian lips off on Montserrat. Not due back for another week. Besides, she's only part-time and doesn't know enough about technical matters to defrag a hard drive."

"What if I quit?"

"You can't."

"My contract says I can. I made sure of that. This was only going to be a trial thing anyway, remember? A goof."

Miles's voice lowers to its snake-charming register. "But you've stayed at it all these months, haven't you? You *like* it. Besides, if you quit, you'll lose your fifty-yard-line seat."

Jesus. "I don't need the aggravation, Miles."

"No? What about your online friends, then? Or should I say lovers? Are you ready to tell them good-bye forever? Your employment contract *does* forbid you from ever trying to contact them in person. If you quit, I'll probably have to remind Elaine Abrams about that clause."

"Fuck you. I quit."

"What about Eleanor Rigby?"

I exhale slowly, my grip tightening on the phone. "What do you know about Eleanor?"

"I know she'd be positively despondent if you dropped off of EROS without explanation."

Miles knows he has me. The truth is, I don't really want to quit. After summoning the nerve to "go public" with my suspicions—and being proved correct—I want resolution. Miles just pisses me off. "I'll stay until Raquel gets back," I tell him, my voice tight.

"Good man. Oh, you'd better start getting your alibis organized. Your FBI friends will be asking, and it can be difficult to remember where one was on so many different nights so many months ago."

"I have nothing to hide," I say firmly. "I'm innocent."

There is a long silence, then a strange, muffled sigh. When Miles finally answers, his voice seems burdened by age beyond his years. "Harper, have you learned so little during your time with EROS? You speak of innocence with such conviction. Are any of us?"

Then he hangs up the phone.

I look around the office at the familiar landmarks of my existence, the EROS computer (custom built by Miles), the Gateway 2000 I use to make my futures trades, two laser printers, the antique laboratory table that functions as my desk, the twin bed I crash on during marathon trading sessions, the guitars hanging over the bed. Lifting my feet from the floor, I spin the swivel chair in a circle. The window flashes past again and again, merging with reflections from framed prints, antique maps, the unsheathed Civil War sword carried by one of my maternal ancestors at Brice's Cross Roads. When I stop spinning I am facing a sport coat.

My father's coat.

It droops from a wire hanger on a nail driven straight into the wall. The jacket appears to be cashmere, with thin vertical stripes of black and wine. It is absolutely motionless. There is a reason for this. The coat is made of wood.

I commissioned this piece from a sculptor I discovered one summer in Florida. He is a big blond guy named Fraser Smith, and he sculpts nothing but clothes, quilts, and old suitcases. The day I met him, I compulsively bought two of his pieces and in the after-sale chatter learned that he was originally from Mississippi. I don't know why his work affects me so strongly, but I don't question it. Things actually worth buying are rare.

My father's taste in clothes was exceptionally bad as a rule—mostly synthetic fabrics in loud colors—but he bought this jacket while serving as an army doctor in Germany in 1960, the year I was born. All I can figure is that the store was out of electric plaids, leaving him no choice but to buy this jewel for warmth. Twenty years later, he gave it to me after I remarked on its quality, and I wore it often. Ten years after that—a year after he died—I carefully boxed it up and sent it UPS to Tampa, Florida, where Smith kept it four months, then shipped both the jacket and the sculpture back to me with a bill for fifteen thousand dollars.

It was worth every cent.

Why, I don't know. Maybe because the jacket says something to me about the permanence of the apparently transitory. For what is that jacket but an articulated memory? As surely as the jacket is here with me, my father is here with me. And for all his failings, which were many, he was a man of principle when it came to the big things. And I know, as I sit here worrying about the consequences of my recent actions, that I am doing only and exactly what my father would have done—the consequences be damned.

Maybe that's Miles's problem. He had no such anchor. Miles's father left him and his mother to fend for themselves when Miles was five. People said Miles was his spitting image, but since Mrs. Turner kept no pictures of "that no-count SOB" in the house, we could never confirm or deny this. He certainly didn't look like his mother, a petite, harried woman. He was tall even as a child, all bones and tendons, which in a small town usually leads to school sports. But Miles was apathy personified. When one coach tried to talk him into playing basketball, he just stared until the man walked away. That was a common adult reaction. Miles's eyes are grayish blue, and you can't see anything in them if he doesn't want you to. They're like background pieces in a stained-glass window. Nothing there but space. Yet, like the sky, they can come alive with everything from thunderheads to blazing blue light.

According to local legend, Miles's father was a mean drunk and a gifted engineer who helped the Army Corps of Engineers figure out how to stop a bad sand boil in the levee west of Mayersville in 1973. Because of that, people said Miles got his brains from his father. Miles hated them for that. He hated anybody who ever said it. I think he took it as some sort of insult to his mother, who was no rocket scientist, to be fair to the gossips. Yet Annie Turner was clever in her own way. She never remarried (or even divorced, for all the town knew) but she did manage to become involved with certain solvent gentlemen (railroad men, for example) who happened to be passing through Rain during times of financial distress.

Miles never talked about any of those men. When they were around, we knew to stay away from his house from noontime on. Once, shooting squirrels out of season, we ran into the Turner kitchen to grab some .22 bullets from the drawer and saw a man standing in the kitchen with his shirt off, drinking milk from a half-gallon carton. He looked old as the hills to us (at twelve) and had milk dribbling down his chin. When we got outside and Miles fumbled the bullets into the .22, his eyes sort of glazed over and he took a couple of steps back toward the house and before I could spit he put two bullets through the top pane of the kitchen window. When I crashed into his back and pulled him down, I felt his shoulders shaking like the flanks of a horse run almost to death. I had to hit him in the face to get the gun away, and then we ran like hell until we couldn't hear anyone screaming behind us. Miles didn't say anything for about two hours after that. We just walked along the weedy turnrows dividing the cotton fields, rapping the hard, knobbed stalks everybody called nigger knockers against the rusty barbed wire. I went home at dark. I don't know if Miles went home at all.

But they made out okay. Annie even managed to pay Miles's way through private school until she realized that the school would pay to have him. Because Miles Turner was a genius. I say that because, though I did well in school without much effort, Miles did not try *at all.* In the ninth grade he could answer "reading" problems in algebra after scanning them once. He never put anything on paper. After we all took the Armed Services Vocational Aptitude Battery, some army major from Washington telephoned down to the school, talked to the principal, and asked to speak to Miles. He said something about Miles having a home in the army just as soon as he came of age. Miles told the major he wouldn't join the army unless Russian paratroopers landed in his mother's yard. The major said that might not be such a remote possibility. He also told Miles that Greenville was a confirmed Russian nuclear target because of its bridge over the Mississippi River. Miles said if the Russians wanted to nuke Greenville, he might consider joining the army after all. The Russian army.

Okay, he was a smart-ass. But that doesn't make him a

killer. He was just born in the wrong town. And he knew it. We both graduated high school as National Merit scholars, and could have gone to college anywhere in the United States for next to nothing. But there our paths diverged. I was so into girls that summer that I hardly gave college a thought, and since my parents were having their own problems at the time—financial and marital—they ignored the issue as well. I'd always done well in school, thus I always would. In the end I went to Ole Miss sight unseen, and because I had waited so long to decide, my father even had to pay for the privilege.

Miles applied for and was awarded a full academic scholarship to the Massachusetts Institute of Technology. While I farted around Oxford, Mississippi, with scatter-brained, Venus-shaped sorority girls and drunken Young Republicans, Miles Turner was fanatically programming, tearing apart, and rebuilding big clumsy metal boxes that I would not even have recognized in 1978.

Computers.

It seems natural now, but at the time it was odd. He spoke the language of bits and drives and floating memory at a time when those words were as foreign to the general public as Attic Greek. The really odd thing is that Miles thinks I'm smarter than he is. I have no idea why. This is not false modesty. I will frankly admit that I have above-average intelligence, just as I will admit I have a poor sense of direction. I can look at a problem, analyze it—for patterns, usually—and given enough time, solve it. Miles doesn't analyze anything. He looks at something, and he *just knows.* He grasps physics and numbers the way I do people and music—wholly by intuition. It's as though his asocial childhood allowed him to tune into some subrational channel of information that is beyond the rest of us.

When I took the sysop job, I was looking forward to getting to know him again. I'd only seen him a handful of times in the past fifteen years. But for whatever reason, it hasn't worked out that way. We occasionally exchange e-mail—sometimes using the satellite video link that his techs installed here when I took the job-slash-hobby—but on balance, I know him no better now than I did when we were kids. Maybe my hopes were misplaced. Maybe you can never know anyone more deeply than you know them in childhood.

By the time Drewe arrives, I've put together a bastardized stir-fry of broccoli and pork and lemon. We eat it on the front porch, which is thick with heat despite the falling darkness, but mercifully free of mosquitoes. As soon as we sit, Drewe asks for a play-by-play of the meeting in New Orleans. I give it to her, glad not to have to keep anything back. She takes in every word with the machinelike precision that carried her through medical school with honors, and when I am done she says nothing. I have held one detail until the end, hoping for a silence like this one.

"What's the pineal gland?" I ask.

She finds my eyes in the gloom. "The pineal body?"

"I guess, yeah."

"It's a small glandular structure at the core of the brain. In the third ventricle, I think. It's about the size of a pea."

"What does it do?"

"Until about thirty years ago, nobody thought it did anything. It was considered a vestigial organ, like the appendix. Scientists knew the pineal made melatonin, but no one knew what melatonin did. What does the pineal have to do with anything?"

"The FBI says the killer cut off Karin Wheat's head to get to her pineal gland."

"What?"

"Sick, huh? The other victims might be missing theirs too, or else their whole heads."

Drewe grimaces.

"Can you think of any reason why someone would want pineal glands? Do they have any medical use?"

"I don't think so. There were some pineal experiments going on at Tulane when I was there, related to breast cancer, I think. But I don't remember what the findings were." She pauses. "You can buy melatonin in health food stores, though. God, this reminds me of those PBS shows where they talk about Oriental medicine. You know, how Japanese men pay poachers hundreds of thousands of dollars for rhinoceros horns and tiger testicles and things. All to cure impotence or restore their lost youth or something."

My opinion of my wife's mental acuity has been reaffirmed yet again. She has already broached a theory that seems more logical than that of the police in California, who believe the EROS murders may be the work of a cult.

"So what *is* melatonin?" I ask. "What does it do?"

"It's a hormone that regulates your sleep cycle. Your circadian rhythms. You know, what causes jet lag. Some people take it to prevent or relieve jet lag symptoms."

"Can you remember anything else about it?"

Drewe touches her forefinger to the tip of her nose and fixes her gaze somewhere out in the darkness. I know this posture well: concentration mode. "I think it controls the release of serotonin, maybe some other hormones. I seem to recall something from one of the journals. Neurobiological stuff. Something to do with the pineal and the aging process. Weird how that fits with the Oriental thing, isn't it? But that doesn't mean anything. Murderers don't read *JAMA* or *Journal of Neuroscience.*"

"Why not?"

"Well . . . I guess it's possible." Drewe grimaces and says, "Men are scum." A routine comic line of hers that doesn't sound so funny tonight.

"So what's the plan?" I ask lightly, falling into our usual banter.

"More dictation." She stretches both arms above her head. "My personal cross to bear." She begins gathering up the plates. "Which reminds me. Tomorrow you face yours."

I feel a sudden chill. "What are you talking about?"

"Take it easy," she says, giving me an odd look. "I meant the biweekly burden. Sunday dinner with your in-laws."

She turns away and moves through the screen door, but my chill does not dissipate. Over her shoulder she says, "Lately you've acted like it's a trip to the dentist or something."

If only it were.

I rise from the porch and head for my office. Combined with the stress of the past weeks, the trip to New Orleans has exhausted me. After months of anxiety, I have finally done what I should have done long ago. For months I've stayed up far too many hours and slept too few, lurking in Level Three in the hope of recognizing the error-free transmissions of David Strobekker. But tonight I will sleep.

As I strip off my clothes, Drewe's last comment echoes in my mind. *Lately you've acted like it's a trip to the dentist or something*. In reality the trip to her parents' house is a trip into a minefield. A place where one wrong word or a too open glance could cause instant devastation. Drewe does not know this. Like the most dangerous mines, these were laid long ago by people who scarcely knew what they were doing. No maps exist, and disarming them is impossible. Once I thought it might be, but now

I know the truth. When we seek to resurrect the past, it eludes us; when we seek to elude the past, it reaches out with fingers that can destroy all we know and love.

Tonight I leave David Strobekker to the FBI.

I have my own demon.

Chapter 7

Dear Father,

We landed near Virginia Beach at dusk, riding the scent of ocean to the earth.

We misdirected taxis to bring us within range of the patient's house, then walked.

No EROS dalliances with this one. She's a Navy girl, young and simple and tough. I was lucky to have Kali with me.

We entered while she showered, and what a specimen she was. Firm pink skin shining in the spray. For a moment I wished we were there for the old protocol.

But—

After her scream died, I tried a little humor. "Hello, Jenny, we're from DonorNet. I'll bet you didn't think we made house calls."

She tried to fight us in the bedroom, making for a dresser (in which I later found a pistol). Kali brought her down with a knife slash to the thigh. Lots of blood, but essentially a superficial wound. It will have no effect on her role in the procedure.

Kali helped her dress, then forced her to give us her car keys. Jenny didn't whine or beg, like some. She was trying to think of a way out.

I drove her car to the airstrip, Kali guarding her in

the backseat. At the plane I'd planned to inject a mild sedative, but despite my reassurances the patient would not submit. I was forced to shoot her with a Ketamine dart. I also had to leave her car at the runway. Eventually it will be found. But there is no record of our landing. No note. No trace of our passing. Another question mark for the police.

Kali has the controls now. My dark Shakti shepherds me through the stars. We hurtle into history at two hundred miles per hour. The patient lies bound behind us, silent as death, as blissfully unaware of the contribution she will make as the monkey that gave Salk his poliomyelitis vaccine.

I've been thinking that I should present an edited version of these letters as an addendum to my official findings, or perhaps they belong with my curriculum vitae. Shocking to the unprepared mind, I suppose, but highly edifying for the medical historian.

But enough of that.

Things are where they are, and,

as fate has willed,

So shall they be fulfilled.

Chapter 8

"It's that damned nigger contractor," says Bob Anderson.

"Robert, not in front of Holly," scolds Margaret, his wife.

Bob Anderson is my father-in-law. He points across his Mexican tile patio toward a small girl child splashing in the shallow end of the swimming pool.

"She can't hear me, Marg. And no matter how you cut it, it all comes back to that *nigger contractor.*"

Patrick Graham, my brother-in-law, rolls his eyes at me while carefully making sure I am the only one who can see him. Patrick and I went to school together and are exactly the same age. An oncologist in Jackson, Mississippi, he is married to Erin, my wife's younger sister. His rolling eyes sum up a feeling too complex for words, one common to our generation of Southerners. They say, *We may not like it but there's nothing we can do about it except argue, and it's not worth arguing about with our father-in-law because he won't ever change no matter what.*

"It" being racism, of course.

"What are you jabbering about, Daddy?" Drewe asks.

My wife is wearing a yellow sundress and standing over the wrought-iron table that holds the remains of the barbecued ribs we just devoured. Erin excluded, of course. My wife's sister is a strict vegetarian, which in Mississippi still rates up there with being a Hare Krishna.

This get-together is a biweekly family ritual, Sunday dinner at the in-laws', who live twenty miles from Rain, on the outskirts of Yazoo City. We do it rain or shine, and today it's shine: ninety-six degrees in the shade.

"Don't get him started, honey," my mother-in-law says wearily. Margaret Anderson has taken refuge from the heat beneath a wide-brimmed straw hat.

"I'm talking about my new office, baby," Bob tells Drewe, ignoring Margaret.

Bob Anderson is a veterinarian and an institution in this part of the Delta. His practice thrives, but that is not what pays for the columned Greek Revival house that towers over the patio we are sitting on. In the last twenty years, Bob has invested with unerring instinct in every scheme that made any money in the Delta, most notably catfish farming. Money from all over the world pours into Mississippi in exchange for farm-raised catfish—enough money to put the long-maligned catfish in the same league with cotton. A not insignificant portion of that money pours into Bob Anderson's pockets. He is a short man but seems tall, even to those who have known him for years. Though he is balding, his forearms are thick and hairy. He walks with a self-assured, forward-leaning tilt, his chin cocked back with a military air. He is a natural hand with all things mechanical. Carpenter work, motors, welding, plumbing, a half dozen sports. It's easy to imagine him with one strong arm buried up to the shoulder in the womb of a mare, a wide grin on his sweaty face. Bob Anderson is a racist; he is also a good father, a faithful husband, and a dead shot with a rifle.

"I took bids on my building," he says, looking back over his shirtless shoulder at Drewe. "All the local boys made their plays, o'course, first-class job like that. And all their bids were close to even. Then I get a bid from this nigger out of Jackson, name of Boyte. His bid was eight thousand less than the lowest of the local boys."

"Did you take it?" Patrick asks.

Erin Graham—Patrick's wife—turns from her perch at poolside. She has been sitting with her tanned back to us, her long legs dangling in the water, watching her three-year-old daughter with an eagle eye. Erin's dark eyes glower at her father, but Bob pretends not to notice.

"Not yet," he says. "See, the local boys somehow got wind of what the nigger bid—"

"Somehow?" Drewe echoes, expressing her suspicion that her father told his cronies about their minority competition.

"Anyhow," Bob plows on, "it turns out the reason this nigger can afford to bid so low is that he's getting some kind of cheap money from the government. Some kind of *incentive*—read handout—which naturally ain't available to your white contractors. Now I ask you, is that fair? I'm all for letting the nigger compete right alongside Jack and Nub, but for the government to use our tax money to help him undercut hardworking men like that—"

"Are you sure the black contractor's getting government help?" Drewe asks.

"Hell yes, I'm sure. Nub told me himself."

"So what are you going to do?" asks Patrick, as if he really cares, which I know he does not.

"What can I do?" Bob says haplessly. "I've got to give it to the nigger, don't I?"

"DADDY, THAT IS ENOUGH!"

Patrick and I look up, startled by the shrill voice. Erin has stood up beside the pool and she is pointing a long finger at her father. "You may do and say as you wish at your house any time you wish—*except* when my daughter is present. Holly will *not* grow up handicapped by the prejudices of this state."

Bob looks at Patrick and me and rolls his eyes, which from long experience we sons-in-law have no trouble translating as, *What do you expect from a girl who ran off to New York City when she turned eighteen and lived among Yankees?*

"Calm down, honey," Bob says. "To you he's an African American. Five years ago he was black, before that a Negro, before that colored. How am I supposed to keep up? To me he's a nigger. His own friends call him nigger. What's the difference? Holly won't remember any of this in five minutes anyway."

To be fair, Bob Anderson would never use this kind of language in mixed company—mixed *racial* company—or in front of whites he did not know and feel comfortable with. Unless, of course, someone made him mad. To Bob Anderson, "politically correct" means you salute the flag, work your butt off, pay your taxes, pray in school, and you by God *go* when Uncle Sam calls you, no questions asked. I could ridicule his views, but I won't. Guys like Bob Anderson fought and died for this country years before I was born. Guys like Bob Anderson liberated Nordhausen and Buchenwald. Bob himself fought in Korea. So I keep my thirty-three-year-old mouth shut.

But Erin doesn't. "Goddamn it, Daddy, I'm serious!" she snaps, her tanned cheeks quivering. "Holly's like a sponge and you know it!"

Bob's face glows pink. He half rises from his reclining lawn chair. "You hear that, Margaret? Your daughter just took the Lord's name in vain, and she's on me for calling a spade a spade! I think any civilized person would agree that blasphemy is *far* worse than saying nigger now and again!"

Margaret Anderson snores beneath her straw hat.

"No it's not, Daddy," Drewe says softly from the table. "But you'll never understand why."

* * *

I am enthralled by the continuing role reversal Erin and Drewe have been undergoing since they were kids. When they were teenagers, it was Drewe who almost daily pushed her father to the point that he locked her in her room or thrashed her with his belt. She constantly tested her limits, proving only that she was as stubborn as he was. Erin was a creature of equanimity, slipping through life with no resistance at all. Yet now that Erin is a mother, it is she who faces down Bob without fear or second thoughts.

As a child Drewe was a tomboy, curious, competitive, and tough. After puberty, she began to soften into a more feminine figure at the same time her intelligence put her at the top of her ninth-grade class. To prevent the inevitable taunts of being "too good" for everyone else, Drewe evolved a unique strategy. She became the wildest girl in the class. Or at least she seemed to. And one of her most convincing moves in this game of social survival was dating the wildest boy in her class—me. And so it was that I alone knew her secret. While the other girls were perpetually awed by the craziness of some of the things Drewe did, I knew, for example, that on those occasions when we managed to spend nearly all night together in bed, she stopped our passionate groping well short of "going all the way." Yet she was perfectly content to let her friends think otherwise. And in the whirlwind of our relationship, no one seemed to notice that she maintained a 99.4 average in all subjects.

Erin was just as deceptive, but she took the opposite tack. A year behind Drewe, she effortlessly convinced every parent and teacher within thirty miles that she was a perfect angel while actually having sex with any guy who took her fancy, from clean-cut quarterbacks to pot-smoking cowboy rebels. Her grades were middling at best, but on the other hand, they were irrelevant.

Erin's secret was her looks.

I gaze past Patrick and Bob: Erin has finally turned back toward the shimmering pool. I am now looking at what was once described as the finest ass in the state of Mississippi, and it still manages to make the one-piece bathing suit that covers it seem more revealing than a thong bikini. Even now, I am convinced that this thirty-two-year-old mother could give any high school senior a run for her money.

During 1979, Erin Anderson's face appeared on the covers of six national magazines. Four days after she graduated from high school, she left Rain, Mississippi, for New York with five hundred dollars and the name of a modeling agent in her purse. Two months later she had signed a contract with the Ford agency. In quick succession came runway work, the six magazine covers, some TV spots. Then came a brief hiatus, and after that it was the inner pages of the magazines. Another hiatus, then mostly they used her hands, feet, breasts, and hair.

No tragic accident had disfigured her face. If looks alone were the criterion, Erin would still be gazing out from the racks at the supermarket checkout instead of gathering up her child from the shallow end of her parents' swimming pool. Erin's problems were inside her head, not outside.

But first the exterior. Where Drewe is fair, Erin is dark. I lay that at the feet of genetics. Bob Anderson came from Scots-English blood, Margaret Cajun French. Drewe got her father's genes, Erin her mother's. And the differences hold true right down the line. Drewe's hair is thick, auburn, and slightly curly. Erin's is fine and straight and so brown it is almost black. Drewe's eyes are green and bright with quick intelligence; Erin's are almond-shaped, as black and deep as smoldering Louisiana bottomland. Drew has a pert nose, while Erin's is long and straight with catlike flared nostrils. And where Drewe's lips are pink, like brush strokes on a Royal

Doulton figurine, Erin's are full and brown, her upper lip dusted with fine tawny down. Both girls are somewhere around five foot nine, but Erin is *long*.

I don't mean to shortchange my wife. Any man with functioning retinas would call Drewe a beauty. She is also demure—except while working—and her strength and smarts give an edge to her elegance. She is a doctor, after all. Erin is a former model turned jet-set girlfriend turned housewife. But as I watch Erin leading her child by the hand to the wrought-iron table, the physical difference comes clear: Drewe is feminine; Erin is feline.

This is a difficult art, watching another woman without your wife noticing. You look with unrestricted freedom for the early part of your life, then suddenly you have to learn to conceal your interest. The battle is hopeless, like a physicist trying to train iron filings not to follow a magnet. But with Erin, I have had lots of practice.

Since I dated Drewe in high school, Erin and I were almost natural enemies. We constantly razzed each other, behaving as if related ourselves. I grew adept at ignoring her stunning legs as we hung around the pool in the summers. But sometimes ignoring her was impossible.

Once, at a high school lake party, some of the seniors got drunk enough to start skinny-dipping. Dusk was falling, and a few of the girls felt safe enough or bold enough to slip off their suits in the growing shadows and dive off the pier into the silver water.

When Drewe saw this, she silently stood up, threw her "wild" act to the winds, and started walking back toward the car. She obviously had no intention of stripping nude in front of strangers, no matter how drunk they might be. Besides, her coolness quotient was secure. She didn't look back at me, but I knew she expected me to follow. And I meant to. But as I stood up, I heard a voice say softly: "Harper."

I turned around to see Erin standing behind me. She

wore the bottom half of a bikini, but her brown-nippled breasts were exposed. With her eyes locked on mine, she hooked a finger in the side of her suit and stepped lazily out of it.

She was glorious. And she knew it. I stood blinking in the dusk, trying to take in what I was seeing. Looking back now, I realize that trying to see—truly *see*—a naked woman in her entirety is like trying to take in the carnage at a traffic accident. Your brain simply cannot process all the input being channeled like floodwater through your eyes. I saw bits of her: collarbones like sculpted braces inside a guitar, her flat brown oiled belly, beaded with pearls of lake water descending to a stark tan line where a lighter brownness descended again to the rough black triangle blurring the wide cleft between her thighs. And always her eyes. How long did I stare? Five seconds? Ten? I heard a long, reverent whistle from the water below the pier. Then Erin's gaze floated above my shoulder and she simply stepped off the pier and dropped into the lake. When I turned around and looked up to the house, I saw no one. But after I reached the car, Drewe remained silent all the way back to Rain.

"Uncle *Harrrrp*—"

Startled, I look away from Erin and into the face of Holly, her daughter. "What is it, punkin?"

"Where's your *git*-tar?"

Bob chuckles.

"I didn't bring it today."

"Play me a *sawng*," commands the three-year-old.

"I can't. I guess I could sing one a cappella. What do you want to hear?"

"Blackbirdie!" she squeals, laughing. She means "Blackbird," by Paul McCartney. Sometimes Patrick whistles birdcalls while I play the song, which drives Holly into fits of laughter.

"Sorry, Scooter," I say. "I need the *git*-tar for that one. What's your second choice?"

"BARNEY!" she screeches.

"Christ," whispers Patrick. "I thought she got over Barney last year."

"Uh, Marg?" Bob says softly. "Didn't you tell me ol' Barney got killed in a car wreck yesterday?"

"What?" Holly asks, her eyes round.

"Daddy!" Drewe snaps.

To prevent bloodshed, I begin the anthem adored by most humans under three and reviled by most above that age. Holly sits entranced. She actually resembles Drewe more than Erin. The Scots-English genes apparently overpowered the Cajun. I give the Barney theme a soul-gospel ending; Holly claps and giggles, and even Margaret lifts the brim of her hat and applauds.

"Did you hear about Karin Wheat?" my mother-in-law asks me softly.

While I consider my answer, she takes a sip of half-melted Bloody Mary, shivers, and says, "Gruesome."

"I did hear about that," I say noncommittally, feeling Drewe's gaze on the back of my neck.

"I was just reading *Isis*," Margaret goes on. "I'll bet one of her crazy fans killed her. That book was chock *full* of perversion."

"Didn't stop you from reading, though, did it?" Bob snickers. "What's happening on the porno box, Harper?"

"Porno box" is Bob's nickname for the EROS computer. "Same old seven and six," I say, though I would give a lot to know whether the Strobekker account has gone active in the last few hours and, if so, whether the FBI was able to trace the connection.

Bob shakes his head. "I still don't get why anybody—even sex maniacs—would pay that much money for a box that won't even transmit pictures."

"Actually, it will now," I tell him. "There was so much demand for it, Jan Krislov decided to give in."

"I'll be damned."

Erin slips on a terry cloth robe and leads Holly away from this conversation onto the perfectly manicured lawn. Bob keeps all eight acres as immaculate as a golf green and does all the work himself.

"I heard on *A Current Affair* that the killer cut off her *head*," Margaret adds.

I force myself to look uninterested.

"This is one time I'm gonna surprise you pinko-liberals," Bob says with good humor. "I'll guarantee you it was a white man killed that writer woman."

Drewe raises her eyebrows. "Why do you say that?"

" 'Cause a nigger don't kill that way," Bob replies seriously. "Oh, they'll cut you, or shoot you. But it's an impulse thing. A nigger gets mad quick, kills quick, gets over it quick. He's likely to be feeling sorry about it five minutes after he did it. White man's different. A white man can nurse a hate a long time. A white man *likes* to hate. Gives him a mission, a reason to live. And a murder like that thing in New Orleans—mutilation, I mean—it takes a long time to build up an anger like that."

We are all staring intently at Bob Anderson.

" 'Course, it was New Orleans," he adds philosophically. "God knows anything can happen there."

After a thoughtful silence, Margaret asks Drewe about some policy change at one of the Jackson hospitals. Drewe and Patrick both have staff privileges there, and strong opinions about the issue. Every now and then Bob chimes in with an unsolicited expert opinion. While they banter back and forth, my eyes wander back to Erin and Holly. They move like exotic animals over the dappled lawn, Erin graceful as a gazelle, Holly like a sprite risen from the grass. As I watch, I let my eyes take on the thoughtful cast I have practiced so often at this gathering.

Everyone assumes I am thinking about bond trades or commodities. Before long, Bob will ask me if I made any killings this week.

But for now I am granted a dispensation.

I try to keep my mind clear, but the effort is vain. As always, my secret rises unbidden. It is always there, beating like a second heart within my brain. The ceaseless tattoo grows louder, pulsing in my ears, throbbing in my temples, causing little storms of numbness along my upper forearms. These are parasthesias; I looked up the symptom late one night in one of Drewe's medical books. Parasthesias are caused by extraordinary levels of stress. Everyone has a different tolerance, I suppose. What would terrify an equestrienne would not faze a bull rider.

I have carried my secret for a long time, and consequently thought I had learned to live with it, like a benign growth of some sort. Then, three months ago, I discovered that my secret had far more frightful consequences than I ever imagined. That my guilt is far greater than my capacity for rationalization.

And my skill at deception is crumbling.

Beyond this, I have an irrational feeling that my secret has taken on a life of its own—that it is *trying to get out.* It flutters at the edge of Patrick's consciousness, polishes the fine blade of Drewe's mistrust. I sometimes wonder whether she knows already but lives in a denial based on fear even greater than mine. Is this possible? No. Drewe could not know this thing and not *act.* Look at her, sitting in the black iron lawn chair, speaking with calm authority, words precise, back straight, green eyes focused.

Erin joins hands with Holly as they dance across the grass, now closer, now farther away. They spin like dervishes in the August heat. The drone of medico-political conversation presses against my eardrums, blending with the sound of Bob's bees in Bob's bushes.

Comparing Drewe and Erin now, I see beyond the physical. Their innermost differences are stark, essential. They can be divided by single words: Drewe is control, Erin chaos. Drewe is achievement, Erin accident. Erin's eyes catch mine for the briefest instant. I try to blank my mind, to shake my preoccupation and smile.

But I cannot.

She spins more slowly, her eyes catching mine each time she turns. What is in those eyes? Compassion? I believe so. In these fleeting moments I sense an intimacy of such painful intensity that it seems almost in danger of arcing between us—of ionizing the air dividing our eyes and bodies and letting that which resides separately in both our souls unite, as someday it inevitably must. What is this power that burns so for unity? That threatens to declare itself without invitation? What is it but the truth? A knowledge that Erin and I alone possess, of *things as they really are.*

And what is the truth of things as they really are?

Holly Graham is my daughter.

Chapter 9

"Did you sense something wrong with Patrick?" asks Drewe.

We are already five miles from her parents' house, rolling down the two-lane blacktop toward our farm, which is still ten miles away. With every mile we cover, my anxiety lessens.

"No," I answer. "He seemed like his usual weekend self. Glad to be away from the hospital, wishing he was playing golf instead of sitting at your parents' house."

Drewe clicks her tongue. "I think he and Erin are having problems."

"What?" I say a little too sharply. In fact, I know Erin and Patrick are having problems. "They seemed fine to me."

Drewe looks at me, but thankfully her gaze is only on half power. "I guess you're right. Sometimes I just get the feeling that Erin's new life—her domesticity, I mean—is really just a front. That in her mind she never really left New York and all that other stuff behind."

"New life? It's been three years, Drewe. That's a lot of commitment just for an act."

She smiles. "You're right. God, Holly gets more beautiful every week, doesn't she?"

"She sure does."

"And Erin's so good with her. Did you hear her jump

on Daddy about his racism? I think she really embarrassed him."

"Impossible."

She punches me on the shoulder. "I was pretty impressed with you, too."

"What do you mean?"

"You had Holly wrapped around your finger."

Here it comes.

"You know," she says—and despite her effort to sound as casual as she did a moment ago, I detect the tonal change—"I've been off the pill over five months now."

I know exactly how long she has been off the pill. I can trace the date by the fight we had when she made this unilateral decision. My wife is not one to equivocate. When she decides on a goal, she takes the shortest path to it. In her mind, the time has come for us to have children. If I am opposed, it must be because I'm nostalgically clinging to my irresponsible youth, which is pointless. Neither of us ever liked using a condom or anything else during sex; thus, she assumed that when she stopped taking the pill it would be only a matter of weeks until she conceived.

The first four months were the grace period required for the artificial hormones to be purged from her system. At that time she had a vested interest—genetic—in keeping our sexual contact to a minimum. But we are at the five-and-a-half-month mark now, and despite her confidence in my uncontrollable lust, Drewe has yet to conceive. This is not due to a flaw in her judgment of my character. It's just that she forgot to reckon EROS into her calculations. The computer forums—and certain women on them—have proved to be a vicarious but satisfactory outlet for my sexual energy. I think Drewe suspects this, and it accounts for her bitter resentment of the time I spend sysoping the forum.

"You love Holly so much," she says, and I feel her

looking right at me. "I can see it. I don't understand why you don't want a child of your own."

"I do want one," I say truthfully. "I want two."

"But what? Just not yet? Harper, I'm thirty-three. At thirty-five, the odds for Down's syndrome and a hundred other things go up dramatically."

As neutrally as possible, I say, "We've had this discussion before, Drewe."

The temperature in the car drops ten degrees. "And now we're having it again."

When I don't respond, she sighs and looks out at the dusty cotton fields drifting by. The ocean of white covers the land as far as the eye can see. "I know I'm pressuring you," she says in measured tones, "but I just don't understand your reasoning."

And I hope you never will.

After a silent mile, she says, "Are we ever going to make love again?"

As if the situation isn't complicated enough. Five minutes after discussing having children and being off the pill, she makes a sexual overture that by her tone I am supposed to interpret as passion?

"I do actually miss it, you know," she says, looking straight through the windshield.

"Me too," I murmur. What else can I say?

"Doubting my motives?"

I can tell by her voice that she has turned to face me again. Hearing a rustle of cloth, I look across the seat. Drewe has opened her blouse. Her bra attaches at the front, and she opens that too. Twice in the past month, advances like this have led to serious arguments. However, her nipples confirm her tone of voice. Maybe this is an honest approach.

She turns sideways in her seat, lifts one bare foot over the Explorer's console, and lets it fall into my lap. She is very good with that foot. Giggling like a schoolgirl, she manages to unfasten the belt, snap, and zipper of my jeans.

"Obviously you miss it too," she says.

"They teach you that in medical school? In case you have a hand injury?"

"Mmm-hm. We practiced on interns. The young, handsome ones."

"Okay, okay."

In one smooth motion she hitches up her sundress and climbs over the console. Then, facing me, she plants a foot on either side of my seat and lowers herself between my body and the steering wheel. I glance away from the road long enough to see her pull aside her white cotton panties and slide effortlessly down onto me.

The sudden grating of gravel under the right front tire tells me we are going off the road. I jerk the wheel left and look up, then floor the accelerator and whip around a mammoth green cotton picker. Drewe is laughing and kissing my neck and pressing down harder.

"Jesus, you're ruthless," I tell her.

"You can pull out," she whispers.

Sure.

We have been home less than ten minutes when the telephone rings. It is Bob Anderson.

"Did we leave something over there?" I ask, feeling my back pocket for my wallet.

"Nothing like that." Bob falls silent. After ten seconds or so, I ask him if anything's wrong.

"I don't know, Harp," he drawls. "But fifteen minutes after you left the house, Bill Buckner called."

"The Yazoo County sheriff?"

"Right. He told me—strictly as a favor—that he got several long-distance calls last night and again today. Calls about you."

Shit. "Me?"

Bob gives me more of the silent treatment. I blink first. "Look, Dr. Anderson, I can probably guess what this is about."

He offers nothing.

"We've had a little trouble on the EROS network."

"Trouble."

"There's been a murder."

"More'n one, from what Bill says. Bad, too."

Drewe is staring at me inquisitively. "Look, Dr. Anderson, I met with the New Orleans police yesterday, and I'm pretty sure everything's under control."

"Bill said a couple of the calls were from the FBI."

"I met with them too."

Bob mulls this over. At length he says, "Harper, do you need help, son?"

"Thanks, Dr. Anderson, but I really think everything's under control."

"I know a lot of people," he says in a voice that makes it clear he does not like talking this way. "In a lot of places."

"I'm sure you do. And if there was real trouble, you'd be the first person I'd call."

Bob waits some more, then says, "Well, I guess you know best," in a tone that says he guesses anything but that. "You keep me posted, son."

"I'll do that."

"And you take care of my little girl."

"Yes, sir."

I hang up.

"Your dad," I tell Drewe.

"What is it?"

"He's worried. The Yazoo County sheriff called him. Buckner's been getting calls from the FBI, asking about me."

Drewe shakes her head, her eyes locked on mine.

"God. Harper, do they actually think you're involved in these murders?"

"I don't know. Miles and I are two of only nine people who have access to the real identities of EROS subscribers. Anybody who has that access is a suspect until they can prove they're innocent."

"That shouldn't be hard for you."

"For three of the murders, no. And with your help, I hope I can prove it for all of them."

"What do you mean? You're always here with me. When did these murders happen?"

"I don't know exactly. They started about a year ago. Most happened within the last nine months. The problem is that for the past few months you and I haven't been spending that much time together."

Drewe looks away quickly. She is an intensely private person, and I know she is wondering what I told the police about our relationship. "Harper, damn you." She closes her hand around my wrist. "No matter what's going on between us, I'm your alibi. Don't you know that?"

"Thank you. But the cops won't necessarily believe you."

"I'll make them believe me."

This from a woman who has told women her mother's age that they have less than a year to live, friends that their newborn babies are deformed or dying. The certainty in her voice is powerful enough to resuscitate my flagging confidence, possibly even enough to sway a jury, if not the FBI.

"Thank you," I say again, trying to distance my mind from the idea of police questioning Drewe. "Your dad offered to use his connections if we need them."

"He must really be upset."

"He's just worried about you. Does he really have connections high enough to help in something like this?"

She shrugs. “He knows the governor. Can a state governor influence the FBI?”

I shake my head. “I don’t know. Let’s hope we never have to find out.”

She goes to the refrigerator and pulls out a lemon pie that a churchy Baptist neighbor brought over yesterday. Drewe was raised Methodist, but since she rarely attends church, her Baptist patients never cease trying to pull her into their fold. They know I’m a hopeless case. Drewe and I attack the pie for a couple of minutes in silence, more than making up for the calories we burned in the truck.

“This is sinful,” she mumbles through a huge bite of pale yellow filling. She always scoops out the filling and leaves the crust.

“Praise God,” I manage to reply in a mocking mushmouth.

She flicks her fork at me, plopping a piece of meringue onto my cheek. When she laughs, her eyes sparkle like stars, and in that moment I feel the weight of my secret lift from my shoulders just long enough to sense the lightness of peace.

Then something closes around my heart with suffocating power. It’s like a Chinese torture: the better things are, the worse they are.

“What’s the matter?” Drewe is studying me as she might a patient having a sudden stroke.

“Nothing. I just remembered something I need to take care of. A couple of long positions in Singapore. Boring but necessary.”

“Oh.”

The realization that tomorrow is a workday instantly manifests itself throughout her frame. Her shoulders hunch slightly, her eyelids fall, she sighs with resignation. But more dispiriting than work is the realization that our unusual moment of closeness is over.

"I'm whipped," she says. "You coming to bed?"

I shake my head, averting my eyes. "I'd better check the Singapore Exchange."

She looks long enough to let me know she knows I am at least partially lying. Then she turns and walks toward the bedroom.

I move quickly toward my office.

I've got to talk to Miles.

Chapter 10

When I check my e-mail, I find two messages from Miles. I click the mouse and open the first. Seeing the length of the text, I push ALT-V to activate the most unique feature on my EROS computer—its voice.

The first time I heard EROS speak I felt strange. Then I realized it was not the first time I had heard a computer talk. The telephone company's computers had been talking to me for years. I had toyed with digital sampling keyboards that could exactly reproduce anything from a thundering bass to a contralto soprano. The voice chip inside the EROS computer is similar. However, it is not voice-recognition technology. Getting a computer to verbalize text displayed on its screen is relatively simple. Getting one to recognize millions of different voices speaking with hundreds of different accents—even in one language—is currently taxing the best brains in the R & D departments of the world's top high-tech firms.

EROS cannot hear.

But it does talk. Its voice can take on any pitch between twenty and twenty thousand hertz, which is slightly superfluous since my multimedia speakers bottom out at around one hundred, and my rock-and-roll-damaged eardrums probably top out at ten thousand. Also, the pitch versatility is misleading. EROS's voice is not unlike Drewe's when she is dictating charts. Whether I select a baritone or tenor frequency, the words will be repeated at that single pitch—a perfect monotone—until the listener believes he is trapped inside the tin-can robot from *Lost in Space.* And vocal monotony is not conducive to sexual fantasy unless your idea of hot sex is having an interspecies relationship with a machine.

EROS's voice program does have what's called a "lexical stress" feature, but it sucks. It makes the voice sound like a saxophone played by a drunk who accents all the wrong notes. A couple of months ago Miles sent me a package containing circuit boards he claimed would give my computer not only a better voice, but also the Holy Grail: voice-recognition capability. Naturally, those circuit boards are still sealed inside their antistatic bags in the box they came in. For my purpose—listening to lengthy e-mail messages—the droning digital voice EROS already has is good enough.

Scanning Miles's messages, I set the frequency to a medium baritone—Miles's register—and lie down on the twin bed to listen.

Hello, snitch. Here's an update from Serial Killer Central. I've finally met the elusive Dr. Arthur Lenz, and I am impressed (though not as impressed as he is with himself).

If you don't already know (and how could you?) there is a massive bureaucratic battle afoot between the FBI and the various police departments involved in what they are vulgarly calling the "EROS murders." (Is "vulgarly" a word? I defer to the grammarians on that.) The instinct of the police (I use "police" collectively for Houston, San Francisco, New Orleans, Minneapolis, et al.) is to shut down EROS for the foreseeable future. This is obviously short-term thinking. They apparently believe that shutting us down will keep "Strobekker" (whoever he really is) off the playing field. The FBI (read Lenz) quite rightly understands that shutting down EROS will only send our predator to greener pastures—or at least different ones. I give Lenz credit for understanding that the digital fields of the Lord are quite expansive, and that our beast at play is well versed in traveling them.

Segue: while writing this I have recalled a bit of high school Emerson.

If the red slayer thinks he slays
Or if the slain thinks he is slain
They know not well the subtle paths
I keep, and pass, and turn again

From "Brahma" I believe. Come to think of it, from now on, when I refer to the killer, I shall call him Brahma. "Strobekker" makes me picture a pasty-faced Minnesotan of Swedish descent, killing with the same knife he uses during the graveyard shift at the meat-packing plant.

I think Lenz plans to lure Brahma to his destruction by somehow manipulating our network. The police argue the obvious: that every minute EROS is up and running is another minute women are at risk. But Lenz has used your session printouts to good advantage. He points out that Brahma not only has a recognizable prose style online, but also that his messages, which are error-free for eighty-five percent of the exchanges with his victims, become full of errors as the dates of the murders approach. Lenz didn't know why that might be, so I decided to throw him a bone. I think Brahma is using an advanced voice-recognition unit, which allows him to simply speak his words rather than type them. Maybe he works for a computer company and has access to prototype equipment. A unit like that might not be easily portable, and he probably couldn't use it remotely because of cellular dropouts. So when he takes his show on the road, he's got to type like everybody else.

Anyway, Lenz realized that the FBI can use this

"error-rate flag" as an early-warning system to know when Brahma is on the move and women are in imminent danger. He also points out that except for Karin Wheat, only women on the blind-draft billing system have been killed so far. This group represents a significant but minority number of total female subscribers, approximately twenty-three percent. Five hundred seventy-eight women.

Lenz also argues that allowing Brahma to continue on EROS will give the FBI time to track him through the phone lines, which Agent Baxter assures both Jan and myself will be but a matter of a day or two. The local police departments seem to have a lot of faith in this argument and will probably relent. Bureaucratic panic always gives weight to the quick-fix solution. But I don't share Baxter's faith in the phone-trace strategy. Brahma has been killing women for some time. He had enough forethought to murder a man for his online identity. Surely he realized that the day would come when the police would attempt to trace him to his lair by phone. N'est-ce pas?

I have my own theories about Brahma's modus operandi, but I choose not to share them with Lenz at this point. The time may come when I need bargaining chips with this man.

Ciao.

Hearing Miles's flamboyant e-mail style repeated by a mindless android voice is singularly unsettling. Yet even through the insectile drone, I heard one thing distinctly: Miles Turner is having fun.

His second message is much briefer.

The Strobekker account went active under the alias "Shiva" at 7:42 p.m. Baxter's techs traced the call from our office through a couple of Internet nodes in the Midwest to New Jersey, through a transatlantic satellite to

London, then back into New Jersey. By that time he'd dropped off. They're pulling out the stops, and they're faster at it than I thought possible, but they don't know much more than they did before they started. The atmosphere is like Mission Impossible—a bunch of guys in suits and ties playing with gadgets. Do you think Brahma wears a tie?

Ciao.

I roll off the bed and sit down at the EROS computer. Feeling more than a little paranoid, I print out hard copies of Miles's messages, then delete them from the computer's memory. Part of me wants to log on to Level Three and lurk in the background, searching for traces of Strobekker or Shiva or Brahma or whoever he is. But something has been itching at the back of my brain since I talked to the FBI. Ever since I realized Baxter and Lenz might leave EROS up and running despite the fact that women are in danger. I have friends on EROS. More than friends. And no matter what Miles or Jan or the FBI think is prudent, I have a duty to warn those people.

My closest friend on EROS is a woman who calls herself Eleanor Rigby. Her choice of alias was probably influenced by one of the stranger informal customs that has developed on EROS. For some reason, wild or obscure code names like "Electric Blue" or "Leather Bitch" or "Phiber Phreak"—so common on other networks—were absent on EROS from the beginning. It wasn't company policy to discourage them, but somehow a loose convention evolved and was enforced by community consensus, more a matter of style than anything else. Apparently EROS subscribers prefer their correspondents to possess actual names for aliases, rather than surreal quasi-identities. All in all I think this has benefited the network; it has kept things more human.

The interesting thing is that while outlandish noms de

plume are discouraged, the practice of assuming names made famous by literary, musical, or film works is very popular. I frequently see messages addressed from Holden Caulfield to Smilla Jaspersen, from the Marquis de Sade to Oscar Wilde, or from Elvis Presley to Polythene Pam. Moreover, it seems that at least some of the subscribers choose their famous (or infamous) pseudonyms to fit their own personalities. In the case of "Eleanor Rigby"—an alias that belongs to a woman named Eleanor Caine Markham—I'm positive the name was chosen out of a deep affinity for the character in the Beatles song. Eleanor Markham is a moderately successful mystery writer from Los Angeles who, except for a second job, rarely leaves her house. The same melancholy sense of loneliness that pervades the Lennon-McCartney tune shadows more than a few of her messages.

Yet Eleanor's second job seems wholly out of character with this first image. To supplement her income, she sometimes works as a body double for major actresses who have reached that exalted status where they do not have to agree to remove their clothes on-screen to win roles. I know it's sexist, but I always imagined women who had these jobs as airheaded blondes with exquisite bodies but common faces who spent their days at the spa working on their legs and abs or at their plastic surgeon's getting their boobs reinflated. I have never seen Eleanor Markham's face—her mystery novels carry no jacket photos—but everything I have learned about her confirms an opposite truth. When Eleanor is not exposing her derriere or breasts or whatever for the camera, she is sitting in her Santa Monica beach house writing very literate, wry whodunits or talking to anonymous friends via her computer.

Her explanation for these seemingly contradictory lifestyles is that she has a sister who is confined to a wheelchair for life by spinal injuries received in a traffic accident. Eleanor feels her sacred duty is to take care of this sister as her parents would have, were they still alive. I cannot fault her reasoning.

All that said, let me confess the obvious: Eleanor Rigby is my online lover. My digital squeeze. What do I know about her other than what I've already revealed? She is thirty years old. She has never had plastic surgery. She describes her face not as plain but as "real"—more Audrey Hepburn than Michelle Pfeiffer, but not as ethereal as Audrey. She has a wit like a razor and she is uniquely gifted at describing sex in words.

She is also generous. Eleanor knows that two-way conversations are fine for foreplay but that typing requires the use of at least one hand. Thus, when she is getting me off, she is quite willing to type endless lines of charged erotica until the moment that I signal her with a relieved and heartfelt banality such as: *Wow.*

I return the favor in a different way.

Eleanor does not usually stimulate herself while online. She prefers that I compose lengthy e-mail messages that she can print out and peruse free from any constraints on time or dexterity. I'm sure the proximity of her disabled sister has something to do with this. This is also why Eleanor is registered to EROS on a blind-draft account. She apparently reads many of my printed messages while locked in the bath.

Tonight I query her the moment I log on. Eleanor frequently lurks in silence, eavesdropping on the conversations of others (searching for material for her novels, she tells me) and so is often present when I send out my usual query. I type:

HARPER> Father MacKenzie calling.

Eleanor is the only EROS client with whom I use my real name. There is a delay of thirty seconds or so, then:

ELEANOR RIGBY> Hello, Harper dear. What are you in the mood for?
HARPER> I need to talk to you.
ELEANOR RIGBY> Talk as in _talk_? <g>

(The <g> symbol stands for "grin." The lines preceding and following a word indicate emphasis, in place of italics.)

HARPER> Yes, just talk. Meet me in Room 64.
ELEANOR RIGBY> Hmm. I guess the little woman talked you into it this week, eh?

Yes, like a corporeal mistress, Eleanor knows my marital situation. Some of it, anyway. With a twinge of guilt I mouse into the private room designated Room 64 and type:

HARPER> No present erection, thank you.
ELEANOR RIGBY> Too bad. Should I sharpen up my pencil?
HARPER> No. This is serious.
ELEANOR RIGBY> How ominous. Is this a Dear John letter?
HARPER> No.
ELEANOR RIGBY> Well, then?
HARPER> You must keep what I am about to tell you absolutely between us.
ELEANOR RIGBY> My lips are sealed. And if you make a horrid male pun I shall disconnect.
HARPER> You're in danger, Eleanor.

She doesn't respond for several beats.

ELEANOR RIGBY> What kind of danger?
HARPER> Physical danger. There's been

I am typing, but suddenly nothing is going through to Eleanor. I stare at the screen in puzzlement until this message appears in large block letters:

SHAME ON YOU, SNITCH

My puzzlement turns to fury. This message can only be from Miles, and its sudden insertion into my private chat with Eleanor tells me something that makes my blood boil. *Miles has the ability to read my private communications whenever he pleases.* I blink as further characters appear.

SORRY TO INTRUDE
BUT WE CAN'T HAVE YOU
SCARING THE PAYING CUSTOMERS
LOOSE CANNON AND ALL THAT
PLEASE FIND SOME OTHER WAY TO GET
ELEANOR
OFF THE NET
IF YOU MUST
CIAO

The next words that appear are:

ELEANOR RIGBY> What just happened?

She must not have seen Miles's message. I type:

HARPER> A glitch in my modem.

What now? Do I ignore Miles? Go ahead and warn Eleanor and a few others? My anger says yes. But what will be the result? A network-wide panic, probably. Eleanor and I are very close, but she has a writer's imagination and love of drama. Could she really keep secret the possibility that there is a murderer stalking the female clients of EROS?

ELEANOR RIGBY> You said I was in danger. Physical danger. What were you talking about?

HARPER> You misunderstood. That was the start of a fantasy file I wrote for you this morning. It was sort of a Mata Hari thing, spies and sex, with you in the lead role.

ELEANOR RIGBY> Well if that's the case, send it through!

HARPER> My modem's on the blink. Pretty embarrassing for the sysop, isn't it? I'll have it fixed by tomorrow. I'll put the file through then. Sorry to interrupt you for nothing.

ELEANOR RIGBY> Wait, Harper. I hate to confess this, but knowing you don't need me right now makes me need you. Could you possibly conjure up some stimulating prose for a lonely 30-year-old spinster with an itch?

HARPER> You mean real-time?

ELEANOR RIGBY> Yes.

HARPER> Unusual for you. How stimulating?

ELEANOR RIGBY> My sister is at a film with her one friend. I have the house all to my selfish self. Please make it hot enough for an online conclusion; i.e. once we get to the good stuff, please don't stop until I signal with a shriek of ecstasy.

I pause, trying to rein in my thoughts. I honestly don't feel like this tonight. Especially after Drewe and I had our actual-reality interlude in the Explorer. But Eleanor has done me this favor many nights.

HARPER> Romantic or dangerous?

ELEANOR RIGBY> Romantic _and_ dangerous.

HARPER> All right. We are finally meeting face to face. Seeing each other for the first time.

ELEANOR RIGBY> Where?

HARPER> The Peabody Hotel. Memphis, Tennessee. We're in the lobby, a huge open room with a bar and a grand piano and ducks and tons of atmosphere.

ELEANOR RIGBY> _Ducks_?

HARPER> Symbol of the hotel. Trust me.

ELEANOR RIGBY> Oh, I do.

HARPER> I'm not as handsome as you have imagined me, but you aren't disappointed. I have a certain power over you that you didn't expect. You want to please me, and this makes you a little angry. You understand?

ELEANOR RIGBY> Perfectly. What do you think of me?

HARPER> Mercy fuck.

ELEANOR RIGBY> Harper!

HARPER> Sorry. ;) You're more beautiful than I imagined. Your body-double's body was a given, but your symmetry still surprises me. Petite, and your face more feminine than I could envision.

ELEANOR RIGBY> Feminine how?

HARPER> The blend of curve and angle. Softs and hards. Cheek and jaw. Defined brows, nebulous eyes. Dusk is falling on the Memphis streets, over the river. Yellow lamps come up inside and light you like a painter's hand.

ELEANOR RIGBY> What am I wearing?

HARPER> White linen. Appropriate for a deflowering.

ELEANOR RIGBY> You give me far too much credit. <g>

HARPER> I intend to boldly go where no man has gone before.

ELEANOR RIGBY> Dare I ask?

HARPER> No.

ELEANOR RIGBY> Yummy.

HARPER> I see shadows of your nipples through the linen. They look more brown than pink.

ELEANOR RIGBY> How do you like my breasts?

HARPER> Champagne-glass size, exquisitely shaped.

ELEANOR RIGBY> What do we talk about?

HARPER> Inanities.

ELEANOR RIGBY> How long do we talk?

HARPER> Not very. We've said all we have to say on EROS, haven't we?

ELEANOR RIGBY> Do we diddle under the table? Victorian teasing?

HARPER> No. I sign the suite number on the bill and lead you by the hand across the high-ceilinged lobby to the bank of elevators. In the elevator we kiss for the first time.

ELEANOR RIGBY> A long kiss?

HARPER> When the door opens, we're still kissing. An older couple is staring at us like we are crazy.

ELEANOR RIGBY> I'm already wet.

HARPER> Not yet.

ELEANOR RIGBY> I'm speaking in the present tense, dear. Off-line.

HARPER> Fine, but we're not going to rush. When the stupid credit card key finally works, I pull you inside the room but do not turn on the light.

ELEANOR RIGBY> We haven't been in the suite until now?

HARPER> No. Before you can say anything, I close the door and slip past you in the darkness, pulling my shoes off as I walk. You call out to me, but I don't answer. I hear you bang your foot into a chair. You curse. We're going to play a game, I say. What kind of game? you ask.

I stop typing for a few moments, letting the images flow freely in my head.

HARPER> A hunting game, I reply. I'm going to hunt you in the dark suite. And the first rule is: we can't talk to each other. Even when I find you, we cannot speak. And there's another catch. I should have mentioned it earlier, but . . . well . . . there's another person in the room.

What? you ask nervously. Who?

Don't be frightened. He—or she—is standing silently—or sitting—somewhere in the room, but only watching. How, you ask? Simple. He's wearing a night-vision headset I brought to the hotel during the afternoon. You giggle nervously, but I'm not joking. This person can see us right now and will watch us when I finally find you.

You don't believe me? Let down the top of your dress.

A few seconds later, a whispered voice from across the room says, Beautiful.

I can almost feel your heart stutter from the shock. Stay calm, I say reassuringly. This person is merely an observer.

All right, you stammer, far from your normally confident self. But who is it? you wonder. Who _is_ it?

Maybe it's your sister, I say.

You bastard, you hiss.

Maybe it's a bellboy I paid a hundred bucks to come upstairs and watch a beautiful woman having sex. Do you want to go on? I ask.

Yes, you say softly.

Even if you are seen?

I can do anything in the dark, you say. Even if the whole city is watching.

And so we begin the hunt. How do you feel now?

ELEANOR RIGBY> >toi bbusy otype<

HARPER> Please do your best to evade me, I tell you. But you should know that I'll be getting a bit of direction from our guest. He/she will whisper "warmer" or "colder" every so often.

You do not answer.

And so I begin the hunt.

The first thing I hear is silence. Blood beating in my ears. The suite is large. I move deeper into the bedroom to give you room to move. Then I wait motionless for two minutes. I sense you becoming more tense with each passing second. You cannot hear me. Very softly I remove my clothes. I feel the air along my body, especially on the places usually covered. I go down on all fours, allowing my body to cover more floor space, increasing my odds of touching you if you try to slip past me. I move slowly at first.

Colder, whispers our guest.

I change direction. Where _are_ you? I ask in a singsong voice.

Warmer, says our guest.

Instinct tells me my back is a few feet from the far corner of the room. You are not behind me. Slowly and soundlessly I work my way across the carpet, pausing occasionally to listen and to try to feel any movement of air against my skin.

Nothing.

There's not much floor space left to cover. Could you have climbed onto one of the beds? No. I'd have heard you.

Wait. A rustle of cloth ahead of me. A few feet away.

Is she naked? I ask.

No reply.

I freeze. There is water running in the bathroom, the sound like a distant cataract in the silence. I rise and move quickly toward the sound—too quickly—and bash my head against the door frame. I'm in the bathroom now, but you aren't. Steam coats my face and body like jungle humidity. When I reach to shut off the tap, I scald my hand. Yet even as I curse, I realize I smell you. In the blackness. The female smell. Strongly enough that I suspect you have left this as a calling card.

This is not turning out the way I'd planned.

As I move out of the bathroom, something swishes past me in the dark. Strangely, it seemed larger than me. Then I hear the bathroom door close. I try the handle but it's locked. Are you really inside? Or is this a diversion?

Where is she? I ask the darkness.

No answer.

Warmer or colder? I ask.

Nothing.

Then, through the bathroom door, I hear new sounds. A woman, softly moaning. A man rhythmically groaning. First I think you are teasing me. Confused, I feel my way to the wall and break a rule. Switch on the light.

My assistant is gone.

The noises are louder. It sounds as though you are using my draftee in the bathroom and have locked me out. This isn't what I had in mind at all, but you sound like you're having the time of your life. I ask what you are doing but he answers insolently, She can't talk with her mouth full. Suddenly I am angry. I kick the door twice near the knob and it splinters open, flooding the bathroom with light. At first glance I feel relief, seeing that you still have your linen dress on. But a millisecond later the positions register: you're sitting on the edge of the tub and you have your hand around him and are working diligently (though your eyes are locked on mine) and he seems very close to release. It's the least I could do for him, you say, but what you're really saying is that you have no intention of letting me manipulate you with some kinky game like this, and I'm standing there with a stupid look on my face while you finish him and he groans and you look into my eyes with barefaced defiance while he squirts copiously and again and you run your hands under the bath tap while he slips out the door of the room but not before he gives me a look like, You must be an idiot to share this lady with _anybody_. And then you lift the linen dress over your head and say, Take me to the bed, please.

So I do. This is finally lovemaking, as you are.

ELEANOR RIGBY> :) Shriek of ecstasy. I'm done. I know that was quick, but I was reading some pretty steamy threads before you queried. At least your fingers won't be too sore.

HARPER> I was just getting to the good part. The part I've really fantasized about.

ELEANOR RIGBY> Sorry. You shouldn't have let me near that insolent voyeur/bellboy/stranger. He was huge in my hand, by the way. I don't like

that in intercourse, FYI, but since I was merely servicing him manually, I liked that my hand wouldn't nearly go all the way around the thickest part of him.

HARPER> You're embellishing my scenario.

ELEANOR RIGBY> Certainly, dear. Don't feel threatened. He was huge, but dumb as a doorpost—as well as being hard as one. <g>

HARPER> Feeling better, I take it?

ELEANOR RIGBY> Lovely. Although I consider that subject sacred, to be honest.

HARPER> What?

ELEANOR RIGBY> Our first f2f meeting. I would never want a third person present for that.

HARPER> Sorry if I tainted your fantasy. I should have realized.

ELEANOR RIGBY> No, it's fine. But you are my secret friend, Harper. That is sacred to me. You have no idea.

HARPER> I do have an idea, Eleanor. You know that.

ELEANOR> Well, don't be a stranger. It was too long between rendezvous this time. Meet me tomorrow.

HARPER> We'll talk soon. And alone this time.

ELEANOR> I like that better. Bye.

HARPER> Bye.

I thrust my chair away from the keyboard and focus on the sculpture of my father's coat. Why *would* I thrust someone between myself and Eleanor like that? I suddenly want to warn her again, but I know Miles is looking over my virtual shoulder.

And then I realize something very disturbing.

The bellboy in the bathroom was Miles.

What the hell is going on in my brain? And how long has that son of a bitch been spying on my e-mail? *Everything's under control,* I hear myself saying to Bob Anderson.

Who do I think I'm kidding?

I've been lying in bed less than five minutes when it hits me: Miles has made a far more serious mistake than reading my e-mail. And I've got to tell him about it. It's an hour later in New York, but I don't really give a damn. He's usually awake all night anyway, monitoring Level Three.

After four rings, he answers "Turner" in a voice that makes it clear he does not like being bothered by mere human beings.

"How long have you been spying on my e-mail, shithead?"

I hear a soft laugh. "Don't worry. I hardly ever look. But since you started talking to the FBI, I figured you might be getting antsy about warning some of your online friends. Which you definitely do not need to do. They're in no danger."

"We'll skip that argument for now. I want to know *how* you've been reading my mail. I've never been able to access yours."

Another laugh. "But you tried, right? There are a couple of system privileges you don't have, Harper. One is called super-postmaster. It's like the postmaster privilege, but it gives you access to sysop mail as well. Even Jan's mail."

"What if Strobekker got the victims' real names by hacking into a sysop account? Into super-postmaster?"

Miles hesitates. "I don't think that's possible. But I'm still assessing the system. It would have taken only one deep penetration to get the master client list, and it could have happened months ago. That makes forensic analysis of the disks very difficult."

"But you don't know it was only one penetration. If he's in the system now, and he has the super-postmaster privilege, that means he could have read your messages to me, which would tell him the FBI was onto him."

There is a long silence. "Brahma is *not* in the system now. But even if he were, he could only have read my messages during the interval between my posting them and your picking them up. Unless you saved them to a file. Did you do that?"

"No. I printed hard copies and deleted them."

"What time did you do that?"

"Just before I talked to Eleanor."

"So stop worrying. And get off my case. All it would take is *basic* postmaster for Brahma to read your warning to Eleanor."

Miles is right. "You just stop looking over my shoulder, goddamn it."

"I can't guarantee that."

At least he's honest. "Miles, I want the super-postmaster privilege and any others I don't know about."

"I can't give you that. Jan has already blocked your access to the accounting database."

"What?"

"What did you expect, Harper?"

"Listen to me. If Strobekker or Brahma or whoever is still roaming our system, I've got to know I can see everything he can. If I can't, I'm off EROS as of now."

"Let me think about it. The FBI phone traces are going nowhere, but I've been going back over some of Brahma's old e-mail—"

"How did you get that?"

"I pulled it out of your computer."

"What?"

"Don't get your panties in a wad. It was necessary. I've got other sources too. The thing is, Brahma's using an anonymous remailer for his e-mail."

"What does that mean in practical terms?"

"Regular e-mail is traceable. You can look at the packet headers and get a user name, or at least take back-bearings and get a rough physical location. But Brahma doesn't use the EROS-mail feature. He sends his e-mail to our servers via the anonymous remailer, which is in Finland, and then through the Internet. The remailer strips off his address and adds a random one. I spoke to its operator about a half hour ago."

"Have you told the FBI?"

"Oh sure, we're like Boris and Natasha here, man."

"Can they get info on Brahma from the remailing service?"

"There's a precedent for getting cooperation from the police in some countries in extreme cases, but the guy who runs this service sounded like a wild man. A real anarchist. He's probably destroying all his records right now."

"That's why Brahma chose him."

"Obviously. Brahma's a clever boy, Harper. Too clever for Baxter's techs, I fear." Miles is clearly enjoying himself. "We've still got FBI agents camped out up here. They're guarding our file vault like it's the tomb of Christ, waiting for the time lock to open and give them the master client list."

"Great. Now we're back to where we were when you changed the subject. Give me the super-postmaster privilege or I'm shutting down my EROS interface."

He doesn't answer for some time. Then he says, "Type S-I-D-D-H-A-R-T-H-A after your password at the sysop prompt. Got it?"

"Siddhartha as in the Herman Hesse novel?"

"As in the Buddha. But that's close enough."

"I think you've gone weird on me, man."

"I always was, Harper. You know that. *Ciao.*"

And he is gone.

I sit thinking in the soft glow of the EROS screen.

Siddhartha? Brahma?

I don't know or care much about Eastern religions, but Miles certainly seems to. And though I do not know the significance of this, or whether it has significance at all, I am suddenly reminded of Drewe's speculation about Oriental medicine and the use of bizarre trophies to restore vitality. I always related such things to Japan, and Buddha fits with Japan, though the Buddha himself was Indian. Brahma and Shiva make me think of India too. I remember from my meeting in New Orleans that the only murder victim who was not Caucasian was Indian. Also that an Indian hair was found at one of the crime scenes. I see no tangible links between these facts, yet I know too well that my knowledge of such things does not even rate as sketchy. They could easily be connected just beyond my myopic mental vision.

Life would be much simpler if the FBI could follow a trail of digital bread crumbs back to the lair of the killer. But Miles has little faith that this will happen, and something tells me he is right. That we have yet to make out even the silhouette of the creature behind these murders.

I hunted when I was a boy. I gave it up the day my cousin put four Number 6 shotgun pellets into my right calf. It was a late February afternoon, and we'd gotten separated. I was following what I thought was a rabbit into a thicket. My cousin heard a noise and thought fate had handed him an out-of-season deer. I don't blame him for shooting. Five seconds later and I might have shot him. Neither of us could see what we were after. That's the way it goes sometimes. But I've often wondered what would have happened had it been something other than rabbits we were chasing. A bear, say. Something that would have seen me lying there bleeding on the ground and come over to finish the job. That's the way it goes sometimes too. It all depends on the quarry you choose to hunt.

Chapter II

Dear Father,

Panikkar telephoned early this morning, saying he had to see me. I feared the worst, and I was not far wrong. When he arrived I was in the basement, settling Jenny in. After I came up, I found him waiting in the study with Kali. Panikkar told me that he and Bhagat had "endured all they could"—his words. I expected next to hear him say that he had gone to the police, who would arrive at any minute.

How wrong I was. Instead of delivering a sermon of moral outrage, he demanded more money. He must have thought I was ripe for fleecing, with the procedure so close. The mendacity of man is his undoing. I was prepared to pay, but when Panikkar mentioned the amount it stunned me. As I tried to explain my position, I saw movement in the shadows behind him. Like a mantis Kali swung her thin brown arm over his shoulder and plunged her dagger into his belly.

There was nothing I could do. It was plain from the spray that the first stroke had pierced the abdominal descending aorta. Before I could utter three sentences she had eviscerated him, while Panikkar stared at his butchered belly in horror.

True to her namesake, Kali removed his head and hung it by the hair from her belt. I realized how dangerous this development was, of course, but it was oddly satisfying after all Panikkar's grousing. Thank God it was him, rather than Bhagat. Anesthesia is a nice luxury, especially for the patient. In future I can do the typing myself.

I feared that when Panikkar did not contact Bhagat with news of our meeting, Bhagat would go to the police. But Kali knew what to do. She called Bhagat and told him the procedure would be performed tonight as planned. Bhagat asked to speak to Panikkar, but Kali told him Panikkar was busy with me in the basement. She said Bhagat could collect the bonus that Panikkar had negotiated, but only after the procedure was completed. When Bhagat expressed anxiety, Kali told him to park outside the rear door. Panikkar would assure him that all was well.

When Bhagat pulled up, Kali switched on the interior light and held Panikkar's severed head up to our door window on a pole. From outside, all Bhagat saw was Panikkar's face (which was never very animated anyway) and a beckoning hand. The fool parked his car and entered with a smile.

Kali sat him down and explained in their language what had transpired, all the while with Panikkar's head hanging from her belt. The expression on Bhagat's face defied description. Not a word passed his lips. When he rose to leave, Kali informed him that the procedure would proceed as scheduled. He had two hours to rest before getting into his scrubs.

Panikkar be damned. Tonight I go in.

Chapter 12

I come awake expecting to see fine blue lines of daylight around my heavy window blinds, but there is only darkness.

My telephone is ringing.

I have to get up to answer it. Sweat cools on my skin as I feel my way across the air-conditioned office to the phone.

"Hello?"

"Is this hopper school?" asks a whisper of a voice.

"What?"

The whisper gets louder. "Is this Harper Cole?"

"Yes. Who the hell is this? If you're a cop, call me in the morning."

"I'm not a cop."

The voice sounds nervous. Nervous and young. "I'm sleeping. What do you want?"

"This is David Charles. Do you remember me?"

"No."

"You talked to me a couple of times on the phone. I'm one of the techs at EROS."

My eyes click open. "Yeah, I remember you."

"No, you don't. That's okay. I'm one of Miles's assistants."

"What can I do for you . . . David?"

"I'm not sure. I just thought I'd better talk to you. You know the FBI is up here, right?"

"Yes. Trying to do phone traces?"

"Yeah. The atmosphere is really tense. They've got agents guarding the file vault, and Miles is acting really weird. He's pretty paranoid about the government."

"I'm listening."

"Well . . . the thing is . . . your access to the accounting database was cut off, right?"

"Yes. Jan Krislov ordered that, if I'm not mistaken."

"You are. Miles did it. I mean, he told me to do it."

I feel a strange giddiness. "What are you trying to tell me, David?"

"Well, I just thought you should know. About two hours ago, I realized that another blind-draft account had been terminated for insufficient funds. It happened this morning. It belonged to a woman—"

I feel my mouth go dry.

"—named Rosalind May. She's from Mill Creek, Michigan. At first I didn't think anything about it. But then I realized she was on a list I saw in Miles's office."

Shit.

"It was a list of blind-draft women who haven't been logging on but are still paying their fees. There are about fifty of them. Anyway, I decided to check and see whether May had logged on at all in the last few months. She seemed to lose interest about three months ago. But then I saw that she'd logged on every night for five nights, starting last week. She dropped off again two nights ago. And then today her secret account was overdrawn. Like she needed to make a deposit but wasn't around to do it. You know?"

Yes, I know—

"And the thing is . . . Miles hasn't told the FBI yet."

"Jesus."

"And since he hasn't told them," Charles says hesitantly, "I don't feel too good about walking up to these suits and volunteering the information. You know? I figured since you first reported the murders, you might know how to handle it."

The weight of this information is too great to absorb quickly.

"Harper?"

"You were right to call me, David. I'll take care of it."

"You will? Wow. Okay, man." The relief in the tech's voice is palpable. "Look, I gotta go. Miles is all over the office right now. I don't think he's been to sleep in like fifty hours."

"Try to get him to rest," I say uselessly.

"Yeah, okay. I will. And, uh . . . try to keep me out of this, okay?"

He hangs up.

I switch on my halogen desk lamp and dig through my wallet for Daniel Baxter's card. I dial the number before I have time to second-guess myself.

"Investigative Support Unit, Quantico," says a crisp female voice.

"I need to speak to Daniel Baxter immediately."

"Your name?"

"Harper Cole. It's about the EROS case."

"Hold, please."

A Muzak confection of old Carpenters tunes assaults my ears for nearly two minutes before Baxter comes on the line. An out-of-tune violin is still ringing in my head when he says, "Cole? What you got?"

"It's five a.m.," I say, looking at my desk clock. "You work all night?"

"It's six a.m. here. What you got? I'm pretty busy."

"You're about to be a lot busier."

Baxter catches his breath. "Spit it out, son."

"I just learned that another blind-draft account went to zero. It was terminated today. It belonged to a woman."

"Jesus Christ. Not this soon. You got a name?"

"Rosalind May. Mill Creek, Michigan."

"Rosalind like in Shakespeare, or Rosalynn like Rosalynn Carter?"

"I don't know."

"How'd you find out about it?"

I remember David Charles's plea for protection. "Worry about that later. Can't you just check the name?"

"I'll do it right now. Anything else I should know?"

"No. As soon as you find out anything, please give me a call. I mean immediately. You owe me that much."

"I'll buzz you. I'm going to call the Mill Creek P.D. right now."

I get up from the halogen glow and walk down the hall to check on Drewe. She left the bedroom door open when she went to bed, a good sign. As she snores softly, I discern her face in the moonlight trickling through the window. Her mouth is slightly open, her skin luminous in the shadows. I don't know how long I stand there, but the muted chirping of my office phone snaps me out of my trance and I slip quickly back up the hall to get it.

"This is Harper."

"It's bad, Cole."

My blood pressure drops so rapidly I grab the desk to steady myself. "She's dead?"

"Worse."

"What? What's worse than dead?"

"Rosalind May has been missing for fifty to sixty hours. That's Rosalind with a D. Two nights ago she was dropped off at her home by a date at eleven p.m. Sometime during the night, she apparently let someone into her house or else voluntarily left to meet them. She hasn't been seen since. In my experience that's worse than dead. It means very painful things."

"Oh, God. You think it was our guy? Strobekker?"

Baxter hesitates. "I don't know. I'd say yes, but there's one thing that doesn't fit. One very big thing."

"What?"

"Rosalind May is fifty years old. She has two grown sons. All the other victims were twenty-six or under."

"Except Karin Wheat," I remind him. "She was forty-seven."

"Yeah. And one other thing."

"What?"

"This UNSUB left a note. The police didn't find it until last night. One of their detectives decided to poke through her computer—"

"There was EROS software on the drive?" I cut in.

"No. Just like the other cases. Anyway, this Michigan detective was poking through her computer, and he found a WordPerfect file he couldn't read."

"It was encrypted?"

"Not digitally. It was in French."

"French? You're sure the UNSUB left it?"

"You tell me. The translation's about a paragraph long, but the end of it reads: 'The dawn is breaking on a new world, a jungle world in which the lean spirits roam with sharp claws. If I am a hyena I am a lean and hungry one: I go forth to fatten myself.' Mean anything to you?"

The skin on the back of my neck is tingling. "Yes. I mean, I recognize the passage. It's Henry Miller."

"The porn author?"

"Miller wasn't really a porn author. Not as you think of it. But that's not important. The passage is from *Tropic of Cancer.*"

"How do you know that? Nobody here did."

"Dr. Lenz must not be there. He would have known it."

"You're right. He's out of pocket just now."

"*Tropic of Cancer* is a classic of erotic literature. I'm sure it's still in print."

"Which means anybody could walk into a bookstore and buy one?"

"Probably not any bookstore. Not the chains. You'd probably find it in stores that cater to a literary crowd, or else in erotic bookstores."

"Thanks. That helps."

"What kind of killer leaves notes in French, Mr. Baxter? You ever see that before?"

"Never. The translator in Michigan said it was probably written by a highly educated French native. Very elegant, he said. I've sent it to a psycholinguistics specialist at Syracuse. He won't be able to look at it before morning, though. The Mill Creek police aren't telling the press about the note, by the way. They're using it to screen false confessions."

"Hey, I'm not talking to a soul."

"I've got a really bad feeling about this one," he says, almost to himself.

"Why?" I ask, not admitting that I have the same feeling.

"The UNSUB has killed all the other victims at the scenes. Now he takes one away, no signs of violence. If this is our guy—and my gut tells me it is—he's varying his behavior more than any killer I've ever seen. He could be starting to come apart, to lose control of what's driving him. But I don't think so. He seems able to choose whatever crime signature he wants, which means he's *not* driven beyond the point of control. If you hadn't called with Rosalind May's name, we never would have connected this crime to the others. You understand?"

"Too well."

"I appreciate the help, Cole. It's nice to know someone at EROS realizes we're the good guys."

I say nothing.

"Talked to your friend Turner lately?"

"No. I mean, not directly. He sent me some e-mail. Nothing important."

Baxter waits. "Right."

"What will you do now?"

"Pray he makes a mistake."

Chapter 13

Dear Father,

The procedure failed.

That is not wholly accurate. I was prevented from finishing by an unrelated accident. As Kali brought out the patient, she showed signs of hysteria. Unlike the Navy girl, Jenny, who adapted quickly, this one seemed not to have settled her nerves since we took her. Kali told me privately that Jenny had attempted to calm and reassure May during the night (quite ironic, considering the respective fates that awaited them) but the older woman would not be comforted. I'd had to sedate her at gunpoint the first night to get her to sleep at all.

I took the precaution of using curare prior to Jenny's euthanization, to prevent her screaming or making any other sounds that might alarm May. But it was no use. As Bhagat and Kali struggled to get May onto the table, she spied a few drops of blood that had resulted from Jenny's procedure. She began to shriek and flail, using her bound hands like a club. Even Kali could not frighten her into submission.

It was then that I made my mistake. I imagined that if I explained the simplicity of the procedure, and the remarkable benefits that would likely accrue to her because of it, May would calm down. But my speech had the opposite effect. When she heard me explain the necessity of opening the sternum, her face went white and she gripped her left arm. Needless to say, I attempted to save her, but it was useless. In four minutes she was dead.

She died of a massive myocardial infarction, and no one could have been more surprised than I. There were no relevant risk factors in her history. As unscientific as it may sound, I believe the woman died of pure terror. When she flatlined, doubt assailed me like a shadow. Should I stop? Should I go on?

Then I thought of Ponce de León, thrashing through the bug-infested jungles of Florida, fighting the mosquitoes and the mud and the alligators and the natives and disease, searching, ever searching for the mystical mythical Fountain of Youth. How the image of it must have burned inside his brain, gushing with pure shining water, liquid with restorative power, holding out its promise to mankind, the possibility of revoking God's harshest decree. And all the time that poor Spaniard was carrying the true fountain with him, inside his head, millimeters from the very space where his seductive vision burned.

We know that now.

Soon I shall stand alone at the pinnacle of the species, the only man with the courage to reach into the fountain.

Soon I shall spit in the face of God.

Chapter 14

It's ten-thirty a.m. and I am tired of talking to cops. Houston cops. L.A. cops. Oregon cops. San Francisco cops. Mill Creek, Michigan, cops. I've repeated the same story I told the New Orleans police and the FBI so many times that I know it like the Lord's Prayer, and to detectives who seemed to be writing each word with the slowness of fourth graders practicing penmanship.

"Stupid sons of bitches!" I shout to my empty office. "You never heard of tape recorders?"

I feel a little better. Some of the cops I talked to want to arrest me, I could tell. Me, Miles, and the other seven people who have access to the master client list. All of them asked why we haven't shut down EROS, and some yelled while they asked me. The Michigan cops were the worst, probably because they're dealing with a kidnapping rather than a murder. I referred them all to Daniel Baxter of the FBI. Let them take their complaints to the Great Stone Face.

When the phone rings again, I grab it as if to smash it against my desk, but I restrain myself and put it to my ear.

"Harper, it's me." Drewe's voice is tight with pent-up emotion.

"What is it? What happened?"

"A lot of things."

A wave of heat rolls up my back and neck as an image of Erin flashes in my mind. "Where are you?"

"Woman's Hospital."

"Can you talk? What is it?"

"The FBI," she says quietly.

"What? They called you?"

"No. They called my bosses. They called my friends."

"What?"

"And not just the FBI. A detective from New Orleans called the hospital administrator and asked permission to question colleagues about me."

Mayeux. "What kind of questions are they asking?"

"Embarrassing ones. Do I drink heavily. Do I ever bring you around the hospital, or even to Jackson. How you and I get along. Why don't we have any kids." Her voice cracks slightly at that. "Harper, this is not acceptable."

"I know, babe. Goddamn it. I'll try to see if I can do something about it."

"You've *got* to do something about it. My world isn't isolated like yours. The good opinion of these people is a prerequisite for keeping my privileges."

"I get the message, Drewe. Let me make some phone calls."

"Please do that. I'm being paged."

And she is gone.

Let me make some phone calls. I said it with such confidence. Who the hell was I kidding? Am I going to call a New Orleans homicide detective and say, "Listen, shrimphead, leave my wife alone or take the fucking consequences!"

No.

Am I going to call Bob Anderson and say, "Dr. Anderson, it turns out I actually can't take care of your little girl so could you please call the governor and ask him to get the FBI off our backs?"

Hell no.

Am I going to call the FBI and say, "Could you please stop questioning my wife about this murder case? She doesn't like it."

Maybe.

I take Baxter's card from my wallet, punch in the number of Quantico, and ask for Agent Baxter.

"Special Agent Baxter is in the field at this time," says a robotic female voice. "Would you like to leave voice mail?"

I decide to wake her up. "My name is Harper Cole," I say too loudly. "I met with Baxter and Dr. Lenz about the Karin Wheat murder, and they told me to call immediately if I remembered anything vital to the case. Well, I have."

"Where are you, Mr. Cole?" says a slightly less controlled voice.

"Home. And I don't have much time."

The voice finally becomes human. "Could you give me your number please? Mr. Cole?"

"Baxter has it," I snap, and hang up the phone. That ought to light a fire under somebody.

I sit down at the EROS computer, log in as SYSOP, and begin scanning the Level Two messages as they are posted. EROS traffic is basically unmoderated, which means we sysops do not screen or censor the communications of clients. This freedom is what allows Miles and me to run the busy service without much help. Certain types of communication are prohibited on EROS, and they are filtered by a simple but efficient program designed by Miles: he calls it "Ward Cleaver." As messages are posted to the various areas of our servers, "Ward" automatically searches out all binary graphic files and references to children and deposits them in a special file called "the Dumpster." (Actually, "Ward" lost his graphic filter three weeks ago.) At his leisure, Miles then attempts—

usually with success—to track down the originators of these forbidden files. He doesn't turn them over to the cops or anything. He just likes letting them know he can find them.

Theoretically, I'm supposed to be monitoring the various areas of EROS on a round-robin basis, doing what I can to assist new clients and helping to foster a sense of online community. But in the past few weeks I have become rather casual about that duty. More than a few of this morning's messages are about Karin Wheat's death. The themes are consistent: shock, denial, anger. Of course, none of the authors of these messages has any idea that Karin was an EROS client. They knew her only through her novels, which would interest most EROS clients, as they dealt with the darker side of the human psyche.

When my phone rings, I pick it up prepared to give Daniel Baxter a piece of my mind, but instead I find myself listening to the flat vowels of Dr. Arthur Lenz.

"You've remembered something of value, Mr. Cole?" he says.

"Where's Baxter?"

"He's not available just now."

"Where are you, Doctor?"

"Is that relevant?"

"Did you go to Minnesota to see Strobekker's body exhumed?"

"Do you doubt that I did?"

"I think you went straight to New York to try to crack Jan Krislov. Didn't you?"

"As a matter of fact, I personally observed the postmortem on David Strobekker."

"Was he missing his pineal gland?"

"Oddly enough, no. Now, what was the purpose of your call?"

"Am I a prime suspect in these murders, Doctor?"

Lenz pauses. "You're a suspect, yes."

"Why?"

"You have access to EROS's master client list. That makes you a member of a very exclusive group."

"Have you got access to the list yet?"

"No."

"Maybe I can help you."

"How?"

"Maybe I have a copy of the list."

"Do you or don't you?"

It's my turn to play coy.

"What do you want?" Lenz asks.

"I want the FBI to stop hassling my wife."

"Ah. Daniel's agents can be clumsy on occasion. They are causing you problems?"

"They're bothering my wife at work."

"I see."

"And anybody who bothers my wife de facto pisses me off."

"Yes."

"What can you do about that?"

Lenz says nothing for a while.

"You realize I could go public with all this at any time," I tell him.

"That would only aggravate the very situation you seek to alleviate. The disruption of your wife's life would increase exponentially."

He's right, of course.

"But perhaps I can be of assistance," he says. "It's true that the various police departments involved in the case—particularly the Michigan department—are ready to have both you and Mr. Turner arrested. I, however, do not share their enthusiasm."

"Get to it, Doctor."

"I think perhaps we can help each other, Mr. Cole. If you will agree to help me in a limited capacity, I think I could have both Bureau and police pressure removed from your life."

"What kind of capacity?"

"I want the master client list, of course. Can you get it?"

"Maybe."

"I'll take that as a no."

Damn this guy. "Why take that as a no?"

"If you had a copy of your own, you would have destroyed it by now. And you no longer have access to the accounting database, which you would need to get a new copy."

How does he know that?

"However, you still have something I want."

"What's that?"

"Your thoughts."

"What?"

And then he tells me. How long he has been planning this, I don't know. Maybe this was the whole point of putting pressure on Drewe. Of not throwing me to the Michigan police. Because Lenz wants exactly what they want. To fly me up to Washington so he can question me with no one else around. He says something about "an informal version of his standard criminal-profiling technique," but I don't really listen. We both know the bottom line. If I want the pressure taken off, I've got to play his game.

"How soon do you want to do this?"

"I'll have a ticket for you waiting in Jackson, Mississippi. It's ten-fifty. Can you get to the airport by noon?"

"Noon *today*?"

"Of course."

If I drop everything and walk out the front door without a toothbrush. Then I remember Drewe's voice, tight with anxiety. "Yeah, I can get there. You think there's a flight?"

"If there isn't a direct flight, you'll find a connecting ticket. Ask for messages at the American Airlines desk."

"Okay. I'd better get going."

"Just a moment. At the meeting in New Orleans, you mentioned that EROS is patronized by many celebrities."

"I can't tell you any names."

"Fine, fine. But what level of celebrities are we talking about?"

"Well . . . Karin Wheat was pretty famous."

"Yes, but authors don't get the kind of adulation that Hollywood stars or sports figures do."

"Not many sports figures on EROS, Doctor. The IQ level tends to run a little higher than that."

"So what level of star are we talking about?"

"The top of the business. And not just actors. Directors, producers, agents, the works."

He digests this in silence.

"Aren't you any different from the paparazzi, Doctor? I thought you were trying to solve these murders, not root up juicy tidbits about Hollywood."

"In all honesty, I find the whole concept of EROS fascinating. However, there is a point to my questions. Jan Krislov refuses to reveal anything about her clients. Thanks to you, I realize she is not grandstanding but prudently shielding people who have a great vested interest in protecting their public images. People who would not hesitate to sue Ms. Krislov and have the funds to pursue such a lawsuit to its bitter end."

"No doubt about it. Hell, there are celebrity *lawyers* on that master client list. Jan Krislov is a lot of things, but she's no fool."

"Do you have any more EROS session printouts?" Lenz asks.

"No more of the murder victims or Strobekker."

"I'll take anything you have. I'm following a rather twisted trail, and I'd like all the signposts I can get."

"I'll bring you what I have."

"Excellent." Lenz says he'll fax me directions to his office in case I miss the FBI agents he plans to have waiting at the Washington airport. Then he says, "May I give you some unsolicited advice, Mr. Cole?"

"People do it all the time."

"You're an experienced futures trader. However, if I were you, I'd clear my current positions. Dump all contracts until this mess is resolved."

"You're not me."

"Quite. Well . . . I'll see you this afternoon."

While Lenz's fax comes through, I call Drewe in Jackson and explain what I'm about to do and why. She warns me to be careful, then goes back to her patients.

I pack a briefcase with a toothbrush, five hundred dollars in cash, and a few EROS folders from my file cabinet. Before I leave the office, I almost pick up the phone and follow Lenz's advice. Getting out of the market now would cost me money, but that's not what keeps me from doing it. The truth is, I feel a simple bullheaded resistance to letting Arthur Lenz tell me what to do. If I lose a few thousand bucks because I'm in a daze, so be it. It's happened before.

I am almost to the Explorer when I remember Lenz's fax. Running back inside to get it, I hear the phone. It's my office line. I debate whether or not to answer, then pick up.

"Hello?"

"Moneypenny? This is Bond. *James* Bond."

"What is it, Miles? I'm in a hurry."

"Brahma went back online five minutes ago."

"Have they traced the call?"

"Yes and no. They took a chance and started at the second Jersey line they wound up at last time. AT&T long line. Anyway, the connection twisted all around the country, but they finally tracked it to Wyoming."

"Wyoming?"

"Yeah. Place called Lake Champion. It's a tiny little nothing of a town."

I feel my heart pumping. "So? Are they going to arrest him or what?"

"Not that easy, I'm afraid. You're not going to believe this. Lake Champion, Wyoming, is one of the last towns in America with electromechanical phone switching. It's like the Dark Ages. They actually have these complicated metal gizmos that spin around making physical connections, and there are rows and rows of them stacked on top of each other, from floor to ceiling."

"What does that mean as far as tracing Brahma?"

Miles chuckles softly. "It means it takes an *actual human being* running up and down the aisles between those switches to trace the connections. With digital tracing, you can move through twenty states in a couple of minutes without getting permission from anybody. But to authorize an actual human being to chase down mechanical connections in one of these little towns, you have to have a court order."

"What?"

Miles is laughing harder. "Here's the brilliant part. To get that court order, you have to prove that a crime is being committed *in the state where that town is*. It's one hell of a buffer system, and Brahma knows it. Rather than going higher and higher tech—which is what most hackers do and which is ultimately a no-win game—he goes to the simplest possible solution. He goes *analog*. It's exactly what I'd do, man."

Exactly what I'd do . . . "So what happens now?"

"Baxter is strong-arming a Wyoming judge as we speak, trying to get permission for a local yokel phone guy to do the trace."

"How long will that take?"

"Hel-lo." Miles sighs with almost sexual satisfaction. "Your question just became academic. The Strobekker account just went dead. Brahma's history." Miles's voice rises to the exaggerated bellow of a game show announcer: "The switches in Wyoming are *no longer connected*!"

I picture blue-suited FBI agents in the EROS office staring at Miles with murder in their eyes. "What alias was he using?"

"Kali this time. I haven't seen that one before."

"C-A-L-I?"

"No. *K*-A-L-I."

"Who's Kali?"

"The Hindu mother goddess, consort of Shiva, which is one of his other aliases. Kali's an ugly black bitch. Wears a belt of skulls, carries a severed head and a knife, has six arms. She's the betrayer, the terrible one of many names. Weird that he'd log on with a female alias."

"Severed head? Christ. Are you an expert in this Eastern stuff or what?"

"I've dabbled. Read the Vedas, the Upanishads, some other things. They make a lot more sense than the chicken-shit dualism of Christianity. You know, you really should—"

"I don't have time for it, Miles."

"Neither do I. Someone just told me the Wise and Wonderful Oz wants me on another line."

"Oz?"

"Arthur Lenz. He's the man behind the curtain on this thing, isn't he?"

"I guess. I've got to run, Miles. Keep me posted. But use my answering machine, not e-mail."

"Don't sweat it. Nobody reads my e-mail if I don't want them to. Not even God."

I tear off Lenz's fax and run for the Explorer. I believe nobody reads Miles's e-mail if he doesn't want them to, but what I'm thinking as I crank the engine is this:

Maybe somebody should.

Chapter 15

I am crossing the Washington Beltway in a yellow taxi driven by a black lay preacher. Lenz told me I would be met at Dulles Airport by FBI agents, but none showed, so I took the cab. The driver tries to make conversation—he still knows a lot of people from "down home," meaning the South—but I am too absorbed in the object of my journey to keep up my end of the exchange.

Lenz's private office is supposed to be in McLean, Virginia. All I know is that my lay preacher is leading me deep into upscale suburbia. Old money suburbia. Colonial homes, Mercedeses, Beemers (700 series), matched Lexi, tasteful retail and office space. The driver pulls into the redbrick courtyard of a three-story building and stops. You could probably buy five acres of Delta farmland for the monthly rent on Lenz's office.

The first floor of the building is deserted but for ferns, its walls covered with abstract paintings that look purchased by the square yard. A bronze-lettered notice board directs me to the third floor. When the elevator door opens on three, I am facing a short corridor with a door at the end. No letters on the door.

Beyond the door I find a small, well-appointed waiting room. There's a lot of indirect light, but the only window faces the billing office. A dark-skinned receptionist sits behind the window. I am not looking at her. I'm looking at a pale, gangly, long-haired young man folded oddly across a wing chair and ottoman. He is snoring.

"Miles?" I say softly.

He does not stir. A Hewlett-Packard notebook computer and a cellular telephone lie on the floor beside him. The computer screen swirls with a psychedelic screensaver program.

"Miles."

The snoring stops. Miles Turner flips the hair out of his eyes and looks up at me without surprise. His eyes are the same distant blue they have always been.

"Hello, snitch," he says. "What's in the briefcase? The names of everybody who works at EROS?"

"Fresh underwear. What the hell are you doing here?"

"Same as you, I guess. The mad doctor wants to pry open my skull, see what he can find. I hope he's in the mood for drama. I certainly am."

"I can't believe you agreed to come."

A fleeting smile touches his lips. "Didn't have any choice, did I? I've got an old drug charge hanging over my head. All Lenz has to do is tell his sidekick—Baxter—to push the button, and I go to jail. Do not pass *GO*, et cetera."

"Jesus."

Miles leans his angular head back with a theatrical flourish and tries to catch the eye of the receptionist. I take the opportunity to study him more closely. It's been four years since I saw him in the flesh. Miles long ago vowed never to set foot in Mississippi again. When I saw him last, in New Orleans, he had short hair and wore fairly conservative clothes. No polo or khakis, of course, but your basic Gap in basic black. He's wearing black again today, but his hair hangs over his shoulders, his sweater is not only torn but looks cheap, and he is *dirty*. I don't smell him—yet—but he plainly hasn't bathed for at least a couple of days.

"Staring is rude," he says, his eyes still on the window to my left. "Don't you read your Amy Vanderbilt? Or is it Gloria Vanderbilt?"

"Miles, what the hell is going on? You look terrible. What's happening with the case?"

He smiles conspiratorially and brings a warning finger to his lips. His eyebrows shimmy up and down as he says in a stage whisper: *"Shhhh. The walls have ears."*

When I stare blankly, he adds, "But then their ears have walls, so perhaps it doesn't matter."

"Are you telling me you think this waiting room is bugged?"

"Why not? Lenz works for the FBI. They could bug this room in the time it took you to wake me up."

"How do you know how long that took?"

"Touché."

"What's the computer for?"

"Keeping up with developments, of course. Baxter just got the court order to do the trace in Wyoming. He must have blackmailed the judge. I think it's a standard FBI tactic."

"Has Brahma logged on again?"

"Once, about an hour ago, but Baxter didn't have the court order then. He was only on for a couple minutes. They did manage to trace digitally back to the Wyoming phone company again. Lake Champion."

"How do you know that?"

Miles smiles with satisfaction, then replies in a vintage Hollywood Nazi accent: "I haf my sources, Herr Cole."

"What about the kidnapping? Rosalind May. Anything on that?"

"Nada. By the way, I didn't know you had a mole among my faithful."

"What are you talking about?"

He smiles again. "How else could the FBI have found out about Rosalind May?"

"Don't you care about these women, Miles?"

"I care about *all* women." Suddenly he is whispering so that I can barely hear. I sit beside him.

"They're going to call one of us in there soon," he says. "Why don't we make a little deal right now? I say nothing to Lenz about you, you say nothing about me."

This shocks me more than anything I've seen or heard yet. "You think you have to spell it out like that? You think I'd tell these people anything about you?"

His lips narrow in a shadow of the smile Jesus must have given Peter when he prophesied the disciple's betrayal. "Humans do strange things under stress, Harper. Why don't we just shake hands on it?"

I look down at the proffered hand and surprise myself by taking it.

"You want to grab a bite to eat after this?" he asks lightly. "Tie on the old feed bag, as they say back home?"

"Sure. I want to find out what the hell's going on with this manhunt."

"Whoever goes first waits for the other. Cool?"

"Sure."

"Mr. Turner?"

The receptionist has slid open her window, but she is seated, and I see only a tight black bun atop her head.

"Dr. Lenz will see you first," she says in a husky, almost luminous voice. "Go through the door and down the corridor. The doctor is waiting."

Miles stands slowly, looks through the billing window, and says, "You have spooky eyes." Then he picks up his computer and his cellular phone and disappears through the door like a tall and undernourished White Rabbit.

Chapter 16

When the receptionist finally calls my name, Miles has not yet reappeared. Perhaps Lenz wants to talk to us together. As I get up and move toward the door that bars the office proper, I turn to get a closer look at the receptionist.

She is no longer there.

The door leads into a short hallway carpeted in royal blue. To my left is the empty receptionist's cubicle, at the end of the hall another door. I open it without knocking.

Arthur Lenz is seated behind a cherry desk in a worn leather chair much like the one my father used in his medical office. But Lenz smells of cigarettes, not cigars. And his office is spartan compared to the Dickensian clutter of my father's sanctum sanctorum.

My first thought when Lenz looks up is that I pegged him wrong in New Orleans. There he seemed a handsomer version of William F. Buckley Jr. Now, seated silently behind the ornate desk with his iron gray hair and gold-rimmed spectacles, he seems to have morphed into a more sinister character—Donald Sutherland in one of his heavier roles. Lenz gives me a perfunctory smile and motions me toward a sleek black couch that reminds me of an orthodontist's chair.

"Did you transport Miles to an alternate dimension?" I ask.

He looks puzzled. "Here are your printouts," I say

quickly, dumping the contents of my briefcase on the center of his desk.

Lenz gives the laser-printed pages a quick scan, then slips them into a desk drawer. "I was about to have some tea sent in," he says. "Care for some?"

So this is how he means to play it: two supercivilized males sitting here sipping tea. "Got any Tabs?"

"Tabs?"

"You know, the drink. *Tab.* Tasted shitty in the seventies, now it's just palatable. That's what I drink."

The psychiatrist's mouth crinkles with distaste. "There's a vending machine in the building next door. I suppose I could send my receptionist over for some."

"Fine. Normally, I'd be gracious, but since you're the one picking my brain, I insist. I need some caffeine."

"Tea has caffeine."

"But it ain't got *fizz.*"

Lenz pushes a button on a desk intercom and makes the request. It reminds me of the old *Bob Newhart Show.* I almost laugh at the memory.

"What's funny, Mr. Cole?"

"Nothing. Everything. You're wasting time talking to me. Your UNSUB could be out there killing another woman right this second."

"Yes, he could. But you don't seem to grasp the fact that you and Mr. Turner are the only direct lines into this case. And as for wasting time, I frequently spend hours interviewing janitors or postmen whose only connection to a case may be that they walked past the crime scene."

I don't respond to this.

Lenz smiles like he's my favorite uncle or something. "I know the couch seems camp. But it does tend to concentrate the mind." He takes a pencil from the pocket of his pinpoint cotton shirt and taps the eraser on a blank notepad in front of him. "Lie back and relax, Mr. Cole."

The soft leather couch wraps itself around my back

like beach sand, which tells me it does anything but concentrate the mind. Lenz's ceiling tiles tell me his roof has leaked before. He modulates his deep voice into a fatherly *Masterpiece Theatre* register, but behind it I sense an unblinking gaze.

"This is not a formal interview," he says. "Psychological profiling is not an exact science. Any wet-nosed FBI trainee could question you about the homicidal triangle: bed-wetting, fire starting, cruelty to animals. I use a different approach. Despite the attempts of thousands to discredit Sigmund Freud, I still believe the old grouch was onto something regarding the importance of sexual experiences."

"Uh-huh."

"Are you familiar with Nietzsche's epigram?"

"That tired old saw about monsters and the abyss?"

"No, this." Suddenly Lenz is speaking harsh German that sounds like Erich von Stroheim in *Five Graves to Cairo.*

"I didn't catch that, Doctor."

"Forgive me. 'The degree and kind of a man's sexuality reach up into the ultimate pinnacle of his spirit.' "

"I've seen that on EROS."

"I happen to believe it. I'm going to ask you some very personal questions. I hope you'll answer frankly. You may feel a bit harried. I tend to jump from subject to subject, following my nose, as it were. Please try to remember that there is no personal motive behind my questions."

Right. You just want to put me in line for a lethal injection. "Fine," I say aloud. "Let's do it."

"What is the worst thing you've ever done, Mr. Cole?"

The question takes me off guard. "I'm not sure I understand."

"What could be simpler? Please answer."

"You don't waste much time on foreplay, do you?"

"What is the worst thing you've ever done?"

"Next question."

Lenz sighs in frustration, but I don't really care. "Very well. What moment are you proudest of in your life?"

"What is this?" I ask, trying to get some idea of how to handle this guy.

"Mr. Cole, did you come here expecting to look at Rorschach blots? Perhaps to say the first thing that popped into your head when I said words like 'breast' or 'hate'?"

"I guess I thought you were going to ask me about EROS."

"EROS, you, Turner—it's all one package, isn't it? For the moment I'm concerned with you personally. Moments of shame and pride are frequently things people keep to themselves. The acts that cause these emotions often illuminate the extreme boundaries of the personality. If I know the extremes, I know the man. So please try to answer frankly. Yes?"

"Okay."

"Would you consider yourself what laymen call a control freak?"

"Yes. I guess that makes two of us."

"Do you masturbate regularly?"

"Don't you?"

"Is that a yes?"

"I'm still waiting for your answer."

Lenz gives a faint smile. "Do you masturbate while communicating on EROS?"

"Occasionally."

"Would you say most subscribers use EROS as an aid to masturbation?"

"I'm sure most of them *have*. I wouldn't say that's their primary use for it. EROS is more for your head than your body."

"What do you think about when you masturbate?"

"That's my business."

"Mr. Cole."

"Women, of course."

"Women doing what?"

"What do you think?"

"That you're being evasive."

"What the hell do you want to know?"

"Do you have violent fantasies?"

"Such as?"

"Women bound, for example."

"No."

"Women making sounds of supplication?"

"No."

"Women in pain?"

"No."

"Do you ever make mental connections between sex and blood?"

"Hell no."

"This may be a sensitive question, but I must ask it. You grew up in a rural area. Have you ever had sex with an animal of any kind?"

"Have you ever had someone pound the living shit out of you? Jesus."

Lenz marks on his notepad. "Would it surprise you to learn that over a third of all males raised in rural areas have had intercourse with some type of animal to the point of orgasm?"

"It's not something I've ever thought about, okay? And I'd like to keep it that way."

"I hope you can control your temper, Mr. Cole. There is a method to my madness, I assure you. Now . . . what is your first sexual memory?"

"What do you mean? Like as a kid?"

"Your first sexual memory of any kind."

"Well . . . trying to peek under my mother's nightgown while she was sleeping, I guess."

"What did you see?"

"Not much. It was dark."

"After that?"

"Playing doctor in a tree house."

"With girls or boys?"

"Girls. One girl."

"The same age as you?"

"Yes."

"What age?"

"I don't know. Definitely little kids. Innocent stuff."

"Any genital touching?"

"Nah. Just show-and-tell."

"What about same-sex play?"

I hesitate. "A little."

"One boy, or several together?"

"Several. Just neighborhood buddies."

"How old were you?"

"Older. Still young, though."

"Any fear that you were a homosexual because of it?"

"We didn't even know what a homosexual was. Discovering my dad's stash of *Playboys* was like unearthing the Rosetta Stone."

"Have you had online sex with other men?"

"Not knowingly."

"What do you mean?"

"A lot of men pretend to be women online. On regular networks it's because there's a shortage of women. But on EROS that doesn't apply. Some men still do it there, so I guess I could unknowingly have fantasized sex with a man."

"But you've never pretended to be a woman online?"

"Once. My wife told me I should try it to see what it felt like. I did, and I didn't like it."

"Why?"

"It's like you're assaulted from every side. Even on EROS, which is the most civilized online service, being a woman means you're constantly approached by men. It's the loss of control, I guess."

"How old were you when you first had sex with a woman?"

"All the way? Complete intercourse?"

"Serious foreplay. Touching of genitals."

"Probably . . . thirteen. With a couple of curious girls the same age. When I was fourteen this other girl and I did pretty much everything but intercourse. We were in love, though. Jesus. Like holding hands and kissing and touching each other was some kind of new religion. An indescribable intensity of feeling. Your heart pounding like it would punch through your chest. She was a year older than me."

"How did that relationship end?"

"She broke my heart after seven months. I still remember that. Funny, huh? Seven months. I was physically sick. I think that warped me. I was never willing to fall totally for a girl after that. I knew what could happen."

"How did that color your relationship with other girls? You were angry?"

"I don't think so."

"When did you first have sexual intercourse?

"Fifteen. The girl was eighteen."

"A one-time experience?"

"Are you kidding? Once I got a taste of that, it was nonstop. Day and night, sneaking out of the house, anywhere we could find a place."

"What kind of places did you usually find?"

"Outside, mostly. Or in the car, you know."

"Not in her parents' house?"

"No. We had a little respect."

"What do you remember most about that relationship?"

I close my eyes. "Later, a couple of years later, I heard she'd become a slut. I'd really started to care for her after a while. She was country, but she read poetry, like that. She was a real person, just a little lost. She had feelings nobody knew about. It was sad."

"What makes you say that?"

"Well . . . I read her diary once."

"She let you read her diary?"

"Not exactly. I went over to her house one time, and nobody answered the door. I went in anyway."

"The door was open?"

"No. The few times I'd sneaked in to see her, I went though her window, so I did that. I looked around the house. Her room, especially. I found this little calendar where she'd written really small in the day spaces, like a diary."

"What had she written?"

"All kinds of things. She had codes. Simple ones. There were Xs on the days when she had her periods, that was easy. Then there were some initials, which I figured out were guys she knew—guys her age. Then there was "M.L." on some days, which stood for "made love." I knew that because I'd been with her on those days."

"All of them?"

"Not all."

"How did you feel reading that diary?"

"Like a spy."

"You put it back where you found it?"

"No. I took it."

"Stole it?"

"Mm-hm. There were a few of them. I just took the one."

"Do you still have it?"

"No."

"When did you get rid of it?"

"Just after I got married. With a bunch of old letters and stuff. I didn't want Drewe finding that kind of thing.

Stuff from old girlfriends, you know? Some of it was pretty explicit. And she knew some of the girls."

"Why did you keep those letters so long?"

"All is vanity, right?"

Lenz scribbles something on his notepad. "How many women have you slept with in your life?"

I pause. "Fifteen."

"Approximately fifteen? Or fifteen exactly?"

"Exactly."

"You could write down all their names? Here and now, I mean?"

"Yeah, but I won't."

"But you've written down their names before."

"Yes."

"Ever rated their performances? Their looks, what they did, things like that?"

"Any guy who says he hasn't is probably lying."

Lenz chuckles, a quick deep rumble. "Odd, isn't it? This compulsion to prove what we have done? Were you in love with these women?"

"I thought I was, with some of them. Some not. I guess I just wanted to know they wanted me enough to do that."

"One-night stands?"

"Not my thing."

Lenz scribbles some more on his pad.

"What experience would you say constitutes the best sex you've ever had?"

"The best sex? Well . . . I guess the best sex—I mean the most uninhibited, unrestrained sex—I had with women who were a little crazy."

"What do you mean?"

"I mean very intense women. Very jealous, or if not jealous, then kind of haunted . . . driven. Doomed, maybe."

"Doomed to what?"

"I don't know. Unhappiness. Unfulfillment."

"Can you elaborate?"

"I'm talking about purely physical sex, now. Not necessarily . . . loving sex. I don't know if I can explain. I think once you start down the road toward pure pleasure, some things get left behind. I know the PC line, how the best sex can only happen in the context of love, all that. But from an existential point of view, I'd disagree. The most intense sex takes place where there is no psychological limit. No moral limit. The word 'no' has never been uttered, so possibility is infinite. And that covers a lot of territory, you know?"

"Please go on."

"I'm talking about exploration, discovery, crossing thresholds. And once you cross some thresholds, I'm not sure you can get back. Sex engages the whole psyche, doesn't it? Self-respect is involved, and your respect for the other person. Love, lust, obsession . . . it all blurs. Some women do things they might never ordinarily do because they want to be unique in your experience. They want to prove they love you more than anyone else ever did or could, and they do that by venturing onto erotically scary territory. And you pretend they're unique, because to tell them the truth would probably deny you the physical pleasure of the act, and also devalue their gift to you in their eyes. Yet . . . these acts, these roads you travel down, aren't a place you want to be all your life. A sexual relationship has an organic curve. The more intense the experience, the shorter the curve."

"You're saying you don't have or want these types of experiences with your wife?"

"I guess I am. Maybe a taste of it now and then. But you can't push sexual limits for thirty or forty years with one person. Eventually you run into a wall. I think you have to come to an accommodation. A nice warm place where there is heat and light, though maybe a little less fire. It sounds provincial as hell, I know, but there's a lot more to marriage than sex."

Lenz taps the end of his pen against his lower lip, which is gray and bloodless. At length, he says, "What are you hiding from your wife?"

My cheeks burning, I try to hide my embarrassment in anger. "What the hell are you talking about?"

He looks at me like a state trooper watching a drunk driver claim he's sober. After tapping the pen some more, he says, "You just described a problem of intimacy with your wife."

"Bullshit."

Another tired sigh. "The intense sexual experiences you described are essentially adolescent in character. The aggrandizement of the self and the depersonalization of the woman in pursuit of physical ecstasy. I've seen a photograph of your wife. She's—"

"Where did you get a picture of my wife?"

"A beautiful woman," he continues. "And obviously intelligent. You've been married only three years and have no children, yet you recall premarital sexual adventures with more than mere wistfulness. Furthermore, you spend a great deal of time pursuing relationships with other women through your computer, acting out virtual sexual fantasies with famous actresses who have no idea you know who they are—"

"Did Miles tell you that?" I heave myself up into a sitting position.

"Mr. Cole, I suggest that there is something preventing you from fully accepting the love of your wife, and thus from entering into a fully mature and satisfying sexual relationship with her. I doubt whether anything you could tell me would do more to exonerate you of these crimes, in my eyes, than what that is."

"Look, Doctor, I've done just about anything sexual I ever wanted to in real life. Do I miss sex for its own sake?

Sure. Married sex is different. It gets weighted down by everyday life. I don't care how imaginative you are. Everybody thinks he's an expert on sex, from the frigid old schoolteacher to the great Arthur Lenz, but everybody has the same problem. Men want more sex and women want more love. We're hardwired differently. Do Drewe and I have a perfect relationship? No. Do we have a good one? Yes. Next question."

Lenz seems about to argue further, then thinks better of it. "Have you ever struck a woman?" he asks.

"Once," I reply, forcing myself to lie back down.

"What prompted it?"

"She tried to kill me."

"Why?"

"Jealousy."

"How did she try to kill you?"

"Once with a car. Another time with a rifle. I don't think she really knew who she wanted to kill, me or her."

"Where is this woman now?"

"Married with kids."

"Do you consider yourself a handsome man?"

"Handsome? In a regular kind of way, I guess. I don't think it was necessarily my looks that attracted women to me, if that's what you're getting at."

"What was it?"

"I knew how to talk to them."

A sudden heightening of awareness. "What do you mean? You were smooth? You had a good line, as they say?"

"God, no. I understood them, is all. I could talk to them like their female friends did, but probably more honestly than their friends *would*. You know what I mean?"

"Tell me."

"Most guys are into things I have no interest in. Sports, hunting, like that. I mean I played sports, but I could care less about watching them, you know? Vicarious thrills aren't for me."

"You like to participate."

"Right."

"Have you ever participated in a murder?"

"Is that your idea of a trick question?"

"Will you answer it, please?"

"Hell no, I've never committed murder."

"Ever thought about it?"

"Sure. I've known a couple of dyed-in-the-wool sons of bitches who deserved it. They never get it, though. It's the good people that get it. Right, Doctor?"

"Define 'good people.' "

"I mean regular folks. People who try to obey the rules. Little kids minding their own business and trying just to grow up. I think anybody that purposefully hurts a person like that has forfeited his right to much consideration. People say the world's gone gray, but that's bullshit. There's still a line. And anybody who crosses that line deserves whatever they get."

"How do you feel about capital punishment?"

"In first-degree murder cases? The murder of a child, like that?"

"Yes."

"Fry the fuckers. Instant karma."

Lenz writes on his notepad again.

"You think I sound like some reactionary Southern redneck, right? Let me tell you, Doctor, where I live I'm considered a *liberal.* If this nut kills a woman down my way, he'd better get clear in a hurry. There's still a lot of Old Testament justice down South. And I'm not sure that's such a bad thing."

"He killed a woman in New Orleans with impunity."

It's my turn to chuckle. "New Orleans isn't the South I'm talking about."

"I get the feeling you believe the killer is not from the South."

"You're right."

"Why?"

"For one thing, he doesn't write like a Southerner."

"He is remarkably literate."

"Fuck you, Doctor. Ever read Faulkner? Thomas Harris?"

"I meant for a serial murderer, Mr. Cole. No need to get defensive."

A soft knock sounds at the door. I look over quickly, half expecting Miles. When the door opens, a slender woman with cinnamon skin enters soundlessly and places a silver tea service on Lenz's desk. The sweating pink Tab can looks incongruous on the gleaming tray. Without meeting my eyes she offers me a glass of ice, but I take only the can, pop the top, and drink half the contents in a few long swallows. Her black eyes rise to mine with disapproval. I try for a moment to guess her race but find myself at a loss. Living in Mississippi doesn't give you much practice for this. There it's either black or white, with a smattering of Vietnamese, Chinese, Lebanese, and Hispanic.

Lenz watches the dark woman pour his tea without comment. After she exits, he says, "Why don't we leave sex and violence for a moment?"

"Fine."

"Do you earn a lot of money?"

"Making money's not a crime yet, is it?"

"Were your parents wealthy?"

I lie back on the couch and focus on the stained ceiling tiles. "My mother grew up on a farm that didn't have electricity until she was fourteen years old. She picked cotton with her own hands all the way through college. In case you don't know, wealthy people don't pick cotton."

"Is money important to you?"

"Is that a serious question?"

"Your friend Mr. Turner seems to think you place an inordinate value on it."

"He talked to you about me?"

"A bit."

I lean up on one elbow. "Tell me one thing he told you."

"He told me you keep a cache of gold buried beneath your land."

"That lying son of a bitch."

"It's not true?"

"About the gold? Yeah, it's true. My grandfather Grant put in a nuclear bomb shelter at the farm during the fifties. Some company was traveling through Mississippi selling plans. Big concrete bastard sunk into the ground. I keep some gold there."

"Why?"

I lie back down and think for several moments. "I was raised by people who grew up during the Depression. I think the memory of that time stayed so real to my parents that it somehow entered me. Not the physical deprivation, but the knowledge that it could *actually happen*. That the whole social and financial structure of this country could implode and leave nothing but hungry and confused people."

"You feel anxiety about something similar happening again?"

"I work in financial markets, Doctor. Most of the guys I know in Chicago have no real conception of the Depression. They know the *word*, but the only mental reference point they have is 1987, and that was over in a couple of days. They leverage positions to the moon, trade derivatives they don't understand, tear apart companies in a day that took decades to build, and don't see any farther than next week's paycheck. You're asking me if I think it could happen again? You should be asking *when*."

"This hoarded gold is insurance against some sort of final collapse?"

"Laugh if you want. Ask the Russians how important gold is right this minute."

"Well, given these apocalyptic feelings, you seem like the last man in the world who'd be playing a game as risky as futures trading."

"I don't mind risk. Because I'm not playing a game."

"What do you mean?"

"No one who trades commodities has any intention of taking delivery of anything they buy or sell. It's all a paper illusion, a numbers game. Until that fatal margin call, anyway. One day I decided I'd take delivery on something, just to find out if any of it was real. I'd heard of an old guy in Baton Rouge who took delivery of a truckload of soybeans for the same reason. I chose gold. They delivered it, too. And right now it's locked in the bottom of that bomb shelter next to some forty-year-old cans of Spam."

"Remarkable."

"What does that tell you about me? Paranoia's in my genes? I've always known that. I consider it a Darwinian advantage."

"Is paranoia the reason a man of your youth and wealth chooses to live in such an isolated place?"

I raise my hands as if echoing his question.

"Let's try another tack. Why did you wait so long to go into the career for which you seem so singularly suited?"

"I don't know."

Lenz's voice swings back at me like a pendulum. "I'm sure you do."

"Does everybody with a green thumb run out and become a gardener?"

He folds his notepad shut and leans back in his chair. "Let's say a man is a gifted mathematician. He may not choose mathematics as his career, but he will likely choose a related field, such as architecture or engineering."

"I didn't."

"Of course you did. Music is fundamentally a mathematical art."

"That's what I've always heard. Usually from people who don't know diddly about music."

"What do you mean?"

"Sure, you can break music down into mathematics. Classical music, especially. But, Doctor, I've sat on the porches of tar-paper shacks with guys playing stuff . . . you wouldn't believe it. Old arthritic black guys playing out-of-tune guitars and just effortlessly bending the notes into tune, playing with their eyes shut and it didn't matter anyway 'cause they couldn't read a note. They play *between* the numbers, man. And that's just blues. Think about jazz. Music is math, what a load of crap."

"You're a romantic, Cole."

"Music is romantic."

"Not all music."

"Mine is. The music of my generation, and the one before. Somebody—Oscar Wilde, I think—said that when trying to describe the act of love, humans have two choices, the language of science or the language of the gutter, both of which are inadequate. But rock and roll split the difference. That's why it endures. It says the unsayable. Rage, angst, alienation, a dozen emotions. But the core of it is sex, Doctor. Sex, love, and obsession."

"An interesting thesis."

"That's no thesis. It's just *life*."

"I'd like to get back to your family for a moment."

"Did we ever leave?"

"Your father was a physician. How did that affect you, growing up?"

"I never had any anxiety about what my dad did for a living. 'What does your dad do? He's a doctor.' End of conversation."

"Negatives?"

I think a moment. "He wasn't home a lot of the time. And when he was, it could be weird. I remember times I cut my legs, needed stitches, stuff like that. I'd run in the house yelling, he'd be watching the Saints play or something. He'd take a look through all the blood, then send me off with my mom to clean it up while he waited for the end of the first half. Then we'd finally go down to his office and sew it up. That bugged me when I was young. But I guess it taught me something too. A lot of injuries that look bad aren't, really. No need to panic, you know?"

"What else?"

"Uh . . . speeding tickets."

"I'm sorry?"

"After I got my driver's license, I'd get stopped by the sheriff or the Yazoo City cops, like every other kid. They'd be writing me a ticket, then they'd look up like they just realized something and say, 'Are you Dr. Cole's son?' Most times they'd just tear up the ticket and let me go my way. At first I thought they were letting me go because they thought my dad was the greatest guy in the world. And some of them did. The black ones, especially. But even the white ones let me go, guys that probably hated my dad. Then I figured out the deal. Dad had been the police doctor for a while. Back several years before. A lot of these guys owed him money. He never would have tried to collect, but they didn't know that. They figured, I write this kid a twenty-dollar ticket, I get a bill for eight hundred bucks or whatever."

"Why did these white police officers hate your father?"

I take a long, weary breath and exhale slowly. "You've

arrived back at your second question, only you don't know it."

"Which question?"

"What am I proudest of."

"Ah. Will you answer it now?"

"I don't see the relevance."

"Please let me decide what's relevant."

"You think I'm going to spill my guts to you in the naive belief that you'd honor doctor-patient confidentiality?"

Lenz straightens at his desk. "I honor patient confidences absolutely."

"Yeah?" Propelled by some contrary impulse, I take out my wallet, withdraw a hundred-dollar bill, cross the room, and stuff the bill into Lenz's breast pocket. "You're hired."

"You're testing my patience, Mr. Cole."

"And I give you a C-minus. You want to turn off the tape recorder now?"

"I do not tape my sessions," he says indignantly.

"Thank you, Doctor Nixon."

Lenz looks genuinely indignant. "You're making me angry, Cole."

I back over to the couch and lie down again. "I'm now officially your patient. What if I tell you I killed those seven women?"

He catches his breath. "Did you?"

"Answer my question first."

Lenz nervously pushes up the nosepiece of his glasses. "If you're telling me that you did . . . well . . . my honest answer would be that I . . . I would try to find some other way of proving your guilt than violating doctor-patient confidentiality."

"What if you couldn't do that? And you knew I was going to kill again?"

"I don't know."

"You could always kill me yourself. Then doctor-patient privilege would no longer be in effect, right?"

"You're as bad as your friend."

"What do you mean?"

"The levels of deviousness. I don't know whether to tell Daniel to arrest Turner or to hire him as a consultant. I think he's already figured out more about the EROS killer than the Bureau has."

"That wouldn't surprise me." Again I wonder if the FBI arrested Miles right on this couch and hauled him off to jail. "On the other hand, maybe Miles knows so much because he *is* the killer."

Lenz doesn't bite.

A telephone on the desk emits a soft chirp and the psychiatrist answers, his eyes still focused on me. He listens, then covers the transmitter and says, "Would you mind leaving the room until I'm done?"

I stand up and step into the hall. Lenz's sonorous voice resumes behind me, muted by the heavy door. The dark-skinned receptionist is still AWOL from the billing office. I open the waiting-room door on the off chance that Miles may be there, but he isn't. Thinking I might catch Drewe on her cellular, I step over to the receptionist's desk. I am reaching for her phone when I notice an envelope with my name on it at the center of the desk. Without hesitation I pick it up and scan the few handwritten words on the paper inside.

Harper,

Brahma just logged back on to EROS under alias "Shiva." With that Wyoming court order, Baxter now has the power he needs to trace the call. I'll talk to you when I can.

Ciao

As I slip the note back into the envelope, the waiting-room door opens and a blond, square-jawed yuppie in a blue business suit steps inside. I crush the envelope into my pants pocket and head back toward Lenz's office.

The psychiatrist almost bowls me over as he hurries up the hallway, tugging on his jacket to the jingle of car keys.

"Sorry, Cole," he says, his voice clipped. "We're going to have to talk on the move. This is Special Agent Peter Schmidt."

I ignore Agent Schmidt as he steps up behind me. "What are you talking about? Where are we going?"

"That was Daniel Baxter on the phone. There's been a new development. I'm needed at Quantico and he told me to bring you along."

"What kind of development?" I ask, thinking of Miles's message.

"They may have found Rosalind May."

My heart thumps. "Dead?"

"We don't know."

"Look, I've got a flight to catch tonight, remember?"

"Cole, need I remind you that you are currently a suspect in seven capital murders?"

"You know I didn't kill those women."

"What I think doesn't matter at this point. A woman's life is at stake."

"You're lying, Doctor. What you think is all that matters."

Lenz looks at Agent Schmidt, then at the floor, then back at me. "Our UNSUB's in Dallas, Texas. It's your choice. Fly home and be out of it, or watch the killer you smoked out get what's coming to him."

In that moment all the hours I spent reading "David Strobekker's" dark seductions alone in my office come back to me. Beyond that, the horror and guilt of watching the first CNN report of Karin Wheat's murder twists in my gut like a strand of barbed wire. I have no choice.

"Let's go."

Chapter 17

Lenz leads Agent Schmidt and me across the parking lot to a midnight blue Mercedes 450SL. Schmidt starts to get in, but the psychiatrist pulls him aside and speaks softly, and he disappears.

Lenz drives with assurance, keeping just under the speed limit as he makes for a distant overpass bristling with green metal signs. Afternoon is wearing toward evening, the gray over our heads fading downward to a deep blue.

"We're about thirty-five miles from Quantico," he says, punching a button on his cellular phone, apparently to make sure it's working.

"If everything's happening in Dallas, why are we going to Quantico?"

"They have certain facilities there." He threads the Mercedes through a thicket of cars. "You'll know more soon."

"Nice ride," I comment.

"A gift from my wife," he says in a taut voice.

At that moment Lenz's cellular rings, and the speed with which he snatches it up betrays the tension he feels. He listens for twenty seconds, says yes twice, and then hangs up.

"Come on," I say sharply. "They traced Strobekker's call through Wyoming to Dallas, right? And they just got an exact address."

He looks over in astonishment. "How . . . ? Ah. Turner, of course." He stares at me another few seconds. "They traced the call from the Lake Champion phone exchange to the WATS line of a mining company in that town. The WATS was connected to Dallas, Texas. To an apartment. Rented under the name of David M. Strobekker."

"Holy shit. What's going to happen?"

"Dallas FBI and police SWAT teams have already surrounded the complex and evacuated the nearby apartments. Strobekker's still online. An FBI Hostage Rescue Team is en route from Kansas City via jet. They were waiting on alert there so that they could reach any U.S. destination in the shortest possible time."

"Don't you need to be in Dallas? In case there's a standoff or something? To try to talk the guy out?"

"Daniel has authorized explosive entry. Rosalind May could be inside, and Strobekker has already proved he'll kill without mercy. Hostage Rescue blows down the doors as soon as they get there. ETA eighty minutes."

"What if Strobekker tries to leave before they get there?"

"Dallas SWAT takes him down."

"You mean they kill him?"

"I hope it doesn't come to that. Where we're going, I'll be able to speak directly to whoever's in the apartment, if necessary."

I sit back heavily in my seat. Ten minutes ago I was angry and tired; now I taste the euphoria of my name being cleared, of my life getting back to its normal anxiety level.

Lenz gooses the Mercedes up an on-ramp and joins the southbound stream of traffic on 495. "Cole, I need your help, and you need mine. The best way for you to avoid trouble in this case is to assist with the investigation. But before I can use you, I have to be sure you're not involved."

"But they're about to nail the guy."

"Perhaps. Perhaps not. The evidence in this case suggests a group of offenders working in concert. Is Strobekker himself in that apartment? Or is it the owner of that Indian hair found at one of the crime scenes?"

Great. "What do you want from me?"

"Answers. I think you're a good man haunted by a bad thing. The question is, is that thing related to this case or not?"

"It's not, okay? Isn't my word enough?"

"I'm afraid not."

"Goddamn it, I reported the murders! And so far all I've gotten for my trouble is more trouble."

The psychiatrist looks away from the darkening road long enough to fix me with a disquieting stare. His face looks like my father's did the first time he confessed money problems to me. One minute I was looking at a man in his prime—responsible, circumspect, in charge—the next at a drawn visage haunted by failure and doubt. A face about to confide secrets that would change my life forever.

"I've been a forensic psychiatrist more than thirty years," Lenz says in a voice stripped of all affect. "Thirty years of listening to men describe how they tortured and violated children. Watching videotapes of men tearing women into bloody pieces in vans and basements." He lowers his head almost defensively. "My work is the benchmark by which others are measured. But not long ago, I reached a point where the compass that had led me thus far no longer functioned. I had problems at home. My work had become an endless round of tedium. Do you have any idea what the Investigative Support Unit actually does, Cole?"

"Catches serial killers, right?"

"Wrong. It does exactly what its title says. Gives *support*. The movie image of FBI agents single-handedly tracking down serial killers is pure fantasy. We advise. Local police do the physical work, make the arrest, and get the credit."

I watch Lenz from the corner of my eye.

"Killers are monotonous, as a rule," he goes on. "Variations on a theme. I testify at their trials, seal their fates, then recede back into the shadows. It's just . . . rote. The whole goddamned profession is being corrupted. By greed, ambition. Men I've trained peddle my ideas to the masses in the form of sensational books, lectures, and Hollywood consulting. None of which I ever had a taste for. I'm a scientist, do you understand? A physician."

The integrity in Lenz's voice is almost embarrassing. "I understand, Doctor."

"The only thing that kept me working was that the prospect of retirement seemed even less appealing."

"You just spoke in the past tense. What changed it?"

"You." Lenz turns to me with new light in his eyes. "The EROS killer has already murdered seven women we know of, with the corpses found in every case. Yet he staged each crime but two in such a way that they were not linked. And homicide detectives *look* for staging, believe me. Were it not for your coming forward—courageously, against the wishes of your company—he would still be killing without any risk of being caught."

Lenz may be manipulating me, but it feels pretty good to finally hear someone recognize my effort.

"Serial murderers normally operate on an emotional cycle," he explains. "They kill, cool off, kill again. Generally, the period between kills gets shorter and shorter until the murderer begins to decompensate, or come unstrung, in layman's terms. This is generally what allows him to be caught. You with me?"

"I'm with you."

"The EROS killer is different. He operates with utter calm and deliberation. He's not even *close* to decompensating. Serial offenders frequently communicate with police. He has not done so."

"What about the Henry Miller quote?"

"That was more staging, not real communication. In the stakes-through-the-eye-sockets case, he smeared the words 'Now she can see' on the bedroom mirror with feces. Pure theater. This man has harnessed computer technology not only to select his victims but also to probe their minds and emotions before he strikes. Miles Turner is a computer genius, yet he cannot or will not explain how Strobekker got hold of the EROS master client list—"

"That's why you suspect Miles," I cut in. "This guy is like Miles would be if he decided to start killing people."

"Exactly. And now he has kidnapped a woman."

"Do you know why?"

"No."

"Something to do with the pineal gland?"

"Almost certainly."

"This may sound crazy, Doctor, but could he be killing these women for some perfectly logical reason? Something we can't understand because we lack the information?"

"Crimes of this type are always eminently logical to the man who commits them, Cole. Keep one thing in mind. In serial murder, selection is everything. How does the killer choose his victims? What fantasy do they fulfill? If you can parse that out, you have your man. Or at least his profile."

"He uses EROS to select them."

"That's merely method. What are his criteria? The printouts you gave me are interesting, but they're basically seductions. They reveal no critical similarities among victims. Neither do studies of the victims' bodies or daily lives."

"They all had pineal glands."

"Yes. But of what sexual importance is the pineal?"

"I don't know. Does it have to be sexual?"

"Ultimately, yes. All murders of this type are sexually motivated. It's just that the sexual component may be deeply repressed. The taking of the pineal conjures images of cults or mad scientists, but in the end, all this will resolve into some variant of old-fashioned lust. Mr. Strobekker is what we called in the bad old days a lust killer, Cole. A sex killer."

"That's why you asked so much about my sex life."

He nods distractedly, his head swaying slightly from side to side as he drives. When he speaks again, his voice carries startling certitude. "I'm the only man alive who can stop him, Cole." He glances over as if to reassure me. "No, I haven't lost my head. All my life I've been training for this moment. You should see some of the profiles the junior men in the Unit have turned in. Not even close. Strobekker has them all chasing their tails. Why? Because he's a new species, Cole. They don't have little crib sheets that fit him."

"And you do?"

"I don't *need* any." Lenz taps his fingers excitedly on the wheel. "I wrote the books. The police won't stop Strobekker because he won't make a conventional mistake. He's not some traumatized human robot composted from the dregs of society. He has a brain. And he's *using* it." Lenz falls silent, apparently lost in a reverie. "This time," he says almost to himself, "I'm going to do something no one in the Unit has ever done. That no psychiatrist has ever done. I'm going to *catch this one myself.*"

I keep my eyes averted, surprised by the emotion he has invested in this case. "Unless Hostage Rescue gets him in"—I glance at my watch—"sixty minutes, you mean."

"Of course," he says, looking at me. "I've been speaking in terms of a single person, but the evidence points to a team-offender situation. That's what underlies the police interest in you and Turner. And that's what makes Dallas such an interesting development. Think about it. Who is inside that apartment?"

"I just don't see what you want from me."

"You will. I've been studying the printouts you gave me, and I'm convinced I can trap Strobekker."

"How?"

"By creating a fictional woman, then becoming that woman on EROS. To be frank, I'm almost done with her."

I am trying to digest Lenz's words, but the implications are too complex to take in at once.

"She fits the new victim profile almost exactly," he adds.

"New profile? You mean you're making her like Karin Wheat instead of the younger victims?"

"Yes. It's rare for a killer to establish so clear a pattern and then break it. If Wheat were merely a crime of opportunity, I'd discard her from the group. But she wasn't. Wheat represents a new paradigm."

"And my function?"

"Smoothing my entry into the EROS community."

"You don't know what you're getting into, Doctor. God only knows what databases this guy can access to check out people who approach him online."

Lenz chuckles. "Don't worry about that. Daniel's men are very good at paperwork. My personal Eliza Doolittle is in the process of coming to official life as we speak. Social Security number, DMV, voter registration, credit cards, credit history, a house, and a car. In a matter of hours she'll be as real as your wife."

"What's this fictitious woman's name?"

"Anne Bridges. But that's irrelevant. It's the alias that matters, correct?"

He's right. "What's the alias?"

"Something primal," Lenz says, obviously pleased with himself. "Archetypal. Biblical."

"What the hell is it?"

"You're interested now? Don't worry, you'll know soon enough. *If* you cooperate."

I could care less about the alias, but I do want to know who is in that Dallas apartment. After all, it was I who first detected Strobekker's deadly passage through the digital universe. "But you don't know anything about how EROS really works," I point out. "There are all kinds of esoteric abbreviations, informal practices, things that are understood only by the members."

Lenz smiles. "You just argued yourself into the job."

"You really think you can fool people—not just people, but *him*—into thinking you're a woman?"

"That's what makes it worthwhile. How much insight do I truly have into the female mind? This will be the acid test."

He blinks his headlights twice and roars past a semi-truck. "We're over halfway to Quantico, Cole. Let's hear your secret. If I decide it's unrelated to the case, you get me started on EROS, then you go home with no more police problems."

I turn and look out the passenger window. Halfway to Quantico. Halfway to the Hostage Rescue Team knocking down Brahma's door in Dallas. Lenz wants answers to his little questions, snapshots of my soul before I'm allowed into the inner circle of the investigation. What am I proudest of? Most ashamed of? The answer to the first question is private but not really secret, and it will get me to Quantico. The other answer can wait until that door goes down in Dallas. It can wait forever.

"I played music professionally for eight years," I say evenly.

Lenz settles back in his seat. "Were you successful?"

"Depends on your definition. I made a living. But as far as reaching my dreams, no. I'm a good songwriter and guitar player, but only a fair singer. Some people thought I was better than I did, but I always felt I needed someone else up front as lead vocalist."

"And this dependence led to conflict? Resentment?"

"Yeah. I'll skip five years of wasted time. The last band I was in had major-label interest. But by the time we'd gotten that far, the group was ready to self-destruct. I was writing the best material, and the singer—a good friend of mine—couldn't stand my getting that part of the glory. Forget that he got all the spotlight time. He wanted it to be him singing his stuff or nothing."

"So?"

"So it was nothing. He's still out there singing his stuff. The clubs are bigger, but he's on the same treadmill. When that group split, I decided I'd never again put myself into a situation where my destiny was controlled to any degree by another person."

"Now I understand the commodities trading," Lenz says. "No messy humans to deal with."

"You got it."

"And you got rich."

"You're damn right."

"You sound angry."

"Good assessment."

Lenz drives silently for a half mile, and I'm glad for the delay. Finally, he says, "And?"

"Before all that, I went to college like most of my friends. Majored in finance, the whole thing. But I'd wanted to play music since I was a kid. I used to ride up to Leland and Clarksdale and play blues with the old black cats—Son Thomas, Sam Chatmon, those guys.

When I got out of college, I went home and told my parents that before I got a job or went to graduate school, I was going to play music for a while."

"How did they respond?"

"Not well. When I was a kid, they were really supportive of my music. But during my senior year of high school, things changed."

"What happened?"

"The second act of a tragedy that started fifteen years before. Summer of sixty-four. The Freedom Summer. The year they killed those three civil rights workers in Neshoba County."

Lenz nods. "Schwerner, Chaney, and Goodman." He says the names softly, as if those long-dead kids were friends of his.

For the first time I suspect Lenz might be Jewish. "Right," I tell him. "Buried them in that dam. Anyway, a New York college sent some civil rights workers down to Cairo County, where our farm is. My dad, being who he was, decided to invite a couple of them over—"

"Excuse me? 'Being who he was?' "

"He wasn't a native Mississippian. He was from Louisiana, down below the hard-shell Baptist parishes. He was raised strict, but not prejudiced, you know? He was a doctor, but he came from working-class people. Grew up working right alongside blacks."

"Go on."

"These civil rights workers would come in from a day of running the back roads, teaching blacks how to answer the voting questionnaire or whatever, and my dad would feed them. He'd talk medicine, they'd talk politics. Or maybe they'd talk baseball. I got this from my mother, you understand, much later."

"Keep going."

"Anyway, the local yahoos, the Klan or whoever, didn't like my dad having these guys over to the house. They warned him, but Dad didn't pay any attention. Then this colored guy got killed at a church outside Itta Bena. They blew him up in his car. He was a patient of my father's. He'd served in action in Korea. Dad put a lot of stock in a man serving his country in battle. He'd turned a blind eye to a lot that the Klan and the Citizens' Council did in those days, like everybody else. But he couldn't stomach the murder of this black vet. He sat down and wrote an editorial that would blister the hide off a rattlesnake. He told it like it was, and he *named names.* He sent that piece to the Greenville paper, the liberal paper owned by Hodding Carter, the paper printed it, and lo, there came a shitstorm."

Lenz smiles in the dark. "I'll be damned."

"My mother just sat around the house waiting to be firebombed. But it didn't happen. Dad had been so public with his accusations that the Klan was afraid to do anything too soon after the piece appeared. The fact that my mother was from an old Delta family helped. It wasn't a wealthy family, but her people—the Grants—had been in the Delta about as long as anybody but the Indians. Quite a few white patients stopped coming to my father, but blacks took their places just as fast, so that didn't matter much. After about a year, it was all forgotten. At least by my family."

"But not by the Klan."

"I wouldn't necessarily say the Klan. The Klan doesn't even exist in Mississippi anymore. Not in any meaningful way. It's just a bunch of bitter old drunks now. Anyway, a lot of time passed. And during that time, another facet of my dad's character emerged, though we knew nothing about it."

I wonder how far we are from Quantico, but I don't dare break the flow to ask. "My dad was a doctor of the old school. All he cared about was treating people's sickness. He never thought about money. Some years he didn't collect fifty percent of what he was owed. And he'd accept anything as payment when he did collect. Green beans, catfish, peaches, venison, collard greens, whatever. He was still making house calls in 1987."

Lenz leans his head back and flips on the Mercedes's headlights. "A dying breed," he says softly.

"A dead breed. And the country's worse off for it. Anyway, his entire financial planning strategy was his belief that if a doctor worked hard in America, he'd make enough money to raise his family and pay for his whiskey and cigars, and send in the next patient please. Get the picture?"

"A common failing among practitioners of his generation."

"Yeah? Well, it didn't take long for that failing to get him into serious trouble. By 1968 he was a year behind on his income taxes. That meant that every April—*every year*—he had to go to the bank and borrow the full amount of his taxes to pay off the government—something like sixty or seventy thousand dollars at whatever the interest rate happened to be. And after he'd paid, he would *still* be a year behind. He did that for twenty years."

"My God."

"Talk about pressure. But he didn't tell a soul about it. It was a secret between him and his banker, who was thrilled by the arrangement, of course. There was enough cash flow that nobody felt the pinch, but it was all an illusion."

"What about an equity loan?" Lenz asks. "A home mortgage?"

"Not a chance. All he could have used as collateral was the farm or the house sitting on it, and both had been in my mother's family for generations. She didn't have any brothers, so hers was the first generation of Grants that hadn't farmed the land. They leased it out. Anyway, Dad felt the debt was his cross to bear. He just worked harder and harder.

"My junior year of high school, things came to a head. The people we leased the farm to had had two bad harvests in a row. Dad's income was stretched to the breaking point. And when he went into the bank and asked for his annual tax loan, they said no. They'd never demanded collateral before, because they knew he could cover the debt. But this time they did. He was stunned. He went to another bank and got the same story. After a while he figured it out. The chickens from 1964 had come home to roost."

Lenz is shaking his head.

"You can see the rest. Dad had to put up the farm as collateral. Carter was president; interest rates were twenty percent. When Dad finally told my mother how things stood, she didn't hesitate to sign the papers. But it almost killed her. Her father had never believed in borrowing money, and she didn't either. I mean *never.* Dad worked harder that year than he ever had in his life. He was nearly fifty then, and he was working hundred-hour weeks. Seventy-two-hour shifts in emergency rooms out of town. Seven months into it, he had a coronary. He survived, but the cash dried up. I worked, my mother worked, but it wasn't any good. The people we leased to had their third bad year, and we lost the farm."

"All of it?"

"We managed to keep the home place. Where my wife and I live now. Everything else the bank took. They put it up for auction, but somehow the bank president himself bought it for about half what it was worth. He was a smug, redneck son of a bitch named Crump. He *loved* taking that land. He was about sixty-five then."

"How did this affect your mother?"

The memory of my mother in those years is something I would prefer to forget. "She became a ghost," I say softly.

"I beg your pardon?"

"A ghost of herself."

Lenz nods silently.

"So you can imagine what happened when I arrived home from college four years later with my honors degree in finance and announced my intention to roam the country playing guitar. They weren't exactly thrilled."

"Yet you did it anyway."

"Not immediately. For a couple of weeks I just moped around. Then I got mad. I saw that their whole view of the world had been warped and beaten down by bastards like Crump. And worse, that it was going to affect my whole life if I let it."

"Did you confront Crump?"

"What good would that have done? I had no leverage, no power. I packed up my clothes, my textbooks, and my life savings—five grand—and took the Amtrak to Chicago. One of my professors wangled me a job at a company with seats on the Board of Trade. After a week of trading for the company, I started trading for myself. And I was *fearless.* I can't explain it. I was trading like I played music, purely on instinct. Balls to the wall, sometimes risking everything on single trades. I'd have a stroke if I tried that now. I'm a system trader—I cover every conceivable angle before I make a move. But back then I was high on rage. Everything I'd ever learned had somehow been recalled and slaved to my anger. I was like Mr. Spock possessed by a pissed-off Captain Kirk. A fucking superman."

My pulse races just remembering that rush.

"The market was different then too. Especially the S&P index. You could leverage your position to an unbelievable point. It was like showing up at the Indy 500 with a Ford Pinto, handing them your keys, and them saying, 'Son, these Pinto keys qualify you to drive a Maserati for the duration of the race. Of course, if you wreck the car, you'll have to pay for it, but we'll worry about that when it happens. Please try not to kill yourself.' And then they let you drive out onto the track."

"And you won the race?"

"I kicked ass, Doctor. After five months, I resigned from the firm, and a twelve-hour train ride later I was back in the Delta. I went straight to the bank and asked to see Crump. I must have looked like shit on a stick after that train ride, but he didn't bat an eye. He was past seventy by then.

"I told him I wanted to buy back our farm. Crump said the land wasn't for sale. I told him I'd give him a good price. He told me not to let the door hit my ass on the way out. I knew what fair market value was, so I named a figure double that—four times what he'd paid for it. Crump said no sale. I was starting to lose my temper, but I didn't show it. I told him he ought to be sensible, that everything had a price. He told me that wasn't always the case.

"That stumped me. I'd been relying on his greed, and he'd made a statement that indicated I might have misjudged him. He was staring at me the way a hunter looks at a treed coon, and I decided then that my only chance was to go for broke. I told that son of a bitch I'd pay him four times market value for the farm—an *eight hundred percent profit*—but that the offer was good for only sixty minutes. I said I'd be back in one hour and if he wanted the money he'd better have the papers ready. I walked out to a cafe, had three slow cups of coffee, took a leak, and walked back to the bank."

"And?"

"And Crump had his lawyer and two witnesses and the contract sitting there waiting for my signature. After I signed the papers, he told me I was the dumbest egg sucker that ever walked through his door. I said maybe I was, but that I had ten thousand bucks left and I'd have given him that and the shirt off my back for that land, and I hoped he died a damned lonely death."

Lenz has turned his head to me. He is staring with new eyes. "Is that story true? It sounds like something from *It's a Wonderful Life.*"

"An R-rated version, maybe. It's true all right. Life doesn't give you many chances like that."

He nods. "Life didn't give you that, Cole. You took it."

"A barber drove me out to the farmhouse. Mom was in the kitchen, smoking a cigarette and drinking a cold cup of coffee. When I laid that deed down on the table in front of her, she stared at it for nearly a minute. Then she looked up and asked me if it was real. If it was *real.* When I told her it was, she broke into pieces. She just . . . it was too much. She was shaking and crying and trying to hug me, and right then . . . goddamn it, I knew what it felt like to be a man. You know? I finally understood that being a man means taking care of the people you love, no matter how you do it. Even if you have to die to do it."

"How did your father take the news?"

"I guess relief was the main thing. For four years he'd lived knowing he'd failed my mother and would never be able to make it right. My getting back the land changed things for the better, but a lot of damage had already been done. Dad had spent four years thinking he was worth more dead than alive to the people he loved. Businesswise, his life insurance policy was about the only thing he'd done right. He figured dying was the only way he could take care of his own. He'd started drinking heavily. It wasn't a perfect happy ending or anything."

Lenz raises a finger and points to a turn in the road at the limit of his high beams. "But the best ending possible under the circumstances, in my view. You have my respect, Cole."

The Mercedes takes the curve with the grace of a racing hound and glides toward a lighted gatehouse in the distance. "A lot of men go through life the way your father did."

"Silent desperation, right?"

"Thoreau knew a thing or two."

"Actually that's James Taylor. Thoreau said *quiet* desperation."

Lenz snorts. "My mistake."

The Mercedes stops at the gate long enough for a uniformed marine to come to the window, check Lenz's pass, and wave us through. Before we've driven fifty yards the rattle of gunfire rolls out of the darkness. I feel as though we're moving through a ghostly skirmish in these historic Virginia woods, but it must be marines on night maneuvers. After we pass a second gate, a complex of lighted buildings much like a college campus appears. Lenz picks up his cellular and hits a speed-dial code, mutters into the phone, then hangs up and makes a sharp turn off the main drive.

"Hostage Rescue touches down in Dallas in twenty minutes," he says. "They'll be at the apartment in thirty-five, maximum. Strobekker's still online."

I shudder with the sudden exhilaration of impending action. "This is unbelievable."

Lenz nods. "And we're going to have a front-row seat."

"What do you mean?"

"Wait." He stops the Mercedes near the rear of a parked semitruck and looks at me. I hear a heavy metallic *ching*, then watch in amazement as the rear panel of the semitrailer rises into the roof and dim red light bleeds out around the silhouette of a man. I have only seen him once in my life, but every fiber of my instinct tells me that black shadow belongs to Daniel Baxter, chief of the Investigative Support Unit.

"We drove all this way to get to a *truck*?"

Lenz chuckles softly. "Don't say that word anywhere near the people you're about to meet. They call this vehicle Doctor Cop. For MDCP—Mobile Digital Command Post. You're about to see interactive media like you never imagined, Cole. As close as the FBI ever gets to Hollywood."

Chapter 18

The silhouette at the back of the truck does belong to Daniel Baxter. After shaking hands with me, he leads us into the strangest environment I have ever entered. The interior of Dr. Cop—the Mobile Digital Command Post—feels like a mobile home from some world's fair exhibition fifty years in the future. It is long and narrow and stuffed to the ceiling with rack-mounted shock-cushioned computers, CRTs, satellite receivers, surveillance gear, and pale technicians with bona fide nerd packs in the pockets of their short-sleeve poly-cotton shirts.

A constant thrumming vibrates the floor of the command post. Soft radio chatter emanates from several sets of speakers, none of it in sync. I assume the nerds are somehow following all of this. Baxter leads us along a cramped walk space to a curved bank of video screens. Most are blank, but two show black-and-white views of what appears to be a detached apartment building much like the ones I lived in during college.

"Is that it?" Lenz asks.

Baxter nods. "Two apartments per unit. Strobekker is six seventy-two. Six seventy-three is empty, thank God."

"Is that a live feed?" I ask.

He nods.

"The resolution's unbelievable."

"Digital video. We're getting it encrypted over a secure channel." Baxter points at a screen. "Notice the windows of the apartment? Covered with aluminum foil on the inside."

"Bad sign," says Lenz. "How long until HRT gets there?"

"Touchdown in five minutes at Love Field. Another ten, give or take, to get on site. The complex is about halfway between Love and Dallas–Fort Worth International, just one in a sea of complexes. Anonymous as you can get."

"Anything I can do before Hostage Rescue goes in?"

Baxter shakes his head. "He's using the only phone, so we can't call and ask him to come out. I don't think I would anyway. He might do the hostage."

Lenz nods. "Mr. Cole and I need to speak privately. Any chance?"

I can't believe Lenz is this persistent. Baxter motions for us to follow him through a narrow door at the end of the aisle. Beyond it is a dim room with six bunks shelved up the walls in groups of three and a microwave kitchenette between.

"I want you with me when they go in, Arthur," Baxter says. "If our UNSUB is as smart as he's been so far, he may catch on and barricade himself."

"Wouldn't miss it," says Lenz.

When the door closes after Baxter, the psychiatrist takes a seat on one of the bottom bunks, pulls a pack of cigarettes from his pocket and lights one, which must be breaking about a dozen rules in this high-tech government vehicle. No alarm goes off. He blows smoke away from us and says, "You talked your way in. Let's finish up."

"Doctor, nothing I could tell you has anything to do with the EROS murders."

"Then the sooner you tell me, the sooner you'll be in the clear."

My eyes remain on his face, but my mind is far away.

He takes another drag in silence, then gets up from the bed and squats before a small refrigerator. The opening door fills the room with sickly fluorescent light. "Eureka," he says in a deadpan voice. "It seems that Daniel's boys share your taste for orally administered carcinogens."

Lenz holds a pink Tab can covered with icy condensation over his shoulder. I take it, pop the top, and suck down half its contents in four quick swallows. The peppery sting of caffeine-spiked carbonation burns my gums and throat and makes my eyes water. I feel twice as good as I did ten seconds ago. I want to tell Lenz that there is no secret, that I've never done anything to really be ashamed of, but of course that would be absurd. He knows there's something there. He knows there's always something.

"You still don't understand what's happening, do you?" he says, sitting back on the bed with a bottle of Evian.

"I know a woman's life is at stake."

His face is a gray outline behind gray smoke. "That's not what I mean. Something's eating you up inside, Cole. I'd say it's been eating at you for a long time. You *need* to tell me this thing. Don't you feel that?"

The maddening thing is that Lenz is right. I don't especially want to tell *him*, but lately some part of me has been bursting to rid itself of this psychic weight.

"Relax," he says. "I carry more secrets around in my head than any ten priests. There's hardly room in there for sins like yours, between the rapes and the child abuse and the murders."

"None of those give you leverage over me," I point out, my voice brittle.

He smiles a little at that. "You think I don't have leverage now?"

I shrug.

In that moment Lenz's eyes look older than any I've ever seen. Older than the eyes of crooked black women in the Delta, older than the eyes of men who've survived combat. "It's your wife's sister," he says softly. "Isn't it."

No feigned reaction will deceive those eyes. Fury at Miles boils like acid up into my chest.

"Don't blame Turner," Lenz says gently. "He doesn't even know he knows. I think he's half in love with the girl himself."

I say nothing.

Lenz takes a drag from his cigarette. "I know you're no murderer." He laughs. "Your sense of guilt is far too well developed for that. What do you think? I'm fishing for information to ruin your marriage? To force you to work for me? Like the threat of arrest or ten years of tax audits wouldn't be enough?"

He stands suddenly and pats me on the shoulder. "Take it easy, Cole. Let's go watch some TV. One way or another, everything's going to look a lot different in a few minutes."

With that he opens the door and leads me back into the main room. A small crowd has gathered around the video bank, but it parts like the Red Sea for Lenz. I slipstream behind him.

One of the nerds has taken up station in a chair before the monitor bank, a headset over his ears, both hands on control knobs. I hear a burst of static, then a Southern-accented voice saying, "This is Deke Smith, Dallas SWAT, advising Hostage Rescue has arrived."

The acknowledgment is lost beneath Daniel Baxter's "Okay, let's do it." He nods anxiously at the screens. "Did they lock and load in the van?"

The nerd in the chair repeats the question like a submarine officer relaying the orders of his captain. He listens to his headset, then replies, "Locked and loaded. Approaching the local command post."

"Damn it, I want to hear everything," snaps Baxter. "Put it all on the squawk box."

The nerd flips a couple of switches, and suddenly the trailer is alive with the voices of the Dallas FBI SWAT team, the Dallas police, an FBI command post, and the wireless communications of the FBI Hostage Rescue Team.

"Bravo Leader, checking in. Testes, testes, one, two."

Someone behind me emits a truncated laugh.

"That's Joe Payne, Hostage Rescue commander," Baxter says, either for my benefit or Lenz's. "They're Bravo Team."

The remainder of Payne's unit checks in, which sounds like between eight and twelve men. It's hard to tell because they all talk at once.

"We live to Alpha?" someone asks over the radio. Payne, I think.

Baxter hits the nerd on the shoulder. The nerd mutters into his headset mike. Someone on-site tells Payne he is live to Alpha.

"Are we Alpha?" I ask.

A tech opposite me rolls his eyes.

"Is the target still on the phone?" asks Payne.

Someone farther along the trailer yells, "Affirmative. An EROS tech in New York confirms UNSUB interacting with a female subscriber."

"Prospective victim number eight," says Baxter.

"No point in waiting," crackles Payne's voice. "Can't see anything through the windows. Let's mount up."

"What about video?" asks Baxter. "You got a camera going in?"

The nerd relays the question, and Payne says, "Camera goes in right after the guns."

Unable to bear the delay, Baxter yanks the headset off the nerd's head and puts it on. "Joe, this is Dan Baxter.

You don't want to slip a pinhole camera under the door and check the layout?"

"Not this time. Dallas P.D. did a good job staying out of sight. I don't think this guy knows the cavalry's here. I don't want anyone approaching that door until we go up with the sledgehammers."

"The manager wouldn't give up a key?"

"Sledgehammers are faster," says Payne. "We're busting off the hinges in case he has hardened dead bolts. I'm holding a floor plan now. Last-minute advice?"

Baxter turns to Lenz. "Arthur?"

"Whoever's in there," says Lenz, "I'd like to see them get out alive. We could learn a lot."

"I heard that," says Payne. "You tell your shrink no guarantees. This guy throws down on us, we take him out."

"Can they go for a disabling wound?" asks Lenz.

Baxter starts to explain something about body armor, but Payne's reply drowns him out. "If my men shoot, they shoot for the head."

"Good luck, Joe," says Baxter.

"I'll watch the reruns with you tonight," says Payne. "You bring the beer."

"You're on."

Suddenly the camaraderie is gone. Now the radio exchanges sound like snippets from a World War II combat movie. Curt questions, clipped replies. I hear several sighs of satisfaction around me as a third video screen lights up. On it is a black-and-white image that looks like it's being shot by a five-year-old. Nothing but black boots. Then the frame rises and focuses on the back of a black UPS-style truck. On the spare wheel housing, stenciled in gold, are six words that make it clear that this truck does not belong to a shipping company:

BAD COMPANY
ANY TIME, ANY PLACE

"Jesus," mutters Baxter, but when he turns to Lenz he is smiling. "The Dallas FBI SWAT motto."

The short ugly snout of a submachine gun passes into the frame, wiggles, and disappears.

"Cameraman's carrying," says a tech.

"Good for him," says Baxter. "He's probably seen those Civil War movies where the flag bearer charges with nothing but a flag. At least he learned something."

The new video image suddenly begins to jerk. A flash of sidewalk, then I'm moving along it the way you do when you're watching a horror film. The camera rises, showing us the back and shoulders of a man walking ahead of it. Then others in file ahead of him. Moving quickly now. They're clad from boots to balaclava helmets in bulky black jumpsuits with ripstop nylon and Kevlar and guns strapped all over them. They look like paratroopers.

"Go, ninjas," whispers someone near the video monitors.

The entire team suddenly appears on one of the static screens. They're standing behind the wall of the apartment building nearest Strobekker's, their backs to the camera. Over their shoulders, Strobekker's front door is clearly visible. It looks no more than twenty feet away, but then I remember how camera angles can distort distance. It's like watching a baseball pitcher from a camera placed behind the catcher; you think you could reach out and touch him, but he's over sixty feet away.

"This is Bravo Leader," says Payne. "Ten seconds."

On the static view the Hostage Rescue Team lines up in a formation not unlike a football team. In front stand two men with black-painted sledgehammers in their hands.

"Five seconds," says Payne.

"Rock and roll," murmurs Baxter.

"GO!"

Payne's barked command seems to propel the two point men across the open ground by volume alone. They move quickly, but anyone who has ever lifted a sledgehammer knows that a full-speed sprint while carrying one is out of the question.

"GO! GO! GO!" someone shouts.

When the lead agents reach Strobekker's door, the mobile video camera begins to move. Everyone in the trailer is racing across the open space with the second element of the assault team. On the static image I see the apartment door go down like a piece of styrofoam.

"FEDERAL AGENTS! FEDERAL AGENTS!" scream wild voices, and by then at least five men have gone through the door.

"DROP YOUR WEAPON! ON THE FLOOR RIGHT NOW!"

"Jesus!" I grab Baxter's coat. "They got him?"

"Shut up, Cole!"

"Camera's in," a tech says softly.

"Holy shit," someone hisses.

The mobile camera shows an apartment as bare as a spinster's cupboard. Men are still yelling "Federal agents!" but as the camera swings around the apartment I see no one but the commandos of the Hostage Rescue Team.

"Locked door!" someone screams.

"Strobekker just went off-line!" shouts a voice from inside the trailer.

I hear a crash as the locked door goes down, but the camera does not follow.

"Don't shoot him!" shouts Lenz. *"For God's sake, don't fire!"*

I am stunned beyond words when Baxter turns and shoves Arthur Lenz out of range of the mike. Brahma's fate is in the hands of soldiers now.

"What the fuck?" says a shocked voice. "Did he go out the window?"

"Negative!" someone answers. "This is Dallas SWAT leader, no rabbits."

"Closet's empty!" screams a shaky young voice.

"What the fuck?"

"Get the camera in there!" yells Baxter. "What's going on, Joe?"

"Alpha, there's nothing in this apartment but a computer and a phone. We've been had."

"What?"

"There's no monitor attached to the computer, but it appears to be powered up. No keyboard either."

"Get the goddamn camera in there!"

Finally the mobile camera squeezes through the crowd of broad black shoulders and shows us the room. Payne is right. There is nothing inside but a harmless-looking white PC sitting on the floor beside a telephone.

"What good's a computer without a monitor or keyboard?" he asks.

"Shit," I say, not wanting to believe what I am seeing. But I am seeing it.

"What?" asks Baxter, turning to me.

"The drive light. The hard drive is active."

"Goddamn it," curses a tech. "The drive's reformatting itself! Erasing itself!"

As I watch the tiny flashing dot of the drive light, I know that the tech is wrong. I don't know why, but I know.

"Pull the plug!" shouts the tech.

"Wait!" I say, holding up my hands. "That's—"

"Joe!" yells Baxter. "Pull the fucking plug!"

"No!" I scream. *"Get your men out! Everybody out now!"*

Baxter whirls on me with fury in his eyes. Then comprehension dawns. He opens his mouth and yells, *"JOE! GET—"*

But he is too late. A black-clad figure has leaped at the

electrical socket with his arm extended, reaching into a white flash that seems to sear the screen as it goes blank.

"Oh my God," says a flat voice.

The two static cameras continue recording as yellow flame blasts out the windows on one side of Strobekker's apartment building. The sound of the explosion is muted after being filtered through countless circuits to arrive here in Quantico, but its effect in the trailer could not be more profound.

Baxter gapes at the video bank while screams of anguish pour from the speakers. Disjointed voices from the Dallas command post shout at each other to call paramedics and the fire department. Other voices—almost unrecognizable from shock and panic—scream to get the wounded out of the smoke-filled building.

"What in God's name just happened?" Baxter asks. Then he snaps out of whatever trance he was in and begins shouting questions and commands over the link to Dallas. The technicians behind him are conspicuously silent. "Was that Joe who reached for the plug?" he asks.

No one volunteers an answer.

On the two remaining live screens, wounded or dead men are being dragged from the smoking apartment. I know some are alive, because their agonized shrieks are being transmitted over the radio net.

"Dan?" croaks a voice. "This is Joe."

Everyone in the trailer freezes. Near the apartment building, a black-suited agent has held up his right arm and waved broadly at one of the static cameras.

"Thank God," mutters Baxter. "What's your situation, Joe?"

"FUBAR. I just wanted to let you know I made it." Payne rips off his balaclava and bends over to catch his breath. "I'm gonna be busy for a few minutes. I'll get back to you when I can."

"Do what you have to do, buddy."

When Daniel Baxter turns around to face the technicians, his rage is fearsome to behold. "What the *hell* just happened?" he asks, his eyes flicking from man to man.

"He knew," I say.

"He couldn't have known."

"Not about this raid. But he knew you'd be coming eventually. And he prepared for it."

One of the nerds says, "Tell them to check the front door, chief. Look for an alarm. Trip wire. Something."

Baxter turns back to the screens but issues no orders. There's no point until the tragic opera on the video bank is brought under control. HRT commandos crouch over their prostrate comrades, giving what help they can from first aid kits. The radio chatter focuses on the danger of fire until some Dallas SWAT officers go in with extinguishers and hose down the apartment's interior with chemical foam. The mood in the trailer reminds me of the hotel lobby I was in when I saw the *Challenger* explode after launch. Suddenly, in a moment of dead air, a broken voice says:

"He's gone."

The radio chatter stutters, dies. On-screen, a crouching FBI agent wipes a hand across his eyes, then removes his coat and lays it over the face of a man on the ground.

"God in heaven," Baxter murmurs.

As the paramedics arrive and load the casualties into ambulance bays, a black-suited commando with bloody hands and a scorched black face steps up to one of the static cameras. The whites of his eyes seem to give off their own light.

"Dan?" he says, panting like a man who has run five miles.

"Right here, Joe. What can I do?"

"I was about to ask you the same thing."

"What's the status of your men?"

"Four took shrapnel. We got everybody out, but Pete

Carelli died on the ground. If it hadn't been for the body armor, we would've had four KIA."

"What about you, Joe?"

"I was outside the bedroom. I caught some stuff in my arms and hands. Nothing to write home about."

"Any way you can get in there to check some things?"

Payne nods wearily, then turns and hustles five men together using hand signals.

Baxter says, "We're looking for trip wires, alarms, you know the drill."

Payne grunts into his mike. There is no mobile camera this time, but seconds later we hear him and his men and tearing through the apartment.

"Son of a bitch!" cries a young voice. "I've got it! Photoelectric beam. Standard alarm kit."

"We're following the wire," says Payne. "Runs along a baseboard."

"Got another beam on the bedroom door," calls out another voice.

"Window too," says a third.

"Okay, Dan," says Payne. "We got a rectangular black box in the closet of the adjoining bedroom."

"Good work, Joe. Gimme a sec." Baxter turns back to his techs. "Somebody lay it out for me."

No one offers anything.

I guess I have the least to lose here. "That apartment's nothing but a wire with tin cans tied to it," I tell him. "A perimeter. Payne's team broke the beam and the black box alerted the computer. The computer sent out a message to Strobekker, wherever he really is—that's why it didn't blow immediately—and then it self-destructed. He knows you're after him now, Mr. Baxter. Or he will soon."

"But how could he not be there? We traced the call to that apartment. He was somewhere else the whole time?"

"You said the apartment next door is empty, right?"

Baxter's eyes narrow. "Joe, did Dallas SWAT check the apartment next door?"

"Negative. The manager said no one lived there, so I issued orders from the plane. Do not approach under any circumstances. Didn't want to risk the UNSUB seeing or hearing anything."

"Check it now. But for God's sake be careful."

"You heard him," says Payne.

We wait in a distinctly uncomfortable silence. Lenz stands sipping his Evian water about five feet from the crowd. When he notices me watching, he gives me a mock salute.

"Goddamn it!" says a voice over the speaker. "There's another phone over here! By the wall adjoining the target apartment. The thing's blasted to hell, but it's a phone. There's a modem too, and some other kind of gray box. Looks homemade."

"I will have someone's ass," says Baxter. "Where's the manager of the complex?"

"Outside, Alpha," says a different voice.

"Put that son of a bitch on camera."

A command is barked. Then two Dallas SWAT officers pull a middle-aged man with dark skin and black hair into view. He looks like an Arab.

"Arrest and Mirandize him," says Baxter.

I stare as a Dallas police officer arrests the terrified apartment manager and reads his Miranda rights.

"Put a headset on him," Baxter orders. When this is done, he asks, "What's your name?"

The man swallows and says, "Patel. Mohandas Patel."

I close my eyes in disbelief. An Indian.

"You manage these apartments, Mr. Patel?"

"I own them. With my brother, resident of Houston."

"One of the murders was in Houston," says one of the nerds.

Baxter asks, "Why did you tell the police that apartment was empty, Mr. Patel?"

"I did not say that. I said no one lived there."

"There's a telephone inside that apartment, sir. Someone must have put it there. Someone who rented the apartment."

Patel's eyes brighten. "Ah, yes, apartment was *rented.* But no one ever moved in. They pay the rent, I don't ask questions. Police ask who lives in that unit, I tell them no one. I tell them correctly, yes?"

Baxter expels air, trying to suppress a fury I can only guess at. "Who rented that apartment, Mr. Patel?"

"Nice lady," he says. "A lady from my own country."

"An Indian woman?"

"Yes, sir."

A sigh of satisfaction from Dr. Lenz's direction.

"How old was she?" asks Baxter.

Patel rocks his head from left to right, estimating from memory. "Between forty and fifty. Hard to tell these days. Well-spoken lady. Very lovely."

"Who rented the other apartment?"

"Mr. Strobekker. Almost a year ago."

"What did he look like?"

"I already described him for the police."

"Describe him again."

Patel hesitates, then looks at each of the officers holding his arms. Both are at least a foot taller than he is. "I believe I would like to call my brother," he says in a shaky voice.

"At least he didn't ask for a lawyer," murmurs a voice behind me.

"My brother is an attorney," adds Patel, driving the final nail into Baxter's interrogation.

"Alpha, this is Bravo Leader," says Payne, his voice cool and professional again. "Dallas police advise they do a lot of business at this complex. High-dollar call girls, drug busts, you name it. The rent is high but it buys privacy."

"Damn," Baxter mutters.

Someone pulls the headset off Patel. "What you want us to do with him?" asks a heavy Texas accent. The voice of a cowboy.

"Book him," says Baxter. "Let him call his brother, then sweat them both. Threaten them with RICO, terrorism, whatever it takes. I'll send my regional profiler over to consult. We've got a hostage out there somewhere. Copy that?"

"Yessir," says the cowboy. "Let's take this one back to the barn, boys."

"This is Bravo, Dan," says Payne, off camera. "You want us back in Kansas City?"

Baxter thinks for a few seconds. "No. Get your wounded squared away, then get back here ASAP. Sorry, buddy."

"No problem. We may doze, but we never close. Mount up, girls."

The video screens wink out.

"Why didn't we trace through to that second phone?" Baxter asks, turning toward the techs.

"He could have blocked it," one answers. "With the right equipment. Some kind of relay. Probably that gray box."

"Equipment notwithstanding," says a calm voice on the periphery, "I believe Mr. Strobekker's ruse worked on a deeper level." It's Lenz, of course. "He led us through a dozen states, overseas, then through that little burg in Wyoming—which we assumed was his pièce de résistance—and finally to the Dallas apartment. That was the first actual residence we tracked him to, so we assumed it was where he lived. I'll bet the technicians didn't even try to look beyond it."

I think I see a couple of sheepish faces among the techs.

"The question," says Baxter, "is can we trace the call now that it's been terminated?"

"There'll definitely be a record," a tech says brightly.

"I don't want to rain on your parade, guys," I chime in, "but I think you're going to find that telephone simply dialed an Internet on-ramp, and from there sent a message to some anonymous bulletin board a thousand miles away. Strobekker dropping off-line during the raid was probably coincidence. He wouldn't risk a direct link to his physical location. If you get the phone records, you can find out where that computer sent its warning message *to*, but if it's a big BBS, thousands of people will log on over the next few days and see it. And you'll never be able to track them all."

Baxter's face tightens with frustration. "We have access to some excellent cryptanalysts. If we could find the message, we might be able to break it down."

"That's not the point. We already know what it says. It might be only one character. It might be a 'test' message, of which there are thousands. It might even say, 'Dear Daddy, somebody just blew me up.' "

"Goddamn it!" curses Baxter, his anger like a kerosene heater in the room.

"You need Miles Turner," I say bluntly. "He can nail this bastard for you."

"Turner may *be* this bastard," says Lenz, stepping through the tech desks.

"Bullshit, Doctor."

Baxter is studying me intently. "Is Turner that good?"

"He is truly scary, Mr. Baxter."

"I'll hire him as a consultant. Plenty of precedent."

"Not Turner," Lenz says firmly.

Baxter waves his hand and the crowd of techs scatter like leaves. When they are sufficiently dispersed, he says on a low voice, "We've taken casualties, Arthur. We've got a hostage out there. Hopefully alive. You've got a proactive plan, but it's a long game. We've got to get this SOB before he kills Rosalind May or anybody else."

"Using Turner would be a mistake, Daniel. If you want an electronics wizard, call the NSA. If you want Strobekker, give me Cole."

Baxter considers this long enough for me to get edgy. Then he says, "The Bureau was slow to get on the computer crime bandwagon, Arthur, and I'm not ready to say we've caught up. Cole came close to saving a life today, and he says Turner's better than he is."

"Daniel," Lenz says evenly, "if my past work means anything to you, trust me now."

Baxter bites his bottom lip and probes Lenz's eyes. A silent conversation is taking place based on years of professional association, and maybe more than that. It might as well be in Farsi. Lenz is the first to speak aloud.

"How's my alter ego coming?"

Baxter does not respond. Then, almost grudgingly, he says, "Another hour should do it. It's tough to get access to some of those offices after hours."

While I have Baxter close, I take a chance. "Mr. Baxter, I'm ready and willing to assist Dr. Lenz, but I'd like to do as much of it as I can from home. There's no reason we can't work together that way. And quite frankly, I promised my wife I'd be back by morning."

Baxter's mind is miles away. "How long do you need Cole to get you started, Arthur?"

"Impossible to say." Lenz glares at me. "He won't make a commercial flight anyway. Not back to Mississippi."

Baxter checks his watch, then looks at Lenz. "I'd prefer not to use the regional SWAT teams for this. At oh-one hundred hours I'm deploying a second Hostage Rescue unit from Quantico to a more southern-lying city. Jan Krislov offered us the use of her corporate jet, and I took her up on it. Cole, you get Dr. Lenz set up and running in three hours, you can hitch with HRT. I'll have the pilot set you down in Jackson. Good enough?"

"That's where my truck is. I appreciate it, sir."

Lenz looks like he might argue, but Baxter doesn't give him the chance. With a curt nod he is away and reaching for a telephone.

Lenz motions me toward the door of the command post. Keeping my arms close to my body, I move carefully down the narrow aisle between the shelves of humming equipment, past Baxter, past the short-sleeve poly-cotton shirts glowing in the pixel light. Someone rises to let me out of the trailer, and when my feet hit the pavement I expel the conditioned air from my lungs and drink in the cool forest breeze.

Hearing the scrape of a shoe behind me, I turn and find the square-jawed face of Special Agent Schmidt staring from the darkness.

"Why don't you wait in the car?" he suggests, opening the door of Lenz's Mercedes.

Two minutes after Schmidt closes me inside, Lenz slides into the driver's seat, holding a fresh Tab in one hand and an Evian in the other. He sets both in a plastic drink caddy, then cranks the engine and closes the door. While I wipe the top of the Tab can on my shirt, he lights a cigarette, then exhales into the Virginia night.

"Very smooth," he says. "Very smooth indeed."

Chapter 19

Dear Father,

The barbarians are at the gate.

It was inevitable, of course. And I have no fear that they will locate me. But I shall have to exercise greater caution when procuring patients. I must assume that the Justice Department will shut down EROS, or that the company will shut itself down for legal reasons. Of course the list makes that academic. I must remember to thank Turner properly.

Or will they shut it down? Perhaps Jan Krislov will resist. It could become quite a cause célèbre. Another battle in her crusade for electronic privacy. Someday I'll have to show her just how private her little universe really is.

My God, such noise from the basement. I should never have let Levy catch sight of the O.R. He should quiet himself, or I'll be forced to send Kali down to quiet him.

But first things first. I need new patients, and I suppose my next move depends on the FBI. Will they enter the digital forests of the night? Or will they simply try to fence me out?

No matter.

I shall burn all the brighter now.

Chapter 20

Lenz's Mercedes shunts us through the night like spores on a wind. He says we're headed back to McLean, Virginia, to an FBI safe house from which his digital decoy operation will be run. In the Delta I can drive for miles at night and see no light but moon and stars, but tonight I'm thankful for the busy interstate. The glaring lights and motion help me to suppress the image of the exploding PC and the screams of wounded men in the Dallas apartment.

"Are we somewhere near the Manassas battlefield?" I ask, recalling a golden summer years ago when my father and I climbed Henry Hill in the chill morning mist to see the spot where Stonewall Jackson earned his nom de guerre.

"Ten or fifteen miles to the west," Lenz replies.

"Is it a Disney World now?"

"No, they finally killed that, thank God."

The first uplifting news of a very long day. "Back there," I say hesitantly. "At the trailer. I was thinking that Strobekker, or whoever he is, didn't really mean to kill anybody."

"What do you mean?"

"I mean the explosion was pretty much confined to the computer. He could have flattened that whole building if he'd wanted to."

Lenz ponders this for a few seconds. "That helps with

the profile, but in the larger scheme it doesn't make a bit of difference. When he killed that Hostage Rescue man, he practically signed his own death warrant. If he doesn't surrender the instant we locate him, he's a corpse."

Lenz lights a fresh cigarette. "Why don't we talk about it?"

"The case?"

"No. This thing that's eating you."

"Jesus, don't you ever let up?"

"Believe it or not, Cole, I'm trying to help you. You fear my knowing anything about you. Having leverage over you. But if you'd really listened to me earlier, you'd know this case means life to me. It's my personal resurrection. Don't you see the leverage that gives *you*? One anonymous e-mail message to Strobekker and he knows 'Anne Bridges' is me. I'd never be able to prove you did it."

"But I'd never do that."

"And I'd never betray a confidence from you." He cracks his window slightly and blows a stream of smoke at the opening. "I respect you, Cole. You risked civil prosecution—maybe financial ruin—to come forward with the names of these women. Turner didn't. Krislov didn't. I don't know that they ever would have, so long as they weren't staring the corpses in the face."

I start to argue, but Lenz may be right.

"Guilt is a funny thing," he says. "A sense of guilt, I mean. It's what separates you from Strobekker. Ironic, isn't it? This cross you bear makes you a better man. I ask you to talk about it only because I know the pain of secrets so intimately. I've seen what it does to people. Don't get me wrong. I don't advocate unburdening yourself to your wife. That would make you feel better, but it would make her feel much worse. The noble thing is to bear the weight yourself. But that doesn't mean you can't share it a little. Even Christ did that."

I study Lenz's face for any trace of cynicism, but he seems sincere. "I don't think I could just tell you. You or anybody. The bare reality of it is . . . I don't know . . . too simple."

"Just start talking. These things have their own rhythm. Anything else is just facts."

"You don't want facts?"

"Facts are for men like Daniel. I'm a truth man. And that's altogether different."

After a slow breath, I push my hands back through my hair and say, "You know my wife is an OB-GYN."

"Yes."

"You probably don't know we were high school sweethearts."

"You've been married that long?"

"No. We were high school sweethearts who got married twelve years after high school. We've only been married three years."

"No other marriages before that?"

"No."

I give Lenz a thumbnail sketch of Erin and Drewe's family history, focusing on the opposite personalities of the sisters and the deceptions they used to hide them. The glow of Lenz's cigarette bobs up and down as I try to describe Erin's unique combination of beauty and sensuality, but I'm not sure he gets it. He seems more interested in Drewe.

"She graduated first in her class at Tulane Medical School?"

"Tied for first."

"No mean accomplishment. You never slept with her in high school?"

"Plenty of times. A lot of making out, fooling around. But we only actually had intercourse once, and it was a disaster. I think she just wanted to get the whole virgin thing out of the way. It was a mistake."

"You didn't have sex with other girls during this time?"

"Too many."

"Did your wife know this?"

"Eventually."

"And she knew some of the girls."

"Like I said, small school."

"Was her sister one of these girls?"

"No. Erin and I were enemies then. Almost like brother and sister."

"What life path did Erin take?"

"Four days after she graduated, she left Mississippi for Manhattan and never looked back. A guy saw her in a restaurant and *wham*, she was a model. She went through the usual celebrity arc—Who's Erin Anderson? Get me Erin Anderson. Get me someone *like* Erin Anderson. Who's Erin Anderson?—but at ten times the usual speed. A year after she left home, she was drying out in a clinic in New Hampshire with a very wealthy 'friend' footing the bill.

"For the next few years she kicked around New York and L.A. on the arms of various actors, artists, musicians. I actually ran into her a couple of times on the road. But we just played the roles we'd played since childhood."

Lenz stubs out his cigarette and lights another. "How so?"

"Friendly but sarcastic. She made fun of Drewe, the saintly sister pursuing her medical degree with the commitment of a nun. She joked about my waiting for Drewe."

"Were you?"

"I don't know. I had affairs during those years. Long, badly ended relationships."

"Did you have sex with Erin then?"

"Hell no. I told you."

"Yes, but it's obvious that there's always been a strong attraction between you and your wife's sister."

"*Any* man who sees my wife's sister feels a strong attraction to her, okay?"

"But Erin doesn't feel reciprocal attraction to these masses of other men, does she? Not the kind of attraction she felt for you."

"I didn't know that at the time."

"Of course you did. Continue."

"No matter what relationships I was in during those years, I always stayed in contact with Drewe. Sometimes a year would go by without our seeing each other. Just a couple of late-night calls. But other times she'd call me in tears about something and I would drop whatever I was doing and drive ten or twelve hours to New Orleans to be with her."

"Still no sex between you?"

"Not in the complete sense. She's a different sort of girl. Very old-fashioned."

"Was she involved with other men during these years?"

"She dated. But it never worked out. I don't think she ever meant for it to. When Drewe didn't put out after a few dates, the guys usually went elsewhere."

"But you weren't holding to a similar code of abstinence."

"Didn't even try. It was the classic dilemma. She wanted total commitment from me before giving up what she held precious. I wanted what she held precious as proof of her love."

"Smart woman."

"Okay, okay. Cut ahead a few years, to when my last band self-destructed. Where do you think I ran to lick my wounds when that happened?"

"New Orleans."

"Naturally. Drewe was entering her final year of residency at Tulane. My career was in flames. It was start over or get out for good. What do you think happened?"

"She started sleeping with you."

"You've heard all this before, I guess."

"Not quite in this way. But I'm starting to feel as though I know your wife." Lenz allows himself a smile. "I like her."

"I asked Drewe to marry me, but she said we had a year before real life started. She said we should use that time to make sure we were sure. What she really meant was, I had a year to make sure *I* was sure."

I reach down to the drink caddy and take a long swig of Tab. "I did a repeat of what I'd done after high school. Packed up my clothes, twenty grand I'd saved from gigging, and headed north to Chicago. I was going to relearn everything I ever forgot about the markets and earn our stake for the future. I took a tiny apartment near the Board of Trade. A bed and a TV. No guitar. Books stacked waist-high everywhere, even in the bathroom. Drewe and I had planned to see each other as often as possible, but we only managed it twice. The timing was too tough. But we talked on the phone constantly."

I feel a last flush of anxiety, but I force myself to go on. "And then it happened."

"Erin appeared magically in Chicago."

"Standing in my hallway in the dead of winter without even a coat. She was flying cross-country with some actor, had a layover in Chicago, and she just walked off the plane."

"As beautiful as ever?"

"More so. White linen blouse buttoned to the throat, black jeans, plain silver earrings, sandals on her tanned feet.

"You slept with her that night?"

"No. We just talked. I lent her a ski jacket and gloves and took her out to dinner. We took a cab up and down

Michigan Avenue, rode the elevator to the top of the Hancock like a couple of tourists. I was lonelier than I knew. I found myself holding Erin's hand as she looked out over Lake Michigan. The intimacy of it was . . . I don't know. Thirty seconds of connectedness in a winter when my only connections had been with greedy assholes and numbers. She didn't look at me while we held hands, but she squeezed hard before she let go and walked back to the elevator."

I stop talking for a moment and watch the constellations of headlights around us, racing toward us, overtaking us from behind. "You want details, or just the Jack Webb version?"

"Oh, details, please. But for the details, *Mourning Becomes Electra* would be no different than the Oresteia."

I grope for the allusions, but all I come up with is an absurd image of Jack Nicholson trying to get Diane Keaton to sleep with him in *Reds.* "We talked some more at the apartment. Sitting on the floor and drinking coffee laced with bourbon to keep warm. We talked about Erin's time in New York, her getting clean, my giving up music. She seemed surprised Drewe and I had only seen each other twice. She had no grasp of the demands of medical school. When she fell asleep, I tucked her in my bed, then slept in an easy chair I'd bought thirdhand from another tenant.

"The next morning I forced myself out of the chair, brushed my teeth, and got in the shower. I felt like hell. I turned the water as hot as I could stand it. Then I felt a quick draft of cold air. The bathroom door had opened and closed. I heard Erin say, 'I couldn't wait.'

"I pulled the shower curtain away from the wall and saw her sitting stark naked on the commode with her elbows on her knees and her chin propped on her hands. She shooed me away with one hand when she realized I was watching. I let go of the curtain and started washing my hair.

"A few seconds later she stepped into the shower. I'd seen her naked once before, in high school, skinny-dipping, and her body looked no older than that in Chicago. Her skin was much darker than mine, her hair almost black. Long and thick falling over those shoulders, and the same . . . you know. Lots of it. She looked up and smiled, then hugged me and laid her cheek against my chest, as if she meant to go back to sleep standing there in the spray. I didn't hug her back, but I wanted to. I'm sure it all sounds calculated now, but then it seemed like the most natural thing in the world. Unavoidable."

Lenz makes no comment.

"She was so casual about it. Like walking in to pee as if I wasn't there. Like we'd been married for years. She just didn't worry about things like that. Propriety. That affected me. Seeing her on the commode like that affected me. Weird maybe, but it's the truth. And she . . . she just wasn't like other women. She kissed my nipples before she ever kissed my mouth. She seemed to sense it had been a long time since I'd had a woman, long enough that any serious lovemaking would have to wait until she'd gotten that first release out of the way. She used her mouth for that, and her hands. She knew before I did where I was, you know? And when I started to finish, she didn't pull away. She just . . ." I trail off, unable to find words to communicate the experience.

"Afterward, she stood up and hugged me again. She didn't speak, but I saw she somehow knew her sister didn't complete that act in the way she just had. I thought of Drewe then, but she seemed removed from all this, wholly apart from it. It was as though Erin and I were meeting in some place where Drewe didn't exist. The way it might be if Erin found herself in grand rounds at the hospital with Drewe. In that environment, Erin simply would not exist. The analogy isn't perfect. Drewe certainly has a sexual identity of her own, but—"

"I understand."

"You want me to skip ahead?"

"It's you or the radio," Lenz says in a strangely thick voice. "Just keep going. From the shower."

A bleak image from *Fahrenheit 451* suddenly passes behind my eyes: I see myself driving through its wooded film location, a living book spouting my soft-core text for Lenz's strange pleasure.

"Look, I can't explain what made Erin so unique. What I said before about exploration, crossing thresholds . . . even that fails with her. I doubt there's any erotic space she's never been. *Except* maybe pure love. But her sexual presence, her magnetism . . . Jesus. Bottomless eyes, scalloped collarbones, small dark-nippled breasts that made a mockery of all the surgically enhanced architecture I saw every day at the Board of Trade. I think she realized I was being overcome by her beauty for the first time, and she was determined to give me access to all of it. She must have seen a lot of men get lost in her like that, but I could tell this meant more to her."

"For more reasons than you could imagine, Cole."

"The first time we made love in the bed, she came about ten seconds before I did. Then she cradled my face in her hands and—I still remember what she said."

Lenz turns to me, his eyes tiny points of light. "I love you?"

"No. She said, 'It's so easy, isn't it?' And then she smiled when I emptied into her. A Mona Lisa smile. No other way to describe it. Like she knew all the secrets of creation."

"How long did she stay in Chicago?"

"Four days. We hardly left the apartment. The most

she ever wore was one of my shirts. She watched movies without comment, unless laughter or tears is comment. Once we saw an eyeliner commercial that had used her eyes. I never once looked up to find her watching me. Yet when I caught myself staring at her, she would turn to me with a half smile that told me she knew I was watching. It was like living with a wild creature. She never once put on a spot of makeup. She seemed to stay perpetually wet. I mean she *never* got—"

"She was a fantasy lover," Lenz says softly.

"No. She was real."

"I meant in the sense that the erotic activity was directed toward your satisfaction rather than hers."

I consider this for a few moments. "I don't think that's true. She got her share of surprises as well."

The car seat groans slightly as Lenz repositions himself. "What do you mean?"

"Sometimes—at the moment of orgasm—she passed out. I mean *out.* We weren't drinking at all, but she would literally lose consciousness. It only happened three times, but the first time I was actually dialing nine-one-one when she woke up."

Lenz chuckles softly. "Your reaction isn't unique."

"It happened to you?"

"Alas, no. I've never seen it personally. *La petite mort.*"

"Does that mean 'little death'?"

"*The* little death. Yes. It's a phrase from French poetry."

"That's what Erin said. She told me it had never happened to her before, but I didn't believe her. I mean, how would she have known about it otherwise? She's not the type to read French poetry."

Lenz makes a noncommittal sound. "In her circle she might have heard it described. Did you enjoy *la petite mort* after that first time?"

"I'm not sure. But I saw how right the expression was.

At the moment of greatest intensity, when her chest was mottled red and her face flushed, she just snapped right out of the world. The last time, when she came out of it, she told me that she'd felt pure peace, one of the only times she'd felt it in her life. As if she had just been spit out of the womb, whole and new. And—"

"Yes?"

"She said she thought being dead might not be a bad thing. She was serious. Later she even talked about her funeral, how she wanted it to be. There was this song of mine she'd heard on a tape I made for Drewe. She'd dubbed a copy for herself. It's called 'All I Want Is Everything.' She said it was about her and that she wanted me to play it at her funeral."

"What did you say?"

"I said sure and changed the subject."

Lenz purses his lips and cuts across two lanes of traffic. The lights of suburbia are almost continuous now, so we must be getting somewhere.

"How long did this erotic interlude last?" he asks.

"Drewe called on the fourth night."

"Ah."

"Erin was lying beside me in the bed. In the time it took Drewe to explain that she was calling from the hospital and that a patient she was close to had just died, Erin became her sister again. Not some ethereal being—Drewe's little sister.

"She'd risen up and was mouthing *Is that Drewe?* while Drewe said something about a pulmonary embolism. I don't remember what I said to get off the phone, but I knew I had failed Drewe in a time of emotional crisis. What I do remember clearly is what Erin said the moment I hung up."

"What?" Lenz asks.

" 'How are we going to tell her?' I wasn't sure I'd heard right, so I asked what she meant. She leaned back against the headboard, exposing those perfect breasts, but for once I wasn't looking at her body. She said, 'How are we going to tell Drewe about *us*?'

"I was in shock. I climbed out of bed and said something like, 'Jesus, where did this come from?' 'Where?' she asked me. 'What have we been doing the last four days? Shaking hands?'

"Before I could answer, she said, 'Fucking?' Then she jerked up the covers and let me have it. 'I thought you were different. I thought you understood some things. About women. About *me*. What do you think I came out to the frozen wastes of Chicago for? Sport sex? I can get all of that I want anywhere on the planet, thank you very much.' And so on.

"I was more stunned by the pain in her voice than by her venom. I thought she'd come out because she was at a place in her life where she needed a friend. After hearing how dumb that sounded, I said, 'What *did* you come out here for?' She let the covers fall, stood up naked on my hardwood floor, and said, 'To marry you, you asshole.' "

"How unfortunate," says Lenz, as if commenting on some distant village destroyed by a typhoon. With a smooth motion he exits from the interstate and turns into a broad avenue. "So, you had an affair with your wife's sister while you were engaged."

"We weren't engaged. Not technically."

"You're splitting hairs. You had committed yourself to Drewe."

"Yes."

"But she never learned of the affair?"

"No."

Lenz shrugs. "I'm missing something. This betrayal weighs heavily upon you? On a daily basis?"

"Oh, you're definitely missing something. That night, Erin left Chicago. Two months later I heard she had married a guy named Patrick Graham. He's an oncologist now, but he went to high school with the rest of us. Everybody knew Patrick had been in love with Erin since we were kids. And by a seeming miracle, his dream girl had suddenly decided she loved him. Erin lost no time getting pregnant and plunging into a domesticity that would shame Martha Stewart. A few months later, I left Chicago and married Drewe. We weren't sure where we wanted to settle, so we moved into my parents' farmhouse in Rain. They were dead by then."

"Quite a detail to omit."

"Nothing Oedipal about it. Anyway, Drewe and I still live in Rain, while Erin and Patrick and Holly, their daughter, live in Jackson. That's the state capital, seventy miles away. We see them a good bit, usually at Drewe and Erin's folks' place in Yazoo City."

"Did you resume your affair with Erin?"

"God, no. I felt queasy from guilt whenever she was around. She seemed stable, but I knew she was capable of anything under stress. I thought she might even blurt out the truth one day in an argument with Drewe or Patrick, just for spite."

"Did she?"

"No. But if I'd known the real truth, I wouldn't have been afraid of that. You see, her child—Holly—is my daughter."

For once Lenz has no comment. He rubs his chin for a few moments, takes a deep drag on his cigarette, and blows out the smoke. "That is a serious problem."

"Try catastrophic."

"How long have you known this?"

"Three months."

"Does Patrick know the child is yours?"

"No."

"Does he know the child is not his?"

"Yes. Erin told him she was pregnant before she

agreed to marry him. But she made him promise never to ask who the father was. Patrick was so blinded by love that he agreed."

Lenz makes another turn, this time onto a wooded two-lane road. "But as time passed, the question began to prey upon his mind."

"That's my guess. Who knows what their problems are? With Erin it could be anything."

"And for the last three months, you've lived in terror that their imploding marriage will spit your dark secret up into the light."

"You got it."

He shakes his head. "I'm surprised you haven't developed hives."

"I'm having some pretty bad headaches. Drewe wants a baby, and she doesn't understand why I don't."

"You don't want a child by your wife?"

"Of course I do. But . . . I feel like taking that step while this other situation is unresolved would be the worst betrayal of all."

"How so?"

"Well, you're married, right?"

"I have a wife and a son. But you don't want to extrapolate from my marital relationship."

"You'll know what I mean, though. You know how when you first get married, even though you're totally in love, there's still this tacit sense that if you both decided it was a horrible mistake, you could just shake hands and walk away? I know that sounds shallow, but my wife is as old-fashioned as they come, and I know she feels this too. Having that first child is the final step, you know? *That's* the true marriage. It's irrevocable. The two of you can never be truly separate again. You're joined in the flesh."

"To wit, Erin and yourself."

"Jesus, don't even talk about it like that."

"But this is why Drewe so passionately wants to have your child. She's an intelligent woman. She senses a formless but disturbing threat. She knows a child will bind the two of you against that."

"I don't think she senses the threat. Well, maybe, but not from Erin. No way. I'm sure of that."

"I think you would be making a mistake to underestimate your wife in any way."

"Hey, I know that better than anybody."

Lenz looks lost in thought.

"Any great insights, Doctor?"

"Well . . . unlike many psychiatric patients, you have a real problem. In the physical sense, I mean. That child is a living symbol of a secret relationship. You love the child, I'm sure. And the mother must—*must*—sometimes look at you and wish that you were the man raising her. In my opinion, the truth will eventually come out, regardless of what you do. You can choose the time, that's all."

Lenz states his opinion with the conviction of an oracle, and the catharsis I'd begun to feel with the act of confession dissipates like smoke in a wind.

"Let me change the subject for a moment," he says. "Would you answer one question about Miles Turner?"

"It sounds like he answered enough about me."

"When I asked him the worst thing he had ever done, he refused to answer. But he did say he would tell me the worst thing that ever happened to him. He said he once spent sixty seconds face-to-face with a pit viper."

I feel the skin on the back of my neck prickle.

"That's all he would say," Lenz adds. "Can you supply any details?"

"That old drug charge wasn't enough to make him tell you?"

Lenz looks genuinely surprised. "Is that what he told you?"

"That you coerced him? Yeah. You didn't?"

"I did. But not with a drug charge. It was assault and battery."

I feel the nausea of a sudden descent. "Assault?"

"Yes. I've reviewed the case file, but the details are sketchy. It happened outside a gay bar in Manhattan. Two men verbally abused a friend of Mr. Turner's—a homosexual friend—and Turner abused back. The sequence of events is unclear after that, but the upshot is that both men were beaten severely by Mr. Turner. He apparently has some martial arts training."

My anger at Miles for talking about me is vanquished by a question that has badgered me for a long time. "Doctor, do you think Miles is gay?"

Lenz smiles with bright irony. "Doctor-patient privilege, Cole. However, there's no legal stricture keeping you from telling me what you know."

I start to refuse, but if Miles didn't want me to talk about it, why did he mention it to Lenz at all?

"We were kids," I say. "Eleven or twelve. Best friends. Miles didn't have many. He was hard to like. Some of the older guys actually hated him. He was twice as smart as they were, and he didn't mind making them look like idiots in school. It was summer. The two of us were hunting for arrowheads on a little Indian mound out in a cotton field. Some kids had built a fort in a stand of trees on the mound. It was just a hole in the ground, with a foot-high wall of logs around it and a scrap-tin roof laid over. The hole stayed full of water most of the time. We were looking at the fort when four older kids came screaming up to us on their bikes. They started teasing us, especially Miles. Miles made a smart-ass remark, and that was it. They hit him a few times. Then the ringleader said he was going to teach Miles a lesson. He said there were water moccasins nesting in the fort, and unless Miles swore by his no-good daddy that he loved sucking nigger dicks, he was going into that hole. Miles was scared to death, but he wouldn't say what they wanted. I think it was the part about his father that got him, not sucking dicks. Finally, they forced him kicking and screaming through the little entrance to the fort. I heard a splash, then nothing. The guy said if Miles came out before dark they'd break his arm.

"It was bad, Doctor. I wanted to help him, but I knew if I tried they'd just throw me in there with him. I was hoping they'd get bored and go away when I heard a sound that froze my blood. There *was* a snake in that pit, but it wasn't any moccasin. Moccasins don't make noise; they just bite you. This was a rattlesnake. Two seconds after it rattled, those assholes jumped on their bikes and hauled tail.

"I screamed at Miles to get out of there, but he didn't come up. Then I heard a tiny little voice whimper, 'I can't.' I jumped down beside the entrance hole and started whispering at him to back slowly toward my voice, but he just kept whimpering. I couldn't see a goddamn thing. After about a minute, I got up my nerve and reached my hand into that hole. I mean *slow.* My whole arm was tingling. Even at eleven years old, I knew a rattlesnake was a pit viper, and they see *heat*, not objects. And I knew my hand was a lot warmer than the wall of that wet hole. I edged my hand along the dirt for what seemed like an hour. Then my fingers felt cotton. I grabbed Miles's arm and yanked him up out of there. His face was covered with tears and his jeans were soaked with piss. He was shaking like an epileptic."

I wipe stinging sweat out of my eyes. "After he calmed down, he told me very quietly that one day those bastards would regret what they'd done to him."

"Are you all right, Cole?"

Orderly rows of soft yellow lights passing my window

finally break through, telling me we're in a residential area. "Sure."

"Is there more to the story?"

I consider holding back, but for whatever reason, I don't. "Several years later, the ringleader of that little gang had a strange accident. He was bitten four times by a cottonmouth water moccasin. Or twice each by two cottonmouths. Anyway, he ended up losing a foot."

Lenz catches his breath. "How did that happen?"

"The guy was going to college at Delta State, about a hundred miles north of Rain. He got into his car late one afternoon and these snakes just started hitting him around the ankles. Somehow they'd got into his car. They were lying under the driver's seat, baking in the hot shade. The guy had left his window open. I guess they just dropped in from a tree limb. They do that, you know."

Lenz stops the Mercedes at a turn and looks at me. "Are you saying Turner put those snakes in that man's car?"

I choose my words carefully. "I'm telling you that if cops could trace snakes, they would have traced them right back to that little fort on the Indian mound."

"My God. How many years after the initial incident was this?"

"Six or seven, at least. That's one thing about Miles. He follows through. I'm not saying he's a killer. After all, those guys had terrorized him. He was just giving back some of what they'd given him. Sort of a Southern tradition."

I crush my Tab can flat and drop it on the floor. "Look, are we there or what? I want to get this over with in time to make that SWAT plane."

Lenz turns onto still another residential street. The houses here are large, not as large as Bob Anderson's, but undoubtedly more expensive. At last he swings the Mercedes into a bricked drive and parks.

"Cole," he says in the sudden silence. "You reported the missing women because you knew something was terribly wrong. Are you ready to help me make it right?"

"Isn't that clear by now?"

He just sits, letting the engine tick. "Even if the trail leads to Miles Turner?"

"Yes. But it won't. Miles could kill, maybe. But not like that. I don't think it's in him. Do you?"

"I'm afraid I haven't ruled it out."

Lenz gets out of the car, and I do the same. But as I follow him around to a side door I see nothing of the house or grounds. I merely track his shoes, using the same trancelike vision that keeps my car on the road when my mind is a million miles from reality. *Can* Lenz count on me if the trail leads to Miles? I answered yes, but it was a reflex response. Because what I was thinking at that moment was how, after that Delta State guy was bitten by the cottonmouths, the state police showed up in Rain to question Annie Turner about her son. They'd heard some strange things about the kid and wanted to know his whereabouts on the day the guy was bitten.

Annie Turner didn't know. But I did. And I did what any friend would do under the circumstances.

I lied.

Chapter 21

When Lenz opens the door to the FBI safe house, what I see in the glow of the porch light bears little resemblance to the mental picture I had. But then I suppose that picture was generated by trash fiction and bad films.

"Pretty swank," I comment. "This is the safe house?"

"No, no," he says in a strangely soft voice. "This is my home. I need some files from my desk, some clothes. I intended to have an agent pick them up, but I left it until too late. My wife's probably sleeping."

"I can wait out here, no problem."

"No . . . no. You shouldn't be out here alone."

"Afraid I'll call a cab from your car phone?"

"Nonsense. Come along."

Lenz creeps through his own house with the stealth of a burglar. I realize I'm doing the same as we pass through a laundry room and into a dark kitchen with copper pots and utensils hanging like ancient weapons above our heads. At the far end of the kitchen stands a wide arch that leads into a breakfast area. A dim bulb in the stove hood throws a yellow pool of light on the floor.

Lenz points to a chair. "I'll only be a minute. Make yourself at home." Then he disappears through the arch.

A low beating sound tells me he is going upstairs.

"Yes, *please* do," says a woman's voice, sending a cold shock up between my shoulder blades.

All my senses on full power, I focus on the table beyond the arch. Against a wall-high curtain, I see the silhouette of a woman sitting in a straight-backed chair. A bar glass glints on the table in front of her. Lenz must have walked right past her.

"Janet?" he calls, and I hear his feet coming back down the stairs. "Janet? Are you awake?"

"No, I'm sleepwalking. Thank God I can still taste my drink. Where the hell have you been for three days?"

I can see the stairwell now. Lenz's face drops below the level of the ceiling. "I'm working a case for Daniel. An important case."

He comes down two more steps and looks at his wife. He seems caught between not wanting to invite me up to his office and not wanting to leave me down here with her. Why the hell didn't he just leave me in the car?

"I'll be right down," he says finally. "Please take care of Mr. Cole." And then he scurries back up the stairwell.

"Oh, I *will*," says the woman in a slurred voice.

As she stands up and moves toward me, light from the stove falls across her. The light is not flattering. Several years older than her husband, Janet Lenz is wearing some kind of sheer wrap over a filmy undergarment. I suppose it's meant to be sexy, but with the smudged mascara and the smell of stale gin and cigarettes wafting across the kitchen, the effect is pathos. She is a thin, Waspish woman with a fading dye job and a spiderwork of wrinkles around her mouth that marks her as a lifelong smoker. Yet her eyes hold a gimlet glow of cleverness, as if her mind retains just enough clarity to be momentarily observant, or cruel. Her voice has an edge reminiscent of schoolteachers who enjoy dispensing discipline a little too much.

"Your accent," she says. "It reminds me of North Carolina. My people are from Philadelphia, but I attended Greensboro, an all-female institution. They used to bus in boys from Duke, though. The most *charming* boys."

"That's nice."

"Oh, it *was*," she says in a lilting drawl about as authentic as Vivien Leigh's Blanche DuBois. "They knew how to be gentlemen, those boys. But they also knew when to *stop* being gentlemen. You know what I mean? Mister Cole?"

My noncommittal "Mmmm" trails off into an averted gaze. Mrs. Lenz demands my attention by tinkling the ice in her glass and clucking her tongue.

"That's something Arthur never learned," she goes on. "He's always *such* a gentleman. But the New England version can be so dull."

"Dr. Lenz doesn't seem like the dull type to me, ma'am."

"Give him time, darling. He makes a terrific first impression. He's *blindingly* analytical. But he's also numbingly predictable."

The uncomfortable silence grows more so as she moves closer and smiles with the yellow brilliance of a cheap diamond. I have the feeling she is circling me, like a scavenger.

"You'd think a man who knows Freud like the back of his hand would know his way around a bedroom, wouldn't you?"

"Uh . . . I don't think that's any of my business."

Still closer. "I must have gotten to know a hundred psychiatrists over the past twenty years," she says. "The coldest bunch of jellyfish you ever shared pâté with. Half of them impotent, the other half queer."

Deliverance arrives at last in the form of Dr. Lenz, who bounds into the kitchen carrying a suit bag and a briefcase. He's probably well aware of what I've been enduring down here. I nearly stumble over my shoes making my escape.

Janet Lenz trails us to the laundry room. As her husband opens the door, she says, "Go play your little mind games. We can't let any of those wicked boys out there have any fun, can we?"

I turn back in time to see Lenz slam the door.

As the Mercedes swallows the driveway with a low-throated growl, Lenz says, "As you can see, we all have our problems. Did she make a nuisance of herself?"

"Not at all. Just idle chitchat."

He makes a curious sound in his throat. "She didn't bring up the relative sizes of Caucasian versus Negroid sex organs?"

"I don't recall it coming up."

"You're lucky."

"What's her problem?"

"Depression. Alcohol. An emotionally distant husband who is frequently an asshole. Not necessarily in that order."

"None of my business."

"Sorry to put you through it, nonetheless."

Lenz is driving well over the speed limit now, fast enough that I grip the seat between my thighs. "We're only a short distance from the safe house," he says. "Makes it easy for me to commute. You can see why I need to be close."

I nod as if I agree, but if I were in his place I'd have chosen a safe house in Los Angeles.

The trip takes less than ten minutes including stops for traffic lights. The safe house is more modest than Lenz's home but easily worth over a hundred thousand in the Mississippi market. God knows what it appraised at here. As the automatic garage door whirs down behind the Mercedes, I decide the FBI chose well. A woman who could afford the fees for EROS wouldn't live in a house less expensive than this.

Inside, I am surprised again. I expected stern FBI agents pacing around drinking coffee, but all I find is pristine cream carpeting, functional furniture, and framed watercolors that look like they were bought from a hotel chain. The place feels like a model home in a tract development.

"Doctor Lenz?" calls a woman's voice.

From a hallway that must lead to the first-floor bedrooms steps a woman in her late twenties. She has auburn hair a little coarser than Drewe's, green eyes, fair skin, and a slim but athletic figure. All in all, she's a slightly harder version of my wife. She takes three steps into the room before I notice the holster and pistol slung tight under her left arm.

"Sherry's in the back," she tells Lenz. "And the guy from Engineering Research is in the spare bedroom upstairs." Her eyes move to me. "Who's this?"

"Special Agent Margie Ressler, meet Harper Cole. He's one of the sysops for EROS. He's going to help me get started tonight. How's trade so far?"

"All I've done so far is send out for pizza. I ordered enough for everybody." Agent Ressler cannot conceal the excitement in her eyes. "I figured since you haven't gone online yet, nobody could be surveiling the house, right?"

When Lenz merely sighs, she adds, "I got supremes. Told them to leave off the anchovies, just in case. You want me to nuke a few slices for you?"

"Not hungry," Lenz says distractedly. "Cole?"

"I'll take some."

"Diet Coke okay?"

"Great."

"Bring it upstairs," Lenz instructs her.

At the bottom of the carpeted staircase, he stops and calls back over his shoulder, "I didn't see a car in the garage!"

Margie Ressler hurries back into the living room.

"They're delivering it tonight. Should be here anytime. It's an Acura Legend, ninety-two model confiscated in a drug raid. Is that okay?"

"Fine. Make sure Sherry shows you everything you need to know."

"Yes, sir."

At the top of the stairs Lenz steps into what must have been designed as a bedroom. Now it sports a wall-size computer cabinet, a Dell desktop PC, a Toshiba subnotebook computer with PCMCIA modem slotted in and connected, a bank of wire telephones, a fax machine, a cellular phone, and a Sony television. Near the bathroom stands a refrigerator-freezer with a microwave oven on top, and against the far wall a twin bed.

"Planning to stay awhile?" I ask as Lenz deposits his suit bag in a closet half filled with men's clothing.

He turns to face me, his gaze eerily intense. "This is where I live until Hostage Rescue carries Mr. Strobekker out in chains."

He stares at me until I break eye contact. "What do you want me to do?" I ask.

"Show me the highways and byways of EROS. I want you to establish my bona fides." He motions to one of two swivel chairs. "You take the Toshiba."

"Have you logged on yet?"

"I didn't want to risk doing anything stupid."

"Lurked any on other services?"

"Lurked?"

"Lurking is logging on but not interacting with anyone. Watching the conversations of other people."

"No."

"But you've installed the EROS software."

"The kid in the spare bedroom did."

"Okay, sit."

Lenz obeys without demur, taking the chair before the Dell.

"Got EROS's eight hundred number entered into both systems?"

"Ready to go."

"Password chosen?"

"Done."

"What is it?"

"You don't need to know that."

"Touchy. Okay, press ENTER and let the system make the connection. It's all automatic, just like CompuServe or AOL."

After checking the Toshiba for a keystroke-recording program (which would allow FBI technicians to replay everything I type on this computer)—and disabling the one I find—I log on and enter my password. "What does your status line say, Doctor?"

"Checking password . . . logging on to EROS at 14,400 bps. Welcome, Lilith."

"Lilith? That's your great alias?"

"Just wait. Where am I?"

"The main page."

"Now it says 'Downloading Image.' That's . . . the bust of Nefertiti. My God, the color and resolution are wonderful."

"She'll start spinning 3-D in a second. See? Okay, hit ENTER and she'll go away. Look at the right side of the main page. See those little icons? That's how you decide where you want to go. Into a live-chat area or forum, maybe the EROS library. You just move your mouse onto the icon you want and click."

"I know how to use a mouse, Cole."

"Congratulations. Look at the top line over the page. That's your menu bar. See the choices? That's where you decide what you want to do in those different locations—again, with your mouse. You can post messages to forums, compose and send e-mail, download files from the library, access the Internet, anything you want. You can even query the system to ask who's in a given room at a given time. Of course, it will only give you their user names in answer."

"You mean we can query the system to ask whether or not Strobekker is online?"

"Not exactly. First of all, you're not supposed to know his legal name—if Strobekker *is* his name. Miles or I can search using the account name, but I can't guarantee Strobekker wouldn't see us looking for him. God only knows what kind of setup he has, wherever he is."

"But I can search using his online aliases?"

"Yes."

"Let's query for Shiva and Kali right now."

"You can only search for one alias at a time. The system will tell you whether the person using that name is online, but not where he or she is. Then you can send the person a message, but there's no guarantee he'll answer. The other way is to enter various chat rooms and ask 'Who's Here?' "

"Will the other people in the room see you ask that?"

"The minute you enter a room, they see your name pop up on a list in a little window on their screen."

"How many rooms are there in the system?"

"Theoretically, an infinite number."

Lenz groans. "I need Strobekker to find me as if by accident. How can we search an infinite number of rooms?"

"It's not as bad as it sounds. The number of active rooms fluctuates anywhere from a couple of dozen on a Monday morning to eight or nine hundred on a Friday night. That includes so-called private rooms that hold only two people at a given time."

"Nine *hundred*? You said you or Turner could do a search by the account name. Can you do that from here?"

"Yes, but I'm sure Miles would already have told the

FBI agents at EROS if the Strobekker account was active."

Lenz gives me a look that makes plain how little faith he has in Miles's motives.

From the Toshiba I log in as SYSOP TWO, give my password, and run an account search for STROBEKKER, DAVID M.

"Not among those present," I say, and push the chair away from the Toshiba. "Look, I really need to call my wife. It won't take more than a couple of minutes."

"Well, get me started at something," Lenz says.

I wave him out of his chair and mouse him into a lobby room with about ten people in it. "Just read what comes up on your screen. Get a feel for the conversational style. If somebody asks you anything, ignore them. I'll be back in no time."

"Use my cellular," he advises. "It's secure. Punch seven-seven-seven-six before you dial your home number. And don't put a one in front of the area code. And don't take too long. I want you right here when I get a nibble."

A *nibble*. I almost laugh as I step into the hall with the cellular. The guy thinks he's fishing. And maybe he is. I punch in the FBI code, then the familiar six-zero-one that encompasses all of Mississippi. Drewe answers after two rings.

"Harper?"

"Yes."

"Thank God."

"Are you okay?"

"I was worried. Are you calling from a plane?"

"No. I'm still in Washington. Virginia, really."

"You sound like you're in a plane."

"It's too complicated to explain. But I should be home before morning. Any more police harassment?"

"No. Whatever you're doing, it's working. I did get one call, though. From that New Orleans detective."

"Mayeux?"

"Yes. He's worried about you. He said he didn't know where you were, but he had a feeling you were with the FBI. He told me to warn you not to trust them, Harper. He said the FBI will use you while they need you, then throw you to the dogs."

I hear a muffled "Cole?" from inside Lenz's room. "I've got to go, Drewe. Tell your dad everything's under control. I know he's worried about all this."

"Not right now he's not. All he can think about right now is Erin."

My heart stutters. "Erin? Why's that?"

"She and Patrick are having problems again. When I got home tonight she was sitting on our steps with Holly. She drove over from Jackson because she didn't want to be there when Patrick got home. We drank coffee and played with Holly for hours. Then she went to Mom and Dad's to spend the night."

Jesus. "Did she tell you what was wrong?"

"She wouldn't be specific, but it's serious. Patrick called four times, and he sounded angrier every time."

"Is Holly okay?"

"She senses the tension, but I think Erin and Patrick know enough not to fight in front of her."

I wonder. The likely source of Patrick's "tension" could turn any man violent.

"Don't worry about that stuff," Drewe says buoyantly. "Just take care of the police problem and get back here. I love you, you know."

"I love you too." A brief silence. "Bye."

"Bye."

I shut off Lenz's cell phone and lean against the wall, my right cheek flush against the cool Sheetrock. *She was sitting on the porch steps with Holly . . . wouldn't be specific . . . he sounded angrier every time—*

"Mr. Cole? You okay?"

Special Agent Margie Ressler is standing before me with a tray piled with sliced pizza, paper towels, a glass of ice, and a Diet Coke. She looks like a waitress in a college town, where restaurants are blessed with a pool of potential employees overqualified in every department.

"You look like you're in a daze," she says.

"I'm fine."

"When was the last time you ate?"

"It's been awhile."

"Here." She holds a slice of pizza within biting distance. Something about Agent Ressler encourages informality, so I lean forward and take a bite. The spicy cheese is a moist explosion in my mouth.

"Mmmm. Better than crawfish étouffée."

She grimaces. "I'd think anything was better than that."

"Ever had it?"

"No."

"Then you don't know what you're slandering."

She laughs lightly. "You don't look like most computer jocks I know."

"That's because I'm not one. I've got a knack for applications, but that's it. I guess it's sort of like driving a car. I'm a good driver, but I couldn't rebuild an engine if my life depended on it."

"I'll bet you can change the oil, though."

"Are we flirting, Agent Ressler?"

She grins. "I guess we are. Call me Margie. I think I'm flirting because I know I might be trapped here for a long time."

"It seems like dangerous duty."

"Decoy work?"

"Yes. I guess you've done it a lot, though."

"No. This is my first time. I've only been out of the academy a couple of years."

"Cole," Lenz calls, his voice like a hand on my sleeve. "Are you out there?"

Margie laughs. "He sounds mad." She drops her voice. "I wouldn't want that bird mad at me. He's a strange one."

"He grows on you." I smile and slip the cell phone into my pants pocket. "I'll take the tray, Margie. You be careful."

"No sweat," she says with a toss of her hair. Then she turns and trots back down the stairs.

At the bedroom door I pause. I'd intended to make one other call while out here. Eleanor Rigby. Miles interrupted my first attempt to warn her off EROS, and I haven't managed to do it since. The hard bulge of the cell phone in my pocket offers a chance, but instinct tells me that any number I call on the "secure" FBI phone could later be identified and traced to a name. I'll have to find another way.

"This is fascinating," Lenz says as I enter the room. "These conversations are a free-for-all."

"You mean threads," I correct him, setting down the tray.

"Threads?"

"That's the online term for conversation, on EROS anyway. On other services 'chat' is the correct term, but on EROS 'thread' covers pretty much any conversation. In special interest forums, a 'thread' is where a few people get on one subject and everyone puts in their two cents' worth. Like 'Coping with AIDS' in the gay forum. Any time of day or night, clients can read what's already been said and post a reply if they want."

I sit down in the swivel chair and begin munching on the pizza. "Let's scan the forum headings, just to give you an idea of what's out there."

I click the mouse on GENERAL INTEREST FORUMS, and the thread headings appear in a column window:

ABORTION RIGHTS UPDATE
ACTS OF LOVE [*GRAPHIC FILE (UNDER CONSTRUCTION) DECODING SOFTWARE REQUIRED*]
ACTORS' STUDIO
ANALISM
BREAST CANCER, NOT THE END OF YOUR SEX LIFE
BREAST REDUCTION/ENLARGEMENT, IS IT SAFE?
BRIEF ENCOUNTERS
CAMILLE [PAGLIA]
CINEMA VÉRITÉ
COPING WITH AIDS

"Paglia?" says Lenz. "Camille Paglia is on EROS?"

"I can't tell you that. But clicking on that heading will lead you to a discussion of her works. There are over a hundred headings, but you get the idea."

I'm reaching for my mouse when Lenz stops my hand and says, "I'd like to see them all."

I can almost see his eyes focus on the more provocative selections. My eyes gravitate to those I know as the more popular or strange.

COPROPHILIA
DE SADE RECONSIDERED
DOMINANT FEMALE
EROTIC FINE ARTS [*GRAPHIC FILE (UNDER CONSTRUCTION) DECODING SOFTWARE REQUIRED*]
EROTIC LITERATURE SALON
EUROTRASH BIN
FEMINISM 101

FETISHISM [23 SUBCATEGORIES]
FROTTEURISM
GAY MAN'S WORLD [28 SUBCATEGORIES]
GOD IN THE BEDROOM
HETS ONLY [HETEROSEXUALS]
HIV POSITIVE?
INCEST SURVIVORS: WOMEN ONLY
ISLAND OF LESBOS [31 SUBCATEGORIES]
JAN KRISLOV [THE CEO ANSWERS YOUR QUESTIONS]
MEDICAL-SEXUAL QUESTIONS [M.D.s RESPOND AS TIME PERMITS]
NECROPHILIA
PHONE SEX, STUCK IN ADOLESCENCE
PRIVACY RIGHTS (14 SUBCATEGORIES)
QUEER NATION
RAPE COUNSELING
ROMANCE
SEX POLICE
UROPHILIA
VOYEURISM
YOUNGER MEN, OLDER WOMEN
ZOOPHILIA

"Many of these are medical terms," Lenz observes.

"Drewe had to bring home a DSM-III-R manual just so I could figure out what some of them meant. Now I name a lot of the threads myself."

"Are there many physicians on EROS?"

"A fair number."

"How many?"

"Over a hundred."

Lenz seems to be thinking. "Are these headings permanent?"

"Some are, but the idea of EROS is to be dynamic, to respond as various needs arise. For example, 'ISLAND

OF LESBOS' is constant, but many of its subcategories change every day. It covers all kinds of lesbian behavior and interests."

"Let's look."

I click the mouse on LESBOS and watch the new window open, revealing another column of thread titles.

"What's 'Penetrating Discussion'?"

"Some lesbians are into penetration, others aren't. They discuss various objects to use for it. What's better, natural versus artificial, like that. I figured you knew all about this stuff."

"I have some lesbian patients who use vegetables for stimulation. I sometimes think about it when I walk through the produce section of a grocery."

"That's garden-variety stuff, pardon the pun. You know what shocked me? They talk about size a lot. One woman said most vegetables were too large for her. She said the perfect thing to use was an Oscar Mayer wiener. Don't laugh—it's true. I said, 'Isn't that too soft for the job?' And you know what she said? 'Not if you freeze it.' If you *freeze* it!"

Lenz beams with the pleasure of a man who is rarely shocked. "But how does she stand the temperature? That could damage her tissues."

"That's exactly what I said. She told me that when she's ready, she just takes one out of the freezer and runs it under hot water for about sixty seconds. Then it's perfect." I shake my head. "I'm telling you, anything you can possibly think of, it's already been done and posted on EROS."

"What about these graphics files?"

"That's Miles's project. Jan Krislov originally wanted EROS to be purely text-based. She saw that as another way to keep the level of discussion high. But the demand for graphics has become so great, and the technology so much better, that she's had to give in. The whole thing is Miles's baby, of course."

While Lenz nods thoughtfully, I click out of the forum and into the live-chat area. "I guess we'd better start checking room by room for prose that sounds like our man."

Lenz takes something from a drawer. "I'm going to tape our session," he says, pressing a button on a small Olympus recorder. "That way I won't have to make notes of any instructions you give me. It'll save—"

The psychiatrist jumps as one of the phones on the desk rings. He looks to see which number it is, then answers. While he turns away and speaks too low for me to hear, I punch up the EROS e-mail window on the Toshiba and compose a quick message to Eleanor Rigby: *Please DO NOT log on to EROS again until you hear from me. Strange things happening. Will send further mail via Internet. HARPER.* Before sending the message, I disable the Auto-File function so that no record of this note will be saved to Lenz's hard drive. Then I click the mouse on SEND NOW. MESSAGE MAILED flashes just as Lenz hangs up the phone.

"That was Daniel Baxter," he says, his voice brimming with excitement.

"What is it?"

"Strobekker just contacted the Bureau."

"What?"

"He sent a message to Daniel's personal e-mail address at Quantico. Could that be possible?"

"Sure, if the Quantico computers are connected to the Internet."

"Some are. But the Unit's computers are supposed to be sealed off from the outside. This message came across the internal e-mail system, the same way a secret case memo would. The Quantico technicians say they can't locate the source of the message. Daniel is rattled. He's faxing us a copy now."

The fax machine rings on cue, and we both stare at the slowly emerging page. When Lenz is sure no more is to come, he tears off the curled sheet and lays it on the desk. It reads:

> PLEASE STOP TRYING TO LOCATE US. YOU CANNOT SUCCEED. YOU WERE NOT EVEN CLOSE TODAY IN DALLAS. AN INNOCENT MAN DIED FOR NOTHING. IF YOU KNEW WHAT WE ARE TRYING TO ACCOMPLISH, YOU WOULD NOT EVEN TRY TO FIND US. YOU WOULD REALIZE THAT OUR WORK WILL ULTIMATELY BENEFIT ALL MANKIND. OUR WORK IS ALMOST COMPLETE. WE WILL SACRIFICE NO MORE LIVES THAN NECESSARY. WHEN THE TIME IS RIGHT WE SHALL COME TO YOU. YOU MUST TRUST US, AND LEAVE US ALONE.
>
> THANK YOU.

"I've never seen anything like this," Lenz says. "Notice the use of the pronoun 'we'? Often that's a ploy, but in this case it fits with the evidence indicating a team offender situation."

"You mean like a cult? Like the California police were assuming?"

"No, no. Forget that drivel you heard in New Orleans. True cult murders are almost nonexistent. Ninety-nine percent of cult homicides are committed for standard motives. For example, a cult leader will mask the elimination of a rival as a ceremonial killing. More often than not, it's lawyers and the media who turn homicides into 'satanic' murders."

Lenz touches the fax with his forefinger. "No, we're dealing with something altogether different here. No threat at all, you notice that? Not even any baiting. The author was simply trying to communicate his thoughts. He really believes we cannot find him—or them, as the case may be."

My gut tells me the author of the note may be right.

"Daniel asked whether this might be the work of a disgruntled employee or prankster inside the Bureau," Lenz muses. "I don't think there's much chance of that."

"But if you've never seen a note like this, maybe the killer *didn't* write it."

"Oh, he wrote it. I perceive the lack of overt threat as *more* dangerous. The work of a more confident, and thus more organized, personality. And here . . . I think he actually believes we might stop hunting him if we understood his 'work,' whatever that is."

I read softly: " 'We will sacrifice no more lives than necessary.' What do you think that means?"

"We're dealing with some degree of megalomania here. A tremendous ego—or group of egos—that believes itself a part of some grandiose or holy mission. That's fairly common. Who knows what kind of twisted logic leads him to think that by killing he is saving the human race. Hitler thought he was sacrificing no more lives than necessary when he murdered six million Jews."

"I don't know," I say, scanning the note again. "The tone is eerie. Like Jonas Salk trying to explain his polio vaccine to a bunch of Stone Age bushmen. You know, 'Some of you may be paralyzed from this, but in the end it's for the greater good.' "

"Albert Sabin had the live vaccine," Lenz says softly. "But you're right."

"Dallas was his early warning system. This is his response. He invaded the FBI's computers to send it. That fact alone is his threat. He's telling you you're not in his league, Doctor."

"He's wrong," Lenz says quietly. He waves his arm at the arrayed technology. "Tonight is the *commencement de la fin.*"

"The what?"

"The beginning of the end."

I memorize the message before Lenz can set it aside.

"I told Daniel I'd get back to him in an hour with an analysis," he says. "We're going to spend that hour on EROS. Are you ready to guide me, Cole?"

Despite my fatigue and my anger at being coerced into my present position, a powerful current of excitement is circulating through me. The man who killed Karin Wheat just issued a direct challenge, and no Southern male is very good at ignoring those. It may be juvenile and atavistic, but it definitely gets the pulse pounding. I take a huge bite of cold pizza and wash it down with Diet Coke.

"Let's nail this arrogant son of a bitch."

Chapter 22

Dr. Lenz and I have been logged on to EROS for nearly two hours. He went into Microsoft Word for five minutes to compose an analysis of the "Strobekker" note and fax it to Daniel Baxter at Quantico, but aside from that, we've been trolling the private chat rooms like bass fishermen on a slow morning, casting spinners under likely looking trees and piers, dragging artificial worms across dark bottoms. With Jan Krislov's conditional approval, Miles has given Lenz the ability to monitor rooms that the subscribers believe to be private. The psychiatrist seems surprised by each new encounter, whether a steamy tryst in Regency England or a postnuclear tête-à-tête in some virtual retropunk dive.

All my system queries on the Strobekker account have come back: *Subscriber not currently logged on.* The characters scrolling across my screen turned to alphabet soup long ago, and the dot matrix printer recording them now sounds like a herd of cocaine-addicted gerbils.

Suddenly my eyes come clear and a numbing tingle heats the back of my arms. "Move over!" I tell Lenz, jumping up from the Toshiba.

Before he can even get out of his chair, I'm clicking the Dell out of the room he was in and into the room I was monitoring.

"What is it?" he asks over my shoulder. "Is it Strobekker?"

"Maybe," I reply, reclaiming my seat at the Toshiba. "Just read and follow along."

Lenz takes his chair and leans forward until his nose is almost against the screen of the Dell. " 'Levon' and 'Sarah'? Those aren't his aliases."

"I think 'Levon' is him."

"Why hasn't Turner called, then?"

"Read the screen, damn it! Read 'Levon.' "

"This stuff about God?"

"Yes! Look how quickly his responses pop up. And not a single error. Now shut up and read!"

I focus on the dialogue moving down my screen:

LEVON> If it were given to you to create God, what qualities or powers would you give him?

SARAH> What do you mean? I can't create God. God already exists.

LEVON> But if he _didn't_ exist. How would you conceive of him?

"What are those marks?" Lenz asks. "I saw them in your printouts. Emphasis?"

"Yeah. Like italics."

SARAH> Well . . . I'd make Him all-powerful, like He is.

LEVON> Is he?

SARAH> Of course.

LEVON> And what of the Devil?

SARAH> What about him?

LEVON> Doesn't Satan have any power?

SARAH> Some. The power to tempt, I guess. But God has more.

LEVON> Then why does evil flourish in the world?

SARAH> Because humans are weak. We choose evil.

LEVON> But why does God _let_ us choose it? Why have evil at all?

SARAH> Well, to test us. Because of free will.

LEVON> But if God made us, Sarah, why must he test us? If God is all-knowing, he must know ahead of time that we are fallible. So the test is meaningless, isn't it?

SARAH> You're confusing me. Not everyone chooses evil. Some choose good.

LEVON> Of course. We all choose good _some_ of the time. But we choose evil sometimes as well. Haven't you done things you were ashamed of?

SARAH> I don't like this conversation.

LEVON> I'm sorry. I'm a nosey parker, aren't I? What about this? If you were creating God, what would hc _look_ like?

SARAH> Well . . . fatherly, I guess. Strong. Strong but fair. Just.

LEVON> Why not motherly? Was your mother not just, Sarah?

SARAH> Of course she was.

LEVON> But . . . ? She wasn't strong?

SARAH> She was strong. In her way. But

LEVON> But what?

SARAH> Not strong like a father. Not strong enough to protect me.

LEVON> Protect you from what? From your father, perhaps?

SARAH> What are you trying to do?

LEVON> I didn't mean to offend you, Sarah. But sometimes I sense things. Pain. I sense pain now. In you I sense something dark. Hurtful. No one likes to think about those spiritual cubbyholes, but we all have them. I would make God very

different than you would, Sarah. I would make God a woman. A mother. A strong mother. Strong enough to make up for the weakness of fathers. Strong enough to _defy_ fathers. There are women like that in the world.

SARAH> Was your mother like that?

LEVON> No. My mother was like a silk veil in a strong wind.

"It *is* him," Lenz whispers, his eyes glued to his monitor. "I remember something like that from your transcripts. Jesus."

"Stay cool, Doctor."

"We've got to trace him!"

"Baxter's guys are taking care of that. I'm a hell of a lot more concerned about this woman he's talking to."

"He's still got a zero error rate," Lenz says. "He's not close to her."

"You'd better fucking hope not."

"Quiet, Cole! We're missing it!"

Suddenly a frightening thought hits me. I tap out a system search on the Toshiba and my fears are confirmed: Brahma isn't using the Strobekker account. I grab Lenz's arm. "Baxter's techs can't trace this connection! It's not Strobekker's account! They don't know what to look for. Call EROS right now and give them the new alias and the name of the room!"

Lenz hits a speed-dial button on the nearest phone. I read as fast as I can to catch up with the text that appeared while we were talking.

LEVON> My name is not Levon, Sarah.

SARAH> I know that.

LEVON> Would you like to know my real name?

SARAH> I don't know. You frighten me a little. I

like talking to you. But you see too much. I'm afraid you want too much.

LEVON> Too much what?

SARAH> Honesty.

LEVON> How can one want too much honesty, Sarah?

SARAH> You know what I mean. It's not human nature. We need little white lies. To get along with each other.

LEVON> And to get along with ourselves?

SARAH> Is that so terrible?

LEVON> Doesn't God demand total honesty, Sarah?

SARAH> That's different.

LEVON> How?

SARAH> God is God. He accepts us no matter what. He forgives us.

LEVON> I would accept you no matter what.

SARAH> That's easy to say. But you don't know. You don't really know me.

LEVON> I don't need to. Nothing you could possibly say or do would offend me.

SARAH> Are you so sure?

LEVON> Yes.

SARAH> But acceptance isn't the same as forgiveness. You can accept someone but still be disappointed in them. You can live with them but never forgive them.

LEVON> Not me, Sarah. I'm not like that.

SARAH> How do you mean?

LEVON> In my eyes you could never do anything that required forgiveness.

SARAH> What do you mean?

LEVON> I mean whatever you could possibly think of doing, and then have will enough to carry through, that would be your nature. I would never wish you to go against your nature.

SARAH> But that's crazy. That's like saying everything is okay. What if I were a mass murderer? Or a rapist?

LEVON> I would accept you.

SARAH> But what if I were a child molester?

LEVON> I would fold you into my arms, Sarah. It's not my duty to judge you. If that is your inclination, so be it. It is someone else's biological imperative to stop you from molesting children. That duty belongs to the parent. And if a parent were to kill you for doing that, I would accept his or her behavior as well.

SARAH> But what if _I_ was the parent? The parent _and_ the molester? That happens, you know.

LEVON> Alas, it is the rule. But then it is the imperative of the other parent to stop it.

SARAH> But what if the other parent _can't_ stop it? What if she's too weak? What if she's afraid?

LEVON> Your tears are scalding my heart. If someone is too weak, they either enlist help or they fail.

SARAH> Help? No one can HELP in situations like that! The police don't DO anything.

LEVON> Who said anything about police? One should always look first inside oneself. That is where help lies.

SARAH> But what can a woman do in that situation? A weak woman? A woman who's afraid of guns?

LEVON> Pour strong whiskey on the father's face and torso while he is sleeping, then set him afire with a cigarette.

SARAH> My God. Did you just think of that?

LEVON> Yes. But I'm sure it's been done many times. There are other ways. So much misery builds up in the world because people are afraid to act. They would rather endure. That is the nature of Homo sapiens. To endure unmitigated hell and hope that if we sit through enough of it things will change for the better. But they never do. Look at the Russian peasants. The Jews in Germany. The Armenians. One must be willing to risk everything at every moment for survival. And the more you have to lose, the more willing you must be to fight at a moment's notice. If a man accosts you on the street, push him away. If he curses you, knock him down. If he is stronger than you and attacks you, shoot him.

SARAH> Are you really like that?

LEVON> I do not tolerate impudence. My father taught me that.

SARAH> Are you very rich?

LEVON> Yes.

SARAH> That explains it.

LEVON> NO! I am rich _because_ I have never taken abuse from anyone.

SARAH> I don't know.

LEVON> You think GOD takes shit from anyone, Sarah?

SARAII> That's sacrilegious!

LEVON> Is it? Isn't that what the Old Testament is really about? Isn't that what the Book of Job says? I AM GOD AND I DON'T TAKE SHIT FROM ANYBODY! I DON'T EVEN TAKE _QUESTIONS_!

SARAH> That's awful!

LEVON> But true, yes? God in the Bible is sort of like Don Corleone, isn't he? He makes people offers they can't refuse. And minor bosses like

Pharaoh have faith in their own power, and they wake up with a horse head in their bed. Or locusts. It's all the same.

SARAH> I can't believe you're writing this. Aren't you afraid?

LEVON> Of what? A lightning bolt? Now that I think of it, God isn't really like Don Corleone. He's more like a film director. We think we're his actors. We think he's in charge of us, that he has a Plan, that he wants good things for us. That he is slowly working toward some divinely inspired vision that we actors are too dim-witted to see. We think that's why we exist. But that isn't it at all, Sarah. We exist because GOD WANTS AN AUDIENCE. What's the point of being the Alpha and the Omega, the be-all and end-all, if there's no one around to applaud? No one to cower in fear or kneel in supplication? Once in a while God shouts like Bob Barker: "SARAH! COME ON DOWN!" And we think we matter for a while. But God is the only actor, Sarah. That is the secret. We are the audience.

"This guy's scary," I say under my breath.

"Shut up, Cole. This is a forensic gold mine."

"Was Miles at EROS when you called?"

"That was him on the phone."

I feel a sudden release of tension, an inexplicable gladness that Miles cannot possibly be the man behind "Levon." Already the prompt looks different to me.

SARAH> I think that kind of talk

LEVON> What? Don't be afraid to speak.

SARAH> It's what the Devil would say! To confuse me!

LEVON> You think I'm Lucifer, Sarah?

SARAH> Maybe you are.

LEVON> I'm flattered. Did you know that Lucifer is Latin for 'light-bringer'? Something to think about.

SARAH> Are you trying to scare me?

LEVON> It would probably frighten you more if I told you I know your real name and address.

"He's never done that," I tell Lenz. "He's *never* told anyone that."

"Shut up, Cole!"

SARAH> This isn't right.

LEVON> Calm down, Sarah. I was only joking.

SARAH> I don't like it. I'm frightened. How do I know you don't know my name?

LEVON> Everyone's protected on EROS, Sarah. That's what we pay all the money for. I just wanted you to feel my strength. To know I mean it when I say I do not take abuse from anyone. And I think you need someone like me. Someone who could take care of you. Protect you.

SARAH> You make me sound so weak.

LEVON> We all have needs, Sarah.

SARAH> What do you need?

LEVON> Love.

SARAH> What kind of love?

LEVON> Unselfish love. The love that a good mother gives her child. Could you love someone like that?

SARAH> I think I could. I have a lot of love to give.

LEVON> I sense that, Sarah.

SARAH> I'm not beautiful, Levon. I want to tell you that now, because I couldn't bear to go further and have you building up all kinds of expectations I couldn't fulfill. I mean, I'm not fat or anything. I'm about five-seven, a hundred and twenty-five pounds.

LEVON> You don't have to tell me this, Sarah.

SARAH> I want to. I _have_ to. I'm forty-six years old. My hair is brown, a little mousy maybe, but I have really good skin.

LEVON> You're a healthy girl, aren't you?

SARAH> I take care of myself, if that's what you mean. All I'm trying to say is that I don't look like Cindy Crawford or anything. But I'm not unattractive. I mean I get asked out at work and everything.

LEVON> Do you accept?

SARAH> Not often. I'm sort of skittish about dating. I got hurt by someone a while back, and I don't think I'm completely over it.

LEVON> Someone at work? A superior?

SARAH> How did you know?

LEVON> A married man.

SARAH> Yes. Though it still hurts to admit it. I feel so guilty about his wife and children. He said he loved me. But he just wanted

LEVON> To use you.

SARAH> Yes. I felt so dirty. Sometimes it seems my whole life has been like that. I try to have faith in men, but it just never works out.

LEVON> You are unstained, Sarah. You cannot be dirtied by such men.

SARAH> It makes me feel nice when you say that.

LEVON> It is but the truth.

SARAH> I don't want you to get the idea that I have something against sex or anything. I mean, from what I said about my skittishness. I mean, I feel strange writing this, but I do get stared at a lot. I mean, because of— Well, men stare at my chest. I'm fairly well endowed in the bosom department. Not that they're huge or anything, but I never had kids, you know, and so they're still, well, firm and high. I'm not conceited about it. I don't even like them sometimes. It's like people don't see me because of them, you know? It alienates female friends too. But I mean, for the right man, if he liked that and all, it might be nice for both of us. Would you like that?

LEVON> The needs of the body are secondary to me, Sarah.

SARAH> Oh. You mean, like sex isn't that big a deal to you?

LEVON> On the contrary. Sex is of primary importance.

SARAH> I'm not sure I understand.

LEVON> I speak of a passion you have yet to experience. Spiritual, refined, prolonged sexual union, a melding of heart and mind and flesh. A marriage of the sacred and the profane.

SARAH> Wow. That sounds, I don't know, poetical or something.

LEVON> But my time has ended for tonight, Sarah. I must go now.

SARAH> Oh. Will you be back tomorrow?

LEVON> Perhaps. I am never far away. Remember, you are far stronger than you believe yourself to be. You need no one.

SARAH> I think I need you. I mean it. Can you tell me some more about this spiritual sex? I mean, like describe it?

LEVON> I must go now, Sarah. When you most need me, I will be there.

SARAH> I'll be waiting.

LEVON> I know you will. Good-bye.

SARAH> Bye. And thank you.

"You see that?" I ask. "Christ. One session and he's got this woman ready to do anything he wants."

"He simply played to her needs," says Lenz. "As I intend to play to his. A little mysticism, a little danger, a little sex."

"Forty-six years old and simpering like a schoolgirl. She was practically begging for a chance to tell him where to get her."

Lenz taps his fingers on the desk and exhales heavily. "That's common with serial killers. Many times the victim acquiesces to a situation that puts her in harm's way. Often when she's in an environment where she feels no immediate danger, such as this one, she makes a critical mistake. The last one she'll ever make."

"It's like she's on standby for murder."

"No question about it."

"What are you going to do?"

"Calm down, Cole. He's not close to her yet. I'll call Turner back and get 'Sarah's' real identity. Then Baxter can have the local police department wherever she lives do a drive-by at her residence, use some pretense to verify that she's okay."

"You really think that's enough?"

Lenz punches the speed-dial code for EROS. "Within four hours we'll have FBI surveillance on her around the clock. If she's in a major city, less than one hour. Daniel's already got the budget approved."

"You're relying on the zero error rate to tell you he isn't close to her. But what if he's changed his methods? He already changed his victim profile, you said. What if he's changed his hunting method too? Shit! We've got to shut down the network!"

"Calm *down*, Cole! You sound like a rookie cop."

"Okay . . . okay. I'm just trying to cover every angle."

Lenz speaks to Miles in measured tones. Even hearing only one side of the conversation, I can tell the phone trace went nowhere. Glancing over to make sure Lenz isn't watching, I send a copy of the entire Levon-Sarah thread to my personal mailbox in EROS's server.

"Sarah's legal name is Phoebe Tyler," announces Lenz, stabbing another speed-dial code. "She is indeed forty-six years old and a resident of Aurora, Illinois. The Chicago field office can have a team at her house in thirty-five minutes. They'll use a ruse to ensure that she's okay, then organize around-the-clock surveillance. Daniel? Arthur here. . . ."

I am eyeing one of the cold pizza slices when Lenz shouts, *"What?"* As I look up, he snaps, "Do it," and hangs up.

"What is it?"

"Strobekker again."

Suddenly the pizza I ate two hours ago burns upward toward the center of my chest. "He hasn't killed Phoebe Tyler. He couldn't have!"

Lenz stands up and leans over the fax machine with his hands on the table. "No. He sent Daniel another message."

I close my eyes in relief. "When?"

"Thirty seconds after the conversation between Levon and Sarah ended."

"Man, does this guy have our number. What did the message say?"

"Daniel's faxing it to us now. This is clearly a reaction to the Bureau's attempts to trace his phone connection, yes?"

"Got to be."

"Could Strobekker have known we were watching his Levon-Sarah exchange?"

"I don't think so. I mean, if he were in the system as a sysop, or had root access, Miles would know about it. But that doesn't mean it's impossible. A lot of people know a hell of a lot more about computers than I do."

The fax machine rings. Lenz picks up the receiver and hits the SEND/RECEIVE key. "Daniel is considering arresting Turner," he says without looking up.

"What?"

His eyes stay on the fax machine. "There's a great deal of pressure from the police departments involved to arrest you both."

"Goddamn it! I'm sick of this intimidation!"

"Don't worry, no one's going to arrest you. But arresting Turner might keep the local gendarmes at bay for a while. Multijurisdictional investigations are always difficult. And this one is worse than most."

I read the new message as it curls out of the fax machine:

> YOU HAVE NOT STOPPED HUNTING US. I ASKED NICELY. IF YOU DO NOT CEASE, I SHALL BE FORCED TO ENTER YOUR GAME, AND AT YOUR LEVEL. I DO NOT THINK YOU WILL LIKE THE RESULT.
>
> REMEMBER DALLAS.

"Now the threat," says Lenz.

"If he's so confident we'll never find him," I ask, "why is he worried about us hunting him?"

"Good point. Notice the pronoun change? The 'I' creeps in now. Note the proper use of 'shall.' And no contractions. I think this man has considerable education."

My eyes glance over the fax paper, all but unseeing. "You know what I think? I think that whole Levon-Sarah thread was bait."

"Mmmm?" Lenz murmurs. "Meaning?"

"Meaning the whole thing was done just to see whether we'd be able to localize him to a chat room or isolate a phone line at EROS, et cetera. To see how far we could get."

"And we did localize him to a room."

"It was luck."

"But he doesn't know that," Lenz points out.

"No, but I don't think you realize what his use of a new alias means. Either he has gained sysop privileges, or he has access to at least one—and possibly hundreds—of other legitimate accounts."

"Wouldn't a legitimate client quickly complain about an unauthorized person using his or her account?"

"No. That's the beauty of EROS. For Strobekker, I mean. We're expensive, but we charge a flat fee. Someone who knows my user name and password could log on for hours as me without me being the wiser or even giving a damn if I was."

"You mean—"

"I mean if Strobekker knows the names and passwords of legitimate account holders—if he really has a copy of the master client list and the clients' passwords—you may *never* be able to trace him. Because the only way we'll know what to trace is by searching room to room for his goddamn prose style. You saw how long it took us tonight, and we were lucky."

Lenz grunts and turns away from me. He stands in silence, like a man in defeat. But then I see a tensing of his posture.

"What is it?" I ask softly.

His right arm rises and points to the Dell's softly glowing monitor. "Levon's back. In a lobby." The psychiatrist drops into his chair and pulls up to the Dell. "How do I approach him?"

"*Don't.* Just watch him."

"You said yourself we'd be lucky to find him."

"And I don't believe in luck."

Lenz clicks his mouse and types something into the Dell.

"Don't bite, Doctor. He's in control right now. I don't see any advantage until we can turn the tables—"

It's no use. Lenz—under the alias "Lilith"—has already invited "Levon" to join him in a private room. My fingers tremble as I wait for Brahma's response. The words appear in a flash without a single error:

LEVON> I don't believe we've met before.

"Got him!" Lenz cries, his fingers flying across the keyboard.

LILITH> I just joined the network. I'm trying to get a feel for what's out here in cyberspace. So far, I must confess I'm a bit disappointed.
LEVON> How so?
LILITH> Most of the talk is conventional. Even the "racy" stuff is fairly pedestrian. I was hoping for more sophisticated fare.
LEVON> You have to know where to look. I'm intrigued by your name, Lilith. Do you know its origin?
LILITH> Do you?
LEVON> Rest assured that I do.

Lenz pauses, then types:

LILITH> Consider it a test.
LEVON> I've always tested very well, Lilith.
LILITH> Amaze me.
LEVON> "Lilith" is a Hebrew word for "demon of the night." It was mistranslated in the Book of Isaiah as "screech owl," which is probably where your parents picked up the name. "Lilith" de-

rives from the Babylonian _lilitu_, which itself derives from the Semitic word for "night." Later rabbis took this "night demon" and from her created "Lilith"—a beautiful woman who became Adam's wife before Eve was created. Perhaps your father was learned in the rabbinical tradition?

Lenz's stunned expression tells me Brahma's information is dead on. I'm still in shock when Lenz's shaking fingers type:

LILITH> I _am_ amazed. I now consider this month's EROS fee well spent.
LEVON> You didn't answer the question about your father.
LILITH> I value my privacy.
LEVON> A sentiment I share. Good luck tonight, and all other nights. I must away.
LILITH> But we only just met.

"Stop!" I hiss at Lenz. "Type B-Y-E."

"But he's right here—"

Before Lenz can type another word, I shove his chair away from the Dell and type:

LILITH> Until we meet again.

"You're absolutely right," Lenz says in a quavering voice. "I lost control for a moment. I felt my fingers on his sleeve."

"You caught buck fever is what you did."

Suddenly Lenz is grinning like a hyena. "By God, it was exhilarating, wasn't it? I think I finally understand the expression 'thrill of the hunt.' "

"Don't mistake what you're doing with hunting, Doctor."

"What am I doing, then?"

"Trapping."

"What's the difference?"

"If you don't know that, you'll never get this guy."

Lenz looks at me like I just kicked his dog. "Explain yourself."

"Well . . . in hunting, the first thing you do is go into the quarry's environment."

"I'm doing that."

"No, you're not. Not really. Because the digital environment is an illusion. It's a virtual world in every sense. You can't reach through that screen and touch him. Remember, somewhere out there this killer actually exists—in the *corporeal* world. That's where he lives, not in this box."

"Keep going."

"When you hunt, you follow an animal's tracks."

"I'm not doing that?"

"No. That's what Baxter's technicians are trying to do. And so far they're failing. You personally don't have even the beginnings of the skill required to track Strobekker's digital footprints. And if he really knows what he's doing, there won't *be* any footprints."

"So, what are you saying?"

"Didn't you ever visit the country when you were a kid? Shoot sparrows with a BB gun or anything?"

"No."

"Jesus. Look, hunting is an aggressive activity. Basically, you take yourself to the quarry's territory, conceal yourself, wait a while, or maybe have dogs or beaters drive the game to you. And when your quarry happens up within range of your gun or your bow, you pop him. *Wham*—he's dead. Trapping is completely different. It's all preparation. It's all about bait. Using the right bait, placing it in your quarry's path, and waiting."

"What's your point?"

"Lilith is the bait."

"I know that."

"And what is the job of the bait, Doctor?"

"The job of the bait? To lure the quarry, of course."

"*Fundamentally,* what is the bait's job?"

Lenz sighs in exasperation. "I guess I don't know."

"To be what it is. That's all, Doctor. To sit there and do nothing but be what it is. You get it? Bait doesn't walk out to the quarry and say, 'Come and get me!' If it's raw meat, it just sits there and looks dead and appetizing. If it's a rabbit tied to a stake, it goes berserk for a while, then freezes in terror. If—"

"This situation is more complex than that."

"No. It's exactly the same. Everything must happen in the quarry's head. Your UNSUB is biologically programmed to want to kill the bait. Your job—your only job—is to be what the killer wants. Forget about Baxter and his geeks, forget about trying to manipulate the killer into *doing* anything. He knows what to do. You just sit here and be that woman. Talk to other users, not him. Build your personality. And then he'll come. In his own time maybe, but he'll come. And you'd better be ready."

Lenz stands up from the chair and stretches with nonchalance so elaborate that it must be feigned. He tears off the stream of paper where it meets the printer and lets it fall to the floor. "I'm sure you're ready to get back home, Cole. If we hurry, you'll just have time to make the Quantico plane. Unless you want to spend the night at a hotel and fly commercial in the morning."

He frowns at me like a flight attendant who's decided he made a mistake by inviting me to sit in the first-class cabin. "Which is it, Cole? A hotel or Ms. Krislov's jet?"

Part of me hates to walk out of this room, to withdraw from a game with stakes so high. Even at the most rarefied level, trading futures risks only money, not human lives.

"The plane," I say, standing up from the Toshiba and walking past him without another look.

He follows me down the stairs. Near the bottom, I ask, "Why did you decide to use a young decoy? I thought you'd decided that Strobekker changed his pattern. That he wanted older women like Karin Wheat."

"That's correct."

I pause at the floor. "But Margie Ressler's only, what, twenty-eight?"

"You should have more faith in me, Cole."

As we move across the den toward the kitchen, I look over the Corian counter and see a full head of brunette hair. Sherry, I presume. She's looking at something through the top window of an electric range. "Pretty soft setup," I say to Lenz. "Cook and everything."

Then the cook turns around and I am looking into the green eyes of Special Agent Margie Ressler. Her eyes are all I recognize. In the past two hours she has aged twenty years. Lines around her eyes and mouth, gray in her hair, a suddenly sagging bosom, and dowdy hips.

"It really works, doesn't it?" she says, her eyes sparkling. "I can tell by your face. Sherry's a *wizard* at this stuff. She told me some of the actors she's worked on, and now I believe her."

"Say farewell to Mr. Cole, Agent Ressler," Lenz says.

"Oh. Hey, I really enjoyed meeting you."

"You too, Margie. Thanks for the pizza. Be careful."

"No sweat. I warmed up some pizza for you, Doctor."

Lenz takes my arm and leads me out to the garage. The Acura Margie mentioned earlier has appeared. Special Agent Schmidt, the ever chipper factotum, steps silently from the door behind us. I turn back as he walks past me and climbs into Lenz's Mercedes.

"I'm going to say it one more time, Doctor. Don't push this guy. If you spook him, you'll never get him. Or worse—he might get you."

"I heard you the first time, Cole." He leads me around to the passenger door and opens it. "The Quantico airstrip, Schmidt. You might have to put some lead in your foot."

I climb into the car, lean back in the seat, and address Lenz through the window. "I don't think Agent Ressler understands how much danger she's in."

He smiles. "Your Southern sexism is creeping in. Ressler is a trained agent."

"How do you train for something like this?"

The psychiatrist straightens up and walks away. He is edging through the narrow margin between the Mercedes's hood and the front wall when a thought hits me. I reach over and beep the horn, startling him into the air like a cartoon character.

"What is it?" he shouts.

I lean out of the passenger window. "Remember the smiling young lady from Niger, Doctor."

He stares at me as if I'm insane.

"She went for a ride on a tiger. After the ride, she wound up inside, with the smile on the face of the tiger."

I tap Special Agent Schmidt on the arm, and he obediently backs the Mercedes out of the garage, leaving Dr. Lenz staring at us from the blue-white glare of the headlights. He does not squint into the beams, as most people would, but simply watches us pull away, the halogen light on his retinas giving him the burning red eyes of a night creature.

Chapter 23

The jet I boarded at Quantico touched down in Jackson, Mississippi, at three a.m. Central Standard Time. Jan Krislov would have broken into a nervous sweat had she seen her precious Gulfstream filled to its porthole windows with angry FBI Hostage Rescue commandos. I sweated a little myself. Three hours cooped up with those guys was like riding a bus full of Southern Baptist ministers on their way to picket a Bourbon Street strip club. Most were trying so hard to be professional that their grim frowns seemed on the verge of splitting into fierce grins of anticipation. I still don't know whether anyone had told them of my status as a suspect, but I didn't volunteer the information. Two agents watched me throughout the flight, their hostile eyes tracking me like those of snipers, which is exactly what they were. I was never told their destination, but by the time the pilot set me down I was damned glad it wasn't my farmhouse.

Two minutes after the jet taxied to a stop, I was standing at a pay phone calling Miles at EROS headquarters to warn him that he might soon be arrested. I feared that he might have been taken while I was airborne, but nighthawk Miles—awakened from a cat nap at his monitor—finally picked up the phone and began joking as if nothing more were happening than the usual bitflow of nocturnal erotica.

He didn't sound surprised by my warning, but he did

thank me for it. He thinks he's safe until EROS's time-locked file vault opens at one p.m. tomorrow. Daniel Baxter apparently believes that Brahma might be a legitimate EROS client. If that's true, the master client list now locked in the vault would allow the FBI to put "brute force" methods into the hunt, making the resolution of the case only a matter of time and manpower. Miles told me at least two agents have been guarding the vault since it slammed shut two days ago, but he seems to think they're in for a big surprise.

After we hung up, I tried again to warn Eleanor Rigby, but all I got was her answering machine. Knowing that her clingy paraplegic sister is the reason she keeps a blind-draft account, I felt I couldn't leave a detailed message without screwing up her personal life. I resigned myself to warning her by snail mail and jogged for my truck.

All that happened an hour ago, but I am still twenty minutes from home, driving a steady sixty-five miles per hour. It feels better than good to be rolling through the dark Delta cotton fields with at least the illusion that I am free from the clutches of Arthur Lenz and Daniel Baxter. Though it's dead hot outside, I roll down the Explorer's windows and let the air whip through the truck. Four-thirty in the morning is about as cool as it ever gets in August in Mississippi. The windshield fogs from the sudden temperature change, but the road is straight as a plumb line here, and I don't even wipe the glass.

There is enough moonlight to turn the cotton into a pale purple sea stretching away from the highway in all directions. I'm glad I won't be picking that cotton. Glad no one will be, except a handful of people on the poorest farms. Twelve hours in the burning sun with bleeding hands and a hundred pounds of itchy sack dragging behind you isn't fit work for man or beast. In the cotton field, if nowhere else, the machine has fulfilled its nineteenth-century billing as the savior of mankind.

At last my headlights illuminate the battered green road sign that announces "RAIN, MS, Home of the 1963 State Basketball Champions" to an indifferent world. Dinged by flung beer bottles, pierced by bullets fired in boredom, drunkenness, or anger, rusted by the heaven-sent water the town was named for, the old double-sided sign still stirs a strange soup of emotions in my chest when I roar past it in either direction. It takes less than a minute to sight the first hints of human habitation, blow past the tiny post office and tinier Laundromat, and sweep back into the long, still fields on the other side of Rain. Somewhere out there children are sleeping. But the men and women are not. They are waking to fry eggs and boil grits and pull on overalls and boots to face the hottest sun in the United States with no more protection than a faded John Deere cap.

I look out to my left and try to sight the crumbling superstructure of the old Edinburgh plantation. At one time this antebellum monolith dominated the land like a feudal castle. All activity for miles around was subordinate to its workings, its long shadow falling across slave and master, mammy and overseer, then sharecropper and bossman, and finally the not-so-slow decay of the gene line. In a burning dry year in the 1890s—a year not unlike this one—a sober gambler won the entire plantation from a dissolute heir in a midnight poker game. The way the story's most often told, the gambler raised the stakes beyond the heir's liquid resources, the heir used the plantation deed to call the bet, and signed a marker in front of a dozen witnesses. When the gambler laid down a flush, the heir fainted. By the time he staggered out of the old slave quarters, the divine deliverance of rain was beating dust devils on the drive, and the tin roof roared as though a hail of Yankee grapeshot had been loosed against the building. The heir went home, tried twice to shoot himself in the head, missed both times, and passed out. He woke up in time to see the gambler nail a board sign to a horse post out front. Painted on the sign was the word "RAIN," which from that day forward became the new name of the plantation and of the indolent crossroads of commerce that passed for a town.

My tin mailbox glints at the left margin of my high beams, which suddenly fluoresce the legend COLE. I slow the Explorer and sigh in exhaustion, knowing I could probably cover the last fifty yards and make the turn with my eyes shut.

The farmhouse stands about forty yards back from the road, shaded by oaks, pines, and a single weeping willow that hovers near the porch like a giant green mushroom. Just as I start to turn, my headlights flash on something farther up the road. Something that shouldn't be there. It's on the left shoulder, where there should be only cotton. I start to ignore it, but the landowner's imperative steels my nerves. I brake, back out of the drive, and accelerate slowly toward the silver reflection.

It's a sport utility vehicle. A Jeep Grand Cherokee. I recognize the distinctive slope of the hood. It's parked about sixty yards from the house. As I move closer, I realize something that chills me more deeply than the idea of poachers. The Jeep has a Hinds County license plate on its front bumper. That plate, and the Jeep, belong to my brother-in-law, Patrick Graham.

Without hesitation I reach under the seat, take out my Smith & Wesson .38, and lay it on my lap. This act would have been unthinkable three months ago, but I know enough about human nature to know that in a domestic dispute, anyone can become a target of deranged fury.

I pull the Explorer across the left lane and stop alongside Patrick's Jeep. Our faces are less than three feet apart, separated only by two sheets of glass. Patrick is handsome, in the fraternity president mold. Short sandy hair parted on the side, scrubbed skin, great teeth. He's one of the few doctors I know who always wears a suit to make evening rounds at the hospital. Even when he dresses casually, his clothes are either Ralph Lauren or something sent UPS from New England.

But tonight he looks like a ghost of himself. He is wearing a polo shirt, but it looks like he pulled it out of a dirty clothes hamper. His hair is longer than usual, and his eyes don't seem able to focus. He faces forward when I roll down my window, studiously ignoring me. I tap on the glass.

At last he rolls down his window.

"What's going on?" I ask in the calmest voice I can muster.

Patrick says nothing.

I tighten my hand around the wooden grip of the .38. "You waiting for somebody?"

"Erin's in there."

"Where? My house?"

He nods.

I say nothing, hoping he'll volunteer information, but he doesn't. "Holly too?"

He nods again. This is like talking to Gary Cooper. "I guess things aren't going so good, huh?"

He keeps staring at the dashboard.

"What's the deal, Pat?"

"I married a slut, that's what."

I blink in disbelief. Hearing these words from Patrick is tantamount to hearing a priest shout "God is dead!" from the pulpit. "That doesn't sound like you. Did something happen? You think she's sleeping around or something?"

He's nodding steadily now, his eyes full of sullen

anger. "She's making a goddamn fool of me. She has been from the start."

"What do you mean?"

"Don't worry about it. It's between her and me."

"I am worried about it. Does she know you're out here?"

He shrugs. I consider asking him to come into the house and sleep in my office, but I have no idea what's transpired in the past few hours. "Well . . . is there anything you want me to tell Erin?"

Suddenly he turns, and his eyes lock onto mine. "Where the fuck have you been all night?"

"Trying to keep the FBI off my ass. This EROS thing is out of control. There's a guy killing people out there. Cutting women's heads off, blowing up FBI agents. You believe that shit?"

He just stares. As I sit clenching the .38, a thought rises unbidden. "You know anything about the pineal gland?"

"The pineal gland?"

"It has something to do with these murders."

Patrick straightens in his seat. "It's a pretty uncommon tumor site. Not long ago pineal tumors were real problems, because they were often inaccessible to neurosurgeons. But with the new microsurgical techniques, that's changed completely."

Typical Patrick. His personal life is going to hell, but one medical question puts him into android-M.D. mode.

"There's a craze right now over one of the hormones it makes," he adds. "Melatonin. Crackpots all over the country are taking it for a dozen different reasons, but it hasn't been approved by the FDA."

"What do you think about it?"

"Homeopathic bullshit."

"That's what I figured. You sure you're okay out here?"

He faces forward again and nods.

I start to pull away, then stop. If Patrick is going to blow a gasket, I'd rather he do it out here while I'm holding a pistol than after I'm asleep inside. "Listen, you're not going to do anything stupid, are you? I mean, Erin loves you. I know she does. You're the best thing that ever happened to her."

His laugh is hollow and cold. "I'm just making sure of something. Don't worry, I'm good at repressing anger. Go inside."

"Okay. Take it easy."

After staring into his eyes a moment longer, I execute a three-point turn and idle back down to the house. I park in the gravel turnaround and get out with my briefcase and my gun. I'm on the second step when I spy the rear end of Erin's Toyota Land Cruiser jutting from behind the right side of the house.

My watch reads five a.m. Drewe and Erin are almost certainly asleep. I slip through the front door and turn left into my office without turning on any lights. As I undress, I realize that Erin and Holly are probably sleeping in the guest room on the other side of my office wall. A hundred thoughts and images flood my brain, but I am too tired to analyze them. I slide the .38 under my mattress, then fall facedown onto my pillow and inhale the welcome scent of home.

But sleep eludes me.

Why is Erin in our house? What is fraying the bonds of her marriage? Not the normal frustration that accretes like rust and eats at every relationship. If it were, Patrick would not be parked outside. So what remains? Other than our secret?

A faint creak causes me to turn over in bed and open my eyes. I sometimes hear this sound when the air conditioner kicks on, but I don't hear the compressor running. Then I realize my door is standing open. And silhouetted in it is a female form too slender and dark to belong to my wife. The white-gowned apparition glides across my floor and stops beside my bed.

Erin.

Without hesitation my wife's sister sits beside me on the twin bed and looks down into my eyes. This is the ruthless directness of woman, to observe no artificial boundaries, to behave as though no time has passed between our coupling three years ago in Chicago and now. I am supremely conscious of my wife, who lies sleeping less than thirty feet away. Yet Erin seems oblivious. She scrunches her left flank into my side, making more room for herself. Her face slowly coalesces in the darkness, oval planes of sculpted bone and tanned skin, eyes a shade darker than her long fine hair. She smells just as she always did, irresistibly feminine.

Then I see tears glinting in the dark. She lowers her head into her hands, stifling a sob. I want to wrap my arms around her and comfort her, but I do not trust myself. After three years of self-inflicted guilt, I should feel no impulse to anything crazy, but the drive that pushed me into Erin's arms the first time had nothing to do with reason, and it remains true to itself.

"What?" I ask softly. "What is it?"

"Everything's coming apart," she says much too loudly.

"What do you mean?"

"It was a mistake, Harper. It was all a mistake."

"You mean you and me? Keeping Holly? What?"

No answer.

"Have you left Patrick?"

She doesn't speak. I take her hand away from her eyes.

"I've tried," she whispers. "To be a good wife, a good mother. To leave everything I was behind."

I squeeze her wrist and force her to look into my eyes. "That's the problem, Erin. You can't leave your past behind. That's *Oprah* bullshit. I've tried it. You have to come to terms with whatever you did, and then move forward."

Her eyes widen, boring into my soul. "Like *you've* come to terms with it? You're living the same lie I am."

I look away. "I know. Look . . . does Patrick know anything specific?"

She covers her eyes and sobs again.

"Erin . . . I've got to tell you. He's outside. Patrick. He's sitting out there in his Jeep."

Her hand grips my wrist like a claw. "*Now*? He's out there?"

I nod. "He looks pretty bad too."

"Oh, God. Oh . . . *God*."

I raise myself enough to put my arms around her and pull her shuddering body to mine. Her arms close around my back as her wet face burrows into my neck. I have a sensation very like falling, but falling through time rather than space, and even as I hold her I feel her kick her way under the covers and mold herself to me. Fear and guilt and arousal surge through me in a flood.

"Erin," I whisper. "Erin—"

"Shhh," she says, her weight pressing down on me, against me, the heat of her long legs electrifying my skin. "I just want it all to go away. Make him go away."

"Erin—"

"I *hate* it!"

I take a deep breath and try to stay calm. I haven't held her like this since Chicago, not even hugs at family dinners. Now, only hours after I tried in vain to describe her unique sensuality to Lenz, the elusive has become all too tangible. Erin is crying softly, her face still buried in the hollow of my neck. With a shaking hand I stroke the silky hair above her ear, as I would a child's. "It's going to be okay," I murmur, even as a taut wire of fear sets to thrumming in my chest.

She sobs, her breast heaving with irregular breaths. It's already hot enough under the covers that I'm sweating. I'm about to try to pull back the bedspread when she lifts her head and looks down into my eyes.

"I'm not going back," she whispers, her mouth inches from mine. "I can't."

"Erin, you—"

She puts a finger to my lips and shakes her head. I feel her other hand slip into the hair at the back of my neck.

"Mama?"

I freeze.

"Mama?"

It's Holly. She's awakened alone in a strange bed.

Erin jerks upright, her head alert and rigid like that of a doe sensing danger.

"Maaammaa!"

Erin slides off the bed with fluid swiftness, her sheer white nightgown flashing across the room. She stops at the door, hovering like a veil. Then she's moving back toward me, quickly, but seemingly uncertain of direction. A bright scythe of light slices across my floor. The hall light.

Drewe.

"Daaadeee!" Holly wails.

Daddy? I grope under the mattress for my .38 while Erin stops in the middle of the floor, obviously torn between protecting her child and being caught in the dark with her sister's husband. Has Patrick broken into the house? Or is Holly calling for him out of habit?

I hear footsteps in the hall.

As I stand with the pistol, Erin vanishes through the door. Seconds later, Holly stops crying. I press my ear to the wall and hear Drewe say, "Everything's okay, punkin. Mama must be in the bathroom." Then Holly's higher voice, crusted with sleep: "Mama went to tee tee, Aunt Drewe?"

As though in answer, the commode flushes down the hall. I hear a quick beat of footsteps, then Erin's voice through the wall: "I'm sorry she woke you up. I had to pee. I didn't think she'd wake up. I guess it's the strange house."

"I didn't see the bathroom light," Drewe replies, ever logical. "I thought something was wrong."

A pause. "I'm used to finding strange bathrooms in the dark."

A longer pause, then, "That makes me sad, Erin."

The shell of my ear aches from the pressure of the wall, but I'm not about to miss this exchange. After a long silence, Drewe says, "Are you okay? Is this all going to work out?"

"I hope so. Let's don't talk about it anymore."

"Talk about what?" Holly asks in a bleary voice.

"Work stuff, honey."

"Tell me a story, Mama."

"We're going back to sleep, punkin."

"I want a story!"

"Lie down," Drewe says. "I'll tell you a story."

And she makes one up on the spot. It is a tale of a king with two daughters, both beautiful and smart, but each of whom believes she lacks one of the two qualities. We all listen spellbound, recognizing the allegory of Drewe and Erin as they struggle through myriad trials, all of us knowing Drewe will ultimately weave the threads into one of the happy endings she so fervently believes in, and all of us glad for it. This is my wife's transcendent gift, her optimism, and in the predawn shadows it is proof against despair. As she speaks, her voice like a lantern in the dark, I realize that Drewe is a living archetype of maternal love. Erin and I struggle in states of arrested growth, uncertain of our natures or fighting acceptance of them. But Drewe radiates heat and nurturing love like a warm spring flowing through bedrock, even without a natural object for her affections. I am the only obstacle to the fulfillment of her dreams, and at the deepest level, I know that if I have a duty to anything in this world, it is to bring those dreams to fruition.

After the two princesses have laid their parents to rest and agreed to jointly rule the "queendom"—a concept of which Hans Christian Andersen was apparently ignorant—Drewe says "night-night" to Holly. I expect her to go back to the master bedroom, but instead she appears at my door, a flannel-clad silhouette against the hall light.

"You back?" she asks softly.

"Yeah. Just got here. Everything's okay. For you and me, anyway. But not Erin. Patrick's outside."

"What?"

"He's parked on the road. I don't think he'll do anything crazy. But wake me up if you hear anything weird."

"This has got to stop," Drewe says with conviction. "I don't think I can get back to sleep now. You want to come in and give me the play-by-play on your trip? I'm going to make coffee."

I have no intention of letting my wife peer into my eyes after the events of the last ten minutes. "I'm pretty wiped out," I tell her. "I should probably get some sleep."

She remains at the door. "I'll throw together some lunch for you," she says finally. "I'm going to try to talk Erin into going home this morning."

"Thanks. Good luck."

"You forgot to close your blinds."

"I'm so tired it doesn't matter."

" 'Night," she says. Then she reaches across the invisible border between our lives and pulls the door shut after her.

Lying motionless in the pale dawn, I am overcome by a terrible certainty that, barring divine intervention, we are all moving toward an explosive revelation of the true and tragic state of affairs. And I am not one to look for divine intervention, at least of the positive sort. Retribution is the only cosmic principle I have ever found the capacity to believe in.

I sleep with the gun under my pillow.

Chapter 24

I slept ten hours last night. When I blinked myself awake at three-thirty this afternoon, I felt like I was stepping out of a recompression chamber after a mild case of the bends. Finding the house empty, I walked out to the road—ostensibly to check our mailbox—and verified that Patrick's Jeep had disappeared as well.

I can hardly believe it's been only four days since I saw the CNN report of Karin Wheat's death. Only three days since I faced the police in New Orleans, and Detective Mayeux ushered me into the fast-forward world of the FBI and its Investigative Support Unit.

Karin's body must be in the ground by now. God only knows where her head is. Her burial was probably a circus, with hundreds of gawkers dressed like kids for Halloween. What a grotesque irony. Karin long believed in—or at least wished for—physical immortality, and now she lies *sans* head in a concrete vault in one of the old French cemeteries that lent Gothic atmosphere to her dark novels.

And in some other place—perhaps just as dark and lonely—a woman named Rosalind May is lying or standing or sitting tied in a chair, and the most any of us can do is pray there is breath in her lungs. The Mill Creek, Michigan, police have probably turned their city upside down, rousting every homeless drunk and sexual offender within their jurisdiction and coming up with zero.

I remember Baxter telling me May had two grown sons. My mind conjures images of them trying to convince themselves that their mother eloped with a secret lover—or even that she was kidnapped by some money-hungry sleazoid—because to accept anything else is to accept that she is beyond mortal succor.

The dazed feeling of decompression sickness will not leave me. Last night, driving home from the Jackson airport, I felt a brief euphoria at successfully extricating myself from the clutches of the FBI. But have I really? Four days ago I disengaged from my normal life with a single phone call, and I have yet to reengage. It's not for lack of trying. Earlier today—as soon as I saw that Patrick was gone—I sat down at my Gateway 2000 to check the status of my futures positions. The layer of dust that had accumulated on the keyboard in my absence told me the news would not be good, and it wasn't. I was several thousand dollars down, and the trend was moving against me. Lenz's suggestion about dumping my contracts looked much better from hindsight. My first thought was, *I'll catch back up. I always do.* Yet the old conviction wasn't there. After a few fruitless minutes of shuffling my options, I stood up, stripped off my clothes, and got into the shower. Thinking about trading was useless. The events of the past days had locked my mind onto a single track.

The mathematics of the situation are simple: one man and seven women are dead; one man killed them all. Rosalind May is missing, probably dead; the same man kidnapped her. The single known element common to all the crimes is EROS, which I know better than anyone on earth save Miles Turner. In some ways—in the human dimension—I may know it better than Miles. But at that point I stop thinking. Because to go further is to admit things I do not want to admit.

Returning from the kitchen with a chicken salad sandwich, I notice the message light blinking on my answering machine. Nine messages. I must have slept like the dead not to hear the phone ringing all day. Taking a bite of my sandwich, I stare at the digital readout, debating whether to play back the tape or just erase the damned thing.

Intuition is a strange thing. The red LED light is inanimate, yet it speaks to me with the urgency of the voices captured as magnetic particles inside that machine. I want to ignore it, but I can't. Somewhere in the fluid circuits of my brain, a certainty has formed. Most of those voices will say little I wish to hear, but at least one will profoundly change my life. Or at least my perception of it. I'll wait as long as I can to play them back.

Suddenly, like God laughing at me, the machine clicks and the *9* changes into a red horizontal line. After a moment's hesitation, I turn up the volume to hear the caller.

"Pick up the goddamn phone, Cole!"

Arthur Lenz. By now his voice rates up there with the shriek of my college alarm clock.

"Your friend Turner has flown the coop, so you're next on the chopping block. You'd better listen to what I have to say."

"I'm here," I say, picking up.

"This isn't Ed McMahon, my friend."

"What did you say about Miles?"

"He's gone AWOL. Slipped his leash."

"What do you mean?"

"He walked out of EROS headquarters and never came back."

"When?"

"About two hours ago."

"How do you know he's not coming back?"

"Trust me. He's history."

Good, I think. "Baxter must have had people following him. How did he get away?"

"That's immaterial."

"It is? I thought Baxter was going to arrest him."

"You warned him, didn't you, Cole?"

I don't give Lenz the satisfaction of hearing me deny it.

"It doesn't matter. A half hour ago Turner's name went out on a nationwide police alert. He'll be arrested the second he's sighted. He's been classified armed and dangerous."

"What! You know Miles isn't armed."

"There's a nine-millimeter pistol registered in his name in New Jersey. Did you know that?"

Goddamn it, Miles. "No. But you know him, Doctor. He's not dangerous."

"I don't know anything today, Cole. I tried to help you two, and against the advice of seasoned police officers. Now you're just about on your own."

"Just about? What does that mean?"

"It means you should listen closely."

Here it comes. "I'm listening."

"I think Turner may run in your direction."

I laugh out loud. "If that's what you think, you're never going to catch him. He'd go to jail before he'd come back to Mississippi. To him it's the same thing."

"And he knows I believe that, which is precisely why I think he might do it. Turner's no fool."

"I'm still listening."

"The situation is fluid now. You're going to notice some surveillance around your house."

"What? Damn it, you said you were taking care of the harassment."

"There's only so much I can do. Daniel must be able to tell the police component of the investigation that he's watching you. It'll be local law enforcement."

"Great. Our felonious sheriff who can't legally carry a gun?"

"No. Your farm is on the line between Cairo and Yazoo counties, so Baxter chose Yazoo. Still, I have my doubts about local cops being able to handle Turner."

"If he did show up, they wouldn't have much trouble spotting him. Miles would be the only guy within sixty miles wearing all black, long hair, and any jewelry besides a ring."

"You know better than that, Cole."

"I still think you're nuts. If I were you, I'd watch the airports in nonextradition islands like Tenerife."

Lenz hesitates. "How do you know about Tenerife?"

"Christ, you're paranoid. I read, okay? And so does Miles."

"Does he have money?"

"You'd know more about that than I would."

The psychiatrist is silent for several moments. "Here's the deal, Cole. If Turner contacts you—especially if he shows up at your door—you call me first, then stall him until someone arrives to pick him up."

"Sorry. You're asking too much. As far as I know, you have zero evidence that Miles has committed any crime."

"We have a warrant for his arrest."

"On what charge?"

"Obstruction of justice."

"Fine. Just don't expect me to do your work for you."

"I think you're forgetting the leverage I hold over you," Lenz says, his voice tight.

"So much for patient confidentiality, eh?"

"Damn it, can't you see what's at stake here?"

"Your career?"

"Rosalind May's life!"

"I think Rosalind May is dead, Doctor. So do you. And you can bet your last buck that if you reveal anything I told you yesterday, this entire Chinese fire drill of an investigation—I mean every pathetic detail starting with the FBI's failure even to connect these murders and ending with the glory-hungry shrink and his hot-pants alky wife—will be on *A Current Affair* by dinnertime tomorrow. And if you think I'm kidding, remember one thing. Miles and I are alike in one very important way. When we say something, we mean it."

Another icy silence. "I'm not happy about this, Cole."

"Call somebody who gives a shit."

This wins me a brief silence. "Let me ask you something, Doctor. What happened today when the EROS file vault opened? I thought you'd sound happier this afternoon."

"What we found in that vault implicates Turner in ways you wouldn't like to think about."

I have no snide response to this, nor any further point to make. "Good-bye, Doctor Lenz. And good luck. I think you're going to need it." I hang up slowly, not wanting him to know he rattled me enough to want to smash the phone into pieces.

So much for normal life. The FBI is throwing its weight around again, and Miles is on the run. I'm surprised he hasn't bolted before now, given his pathological mistrust of authority. What bothers me is that he hasn't yet discovered how Brahma stole our master client list, or else hasn't told me that he has. The latter is more likely. Miles is God of the EROS universe, and if a digital sparrow falls within its bounds, he knows it.

Suddenly my office feels about five sizes too small. I grab what's left of the sandwich, a cold Tab, and my keys and hit the front door at a trot. The Explorer roars at the pressure of my foot on the accelerator and fishtails up the gravel drive toward the blacktop.

Two hundred yards to my right, parked on the wrong shoulder at the first gentle curve in the road, sits a boxy sedan with a gumball light on the roof. I look left but see no car there, only a turboprop crop duster buzzing over the power lines that border our leased cotton fields. My neighbor finished his aerial defoliation several days ago, but duster pilots have an affinity for flying on the deck, so it may be a pilot in transit.

My adrenaline surging, I gun the motor and drive straight toward the parked car. As I draw near I make out the white silhouette of a Yazoo County sheriff's department cruiser. I keep the Explorer at fifty-five until I'm almost on top of the car, then squeal to a stop beside the driver's window. The face is a chubby blur behind the glass. Slowly, the motorized window lowers into the door, and a reddish young face with a wad of Skoal tucked behind its lower lip smiles at me.

"Hey, Harp."

I know this guy. I played football against him in high school. "Strange place for a speed trap, Billy."

Deputy Billy smiles wider, then spits in the no-man's-land between our vehicles.

"Gonna get hot out here before long," I comment.

"Already hot. Ground's so goddamn dry it's grateful if you take a piss on it."

I give him a courtesy laugh. "You know why you're out here, Billy?"

He bites one side of his distended lower lip and looks down at my front tire. "Waitin' for Turner to show up, ain't I?"

"You remember him from school?"

Billy shrugs. "Saw him around. Never cared much for the sumbitch myself. Acted half queer."

This is about what I expected. "You really think he'd come back?"

"Can't ever tell. Folks do strange things on the run. Sometimes they get the homing instinct, like a sick dog."

"Not Miles. He hated this place."

Billy nods distractedly, then fiddles with the laser speed gun mounted on his door panel.

"Let me ask you something, Billy. Straight, okay?"

He looks up a little suspiciously. "Okay."

"Are you here just to watch for Miles, or are you supposed to keep tabs on me too?"

He takes a while with this one, his beardless chin working around the snuff. "Can't really say. Sheriff ain't talkin' much. Somebody wants Turner's ass bad, though. You, I don't know. But they're talkin' 'bout you some. Talking to people who know you."

"Like you?"

He smiles again. "I told 'em you was all right. Had a hell of a forearm on you back in seventy-seven."

"Not enough to handle you, though, was it?"

He grins wide at this.

"Look, do you have orders to follow me or not?"

Billy's answer is the eternally inscrutable smile of the Southern law enforcement officer. I guess there's only one way to find out. I stomp the accelerator of the Explorer and leave six feet of smoking rubber beside the door of his cruiser. When the speedometer pegs seventy, I look in my rearview mirror. Billy's Caprice is still sitting where it was. He's probably still grinning like Junior Samples. But at least he's not following me.

Driving back from a long and pissed-off run through the cotton fields, it occurs to me that Deputy Billy—if he hasn't handed off his stakeout position and headed home for supper—might stop me and demand to look in the cargo area of my Explorer. He wouldn't have to open the vehicle to do this, so I don't suppose he'd need a warrant. But if I took Drewe's Acura out for a drive one night, the only way anyone could be sure I didn't have Miles stuffed in the trunk would be to stop me and check. Would that be legal? Would I resist? It's academic now, of course. But will it remain that way?

Earlier this afternoon, I shifted the Explorer into four-wheel drive and fought my way across three hundred yards of grassed-over tractor ruts that ended at a wide flat bump in the fields. This was the Indian mound where Miles was bullied down into the fort with the rattlesnake. I could still see a low pile of deadfall and undergrowth where the fort had been. I got out and walked around the mound, half looking for arrowheads, and tried to remember what it felt like to be that young and have a friend I trusted like I trusted Miles Turner. I couldn't quite do it. I'm a different person now, and Miles is too. We're grown men. Yet somewhere inside, he must carry the tough little boy I knew back then, just as I carry my own. And while he is running for his freedom in New York or Tenerife or God-knows-where, what that little boy sees in the FBI, I am sure, is another gang of stupid bullies who want to scare him or hurt him or worse. And that makes me afraid of what he might do if they corner him.

As hard as the murders hit me, my experiences with the FBI disturb me more. Even with their vast material resources, they seem powerless to locate Brahma using technical or conventional methods. Daniel Baxter as much as admitted to me that they are waiting for the killer to make a mistake. But after several months of observing Brahma on EROS, I have no reason to think he will make one. Dr. Lenz seems to recognize this. Yet his response seems more than a little naive. His reasoning is sound: the surest way to stop a man who cannot be hunted down is to lure him from concealment. But is Lenz the man to do it? Could *any* man do it? Brahma is the most intuitive person I have ever seen on EROS. The odds that a man could trick him into believing he was talking to a woman for any length of time are probably nil. Worse, Lenz is a neophyte when it comes to EROS. He knows little about its social customs and nothing about its system architecture.

If anyone can trap Brahma using EROS, it's those who know the system best. Miles and me. I've spent the better part of nine months exploring the digital world that is EROS, interacting with women, lurking over supposedly private conversations, learning secrets that caused magnitudinal shifts in my perception of human nature, shepherding the evolution of a shadow community built on anonymity and desire. Miles has done this and more: he built the system from the test bench up.

And there lies the problem.

Miles is the digital sorcerer; I am not even an apprentice. And so far Miles has resisted helping the FBI. Brahma has already proved himself adept with computers; until the riddle of the stolen master client list is solved, I have to assume that he may be as proficient as—or more proficient than—Miles himself. The idea that I could attempt to deceive Brahma online without Miles's help is ludicrous. It was this realization that finally brought me some peace on the Indian mound.

Dusk is falling as I take the gentle curve going toward our house. Billy has indeed changed shifts with another deputy. Just to be an ass, I honk and wave as I pass the new guy. He replies with a sullen stare.

Braking for the driveway turn, I see the low cross-section of Drewe's Acura coming from the other direction like a cruise missile. She blinks her headlights European style, then cuts in front of my grille and into the drive. By the time I roll in behind her, she is standing on the porch holding her purse and a covered metal pot. She's dressed in khakis tapered to the ankles and an embroidered white blouse. Silver loops dangle from her earlobes, an unusual accessory for her.

"Where you been?" I call.

"Mom's."

I trot to the steps, hug her around the waist, and kiss her cheek. "Erin and Holly there too?" I ask, recalling Erin's vow that she would not return home.

"No, they left for Jackson a half hour ago. I hope Erin doesn't get halfway home and then turn around."

I push open the door and follow Drewe to the kitchen. "What's in the dish?"

"Chicken and dumplings. Anna made them."

"Yes!" Anna is the maid who raised Drewe and Erin from infancy. Even at seventy-eight, her cooking beats damn near any woman's in the county.

"I've been thinking about your case," Drewe says as she sets the pot on the stove.

"My case?"

"The EROS murders."

"Really? What about them?"

"The pineal gland, remember?"

"What about it?"

She surveys me from head to toe. "Why don't you jump in the shower while I heat this up? I'll tell you when you get out."

I look down at my clothes. I took a shower earlier, but my walk in the cotton fields soaked me with sweat. "I definitely need one," I admit. "I'll see you in a minute."

In my office bathroom, I strip, then switch on the special exhaust fan I installed to keep steam from escaping around the door. Mississippi humidity is bad enough for computers, but with shower steam thrown in, mine would be a lost cause.

I bang a switch on my waterproof ghetto blaster, sending the razor-clean guitar riffs of Steely Dan's "My Old School" bouncing around the cubicle. With the water set as hot as I can stand it, I let the spray scald my back as I sway in time to the horn parts. The knowledge that Erin has returned home lifts my spirit as much as anything could today, except maybe Brahma being caught. I've almost succeeded in working myself into a good mood when I feel a cold draft of air around the shower curtain. Drewe's voice rises above Donald Fagen's.

"You'd better get out here, Harper."

Her tone says trouble. I pull back the curtain and see something I rarely see on her face—alarm.

"What is it?"

"We've got company."

"Cops?"

"Just hurry."

I snatch a towel off the rack and shut off the boom box. Pulling on some jeans, I get a quick premonition that our "company" is Michael Mayeux, the New Orleans police detective. But when I peek around my window curtains I see no strange car outside. Geared up for anything, I stalk barefoot down the hallway to the kitchen.

There is a stranger waiting for me. He's tall and thin and clad in Levi's, western shirt, Red Wing work boots, and an oil-stained Treflan cap pulled over a sidewall crew cut. He stands with his back to me, facing Drewe, who watches him warily from the hot stove. Two seconds is all I need to place him as one of our lease farmers, probably coming to me with some preharvest catastrophe, a mutilated worker or some other nightmare that will bring endless years of lawsuits.

"Here he is," says Drewe, announcing my arrival.

When the guy turns around, it takes me a minute to understand what I am seeing. My skin heats with apprehension. Impossibly, incredibly, from beneath the bill of the Treflan cap beam the brilliant blue eyes of Miles Turner.

"Like the haircut?" he asks.

"You crazy son of a bitch."

His mouth breaks into a wide smile. I glance at the window to make sure the curtains are drawn, but Drewe has already taken care of it. "How the hell did you get here?"

"He almost gave me a coronary," Drewe snaps.

Miles makes an effort to look contrite. "The place is surrounded. I had to use an unorthodox entry."

My puzzlement speaks for itself.

"The bomb shelter," Drewe explains. "He came through the tunnel in the backyard."

This I can't believe. "You came through the old tunnel? In the dark? Mice and roaches and God knows what down there?"

"No choice. I moved fast. You know how I feel about closed spaces."

With the initial shock wearing off, Drewe's anger boils over. "My back was to the stove when he popped the latch on the trapdoor in the pantry. I almost dumped hot chicken broth all over myself."

"How did you get here so fast?" I ask, still not believing my eyes.

Wisely directing his attention to Drewe, Miles points at our kitchen table and silently asks permission to sit.

She nods grudgingly.

He sits the way a man sits after ten hours' plowing behind a mule. After taking a moment to collect himself, he says, "I rode the train to Newark Airport. Paid cash for a Delta ticket to Atlanta under a false name. In Atlanta I bought a ticket on a commuter flight to Mobile under another name. Then I gave a Mobile cabbie fifty bucks to take me to a juke joint where charter pilots hang out. It took about thirty minutes to find a guy who would fly me up here. Cost me fifteen hundred bucks. He thought I was running coke or something."

"Where did you land? Yazoo City?"

"Hell no. We found a grass strip about two miles north of here."

"I saw you! A turboprop plane? Looked like a new crop duster?"

He nods and laughs.

"You landed at the old Thornhill place? That strip is still good?"

"It's not *good*, but it's usable. I saw the sheriff's cars from the air. There's one parked to the east of you, another to the west, out of sight. From the strip I walked turnrows till I got within a half mile of your place. Then I went down on my hands and knees, below the cotton. I'm glad the bomb shelter wasn't locked. They can see your front and back doors with field glasses."

"I don't understand this," says Drewe. "Who's after you?"

"The FBI put out a warrant for his arrest," I explain.

"But why?"

"A lot of reasons," says Miles. "All bullshit. The warrant probably says obstruction of justice."

"It does."

"You both have some explaining to do," Drewe says.

"Lenz called today," I tell Miles. "He thought you'd run here. I told him he was crazy. I didn't think you'd ever come back."

"It wasn't easy."

"What happened when the vault opened at EROS?"

His malicious delight shines through his fatigue. "I told you they were guarding that vault like the tomb of Christ, didn't I?"

"Yeah."

"Why do you think I chose that simile?"

"Because the time lock was set for seventy-two hours?"

"You're half right. What did they find after the stone was rolled away from Jesus' tomb?"

"Nothing?"

Miles grins. *"Nada."*

"But you told me Jan sealed the vault when the FBI showed up with the search warrant."

"What did you think? She rolled a two-hundred-pound file cabinet in on a dolly? The files are on disk, man. Portable hard drive. Updated daily and then dumped to the master drive."

"Where's the master drive?"

"On the Sun workstation that sits in the file vault."

"Son of a bitch. She ran in there and plugged in the drive, then locked the vault?"

"Uh-huh. And one hour later, after Agents Moe, Larry, and Curly took up station at the vault door, I downloaded every byte of information through the fiber-optic cables that run out of a discreet hole in the floor of the vault. I exported them to a computer off-site, then remotely wiped out everything on the Sun."

"Just like Brahma did in Dallas."

"I didn't blow it up, but I definitely put that puppy into Helen Keller mode. Great minds think alike."

"Jesus, don't say that."

"Who's Brahma?" asks Drewe.

"The guy who's killing these women," I answer. "That's what Miles calls him. The FBI calls him UN-SUB, for 'unknown subject.' "

She gives Miles a look of distaste. "You name a serial killer after a god? I guess he's your hero or something."

"No. But I do admire his skill."

"You look wiped out," I cut in, stating the obvious in an attempt to head off useless squabbling.

Miles rubs both hands through his new flattop and sighs. "I'm as tired as a pair of jumper cables at a nigger funeral."

Drewe and I gape at each other: this slur from the most liberal white boy who ever left Mississippi. But Miles is grinning under the Treflan cap. "Just practicing my cover," he says. "I guess being a redneck is like riding a bicycle."

"You were never a redneck."

"My dad was."

This easy reference to his father surprises me. "How long have you been awake?"

"Three, four days."

"How did you get out of the EROS offices? Weren't Baxter's people all over the place?"

"It wasn't hard. Just before the vault opened, I switched shirts with one of my long-haired assistants. Then I went into the bathroom with a pair of scissors and a Ziploc and lopped off most of my hair. When the vault opened and the shit hit the fan, my assistant made a break for the front door, just as I'd told him to. While they chased the long-haired guy wearing black, I slipped out through Jan's private exit, got into a service elevator and *hasta la vista*, baby."

"You're whacked, man. You're nuts."

"You want some chicken and dumplings?" Drewe asks with her usual practicality.

Miles laughs again. "Since I haven't had any for at least ten years, I might as well. What I really need is some coffee, though. A whole pot. We've got a lot to talk about."

His eyes wander toward the pantry. There are two cases standing by the door. One is an expensive briefcase, the other a large leather computer bag with multiple compartments.

"What's all that?" I ask.

Drewe sloshes water into the coffeemaker.

"The whole stinking thing," Miles says softly. "The whole case. As much as I could get, anyway. Police reports, FBI interview transcripts, e-mail, lab findings, you name it."

"Don't even tell me where you got that shit."

"I've got to." His eyes glaze with sudden desperation. "I need your help."

"To do what?"

"To save myself."

Chapter 25

Miles has already drunk two cups of coffee, Drewe and I one each. It took me that long to recount my experiences with the FBI, even with heavy editing. I dwelt mostly on the tragic raid in Dallas and played down Lenz's plan of luring the killer to the Virginia safe house. Miles seems more concerned with the psychiatrist's suspicion that he might be the killer. I admit that Lenz still suspects him, but before I can qualify my words, Drewe starts asking questions about the murder victims.

In answer, Miles opens his briefcase on our kitchen table. Inside are neatly banded stacks of laser-printed paper covered with the hieroglyphics of command-line communications between computers. In short, Drewe and I are looking at a cornucopia of the fruits of virtuoso computer hacking.

"I have a lot of information here," he says, squeezing back into the narrow space between the table and the wall. "I started as soon as the deaths were confirmed. It's not nearly everything, but what I have is color coded. Green for city police reports. Orange for crime lab findings. Blue for witness interviews. Red for general FBI stuff—"

"You've been into the FBI's computer?" I interrupt.

"Computers, plural. Their acronym for the case is ERMURS—for EROS murders."

"No wonder they want to arrest you. Have you broken into their personal e-mail system?"

"I've seen it. Got some printouts here. I've also been in the National Crime Information Center computer, and some new thing called NEMESIS. Stands for *Nonlinear Evaluation/Manipulation of Evidence System*. That's the only system they have that's really elegant, and it's not officially online. The rest are crufty as hell."

"But why take these risks?" Drewe asks. "Can't you just keep your head down until this is all over?"

"No. Because Baxter and Lenz aren't going to catch Brahma any time soon. And in the absence of real leads, the great god Momentum will cause them to cast around for the most likely suspect. In their book that's me."

"But—"

"The only way for me to get these guys off my back is to catch Brahma myself."

Something ripples through my chest, like a pebble dropping into a still pool miles from anywhere.

"Besides," he goes on, "Brahma is fucking with my network. *My* system. I set it up, created it ex nihilo, and he's treating it like his personal sandbox. Not acceptable."

"Have you figured out yet how he got in?" I ask. "How he got the master client list?"

Miles stares furiously at the table. "No."

I find this almost impossible to believe, but I don't want to press him in front of Drewe. "What about alibis? You must have alibis for at least some of the nights the killings took place. Hell, I can't remember a night when you weren't sysoping the network."

He gives me a sidelong glance. "I don't have to be at the office to sysop. You know that. All I need is a laptop and a phone connection. Beyond that, I don't care to discuss it."

Drewe and I share a look. She takes a sip of coffee and

says, "Couldn't you just turn yourself in and put up with whatever hassle they give you until the murderer kills again? That would prove you're innocent."

"It's not that simple. If I'm arrested, Brahma could decide not to kill again for a while. Or if he kept killing, the FBI could say a copycat had joined the game. They could claim I was part of a group, and try to prosecute me on that basis."

"But surely they can't have enough evidence to prosecute you?"

Miles shrugs. "There are some lab findings that are consistent with my blood. There's other stuff as well."

"Not DNA?"

"They can't have that," he says sharply. "Not legitimately. But Brahma has successfully planted misleading physical evidence at every murder. I have to assume he knows who I am from EROS. Who's to say he hasn't planted something of mine that could give them a DNA sample?"

"That's impossible," Drewe says.

"Nothing's impossible. And don't think the FBI is above juggling samples to create DNA evidence against me, given enough pressure to close this case."

He slides some dark sheets from beneath his pile of paper and spreads them faceup across the table like playing cards. "These are the victims."

None of us speak. The sheets are laser-printed grayscale photographs. All six show side-by-side photographs of young women: two blondes, three brunettes, one Indian. In the left-hand photos, the eyes are open and glowing with life, the lips smiling, the hair well fixed; in the right-hand ones the faces—those that are there—are gray and shapeless, the eyes open but blank with glassy stares. One of the right-hand photos shows a decapitated torso, another a head that looks as though it was put through an airplane propeller. One shows a face like something from a vampire film, with wooden stakes protruding from bloody eye sockets. Before we take in too much, Miles sweeps the pages out of sight and says, "I got these out of NEMESIS. I've got crime scene photos too, but you don't want to see them."

He's right. Drewe is still staring at the blank spot where the images lay. After a few moments, she blinks, then rises and pours Miles a third cup of coffee.

In a remote voice, she asks, "What do the police think drives this man to murder these women?"

Miles drinks deeply from his steaming cup, finishing with an audible swallow. "The case has been running for five days. Ever since Harper called the New Orleans police and linked Karin Wheat's murder to six unsolved cases in other parts of the country."

"What parts?"

"Portland, Oregon. New York, Houston, Los Angeles, Nashville, and San Francisco. Of course the first killing was David Strobekker, the man who was murdered for his identity. That was Minnesota."

"The first one we know about," I correct him.

He nods. "Rosalind May, the kidnapped attorney, was taken from Mill Creek, Michigan. She's still missing, and there's been no ransom note."

"I think she's dead," I tell him.

"Ditto."

"I don't," Drewe says, firmly enough to draw looks from both of us. "At least she might not be."

"Why do you say that?" asks Miles.

"A theory I'd prefer to keep to myself right now. How was each of the women killed? I mean, I saw the photos, but what did the autopsies say?"

Miles watches her from the corner of his eye. Brilliant as he is, he remembers being aced by my wife many times in school. "The first—near Portland—was initially ruled an accidental death. She was a rock climber. Took a fall climbing solo, fractured her skull."

"Was she missing her pineal gland?"

Miles's eyes narrow. "She was exposed for a couple of days before they found her. Coyotes got to her. She was missing a lot more than her pineal gland."

"And the other murders?"

"Shotgun blast to the face in New York. Strangulation and beheading in Houston. Claw hammer in Los Angeles. Pistol shot in Nashville. Strangulation in San Francisco, with the eyes removed and stakes driven through the sockets."

"The pistol shot was also to the head?"

"Right."

"And every woman was missing her pineal gland or her entire head?"

"It isn't certain. With the shotgun victim it was impossible to tell. Some victims were missing only part of the gland. But the FBI consensus says yes."

"And they assume Karin Wheat was also."

"No."

"No?"

"Karin's head was found this morning."

"What?" I cry. "Where?"

"Some Cajun fishermen found it wedged in a cypress stump in the Bonnet Carre Spillway. The police figure the killer tossed it out his window while driving across the causeway toward La Place. That means he drove past the airport going out of town. And her pineal gland *was* missing."

"How was it removed?" Drewe asks, her eyes bright.

"Does that matter?" I ask as the reality of Karin's death hits me all over again.

"Of course. Did someone just reach in with a dull spoon and dig it out, or did he know what he was doing?"

"I don't know what tool was used," Miles says. "I didn't see an actual autopsy report, just an FBI memo. It said the gland was removed through a hole under Wheat's upper lip. Like Brahma punched through the sinuses and up into the brain."

"Jesus," I mutter.

"How big was the hole?" Drewe asks.

Miles checks his papers. "Seven millimeters wide. Damn. That's pretty small, isn't it?"

Drewe is smiling with satisfaction. "That's it," she says.

"That's what?" asks Miles.

"All those traumatic head wounds were meant to mask the killer's real intent. But Karin Wheat's head was never meant to be found. Her wound gives us the truth."

"What do you mean? What truth?"

"Tell me the angle of the pistol shot that killed the woman in Nashville."

Miles consults his papers. "It was fired into the back of her neck at an upward angle, near the first cervical vertebra."

Drewe nods and smiles again. "Have you ever seen anyone who was attacked with a claw hammer, Miles?"

He grimaces. "Have you?"

"Yes. During my residency. It puts big holes through the skull, and the brain squeezes out through the holes like toothpaste from a tube."

Miles and I look at each other in bewildered horror.

"That seven-millimeter hole beneath Karin Wheat's upper lip," Drewe says. "The one that went all the way up into her brain? A neurosurgeon would call that the sublabial transsphenoidal route."

"What?" Miles asks.

"It's a standard method of removing pituitary tumors. The pituitary gland isn't that close to the pineal in neurological terms, but in a dead person you could probably punch right through the pituitary and get where you wanted to go."

"You're saying a doctor could be doing this?" I ask.

"I'm saying a doctor *is* doing it. The stakes through the eyes? A surgeon could go through the optic foramen—where the optic nerve passes through the skull into the brain—veer to the midline, and go straight for the pineal. With the claw hammer and the rock fall, he could practically reach in and pull the gland out. The gunshot wound in Nashville? He goes up through the foramen magnum, the big opening in the bottom of your skull, and into the brain. The traumatic wounds cover up his tracks."

"The track in Wheat was pretty small," Miles says. "How do you pull out the gland through such a small hole? Would that be the reason he only got part of it sometimes?"

"The pineal is about the size of a pea," Drewe explains. "The problem wouldn't be getting it out but seeing it at all."

"What about a flexible probe with a fiber-optic camera and a cutting tool?" asks Miles.

"You're talking about an endoscope. I don't think they have those for neurosurgery. But I guess you could use any endoscope if the patient was dead. I assume the FBI is looking at doctors as suspects?"

Miles nods. "But doctors are only part of a much wider suspect group. Every police department has a different theory. The California police are working a cult angle. They've seen cult murders in the past where certain body parts were taken. No pineal glands, but adrenals, ovaries, testicles, all kinds of things."

"Dr. Lenz pretty much dismisses cult murders," I tell them. "Almost all of them are committed for some conventional motive."

"Baxter has officially classified these murders as normal sexual homicides," Miles says, "if there is such a thing. All the murdered women were raped after they were dead."

A short intake of breath from Drewe.

"There's a ton of forensic evidence," he goes on, consulting his printouts. "Bite marks in some cases, not others. The marks don't match. In one case they may have been made by a woman. With a couple of victims there was severe skin mutilation. The weird thing is that semen samples were found and analyzed in every case, and with seven victims they've found semen from at least four different men. Sometimes near the victim, other times inside the vagina. They're waiting on DNA tests now. To compare to mine, no doubt."

The hair on my forearms is standing. "You mean four men raped each victim?"

"No, no. Four men spread over all seven cases. Though in two victims there were two different semen samples found." Miles shakes his head at Drewe. "I know what you're thinking—one sample from a boyfriend or husband, the other from the killer, right? Wrong. Both samples in each woman were the result of postmortem sex."

"Good God," I whisper.

Miles takes a sip of coffee. "The problem with physical evidence is that the Behavioral Science people basically use a connect-the-dots approach to murder. They have checklists for cops to fill out. Condition of the body. Restraints, no restraints. Type of weapon. Cause of death. Post-offense behavior. Antemortem rape or postmortem rape? Penetration or just masturbation? All these things produce vastly differing profiles." Miles sounds almost saddened by the imperfection of the system. "A guy who knows the system can put a few extra dots at each crime scene and distort the picture. If he puts in enough dots—or takes them away—there's no picture at all."

"Like the radically different head wounds," Drewe says. She pulls at the corner of her mouth with her forefinger. "What about the physician angle?"

Miles shuffles his papers. "The current Unit profile includes butchers, dentists, doctors, male nurses, taxidermists, veterinarians, even people who've worked in slaughterhouses. They figure somebody's expanding his horizons in new and exciting ways—with help, of course."

Drewe wrinkles her mouth in distaste. "Does anyone think just one man might be responsible for the crimes?"

"Yes, but that presupposes an individual of staggering abilities. He'd not only have to have medical skill and access to things like blood and semen, but also detailed knowledge of law enforcement methods, forensics, locks, security systems, not to mention psychology and computers. It's hard to picture one man—particularly a serial killer—having that kind of ability."

"Why? Wasn't Ted Bundy a really smart guy?"

"Not really. I did a Nexis search on serial killers, and I learned a lot. Bundy looks clever compared to the mean of his group—serial killers—but put him on a scale with the general population and he was nothing special. We're talking about a guy who dug up women he'd killed weeks before to have sex with their corpses. He got a lot of press because he looked halfway preppie and could convince women to trust him. The truth is, most serial killers are genetic debris."

"Not Brahma," I say. "You've read some of his stuff, haven't you? He's erudite as hell. And he can exploit insecurity like no one I've ever seen."

Drewe looks at Miles. "You agree with that?"

"Yes. But I don't think he's a doctor. His computer skill level's too high for that. Some doctors know computers, but not at the level I'm seeing."

"So what do you think?" I ask. "You think he's a hacker?"

"No. I think he might be a Real Programmer."

This silences me.

"What's that?" asks Drewe.

"What Miles used to be. At MIT. People the media call 'hackers' get to know operating systems like UNIX and DOS and VMS very well, their design quirks and flaws. But Real Programmers can *build* operating systems. They're supercoders. They call it programming on bare metal. They're the demigods of hackerdom."

"The problem with that theory," Miles interrupts, "is that a Real Programmer killing people doesn't make sense. We're talking about a dogmatically nonviolent personality type. His entire life is lived between silicon, metal, and bits. Someone who's read *The Lord of the Rings* sixteen times and who'd be glad to spend an evening trying to conjugate Elvish verbs with you."

"You're generalizing," I tell him. "If this is a sexual thing, it doesn't matter what his career is. You should know that better than anybody. Brahma doesn't have control over what's driving him. He could be a priest, for God's sake."

"I think he does have control," Drewe says quietly. "Most of the time anyway."

I suddenly recall Lenz telling me the same thing.

"Why?" asks Miles.

"Because the murders have an ultimate object," she says. "The pineal gland. And because the killer has expended great effort to conceal that fact."

"Keep going."

"The fact that the women were raped throws me. But drop that from the equation for a minute. The pineal gland is the primary object because the killer takes it away with him. I mean, if his goal were merely to rape dead women, he could kill just about anybody and do that."

"So . . . ?"

"So the killer is a doctor."

Miles looks disappointed. "Proof?"

"Occam's razor," Drewe counters. "It's the simplest answer, therefore the most likely. You're resisting it because you're biased against doctors."

"I am not."

Drewe laughs. "The killer broke into your computer system and you don't know how. Therefore, you assume he must be a member of the secret fraternity of the world's smartest people—those who do what you do. But you're shortchanging doctors."

Miles's face is red. "I think you're wrong."

"Why else should the killer hide the fact that he's taking pineal glands? Unless it could somehow lead to him? And who does the pineal lead to? You said there were no cults known for taking the pineal. And in the one victim where there was no major head wound, the gland was removed using a standard neurosurgical approach that, despite the fantasies of the FBI, would not be the likely one chosen by a butcher or dentist."

Drewe begins walking around the kitchen, seemingly propelled by the tide of her reasoning. "Look at the areas of expertise you mentioned. Postulate a brilliant surgeon and medicine is taken care of. Law enforcement is a technical undertaking usually handled by men from . . . what? The fiftieth to eightieth percentile of intelligence?"

Miles and I watch her with fascination. The logical ruthlessness of a smart woman can be chilling.

"Who better than a doctor could plant false biological evidence at crime scenes? He could get blood, urine, semen, stool samples, hair. Locks and security systems are child's play compared to microsurgery. Human psychology? Again, an experienced physician. That leaves—"

"Computers," Miles finishes.

Drewe stops beside the stove. "Yes. Now please listen, Miles. If I were to drop all my personal prejudices, I'd have to admit that a person like you, a computer genius, could have been a brilliant surgeon had he chosen that path. And because I believe that, I must believe the reverse could be true."

He looks unconvinced. "I understand your reasoning, but you just don't see that in real life."

"I'll tell you why you don't see computer experts becoming surgeons. Because it requires a minimum of nine, sometimes eleven years of postgraduate training. The learning curve on computers is much shorter. You can jump in and begin working almost immediately, because if you screw up, you've only killed a machine or a program, not a person."

Miles stares stubbornly at the table.

"But once you're really seduced by computers," she continues, "it's too late for medicine. You're into hardware and software, not wetware."

Her accurate use of this computer term for the human brain, and by extension human beings, surprises us both.

"But surgeon as computer expert?" she asks, moving across the floor again. "The stereotype of no spare time in medical school is false. People do get married, have hobbies. If we posit a medical student who had little or no social life but an obsession with computers, I can easily see him attaining the skill level you're talking about. Especially if he has the aptitude. And a practicing surgeon would have whatever spare time he wanted, plus the money to pursue his obsessions."

Miles looks up in defeat.

"The question," Drewe concludes, "is what is he taking the pineal gland *for*? What does he do with it? What does the FBI think?"

Miles drums his long fingers on the table and scans a new sheet of paper. "Possibilities range from eating it to burning it to selling it to Asians who render certain hormones from it."

Drewe stops again. "Melatonin."

"That's right," says Miles.

"Do you know what melatonin does?"

"It regulates the sleep cycle. There's apparently a craze right now where people use it as a natural sleeping pill. Some think it's a magic antiaging pill. I know a few computer people who take it, along with a hundred other vitamins and herbs."

Drewe finally comes to the table and takes a seat. "After Harper got back from New Orleans," she says, "he told me about the pineals being taken. The next day, I punched a few queries into the Medline computer at University Hospital. It told me more than I knew before, but not a lot. Just enough to lead me in the right direction. There's a neurobiologist on staff at University; he hasn't been there long, but he's good. You should have seen him come to life when I asked about the pineal gland. He was still jabbering when I left forty-five minutes later.

"Melatonin is hot right now because research teams in different parts of the world have recently come up with some startling new findings on it. But before I tell you what they're doing, I'm going to tell you why these women are being killed."

Miles stares at Drewe with the wonder of a kid watching a magic show.

"Let me ask one question first," she says. "What were the ages of each of the victims?"

Miles's eidetic memory spits out the digits like bingo numbers. "26, 23, 24, 25, 26, 25, 47."

"Is that in order? By date of death?"

"Yes."

"How old is the kidnapped woman? Rosalind whatever?"

"Fifty."

Drewe smiles. "There it is. Someone is trying to transplant pineal glands between human beings."

"What?" Miles cries.

"Why?" I ask.

"To add fifteen to twenty vital years to the human life span. Perhaps ultimately to his own life."

Miles and I are silent.

"According to the neurobiologist," Drewe says, "foreign researchers working on the pineal began by focusing on melatonin as a dietary supplement, just the way people are taking it now. They found that mice ingesting a regular regimen of the hormone were not only healthier but also lived longer than the control mice. This prompted them to try a more radical approach. They had microsurgeons transplant pineal glands between mice—the pineals of young mice into old mice and vice versa. The results were astounding. *Far* more dramatic than oral dosages. The coats of the old mice regained their luster, the animals regained their sexual appetite and ability, T-cell counts went up, certain tumors disappeared, and a dozen other results, all positive."

"And the young mice?" Miles asks.

"They immediately began to age rapidly. But the most fascinating thing is that the old mice with transplanted pineals maintained their reinvigorated state almost up to the point of death. To put it simply, they never got old. They just died."

The kitchen is so quiet that the *cheeep* of crickets outside sounds like a roar.

"If that were true," I say finally, "American pharmaceutical companies would be researching melatonin twenty-four hours a day."

"How do you know they're not? They may be duplicating these experiments right now. It just might be that a gland thought vestigial until 1963 is the engine that controls the human aging process. The number of people taking melatonin nationwide is staggering. It's also frightening, because no one knows what its effects are over time. The pineal gland basically rules the endocrine system, Harper. It controls sexual development by regulating other hormones. It affects body temperature, kidney function, immunity. It controls hibernation in mammals, migration in birds, it changes skin color in chameleons. All this was new to me. When the neurobiologist started asking why I was so interested, I made excuses and got out of there. But by then it was clear to me."

Miles is tapping his fingertips together. "You're saying the age disparity between the first six victims and Karin Wheat is explained by the fact that the killer was taking—"

"Harvesting," Drewe corrects him.

"*Harvesting* the pineal glands of young women for transplant? You're saying he put these first few glands in the freezer until he got ready to start kidnapping older women to test his theory on?"

She shakes her head. "I think the first murders were part of a training program. Transplantation of a human pineal has never been tried. The pineal gland has the highest blood flow by weight of any organ other than the kidneys. A transplant would be fantastically difficult, probably impossible. Lots of microvascular stuff, severing and reattaching minute blood vessels. We're talking groundbreaking neurosurgery. I think whoever's doing this knew he would need practice in the vasculature surrounding a pineal gland—probably a pineal as close to the living state as he could get it."

"So according to your theory," says Miles, "just prior to the murder of Karin Wheat, this mad doctor decided he was ready to make a transplant attempt?"

"Karin Wheat is the flaw in my reasoning," Drewe says quickly. "To make a transplant attempt, the surgeon would obviously need his recipient alive in an operating room, not dead in New Orleans. But I still think the last young woman killed prior to Wheat was meant to be a transplant donor. What was the elapsed time between her death and Karin Wheat's murder?"

"Six weeks," I reply.

She sighs in frustration. "That's too long. No way a gland would remain viable that long."

"Oh no," I nearly moan.

"What?" Miles asks.

"Brahma's primary topic of conversation with Karin Wheat was immortality. That was the subject of her last novel. They both seemed obsessed with it."

"Score one for my theory," says Drewe.

"But he didn't kidnap Karin Wheat," Miles reminds her. "He murdered her."

"But he *did* kidnap Rosalind May," she counters. "And May was almost the same age as Wheat, right? Fifty is definitely the downhill side of the hormonal roller coaster. Perfect candidate for what I'm talking about."

"Maybe the killer *wanted* to kidnap Wheat," I suggest. "But something went wrong."

"Maybe," Miles allows. "She was the only victim who died with a drug in her system. Ketamine. It's an animal tranquilizer."

"Your tech called me two nights ago. Baxter said May had been missing for two days. That means she was kidnapped—"

"The night after Wheat was murdered."

I nod. "They wanted to kidnap Wheat, somehow bungled it, and decided to go for May as a substitute."

"A preplanned backup," Miles suggests.

"But what went wrong with the Wheat scenario? Why kill her?"

Drewe slaps the tabletop, stunning us both. "There's another victim," she says.

"What?" Miles asks.

"There has to be. Wheat was the intended transplant recipient. Something went wrong, so they took Rosalind May the next night. But who's the *donor*? The last murder of a young girl—that we know about—was six weeks before Wheat's death. That's too long for a harvested pineal to remain medically viable. That means another young woman was kidnapped in the interval, or is about to be. *She's* the donor."

"My God," I whisper, starting to believe for the first time.

Drewe looks at me. "How long does it take you to find out an EROS woman is dead or missing?"

"Weeks, usually. I only found out about Karin so fast because she was a celebrity."

"What about Rosalind May? She was only taken days ago."

"It's complicated, but it comes down to coincidence. She was a blind-draft account holder who hadn't been active for a while but was still paying her fees. When her account went to zero, one of Miles's techs started poking around. A week ago, her account went active again. It looks like she was talking to Brahma right up until the second he took her."

"My God. Are there more accounts like that?"

"About fifty."

Drewe goes still. "The donor is one of those fifty. Only her account hasn't dropped to zero yet, so nobody but the killer knows she's part of this. Both she and May could be lying on an operating table right now, waiting for—"

"Wait a minute," says Miles, holding up his hands. "We're going off the deep end here. If your surgeon is a he—like almost all serial killers—and he wants to prolong his own life, wouldn't he be kidnapping men?"

"Sex doesn't matter in organ transplants."

"But why is he *raping* them, for God's sake? After

they're dead, no less? According to your theory, this surgeon would be motivated by a semblance of rationality. Is raping corpses the act of a rational man? On EROS I once saw a quote about necrophilia taken from a psychiatric textbook. 'In necrophilia, the diagnosis of psychosis is considered justified in all cases.' I laughed about that for two days. Talk about understatement. I'm no missionary, but bonking corpses is definitely off the reservation."

"I can't explain that part of it," Drewe confesses. "But I stand by my theory. And I'll tell you something else. One glance at those pictures you flashed tells me these murders weren't committed for purely sexual reasons."

"Why?"

"Every one of those women looked different from the others. Different hair, complexion, bone structure, and enough difference in cosmetics show different personalities. Men are visually motivated. The only connection between those girls was that they were young. And Karin Wheat and Rosalind May weren't."

Miles flattens his hands on his papers. "Okay, let's look at your surgeon for a minute. If he intended to try this transplant, wouldn't he need the victim's blood type, tissue type, things like that?"

"I assume so," Drewe says, "but I don't know. I'm an obstetrician. I know virtually nothing about transplantation. There are very good antirejection agents now."

"How would he do it? He's got to remove a gland from the center of the brain, then put the new one right back in that spot? Or could it go somewhere else?"

"I would say reattachment in situ is impossible. Damaged central nervous system tissue will not grow—that's axiomatic. The pineal is attached to a stalk through which all kinds of chemicals flow. Once you sever that stalk, it's over. Maybe he could park it in a kidney or something."

"A kidney?" I ask.

"In the early mouse transplants, the surgeons placed the new pineal inside the thymus, which is behind the sternum. They did that because both glands were connected to the same nerve center in the brain. And the transplanted gland functioned. But in the later mouse transplants, the new pineals were put right into the brain after the old glands were removed. How, I don't know. And I don't see how you could do that with humans."

"How long would an operation like this take?" Miles asks.

Drewe opens her hands. "Removing a pituitary tumor takes two or three hours. But that's simply an excision of tumor tissue. This would take much longer."

"But you know for a fact that it worked on mice?"

"Yes. But you see the difference, don't you? The doctors working on mice were studying only the aging process. Who knows how much brain function they destroyed in the process of transplanting the pineals?"

A horrifying thought hits me. "Who's to say Brahma didn't take the pineals from those first victims and transplant them into living recipients? There's no reason to think we know about all his victims. He could be taking women from other online services. He could be taking homeless women off the street."

"Shit," mutters Miles.

"And if he is, he might not care any more than those mouse doctors about what mental functions he destroyed."

"Oh God," Drewe whispers. *"God."*

"Maybe Rosalind May is alive," Miles says, getting to his feet. "How many people would it take to do what you're talking about? Bare minimum. Double up any functions that allow it."

"Mmm . . . five. Two surgeons, two nurses, and an anesthetist."

"That sounds high," I tell her. "Think about battlefield surgery. The Civil War. Doctors have performed operations with almost nonexistent resources when they had no alternative."

"Okay, ditch one nurse. But this isn't some macho deal where they do without sedative and cut with a kitchen knife and someone calls it a miracle because they got muddy doing it. You're talking about a transplant. A *glandular transplant at the core of the brain.* It has *never* been done. If anything, it would take more hands than usual. Plus a state-of-the-art operating room. You'd need an operating microscope, a C-arm fluoroscope, all kinds of stuff. It might take surgeons working in shifts. Some neurosurgical operations take more than twelve hours."

"So even if he is a surgeon," Miles says, "he needs serious help. Trained people. We're talking a lot of money here. The ultimate object might even be money."

I start to argue, but he holds up his hand. "I agree that Drewe's estimate of five is high. We're talking about someone who has access to state-of-the-art voice-recognition technology." Miles quickly explains to Drewe the theory behind Strobekker's zero typographical error rate. "So who's to say he doesn't have access to computer-assisted robotic surgery, or whatever else he needs? I've seen some prototype medical equipment that's unbelievable. I mean, we don't know *who* we're dealing with. It could be the chief of neurosurgery at a major medical school."

"No way," Drewe objects.

"Where's the best neurosurgery department in the world?" I ask.

"Columbia," she replies without hesitation.

"Where else is good?"

"Not the places you'd think. The University of Washington, Michigan, the Barrow Institute in Arizona. But

Columbia turns out the majority of academic neurosurgeons in the U.S."

"I'm getting something from this," Miles says.

"What? Columbia?"

"I don't know. It might come to me in a second. Might take ten years. This is where the brain is truly inferior to the computer. I've lost a file in my own head, and I can't retrieve it no matter how hard I try."

Memories of Lenz's verbal primer on the psychology of serial killers flash through my mind. "You really think the motive could just be money?"

"*Just* money?" Miles barks. "Man, you must be even richer than I thought. My only question is *how* Brahma could ever make money off the procedure. Even if he succeeded at the transplant, he'd be guilty of murder."

"True," says Drewe. "But if it worked, legitimate surgeons might begin working on the procedure."

"How?"

"Same as any transplant. Pineals could be harvested from recently deceased persons. Your Brahma can't access legitimate donor networks because his research is illegal. That's why he has to kidnap or kill to get donors. But if pineal transplants were proven to counter the aging process, the demand for the procedure would be unimaginable."

"But *personally* he'd never make a dime," I point out.

"He'd be famous, though," says Miles. "And with the current legal climate, he might just get off and do a multimillion-dollar book deal."

"Money and fame," murmurs Drewe. "The twin gods of our society. Pretty strong motivation for the right person."

"I just don't buy it," I insist.

"Well, obviously there's the metaphysical side," says Miles. "I mean, whoever pulled this off would be accomplishing what no one in history ever has. If you forget morality, his quest is heroic. Even noble."

"Noble!"

"Hell, yes! Melvillian in scope. Captain Ahab with a scalpel. Mary Shelley unbound. One of his aliases *is* Prometheus, remember? I'll tell you something else. The three of us are under thirty-five. But one day we're going to look down at parchment skin, shriveled breasts, limp dicks, and swollen joints that creak like ratchets when we try to move. And on that day I think we'll understand the fountain-of-youth motive much better than we do now."

Drewe wrinkles her nose. "I think you're crude but also right. That tells us that the killer must be at least . . . what?"

"Forty-five," says Miles.

"That's the upper range limit for a serial killer," I tell them. "And you're using it as a lower limit. At least that's what I got from my research."

"If we go with Drewe's theory," says Miles, "I don't think Brahma *is* a serial killer, except by after-the-fact definition. He's a doctor, period. A scientist. Lumping him in with Jeffrey Dahmer and John Wayne Gacy is like grouping Denton Cooley with Doc Adams from *Gunsmoke*."

"Forty-five sounds good," Drewe agrees. "Surgery is an acquired skill. Even gifted cutters need to be tempered."

In that instant my mind skips off track, giving me a new perspective. "We're missing the forest!" I declare, startling both of them. "If Drewe could find out all this about the pineal gland, surely the FBI has as well?"

She looks put out at my devaluation of her detective work. "What do your papers say?" she asks Miles.

"As of last night, they weren't giving more weight to

doctors than to any other group. That may have changed after Wheat's head was autopsied."

"I doubt it," I tell them. "Do you know why?"

My oracles are silent.

"We've created a single suspect brilliant enough to actually pull off this transplant thing. But that's flawed logic. It isn't necessary that he be capable of it, or that it even be possible. You see? All that's necessary is that he know about the pineal research and that he *believe* he's capable of doing a transplant. That's what lets in the psychotic taxidermists and dentists and all the rest."

"But his computer skill proves he's brilliant," argues Miles.

"Brilliant with computers," says Drewe. "Not necessarily medicine."

"Let's say a surgeon is the brains behind this," I cut in. "He trolls EROS himself, but he needs a hacker to get at our master client list, plus medical information from health insurance computers, God knows what else. Then he hires muscle to do the actual killings—"

"That explains the rapes!" cries Drewe. "It's not the surgeon, it's his hired thugs. Some sleazeballs are raping the women, and the surgeon doesn't care so long as he gets his pineal glands. He's probably glad his thugs are confusing the crime scenes!"

Miles is nodding. "Division of labor. A surgeon could easily afford a cracker and some hired muscle."

"Gross income for a neurosurgeon is nearly half a million," Drewe says. "And that's an *average.*"

"I'm definitely in the wrong business," Miles mutters.

"But that theory works only if Brahma's a flake," I point out. "If we postulate a man with a real chance of success, he needs a team of medical specialists to help with the operation."

"And they'd realize what he was up to," says Drewe.

"Eventually. I don't think money would be enough motivation for medical people to take part in murder."

Miles laughs bitterly. "Money is always enough motivation for some people. You two have so much of it now you've forgotten what it's like to really need it."

"Whether it's a nut or a serious surgeon," I say irritably, "it's clear why you and I are suspects. You could easily be the paid hacker. You'd be guilty of murder even though you were never at a single crime scene."

He nods soberly.

I shove back my chair, climb onto its wooden back, and perch there with my feet on the seat. "I'd say we've come up with some significant reasoning here. The question is, do we tell the FBI?"

"Fuck no," Miles says savagely. "They've got me cast for the remake of *Midnight Express*."

I look to Drewe, but she is gazing at the kitchen curtains drawn shut against prying eyes. "They know most of this already," she says softly. "They must. If they don't, I don't have much faith in them."

"What do you think?" I ask Miles. "Do they?"

He averts his eyes. "The groundwork is there."

"They don't suspect there's an unknown victim," I press him.

He shakes his head.

"We've got to tell them about the fifty blind-draft women," Drewe says flatly. "That's nonnegotiable. One of them is dead or missing right now."

"Drewe," Miles says carefully, "women set up blind-draft accounts precisely because their use of EROS might cause problems or even physical danger in their homes. I can't sic the FBI on them without any warning."

She is clearly upset by this. "Privacy means more to you than a human life? You think those women value it over their lives?"

"It's more complicated than that. You just came up

with this unknown-victim idea. And if we accept our own logic, she's already dead. Right? I mean, we're pegging her as a donor."

"Not necessarily dead. She could be lying on an operating table right now."

Miles is thinking. "What if I call Jan Krislov and tell her to order my techs to start contacting those fifty women? To verify that they're alive and okay?"

"*Every* woman with a blind-draft account," Drewe insists.

"That's over five hundred women," I tell her.

"Closer to six," Miles says. "It might cause a panic, but we could do it." He pauses again, weighing the risks. "Okay. I'll tell Jan to put four techs on it. They'll start with the fifty women who aren't active but are still paying their fees. Good enough?"

Drewe bites her bottom lip.

I feel a strange fluttering below my diaphragm. "Miles, maybe it's time to come clean with Baxter and Lenz. You talked me out of pursuing this thing once, and the result was very bad."

He lets out a frustrated sigh. "Harper, the three of us are buying into a scenario we came up with off-the-cuff, and a pretty damned wild one at that. The FBI has twice the raw data we do, but *they're* not buying the doctor theory yet. Because they can't afford to. It's their responsibility to catch this guy. We're just three people talking. You see?"

At my core I know this is a lie. We are not "just three people talking." We are bright people with specialized knowledge and personal stakes in the case. Even Drewe seems to have attacked the problem with proprietary intensity.

The blaring ring of the kitchen telephone freezes us all in place. Drewe looks to me for a sign.

"I'm here," I tell her. "Miles definitely isn't."

She takes a deep breath, then picks up the receiver and says, "Dr. Cole."

She listens intently for about ten seconds, then cuts her eyes at us and smiles tightly. "Hang on," she says, and puts her palm over the mouthpiece. "It's Mom. It's about Erin. This is going to be a long one. You want me to go to the bedroom phone?"

"We'll get out." I spring off the chairback and land on my feet. "What about telling the FBI?"

She gives me a searching look, and while it lasts Miles does not exist. After some mental process I cannot divine, she says, "They have the same facts we do. As long as you start checking the blind-draft women, I see no point in calling attention to ourselves tonight."

A sigh of relief escapes Miles's lips.

"But if one turns up missing," Drewe adds, "we go straight to the FBI."

Miles nods, then quickly gathers his papers into his briefcase. I kiss Drewe on the cheek and lead him down the hall to my office—the domain of secrets, and of the EROS computer.

Chapter 26

Sitting in a half-lotus position on a stool before the EROS computer, his hands flying across the keyboard, Miles says, "I'd forgotten how quick Drewe is."

"You really think there's another blind-draft woman missing?" I ask, staring over his shoulder. The cover is off the computer, and its electronic guts look very different than they did thirty minutes ago.

"We'll know soon," he says.

Typical Miles. He's already e-mailed his techs and instructed them to begin a discreet check on the safety of all female blind-draft account holders; thus, predictions are pointless.

He stares at the monitor, his hands suspended over the keys. "I can't believe you never installed this card, man. I sent it to you two months ago."

He's referring to a large rectangular circuit board designed for voice synthesis and recognition. The voice-rec/synth card is the most densely packed PC card I've ever seen.

"I don't use the voice much," I tell him.

"That's because the one you have sucks. The new one has unbelievable inflection control. It really sounds human."

"Let's hear it."

He drops his hands to his sides. "Put the cover on, Bwana. You just entered the twenty-first century."

With a hard shove, I press the metal cover back onto the chassis. "You got a demo for it?"

Miles shakes his head. "Call up a file. An EROS file. These cards only work properly with the EROS format."

I lean over his shoulder, click the mouse, and retrieve the top file in my electronic filing cabinet. The text of a typical exchange between myself and Eleanor Rigby fills the screen. Miles hits ALT-V—a key combination called a macro that simultaneously carries out several functions—and a rectangular window appears in the lower left corner of the screen.

	MALE	FEMALE	
VOICE ONE:			**Hz**
VOICE TWO:			**Hz**

Using the mouse, Miles clicks on the first HARPER> prompt, drags the mouse over to VOICE ONE, and clicks again. Then he selects a frequency under the male range. He does the same with ELEANOR RIGBY> but selects a frequency in the female range. Beneath the frequency range display is a group of controls much like those on a tape recorder. Miles uses the mouse to select PLAY.

"Your turn tonight," says a voice not so different from mine, but without any accent. The voice came from my computer's multimedia speakers, but it sounded as natural as a third person in the room. I squeeze Miles's shoulder in disbelief. He just laughs.

"I'm ready," answers a female voice, its timbre not exactly sensual, but definitely feminine. *"We are standing naked on cool black rock, volcanic rock, staring across a vast expanse of primeval ocean. An orange explosion of sunset burns itself out beneath a purple horizon, leaving us stranded beneath white points of stars. Our blood pulses in sidereal time as our eyes dilate to adapt to the newly dark world, pupils ex-*

panding to expose underused receptors, until the very glow of our skins massages the nerve pathways leading to our brains, the first touch not a touch, and yet as real as any language in this—"

"Unbelievable," I say over the hypnotic canticle. "All the subscribers will get this?"

"Not for a while." Miles chuckles with the affection of a proud father. "This part of the package isn't that complicated or expensive. It's the other half that puts it out of reach."

"What? Video?"

"No, quality voice recognition. It's much more complex than real-time video. Which you should know, since you've had video by satellite uplink for six months."

"Which I hardly use either."

"Krislov thanks you. It's too fucking expensive."

He stands up from the stool and hands me a black plastic headset exactly like those worn by telephone operators and receptionists. "I guess this will count as the first field test. The earphones don't work. I picked up the wrong set when I split the office. The mike works fine, though."

"Just talk into it?"

"Hang on." He clicks RECORD/CHAT with the mouse, and the Harper–Eleanor Rigby file vanishes.

"Okay. The real test is whether the program will recognize your voice. If it won't, this thing is useless to you until we train it with your voice."

"How do you train it?"

"By reading many long and boring passages into it, Grasshopper. I've modified the program to be as tolerant as I can make it. Out of six techs at EROS, it accepts four as me."

I sit before the computer and, rather tentatively, say, "Hello?"

On the screen appears:

MILES> Hello.

"I'll be damned!"

"Hello is easy," says Miles. "It displayed the 'Miles' prompt because I logged on as me. I'll set it to read whatever screen name you're using at the time. Try a sentence."

"Okay." As clearly as I can, I recite, "Now is the time for all good men to come to the aid of their country."

On the screen we see:

MILES> Okay. Now is the time four all good men to come two the aid of there country.

"Shit," says Miles, his voice weary. "Actually that's not bad, considering you never trained with it. If you'll consciously avoid your Southern accent, you'll probably get better results."

"*I* have an accent?" I ask, laughing.

Now that he's neutralized the stress he felt at being around a computer that was not quite state-of-the-art, Miles walks away from the EROS table and examines various objects around the room with distracted interest. My guitars, the Civil War sword, the sculpture of my father's coat.

"You glossed right over Lenz's plan to lure Brahma by pretending to be a woman," he says, leaning across the twin bed and rubbing the side pocket of the coat. "I let it slide because you sounded like you didn't want to go into detail about EROS in front of Drewe."

"Good instinct."

"I can't believe this is made of wood," he says, running his fingertips over the sculpture. "I thought Drewe was into EROS."

"She was until about three months ago. Now she can't stand it. She hasn't stepped into this room in six weeks."

He sits down on the bed and peers at me with open curiosity. "Why the change? She find out about Eleanor Rigby?"

"No. She's ready to have kids, Miles. But that's only part of it. I'd rather not go into it right now."

"And Erin? Problems with her husband?"

"Same story. Skip it." I get up from the stool and roll my swivel chair opposite him.

"The last time I saw her was in New York," he says as I sit down.

"You saw Erin?"

"Yeah. This was years ago. She looked seriously medicated."

"She finally kicked that."

He raises a skeptical eyebrow. "She got kids now?"

"One."

His gaze is too direct for me to dissemble on that subject, so I push him straight to our mutual problem. "What do you think about Lenz's plan?"

"I think it might work."

"Really?"

"The logic is sound. There wasn't a word about it in any of the FBI or police computers. Not even on Baxter's personal e-mail. If they're keeping it that secret, Baxter must think Lenz is devious enough to pull it off."

"He may, but I don't."

"Why?"

"Because it's not that easy to pretend to be a sex other than the one you are. Especially for a man to pretend to be a woman. I see people try it all the time, and I can always tell. Can't you?"

Miles runs a finger down his aquiline nose. "Sometimes. But if I couldn't tell—and I couldn't peek at the master client list—how would I know I was being fooled?"

"Granted. But what about the trip-up questions like

'What does a speculum look like?' Or 'What brand of feminine protection do you use and why?' "

"Lenz is a doctor. He can handle that stuff."

"Maybe. But when someone starts writing their innermost thoughts to you—live, on computer—you begin to form an emotional picture of who they are. And when something rings false, you get a little twinge somewhere, like hearing a dissonant voice in a choir."

Miles laughs softly. "Harper, you're more perceptive than almost anyone I know. But even you can be fooled."

His tone stops me; he is not speaking in theoretical terms. "What do you mean?"

"People are fooled about sexual identity every day on EROS, and I can prove it to you."

"How?"

"You won't like it."

Spider legs of apprehension creep along my shoulders. "Why?"

"It involves someone you care about."

"What are you telling me, Miles?"

"Eleanor Rigby."

I am utterly still. "No way she's a man. I know who she is. She's Eleanor Caine Markham, a mystery writer."

An odd smile narrows his lips. "Who also works as a body double in Hollywood? And has a crippled sister in a wheelchair who resents her personal life?"

I am too stunned to respond immediately. Miles's invasion of my privacy is momentarily forgotten as I try to guess what shocking revelation he is about to drop on me.

"Harper," he says, his tone like that of a teacher urging a child toward the answer to a simple question. "Eleanor Rigby *is* the sister in the wheelchair."

This statement hits me with physical force, as though my parents had sat me down and told me I was adopted.

"You never considered that?" he asks gently. "A woman

with the brains to be a successful mystery writer also has a body that major directors pay to put on film? Possible, but not likely."

It seems so obvious now. But sixty seconds ago I had no clue. "It just—everything she said seemed so heartfelt."

"It *was*. Each part of 'Eleanor Rigby' is based in objective and emotional truth. She just shuffled the parts on you, mixed the roles. She lives vicariously, through her novels and through talking to people like you on EROS. You're her sex life, Harper. You truly are her lover, maybe the greatest of her life. Sad, isn't it?"

A shapeless flood of anger courses through me, and for lack of a better target I direct it at Miles. "Who gave you the right to go prowling through my life, goddamn it? *You're* the one who doesn't have a life."

"We're all voyeurs," he says in a neutral tone. "It's the new American pastime. Pretty pathetic, I guess, but that's where we are."

"That's a cop-out, Miles."

"Maybe. If you want to know the truth, I checked out Eleanor because I saw you getting tight with her. Maybe even risking your marriage, if Drewe happened to see the stuff you two were writing. I wanted to make sure she wasn't some basket case. You know, the kind that shows up and starts boiling rabbits on your stove."

"How can I ever thank you." Though I am spitting sarcasm, my inner voice tells me that Miles does care what happens to me. But still I feel the urge to strike back. Before I know it, I am asking him the one question I have spared him up until now.

"Miles," I say in my father's voice, "are you involved in these murders in any way?"

He blinks in surprise.

"In *any* way."

He looks away, then back at me. "Anything else you

want to ask while you're at it? Am I queer? You've been wondering that too, haven't you?"

"You're avoiding my question. That scares me."

"Fuck no! I am not now nor have I ever been a corpse-fucking killer, okay? Good enough?"

I watch him impassively.

"I can't believe you asked me that."

I feel the peculiarly human satisfaction of knowing I have made him as angry as I am. "You'd better get used to it. I'm on your side, and I had to ask. What do you think the FBI will think?"

"Hey, I *know* what they think. That's why I have to catch this asshole."

I slowly roll my chair forward and back with my feet. "I agree. Do you have a plan?"

"You think I came back to this cultural wasteland for the sights? Of course I have a plan."

My pulse quickens. "What is it? You've got a way to trace his phone connections?"

He shakes his head. "I might be able to, if I had the help of AT&T and the major cellular companies. But I don't, do I?"

"So?"

He slides off the bed and stands, his uncovered crew cut a mere shadow against his scalp. He runs a hand through it like a man feeling the stump of an amputated limb, then begins pacing out invisible patterns on the floor.

"This is what will happen," he says. "For a while, Brahma will communicate just as he has, in live-chat mode. How long depends on the telephone tricks he has up his sleeve. It's not easy to avoid being traced these days. Once they get close to him, he can keep using live-chat mode by switching between authorized accounts to which he has the passwords. According to you, he's already done this once, talking to Lenz. But if the FBI techs are smart—and that's open to question—there's a way to track those legitimate accounts."

Miles has paused, so I oblige him with a "How?"

"You gave Lenz some transcripts of some of Brahma's dialogues with his victims, right? Using those, the FBI should be able to build a search engine that will sift through EROS for his most common prose patterns. It will take less and less time for them to begin their traces."

"And?"

"Eventually Brahma will switch from live chat to e-mail."

"Does that help us?"

"Think, Harper. What's the essential difference between chat mode and e-mail?"

"Well . . . I don't know."

"Sure you do. Think real estate. Location, location, location."

Suddenly I have it. "In chat mode, each person is sending his side of the conversation to one of our servers in New York. In essence, each is viewing the conversation by long distance."

"Whereas e-mail?"

"Is an actual file that the user downloads from our computer into his own. Usually, anyway."

He grants me a smile patronizing enough to make me feel I'm back in the third grade. "That's how I'm going to get him."

I try to see farther down the logical track. "How? You're going to give his computer a virus? Destroy all his files? What will that accomplish?"

"I'm not going to do either."

"What, then?"

"A Trojan Horse."

I sit back and ponder this. A Trojan Horse is a program that a hacker plants inside someone else's computer, usually to facilitate the burglary of passwords. It resides in some neutral area of the host computer's memory, waiting patiently until a legitimate user logs on and enters his or her password. When that happens, the Trojan Horse copies the user's password into a secret file before allowing him access to the computer. After a day or a week or a month, the hacker dials back into the computer, opens his Trojan Horse program, and removes a hefty new file filled with legitimate passwords. Then he deletes his Trojan Horse so that no one will ever know it was there. After that, he can gain illegal access to that system whenever he wishes by using the legitimate passwords. The Trojan Horse, true to its name, has opened the gates to the city.

"I don't see your reasoning," I tell Miles. "You're not trying to break into Brahma's computer."

"This isn't going to be a traditional Trojan Horse. *If* I can build it. This will be a *real* Trojan Horse."

"I don't understand."

"You remember how the Trojan Horse got inside the walls of Troy?"

"Sure. The Greeks built it, pulled it up to the gates of Troy, and pretended to sail away. The Trojans thought the horse was a gift and pulled it inside their walls."

Miles nods. "Which is exactly what Brahma is going to do."

"Why should he do that?"

"Trust me. He will. What happened after the Trojans pulled the horse into the city?"

"The Greek soldiers hidden inside climbed out that night and killed them all."

Miles chuckles softly. "My plan is slightly different from that. But the result will be the same."

"But you can't even roll your Trojan Horse up to the city walls. You don't know where it is."

"I'm not going to," he says calmly. "You are."

And then I see it. Miles has arrived at the same conclusion I did at the Indian mound this afternoon, only he probably did it three days ago. "You want me to do what Lenz is doing. Pretend to be a woman. Engage Brahma online."

He smiles. "Don't tell me you haven't thought about it. And I know you can do it, Harper. Much better than Lenz. You're a songwriter, for God sake. A fucking pied piper with words."

"Not exactly a successful one."

"For reasons wholly unrelated to your talent. And you have more empathy with women than anyone I know. Every girl we ever knew confessed her darkest secrets to you at some time in her life. Am I wrong?"

He's right, but I'm in no mood to admit it. "I'm not saying I haven't thought about it. But Lenz has some advantages we don't. Like a SWAT team to take Brahma out if he shows up."

"We don't need that! We're not trying to lure him here. We have three simple goals, all based around the Trojan Horse. One, get Brahma to believe in you. Two, keep up the relationship until he switches from live chat to e-mail. Three, get him excited enough that he doesn't examine every bit of information flowing down the pipe from you to him."

"You're going to bury your Trojan Horse program in my e-mail and hope he downloads it into his computer?"

"That's one possibility."

"But won't he see the program? An executable file piggybacked with e-mail?"

"I don't know. I'm not sure I can do what I want to do with e-mail. But I have an advantage. I designed EROS's e-mail system. We want a situation where the two of you are exchanging long letters, sexual fantasies, anything that requires a lot of bits. If I can't do it with e-mail, you'll have to convince him to download some program you say you're wild about. Some sexual thing I could kluge up fast. Maybe with a video file or something."

"What if Brahma doesn't switch to e-mail?"

"Then *you* make the switch. Tell him you get nervous live. You like to compose your letters in romantic contemplation, or some such bullshit."

I consider the plan, searching for faults. "Exactly what kind of special Trojan Horse is this going to be?"

The serene smile of a Zen master smooths Miles's face. "A masterpiece. Almost invisible, but deadly in its own way. A study in elegance."

I want to press him, but I know it would be useless. "How long will it take?"

He shrugs. "I don't know. I never know that. Bumming code isn't linear work. I mean, I might hack through it line by line, but more likely I'll stare at the TV for two days, then cop to the right thing when I'm not thinking about it."

Reaching across the twin bed, he pulls down one of my old Martins. He studies the guitar's scarred face, then cradles it under his arm and puts his fingers to the strings. A halting rendition of Neil Young's "The Needle and the Damage Done" tinkles from the sound hole. I taught him to pick that tune sometime around 1974. At fourteen Miles was growing his own marijuana, and he drove me crazy to teach him the song. As far as I know, it's the only thing he can play.

"How long since you played that?" I ask.

"I've picked it out on every guitar I ever found leaning against a wall in someone's apartment."

I laugh with him. The bonds of friendship are strange, and the moment emboldens me to be painfully honest. "Miles, what we're talking about could take a while. You know as well as I do that one of those sheriff's cars could pull up outside with a search warrant any time. And we'd both be arrested."

He nods soberly. "If that happens, I'll go back out through the tunnel, just like I came in. And I won't come back."

"Drewe isn't going to like this."

"I know. But I don't think she wants me in jail, either."

"She'd rather it be you than me."

He hangs the guitar back on its pegs and unfolds his long frame on the bed. Sighing deeply, he turns his head to face me. Exhaustion clouds his eyes like smudges on a camera lens.

"We could go two different ways," he says, as if I've already agreed to his scheme. "Use the identity of a real EROS client, a woman with a blind-draft account. Or we can create a fictional woman, totally from scratch."

After a useless moment of internal resistance, I ask, "Which is better?"

"A real woman is easier from a technical standpoint. But there are disadvantages. You won't know much about her. Brahma might discover real information that conflicted with what you were telling him. Also, if Brahma's selection criteria *are* medical, we don't know what they are. A real woman has real medical records, and if he got access to them, he might disqualify her on that basis alone. Plus, we'd be putting her life at risk. Without her consent. Unless someone like Eleanor Rigby would let us—"

"No," I say, cutting him off. Miles's manipulative tendencies are never far from the surface. As I consider his words, an image of Agent Margie Ressler's gamine face comes into my mind. "What about a fictional woman?"

"The plus is that she can be whatever you want. The negative is that she won't really exist. Which means I'll have to create her."

"What do you mean?"

"Bureaucracy. Social Security card, driver's license,

motor vehicle records, address. I'm sure the FBI faked credit cards and everything else for Lenz's decoy."

"They did," I confirm, recalling Lenz's boasts in his car. "Can you do that?"

Miles yawns heroically. "Sure. Only I don't have the help they do. If we go that way, I'll keep it simple. No medical records at *all*. That way, Brahma has to go with whatever you tell him."

Despite anxiety about the risks, I'm fascinated by Miles's proposal. Rather than trying to lure a predator toward us in the hopes of trapping him—which is basically Lenz's plan—Miles means to trick him into swallowing a hand grenade. As his eyes close, I say, "Those goals you mentioned? Contacting Brahma, keeping the relationship going long enough for him to switch to e-mail, all that?"

"Yeah?" He opens one eye.

"You forgot one."

Both eyes are open now. "What?"

"Catching the son of a bitch before he decides to kill me."

He smiles; then both eyes close.

Miles is snoring softly—with three cups of coffee in him, no less—while I sit at my desk with the contents of his briefcase spread in front of me. Drewe is still on the phone with her mother. Occasionally her voice rises above the hum of air conditioner and computer.

There's enough stolen information on my desk to fill twelve hours with steady reading. Not merely Nexis newspaper stories, but lab results and detectives' case notes, things that would put Miles under a jail were they ever entered as evidence in a court of law. Yet all of it pales into insignificance beside the photographs of the victims.

Confucius was right about pictures and words. All the

words on the paper in this pile add up to mere statistics, but the faces are real. The faces are *people.* A more analytical man might look at those statistics and see gold, see his destiny, might feel certain that after enough solitary study of those lines and squiggles, a new relationship would emerge like a hologram from the chaos and point him toward the killer. But my analytical gift ends at murder. I feel too much empathy with the women in these searing images to place myself at the appropriate remove for objective study. Perhaps this is the reason I first strayed out of my father's footsteps.

Drewe has that capacity for distance. It may well be what allowed her to make logical leaps about Brahma while Miles and I plodded along like boys following bread crumbs. Strange that emotional distance would be a requirement for those who heal, whereas I, who feel others' pain more keenly than most, have hurt far more people than I have helped.

What can I do for these poor women? What do they need? Someone to avenge them? They're certainly past hurting now. As this thought dies, I realize what holds my gaze to their haunted faces. They are eternally unattainable. Like Keats's Grecian figures, they will possess their mystery, and thus their beauty, forever. I can never touch them. And if I can never touch them, I can never hurt them. Granting myself that reprieve, I am able to admit that I do know what they need. They need justice.

But justice cannot be served until their killer has been hounded to his lair, chained, and brought to a place of judgment. It may be that Miles and I can assist with the first task. Yet my logic remains sound enough to comprehend the scale of the problem. For almost a year Brahma has gone about his business without hindrance. In all the world, I alone—because of a few ripples in the EROS net—perceived the foul wake of his passing. I reacted late, but I reacted, and by so doing created a window of opportunity. And then in Dallas the FBI squandered forever the only advantage it would ever have—surprise.

Now Brahma is hiding. And he has an infinite matrix in which to conceal himself. I once thought the vastness of America was geographic, that miles of space or denseness of wood made massive measure. Then, on an icy Chicago street, I met a man and woman searching for their stolen child. After a single conversation, a couple of long looks into their hollow eyes, I saw that every mountain Lewis and Clark traversed, every steaming swamp De Soto pushed through, every plain the pioneers crossed has been transected by the compass, riven by the surveyor's level, scarred by roads, photographed by satellites, and reduced to a thing you can fold into your glove compartment. But those lost parents stared across an uncharted sea of people, praying in vain for the phosphorous glow of a long-vanished trail, each town an eddy, each city a whirlpool that could swallow a hundred children without trace. And across that sea float the millions of milk cartons carrying photographs of the missing like messages in bottles, bound for garbage cans as surely as the ruins of last night's dinner.

Looking at Miles's stolen photographs, I know that somewhere in that same sea moves a man who saw final agony twist the faces of these women, who heard the last word or plea or wail that passed their lips. He moves comfortably, in the knowledge that maps do not exist to lead men to him. That he can do his grisly work in peace. That he can taunt his hunters. That only an accident will raise his head above the mob and mark him as a son of Cain.

Chapter 27

I found Brahma at eleven thirty p.m.

To my surprise, he was deep in conversation with "Lilith"—Dr. Lenz's personal Eliza Doolittle.

I'd been looking for him for about an hour, stopping occasionally to run a global search of EROS, checking for "Anne Bridges," the account name that backed up Lenz's "Lilith." I also searched a few chat lobbies for "Shiva" and "Levon" and "Prometheus" and "Kali." As I searched, I wondered whether Brahma, like me, could roam behind the digital walls that appear solid to EROS's subscribers but yield like curtains to its system operators. If so, he could see me searching. Yet I had no choice if I wanted to find him. After a while, Drewe leaned in, saw Miles sleeping, said good night, and padded away without offering a summation of Erin's problems. I wasn't about to ask for one.

And then I got the hit.

At first I didn't understand what I was seeing. The alias interacting on-screen with "Lilith" was not "Shiva" or any of the other familiar noms de plume. It was "Maxwell." Yet after reading less than twenty lines of text, I knew "Maxwell" was Brahma. My excitement made me clumsy when I tried to activate the new voice-synthesis program, but I finally got it going.

Now my LaserJet printer hums and whispers as it records the conversation, while the digital voices of "Lilith" and "Maxwell" spar and weave and intertwine like mating serpents. They seem to be discussing a sexual incident that sounds like a cross between a group sex encounter and a gang rape.

LILITH> It _was_ my decision.
MAXWELL> I don't accept that. Why did you let nine men have their way with you?
LILITH> It's not easy to explain.
MAXWELL> Was it you who suggested it?
LILITH> It wasn't that clear-cut.
MAXWELL> Wasn't it suggested by the first man? The one who took you upstairs?
LILITH> Why do you think it was upstairs?
MAXWELL> It always is. Or else in a basement.
LILITH> It was upstairs. At a fraternity house. And I don't remember exactly. It was like . . . we were doing it, my date and I, on this bottom bunk. And then this other guy walks in. A boy really. He said, "Hey, I'm really drunk, I need to crash." And then he climbed up on the top bunk to sleep.
MAXWELL> But he didn't sleep.
LILITH> No. In a minute or so I opened my eyes and saw his head leaning off the edge of the top bunk, looking down, watching us. Looking into my eyes. He looked like he was watching God or something. Wide-eyed like a kid. And then his head disappeared and I noticed the top bunk was moving too. And like I knew what he was doing up there. He couldn't help himself. And when my date finished a second later, I said, I think your friend is frustrated. He looked at me funny—he was pretty drunk, too—and he said, you wanna help him out or something? And I just laughed and said I felt sorry for him. Why

not? I swear to God I'll never know why I did that. So my date got up and laughed, and the kid from the top bunk came down. He was really timid at first, really gentle, but then he started thrashing and moaning. It took him like a minute and a half to finish. And by the time he did, I noticed the first guy was gone and there were two other guys standing by the door.

MAXWELL> Inside the room?

LILITH> Yes. The door was half open. And I don't know why, but I just sat up and said, Who's next? And they practically fought each other right there. It was like wild animals or something. After that it was all sort of a blur.

MAXWELL> Nine men in a row?

LILITH> Does this turn you on or something?

MAXWELL> It saddens me, Lilith.

LILITH> It shouldn't. Don't you understand what I told you? It's what finally _liberated_ me.

MAXWELL> I don't believe that.

LILITH> Because you don't understand it. All these guys, these boys whose whole lives were wrapped up in their egos and the size of their penises, this macho thing, every one of them was the same. You see? They all wanted the same thing, me, and none was any better than the others, or any worse, and I could take whatever they dished out and reduce them to nothing. They came in like lions and went out like lambs.

MAXWELL> You're not telling the complete truth, Lilith. I _know_ it was degrading. Did they stand around watching each other do it to you?

LILITH> I wouldn't allow that. One at a time.

MAXWELL> Was the room dark or light?

LILITH> Dark.

MAXWELL> Did they all have you the same way? Missionary position?

LILITH> A couple tried to turn me over, but I knew better.

MAXWELL> How long did each one last?

LILITH> Why do you want to dwell on this stuff?

MAXWELL> Lilith.

LILITH> Some lasted a few minutes, others fifteen seconds. Most around two minutes, I guess.

MAXWELL> So it was just twenty minutes out of your life. No big deal. That's what you're telling me?

LILITH> No! I'm telling you it _was_ a big deal. But not in the way you think. After it happened, I no longer felt that stupid sense of obligation to satisfy whoever happened to want me. A guy has an erection, so what. That's his problem. When I was younger I didn't understand that. It may sound naive, but I didn't.

There is a sudden silence. I wait with my hands gripping the arms of my chair. Where is Lenz getting this stuff? Despite my assertions to the contrary with Miles, I'm having a hard time remembering that "Lilith" is a middle-aged psychiatrist sitting in McLean, Virginia. The "female" voice synthesized by the computer probably contributes to the illusion, but Lenz's nightmarish story is freighted with the pain of real experience. As I begin to worry that he has somehow blown it, "Maxwell's" voice and text resume.

MAXWELL> You say you didn't know any of these men?

LILITH> I knew the first guy. He was the guy who asked me to the party. My date. Hah.
MAXWELL> I think you knew someone else at the party, Lilith.
LILITH> Like who?
MAXWELL> A former lover?

Another caesura, then:

MAXWELL> Lilith?
LILITH> I'm here.
MAXWELL> I think you let these men have sex with you not to liberate yourself but to hurt someone else.
LILITH> You don't understand anything.
MAXWELL> Be honest. Only truth can free you.
LILITH> You think you'rc pretty damned smart, don't you?
MAXWELL> I see what is. I sense pain.
LILITH> Yes, he was there.
MAXWELL> A former lover?
LILITH> Yes.
MAXWELL> He'd thrown you away for someone else?
LILITH> Yes.
MAXWELL> Was this someone else at the party too?
LILITH> No.
MAXWELL> Did this young man learn what you were doing upstairs? That you were servicing his friends?
LILITH> Yes.
MAXWELL> Did he come upstairs?

The longest silence yet kicks up my pulse rate. But finally "Lilith" responds.

LILITH> Yes. Someone pushed him into the room. They were yelling at him. Telling him to take a turn.

MAXWELL> Did he?

LILITH> No.

MAXWELL> What did he do?

LILITH> He started crying.

MAXWELL> Really.

LILITH> Yes.

MAXWELL> And?

LILITH> I told him if he wanted me, he'd have to wait in line.

MAXWELL> Someone was fucking you while you said this?

LILITH> Yes.

MAXWELL> What happened then?

LILITH> He tried to stop it.

MAXWELL> Did it stop?

LILITH> No. They beat him up and threw him out.

MAXWELL> How did you feel after that? After he left?

LILITH> I wanted it to stop then. I wanted to go after him.

MAXWELL> To explain? To tell him how badly he'd hurt you?

LILITH> Yes. And how I'd wanted to hurt him back, so he'd understand what he'd done to me.

MAXWELL> Did it stop?

LILITH> No.

MAXWELL> Why not?

LILITH> I was trapped.

MAXWELL> By your own perversity.

LILITH> I guess. I don't like to think about that part of it.

MAXWELL> The door to the room was open, wasn't it?

LILITH> Yes.

MAXWELL> People were watching.

LILITH> Yes.

MAXWELL> How many, Lilith?

LILITH> I don't know.

MAXWELL> How many had you?

LILITH> I don't KNOW! Some got in line two or three times.

MAXWELL> And what was it like?

LILITH> Horrible.

MAXWELL> What was it _like_, Lilith?

LILITH> Like drowning. Like they were holding my head under water. I couldn't . . . fight. They were too strong.

MAXWELL> Did you call out for help?

LILITH> Yes.

MAXWELL> To whom? Your mother?

LILITH> No. If my mother had seen me that way I would have killed myself.

MAXWELL> Your father?

LILITH> My father was dead. There was no one.

MAXWELL> The police?

LILITH> I didn't report it.

MAXWELL> You couldn't, could you? You'd agreed to have sex with more than one man. At what point did it become rape?

LILITH> I knew that's how a cop would see it. How men would see it.

MAXWELL> Women too, Lilith. Women are far more cruel judges of female character than men, I assure you.

LILITH> You don't have to tell me that. But I meant what I said before about how it changed me. At some point during the thing, I just rose above it all. Like I died and rose ten feet above the bed and hovered there, and saw myself being humped by these brainless bastards.

MAXWELL> How did you feel about them?

LILITH> I didn't feel anything. I saw them like a pack of wolves. Biological jello in the evolutionary chain. Consciously, they were just animals trying to show off to each other. Unconsciously they were trying to spread their genes. I just thank God I didn't get pregnant from it. I might have killed myself.

MAXWELL> You talk a lot about killing yourself.

LILITH> I used to think about it a lot. Before that night, anyway. Like after a date when I had let a guy screw me, and then he wouldn't call. That kind of purgatory feeling when all the other girls are out with their boyfriends, and you know they're holding out for that letter jacket or that pin or that wedding ring, "Oh no, Jimmy, not there, not yet, just on the outside of my panties. I'm so sorry, sweetie. I can help you though, I'll just use my hand, okay?"

MAXWELL> It sounds like you've been there yourself.

LILITH> Guys have told me that stuff.

MAXWELL> And you never held out for anything?

LILITH> Not back then. I dropped my panties for any good-looking guy with a hard-on.

MAXWELL> And now?

LILITH> I still don't "hold out." Because someone who holds out is on the defensive. I'm not on the defensive anymore.

MAXWELL> No?

LILITH> No. I fight for what I want, and I get it.

I'll bet I make more money than any of those idiot jocks who raped me.

MAXWELL> I wouldn't be surprised, Lilith. There's just one thing I want to know.

LILITH> My address, right? Or what color is my pubic hair? Christ, you're all alike.

MAXWELL> Not at all. I would like to know what you're doing on EROS.

I am praying Lenz will reply quickly, but the next voice that speaks is not his.

MAXWELL> It doesn't seem to me that someone who has experienced what you say you have, and grown spiritually from it, would be spending time on a sexual online service. N'est-ce pas?

LILITH> I'm not a sexual being anymore? Is that your point? Maybe you'll figure it out eventually. Maybe you'll see me again here. Maybe you won't.

MAXWELL> I'm sure I will.

LILITH> I have a question for you, Max.

MAXWELL> Yes?

LILITH> How long is your cock?

MAXWELL> I shall not dignify that.

LILITH> I mean it. I like them thick at the bottom. Think you can follow fifteen guys in one night?

MAXWELL> Not to my taste, thank you. I'm a fastidious man.

LILITH> You're a liar. I'll bet you're playing with yourself right now.

MAXWELL> You're a hostile person, Lilith. Where did all that rage begin?

LILITH> You'll never know.

MAXWELL> Someday I shall. Tell me, did you climax at any time during this forced bacchanal?

LILITH> I've never had a climax with a man in my life.

MAXWELL> What about masturbation?

LILITH> When I was very young. Not later.

MAXWELL> But you experienced some heightened state on that night.

LILITH> That night? I told you. It was . . . an elevated awareness. Like the more animalistic the situation got, the less individual I was, the less guilt I had, the less I had to worry about anything. Beyond some point, I knew nothing was my fault. And the men seemed almost in some kind of trance state. Like a frenzy. Something about their madness—it was a sexual madness, I think—passed into me somehow, like I was just a vessel for their anger and their fear.

MAXWELL> Why do you say fear?

LILITH> That's what I felt, I guess. That underneath all their thrusting and heaving was some kind of awful terror, something they were running away from, something . . . worse than anything in the world.

MAXWELL> Death?

LILITH> Worse than that. And the harder they tried to come, the closer that thing was getting to them. It was insane, really. I'm not sure I could live through it again.

MAXWELL> What do you mean?

LILITH> I think my heart might stop. Or just explode. I would probably kill one of them or die myself.

MAXWELL> That was the next natural step wasn't it, Lilith? Death? From this sexual frenzy to death?

LILITH> I suppose it was. Violence was all over that room.

MAXWELL> Did you ever feel, while it was going on, that the young men might kill you?

LILITH> I don't know. I was scared. Scared enough to help them finish. I mean, I didn't just lie there. I figured the faster I moved, the faster they'd finish and the safer I'd be.

MAXWELL> You were frightened that they'd hurt you?

LILITH> They _were_ hurting me. You asked if I was scared they'd kill me.

MAXWELL> And?

LILITH> No. They weren't . . . at that level, you know? They were like, these suburban white guys. There were moments when they'd all . . . like realize what they were doing, that it was a crime or whatever. I think it was only the fact that they were all together that gave them the guts to keep going. Individually, they'd never really crossed the line.

MAXWELL> What line?

LILITH> You know. I've dated guys who've really been to the edge. Guys who could have killed every kid in that room and never given it another thought.

MAXWELL> You exaggerate, Lilith.

LILITH> No. There are men like that. I like men like that.

MAXWELL> Men who have killed?

LILITH> Not necessarily. But men who *could* kill, and damned quickly, if they had to.

MAXWELL> All men can kill, Lilith, if pushed far enough.

LILITH> I disagree. Physically, yes. But spiritually? No. Just as every man with a penis could technically have raped me that night, but mentally and spiritually some could not have. People are different.

MAXWELL> You are an interesting person.

LILITH> What would you have done if you'd walked into that room that night?

MAXWELL> I would have stopped it.

LILITH> You couldn't have. My old boyfriend was there and he couldn't. They beat him to a pulp.

MAXWELL> I am not your old boyfriend.

LILITH> How would you have stopped it?

MAXWELL> By deciding to. I am like John Galt. I can stop the motor of the world if I so choose.

LILITH> Who is John Galt?

Lenz must be reveling in the delicious irony of typing those words, that question, as though he had never heard of that literary character.

MAXWELL> A fictional hero in a magnificent but ultimately silly novel by Ayn Rand. The allusion seemed appropriate ten seconds ago.

LILITH> What are you really like, Maxwell? I want to know more about you. I'm curious.

MAXWELL> Curiosity kills cats.

"Here we go," I say softly. "Here it comes."

LILITH> Are you threatening me?

MAXWELL> Do you respond to threats?

LILITH> Not well. Why shouldn't I be curious? You've been interrogating me as you please.

MAXWELL> What do you wish to know?

LILITH> How old are you?

MAXWELL> Forty-seven.

"Holy shit." I glance right to make sure the printer is still recording every word. Is Brahma telling the truth? Turning toward the bed, I call, "Miles, wake up!" Then I turn up the voices.

LILITH> That's a good age.
MAXWELL> How so?
LILITH> Old enough to know what you're doing, not too old to do it.
MAXWELL> To what are you referring?
LILITH> Whatever you like in life. Do you like your work?
MAXWELL> I focus more on my avocation.
LILITH> You have your own company or something?
MAXWELL> I own several companies, but they're merely paperwork. What most people call careers, I call glorified secretarial work.
LILITH> Do I sense an attitude?
MAXWELL> I do not suffer fools gladly.
LILITH> So—what's your real work?
MAXWELL> I'm in the medical field.

"Score one for Drewe," Miles says from behind me.

"You were right," I admit. "Lenz seems to be pulling it off. He's damned good at it."

"I thought he might be."

LILITH> Are you a doctor?
MAXWELL> Please do not pry too much. We don't know each other well enough.
LILITH> How much closer can we get? I've already told you my darkest secret.
MAXWELL> Really? There must be more in your past than a postadolescent gang rape, however tragic. A woman who will ask "Who's next?" to

drunken fraternity boys has more in her closet than that.

LILITH> I don't care for your attitude.

MAXWELL> You can always log off.

"Do it," I say sharply, though Lenz is a thousand miles away.

"Log off, asshole!" Miles spits at the monitor.

But Lenz is greedy.

LILITH> Why do you want to bully me like that?

MAXWELL> I thought you didn't put up with bullying anymore.

LILITH> I'm not made of stone.

"Inconsistent," says Miles. "He's losing it. Goddamn it, log off!"

LILITH> I haven't let a man into my life for some time. But I had a new feeling tonight.

MAXWELL> I must go now. Perhaps we'll speak again.

LILITH> How will I find you?

"Stop pushing!" I yell.

MAXWELL> I'll find you. _Auf Wiedersehen_.

"He knows," says Miles, staring at the letters still glowing on the screen. "Lenz spooked him and he split."

"Maybe not. A lot of exchanges get like that at the end. One person is always needier than the other."

"Maxwell," Miles murmurs. "Brahma's playing games all over the place, man."

"What do you mean?"

"The name. What's the first 'Maxwell' that pops into your head?"

"Maxwell Smart?"

He shakes his head. "Think Beatles. *Abbey Road.*"

"*Abbey Road* . . . 'Maxwell's Silver Hammer'!"

Miles begins to sing: "Joan was quizzical, studied pataphysical science in the home. Late nights all alone with her test tubes, oh-ohoh-oh. . . ."

I follow with, "Maxwell Edison, majoring in medicine, calls her on the phone—"

"Whoa," he cuts in. "Maxwell was a doctor."

"And the chorus. Jesus."

Together we chant the now chilling words: "Bang-bang Maxwell's silver hammer came down upon her head. Bang-bang Maxwell's silver hammer made sure that she was dead."

We stare at each other in numb silence.

"That's a big leap," I tell him.

"Except that his other aliases were Shiva, Kali, Levon. Shiva is the Destroyer. Kali is a goddess of blood and death."

"Levon wasn't a killer."

"He wasn't exactly Santa Claus either: 'He was born a pauper to a pawn on a Christmas Day when the *New York Times* said "God is dead" and the war's begun. . . .' "

"This is creepy, Miles."

He scans the printouts again. "Lenz had the son of a bitch and he blew it."

"I thought he'd try to mimic Karin Wheat's personality more. Get into immortality and the occult and all that."

Miles shakes his head. "Lenz is in a hurry. He's trying to cover all the bases at once. He's giving Brahma a woman who's both strong and weak. But if we go with Drewe's scenario, Lenz's approach is useless. It's designed to provoke by being overtly sexual, whereas Brahma's criteria may be medical."

"What choice does Lenz have? He can't log on and say, 'Forty-seven-year-old female seeks succulent twenty-three-year-old pineal gland. Please send photo.' "

Miles's laugh is terminated by the ring of the phone. The impulse to flight flashes in his eyes.

"We'll screen it," I tell him.

After two rings the machine answers, my outgoing message plays, and a beep prompts the caller.

"Cole, pick up the phone," says a deep voice.

"Lenz," says Miles. He crosses the room, picks up the cordless, trots back to me, and hands me the phone.

"I'm here."

"Did you see?" the psychiatrist asks, his voice brimming with excitement.

"I saw it. Not bad, Doctor."

"I had him going, didn't I?"

Has Lenz called merely to rehash his triumph? Like a high school kid talking about his football game? Maybe he thinks I'm the only person who truly understands the parameters of his strange quest.

"You saw his age?" he asks. "Forty-seven?"

"Yes."

"And admitting that he's in the medical field! Cole, it's working."

Miles leans over the answering machine.

"What about the bit at the end?" Lenz asks, suddenly penitent. "Did I go too far?"

"Hard to say."

"I know I pushed him, but I'm fighting time here."

Miles punches me in the side.

"I guess Baxter's pressing you to nail him before he kills again, huh?"

"I'm speaking of the phone traces."

Miles punches me again; this time I punch back. "You mean they're close to tracing him?"

"No. They're no longer trying to trace him."

"What?"

"Before we put the decoy plan into action, we realized we were facing an either-or situation. If they tried to trace the UNSUB every time we conversed online, it would be obvious I was helping the FBI. You see?"

"Oh, I see. But I can't believe Baxter stopped the traces."

"It's not indefinite. He's given me seven days."

"Then they start the traces again?"

"Now you see why I'm having to push harder than I'd like."

"Is there anything else you needed?"

"Yes," Lenz says in a strange voice. "I'm wondering why you haven't asked me about Turner."

I look at Miles. "I figure you'd be crowing about it already if you'd caught him."

"If you know where he is, Cole, do yourself and your wife a favor. Turner wouldn't hang his ass out to protect yours."

I sense the heat of Miles's rage from a foot away. "Yeah, well, opinions are like assholes."

"Everybody's got one," Lenz finishes. "Only a lot of people pay a lot of money for mine."

"There's a sucker born every minute."

"Good night, Cole."

I carry the cordless back across the room and set it in its cradle. "Nice guy, huh?"

"He's better than some," says Miles. He points at the red *21* in the LED window of my answering machine. "Have you listened to all those messages?"

"I didn't want them banging around in my head."

He raises his eyebrows and, getting no objection from me, hits the REWIND button. A minute later the tape begins playing back the messages. Most are from various police departments. A couple are from old friends, warning me that they've been questioned about me by police. One is a sales pitch from a credit card company. And six are from Detective Michael Mayeux of the New Orleans Police Department. Miles and I listen to his final message in rapt silence.

"Mr. Cole, I don't know where you are, but you'd better start checking your messages. You may not believe this, but I'm worried about you. If the FBI has pressured you into some kind of cooperation, you better be damn careful. This case got weird fast. There's a lot of bad feeling in all the P.D.s involved. These days the Bureau's pretty good about sharing information, but right now they're acting like they did back in the seventies. Some people are saying they've already screwed up the investigation. That isn't your problem, I know. All I'm saying is things could reach a point where the departments involved just get fed up and decide to do what they've been wanting to do all along, which is blow the whistle, shut down EROS, and arrest you and Turner. You gotta admit I treated you okay when you came to us. If you need help—and, brother, you do—I'm your man. Now give me a call."

Miles has wandered away from me. "What do you think about that?" I ask.

"Never happen," he says distantly. "Going public and shutting down EROS, I mean. City cops aren't going to risk pissing off the feds to that degree."

"Could we use Mayeux to our advantage?"

"Things haven't progressed that far yet. Just ignore him."

"I'm glad he's not a Mississippi cop. He'd be sitting on my doorstep right now."

Miles plunks himself down on the edge of my bed and sighs.

"You said they found Karin Wheat's head near the Bonnet Carre causeway," I remind him. "Headed toward La Place. That means he passed the New Orleans airport. But from the distances between the previous murder cities, I always assumed Brahma was flying."

"He could have flown out of Baton Rouge," Miles points out. "It's only an hour away, and you go through La Place to get there. Or he could have driven to La Place just to toss out the head, then turned around and driven back to the airport. The FBI doesn't know how he's getting around. Common sense says flying, but there's enough elapsed time between the murders for him to have ridden a goddamn Trailways bus."

"Except the one-night interval between Karin's death and Rosalind May's abduction."

He nods. "They're searching airline records, trying to match passenger manifests for the murder cities on given dates, but all matches so far have been legitimate."

"He could have taken a private plane," I suggest, "like you did to get here."

"They're checking that." He looks up and searches my face. "You got something you want to say?"

"Take it easy. I'm just thinking out loud."

He runs both hands over his freshly skinned scalp and focuses somewhere beyond me. "You been thinking about what we talked about? The Trojan Horse?"

"Some."

"And?"

"I'm up for it."

A broad smile lights his face. "All *right*. Now we're cooking with gas."

Miles's occasional regressions to Southern idiom surprise me, but I guess every refugee carries cultural baggage.

"Have you decided which way you want to go?" he

asks. "I mean, a real EROS client or totally from scratch?"

"Not a real client," I tell him. "I don't want to put anybody at risk like that. But I don't want to start totally from scratch, either."

His eyes narrow. "I don't get you."

I move closer to the bed and look down at him. "I'm going to explain this to you once. After that you don't ask me about it."

"Sure. You've got a name in mind?"

"Yes."

"What is it?"

"Erin."

He blinks.

"No questions?"

"I don't get it. You're picking that name out of the blue, or you're talking about our Erin?"

"My wife's sister."

He lets out a low whistle.

"If this is going to work, Miles, it's got to be authentic. That over-the-top stuff Lenz is doing won't fool Brahma long. I mean, I think that gang rape stuff really happened to somebody, but not to *Lenz*. You know? Probably one of his patients. Brahma feeds on the pathos of real human beings. And Erin's the one. I know things about her . . . things that could help me play her very well."

"Whatever you want," Miles says quietly. "I trust your instincts."

"Lenz thinks Brahma is targeting older women now. That's why he made 'Lilith' forty-eight. But I can't play a forty-eight-year-old woman convincingly. We'll just have to hope he's still interested in donors as well as recipients."

He opens his hands. "Whatever you say. But I've got

to ask. Are you saying you want 'Erin' as your online alias, or the real name behind the alias?"

"Online alias. You can make her legal name anything you want."

Miles digests this slowly. "I'm not even going to ask where this is coming from. You're playing the role, you pick the costume. But aren't you worried that using Erin might somehow lead Brahma to her?"

"No. Because it won't really be Erin. It's going to be a blend of Erin's personality and mine. A hybrid. And the fact that the alias is 'Erin' should make Brahma think her real name is anything *but* Erin."

"You're right," he says, looking impressed for once.

"It's your job to create a fake identity that's untraceable. And the address worries me. I know you can do a lot by hacking, but you can't change where we are. What if Brahma can actually trace the phone connections?"

"I don't think he can. Not easily, anyway. But even if he tries, I'll have it covered."

"How?"

"I'm going to hack into AT&T's Jackson switching station, change around some number and address data. Then I'll make that data match the 'Erin' stuff I put into the DMV computer and everywhere else."

"I thought telephone switching stations had gotten practically impenetrable."

"Some have. But I'll bet Mississippi's had the fewest attempted penetrations of any state in the U.S." He smiles. "And they definitely aren't ready for me, Grasshopper."

"I'm asking for one promise, Miles."

"What?"

"Drewe knows nothing about what we're trying to do. Nothing. I don't care what we tell her, but it's not going to be this."

He holds up his hands. "You think I'm nuts?"

"This is illegal and we both know it."

"Yeah. But we've got to do it." Wicked blue light flashes in his eyes. "And it's going to be the motherfucking rush of all time. *Wow.*"

A surge of adrenaline pushes me over to the left front window. I have to fight the urge to peek around the blinds to see whether there are any deputies standing in the dark yard.

"Can I ask you one thing?" Miles says. "One thing, then I shut up for good."

"One thing," I say to the window blind.

"This Erin thing. We're talking about something in the past, right? You and her."

"Yes."

"I thought so."

I turn from the window to ask how far back in time his suspicions began, but he is already hunched over the keyboard at my desk. By tomorrow morning a digital human being that backs up my "Erin" will exist in the bureaucratic agar that forms the basis of legal existence in America. Miles's groundwork will accomplish Brahma's initial suspension of disbelief. But far more important than a Social Security number or address will be the woman I carry in my mind and heart. A carnal phantom called Erin still wanders unbidden through my dreams, and though I am not sure how or why, I know that through me, she can haunt the ruthless killer we have christened Brahma to his grave.

Chapter 28

My chief fascination in the days following Miles's appearance was listening to the baroque mating ritual between "Maxwell" and "Lilith." From the worldly wise but bitter woman who endured a college gang bang, Lenz quickly expanded his creation into a multidimensional character worthy of a Christmas appearance on *Oprah*. Sometimes "Lilith" taunted "Maxwell," other times she passively answered whatever questions he put to her, however personal. I decided Lenz must be drawing his emotional raw material from actual case histories; much of it had the outrageous ring of truth that only reality can provide, incidents that would get any decent fiction writer drummed out of his profession. Through it all, "Maxwell" probed "Lilith's" past with lapidary precision, a twist here, a light tap there, gradually forming a picture of the "woman" who lay behind the alias.

Miles spent most of the first day building the digital skeleton that would support my fictional "Erin." We chose the "legal" name Cynthia Griffin and decided to place her address in Vicksburg, which lies forty miles southwest of Rain. We discussed the chance that a Mississippi address might give Brahma's intuition a tickle, but word of mouth among my old friends had brought the number of Mississippi EROS clients to more than thirty. Miles thought that was more than enough to make one new addition quite natural.

Once "Cynthia's" personal information had been hacked into the proper government computers—and an EROS account opened in her name—Miles began coding away at his Trojan Horse program, consuming massive amounts of Mountain Dew and granola bars ferried by Drewe from the Yazoo City K-Mart. He rarely sat in front of his computer to do his coding. After Drewe left for work each morning, he would commandeer an easy chair in the darkened den and, fortified by junk food, sit glassy-eyed through three or four old movies on the satellite channels. His favorites seemed to be disaster movies from the nineteen-seventies, à la *Airport* and *The Towering Inferno*, melodramatic extravaganzas featuring faded Hollywood legends. Now and then he would jump up and hurry into my office, sit down before his laptop, and punch in a few keystrokes, cocking his head at odd angles and murmuring to himself.

Drewe worked every day, but she called frequently to see how the check on the female blind-draft account holders was going. About midnight on the second night, Jan Krislov e-mailed us, saying that the fifty-two blind-draft women showing low account activity in the past months had all been verified as alive and well. So had more than three hundred of the remaining blind-draft women. This punched a gaping hole in Drewe's theory of another missing woman, and by extension her pineal transplant theory. Or so we thought.

When we told Drewe about Jan's message, she was standing at my office door, about to leave for work. She looked blank for about thirty seconds; then her eyes flickered with knowledge.

"I was so *stupid*," she said. "The missing woman couldn't be an EROS client. The EROS population isn't large enough to allow selection of tissue-matched donors. You see? The killer could do all the surgical practice he wanted on EROS women, but when it came time to match a donor to a recipient, he had to search a much larger population."

"Why?" asked Miles.

"Probability. Donor networks require pools of thousands—*tens* of thousands—of potential donors, so that exact matches can be found for those in need of organs or tissue. After the killer kidnapped Rosalind May—his intended recipient—he had to tissue-type her, then find a donor of the right age who was a match. The twenty-five hundred women on EROS aren't nearly a large enough group to get a match. Actually, he would need a tissue donor registry. Like for bone marrow. Transplant networks list people who *need* organs, not people who want to donate them. And driver's license computers might list organ donors, but not any of the medical information the killer needs."

"So where would he find a group like that?" Miles asked.

Drewe shrugged. "A legitimate tissue donor network. Or directed donors listed with blood banks. Those are the only kinds of databases that would have the medical information he'd need."

While Miles pondered this, Drewe stared at me as if waiting for me to say something. When I didn't, she looked at Miles and said, "We've got to tell the FBI to start checking tissue donor registries."

He looked at me, clearly uncomfortable with the idea of contacting the FBI.

"Can we do it anonymously?" I asked her.

She sighed deeply, then pulled her keys from her pocket and walked away. She slammed the front door on her way out.

At my request, Miles agreed to compose a summary of Drewe's theory and sneak it into the Quantico computer. I suggested using an anonymous remailing service to send the message, but Miles thought the FBI could get at us through the operator if they tried hard enough.

Later that day, a running argument developed between us as to whether Brahma was actually being taken in by Lenz, or whether he was making a fool of him. I'd begun to notice what I thought was dry humor in "Maxwell's" conversations with "Lilith." Most of it was double entendre so subtle as to be arguable, yet I believed it significant. Ever since Miles pointed out the "Maxwell's Silver Hammer" and "Levon" connections, I'd felt Brahma was toying with us. Not just Lenz, but everyone who had committed the hubris of stepping up to the plate against him.

Miles, on the other hand, thought Lenz was doing very well, considering the time pressure he was under, and pointed out that I had yet to draw Brahma into a single online conversation. To speed up this process, he carried his laptop to the easy chair in the front room and, during an encore showing of *The Thomas Crown Affair* on A&E, hammered out a search program based on Brahma's most common figures of speech. He claimed it would locate Brahma online regardless of the alias he was using, and it did. However, it could not draw him into conversation with me.

The police surveillance of our house continued, and by the third day cabin fever had set in. Miles insisted that my phones were tapped. And it wasn't enough that he remain indoors. He demanded that I check one window on each side of the house every half hour and also that I leave the house occasionally to create the appearance of normalcy. I understood the necessity, but it became a major pain to constantly jump up from my computer while he sat watching *The Poseidon Adventure* like some Arabian potentate.

Yet it was tougher on him than on me. He'd promised

Drewe that he would clear out at the first sign of trouble, and I knew he meant it. Like a fireman or a fighter pilot, he had to stay pumped enough to jump up from a dead sleep and race into the kitchen pantry for the trapdoor that led to the bomb shelter.

So it was almost a divine deliverance when, at eleven p.m. on the third night, the long-awaited invitation from Brahma arrived. I'd been in the "lobby" of one of EROS's conference areas, politely fending off not-so-polite advances from a man calling himself "Billy Pilgrim," when a small window opened on my screen. The words inside it read:

MAXWELL> Hello, Erin. I notice that your conversations have a particular type of error pattern. Are you using a voice-recognition unit?

My heartbeat racing, I tried to think clearly. I'd debated whether or not to use the voice-recognition unit. Ultimately, I decided that being able to speak my thoughts into the computer rather than type them was worth arousing whatever suspicion Miles's voice-rec program might cause in Brahma. Speaking as clearly as I could, I said, "Yes. How did you know?"

On the screen appeared:

ERIN> Yes. How did you know?

There was a brief silence. Then three new lines of text appeared, and the voice I'd selected for Brahma said:

MAXWELL> I'm quite familiar with such systems. You're the first person I've seen using one on EROS. Where did you come by it? Quality systems are prohibitively expensive.

Miles had given me good ammunition for this question.

ERIN> My husband is a physician. He's using a new system that was designed for medical dictation. A friend of his works for the company that designed it. He put a version on our computer so we could try it out. I like it. I like having my hands free.

MAXWELL> Yes. What company does this friend work for?

ERIN> Sorry. It's proprietary technology, still in the testing stage. He'd go ballistic if I talked about it. Mostly because of the company's stock price.

MAXWELL> I see. Would you like to join me in the Blue Room?

My heart thudded against my breastbone. After saying yes, I sent a rude kiss-off to "Billy Pilgrim," then clicked my way into digital privacy with a man who had killed at least eight people, and probably more.

Brahma was waiting when I arrived.

MAXWELL> I've been watching you. You spurn attention as though it burns you. What are you looking for?

I paused to compose myself. During the long days of waiting, I'd given much thought to how I would approach Brahma. In the end, I knew, I would have to fly purely on instinct. But as with any new relationship, my opening was critical.

ERIN> Something that doesn't exist.

MAXWELL> What could that be?

ERIN> A man with the soul of a woman.

MAXWELL> There are many of those.

ERIN> A man who has the soul of a woman but remains a man.

MAXWELL> Ah. This is rarer. Why do you seek this?

ERIN> I'm unfulfilled, obviously.

MAXWELL> Man desires all things, thus he is eternally unfulfilled.

ERIN> But woman can be fulfilled.

MAXWELL> I speak of Man in the collective sense.

ERIN> There is no collective sense that includes both man and woman. They are poles of existence.

MAXWELL> You speak wisely. You have much experience?

ERIN> Is that a nice way of asking how old I am?

MAXWELL> Take it as you will.

ERIN> I just passed my thirtieth birthday.

MAXWELL> You are married?

ERIN> Yes.

MAXWELL> Your only marriage?

ERIN> Yes.

MAXWELL> You have children?

ERIN> A son.

MAXWELL> There are problems?

ERIN> Not the usual sort.

MAXWELL> You are sexually content?

ERIN> No. I've lost my passion for the physical.

MAXWELL> But you once enjoyed it?

ERIN> I lived by it.

The speakers fell silent. Then Maxwell resumed his questioning.

MAXWELL> Why do you seek a man with the soul of a woman?

ERIN> Men don't understand me.

MAXWELL> A common female complaint.

ERIN> My problem is different from most. Men can't see me as I am.

MAXWELL> How so?

ERIN> I have the curse for which no one feels sympathy.

MAXWELL> You are rich.

ERIN> I'm not speaking of that. I was speaking of beauty.

MAXWELL> You are beautiful?

ERIN> Yes.

MAXWELL> Many say that here, in this faceless environment. They rub balm into their insecurities by playing at characters they are not.

ERIN> My fantasies have nothing to do with appearance.

MAXWELL> Then perhaps you are what you say you are.

ERIN> You don't believe me. You resist the idea that a physically beautiful woman has the intelligence to step outside herself long enough to analyze herself.

MAXWELL> You assume too much. I can accept that. But it seems to me you share the problem of the wealthy woman—no one ever looks past her money.

ERIN> It's not the same at all.

MAXWELL> Why not?

ERIN> Because physically beautiful people can become rich, but most rich people can never become beautiful. Not with all the plastic surgery in the world.

MAXWELL> I appreciate that distinction. I understand it too well.

ERIN> Are you rich and unattractive?

MAXWELL> You don't use much tact, do you?

ERIN> I don't have time for games.

MAXWELL> Nor do I. I am rich in material things, but I'm not at all unattractive.

ERIN> Is that your opinion?

MAXWELL> One long confirmed by others. But I understand your problem better than you might think.

ERIN> How so?

MAXWELL> I was born a genius.

ERIN> Really.

MAXWELL> Yes.

ERIN> Can you prove it?

MAXWELL> Can you prove you are beautiful?

ERIN> I see what you mean.

MAXWELL> Actually, I could prove my genius in this environment much easier than you could prove your beauty. But what would be the point? Anything I wrote at that level, you would not understand.

ERIN> All right, all right, I believe you.

MAXWELL> Would you mind telling me whether you are fair-skinned or dark?

ERIN> I guess not. In winter I'm fair. In summer I'm brown.

MAXWELL> Your ancestry?

ERIN> My _ancestry_? French and English. Why?

MAXWELL> Mixed on both sides?

ERIN> Father Scots-English blood, mother Cajun French.

MAXWELL> Ah. An interesting roux.

ERIN> Interesting home life, anyway.

MAXWELL> What appeals to you about the female soul, as you called it?

ERIN> Women understand that the past can be left behind. Men don't. Men are haunted by the past.

MAXWELL> Are you speaking of one's own past or the past of a mate?

ERIN> Either.

MAXWELL> Your husband does not allow you to forget your past?

ERIN> Correct.

MAXWELL> You had many adventures?

ERIN> Many lovers.

MAXWELL> From a young age?

ERIN> Fourteen.

MAXWELL> The first was a man or a woman?

ERIN> A man. I've never felt drawn to women's bodies, regrettably.

MAXWELL> You enjoyed these many lovers? Or merely allowed them to take pleasure from you?

ERIN> I learned to take my own pleasure early. And to give it. I felt no inhibition. I shocked men, made them afraid. Men fantasize about wanton women, but when they meet one, they're paralyzed by fear.

MAXWELL> Can you elaborate?

ERIN> Men like easy women so long as they can mentally classify them as sluts or whores. But a highly sexual woman who is beautiful, who has her pick of males, doesn't fit that puritanical equation. And if she has intelligence as well, she is feared, and thus hated.

MAXWELL> Your point of view intrigues me.

ERIN> The bitter fruit of experience.

MAXWELL> You never found a man who gave you the understanding you needed?

ERIN> I thought I had, once. But I was wrong.

MAXWELL> Who was he?

ERIN> I don't have time to tell that story now. In fact, it's later than I thought. I need to log off. I enjoyed our conversation. Good-bye.

MAXWELL> Please wait. Would you answer one question before you go?

ERIN> If it's quick.

MAXWELL> You said you descended from French and English blood. Also that you tan in the summer. From this I deduce that you are more dark than fair. Does the English trait show up elsewhere in your family? Very fair skin, I mean?

Brahma's interest in skin was starting to sound pathological. I was about to answer based on Erin's dark complexion when something stopped me. All of Brahma's victims but one—the Indian woman—were Caucasian.

ERIN> What an odd question. As a matter of fact, I'm not more dark than fair. I have a sister with a peaches and cream complexion, and I'm only a shade darker. It's just that I tan in the summer rather than burn. It's a nice bonus.

MAXWELL> Thank you.

ERIN> Good-bye.

MAXWELL> Au revoir.

"You played that just right," Miles said from behind me. The synthesized voices had drawn him from his throne in the den. "Make an impression, then vanish like the Cheshire cat. You should give Lenz lessons."

"Time will tell."

"Where did you get that 'female soul' stuff?"

"I don't know. I've been trying to put myself inside

Erin's head. When he asked what I was looking for, that seemed right."

"It was. Perfect."

Miles picked up the printouts and scanned them. "What's this? You're ripping off hair color ads now?" In a terrible French accent he cooed, "Don't hate me because I'm beautiful."

"Think about Erin. One thing overrides everything else. Her beauty. It's the central fact of her life. It shaped her whole character. But to her—inside—it must be nothing, you know? I mean, nothing and yet everything. At the same time. Just like you being smart."

Miles ran a hand over his flattop. "I was right about one thing, anyway."

"What?"

"You can do this. You've got him going."

"One conversation is nothing, and you know it."

"Oh, it's something. He likes you."

"You mean he likes Erin."

He gave me a sidelong glance. "If you say so."

"What does that mean?"

"It means you can think what you want, but Erin Anderson—I mean Graham—couldn't have written that conversation if her life depended on it. I mean, she might *feel* those things, but she could never express them. Just like you said. She couldn't step outside herself and analyze her own feelings."

"You don't know her that well, Miles. She's a lot brighter than anyone ever gave her credit for."

"I know her better than you think."

"What does that mean?"

He put down the printouts and looked away. "Nothing. I'm talking out of my ass."

I grabbed his sleeve. "Don't try to crawfish on that line. You said you saw her in New York. Is this something to do with that?"

He studied the floor for several moments. Then he looked up, his blue eyes flat with defiance. "Look, I fucked her, okay?"

My train of thought momentarily derailed. I knew Erin had been promiscuous, but this was a shock. "When was this? In New York?"

"Yeah. Let go of my arm."

He tried to pull away, but I squeezed tighter, at the same time recalling what Lenz said about Miles battering some guy outside a gay bar with martial arts. But the rigidity went out of him, and he broke eye contact again.

"It was just one time, okay? Erin showed up at this party I was at in the Village. She was with this singer, a real asshole. She was high, but he was almost comatose. She said hello to me, then walked away. About an hour later she came back and asked if I could give her a ride. She didn't want to go back to their hotel. We ended up at my place."

"And?"

"And *what*, man? You want gory details?"

"Yes."

He took a deep breath, then blew it out in one hard rush. "We talked for a long time. She told me she'd always thought I was gay."

I was sorry I'd asked the question, but too late. Miles was reliving the moment.

"If anyone else from home had suggested that, I'd have flipped out, brained them. But not her. She was so frank about it. She wasn't judgmental at all, just interested. We talked about it for a while, and then . . . she made love to me. It was unbelievable. Harper, she was everything I'd ever longed for in a woman and had never found."

"Miles—"

"No, let me finish. I think . . . she sensed the pain I was in at that time, and she was trying to heal me. Isn't that funny? Because she was twice as screwed up as I was. Her whole life has been a tragedy, if you ask me. But that was her nature, I could tell. She was whatever people needed. As if through her, they could move to some better place. You know what I mean?"

"Yes."

"God knows what kind of degrading crap she put up with from assholes like that singer."

"And she just left you after that?"

"The next morning she woke up looking like an angel that had crash-landed in my apartment by mistake. She called a cab, kissed me on the forehead, and disappeared from my life forever."

I shook my head in wonder.

"That's why I knew that female soul stuff was right on. That's her, man. That's what she needs."

"She told you that?"

"Not in those words. Like I said, she was . . . I don't know, emotionally farsighted, maybe. She could see other people's problems clearly but couldn't focus on her own."

"That's her, all right."

He smiled with compassion. "I won't ask where you got your insights."

"It was different with us, but not too different. It's like a dream sequence in the middle of my life."

"And it never goes away."

"Not completely, no."

"That's why you picked her, isn't it?"

"What do you mean?"

"Because she's haunting. Tragic. She has this unresolvable tension. She pulls men like a force of gravity."

After this strange moment of communion, Miles picked up the transcripts and shuffled through them. "Printer's low on toner," he said, holding up a sheet with letters so faint I could barely read them. "Got another cartridge?"

"No."

"We can take the cartridge from the printer on your Gateway. Good thing they're both LaserJets."

"We don't have to," I told him, glad to be able to hide my awkwardness in a mechanical task. I walked to a shelf and took down a tall white plastic bottle.

"What's that?" he asked. "Toner?"

"Yep."

"You refill your own cartridges?"

"Out here in the boonies, it's the only way to fly."

"Isn't it a pain?"

I shook my head. With Miles staring in rapt attention, I removed and partially disassembled the wedge-shaped toner cartridge from the Hewlett-Packard printer with a tool called a screw starter. Then, so as not to end up looking like a coal miner after a cave-in, I very carefully removed the plug from the toner reservoir and refilled the empty space with the ultrafine black powder that constitutes the "ink" of a laser printer.

"That's it?" Miles asked.

I replugged the reservoir and replaced the cartridge cover. "Ready to go."

As I reloaded the cartridge into the printer, he pretended to write a note on his palm and said, "A new job for my assistants."

But the fallout from his earlier revelation still hung in the air, like ozone after a lightning strike. I walked over to my minifridge and took out a Tab.

"Why don't you scan for Brahma?" he suggested.

"I doubt he's still on."

"You're the one who broke contact. No reason to think he's closed up shop."

Using Miles's search program, it took less than a minute to locate "Maxwell" in another private room.

There, true to his habits of the past three days, he was conversing with "Lilith." Again the voices confirmed my suspicion: there was a lot more information flowing from Dr. Lenz to Brahma than the other way around.

"Lenz's plan isn't working," I said over my shoulder.

"Why do you say that?"

"Because he's not learning a damn thing about Brahma."

"He's not supposed to, is he? He's just laying out bait, hoping to provoke Brahma to come after him."

"But he *is* trying to find out things. In between his neo-Gothic revelations, anyway. Listen to him. The stuff he spews out makes *Deliverance* look like a Disney film."

Miles shrugged as if to say, "What can I do about it?"

I half listened to "Lilith" for a minute, but my mind was elsewhere. "How's your Trojan Horse coming?"

"It's got tendinitis," Miles said sullenly.

"What?"

"I'll get there."

"You going to tell me how it works?"

"Until you get Brahma heated up, it doesn't really matter, does it?"

I was about to tell him to kiss off when he sighed an apology. "Look, it'll work or it won't, okay? Let's take a break."

I held up my hands for a truce. In the background, Lilith's voice droned on, dredging up dark sexual secrets from "her" past and clumsily—to my ear, at least—pressing "Maxwell" to respond in kind. Brahma tolerated the probes with uncharacteristic docility, but he refused to be drawn out. As the conversation progressed, I could not escape the feeling that Dr. Lenz was greedily reeling in not valuable information but rope.

Just enough to hang himself.

Chapter 29

Last night I dreamed of Erin making love to Miles. My memory is a traitor that way. The images I'd most like to wipe away cling to life with the tenacity of weeds, while those I want to treasure fade like the blush on a rose.

This morning Drewe left before I woke up. I fought to stay asleep while Miles fixed himself an omelette and commandeered the television in the den, but it was no use. He had me checking windows and trolling EROS before I could even get a bowl of cereal.

Brahma logged on as "Maxwell" early, but when "Lilith" started into one of her long monologues, he cut the conversation short and logged off. Miles wandered in and did some coding at his laptop, then drifted back to the TV. After watching CNN for a while, I walked into the backyard to verify that the tomatoes in our garden were as scorched as they'd been last week. They were. Then I walked around front and stared up the highway long enough to make sure Deputy Billy was at his post. He was.

About ten-thirty, I logged back onto EROS as SYSOP. I didn't expect much. Morning traffic is mostly Level One stuff, medical questions or lonely hearts looking for a shoulder to cry on. A quick cruise through Level Two also showed what I expected: soft-core exchanges involving roguish dukes and hard-won ladies (which I knew from long experience were frequently two women taking opposite sides of a romantic fantasy).

Then I clicked into Level Three. The lobbies were mostly empty. Out of curiosity, I peeked into some private rooms. Most of it was gay action—men in some rooms, women in others—plus a few dominance sessions. Then, in a gossip lobby I rarely visited, I found some people discussing the murder of Karin Wheat. They were obviously fans, and speculation about who had killed the author ranged from her jealous and grossly overweight ex-husband to a crazed fan who lost sight of the line between fact and fiction. Meaning to join the conversation, I logged in as "Erin." Ten seconds later a window appeared in the center of my screen. In it was a prompt followed by single line of text, which EROS's voice duly read:

PROMETHEUS> Would you like to join me in the Blue Room?

My skin went cold. I sat paralyzed for a moment. Then I looked at the window on the left of my screen, which listed the code names of everyone in the lobby. Sure enough, "Prometheus" was there. I had got so used to looking at "Maxwell" that this older alias of Brahma's had slipped right by me.

Yanking off the headset, I sealed its mike shut with my thumb and shouted, "Miles! Get your ass in here!" Then I put the headset back on, said "yes" into the mike, and clicked into the Blue Room. Instantaneously, these words appeared:

MAXWELL> I've been waiting for you.

Even as I heard Miles's feet pounding the floor, I answered into the mike and watched my words appear onscreen:

ERIN> I think we're about to be interrupted by someone who calls himself Prometheus.

Miles was standing beside me by then. "Hit the space bar if you want to tell me something," he whispered in my ear. "It mutes the mike."

MAXWELL> I am Prometheus, Erin. I use many names. But Prometheus fits me in many ways.
ERIN> Why use Maxwell if you like Prometheus so much?
MAXWELL> "Maxwell" has its own significance.

I was tempted to ask him about the Beatles reference, but instead I pressed the space bar and said, "Miles, this guy—"

"Say something to him!" Miles snapped, popping me on the shoulder.

I fired an elbow into his leg and held down the space bar. "Listen, goddamn it! I just figured something out."

"What?"

"I logged on first as SYSOP, not Erin, and he didn't see me spying on the lobby he was in. It was only when I switched to Erin that he noticed me."

MAXWELL> Are you there, Erin?

"He wasn't aware you were lurking as SYSOP?"

"Exactly."

"That means he probably doesn't have SYSOP access himself!"

"I know. Now get out of here. I need quiet."

"Remember the Trojan Horse," Miles said, walking backward. "Make him want you." Then he stepped out of the office and closed the door behind him.

Brahma's voice pulled my attention back to the screen.

MAXWELL> Erin?
ERIN> Sorry. The newspaper man came to my door.
MAXWELL> Ah. You follow current events?
ERIN> No, the obituaries.

This was true. Twice during our interlude in Chicago, Erin sat in bed reading the *Tribune* obits aloud and making up outrageous stories that supposedly lay behind the sanitized life summaries of the rich and prominent.

MAXWELL> The obituaries?
ERIN> I'm eccentric.
MAXWELL> You are interested in the death of Karin Wheat?
ERIN> I barely even saw what they were talking about before you invited me here. It does seem interesting, though. Her death sounded so gory.
MAXWELL> I'm sure that was exaggerated. The press makes its money pandering the prurient and the morbid. I was hoping we could continue last night's conversation.
ERIN> I'm tired of the mental sparring on this network. It's all so juvenile.
MAXWELL> What do you want from EROS?
ERIN> I told you, I'm looking for someone.
MAXWELL> The man with the soul of a woman?
ERIN> That's what I called it last night. It's nothing that definite. It's just a yearning I have.
MAXWELL> Do you mean you wish to find this person and then meet him in real life?
ERIN> Why not?
MAXWELL> Most are afraid to transmit real information about themselves over the Net. It may be a wise precaution. The world is full of disturbed individuals.

ERIN> I'm pragmatic about that kind of thing. I figure when my time's up, there's nothing I can do about it anyway. Until then, enjoy.

MAXWELL> You believe in predestination?

ERIN> No. Fate.

MAXWELL> What's the difference?

ERIN> Not sure. Maybe it's one of degree. With predestination, everything's laid out from square one. With fate, those ladies are up there weaving, but you have a certain amount of power to tangle the threads.

MAXWELL> Yes? And death?

ERIN> Well, I mean, you have some power to tangle, but the _length_ of the thread is predetermined from the start.

MAXWELL> How interesting. You know mythology?

ERIN> A nodding acquaintance. You?

MAXWELL> All life is myth, when viewed from the proper perspective.

ERIN> Whatever you say. You're supposed to be the genius.

MAXWELL> Please forget that. A little fillip of ego. In our last conversation you spoke of having no inhibitions. As though you have no shame.

ERIN> I have shame.

MAXWELL> Of what act in your life are you most ashamed?

Déjà vu prickled across my neck and arms. For a moment I saw Arthur Lenz sitting at his computer in Virginia, pretending to be "Maxwell" as easily as he pretended to be "Lilith." Then I remembered that Lenz had used the same shrink routine on Brahma. Brahma could merely be echoing the psychiatrist's questions with me, consciously or not. Maybe Lenz provoked more of a response in him than I thought.

ERIN> Would you answer the same question coming from me?

MAXWELL> Yes. I have never committed an act for which I felt regret. All life is exploration, thus all acts are justified.

ERIN> I don't agree with that.

MAXWELL> Ah. You believe in sin?

ERIN> I don't know about that. But there are certainly wrong choices.

MAXWELL> No, only poor choices. And only from a given perspective.

ERIN> But isn't the idea of sin one of the oldest creations of mankind? It was there in Greek mythology just as much as in the Bible.

MAXWELL> You answered your own question! Sin is a creation of man's intellect. A Herculean effort to explain the eternal condition of sorrow in which he has found himself from the dawn of time. Look at Oedipus. The poor lad did all he could to avoid sin, yet ended up killing his father and sleeping with his mother. Murder and incest, all to illustrate the inevitability of man's fate. The same with Job. Nothing was his fault. It was God having a wager with Satan.

ERIN> No mortal act deserves punishment?

MAXWELL> That's a different question. Sin occurs in relation to God, not man. Look at Prometheus. He ridiculed the gods and their power, and he acted accordingly. He stole divine fire and gave it to man as a gift. He sinned against the gods, but blessed man forever.

ERIN> And look what happened to him. Chained

to a rock with his liver eaten by eagles for thirty years. And the liver grew back each night.

MAXWELL> A nodding acquaintance, indeed! But remember, after paying that price, Prometheus was taken up to Olympus, where he resided forever among the gods.

ERIN> Does that have something to do with why you use the name Prometheus?

MAXWELL> Just so. Heroic men must often endure a period of suffering or darkness before their work is recognized.

ERIN> You sound bitter.

MAXWELL> I'm tired of dealing with squalid little souls. I yearn for a society of Ahabs but inhabit a world of Walter Mittys.

ERIN> Now you sound like some kind of super-race nut.

MAXWELL> I have my moments. Do you know Nietzsche's quote about society? A people is a detour of Nature to get six or seven great men.

ERIN> Yes, but that's not the whole quote. The rest is, Yes, and then to get around them. Or something like that.

MAXWELL> You amaze me.

ERIN> Sometimes I amaze myself. I suppose you're one of the six or seven?

MAXWELL> Only time will tell.

ERIN> I suppose women don't fit into that equation of greatness?

MAXWELL> Of course they do. Women are the gateway of the Absolute. From an evolutionary perspective, as critical as the male. They provide half the genetic code.

ERIN> What do you mean, the gateway of the Absolute?

MAXWELL> You have a child. A son, I believe. Did you deliver vaginally?

ERIN> Yes.

MAXWELL> Did you not feel, when your cervix dilated and the cramps exploded in your belly and your anal sphincter let go and the pain was like a scaly hand ripping you apart that you had been possessed—hijacked, if you will—by something infinitely larger than yourself?

ERIN> Don't remind me. But the answer is yes. It was like . . . I don't know.

MAXWELL> That was LIFE, Erin. LIFE seizing every cell in your body and bending you to its single-purposed will. LIFE is violent and uncontrollable and indescribably beautiful. Don't you sometimes walk naked into the nurturing sun and scream I AM ALIVE?

ERIN> I'm not usually that demonstrative about it.

MAXWELL> You should be. LIFE IS EVERYTHING.

ERIN> You don't believe in an afterlife?

MAXWELL> You do?

ERIN> No. I told you about the thread, remember? When the thread runs out, it's over. I just wanted to know what you thought.

MAXWELL> For a moment I thought we had gone as far as we could go.

ERIN> Are you married?

MAXWELL> No.

ERIN> Ever been?

MAXWELL> No.

ERIN> How old are you?

MAXWELL> How old would you guess?

ERIN> If you've really never been married, you must be young. Or gay.

MAXWELL> I am not _gay_. I defy Nature in far

more profound ways than that. How old a man are you looking for?

ERIN> Age doesn't matter.

MAXWELL> Not in the man, you are right. But the woman must be of childbearing age.

ERIN> You're a real sexist, aren't you?

MAXWELL> A Darwinian sexist, perhaps. What do you visualize happening with this man you seek? You already have a son. Do you see yourself abandoning him for this man?

ERIN> I don't want to talk about that.

MAXWELL> Your family?

ERIN> My son. I don't mind talking about my husband.

MAXWELL> Why the selective affection?

ERIN> It's something to do with what we discussed before.

MAXWELL> Sin?

ERIN> Being ashamed. Having regrets.

MAXWELL> You are ashamed of your son? You regret having him?

ERIN> No. Only the way he was conceived. I guess you could say he was conceived in sin.

MAXWELL> Through an adulterous relationship?

ERIN> Not exactly. Worse, really.

MAXWELL> I don't understand.

ERIN> It's something to do with a sin you mentioned earlier.

MAXWELL> I mentioned? But what? Murder?

I didn't respond. He'd get it fast enough.

MAXWELL> Your son was conceived through _incest_?

ERIN> Not exactly. It's complicated.

MAXWELL> But I must know!

ERIN> I've said too much already.

MAXWELL> But Erin, I can help you with this. I have specialized knowledge. We must explore this!

ERIN> I need time to think.

MAXWELL> Of course. Yes. I understand. But we must speak again. The soonest possible time for me would be late tonight. Possibly very early tomorrow morning. Is either of these times good for you?

ERIN> Maybe. If I'm online, I'll check the Blue Room. You can find me there.

MAXWELL> And if not?

ERIN> We'll leave it to fate.

MAXWELL> How very appropriate.

ERIN> Good-bye.

MAXWELL> Yes. Good-bye.

After a giddy few moments staring at the screen, I called Miles back into the office. He snatched up the printouts of the conversation and read them with stunning speed.

"You've hooked him," he announced, setting down the pages. "You know, Brahma sounds a long way from crazy to me. I feel exactly like he does sometimes."

I took off the headset and pushed back from the computer. "Our conversations don't have quite the same feel as his conversations with the other victims. I can't put my finger on why."

"I know. I don't think he's looking at you as a potential victim. A donor or whatever. He's interested in some other way. Just keep stringing him along. By tomorrow I should be finished with the Trojan Horse, and we'll be ready for Phase Two."

"You sound like a bad movie."

He grinned. "I like bad movies."

* * *

That exchange happened four hours ago.

Since then Miles has been coding more or less steadily. He seems to have scented the finish line, and only stops for fresh Mountain Dew. Now and then he'll shout something like "FMH!"—which he explained was a polite form of "Fuck me harder!"—a hacker curse usually directed at some particularly annoying piece of software that refuses to behave as it should, in this case his Trojan Horse.

I've read half a paperback novel, cleaned up the kitchen, and driven to Yazoo City and back, all in an attempt to keep my nerves steady. Knowing that the man we call Brahma is looking forward to his next conversation with me is more than a little unsettling. This connection is what I set out to establish, but now that I have, all I want is for Miles to finish his Trojan Horse so we can get the whole thing over with.

Around five-thirty it strikes me that Drewe might like it if I whipped up some dinner before she gets home. She might like it a lot. I have a vision of fresh tomatoes from our garden, then remember the heat-shriveled specimens I saw this morning. Without intravenous therapy they'll never be fit for a dinner table. As usual, it's too late to thaw anything out. I am nearly reconciled to tuna on toast when Miles walks into the kitchen with his laptop and says, "Why don't you fire up the search engine?"

I start to remind him that Brahma said he wouldn't be back online until late tonight, but arguing with Miles is useless. I expel the air from my lungs with a disgusted plosive, walk back into the office, and sit down at the EROS computer.

The search program begins its monotonous task with an efficient clicking of the hard drive. Searching for Brahma's prose patterns takes much longer than a search for an account name. After a few distracted minutes of playing guitar on my bed, I look over at the computer. The monitor shows the screen format of a private room. The prompt at the top of the page reads: **MAXWELL>**. The answering prompt reads: **LILITH>**.

First I yell for Miles. Then I rehang my guitar on the wall and sit down before the EROS computer.

"He lied to me," I say when Miles comes in. "He's back on. He's talking to Lenz again."

"I thought he might. Same old shit from Lenz? Freud dispensed at the level of Sally Jessy Raphael?"

"Looks like it. Want me to turn up the sound?"

"Nah." He sits on the bed and opens his laptop.

As I skim the usual purple prose, a wave of heat suffuses my face. My eyes have locked onto one passage like a laser sight.

MAXWELL> I understand too well. The majority of men are asshoels.

I reread the text above this line, but everything looks normal. Then this appears:

MAXWELL> We've discussed HIV in abstract terms, but we've neveer asked each other the one iportant question.

I try to yell "Miles!" but my voice comes out a whisper.

"You say something?" he asks.

"Typos! Look at this!"

In seconds he's reading the screen over my shoulder.

"He keeps making them," I murmur.

"He's not using his voice recognition unit." Miles grips my shoulder. "He's on the move!"

My chest feels hollow. "Lenz knows that, right?"

"Got to. The FBI agents at EROS probably saw the

typos before you did. Scroll back up. I'll bet he's been making errors during the whole exchange."

I scroll through the previous lines and verify that Miles is correct. "Okay," I say, trying to calm down. "Okay, they must have seen that. Too many to miss."

"Damn," Miles says softly. "Lenz pulled it off. I'll bet an FBI SWAT team is greasing its guns right now."

"Brahma goes mobile two or three days before a kill," I remind him. "Based on his error rate and the old murder dates, anyway."

"Reconnaissance," says Miles. "He's out there right now using a laptop and a cellular. I wonder how close he is to that safe house."

"I'm calling Lenz," I decide aloud.

"Why? The FBI's gearing up to slam this guy down right now." Miles runs one hand over his still ridiculous crew cut. "You know, now's the time to trace him."

"Why?"

"Because he's on a cellular, and we know where he's headed."

"I'm calling the safe house, Miles."

"Go ahead, but they're just going to blow you off."

"Fine." Scrounging in my wallet for the number Lenz gave me, I find it and drop it by the phone. My call is answered on the second ring.

"Yes?" says a female voice.

"This is Harper Cole. I need to talk to Dr. Lenz."

"You shouldn't have called here."

"I need to make sure he knows something important."

"He knows. Harper, this is Margie Ressler."

"Margie." The decoy. "Is everything okay?"

"Yes, but we can't tie up this line right now."

"I've got to tell Lenz about something."

"About the errors?"

"You know about that?"

"Everything's under control. Really. Take it easy."

Relief washes over me. "Okay. I just wanted to make sure you guys weren't going to be surprised."

"We're the FBI, Harper. We're not going to be surprised." Her voice goes quiet. "You'd better keep *your* eyes open, though. Did you or Miles Turner send e-mail to Mr. Baxter warning him to check tissue donor networks?"

"Margie—" I stop, unwilling to implicate myself on a phone that might be tapped.

As if reading my mind, she says, "All I'm going to tell you is that the shit hit the fan after they started checking. You'd better watch your butt."

"Thanks. And you'd better take your own advice."

"He won't come tonight. Not if the record's any indication."

Suddenly I hear a babble of male voices.

"Sir!" Margie answers like a boot camp recruit.

The phone goes dead in my hand.

"Well?" asks Miles, back on the bed now.

"They know."

He gives me his dour I-told-you-so look.

"She also said they got your note about transplant networks."

Now he's paying attention.

"She said the shit hit the fan when they started checking."

Miles ponders this for a few seconds. "Then Drewe must be right. There must be another missing woman."

"Jesus. What are we going to do?"

He takes a deep breath, looks at the floor for a few seconds, then says, "I'm going to code until seven, which is when TBS is showing *I Walk the Line*, with Gregory Peck and Tuesday Weld."

"You're kidding."

"Nope. I *love* Tuesday Weld. Did you see *Who'll Stop*

the Rain? From Robert Stone's book? Even Nolte was great in that."

"Miles—"

"Tuesday Weld should have played Holly Golightly in *Breakfast at Tiffany's*, not Audrey Hepburn. Even Capote said that. Of course, he said a *young* Tuesday Weld. With her we wouldn't have gotten that bullshit Hollywood ending. Holly would have—"

"Miles!"

He looks up irritably. "What?"

"Don't you care what happens at the safe house?"

"Of course. But it's not in my power to affect the outcome."

"Isn't there some way to at least monitor the action? Hack into a Bureau computer or something?"

"Harper, a stakeout is just some guys on the radio. They're probably not even talking a whole lot."

"So?"

"There's no computer angle to it. Baxter will want to be there for the collar, so he's probably at the safe house already, or else on his way. Nothing will have to be relayed to him, *ergo* we can't intercept anything digital."

"What about radio, then?"

Miles laughs. "We can't monitor police radio from a thousand miles away."

"Why not?"

"Because it's *analog*, man. Radio waves that die after a few miles."

Smugness is one of my pet peeves. At times like this I want to smack Miles on the side of the head. And somewhere between staring at his arrogant expression and clenching my right fist, a solution arcs through my brain like a Roman candle. As Miles stares, I sit down at my Gateway 2000 and switch on my modem.

"What are you doing?" he asks.

"Logging on to CompuServe."

"Why?"

"To eavesdrop on the stakeout."

"How?"

I click the mouse rapidly. "By talking somebody local into doing it for us."

"Who's going to do that?"

"Ever hear of ham radio?"

It takes less than five seconds for Miles to see where I'm going. "But ham radio is a totally different frequency spectrum than law enforcement stuff," he says.

I don't even respond. I know he's kicking himself for not thinking of this first.

"Ham operators hang out on CompuServe?" he asks, getting up and looking over my shoulder.

"Either here or AOL. One of my neighbors is a ham nut. He's mentioned a forum before, and I think it's on CompuServe. I'm doing a *Find* for the word 'radio.' "

Suddenly a neat column of words appears on my screen:

Broadcast Professionals
CB Handle
CE Audio Forum
HamNet Forum
IQuest($)
National Public Radio

"Ha! You see that?"

"HamNet," Miles says. "That's it?"

"Let's see."

Seconds later we're staring at the multicolored logo of a computer forum dedicated exclusively to the arcane joys of ham radio. I click the mouse, and topic headings like "Amateur Satellites," "Swap Shop," "Utility DX'ing," and "Hardware/Homebrew" appear.

"Miles, I guarantee you some of these guys are into a

lot more than ham radio. That *Tom Swift* crap with cigar boxes full of vacuum tubes is history. These guys are high-tech now."

"A couple of old hackers at MIT were into ham," he says, and I sense how badly he wants to move me out of the chair and take over this job.

"The only question," I muse, "is will somebody with the right equipment be close enough to McLean, Virginia, to do it?"

"Definitely," Miles says excitedly. "McLean's the D.C. metro area, not far from Langley. Bound to be somebody there. I'll bet some of these guys have wet dreams about intercepting CIA and FBI communications."

"I don't know," I say, reading the screen more closely. "Look at some of these topics. "FCC Compliance" and "Proper Certification." Maybe they're not into that kind of stuff."

"Why don't you let me talk to them?" Miles suggests, standing so close that I feel uncomfortable.

"It's all yours," I tell him, rising from the chair.

He sits and immediately begins composing a forum message. "We just have to approach it right. I'm not a federal fugitive, I'm . . . a reporter. For the *Times-Picayune.* So are you." He pauses, thinking. "We just got a tip about a rogue FBI operation in D.C. It might even involve the ATF. How does that sound?"

"Like another bad movie."

He laughs. "This is great, man. Within two hours we'll have real-time coverage of Lenz's little trap, right through your telephone. Just like two tin cans on a thousand-mile string."

"What if my phone's really tapped?"

"Oh, yeah," he says, his brow furrowing. "Well . . . I'll just have to figure something out."

The bang of the front door catapults Miles out of his

seat and to the nearest window. "Go check!" he commands.

"Harper, it's me."

"Drewe," I reassure him. "It's just Drewe."

He steps away from the window and leans against the wall, one hand over his heart. "This is major stress, man. What did I do to deserve this?"

"I won't answer that." I start toward the door. "I'd better fix us some supper."

The office door opens before I reach it.

Drewe stands in the hall holding a large brown paper bag. She is smiling, and her radiance gives me an unexpected lift. Yet it is plain that she does not intend to cross the threshold. Instead, she reaches into the bag and pulls out a paper box printed with red curlicues and an alarmingly orange fluid dribbling down its side.

"Chinese," she says. "I figured we were due for a change."

"You are a *goddess*," Miles says with genuine reverence. "I shall kiss your feet and worship forever at the altar of your infinite kindness."

Drewe laughs. "Just chew with your mouth closed, and I'll be satisfied."

As she walks away, Miles sits back down at the Gateway.

"You coming?" I ask.

He waves one hand. "Just let me post this message. Be right there."

As I pass through the door, I hear him say, "This is going to be better than sex." This from a man who has seen, heard, and perhaps participated in just about every carnal activity the human mind can imagine. I turn and look back. It is the new sight for this century, I think, a man in digital bliss. And yet it is as old as the first hominid who stared mesmerized into a campfire.

We are fascinated by that which can destroy us.

Chapter 30

Miles beat his own prediction by over an hour. By the time we finished supper, three ham radio operators in the Washington, D.C. area expressed interest in helping us monitor the communications of the FBI (in the interest of the public's hallowed right to know, of course). One of these—an ex-marine named Sid Moroney—admitted that he often monitored CIA training exercises on the streets of Washington and its suburbs, and boasted that he maintained a notebook containing the frequencies most commonly used by the government's more aggressive acronymic agencies. This resource put him over the top, and Miles told him we would e-mail our requirements to him ASAP.

We spent fifteen minutes arguing about the best way for Moroney to relay what he overheard to us. We wanted it in real time, but we also knew my phones might be tapped. We decided I would stay linked to Sid Moroney via CompuServe on the Gateway, while Miles monitored the EROS computer for any "Lilith"-"Maxwell" activity. Sid could update me on the stakeout by tapping messages into a private room on a CompuServe chat channel. If anything radical started to happen, he was to call my office number and press the mouthpiece of his telephone to his radio receiver, so that we could hear the traffic ourselves. This was a risk, but Miles figured anything serious enough to warrant a call would probably be the climax of the manhunt—which would exonerate us both.

So far the wait has been anything but climactic. Moroney has intercepted communications indicating a stakeout in progress in the vicinity of the McLean safe house. So far I've received six reports from him via CompuServe, transcribing such bloodcurdling radio traffic as: *"Alpha? Red here. Kensington quiet." "Ten four, Red. Yellow? You there?" "Affirmative, Alpha. Wimbledon clear. Tomorrow must be garbage pickup, everybody's coming out in their robes to put out the cans." "Button it, Yellow. Out."* And so on for the past three and a half hours. The use of "Alpha" reminds me of Daniel Baxter in the trailer at Quantico, but since I can't hear the voice, there's no way to tell.

This time I let Drewe in on what we were doing, since clearing our names seemed possible. But when eleven p.m. came and went, she raised a white flag and retired to the bedroom. I worried that Moroney would get bored and do the same, but after a few queries I found out he keeps a cot in his radio room and, like a good marine, has developed the capacity to detect significant radio traffic even while sleeping.

I am half asleep myself when the balloon goes up.

Miles, sitting six feet behind me at the EROS computer, says, "Hello." As I turn in my seat before the Gateway, he raises his hand, forbidding any interruption.

"Brahma just logged on," he says in a monotone. "He's using 'Maxwell.' "

"What's he doing?" I ask, rubbing my eyes and straightening up in my chair.

"Looking for 'Lilith.' "

"Where?"

His shoulders stiffen. "Lenz is there now. They're going into a private room. I'm turning up the sound."

Brahma's digital baritone fills the office with an almost calming cadence.

"What about his error rate?" I ask.

"I'm looking. Three typos already. He's definitely not using his voice-rec unit."

Miles adjusts the speakers, then looks over at me. Already this conversation seems different from the ones we've become used to. This time Brahma is taking the lead.

"Is Lenz showing a little restraint at last?" I ask.

"Looks like it. I guess we wait now."

We don't wait long. In less than five minutes, a message from Sid Moroney flashes onto the screen of the Gateway.

Just heard some fast chatter. "This is Alpha. All units be advised we have a cellular trace on the UNSUB. He's definitely in the Washington metro area. He's using a rented phone. We're holding off on a pinpoint trace, but UNSUB is close by. Look sharp."

"Miles, the FBI is trying to trace him now."

When he doesn't respond, I turn. He's listening closely to Lenz and Brahma. "Baxter was supposed to give Lenz a week without trying to trace Brahma," I remind him. "Why do it now and risk blowing the whole operation?"

"Momentum," Miles replies, not bothering to turn. "This is like any big business deal. At first everybody's lovey-dovey. But when closing time comes, major egos are involved. The FBI knows Brahma is close. They've got the capability to trace him, therefore they trace him. It's not even a question."

"Moroney says they're holding off on a pinpoint trace, whatever that means."

"Brahma's probably moving between cells, and they don't want to put out scanning vehicles for fear of spooking him."

"But why not just stop his car and arrest him, if they can find him?"

At last Miles turns to me, his look contemptuous. "Arrest him for what? Riding around with a laptop computer and a cell phone and typing sex talk?"

"Couldn't they backtrack over his movements, compare them to the murder dates, stuff like that? Why risk him getting away?"

"There's no reason to think he'll try. He's following an established pattern. He'll shadow the decoy agent for two or three days, then make his move on the house."

"Right," I say, unconvinced.

Suddenly the speakers fall silent. Miles checks his screen. "Brahma just logged off."

"Shit. You think he found out they were trying to trace him?"

"Maybe. He's got guts, this guy. I wonder if he might actually try to hit her the first night."

"That's the feeling I have, Miles. Don't ask me why. Like something's wrong. Really wrong."

"Like what? What could be wrong?"

"I think Brahma's about to make a fool out of everybody. He's been three steps ahead of us all the way. Why should he act like an idiot now? Why walk into a trap?"

"Tell me."

"I don't know, damn it!"

Miles looks thoughtful. "Okay, say you're right. How could he make a fool out of everybody?"

"I don't *know.*" My mind is fuzzy with anxiety and fatigue. "By doing the unexpected?"

"And what's that?"

"Maybe he knows 'Lilith' is a trap, but he's figured a way to kill the decoy anyway. You know, the girl I told you about. Margie Ressler."

"Harper, right this second a dozen SWAT guys are perched in trees and on rooftops around that safe house.

They can shoot the balls off a hamster at five hundred yards, and the range is probably less than forty. If Brahma shows up there, he's dog meat."

"But Brahma doesn't think like other people. Remember Dallas? He won't walk up with a target painted on his shirt. They won't even see him. Or if they do, they'll think they know who he is. One of them maybe. He'll do his thing and split before they even know what hit them."

Miles bites his lower lip. "Shit," he says finally.

"Miles?"

"What?"

"What if Brahma's not even going there? What if he's after someone else?"

"Like who?"

" 'Eleanor Rigby.' "

"That's nuts. She lives in California. We know Brahma's in D.C. or Virginia."

"No, we don't. We know *somebody's* in D.C. or Virginia, logging on as 'Maxwell.' Remember the team-offender theory? If there's really a group behind this, Brahma himself could be anywhere. He could be in California right now. He could be *here*, man."

Miles shakes his head. "Calm down. He has no idea this place exists. And why in God's name would he pick 'Eleanor Rigby' out of thousands?"

"Not thousands. Six hundred. She's a blind-draft account, remember?"

"The odds are still ridiculous. Give me one shred of logic."

" 'Maxwell's Silver Hammer,' remember? A Beatles song. And she's 'Eleanor Rigby.' There's death in that song too. Wouldn't he gravitate to that?"

Miles purses his lips in concentration. "Maybe."

"Is there some central data bank where all EROS conversations are stored? An archive or something? I know you told the FBI there wasn't, but—"

"There's a sixty-day record. Every word is automatically filed to disk for sixty days. Then it's erased. We do it for legal protection, in case of things like crimes against children ricocheting back on us. One of my techs handles it."

"I want you to check it. Right now."

"Why?"

"To find out whether Brahma has talked to 'Eleanor' recently."

"But—"

"If you don't, I'm going to call Eleanor myself. And that's the first step to the whole story coming out."

He clicks angrily at his mouse, then types a brief e-mail message and transmits it to New York. "I told them it was urgent, but it might take a while."

"Thank you."

We sit in uncomfortable silence for a few minutes. I watch the screen of the Gateway, but Sid Moroney sends nothing through.

"Here we go," Miles says. " 'Eleanor Rigby' spoke to 'Maxwell' in a private room three days ago. The conversation lasted eight minutes. You want me to get the text from them?"

My heart is in my throat as I pick up the phone.

"Hey, what are you doing?" Miles asks.

"Warning Eleanor."

"Let's at least look at the file first!"

"Forget it."

Eleanor's line is busy. I set down the phone, an image of a lonely young woman in a wheelchair burning behind my closed eyes.

"Busy," I say quietly.

"Thank God. That would have started a network-wide panic."

I slap the desk with my right hand. "Like I give a shit, okay? We're talking about life and death here! I don't care if the whole goddamn company implodes. Everybody will just have to go back to using magazines to jack off."

Miles looks at me like a scientist observing some rare protozoan, then blinks and goes back to his screen. When I turn back to mine, I find a message from Sid Moroney awaiting my attention.

Just picked up a secondary frequency in the area. Could be another stakeout, DEA or local cops, but I don't think so. It's scrambled. I also heard a couple of references to "Gamma Team" on the primary frequency. No Gamma before that. What are all these guys waiting for? Could it be a dangerous fugitive or something like that?

Without consulting Miles, I type a quick confirmation that the subject of this stakeout could be *very* dangerous. By the time Miles asks what I typed, I've sent the message; by the time I finish explaining the situation, I've received a reply from Moroney.

My guess is that the scrambled freq is being used by a sniper team. That's Gamma Team. A regular stakeout doesn't mean much to eavesdroppers in this city, but people talking about lines of fire, rules of engagement, and stuff like that would have a TV truck over here like lightning. That's why it's scrambled. I'm working on unscrambling it, but the odds are one in a million. This is heavy stuff, guys. Thanks for the invite.

My pulse has settled into a rhythm far above its normal rate. "You were right, Miles! They've got sharpshooters up there."

"Can Moroney hear what they're saying?"

"No. It's scrambled."

He shakes his head, obviously disgusted. "That's about what I'd expect from the FBI."

"What do you mean?"

"Using encrypted radio traffic around the safe house is stupid. You think Brahma won't have scanning equipment? Scrambled chatter is like a neon sign screaming 'COPS.' "

"What choice do they have?"

"Radio silence. Or they could use fake radio chatter, like they've got a drug bust set up near there."

"Should we try to warn them?"

"Way too late."

We stare at each other in silence. Then a familiar male voice floats out of the speakers, and the printer behind Miles begins humming.

"Brahma's back," he says, turning. "Same room."

By the time Brahma finishes his first sentence, Miles and I have frozen like ice sculptures.

MAXWELL> Greetings, Dr. Lenz. I'd actually planned a more dramatic revelation than this, but now it seems juvenile. After Dallas, I warned your agency not to interfere with my work. Yet you persisted. By putting my life at risk, you implicitly risked your own, and also those under your protection. Learning one's limitations is always a painful lesson, but it is only through pain that we grow. Perhaps now you will understand that some "lawbreakers" are best left alone. (Besides, considering what you were forced to endure each night in the name of love, perhaps I did you a favor.) We shall not speak again. My condolences in advance.

"He killed somebody," Miles says in a flat voice. "Right now, somebody close to Lenz is dead or dying."

My hands are shaking. Before I can speak, my office line rings.

"Don't answer it!" Miles commands.

"It's Moroney," I reply in a hoarse whisper. "The machine'll get it."

I steel myself against dreadful news.

After my outgoing message ends, a voice says: "Hello? Guys? Guys! This is Sid! All hell's breaking loose up here!"

I am rooted where I sit, but Miles reaches the phone in three lightning strides. "Keep talking, Sid, what's happening?"

"I'm going to hold the phone to the radio."

Static-filled radio chatter bursts from the tinny speaker of my answering machine: *"Alpha, what the hell? What's going on in there?"* More static, then: *"Stand by, Green, stand—shit! Stop him, Ressler, goddamn it!"*

"That's Baxter!" I cry. "I recognize his voice. Alpha is Daniel Baxter!"

The first voice comes back: *"Alpha, we've got a guy running down the walk, wait—he's turning back for the garage."* Then a new voice, eerily calm: *"Alpha, this is Gamma Leader. I have a male adult in my scope. Looks like your shrink."*

The voices merge into a babel of confusion. *"All units, this is Alpha. That's Dr. Lenz outside. Repeat, friendly personnel outside the house. What the hell's going on, sir? Uncertain, Green. He's in the Acura, Alpha! He's burning rubber out of the driveway! Please advise! Green, follow the doctor but do not attempt to apprehend. Gamma Leader, this is Alpha. I am standing on the sidewalk. Stand down until the car is clear, then converge on the house and secure it. Green, don't let the doctor hurt himself, we don't know what's happening. Roger, Alpha, in pursuit. He's turning onto Dolley Madison.*

Yellow here, Alpha. What about the UNSUB? Contact too brief, Yellow. No useful bearings. UNSUB could be anywhere. Stay sharp. Green, stick to the doctor's tail. We're there, Alpha, turning onto Chain Bridge Road . . ."

A flurry of street names fills the airwaves.

"Does Lenz have any kids?" Miles asks.

"Yes." I'm still too stunned to move. "A son, I think he said."

"Where does he live?"

"I don't know. It's not the kid, though."

"Who is it?"

"It's his wife."

Miles looks at me. "How do you know that?"

"When I was up there, we stopped off at Lenz's house for a few minutes so he could get some papers and clothes. She actually hit on me while Lenz was upstairs."

"And?"

"She's a bad drunk. That's what the end of Brahma's message was about."

"Christ. Where does she live?"

"Ten minutes from the safe house. That's why Lenz chose that location."

The disjointed radio chatter is suddenly interrupted by Sid Moroney's voice. "You guys got any idea what the hell's going on up here?"

"No," Miles says into the phone, his eyes still on me.

"I got traffic on the regular police band. They just dispatched two patrol units to an address not far from the stakeout. That anything to do with us?"

"Could be," says Miles. "Don't hang up, Sid."

"You kidding? I'm putting the phone back to the receiver. I'll give you whichever channels have the most traffic."

The ensuing chatter tells a simple story of pursuit, very like an episode of *Cops*, but for the profanity of the FBI agents attempting to stay up with the racing Acura. After four minutes by my watch, we hear the denouement.

"He's stopping, Alpha. Six-fifteen Whitehall. Repeat, Six-fifteen Whitehall. Large residential house. The doc just parked in a closed garage. We have Fairfax County blue-and-whites arriving at the scene. What do you want us to do?"

"Green, this is Alpha. I'm en route now. Get inside that house. One of you follow Dr. Lenz, the other tell the locals what's what. Move it."

"Understood."

"Green, make SURE the locals know Lenz is a white hat. Whoever goes in the house, give me play-by-play. I'll take over when I get there."

"Alpha, this is Green. I'm in the garage. I'm ahead of the police. It's dark . . . my weapon is out. I'm moving through a slightly open door. It's a laundry room. No sign of anybody. Wait . . . Alpha, somebody's yelling. Screaming. I think it's a man. I have a man screaming—howling really. He . . . oh sweet Jesus . . . oh my God, we got a body here, sir. We have a female down. She's—Jesus, she's on a kitchen table. She's naked. The doctor's giving her CPR, but . . . I think she's dead, Dan. She's got to be dead because her—her head. Jesus, I've never seen one this bad—"

"Terminate contact," snaps a rigidly composed voice. *"I'll be at the scene in less than a minute. Is that understood? IS THAT UNDERSTOOD?"*

"Understood, sir. Sorry I lost my head . . . Green out."

There's another long burst of static. Then Sid Moroney's voice drifts through my office in a hushed interrogative:

"You guys heard that?"

Miles doesn't answer.

"Guys? Hey. Somebody just got wasted. A lady just got wasted. I, uh . . . wasn't expecting that. I think maybe you guys better tell me what's going on, huh?"

Miles shakes his head and puts his mouth to the telephone. "We didn't expect it either, Sid. We knew it was serious, but nothing like this. Don't worry, you're not in trouble."

"The hell I'm not. I've already broken about fifteen statutes that I know of. Now what the hell is this about? You guys really working for a newspaper or what?"

"Yes, Sid. The *Times-Picayune,* out of New Orleans. You can call the office and check us out. But please tell me first what's happening on the radio."

After a moment, Moroney says, "Nothing on the FBI channel. I got some McLean P.D. stuff. They're reporting a one-eighty-seven—a homicide—at Six-fifteen Whitehall."

"Did they mention a name?"

"They don't do that on the radio. Female Caucasian is all. They've alerted paramedics. Some patrolman's asking for brass on the scene, complaining about the FBI. And um . . . uh . . . I think that's about it for me, guys. Next time call somebody else, okay?"

"Thanks for your assistance, Mr. Moroney," Miles says with overdone formality. Then he hangs up.

"This is bad," he says.

Only now do I realize that Miles was consciously disguising his voice on the phone, adding the drawled Southern rhythms he worked so hard to eradicate during the past few years. "Bad?" I echo. "It's a goddamn nightmare."

"I meant the telephone call. It won't be long before Baxter finds out we were monitoring what happened."

"You mean that *I* was. We were using my phone."

"I may have to split," he says, rocking in place like a nervous sprinter. "We've got to accelerate the plan."

"What? We're out of this shit, Miles! As of now."

"What do you mean?"

"I mean no more games. No more 'Erin' and 'Maxwell.' You saw Brahma's note to Lenz. He's knows exactly what's up."

"Just because he caught on to Lenz doesn't mean he suspects you. Have you sensed a single false note in his communications with you?"

I pause. "No, but—"

"Any subtle humor at your expense?"

"Not yet, but—"

"It's totally different! He believes in Erin. Why is anybody's guess. But he does."

"Miles, you're missing the main point here, and that scares me."

"What main point?"

"How did Brahma find Lenz?"

His mouth remains half open.

"Through the telephone system, right?"

Miles's brain is operating at a speed I cannot begin to comprehend. I say nothing while he works out the possibilities. Finally, he says, "Unless new information on Lenz's decoy plan was entered into FBI computers in the last thirty-six hours, I'd have to say yes."

"So he can trace us too."

Miles stares at me without speaking, his face masklike in its lack of humanity. "No," he says at length. "If Brahma checks the phone company's computers, he'll find the Vicksburg address coupled with your line. Any other digital data he can turn up will verify that. He can't check actual land ownership because in Mississippi nothing like that is on computer, and probably won't be for another fifty years."

Something in Miles's tone makes me work through his answer step by step, but it checks out.

"Lenz's problem was that he was at the physical address that went with his phone line. Not so with us." Miles pauses. "What I don't understand is how Brahma knew Lenz *personally* was behind 'Lilith.' I mean, he attacked Lenz's wife, not the safe house. So maybe he did get his information from some FBI computer. Maybe somebody got careless."

"We're still out of it, Miles. Until tonight we were fooling around in a bad situation. Now it's a Force-Ten clusterfuck. Fate just tapped us on the shoulder."

"You want to leave it to the so-called experts now?" he asks angrily. "You just saw their incompetence tragically demonstrated. How many women are we going to watch die because we're scared to take Brahma to the wall?"

"It's not our fight."

"The hell it isn't! You think tonight changed my situation for the better?"

"You couldn't have killed Mrs. Lenz. I can swear you were right beside me. Let's just come clean with them."

"Come clean? A minute ago you threw the team-offender theory up at me. Don't you see it's going to be more popular than ever now?"

"Why?"

"Because unless Brahma was transmitting his first message from Lenz's home, someone else killed his wife. Brahma knew the safe house was a trap. He knew they'd be following his cellular, so he drove around typing messages to Lenz while someone else did his wife. Then he logged off, swung back, picked up the killer, and was already out of town when he transmitted that final message."

As much as I want to argue, the scenario makes sense.

Miles rubs his eyes and walks over to my minifridge for a Mountain Dew. "Do you realize what just happened? A serial killer murdered the wife of an FBI agent."

"Lenz was a shrink, not an agent."

"You think that matters? He was one of the stars of the Investigative Support Unit. And Brahma already took out a Hostage Rescue Team member. We're about to see one of the biggest manhunts in American history."

I feel a sudden urge to set the air conditioner at sixty-five degrees, climb into bed, and sleep for twenty hours.

Miles drains the Mountain Dew like a man dying of thirst. "If I turned myself in now, I'd be asking for a legal reaming the likes of which hasn't been seen since Sacco and Vanzetti."

While I marshal my arguments, he drops the empty can, picks up the TV remote control, aims it over my shoulder and switches on my office television.

"What are you doing?"

"Seeing what's on TV."

"What?"

"My time's almost up, Harper." He gazes past me, surfing through channels at superhuman speed. "I'm going to find a movie that'll induce deep hack mode, then lie down and finish my stupid Trojan Horse. The e-mail thing isn't going to work. Too short a time frame now."

"I meant what I said, Miles. I'm through with Brahma."

"I heard you."

Suddenly a wide and placid smile soothes the lines from his face. His eyes glaze with almost religious receptivity.

"What is it?" I ask, looking over my shoulder.

"*This Gun for Hire.* Alan Ladd and Veronica Lake. Ladd's first big break, and he was playing a killer. It's only been on a few minutes. This is like the fourth scene."

"Film noir? I thought you liked seventies trash."

"I'm eclectic. This is perfect. We're living noir right this second. Digital noir."

He gives me a buck-toothed imitation of Humphrey Bogart, and for a moment I actually doubt his sanity. But then he clicks off the halogen lamp, sits on my bed with his back against the headboard, and props his laptop on his thighs. The black-and-white light of the television flickers over his features like shadows of clouds on the face of a cliff. Whatever anyone may think of Miles Turner, he is a man doing what he was born to do. Not many of us can say that.

"I'll sleep on the couch in the den," I tell him.

He nods slightly, or perhaps not at all. In Miles's universe, I am already running in a minimized format.

Chapter 31

"Harper! Wake up!"

"Huh?"

"Wake up!"

My eyelids are sealed shut with epoxy.

I rub my fists into them. The first image that materializes is Miles's face hovering inches from my own in the dark. I remember now. I'm lying on the couch in the den. Miles shakes me again.

"Wake *up*!"

A bolus of adrenaline sprays through my system, bringing me into a sitting position. "Are the cops here?"

"No. Come to the office."

"I had a nightmare . . . Jesus. What's going on?"

Miles is no longer there. I rise and stumble toward the office, noticing faint blue lines around the edges of the blinds. I must have slept through the night. The muted cyclone of Drewe's electric hair dryer whirs from the end of the hall as I pass across it and through the office door.

Miles is seated before the EROS computer. "You've got e-mail," he says.

"From who?"

"Look."

I rub my eyes again and peer at the screen.

TO: ERIN
SENDER: UNAVAILABLE

I must talk to you. You know who I am. I shall check the Blue Room every half hour by the clock.

"It came in about two hours ago," Miles informs me. "I let you sleep as long as I could. Notice anything interesting?"

"No."

"The momentum of the relationship has shifted. Brahma's desperate to talk to you."

"So?"

"You've got to answer him."

A knock at the door lifts Miles an inch off his seat.

"We're awake!" I call.

Drewe opens the door and smiles. She's dressed for work, in dark slacks and a white Liz Claiborne blouse. "I'm having cereal for breakfast," she says. "Best I can do this morning. You guys want any?"

"No thanks," says Miles, trying to look nonchalant.

"Harper?"

"Sounds good. I'm starved."

I ignore Miles's angry expulsion of breath and follow Drewe into the kitchen, glancing at my watch as I go. Seven-twenty a.m. Miles must have figured it would take ten minutes to convince me to answer Brahma's message. I'm definitely not going back into the office before seven-thirty.

Drewe pours two bowls of raisin bran and slices a navel orange into bright crescents. I go straight for the coffeepot. It's Community dark roast with chicory, and I savor the kick.

"You look rough," Drewe says.

"You look like an ad for Ivory Snow."

"Thanks. Long night?"

"Worse."

"What happened?"

I take another scalding sip of coffee and tell her about

the tragedy in Virginia. I can't tell if she's stunned or furious or both. After a long silence, she says, "Is Miles in there trying to track this nut down?"

I shrug. "He's got a few ideas."

Unable to read her eyes, I twirl the spoon in my cereal bowl. The flakes are already soggy.

"Did Miles tell the FBI to start checking tissue donor networks?" she asks.

"Yes. And it looks like you were right. There's probably another missing woman."

Drewe puts down her spoon. "Then it's time to tell the FBI everything."

I have no answer but the truth. "I can't do it with Miles here."

She gives me a pointed look that I have no trouble translating: *Maybe that's our real problem.*

"Maybe I should call them," she says. "From my office. Tell them I came up with the whole transplant theory."

"Drewe . . ."

She wraps both hands around her coffee cup and stares into it. "I know Miles is our friend, Harper. But it's not fair to us." She looks up. "Jail is not my idea of a future."

I reach across the table and close my right hand around her left. "Nor mine. Miles knows what's going on. I just don't think he knows where to go. I'll talk to him."

She squeezes my hand, then stands. Drewe enjoyed theorizing about the murders when they were a technical abstraction, but she does not share Miles's moral ambivalence about duty. Taking a last swallow of coffee, she smooths her slacks, then bends and kisses me on the forehead. "If he tells the FBI everything, he can stay as long as he wants to. If not, tell him I enjoyed seeing him. I've got to go. See you tonight."

She hurries out of the kitchen, car keys jingling, Coach purse swinging from her shoulder. When the front door bangs shut, I put down my coffee and check my watch. Seven thirty-two.

I take my time with the orange slices.

Miles is sitting on the edge of the bed, typing on his laptop. He doesn't look up or speak, so I take the initiative.

"You're not going to try to talk me into answering Brahma?"

"I answered for you." His eyes never leave the screen. "I told him your husband hadn't left for work yet, but you'd be in the Blue Room at nine."

"What?"

He keeps typing. I had thought he was coding, but he's typing too rapidly for that. "You logged on as 'Erin'?"

"Brahma didn't know the difference. He's desperate to talk to you."

"Goddamn it, Miles, this is dangerous!"

"It's been dangerous ever since you called the police. I always knew that. It was you and Drewe who saw it as some kind of *McMillan and Wife* episode."

I start to cuss him from hell to breakfast, but I stop myself. "Miles, I've got to tell you something. You—"

"I've got to tell *you* something," he cuts in, looking up from the computer at last. "I finished the Trojan Horse."

My mind goes blank. "You did?"

"After what happened last night, I thought it was too late. But once I saw Brahma's message, I knew what to do. The hard part was—"

A roar of motors and flying gravel drowns his voice. Before he resumes typing, his fingers flying across the keyboard, I leap to a window and peek around the blinds. Four Yazoo County sheriff's cruisers have blocked my drive. Their doors are open, and at least six uniformed men are rushing toward the porch.

"It's the cops!"

Miles is still typing like a madman when five fast knocks boom through the house.

"Get your ass into the bomb shelter!" I tell him.

"Keep your voice down," he says calmly. "I need thirty seconds. Stall them."

"They'll break the door down!"

"No they won't. I'll hide the disk where you can find it. *Go on.*"

With a lump the size of a cue ball in my throat, I walk slowly toward the front door in my sock feet.

"Sheriff's department!" shouts a voice. *"Open up!"*

"I'm coming! Hang on a second!"

Thanking God for the Scottish fortress mentality that kept my grandfather from putting windows in or around our front door, I reach for the chain lock and jiggle it loudly.

"Gimme a sec! Chain's stuck!"

"Open up or we break it down!"

As I jiggle the chain again, I have a fleeting impression of something passing across the hall behind me. Praying it was Miles, I count slowly to five, then unlatch the chain and open the door.

Someone in a white polyester shirt shoves a piece of paper in my face and starts reciting legalese while three tan and brown uniforms push past me and fan out into the house. Before the voice stops, another deputy goes by me. Then the plainclothes man who was reading shoves past, and Deputy Billy climbs the steps to the porch. He looks a little sheepish.

"What the hell's going on, Billy?"

"FBI thinks Turner's here."

"You've had the house staked out for a week. How could he be here?"

"Hey, we waited till your wife left, okay? That's better treatment than most people get."

This mollifies me a little, but then I realize that common decency isn't what made them wait. "Sheriff Buckner's scared of pissing off Drewe's father, right?"

Billy gives me his worldly look. "Bob Anderson pulls a lot of weight in this state."

"Who's the guy who read the warrant?"

"Sheriff's detective."

Summoning as much indignation as possible, I stalk into my office and shout, "Well? Did you find him?"

A stumpy red-faced deputy gives me an eat-shit look and continues tearing out the contents of my closet. A rumbling from overhead alarms me until I realize that somebody must be fighting his way through our attic with a flashlight, an invasion of privacy that is its own punishment.

A muffled conference in the hall draws me to the door. Then sharp banging noises pull me across it to the den. I want to laugh. A gangly deputy is hammering his hand along the wall like a man searching for a stud in which to place a nail.

"Looking for secret passages?" I ask.

"Why don't you wait outside?" he says coldly.

"Because this is my property."

"Yeah? B.F. deal."

I can't resist rattling his cage. "Why don't you introduce yourself, so I can be sure to get your name right when Bob Anderson asks me who was here?"

His hand stops in midstroke. He looks at me with naked hatred, then continues his pounding, albeit more softly.

"Got something!" shouts a deep voice from the kitchen.

A wolf's grin spreads across the deputy's face. I fight

the insane urge to trip him as he bulls past me with one hand on the pistol grip of a nickel-plated revolver.

In the kitchen, my heart jumps in my chest. Three deputies have crowded up to the pantry door. They have discovered either Miles or the trapdoor leading to the bomb shelter.

"Whose is this?" asks the sheriff's detective.

Red-nosed and beagle-eyed, he steps out of the group holding a dark suit jacket. It takes only a second to recognize the cashmere coat my father brought back from Germany, the one reproduced perfectly as a sculpture in my office.

"Well?" he says.

"Mine," I confess, still dazed. That jacket hasn't been out of my closet in months.

"Sorta hot for a jacket today, ain't it?"

As I meet his stare, something else rises slowly into my line of sight. Gripped between the detective's tobacco-stained thumb and forefinger is a 3.5-inch floppy disk. Why or how this man zeroed in on this disk rather than the hundreds in my office, I don't know. But I have no doubt that he is brandishing the results of Miles's marathon of coding—the Trojan Horse.

"What about this?" he asks, shaking the disk in my face.

I'll hide the disk where you can find it . . .

"What about it?" I ask, praying that he's smeared Miles's fingerprints beyond recognition.

"What's on it?"

"I don't know. Where'd you get it?"

He looks at the deputies, then back at me. I feel more men squeezing in behind me, but I don't break eye contact.

"Your pantry's a wreck," he says. "Cans all over the floor. And the back door was open." He nods through our laundry room, toward the exterior door. "The jacket was on the floor by the door. This disk was in the inside pocket."

"My wife was mending it," I tell him. "It's old. Nothing but mending thread keeping it together."

A quick examination of the coat confirms my answer. "You can't buy nothing like this around here," he says doggedly.

"My dad bought it overseas. When he was in the army."

Someone behind me grunts as though serving in the army constituted some kind of subversive activity.

"What about the disk?"

I shrug. "I've got a million of them. For all I know, that one's been in that coat since last year."

"Says you, bud." The beagle eyes do not waver. "We'll find out soon enough what's on it."

"We can find out right now," says the lanky deputy I met in the den. "He's got computers out the ass in his bedroom."

"Leave 'em be," says the detective, his drooping eyes still on me. "Sure you don't want to change your story?"

The truth is, I'd like nothing better. But right now Miles is either crouched in the dark tunnel beneath our house or snaking through the cotton fields on his belly, dragging his briefcase and computer bag behind him. He needs time. "I suggest you be careful with that coat," I say mildly. "It has a lot of sentimental value."

The detective blinks, then folds the coat over his arm and hands the disk to a deputy, who slips it into a transparent plastic bag. "Don't you worry, sonny. We'll take plenty good care of it."

He turns and walks through the laundry room and pulls open the back door. I see more brown uniforms in the sunlight beyond him.

"Anybody make a break for it?" he calls.

"Nossir," answers a chorus of voices. "Windows or doors."

He sighs interminably. "Le's go, boys."

He shoves roughly past me and plows through the deputies toward the hall. My eyes track the cashmere coat until it disappears through the kitchen door.

When the front door finally bangs shut, I take a slow walk through the house. Every closet door is open, with shoes and boots and clothing strewn across the floors. The attic door hangs down on sprung hinges. Heavy Detroit engines rumble out front as I make my way back to the kitchen. After checking to be sure the back door is shut and its curtain pulled, I open the trapdoor in the pantry floor. The odor of mildew and insecticide hits me in a wave.

"Miles?"

No answer.

"Miles! You down there?"

Nothing.

Leaving the trapdoor raised, I return to the back door and open it. Across our backyard stands the long open toolshed where my grandfather kept his tractor and plow and disc and hand tools. The rusted brick-and-tin structure has fallen into ruin and now serves mostly as a picturesque prop for the huge fig trees that surround it. Miles could be hiding there, but I doubt it. The exterior entrance of the bomb shelter opens twenty feet beyond the shed, in the field. If Miles came out there, he would have crawled deeper into the enveloping cotton.

My gaze wanders across the dusty white sea, already shimmering with heat at eight in the morning. I half expect to see Miles rise up like a scarecrow from the middle of the field, but he doesn't. Maybe he's still hunched over his briefcase in a corner of the bomb shelter. But at some level I know he is not. He promised Drewe that if the police came for him, he would leave and not come back. And Miles keeps his word.

A movement at the far edge of the field catches my eye, but when I try to focus it disappears. Miles? It could just as easily have been a deer.

After locking the door, I pour a cup of scorched coffee and sit at the kitchen table. I can just see the propped-up trapdoor in the open pantry closet. I'll give Miles another half hour before I close it.

As I sit drinking, I ponder the morning's riddles. Why didn't the police confiscate my computers? I can think of two answers. One: the FBI ordered the raid on my house, but instructed the sheriff's department not to touch my computers. That would mean Baxter still wants me working as sysop, which suggests he might try a repeat of Lenz's ill-advised EROS strategy. Two: last night's debacle in Virginia convinced the nonfederal police agencies involved in the case that the FBI has lost control of the investigation. They told Sheriff Buckner to find out once and for all whether Miles was here or not. Leaving my computers alone suggests that while Buckner doesn't mind thumbing his nose at federal authority, he won't risk screwing up an FBI investigation by interrupting the running of EROS.

This leaves me with the enigma of the cashmere jacket and the disk. Why in God's name would Miles take my coat, hide the Trojan Horse disk in it, then leave both behind? Did he run to the back door thinking he could break for the fields and avoid the claustrophobic tunnel altogether? Did he nearly run smack into the deputies who must have been waiting in the backyard even as Drewe and I ate breakfast? Would that have frightened him enough to make him drop the jacket and dart down the tunnel without it? No. Would he take one of my treasured possessions without asking? I remember him admiring the coat sculpture in my office, but—

I'll hide the disk where you can find it.

I stand suddenly. As though sleepwalking, I move up the hallway to my office. I can't believe the deputies did so much damage in so little time. They dragged furniture away from the walls, pulled guitar cases out from under my bed, and generally trashed anything large enough to conceal a hamster.

But the sculpture of my father's coat—mounted on long bolts driven into wall studs—remains pristine and untouched, just as Miles must have guessed it would. I stand before it like a votary before an icon, wondering whether this inanimate object that has so long preserved my father's memory could have provided the spark Miles sought during a desperate moment. The coat sculpture looks impossibly real, the wine-colored "cashmere" slightly wrinkled, as though the coat had just been slipped off after a night of music-making in a smoky club. Even the fine stitching is rendered in the wood. The outer pockets have flaps, but they do not open. One of the deputies probably bruised his knuckles trying to check them.

But the inside breast pocket—thanks to the sculptor's painstaking technique—is there, somehow cut into the black "silk" lining. With a steady-handed certainty unlike any I've ever known, I reach between the wooden lapels and slip two fingers down into that pocket. A thin edge of plastic slides perfectly between my fingertips. When I withdraw my hand, it holds a 3.5-inch floppy disk labeled "TROJAN HORSE."

"Son of a bitch," I whisper.

Without hesitation I take the disk over to my Gateway, push it into the floppy drive, and scan the contents of the disk. It contains only two files. One is a WordPerfect file of 10,432 bytes called "Harper." The other is labeled "E.jpg"—the ".jpg" signifying a graphic file encoded by the standards of the Joint Photographic Experts Group. This must be the Trojan Horse. Hoping for an explanation, I boot up WordPerfect, hit SHIFT, F-10 and retrieve "Harper." The page-long letter begins:

Harpe , Thabk God i type the upload instructionsbeofr the cops giot here. Jsut get Brahma to downolad this JPEG and we;ve got him. You candoiit TIA!

"Thanks in advance," I mutter. "Thanks but no thanks."

The rest of the letter gives detailed instructions for transmitting the JPEG file via EROS. There are almost no typos in that section; Miles must have typed it as soon as he finished the Trojan Horse. Though he doesn't explain exactly what the Trojan Horse is designed to do, he does say that he based his plan around the likelihood that Brahma would use the new EROS UUEncoder-Decoder program to decode the image file. The Trojan Horse code will probably be visible as a small black line somewhere in the photo when Brahma views it, which I am to explain ahead of time by saying that the picture was digitized with an inexpensive hand scanner.

The problem is that Miles omitted the most crucial fact from his letter: a description of the image contained in the JPEG file. My EROS program will decode JPEG images, but since the Trojan Horse is buried inside this particular file—and I have no idea what destructive function it is designed to carry out—I have no intention of disabling either of my computers by trying to view it.

Since Miles didn't tell me what the image was, he must have thought the answer would be self-evident. What image could Brahma want badly enough to download into his computer?

E.jpg.

A chill races across my shoulders. Would Miles really suggest that I send a photo of my sister-in-law to Brahma? He would. I was willing to use Erin's personality—at least parts of it—to seduce Brahma, and Miles hasn't half my moral scruples. But even if he *wanted* to use her photo, how could he? There are no digital photographs of Erin in this house.

Then it hits me. He wouldn't have to use the real Erin. Miles's latest project was expanding EROS's software interface to facilitate transmission of graphic images between subscribers. He probably had dozens of digital photos on his hard drive or on disks in his computer bag. As long as one showed a beautiful woman who looked something like I described "Erin," he would have been set.

Despite my assertions to Miles that our game with Brahma is through, I feel a quickening in my blood. It's 8:50. Brahma will be checking the Blue Room for "Erin" in ten minutes. I shove my chair away from the Gateway and stand up. The closed-in feeling is on me again, and the disordered room only adds to my anxiety. The closets are the worst. Worthless guitar pedal effects and expensive rack-mount units have been spilled out with equal disregard. Even my video camera lies on the floor beneath a pile of old shoes and boots.

As I pick up the camera, I wonder what it was doing in my closet. We usually keep it on the top shelf in the hall closet, within easy reach if we want to tape Holly during a visit. Drewe couldn't have put it here; she doesn't even put *herself* in my office. That leaves Buckner's deputies.

And Miles.

With a hollow feeling in my chest, I pan my eyes across the room. The scattered junk looks indigenous to my office, much of it stuff I've sworn a dozen times to throw out, then kept for no defensible reason. But something must not fit this picture.

There. On the right side of the EROS computer table lies a photo album that belongs in the den with all the other albums Drewe meticulously maintains. But this is no ordinary family album. It's a portfolio from Erin's modeling days.

I cross the room and open the portfolio with a familiar twinge of guilty knowledge and discovery. A few nights over the past three months—since Erin told me the truth about Holly—I have slipped quietly into the den and brought this album back to my office, where I pored over its pages in a state of time dislocation. It is a strange and terrible thing to know your genes have blended with another's in the person of a beautiful child that can never be acknowledged.

I know every photograph in the portfolio intimately. The first pages are magazine covers: *Glamour*, *Harper's Bazaar*, *Vogue*. Then comes a full-page ad that ran in the French edition of *Elle*. "Miles," I murmur, lingering over the seminude lingerie shot. Erin stares up from the page with startling prepossession. How many models have I seen in my lifetime? They stare out from behind glaring type, straining for aloofness, stretching for sincerity and never quite making it. *Look at me,* they implore. *I am a special creature, one of the chosen.* Yet with most, a look that lingers longer than the time it takes to check your groceries pierces their transparent glamour.

Not so with Erin.

Miles was right, the bastard. The feeling never goes away. It never goes away because Erin is life lived too close to the cycle of birth and sex and death that we in the West have tried to deny for too many centuries. A woman who walks among repressed twentieth-century males projecting the tidal power of the moon and the sexual energy of the harvest is like a human low pressure zone. An eye waiting for a hurricane. And I, like so many others, was sucked into it as inexorably as a palm uprooted from an island shore.

Paging quickly through the portfolio, I come to an

empty plastic sleeve. I know what belongs here, and I find it at the back of the portfolio, torn by a hasty reinsertion. It's an eight-by-ten-inch black-and-white photograph. In it, Erin stands in quarter profile on wet stone steps before an arched doorway. She wears a diaphanous black gown, a silver necklace, and silver earrings. Her hair is gathered upon her head, revealing her graceful neck, bare shoulders, and seemingly virginal bosom. Both arms are extended toward the door, offering a silver chalice to a shadowy figure standing just inside the arch. One pale hand is visible in the blackness, waiting to receive the chalice. The great stones forming the arch suggest a castle or cathedral, and they seem to suck the very light from the air, so that even Erin's dark skin, hair, and eyes appear translucent, as though limned by some inner radiance. The image is a study in contradiction: the gaze of a saint on the face of a harlot, a black gown on a bridal body, warm light flowing from darkness in a scene of carnal communion. The image projects a timeless power that Miles must have recognized the instant he saw it.

I let the album fall shut with a sigh.

My video camera is lying out because Miles used it to reproduce this photograph in digital form. Then he somehow transferred that video image—one frame of it—onto the floppy disk I found in the sculpted coat. He probably had some kind of video-capture device in his computer bag. Miles said his Trojan Horse would be true to its name, and he meant it. The image of Erin is his horse, and hidden inside its seemingly harmless code—as deadly as any Greek army—is whatever program he designed to destroy Brahma.

A raucous buzzing suddenly fills the office. I drop into a crouch, trying frantically to locate the source of the sound.

My alarm clock. In the past year I might have set it

twice, so its sound is now as unfamiliar as an air raid siren.

The clock reads 8:59.

Miles obviously set it so that Brahma's next log-on wouldn't pass unnoticed. As if impelled by Miles's will, I shut off the alarm, then move to the EROS computer and stare at its screen saver, the bust of Nefertiti turning hypnotically in the field of black. The urge to touch the keyboard, to move forward on the path to knowledge, no matter how dangerous, is nearly irresistible.

"Damn you, Miles."

Flexing my fingers like a violinist warming up for a concert, I tap a few keys, killing the screen saver and logging on to EROS as SYSOP. From my bird's-eye view of the system, I scan the block of private rooms that contains the Blue Room.

Brahma is there.

MAXWELL> Erin? The dry earth awaits the rain.

The nerves in my arms dance needle points on my skin. I feel like I just opened my bathroom door and found a stranger waiting behind the shower curtain. With a quick click of the mouse I log off and sit staring at the black screen.

Nefertiti soon reappears. She is beautiful but cold. Somehow, across the ages, she whispers to me how trivial is all this, my concern with who lives and who dies. She is another face of the man who awaits me in the Blue Room, and a reckless humour in my blood stirs me to challenge. I stand and walk to the Gateway, pick up Miles's Trojan Horse disk, set it beside the EROS keyboard, and sit back down.

"Okay, shithead," I whisper, pulling on the headset. "Come to papa."

With savage pleasure I stab the keys that transform me

into "Erin" and take me to the Blue Room, where "Maxwell's" prompt still glows softly. I feel a sudden consciousness of the conditioned chill in the house, the dead heat outside, the burning cotton in the fields and Miles crashing through its leaves somewhere, the violated bodies of women lying headless in dry crypts beneath the ground, and Lenz's pathetic shell of a wife, also dead now, and Rosalind May, who might still be alive and worse off for it. With all this and more coursing through me, I activate the voice-recognition program, speak softly into the microphone, and watch my words appear on-screen:

ERIN> I am the rain.

Chapter 32

MAXWELL> I'm so glad you came back.

Brahma's digital voice floats from the speakers with chilling familiarity. His previous communications have imprinted it in my memory as indelibly as that of Douglas Rain, the voice of HAL 9000 in Stanley Kubrick's *2001: A Space Odyssey.* I'm tempted to assign a different frequency to Brahma, but I don't. The familiarity will help me to visualize him as a man, which of course he is. Somewhere he sits just as I do, facing a glowing screen, preparing to speak his inmost thoughts into a machine. When he does, I follow the letters across the monitor to be sure I do not mistake his meaning.

MAXWELL> But it's you who are the dry earth, Erin. _I_ am the rain.
ERIN> I think the opposite. But I'm not ashamed of need. You may be right.
MAXWELL> Perhaps I am. Ashamed of need, I mean. I have been lonely for so long. Not alone, but lonely.
ERIN> The lot of most people, I'm afraid.
MAXWELL> I am not like most people.
ERIN> No one ever thinks they are.
MAXWELL> Soon you will know that I am not.
ERIN> How?

MAXWELL> Today I'm going to do something I have never done.

ERIN> What?

MAXWELL> Tell my story. And then you will know.

ERIN> Why do you want to tell me? Because I told you I was beautiful and you believed me?

MAXWELL> Beauty is important, but it is not enough. Look at the actors and actresses on EROS. Their pathetic fantasies are encyclopedias of insecurity. You said things yesterday that intrigued me. The way you spoke of sin and fate. To find beauty married with character and intelligence is very rare. I possess all these, so I know. Many seek to know me, but I reveal nothing. I live within myself. I believe you do the same. Thus I long to know you. I sense something deep in you. But I shall not ask you to reveal it without also revealing myself. I ask only one favor of you. If the things I tell you shock you too much, tell me. In this way shall we know we were meant to go no further.

ERIN> All right.

MAXWELL> And please forgive me if I take liberties with specifics such as places or names.

ERIN> Lie about the little things, but tell the truth about the big things?

MAXWELL> Just so. I must start in a time before you were born. For my destiny began then.

ERIN> I'm ready.

MAXWELL> In the latter years of the last century, my paternal grandfather was born into a prominent family in Germany. Call him Rudolf. Rudolf was given a first-class education, and became a distinguished surgeon in Berlin. When he was twenty-five, his parents died in a fire. His

elder brother Karl, also a surgeon, was his only surviving relation. Rudolf was a bull of a man, Prussian to his boots, but he married a small, frail woman. She was porcelain pale, with fine features and sea blue eyes.

When the kaiser began rattling his saber, my grandfather decided to emigrate to America. Karl begged him to remain during what he called "the Fatherland's hour of need," but Rudolf took his inheritance and settled his wife in

Here the speakers fall silent, but after a brief delay Brahma picks up again.

a large American city and quickly established himself as surgeon to an upper-class clientele. Their first child was a son. We'll call him Richard.

Richard was something of a Byronic figure, even as an infant. He'd inherited his mother's slight bones, pale skin, and blue eyes, but his father's dark hair, intellect, and relentless will. A year later a daughter was born. Catherine. At that time it was discovered that Richard suffered from hemophilia. His condition was controllable, so long as he was protected from traumatic injury, but his "handicap" completed his Byronic persona.

Early on, Richard showed signs of genius. He was given a peerless education by private tutors, while Catherine received instruction in music and ballet from the age of four. The family led an idyllic existence until 1929. When the stock market crashed, Rudolf lost his fortune overnight. He could still practice medicine, but suddenly it was a means of survival rather than a lucrative hobby. When several friends committed suicide,

he fell into severe depression. His behavior became erratic, he practically imprisoned himself and his family in

The speakers are silent again. Unsure of what to do, I finally type:

ERIN> What's the matter? Are you all right?

MAXWELL> Yes. It's proving harder than I thought to tell the story without giving away too much.

ERIN> What are you afraid of?

MAXWELL> When I'm finished, you will understand. I'm under a great deal of pressure just now. I am working on a great enterprise. Certain people would like to stop me. They don't understand my work.

ERIN> But you believe I will?

MAXWELL> You might. I'm not sure.

ERIN> I've got to tell you, I'm under a lot of strain myself. Almost breakdown level, to be honest. Don't tell me anything you don't want to, but getting it out might do you some good. I know what it means to keep a secret bottled up for too long.

MAXWELL> If I go on, you must remember something. Knowledge is a burden. It has a price. Remember the Garden of Eden.

ERIN> Don't worry. I'd make a very good Eve. I'd blame Adam or Satan for picking the apple while I made apple wine for God. This is the kind of conversation I subscribed to EROS for in the first place.

MAXWELL> You actually made me laugh. I shall continue then.

After losing his fortune, Rudolf practically impris-

oned his family in their brownstone in the city. He practiced only enough medicine to keep food on the table. The staple of home life was continuing Richard's studies, particularly in anatomy and physiology. My grandmother taught Catherine piano on their Bösendorfer. After five long years of depression, both small and capital D, Rudolf locked himself in his study and put a bullet through his brain.

Richard discovered the body. Though but twelve, he became the psychological head of the family. He wrote to Germany for help, and Uncle Karl obliged with money, stating that Richard should use it to return the family to Berlin. But Richard knew that if he did, his uncle would quickly take his father's place. He convinced his mother they should try to hold on in America. Doling out Karl's money like a man rationing water to lifeboat passengers, Richard continued his studies alone, using his father's magnificent library. He became driven, his solitary goal to regain the status and fortune his father had lost.

Imagine the scene. A shadowy mansion, empty but for three people. A beautiful boy seated at an oil lamp reading Gray's Anatomy and Aeschylus until his eyes blurred. A senile mother rapping her daughter's fingers with a ruler when she made mistakes at her Beethoven, speaking only German, the boy keeping up his sister's English while the mother slept. Their survival was a miracle. The only food was that which Richard could buy cheaply or steal on the streets, while a city and nation starved outside. Rudolf had taught his son how to manage his hemophilia, how to go to hospitals and clandestinely purchase whole blood, how to give himself transfusions. And the boy did it! He survived! It was within this dark and insular realm that Richard came into his sexual awakening.

Virtually cut off from outside contact, he turned to his younger sister for comfort. Bereaved by the death of her father and by the emotional withdrawal of her mother, Catherine accepted Richard's advances, even welcomed them. All the studies tell us incest skyrockets in situations of overcrowding, isolation, or poverty, but I make no excuses. This relationship was a great gift for Richard. His immense powers of concentration were never diverted by petty romances, nor did he risk genetic union with an inferior partner. My grandmother must have known and understood, because the children lived as lovers under that enormous roof, sleeping in the same bed, exploring the limits of physical and spiritual experience.

Have I shocked you, Erin?

ERIN> I'd be lying if I said no. But I'm fascinated too. I've never heard anything like this before.

MAXWELL> It's like reading about young gods, isn't it?

ERIN> In a way. But I know what's coming. Richard left Catherine, didn't he?

MAXWELL> Did he? When still quite young, Richard passed the examinations required to enter university. Desperately short of money, he wrote again to Uncle Karl. He blamed Jewish thieves and anti-German persecution for the family's failure to appear in Berlin. War was looming again, and Karl immediately forwarded funds sufficient for a sea passage. Of course Richard used the money to enter university. He became an academic star, his tuition paid by scholarship. And since his hemophilia exempted him from the draft, he was able to accept a scholarship to medical school three years later.

During this time, Catherine had begun meeting men outside the family, but no relationships developed. My grandmother discouraged her, saying that this or that suitor could never "measure up to the family standard," which of course meant Richard. For his part, Richard had several outside relationships, with both women and men. But none supplanted Catherine in his heart.

ERIN> I feel sorry for Catherine. She never had a chance to find out what she really wanted.

MAXWELL> She was marked by destiny, Erin. Does that idea make you uncomfortable?

ERIN> Why don't you tell me her destiny first?

MAXWELL> While in medical school, Richard decided for Machiavellian reasons that the time had come to marry, and to marry well. His opportunity arrived in the form of the disgraced daughter of a wealthy professor. I always called her the Gorgon. Pregnant before her first marriage, this woman lost the baby immediately after it, then went through a nasty and public divorce. No longer suitable for men of her own class, she was convinced by her father to give a brilliant medical student a chance. Richard wasted no time. Realizing that his plan would be a shock to his sister, he broke the news gently, stressing his mercenary motives, but to no avail. Catherine was devastated. Over the next two weeks she pleaded madly with him and twice seduced him, telling him that no other woman could ever love or understand him as she did. When he refused to yield, she blurted out that no other woman could ever give him the child she could. Richard ignored her and pushed ahead with his plans.

The day before the wedding, Catherine left the city with all the money Richard had in the world. Worried near to collapse, he told everyone she had gone west to seek relief for fragile lungs. If he had known the truth, he would undoubtedly have followed her. Like a homing bird, Catherine had gone in search of their one blood relative, Uncle Karl. This was during the war, remember. She traveled first to neutral Spain and befriended members of the German émigré community there. With their reluctant assistance, she managed finally to reach Berlin. There, during an air raid, cowering with strangers in the basement of a hospital, she delivered the child she had conceived in America, the child of her brother. It was a son.

That child was me.

In the silence that follows these words, my composure begins to fray. During the last few minutes Brahma has told me more about himself than he told Lenz in a dozen conversations. The fantastic character of his story fills me with wonder, and also dread, but I cannot stop to analyze any of it. Time is draining away like water through my hands.

ERIN> I don't know what to say.

MAXWELL> Now you understand my special knowledge of incest. I have gone as far as I will for now. I believe I have earned the right to your story. Or at least part of it.

ERIN> I'm embarrassed. I don't have a dramatic family saga like yours.

MAXWELL> All family histories are dramatic.

Freud showed us that. In some families the struggle merely occurs beneath the surface, like battles under primeval seas.

Brahma has an answer for everything.

He wants a story. And for days I've planned to tell him one. Only now that the moment is at hand, I am paralyzed. How much truth do I tell? How much fiction? Earlier this week, it seemed to me that deception was mostly a matter of facts, with continuity the key to success. Now I see how foolish I was. Successful lies are not based on fact, but instinct. Emotion. If I tell a story that *I* believe, Brahma must believe too.

Closing my eyes, I fill my mind with images of Erin: a child laughing in the bathtub with Drewe in grainy home movies; a girl smoking cigarettes behind bushes in a Girl Scout uniform; a teenager riding pillion behind a Harley-crazed pothead, her long hair flying in the wind; a high school junior standing naked on a pier; a young woman, glossy-faced in the magazines, moving urgently beneath me in Chicago; a bride draped in white and kissing Patrick at her wedding, eyes open and looking down the row of groomsmen, to where I stand. This is like performing a classic song. You don't just sing and play the notes; you open yourself to the subliminal power of the whole, the fluid biopsy of personality that was somehow captured in the words and music of the original recording. And if you're lucky, for one small slice of time, you become Otis or Muddy or Jimi or Janis or Lennon.

I have done that.

And if I can do that, I can do this.

When I speak, I hear my voice as Erin's hypnotic contralto. The sound soothes my nerves. Using stories told me long ago by Bob Anderson, I begin weaving a history of Drewe and Erin's ancestors, then slowly draw it into a New South tale worthy of Margaret Mitchell. My reason tells me I shouldn't use too much truth, but instinct tells me that straying too far from it will destroy my credibility. The lives I use for thread are like my own, are in fact part of my own, and the tapestry that results will not be pulled apart, not even by Brahma. Yet as my story moves into the recent past, he begins asking questions.

MAXWELL> You do not get along with your sister now?

ERIN> We get along. How can you not get along with the most perfect person in the world?

MAXWELL> Obviously you don't believe that about her.

ERIN> Sometimes I do. She's a doctor now, but everybody knew she'd be an astronaut or something like that even when she was a kid. You'd probably love her.

MAXWELL> I doubt it. I know many female superachievers, and the image rarely reflects the reality beneath.

ERIN> In this case it does. My sister's life could be a movie, only it would be too boring. It's more like a TV commercial.

MAXWELL> Is she attractive?

ERIN> Yes.

MAXWELL> But you are more so.

ERIN> Physically.

MAXWELL> She was jealous of your beauty?

ERIN> If she was, she never showed it. If she'd tried, she could have gotten as much male attention as I did. But while I was cutting class, she was dissecting fetal pigs.

MAXWELL> Did you go to university?

ERIN> No, New York.

MAXWELL> Ah. What did you do there?

I pause. It's time to bend the truth a little.

ERIN> I was a singer.

MAXWELL> What kind of singer? Opera? Broadway?

ERIN> A folksinger. Sort of Joni Mitchell, but with more edge. I changed my name so my family couldn't find me. My father had told me I'd end up turning tricks to eat, but I was signed pretty quickly. I was wined and dined and photographed and flown to Montserrat to cut a CD. Then my A&R guy got fired for signing too many acts that flopped. I think he only signed me because he wanted to sleep with me. Nobody else at the label cared whether I lived or died. My CD was never even mastered. I got depressed, did more coke than Sherlock Holmes and Freud put together, and crashed in less than a year.

MAXWELL> Crashed?

ERIN> Lost my bearings. Did too many drugs, slept with too many men, even started losing my looks. They're back now, thank God. I'm vain enough to appreciate that.

MAXWELL> Vanity may be what saved you. But don't you think it's time we went back a bit further? Perhaps discussed your father a bit more?

ERIN> Why?

MAXWELL> I think you know. It's the oldest story in the world, Erin. Let yourself be rid of the weight.

ERIN> You think my father tried to screw me or something?

MAXWELL> Not necessarily. Most adult-child sex involves oral or manual stimulation, not penetration.

ERIN> My God. You've got it ALL wrong.

MAXWELL> That sounds like denial to me.

ERIN> And you sound like every stupid shrink I ever went to. My problem has nothing to do with my father. It's my sister.

MAXWELL> Your sister? Are you telling me you had a lesbian affair with your sister? That you're haunted by some silly adolescent cunnilingus or suchlike?

ERIN> Or _suchlike_? How old are you really?

MAXWELL> Forty-seven.

ERIN> God. I'm not sure whether we can talk or not. Different cultural vocabularies.

MAXWELL> I transcend generations, Erin.

ERIN> Right. Do you keep yourself in shape?

MAXWELL> Cellini's Perseus is my ideal.

ERIN> I've never seen it, but I get the idea. How close do you come to your ideal?

MAXWELL> Perhaps one day you will judge. Let's return to your sister. What is this thing you try so to avoid telling me?

ERIN> It's her husband.

MAXWELL> You are bedding her husband?

ERIN> _Bedding?_ No. Worse than that. I have a child by him. A son.

In the ensuing silence, I sense Brahma's heightened interest like a leopard raising its head.

MAXWELL> Your sister is still married to him?

ERIN> Yes. She does _not_ know he's the father of my child.

MAXWELL> Ah. Does he know?

ERIN> Yes. I told him three months ago.

MAXWELL> How old is your son?

ERIN> Three.

MAXWELL> How did this happen, Erin?

With a fluidity that surprises me, I give Brahma a condensed history of the relationships between myself, Drewe, and Erin—but from Erin's perspective. The names I change, yet the eternal triangle retains its mythic power. Brahma seems particularly interested in the diametric personalities of Erin and Drewe. When I arrive at the incident in Chicago, he asks:

MAXWELL> What was the sex like between you?

How do I describe sex with myself from Erin's point of view? This may be the obstacle that finally trips me.

ERIN> It was the consummation of years of suppressed desire. In a certain way, it was unique. I'd been disillusioned by men very early. Men see women as saints or whores, and at that time I saw men in similar terms. Bastards or wimps. The bastards I was always attracted to tried to destroy me, and the nice guys _I_ destroyed. That's what's happening to my husband now.

MAXWELL> Which type was your sister's husband?

ERIN> Neither. That was the unique thing. With him I responded like I had with my bastard lovers, but he wasn't one. He was gentle. He was a musician, a songwriter.

MAXWELL> But this is the root of your desire for a man with the soul of a woman. Artists are the bridge between the male and female poles. They are spiritually hermaphroditic.

ERIN> Maybe that's it. Because he took me to a different place than I'd ever been. Sometimes when we made love, I achieved something more than an orgasm. It was a total obliteration of consciousness. The waves would start, and then

suddenly I'd reach this hyperaware plateau, a clear white space like a liquid dream. And then I'd black out. Absolutely. When I woke up, I felt something I never had before. Peace. I felt I'd known what it was to be dead, or at least beyond life. And I _liked_ it, you know? I wanted that peace. Later I found out the French call that "the little death."

MAXWELL> Sex and death are opposite sides of the same coin, Erin. We in the West repress this, but the East has always known it. Death without sex means extinction, sex without death the same. Orgasm is a bridge between the two states, a temporary annihilation of the self, a momentary return to the womb waters, to the mindless timeless flux of nature. It was into this infinite province that he took you.

ERIN> You sound like you know a lot about it.

MAXWELL> Death and life? Yes. I know them well. But you should not long for that annihilation. We all get there too soon. Tell me, why did you not marry this unique lover?

As I describe Erin's marriage of convenience to Patrick, and his promise never to ask about Holly's father, I am forced to look into an abyss I have not allowed myself to think about for the past three months. The dark hole where Dr. Patrick Graham has become unhinged, obsessed by a shadow face that lurks in his dreams like a grinning demon that will never grant him peace.

My face.

MAXWELL> Has your husband ever struck you during these arguments?

ERIN> No. Not that I haven't deserved it. But I'm starting to understand him now. I once thought he could grow to love my child as part of me. But men aren't built that way. In the animal world, males try to kill the offspring of other males. At some primitive level, I think the same thing is happening in my husband's brain. The more he loves my son, the more he hates him.

MAXWELL> Yes. And what is your solution to all this?

ERIN> I haven't got one.

MAXWELL> Of course you do. You simply haven't found the strength to admit it. You don't love your husband, do you?

ERIN> No. He's a good father, though. I picked well in that department, even in desperation.

MAXWELL> Do you love your sister's husband?

ERIN> I don't think so. I don't know.

MAXWELL> If you knew you were going to die tonight, how would you feel about him?

ERIN> I don't know. I'd be angry that he was going to be left with my sister. Be free of me and my son. I guess I must resent his happiness.

MAXWELL> And your sister's.

ERIN> No. I was never jealous of my sister. My parents always loved some Nancy Drew idea of me, but my sister really knew me. And she loved me anyway. She still does.

MAXWELL> So why resent her husband's happiness?

ERIN> Maybe because he's the only man who ever made both of us love him. He got to screw Mary Magdalene and deflower the Virgin Mary too, all without taking any consequences. I mean _I_ certainly had to take consequences.

MAXWELL> You want your sister to know the truth.

ERIN> I don't know. But I'm not sure I can keep the secret regardless. My husband is forcing the issue. What if he leaves me? Should I end up alone with my son while his real father lives an idyllic life with my sister? Is that fair? It makes me crazy! I hate him when I think like that.

MAXWELL> Has he asked you for sex since Chicago?

ERIN> No. But he's still haunted by me. I feel it whenever I'm around him. And now that he knows about our son, he's really going out of his way to see us. God. Everything is going to hell and I have no control over it. My sister wants a baby of her own. My son is like an unexploded bomb lying between our two families. My husband's going crazy, my sister's husband's going crazy, I'm going crazy.

MAXWELL> Calm down. Tell me one thing only. What do you want?

Out of five different impulses, the right answer comes to me like divine revelation.

ERIN> I want out.

MAXWELL> That's simply another way of saying you haven't the courage to try to get what you want, which is your sister's husband.

ERIN> No! I WANT OUT!

MAXWELL> Out of what? Out of your situation? Out of life?

ERIN> It's hard for me to admit this, but I still dream of the magical, mystical man out there somewhere who is what I've always wanted. Like Snow White. Someday my prince will come. Go ahead. Tell me I'm pathetic and unliberated and

everything else. I could care less. That's what I want. I want to be saved.

MAXWELL> Describe your prince for me.

I close my eyes.

Out of the luminescent afterimage of the computer screen, something is moving toward me. It is formless yet threatening, faceless yet drawing into focus. It is not one thing. It's a mass of shadows. An army of ghosts, walking with their eyes shut. Ghosts of all the blind men who used Erin throughout her life. And my ghost walks among them. But behind those pale shadows I see something else. A shining obsidian darkness. And within that darkness floats a single pair of open eyes. Terrible cobalt eyes framed by long lashes, eyes that stare into my soul with phallic intent.

Brahma's eyes.

ERIN> I think my prince is a Dark Prince. He terrifies most women, but not me. He knows the ways of the world, but he's not _of_ the world. Do you know what I mean?

MAXWELL> Go on.

ERIN> He inspires awe in men, yet abases himself before me, as I abase myself before him. He knows that all men who ever touched me were like slaves who tended me until his arrival. He knows that earthly defilement confers a certain kind of purity. He knows I possess immeasurable love, but that the edge of my love is terrible and cold, and he welcomes that. He can make me scream in the night, loose me from everything that holds me to the earth, cause an explosion in my head that dwarfs the orgasm of my body. He loves me so desperately that he wants to kill me, but that is the one act he hasn't the power to

commit. Because at the hot core of his strength, he fears me. THAT'S what I want!
MAXWELL> Be at peace, child. I AM COME.

A drop of stinging sweat falls into my eye. Somewhere on this planet a man sits in the glow of a computer screen, speaking these words to me and fantasizing a future I do not even want to crack the door on. I am miles farther down the road Dr. Lenz tried to walk, and the only way home is forward.

ERIN> I don't know what to say. Your words are powerful. I won't deny that I'm drawn to you. But I know the reality. You're nearly fifty years old, and you're sitting somewhere dreaming about _bedding_ this beautiful young girl you've found online. I don't think you're my savior.
MAXWELL> I am more than savior, Erin. I am a second sun burning above the teeming earth. But even suns need sustenance. They consume themselves, as I have done for so long. I am subject to one god above me, and that god is TIME.
ERIN> You sound like you've gone a little far with this.
MAXWELL> We are come to the fork in the road. To the time of choosing. You must decide whether to remain where you are, dwelling in darkness, or to journey to the place of understanding. Remember that knowledge is a burden. Knowledge has a price.

My mind has finally gone blank.

ERIN> I need a few minutes to think about this. It's a lot to take in at once.
MAXWELL> No.

ERIN> Why not? To be perfectly honest, I need to pee. You've made me nervous.

MAXWELL> Urinate where you sit. It will bring your mortality home to you.

ERIN> I'm perfectly convinced of my mortality, thank you. I'm going to leave this terminal for five minutes. I do want to know about your life. I do believe you're different. You might even be the one. But I have to pee, and I want to compose myself. If you're here when I get back, I'll be glad. If you're not, I'll be sorry.

And with that—with my heart beating like a trip-hammer and my hair soaked with sweat—I log off.

Chapter 33

I spent most of the five-minute rest I gave myself from Brahma in the bathroom, wiping my neck and arms with a steaming washrag and staring at my stunned face in the mirror. Brahma's life story—what I've heard of it—is stranger than anything I ever imagined, and I have a sense that it will only get more so. But is he telling the truth? Am I learning the genesis of a murderer? Or is he merely playing me for a fool, as he did so expertly with Dr. Lenz?

I don't think so. A small voice in my mind is telling me to call Daniel Baxter—or even Lenz himself—but I am not ready to do that. Having brought Brahma to the point that he wants to pour out his twisted past to "Erin," I must push on to the end.

Sitting back down at the computer, I pull on the headset and take a long pull from a fresh Tab. On the screen are the last sentences I spoke: *If you're here when I get back, I'll be glad. If you're not, I'll be sorry.* I decide to make him wait another minute, just to keep the authority on my side. After finishing the Tab, I speak again, and EROS faithfully transcribes.

ERIN> Are you still here, Max?
MAXWELL> Yes.
ERIN> You haven't scared me off yet. Let's go.
MAXWELL> Go?

ERIN> I'm ready to hear the rest of your story.

MAXWELL> But we were discussing you.

ERIN> You told me a secret, I told you one. It's your turn again.

MAXWELL> Such children we are. Very well. Where was I?

ERIN> Incest. Your father married a woman in America for her money and position, while his sister—your mother—ran off to Germany and gave birth to you during the war.

MAXWELL> Skip ahead six years. Richard had achieved his childhood dream. He was a prominent psychiatrist in one of America's greatest cities. His wife had money but he earned plenty of his own. Yet he had one regret. The Gorgon had no intention of inhibiting her social life with the drudgery of rearing a child. So Richard lost himself in his work, and became more renowned and controversial with each passing year. His approach was simple. He encouraged people to accept their natures. He used Freud and Jung and the rest to legitimize so-called "aberrant" behavior. I find a humorous parallel with a maxim of the computer industry: "That's not a bug, it's a feature."

Richard relieved his rather exotic sexual needs away from home in a variety of ways, but he managed to stay clear of both the press and the police. When Catherine appeared on his doorstep (the old family brownstone, now fantastically refurbished) with a six-year-old boy at her side, he was stunned. I was a mirror image of him. Dark-haired, pale-skinned, classically beautiful. Mother explained the similarities with the fiction that I was Richard's "nephew." To explain my fatherless existence, Catherine told a harrowing tale of an impulsive marriage to a young German soldier who was quickly killed on the Russian front, then three terrible years in a displaced persons camp with Uncle Karl. The D.P. camp was real enough. The cold there lodged in my bones like tumors of ice. Catherine also revealed that I suffered from hemophilia, the same type Richard had. This made the Gorgon vaguely suspicious, but since hemophilia is passed down through females only, her suspicions were allayed.

When Richard and Catherine were finally alone, Mother confessed the truth. There was never any German soldier. I was Richard's son, though I did not know it. Half mad from exhaustion, Mother told Richard she'd managed to survive only by vowing to deliver me to him before she died. In her eyes Richard saw the glazed apartness that had lighted his father's eyes shortly before he shot himself.

Sweeping aside the Gorgon's opposition, Richard took us into his home. Tension between the two women grew quickly, and one cold morning Richard found Catherine dead in her bed. She'd taken an overdose of morphine from his medical bag. She lay in state in the house for two days, resting in a bronze coffin, her delicate hands folded across her still breasts like those of a fallen martyr. I did not leave her side except to urinate, and I ate no food at all. Nor did I sleep. When Catherine's body passed into the crematorium, I collapsed and had to be admitted to the hospital.

When Richard announced that he would legally adopt his "nephew," the Gorgon's lack of opposition surprised him. He didn't realize that I—without Catherine—was the answer to the

Gorgon's prayers as well as his own. I freed her forever from the pressure to bear a child. Yet things did not turn out quite as she hoped.

In me, Richard had gained more than a son. For what was I but a genetic reconstitution of himself and his sister? The male and female halves united in one being. I was his father reborn. He educated me in the manner he had enjoyed before the Crash—private tutors focusing on the hard sciences—and I did not disappoint. As I surpassed each new expectation, Richard came to realize that his sister had been right. No other woman could have loved him as she did, or given him such a child. He came to believe that fate was acting through our bloodline to bring about a higher order of humanity. Without even being conscious of it, he began to eulogize Catherine as a saint.

As the years passed, the Gorgon grew more resentful of me. From the beginning she'd had suspicions too deep to put a name to, and one night, after consuming a staggering amount of gin, she stumbled upstairs to Richard's private bedroom and confronted him. She disparaged my mother in a long tirade. She'd done this before, but for some reason, on this night, Richard snapped. He told the Gorgon the truth. At first she misinterpreted, shouting that she'd always known I was a bastard, that Catherine's "dead German soldier" was a lie to hide her whoredom. When she finally comprehended the true state of affairs and began wailing about "that demon child," Richard lifted her off her feet, carried her to the second floor landing, and threw her over the rail to the marble floor below.

I was fourteen then, and I saw it happen. The shouting had drawn me to the head of the stairs.

Richard was terrified, not that I would report him to the police, but that he might have lost me forever by committing murder before my eyes. I remember my reaction to this day. I said, "It's about time you did something about that shrew, Uncle."

Do you think me cold, Erin?

In the silence of the hanging question, I force myself to take no position at all, to draw no moral line that might stop Brahma's flood tide of confession.

ERIN> It's almost like a film. I see it all happening in my mind's eye. Is it real? Really real?

MAXWELL> Absolutely. That night, Richard took me into his study to try to explain what had happened. For once, he found himself at a loss for words. He realized he had reached the point where he must risk all—either gain a son or lose me forever. He told me the truth. He was not my uncle but my father. Uncle AND father. He told me of the forbidden union between himself and his sister, how through that sacral/sexual union an immeasurable strength and talent had been created—me.

We had always felt an intense kinship, partly because we were so similar, but also because of our shared disease. During that hour in the study our bond was consecrated. We vowed to stand together on the matter of the Gorgon's "accidental" death, and from that moment forward shared a conviction that we were beyond moral constraint. I was reborn that night, Erin. Incest and murder were my nativity.

ERIN> You were fourteen when this happened?

MAXWELL> Yes. I had wished this thing to be

real for so long, and suddenly it was. It had never seemed possible that I'd been sired by some anonymous German soldier too stupid or unlucky to survive a war. Of _course_ my father was a renowned psychiatrist. If I was a little too ready to see myself as the Übermensch Richard claimed I was, fate has proved him right. Three years later I entered medical school.

Despite my determination to remain calm, I clench my right fist in triumph. Drewe's theory looks more likely with each passing minute.

ERIN> So you _are_ a doctor. I had a feeling you were.

MAXWELL> Yes. But I do not wish to speak about that.

ERIN> What do you want to say?

MAXWELL> I have a perverse impulse to tell you of my failings. My wounds. My darkest journeys.

ERIN> Why focus on your failings?

MAXWELL> Do you understand the essential difference between man and woman? Woman can simply BE. She gains identity through existence itself, through the biological imperative. She merely waits for completion, as you do. But man must BECOME. He must create himself. He must tear himself away from his mother, sever the umbilical, and project himself into the world BEYOND that wholeness. Man must exile himself from comfort and completion. You see that, don't you?

ERIN> I suppose so.

MAXWELL> It can be a dark journey. I was no normal adolescent, Erin. I saw Elvis Presley as a cartoon Dionysus for bourgeois America. When

the Beatles burst on the scene I ignored them. Too chipper, too happy. But then the world changed. The Rolling Stones, the Doors, Hendrix. I immersed myself in the drug subculture. Richard had always been a libertine, and by profession was an expert on pharmacology. He'd traveled down the hallucinogenic highway before Leary ever heard of LSD. He shepherded me in this, as in all things. I was the right age for Vietnam, but my hemophilia disqualified me from the draft, as it had my father before me. I was wealthy, in an Ivy League school, on the fast track for medicine. But in one area I remained unfulfilled. The area which EROS exists to explore.

ERIN> Sex?

MAXWELL> Yes. We are all slaves to our childhoods, and I was no exception. Because my hemophilia was my only limitation, it grew to terrifying scale in my mind. I strengthened my body through ceaseless swimming, a sport in which the chance of sustaining a bleeding injury was very low. My mention of Cellini's Perseus was no idle comment. It was truly my goal, and through years of swimming I attained it. If you saw me in clothes, you would notice only exquisite proportion. But if you saw me naked, you would understand.

My body attracted women, but whenever matters progressed to an overtly sexual level, I found myself put off by their carnality, by their very vitality. I felt revulsion, fear, nausea, and did not understand why. My father's erotic exploits proved that sex was possible for men like us. I masturbated, albeit carefully, and for two semesters in college I had a male roommate who would suck me to climax whenever I needed relief. He disgusted me, but it accomplished the goal. Still, I feared what might happen in the unguarded thrusting and writhing of real sex.

Then, at a college party, I mistakenly walked into a bedroom where a drunken girl had passed out. As I stared at her closed eyelids, the near-motionless breasts beneath her sweater, I felt my pulse quickening, a twinge of tumescence. I closed the door, moved to her, and pushed my hands clumsily under her sweater as my heart thundered in my chest. Terrified that someone would come in, I groped beneath her clothing for a few moments, soiled my trousers, then fled from the house. It sounds pathetic, doesn't it?

ERIN> I've heard stranger things.

MAXWELL> Naturally I found a way to put myself into a similar situation again, only this time I removed the girl's pants and actually penetrated her. The third time, the chosen girl awakened and I ran. She was unable to identify me, but the experience frightened me enough to make me stop. It also forced me to diagnose my own neurosis. All my life, I had been carrying around a psychosexual template of my dead mother in my head. It was my last vision of her, lying motionless in her coffin, pale and perfect, waiting for the flames of cremation. These women I had touched were but gross reflections of the anima in my mind. Of course, diagnosis and cure are different things. An acrophobe who knows he is afraid of heights cannot suddenly shed his fear. My anima remained with me, and it had faces I had yet to perceive.

ERIN> In four years of college you never once fell in love?

MAXWELL> Love? My mind was in chains! Whenever I thought I was making progress, another incident would occur. In medical school, seven other students and I were paraded into an operating room where an anesthetized young woman was about to be given a hysterectomy. We were to practice vaginal examinations, using her as our patient. This is common practice in teaching hospitals, if your husband hasn't told you. As I stood in line, watching my fellow students force their gloved fingers into the pale, still body, I felt fury at the institutional violation of this defenseless woman. But then I sensed a terrific pressure beneath my lab coat. When my turn came to examine her, my hands were trembling. This was so out of character that the attending physician remarked on it. I bumbled through the exam, then raced into a restroom to relieve my distress. As I did, I visualized the anesthetized woman, the most perfect image I had yet encountered of my mother. I knew then that I was not yet free—that I might never be free—of her.

ERIN> Your father never sensed your problems?

MAXWELL> Of course he did! Richard blamed himself completely! For eulogizing my mother long after her death. For not having the courage to marry the woman he loved. If he had, he knew, he might have given me the gift he'd been granted—a sister with whom I could share all. Worse, by denying me that sister, he had also crippled the powerful gene line that had been concentrated in me. He begged me to turn outward, to search for someone who might fill the need he had not provided for, and give me heirs worthy of our genes.

ERIN> Did you?

MAXWELL> I tried. But I was meant to walk a different path, Erin. Summers during college, I began to travel abroad with my father. I had been to Europe, of course, but never to the East. And the East was Richard's great passion. He was obsessed with the fertility cults of the Indus Valley cities, the bloody rituals of sex and death around which Indian culture had developed. He'd been raised by an authoritarian father, a paragon of the sky cult of Christianity, which of course had been grafted onto the sky cult of Germanic warrior culture. Yet he had seen his father break, and commit suicide under the stress of bad fortune. Richard sought a greater strength. Thus was he drawn to India, the great fount and faithful preserver of the Mother principle.

In India my illusions were stripped away. The strong ruled, the weak served or perished. I found women there who would do anything I wished for pitiful sums. The fact that I would be miles away the next day allowed me to overcome my anxieties and couple with them, but always there was a problem. Indian women are dark of skin and hair. They did not fit my template, ethereal Catherine lying in her martyr's coffin.

Back in America, my sexual problems continued, but they did not interfere with my academic advancement. I was like a man aflame. Even as my genius was proclaimed from the heights, I was hiring prostitutes to lie passive in white gowns while I gently mounted them. I believe I was going slowly mad. Even those whores, who had seen so much depravity, were frightened by something in me. One lost her composure during the act and attacked me, and I had to be hospitalized for clotting factor therapy. Suicidal thoughts possessed me. It was then that Richard intervened. He stuffed me with amphetamines, whisked me off to India, and changed my life forever.

ERIN> What was different about that trip?

MAXWELL> I found someone.

ERIN> A woman?

MAXWELL> Yes.

ERIN> Like your mother?

MAXWELL> No. I found a woman who was death in life. Do you understand? Christianity preaches eternal life through death, but that is a false and exhausted dream. It is on the road of death that we find life eternal.

Here we go, I say silently. *Jesus Christ.*

ERIN> I'm not sure I understand.

MAXWELL> You will. On that final trip to India, we crisscrossed the subcontinent in search of rituals and cults which had been outlawed by the British long before, but which rumor claimed still flourished in remote areas. Richard was no Western dilettante. He had friends all over the country, from the teeming cities to the village-dotted plains. At an isolated tribal village we were allowed to see a young boy dragged through the fields while a crowd of farmers hacked the flesh from his body in strips, which they then buried in their fields to ensure fertility.

From there, we trekked to a high village where a certain Shakti cult was known to practice Tantrism of the Left Hand. Most Indian holy men practice asceticism as the route to what Westerners would call salvation. But Tantrics of the Left Hand Path are adepts. For them, self-denial brings pleasure. Their sacrament requires_breaking_each taboo in ritual fashion. No Westerner had ever witnessed these rites. Yet Richard, with the help of a guru, gained us admittance. At midnight in a cremation ground, eleven couples were seated in a circle. At their center sat a young woman, nude. There was chanting of mantras, then the woman was sprinkled with taboo substances such as meat and alcohol, which were shared by all. Then the remaining women removed their vests, which were placed by the guru in a box. Each man approached the box and selected a vest. His choice of vest determined the woman with whom he would couple during the ritual. As we stared from without the circle, the participants disrobed and began to copulate around us. No taboo of class or law was observed during this rite. If a man chose the vest of his sister, they made love as strangers, honoring the goddess by their rapture. For my father the experience was an epiphany, a validation of his life history. For me it was electrifying, the spiritual antithesis of a Roman orgy. It was holy sex. When the men and women around us finally began to allow themselves the release of orgasm—which we had believed forbidden—I realized that this journey was not like the others. Time was funneling in upon itself, sucking me toward some great reversal.

Encouraged by our successes, we pushed farther into the interior. Our only protection in that hard land was our wits, our money, and the strength in our limbs. My father had a very bad time. Hemophilia deteriorates the joints, and Richard's were failing fast. But like mad white hunters pursuing elephants in search of the mythical ivory graveyard, we trod endless miles of grass and rock in search of the one significant cult of which Richard had found no extant trace. The Thuggee.

The Thugs were a robber caste which had flourished in India for centuries. They earned their livelihood by falling in with groups of travelers on the roads and then strangling them in their sleep. They stole all money and belongings, then expertly concealed the corpses. Nothing remarkable in that, of course. What made the Thuggee unique was that the murders they committed were part of their religion. They worshiped Kali—the goddess of death and destruction—in her many forms. Kali the Black One, the Betrayer, the Difficult of Approach. For them, murder was a sacrament, and the profit gained their rightful due. The British claimed to have wiped out the Thugs by the end of the nineteenth century, but my father believed no cult which had thrived for centuries could be utterly stamped out in one.

He was right. After many weeks of following whispered directions bought too dearly and warnings shouted free of charge, we were admitted to the home of a man who confessed that Kali's cult of murder still existed. After a sleepless night talking to Richard (during which a considerable amount of money changed hands) the man admitted that he himself worshiped Kali and had been trained in the ways of the Thugs. For my father it was the culmination of a life's work. But as he greedily absorbed the most arcane of Eastern secrets, I was striking up a relationship of my own.

The Thug had three daughters. Two chattered endlessly, but the middle daughter was silent. She was dark-skinned, of course, but also unutterably beautiful. She watched me wherever I went, and I watched her. On the third night she came to my pallet. It was the first consensual sex in my life with a woman who was not a whore. I did not have to speak. The first time she lay as motionless as the dead beneath me. The second, she rose above me like a black goddess and chanted words that cleft my mind like a scimitar: "Is Kali, my Divine Mother, of a black complexion? She appears black from a distance, but when intimately known she is no longer so. Bondage and liberation are both of her making. She must always have her way." In that instant this young girl smashed my spiritual chains and brought me to fierce, bursting climax. I was a man transformed.

In the morning I was amazed to learn that this proud girl spoke English, which was rare in the province. She had been taught it as a way to lull travelers into feeling safe. For three nights she initiated me into wonders I had never imagined, or had been sickened by when I did. I saw that all my life had been an obsessive exercise in compensation. I had been born with an incurable disease, cursed with fragility. I'd watched my delicate mother perish for love, then sought a woman equal to her. But the daughter of the Thug was Catherine's antithesis. Cold and hard outside, yet soft and fathomless at her core. I had feared unrestrained sex for so long. In my mind the "yoni"—the opening in the woman—was a crevice through which a man would fall back into the mindless black maw of Nature. The women who had wanted me sought to enslave me, to bear children unworthy of my line. But the daughter of the Thug allayed my fears. She taught me that semen, once ejaculated into the fire of the yoni, could still be arrested and returned. That I would not be dissolved into her but rather purge myself of earthly lust and touch the stars. She was Death rendered tangible in flesh.

On the night before my father and I were to leave, I spoke out at the dinner table. In my best attempt at his dialect, I humbly asked the Thug for his daughter's hand in marriage. He opened his stinking mouth and belly-laughed in my face. I was humiliated, blinded by rage and embarrassment. But of course Richard knew exactly what to do. With a bemused smile he removed a leather case from his robe, laid a thousand British pounds on the table, and told the fat man he wanted the girl for me. The Thug snapped up the money and agreed without demur. At first I did not understand. I thought some exorbitant fee for sex had been arranged. But just as I was about to make a fool of myself, the situation became clear. My father had bought the girl outright. Not for the night, but for life.

ERIN> You mean like a _slave_?

MAXWELL> Exactly. The Thug had sold his daughter for two thousand dollars. I had no idea how she would react to this arrangement, but when we departed the next morning, she fell in behind us with a cotton bag hanging from her hand.

A fortnight later, waiting in the Delhi airport for the first leg of our flight home, my father collapsed. At fifty-five he had already outlived most hemophiliacs of his generation, and the strain of the journey had finally caused a terminal bleeding incident. I married the Thuggee's daughter to gain her U.S. citizenship. At the ceremony I told an Indian magistrate that her name was Kali, and no one objected. Kali I have called her to this day. We watched over Richard as he died, then spread his ashes over the Ganges and took the next plane out of the country.

This is my early life, Erin. The seed of my becoming. My strengths I have passed over in silence. Kali remains with me still, as my concubine. Understanding that I could never bear children by her, she allowed me to sterilize her. In this pure form she has purged the lust from my body, watched over me, held my subconscious at bay while assisting in my life's work.

How do you judge me, Erin?

A dozen loose ends from Miles's recitation of the EROS murder scenes begin clicking into place: the Indian hair; the possibly female bite mark; the postmortem rapes, brutal fallout from Brahma's dead mother fixation; even Mrs. Lenz's death, which must have been carried out by Kali while Brahma led the FBI around McLean with his cellular phone.

MAXWELL> Are you there, Erin?

ERIN> You lied to me, Max.

MAXWELL> How did I lie?

ERIN> You told me you'd never been married. But you married Kali. You're still married to her.

MAXWELL> Only as a convenience! To gain her entrance into the U.S.

ERIN> It's obviously more than that.

MAXWELL> It was the only thing I could do

under the circumstances. Just as you did when you married!

ERIN> I know. Just don't lie anymore, okay?

In the silence that follows, I realize that I have put myself into a position where action is a necessity but options are few. No matter what my gut says, I have no guarantee that the tale of Richard and Kali and the rest is anything but the delusion of a madman. Brahma seems to be wrapped around "Erin's" finger, but what is the value of that? He's already proved that he can evade telephone traces. How can I use our strange relationship to stop him? Try the Lenz gambit? Set up a meeting and inform the FBI so that Hostage Rescue can try to ambush him? It sounds workable, until I factor the debacles in Dallas and McLean into the equation.

Like it or not, I have only one trump card to play, and it was dealt by Miles Turner.

The Trojan Horse.

The 3.5-inch disk that contains it lies just to the right of my keyboard. Inside that black plastic, painstakingly woven into a graphic file that can be decompressed into the stunning photograph of Erin holding the chalice, are a few lines of code that Miles designed to stop Brahma as surely as a stake through the heart. I don't know exactly *how* they can do that, but I don't have to know. In matters digital I trust Miles absolutely.

The risk of sending Brahma that photo of Erin—though theoretically almost nil—inflates a large and corrosive bubble beneath my diaphragm. But my choices are few. And the stakes have been life and death for a long time now.

ERIN> Are you there, Max? Jesus, I didn't realize the time. This is my husband's afternoon off. He could get home any minute. I had a gift for you,

something I thought you'd like. But I guess it will have to wait.

MAXWELL> What is this gift you speak of?

ERIN> A photograph of myself. For you. I told you I'd been looking for someone here. And I wanted to be ready if I found him. And you seem to think I have. What I told you is true. The truly transcendent aspect of my existence is my beauty. I know that. A famous writer once asked me a question he said I wouldn't accept at face value, but one that was born from honest curiosity. The question was, What does it feel like to inhabit such a beautiful body? And the thing I tried to make him understand is that I don't _inhabit_ my body. I AM my body. And I want to give that as a gift to you. As a beginning. I may not be as fair-skinned as your mother, but I know I'm fairer than your Indian girl. _Much_ fairer. Maybe I'm too vain, but right now it seems the only thing I can give you to match what you've given me.

MAXWELL> How can you give this photograph to me?

ERIN> I have it on a disk. In a special kind of file. A JPEG file.

MAXWELL> You know how to encode and transmit a JPEG file?

ERIN> I do now. A friend showed me how. She scanned my photo with a hand scanner. The quality of the image isn't that great, but the photo itself I like. If you want to see it, we've got to do it right now, though, or else wait until at least tomorrow.

MAXWELL> I wish very much to see it. Let me give you my e-mail address.

ERIN> Can't I just send it to Maxwell?

MAXWELL> No. Send it to Q69@nowhere .hel.fi—do you have that?

ERIN> I'm printing my screen. Where's that? It's not an EROS address.

MAXWELL> It's in Finland. I'll get it, though.

ERIN> Well, if you don't, assume that my husband got home. Don't try to contact me. No e-mail or anything. I'll try again the next chance I get.

MAXWELL> Perhaps tonight?

ERIN> I doubt it. What you told me is a lot to absorb. You must know that.

MAXWELL> I have faith in you.

ERIN> Remember one thing, Max. I'm worthy of my Dark Prince. After you've seen my photograph, you'll know that. The next question is, are you worthy of me?

MAXWELL> You still have no idea whom you are talking to. You're like the desert traveler who stooped to touch a glimmer of gold in the sand. When he tried to pick it up, he found it would not move. Only when tons of earth-moving equipment had been hauled in did he realize that he had touched the finger of an enormous golden Buddha buried in the sand. That is what you have done today. You have touched the tip of my finger.

ERIN> Good-bye, Max. Sweet dreams.

Shaking with fatigue and excitement, I log out of the chat room and slide Miles's Trojan Horse disk into the floppy drive. The instructions he left me are simple. First I open the EROS UUEncoder program and convert the .jpg file into a .uue file, which comes out to twenty-one pages of indecipherable text. Then I watch the file-status indicator changing slowly as the .uue file is transmitted to Finland as e-mail: 18% . . . 39% . . . 58% . . . 79% . . . 98% . . . then:

MESSAGE SENT
UPLOAD ADDITIONAL FILES?
Y? N?

I press N and stare at the glowing monitor until the bust of Nefertiti swirls into sight. My hands are still shaking. Standing slowly, I look into the tray of the LaserJet III. A neat stack of paper chronicles every unbelievable word Brahma spoke during the past hour. But does it matter? Very soon he will download Miles's Trojan Horse. As images from his twisted tale tumble through my brain, a voice speaks from a still place inside me. It is Arthur Lenz's voice, echoing the French phrase he uttered prematurely at the safe house in Virginia: *commencement de la fin*.

The beginning of the end.

Maybe now the words are true.

Chapter 34

I am highlighting passages from the Brahma printouts when the high-pitched ring that announces a satellite video linkup with EROS headquarters in New York chimes through the office. On the screen of the EROS computer, Nefertiti's head evaporates, and the face of Jan Krislov materializes in its place. A small window opens near Jan's left ear, giving a running status report of the video link.

"Hello, Harper," Jan says in her cool voice. Her moving lips have the jerky quality of low-speed digital video, but the audio is clear. I pull on the headset mike.

"Hello, Jan."

"Someone wants to speak with you," she says. "Just a moment." She looks away from the camera. "All right, go."

Jan's face remains on my screen, but after a harsh click, a static-ridden voice says, "Harper?"

"I'm here, Miles."

"Did you find the Trojan Horse?"

"I found it."

"Did those goddamn deputies confiscate your computers?"

"No."

"Thank God. Or Daniel Baxter, rather. The locals knew he'd been using EROS to try to trap Brahma, and they didn't want to risk crashing the system by screwing with your end of it."

"What the hell were you doing using a real picture of Erin to mask your Trojan Horse?"

"It was the right thing, Harper. You know it. She's not in any danger. Absolutely nothing we've done leads to the real Erin. She's not even on the map." He pauses. "You used it, didn't you?"

I say nothing.

"Did the cops find the dummy disk I left in the coat?"

"Yes."

He laughs sharply through the static. "Come on. You got him to download Erin's photo, didn't you?"

"Like I had a fucking choice?"

"Yes!" he exults. "I knew you could do it. What happened?"

"Brahma told me his whole life story going back three generations. It was like he'd been holding it in forever. And it's some kind of story."

"Well?"

"He's a doctor, just like Drewe guessed. Third generation, actually. There's way too much to tell, Miles."

"Give me a summary."

Looking down at my highlighted pages, I quickly sketch Brahma's journey from incestuous birth to his marriage to Kali. I quote some of his more chilling passages, but Miles absorbs them all in silence. The only thing that elicits a shocked comment is Brahma's hemophilia.

"Harper, you realize that most hemophiliacs born before 1985 got AIDS from tainted blood transfusions?"

"Brahma's a doctor. Maybe he suspected early that there was a problem with the blood supply and acted preventively. Don't ask me how. I think the disease had a lot to do with shaping his character, though. Hey, what's Cellini's *Perseus*? A painting?"

"A sculpture. The Renaissance version of Arnold Schwarzenegger. Mikhail Baryshnikov with better muscles. He's holding a sword and the severed head of Medusa."

"Severed head . . . wow. Lenz will flip over this guy. Miles, I know there's enough here for Baxter's people to figure out who Brahma is. After I black out some of the stuff I had to say to get him to talk, I'm going to fax copies to Quantico."

"They may not need it."

"What? Why not?"

"I think they may have figured out who Brahma is."

"*What?* How?"

"Maybe the organ donor registries. As soon as the FBI started checking donor networks, they turned up two kidnappings, both from the same registry. It's called DonorNet. One was a long-standing missing persons case that had basically been written off. The victim disappeared about eight months ago in Florida. It was a man."

"A man?"

"Yep. A guy named Peter Levy. The other happened the night after Rosalind May was kidnapped. Virginia Beach, Virginia. Jenny something or other. Drewe hit it right on the head."

"And you think this somehow led Baxter to Brahma?"

"I don't know. I do know that an hour ago Baxter asked Jan to temporarily shut down EROS."

"Did he say why?"

"He *said* it was because the media has picked up on what we've been doing, because of Mrs. Lenz's death. He told Jan that staying online any longer would be counterproductive, even to catch Brahma. The perception of risk to our clients would be too great."

"The *perception* of risk?"

"Baxter's words, not mine."

"But with EROS down . . . and with potential hostages, they'll need my information more than ever."

"Maybe. But I think Baxter told us to shut down because he knows who Brahma is, and he's trying to cover up the Lenz fuckup as thoroughly as he can, however late it might be. He threatened us with an injunction if we didn't go off-line."

"And?"

"Jan decided to comply. The risk of client lawsuits is pretty high at this point. When the FBI wanted us online, we could pass the buck to them. Now that shield is gone."

"Miles, I've got to pass this stuff along. How many hemophiliac doctors can there be?"

"I don't know. Go ahead and pass it on. But even if Baxter has a name on Brahma, catching him could be a whole different thing. Why don't you fax me the printouts of your conversation? Fax them to Jan at EROS. She'll get them to me."

I hesitate. "I will if you'll answer one question. The one you've been avoiding from the beginning."

"What?"

"How did Brahma get into the system? How did he get the master client list?"

A flicker of interest on Jan Krislov's inscrutable face.

"I don't know," Miles says simply. "I may never know. But every account Brahma hijacked is over a year old. He could have done everything he's done so far by breaking into the system a single time over a year ago and downloading the list. And there's just no way to check that now."

"How good was your security a year ago?"

"As good as anybody's."

"Like what? A firewall?"

"Give me a break. That's corporate pacifier stuff. I use traps, filters, alarms, other things."

"Logs?"

"Yes."

"You know what I'm thinking?"

"Yes." Miles's voice is strangely flat. "Brahma got physical access to a company computer, either in the office or in one of our homes, and printed out the list."

"Right. Any break-ins at the office?"

"No."

"Your house? Jan's? The techs'?"

Krislov shakes her head. Miles says, "One of my techs had a burglary seven months ago, but that's too recent."

I'm mulling this over when he adds, "There is one other possibility."

"What?"

"It's a little uncomfortable to talk about."

"People are dying, Miles. Spit it out."

"Can you hear me, Jan?"

Krislov's lips move jerkily, but I hear nothing.

"Okay," Miles says. "You're a widow. You date men of the age we're considering as suspects. It's possible that Brahma could have begun a relationship with you just to get access to your house. Your computer."

Even before he stops speaking, I know he's found the truth. His words seem to hit Krislov with physical force.

"That's got to be it!" I tell him.

"Except," he says quickly, "Jan doesn't exactly date guys off the street. She dates corporate people, architects—"

"Doctors?" I cut in.

The static closes around me like a malevolent embrace. Jan's lips are moving again, her eyes wide in anger or fear as she talks to Miles. It's over a minute before he speaks again.

"You going to fax that stuff through, Harper?"

"One more question. How is your Trojan Horse supposed to work? Can it really nail Brahma by itself?"

"If he uses the EROS UUEncoder-Decoder software, there's no doubt about it."

"So how does it work?"

"Just be patient, okay? I don't want to jinx it."

"Shit. Then *when* is it going to happen?"

"I can't predict that exactly. But it will."

"Damn it, Miles!" I want to push harder, but I know it's useless. "All right. Just keep your head down."

"Harper, wait. Did Brahma's messages show any typos during the time you talked to him?"

"I didn't notice any."

"Not during the entire exchange?"

"No, but I'll check again. You think he's on the move?"

"I just want to be careful."

"He can't trace anything to my house, right?"

"No way. I'm just being paranoid. Even if Baxter hasn't identified Brahma, the Trojan Horse will have sealed his fate by dawn tomorrow."

"Tomorrow! Miles—"

"Tell Drewe thanks for letting me stay there," he says, his voice full of hacker's glee. "And fax your stuff to Jan. Ciao."

The static ends.

I can tell from Krislov's face that she wants to speak to me, but I am not interested. Our professional relationship will very soon be over. I terminate the video link, walk over to my desk, and get the number of Investigative Support at Quantico. My name gets me quickly past the operator, but instead of the person I asked for, I get voice mail.

"Dr. Lenz is on compassionate leave at this time," says a sterile female voice. "His calls are being handled by Dr. Weaver of the Behavioral Sciences Instruction Unit. If you need further assistance, please remain on the line."

When the operator comes back, I tell her I want Daniel Baxter. She says he's unavailable. Two minutes after I tell her it's life-or-death and the EROS case, Baxter comes on the line.

"Cole?" he shouts, like a man in the pit of a mine. *"Talk fast, I'm in a hurry."*

"I heard you're shutting down EROS. Is that right?"

"Yes. Speak up!"

"How do you plan to catch the killer without it?"

"The old-fashioned way."

"What?"

"We know who he is, Cole. Our UNSUB is no longer *UN*."

So Miles was right. "How? I mean, who is he?"

"I can't tell you that."

"Well, I just talked to him."

"You mean the killer?"

"Yes. For over an hour, via EROS. He thought I was a woman. I've got pages of stuff, practically his whole life story."

"I'll be damned. You have any idea where he was when he was talking to you?"

"No. But if he was at home, my guess would be New York, or some other large city that has brownstone houses."

A brief pause. "That's consistent with what we know."

"I really think you should look at this stuff I've got."

"Cole, you've been a big help and a pain in the ass. But the game's over. We're about to arrest the guy."

A charge of excitement races over my skin, but my experience with Brahma tells me such statements are premature. "Let me ask you something, Mr. Baxter. You don't have to answer unless I'm right, okay? Is this man you're arresting a doctor?"

"How did you know that?"

"I know a lot more than that."

"Fax everything you have to Quantico. We may need it

if we have hostages, and we'll definitely use it to build the case against him."

"I'll do that if you tell me one thing. How'd you figure out who the guy is? Was it the organ donor stuff?"

Silence. Then Baxter says, "I knew that had to be you. You and Turner, right?"

"No comment."

"It wasn't that. It was flight records. He flew to all the crime scenes."

"Commercial flights?"

"Private. A Beechcraft Baron. Ever since you linked the murders, we've been checking everything that moved in or out of each murder city near the death dates. We finally found a private plane that had flown into tiny airports near three of the cities."

Baxter pauses so long that I think we've lost our connection. Then he says, "Okay listen, Cole. The plane is owned by a doctor from New York. We've got him under surveillance now. Hostage Rescue is going to arrest him as soon as I land, to eliminate any chance of a barricade situation. Did the UNSUB reveal anything to you that might have bearing on a plan like this?"

A doctor from New York. Miles's home territory. "He's got a woman helping him. An Indian woman. In our conversations he called her Kali, but I can't be sure that's her real name. I'm almost positive she's the real killer."

"Good. What else?"

"Is this doctor a neurosurgeon, Mr. Baxter?"

"No. Why?"

"What kind of doctor is he?"

"He's an anesthetist."

"You mean an anesthesiologist? An anesthetist is just a technician."

"Anesthesiologist, right. He's an M.D."

"Is he married?"

"I can't tell you anything else. This thing's about to explode in the media. I want this guy hog-tied and any hostages freed by the time RBJ open their mouths tonight."

"RBJ?"

"Rather, Brokaw, and Jennings. Gotta go, Cole. Fax your stuff through."

"Wait! Is Dr. Lenz okay? He doesn't seem like the type to take compassionate leave."

"I made it compulsory. His wife's murder put him over the edge. Now that's it. I'll see you at the trial, if there is one."

And he's gone.

If there is one. A sudden memory sends a chill across the back of my neck. I am sitting in the New Orleans police station telling the FBI that I know who the killer is: David M. Strobekker. And I have the strangest feeling that this New York doctor Baxter thinks he's about to arrest or "take out" will turn out to be as dead as Strobekker was. But of course he can't be.

Baxter said they have him under surveillance.

Chapter 35

Blackness explodes into light and pain, a burst of brightness cored with shimmering dark. I spring up from something soft, sure I'm in a nightmare until the light resolves into a figure standing in a doorway with one hand on a light switch.

Drewe.

"Are you okay?" she asks.

I rub my fingers hard through my hair to get the blood flowing. I'm on the den couch again. "I guess I fell asleep. I don't even remember how I got in here."

She smiles tightly and moves down the hall toward the kitchen. Still disoriented, I follow and sit down at the table. Drewe stands at the sink, drinking water from a glass. There's an aspirin bottle on the counter. With a quick movement she puts it back into the cabinet over the sink.

"Headache?"

She nods but doesn't speak.

"Bad day?"

She opens the refrigerator and takes out a diet Dr Pepper. Looking at the drink can, she says, "Is Miles still here?"

"No."

"So he wouldn't tell the FBI anything."

"That's not it. The police showed up right after you left this morning. He barely got away."

She's looking at me now.

"It doesn't matter anyway. The FBI called. They've identified the killer. They've probably arrested him by now."

"Really?" Marginal interest.

"He's a doctor, just like you guessed."

She nods, looks back down at the Dr Pepper can.

"Drewe, what's the matter?"

She shakes her head silently.

"Drewe?"

The sight of my wife bowing her head into her hands to hide tears is something I haven't seen in a very long time. I come to my feet, my stomach churning with anxiety. "What's going on? Did somebody die? Is it your parents?"

She shakes her head violently.

"What then?"

She drops her hands from her wet face and stares at me as though pleading for an explanation. "Patrick beat up Erin."

"What?"

"Patrick hit Erin! Last night. More than once."

"But . . . why? What happened?"

"She won't tell me. I stopped by their house on my way out of Jackson. I saw the bruises the second she answered the door."

I cannot think. White-hot rage blots out all reason. Before I know what I'm doing, I've snatched Drewe's car keys off the counter and started for the hall.

"Where are you going?" she asks, grabbing my arm.

"To rip that son of a bitch a new asshole."

"Harper, don't! That's not the way!"

"It isn't?"

"What would it solve?"

"He won't hit her anymore."

"You don't know that. If I wanted revenge, I'd tell

Daddy what happened and he'd drive to Jackson and blow Patrick's head off. Then where would Erin and Holly be?"

I stop trying to pull free. "Where *is* Holly? Is she okay?"

Drewe drops her arm and retreats back into the U of the kitchen. "Patrick wouldn't hurt Holly. You know that."

"I don't know anything. Where is she?"

"Home, I'm sure."

"Is Patrick there too?"

"I assume he'll go there after he finishes his rounds."

"Drewe, what the hell is going on?"

"I don't *know*. They had an argument last night, the worst yet, but she won't say what it was about. All I know is that Erin believes the beating was her fault."

"Nothing justifies beating your wife."

Drewe meets my eyes with a piercing gaze. "Erin says she deserved it."

How quickly anger can give way to fear. This can only be about one thing.

"Harper," she says quietly. "I think she's having an affair."

I have stopped breathing. My effort to look normal is wasted. Drewe has turned away and begun poking listlessly through the refrigerator, seemingly oblivious to the thunderclap reaction in me.

"Did she tell you that?" I ask.

"No, but it's the only thing that makes sense. We all know how she used to be." A plate of leftover chicken rattles on the counter. "The only thing I can guess is that after three years of trying to be faithful, she found she couldn't. What else could make her feel guilty enough to stay with Patrick after he beat her?"

You don't want to know.

Drewe shakes her head again. "Still . . . Patrick is the

last man I would expect to lose control over something like that."

I nod like a robot.

"Harper . . ."

Jesus.

"I want to ask you something."

I am looking straight into the most vulnerable expression I have ever seen on my wife's face.

"Are you sleeping with Erin?"

The directness of the question almost breaks my composure. For three years I have prayed this suspicion would never be voiced; now it cleaves the air between us like the blade of a guillotine.

"What the hell are you talking about?"

"I'm sorry," she says quickly. "You don't have to deny it."

"You think I *am* having an affair with her? How can you even ask that?"

Drewe's face is pale. "It's the only thing I can see making Patrick mad enough to hit Erin! Once the thought got into my head, I couldn't make it go away. And you and I haven't been making love because of . . . of me getting off the pill."

"Jesus, Drewe! I'm not sleeping with your sister."

"I know she's attractive. Sexually, I mean—"

"Drewe!"

"Don't lie to me, Harper." Her lower lip is quivering. "That's all I ask. Just don't lie."

Just don't lie. How many times have I heard that phrase, and from how many women? Drewe is poised like a teacup on the edge of a table. The slightest touch will shatter her into irrecoverable fragments. When I answer, I enunciate each word, my voice filled with the conviction of an apostle.

"I'm not sleeping with Erin, Drewe. I wouldn't screw

her if she climbed naked into my bed at three in the morning."

Like sunlight burning through fog, belief lights Drewe's eyes. She bows her head again and wipes away new tears. "God, I don't know what I'm saying. I think seeing those bruises just about did me in."

I hesitate, then lean forward and hug her as tightly as I can. "It's going to be all right," I murmur, rocking her gently. "They'll get it straightened out."

"I don't know. Whatever it is, it may have gone too far."

Please, God, no. "You can't do anything about it tonight. Why don't you take a Valium or something from your bag? Just climb under the covers and blank your mind."

"You know I never take sedatives."

"Maybe today rates an exception."

She shakes her head and pulls back enough to look into my eyes. "You know what would make me feel better?"

"What?"

"If you'd sleep with me. Forget about those damned murders and just curl up with me."

I feel about as sleepy as a strung-out addict, but I am not stupid. "That's the best suggestion I've heard in a month. Go on and wash your face. I'll be there in a minute."

"Shouldn't we eat something?"

"I'll make some sandwiches and bring them to the bedroom."

She smiles.

As she walks down the hall, I sag back against the counter. For the first time, calling the police after Karin's death feels like a mistake. Though I see no connection, it seems that my involvement in the hunt for Brahma somehow accelerated the implosion of Erin and Patrick's marriage—to the point that I stand here now in fear that my own will not survive the week.

Just don't lie to me. That line should be added to the Three Biggest Lies in the World. All women say it, but none of them mean it. They *think* they mean it. But what they really mean is that they want there to be nothing for you to have to lie about. More sobering still, this plea forms the rationale for a very dangerous act. Just come clean, says your conscience, confess now, and everything will finally be all right. The way it used to be.

But it won't.

Women are human beings, and it's not human nature to forget any more than it is to forgive. Once the soft circuits of human memory are inflamed with carnal images, they can never be erased. More often they grow and metastasize until they take on more passion than mortal bodies could ever experience, and flay the soul of the betrayed with pain as unbearable as any physical torture.

Of course, keeping back a guilty secret has its own consequences, as I know too well. It is a slow poison, and thorough. Yet it does its work primarily on the betrayer. If one bears up under the strain, almost everything can be salvaged.

My reasoning is simple. Every time in my life I ever confessed anything, no good came of it. The truth was known, hallelujah, and everybody was miserable. The lesson was plain: deny, deny, deny. And two minutes ago, when put to the test I've feared so long, I held true to my belief. I did the best thing for everybody.

So why do I feel like shit?

Drewe and I never finished our sandwiches. We never even started them. When I climbed onto the bed with the plate, she pushed aside the covers and without words pulled me under them with her. She was naked, she quickly made me that way, and for the first time in months I had not the slightest suspicion that her desire had anything to do with her quest to become pregnant.

All I sensed was a desperate flight from everything conscious, a willful narrowing of the external world, a plunge into the only fire that can truly expunge grief and pain.

Drewe was not Drewe. She was a woman who looked like Drewe, yet moved and urged and cried out without any of the baggage Drewe carries through everyday life—duty and self-reproach and second-guessing and obligation to family—only wide green eyes and pale smooth skin and the unruly auburn hair she was born with. All through it, I knew that this intensity so long withheld, this energy repressed, was what I had always been drawn to in her, had believed that I could bring out in time. But I never did. It took the shattering of routine to do it. An eruption of violence and fear into her rigidly defined existence. A shock sufficient to cut her moorings and force her into uncharted water.

And it will not last. For all the power of her latent passion, Drewe is a creature of equilibrium. Even now, her regular breathing fills the room like the sound of an organic clock measuring the half-life of dreams.

I've rested fitfully, in desultory lapses of consciousness that never quite dissolve into sleep. A while ago, I had an absurd dream. I was a young whale thrashing in the shallows near a volcanic beach, kicking and rolling toward deeper water, yet unable to reach the ledge of the great rock shelf and drop into the blue-black haven of peace and forgetfulness. I'm only thankful the air conditioner is holding its own against the night heat.

The ring of the phone stuns me like a klaxon, and I grab for it, hoping to keep it from waking Drewe.

"Cole?"

"Yes. Who's this?"

"Daniel Baxter."

"What is it? You got Brahma?"

"Brahma?"

"The killer. The UNSUB."

"No. We didn't."

I sit up on the edge of the bed, a strange buzzing in the back of my head. Drewe's clock reads two a.m. "You missed him?"

"No, we got the guy we were watching. He was the wrong guy."

"But you said you traced the plane."

"We did. And it was owned by this doctor. Right identification numbers, everything. Only this plane hasn't been off the ground for six months. This guy's a classic doctor. Takes up a new hobby every six months, buys all the best equipment, then gets bored and moves on to the next one. Right now he's into high-tech scuba diving."

"You're sure it's the wrong guy?"

"Absolutely. We nailed him as he was walking up to a house. Turns out he was best man at a wedding inside. His brother's wedding. He had alibis for every single murder. He's also got one of the best lawyers in New York, and he's already said publicly that he'll sue for wrongful arrest."

"I don't get it. What explains the plane?"

"Here's what I think. The UNSUB has his own plane. He wants to use it to get to his killing sites, but he doesn't want it traceable to him. He could try using fake registration number decals, but in real life that kind of stuff never works. So he asks around, and eventually he finds a guy who has the same model plane he does, but doesn't fly much. Like a doctor. Then he finds an out-of-the-way airstrip to house his plane. The first time he takes it there, it's already painted with the numbers of this doctor's plane. Not only that, he's dummied up a license in the doctor's name as well. See? Once the original scene is played, he doesn't have to fake anything. Whenever he goes to that strip, he's Doctor So-and-So, not himself. You there, Cole?"

Fully awake now, I speak softly so as not to wake Drewe. "I can see that working. But can't you just search airports until you find another Beechcraft with those numbers? Or trace every sale of that model for the past twenty years?"

"We're trying now. I'm calling because my people say you never faxed us the printouts of your sessions with the killer."

I feel a wave of confusion like the one I felt when Drewe startled me awake in the living room. "Jesus, I'm sorry. When you told me you practically had the guy, it just knocked out all the tension of the past week. I crashed."

"I know how you feel. But I need everything you have. Right now."

Glancing back at Drewe, I memorize the fax number Baxter reads off. "If the stuff he told me is true, you might have enough to ID him just from the printouts."

"I hope so. One other thing, Cole."

"What?"

"Where's Miles Turner?"

I sigh angrily. "I don't know and I'm tired of being asked."

"Don't make it worse on yourself. You hid him out. You aided and abetted."

"You're right. I aided and abetted a friend who has nothing to do with these murders. He was trying to solve the goddamn things for you, and he still may do it."

"What does that mean? What's he doing?"

"Whatever it is, it's over my head."

"Is he the one who came up with the tissue donor network angle?"

Actually that was my wife, I think, looking at Drewe bundled under the covers. But I'm not about to put her on the FBI's agenda. "Yes," I say evenly. "Anything else?"

"Not for now. Just fax that stuff through."

"You'll get it. What about EROS? You going to leave it shut down?"

"We're discussing that right now."

"I'm out of it now, Mr. Baxter. Just remember that."

As lightly as I can, I get up from the bed and go to my office. It's still a wreck. I remove the Brahma printouts from the bottom drawer of my filing cabinet, where I'd hidden them in case Drewe broke her own rule and entered the office. Walking to the fax machine, I notice that I forgot to edit out the details of Erin's liaison with "her sister's husband." Baxter may not recognize the truth behind that story, but eventually someone in the Unit will put it together, even without Lenz's help. With a black Magic Marker, I blot out the lines that contain my personal revelations, then gather up the mess and begin loading pages into the fax machine.

It takes a while to feed them all through, long enough to develop a cramp in my back from bending over the machine. When I'm done, I realize I promised to fax copies to Miles as well. I stretch my back and repeat the process. As the last group of pages starts to go through, my office telephone rings. Normally I'd let the machine get it, but it's late enough now that the possible callers are pretty limited.

"It me," says Miles when I pick up the cordless.

"You safe?"

"Going with the flow."

"What's up?"

"The Trojan Horse didn't work." He says this as though his best friend just died.

"Design flaw?"

"Hell no. A timing thing."

"What do you mean?"

"Can't tell you."

"I'm hanging up now."

"Wait a minute—"

"Cut the bullshit, then."

"Your phone could be tapped, man."

"I no longer care. The FBI missed Brahma, by the way. They arrested the wrong guy."

Miles hesitates. "I'm aware."

I say nothing.

"You never faxed me the Brahma stuff," he says.

"I just put it through to EROS. Now tell me about the Trojan Horse."

After a long silence, he begins to speak in the Mister Rogers tone he uses to explain technical matters to people like me. "The code I wrote is hidden in the compressed data of Erin's JPEG photo, right? When Brahma downloaded the JPEG to his computer, he pulled the horse into his city. When he tried to view it, Erin's photo went up onto the screen just fine. But right before it did, my program slipped away and made a nest in another part of his computer. Once every twenty-four hours—at one-thirty a.m.—that program will wake up and use Brahma's EROS interface to dial my EROS mailbox. Once the connection is made, it'll download a copy of whatever it finds on Brahma's hard drive. And I'd be very surprised if his name wasn't in there somewhere."

I feel a sudden rush of hope. "That's actually possible?"

"Unless Brahma got suspicious of the single black line in the image and detected the hidden code, it's going to happen. The only question is how soon."

"How obvious is this black line?"

"It's practically invisible. I fixed it so it's hidden by the dark stone at the bottom of the photo."

I'm marching around the office with the cordless. "You're a genius, man! You're going to get him!"

"We'll see," Miles says with uncharacteristic modesty.

"How did you come up with one-thirty a.m.?"

"Analyzed Brahma's recent traffic patterns. That was one of his least active times."

"Does his computer have to be on for this to work?"

"Yes."

"If he's at his computer when it happens, will he see it?"

"No. If there's another program running, the Trojan Horse won't activate."

"But if his computer's off, it can't activate?"

"Right. But I figure he leaves all his computers on, just like me and anybody else who knows anything about computers. Unless it's a notebook."

"So tonight he was working at his computer at one-thirty?"

"Bet on it."

"Damn. You're going to crack this thing. You're going to—" I stop in the center of the room, staring at the EROS computer screen.

"Harper?"

"I've got e-mail. EROS mail."

"Who from?"

I walk to the computer and click the mouse on the e-mail icon. "It's Brahma. He's using 'Maxwell.' I thought EROS was shut down."

"What's the time stamp on the message?"

"Thirty minutes ago."

"Damn!"

"How can he be in the system if it's shut down?"

"Shut down doesn't mean switched off. It just means the servers are closed to subscribers. They're still running."

"So he's in the system?"

"He obviously got an e-mail message through. I'll start checking. What does the message say?"

I read it aloud into the phone: "Erin, I know you told me not to send e-mail, but I had to. I cannot express what I feel at this moment. I received the photograph, and it was astounding. Everything you said was true. I stored the image in a program that allows me to view it from any angle, to modify it as I wish, even create a moving montage. Yet every modification, every turn or inversion, is a desecration of the original. I can only imagine what it must be to behold you in three dimensions. Reflect on all I told you. Imagine what I withheld. Be assured that I am your deliverance. Your Dark Prince."

"That's it!" Miles yells. "We've got him going and coming, and he has no idea."

"Maybe," I allow, strangely sobered by Brahma's reappearance in my life. "What about the master client list? Did Jan remember dating anybody who seemed suspicious?"

"She's been out with a couple of doctors, but they're not likely candidates. She's hired private investigators to check them out, though. How are you going to answer Brahma's message?"

"I'm not."

He sighs unhappily. "Any typos in the message?"

"No. It's pretty short, though. Why do you keep asking me that?"

"If he's using voice-rec, he's back at his home base. And I think that's New York."

"Why?"

"The false airplane registration, for one thing. The way that was set up."

"How do you know about that?"

He ignores the question. "Brahma had to know about this anesthesiologist to pick his plane for a front. Other things point to New York, though. I also happen to like the idea. Know what I mean?"

I make an affirmative noise, not wanting to state the obvious. If Miles is glad Brahma's home base is New York, it's not because innocent women are unlikely to die in the next couple of days but because Miles has managed to get back there himself. And if his Trojan Horse works as planned tomorrow night, he can be there for the endgame. I am about to ring off when he speaks again, unable to resist letting me know how deeply this hunt has worked itself into his blood.

"You know what English fox hunters used to say, don't you?"

"Enlighten me."

"In at the death."

I grunt neutrally. "Just remember something. Brahma's no fox."

He laughs. "And I'm no Englishman. Ciao."

After putting down the phone, I save Brahma's message, then sit down on the bed. It's a mistake. In seconds I am lying on my back, half conscious and fading fast. As sleep washes over me, I see red-coated men riding horses through misty fields of dying cotton, their horses' legs thrashing and crackling through the dried brown stalks. Far out in front dogs howl madly as the horses close the gap and then gather in a ring around a tiny hole in a grass-covered hill. Someone lights a bundle of straw, then sets it by the hole while the dogs guard the back entrance to the den. The men on horses swig Scotch and congratulate each other, saying, *In at the death, old man. In at the death.* Then someone says they've made a mistake, the den is empty, and the dogs tear off across the fields again and I sit there on my horse like the others, drinking Scotch with the sun on my back, watching a shadow grow longer and broader on the ground in front of us. I want to turn around to see what is making that shadow, but I can't seem to move. I can hear, though. And what I hear is a wild black animal voice making human sounds for the first time, mangling the simple syllables, trying again and again until they become distinct and form the sound their maker intended.

Laughter.

Chapter 36

Cotton picking began this morning. Not the full harvest, but scattered bands of men and machines controlled by farmers who got fed up with staring at stunted cotton that would grow no more before the drought finally broke and soaking rain flooded the scorched fields and a money-eating rot set in. Men who felt like fools for gambling against God by putting out growth regulators at the wrong times and who finally just said fuck it and called their hands and fired up the four-row pickers to try to salvage what they could.

From my front porch I watch gunmetal clouds gathering over my neighbors' fields. They hover with mocking heaviness, unmoved by wind or by the drone of the mechanical pickers. Drewe left early this morning for her clinic in Yazoo City. I've passed most of the day walking from room to room, avoiding my office. No one has called, few cars have passed on the road, and despite the slow dusty progress of the pickers, the whole world seems to be waiting.

The ring of my office phone is almost a welcome sound. I trot through the front door and veer left, expecting Daniel Baxter's voice from the machine, or Miles's, but I hear neither. It's Drewe, and she sounds shaken.

"I'm here!" I say, picking up.

"Harper, I need you to drive to Jackson right now."

"What? What's wrong?"

"I'm afraid Erin might hurt herself."

"*What*? She threatened to kill herself?"

"No, she told me everything was fine."

"Then what—?"

"Everything is *not* fine. We know that. But she told me she'd found a way to solve all her problems. She said it might be painful for everyone for a while, but in the end it would be for the best."

I feel like my body temperature is plummeting.

"I want you to go right now."

"Wouldn't she rather see you?" I ask.

"She doesn't want me there. I'd go anyway, but I've got a difficult delivery on my hands. It could be a while."

"Drewe, I'm the last person Erin wants butting into her problems. She doesn't even like me."

"Harper, please. Erin respects you more than any man she knows."

"You've got to be kidding."

"Then why did she tell me that? Now get your butt over to Jackson and talk her out of doing anything stupid. Get her out of there if you have to."

"And take her where?"

"Bring her to our house. Do whatever you have to do."

"And if she won't come?"

"Figure something out. *Please* get going."

"I'm on my way."

"Call me if it gets crazy, and I'll find someone to handle this delivery."

If it gets crazy? I set down the phone and glance around the office for my keys. This situation is long past crazy, and I have a feeling it's going to get worse.

Erin and Patrick live in the Belhaven district of Jackson. Most people at their income level long ago moved out to the enclaves of Ridgeland and Madison, but Patrick took advantage of white flight to trade up to palatial quarters for a bourgeois price. I managed to make the whole hour-and-twenty-minute drive from Rain without thinking. I popped in Joni Mitchell's *Hejira* and turned it up to the pain threshold, following Jaco Pastorius's fretless bass as it wound through the spaces between Larry Carlton's guitar and the soaring vocal. But now I'm here.

The front door of the house has one of those burled finishes you'd expect to find at a Victorian men's club. I hammer the big brass knocker and wait, listening to the blows reverberate over the slate and hardwood floors inside. At least a minute passes before I hear heels clacking. There's a rustle at the curtained windows to one side of the door, then stillness again.

I try the handle, then push open the door.

Erin stands just inside, looking at me with preternatural calm. Her facial bruises are yellow at the edges, setting them off from the tanned skin that might otherwise have masked the damage. The orbit of her left eye is a continuous contusion, like an indigo map of an island. Flecks of blood dot the corner of the eye itself. A closed fist delivered that blow.

She's wearing a linen sundress, the color of lilac. It lies as smoothly against her upper body as a silk camisole, billows slightly at her waist. Another bruise marks her left breast where it disappears into the dress. Her hair is tied up, with a dark spray falling around the back of her neck. She wears no shoes, earrings, or wristwatch. No wedding ring.

"Come in," she says, turning away and walking through the entrance hall. "We're in the TV room."

"Is Patrick here?"

The back of her head turns once from side to side.

As she moves deeper into the house, I fear that Drewe

may be right about the danger here. The air conditioner is not running, which on this day is evidence enough of mental instability. Ahead of me, Erin walks with the grace she always possessed, yet her fluidity seems oddly exaggerated. The dimness and heat increase with each step I take. I have a disturbing vision of myself following an Egyptian girl into a tomb.

What do I sense here?

Resolve. Some decision has been taken. A choice has been made in cold deliberation, and the weight of it is tangible. As Erin steps out of the dark hallway and into a blue glow, fear suffuses me. Not for myself, but for what I might find at the end of this brief journey. *Where is Holly?* screams my brain. I quicken my steps, hurrying after Erin, hoping to prevent any madness that might remain unconsummated.

Then I see Holly. She's propped on thick pillows in front of Patrick's treasured fifty-two-inch television. Her back is to me, and she doesn't seem to be moving. I don't see Erin at first; then my eyes pick her out of the shadows, seated in a cushioned chair against the wall to my left, her long bare legs stretched across an ottoman. I move quickly to Holly and lean over her. Her eyes are barely open. I stare with frantic intensity at the little belly beneath the "Precious Cargo" T-shirt, watching for the rise and fall of respiration.

She is breathing. With relief cascading through me, I swoop her up from the floor as though she were weightless.

"You're going to wake her up," Erin says.

I lay Holly's head on my left shoulder and begin rocking her gently as I walk around the room.

"Put her down," Erin insists. "It's nap time. She'll be comatose by the time Ursula the Sea Witch shows up."

I turn toward the TV and see the comforting yellow

splash that is Flounder, then the orange hair of Ariel, the Little Mermaid. "What's going on, Erin?"

"What do you mean?"

"Turn on the lights."

"They'll wake up Holly."

"I don't care."

"You're not her mother."

"I—"

"You're not that either," she snaps. "Except in the genetic sense. You're the sperm donor. What are you doing here anyway?"

"Drewe called me. She's worried about you."

Erin gets to her feet and moves toward me. "Give her to me. She's already asleep."

"First tell me nothing crazy is going on here. That Holly's okay."

"What?" Her voice drops to a threatening whisper. "*You—give—me—my—child.* This *instant!*"

Reluctantly, I release the little body that is flesh of my flesh yet resides under another man's roof, under another man's protection. Erin leaves the room with her.

When she returns, she is alone. She clicks on the overhead light, stretches out on the chair and ottoman, and studies me as if I am some nonhuman creature of trifling interest.

"Now," she says. "What are you doing here?"

I grope for words that will not sound pompous, but find none. Talk about a fool's errand. Content to let me suffer in silence, Erin says nothing. Who are we? I wonder. Two people who three years ago thrashed around a bed in Chicago for three days and somehow produced the beautiful child who now stands unknowing in the eye of a gathering emotional hurricane?

One thing is certain: whatever we shared is finally gone. A few nights ago, when Erin sat down on my bed and began crying, I felt a response, a pulling toward her.

Even through her despair, I sensed desire, a possibility of consummation, however mad it would have been. But today there is nothing. If a landscape of her emotions could somehow be superimposed upon this room, we would be sitting in a blasted gray ruin, devoid of vegetation and fast running out of water.

"It's probably good that you're here," she says finally. "It'll make things simpler."

"How?"

"Patrick and I have been having some discussions."

"Violent ones."

"That's completely irrelevant and all my fault."

"I doubt that."

"Don't."

"Has my name come up during these . . . discussions?"

A faint smile touches her lips. "God, you're so predictable. All you're worried about is yourself. Or maybe Drewe's precious illusions being shattered. Right? That's all anybody ever worries about."

"I'm worried about you too. And Holly."

"Spare me, okay? You're here because Drewe told you to come, and you couldn't get out of it without telling her the truth about us. Right?"

She doesn't wait for verification. "Let me put your mind at rest. Your worst fear is right on target. The problems between Patrick and me are about Holly's father, nothing else."

I'm not sure what is happening to my face, but it must be funny in an awful sort of way, because Erin is laughing at me. "You'd better sit down," she advises.

I back gingerly to a sofa and drop onto it.

"It's all going to come out," she says in a matter-of-fact voice.

I peer across the shadowed room at her face, a study in self-possession. "Why is that?"

"Because it has to. We were stupid to ever think it

wouldn't." She makes a steeple of her long fingers and studies me over it. "You're terrified that Drewe can't take the truth, aren't you?"

"You think she can?"

Erin suddenly begins speaking in Drewe's voice, quoting lines I'm sure Drewe has never spoken. " 'Erin screwed every good-looking guy in school, but dear sweet Harper was above it.' That's what she thinks, isn't it?"

"She knows I'm not above that."

"Oh, you diddled some cheerleaders. But that's not the same, is it? After all, Princess Drewe wasn't putting out, was she? But to come to me, that's another thing."

"I didn't come to you, Erin. You came to me. And it was ten years after high school."

"In her eyes that's *worse*, stupid. You weren't a horny little seventeen-year-old then. You were supposed to be committed to her. You were supposed to have judgment."

"I think Drewe may know us better than we think. I doubt the attraction between us was as secret as we always thought. I think maybe she's knows we're not above it, but she hopes we wouldn't do it."

"But we did, didn't we?"

I say nothing.

She shakes her head. "You still think about it, don't you?"

"What? Chicago?"

"I know you, Harper. You tell yourself you'd sell your soul never to have done it. You lie awake at night, sweating, promising the dark that if only something would make it all unhappen, you'd never do anything like that again. And five minutes after that you're standing in the bathroom making yourself come, thinking about how it felt to be inside me. How it felt to have supermodel Erin sucking your precious weenie."

"Erin—"

I gape as she hikes the lilac sundress up to her hips with a fierce flourish. "Well? There it is. That's what it's all about for you, isn't it?"

She is wearing sky blue panties, but they are sheer, and the black tangle beneath them is obvious. In spite of everything, my eyes lock there with three million years of evolutionary focus. Then the lilac veil falls and she is up on her feet with her hands in the air.

"That's all men ever think about with me!" she cries, turning away in anger. "Because I'm not the girl you marry, am I? My past is just too much. Except for someone like Patrick. Sweet, hardworking, rich, impotent Patrick."

My mouth falls open again.

"Oh, we're way past spats in the kitchen," she says, turning back. "When his obsession hit critical mass, Patrick's plumbing stopped functioning. In the last two months we've made love twice. If you could call it that. Both times he came home drunk at midnight, climbed on top of me, and started flailing away before I could even wake up. If I hadn't known what was making him crazy, I would have hit him in the head with the telephone. But you know what I did? I told him I loved him and begged for more. And as soon as I did that, it was over. He couldn't finish. He doesn't have meanness like that in him." She leans back and touches her bruised eye, and I realize she is on the verge of tears. "And you know what?"

"What?"

"He deserves better than me."

"That's not true, Erin."

"Better than what I've been giving him, then. I was a fool to make him promise never to ask who the father was." She laughs. "I actually thought he was Dr. Pretorius."

She's lost me. "Who's that? Somebody from New York?"

"No, stupid. Dr. Pretorius was Cary Grant."

"What?"

"It's a movie. I thought you knew every movie ever made. Cary Grant plays this wonderful doctor who marries a woman who's pregnant by another man. And it all works out."

"Oh."

"I was actually dumb enough to think a Cary Grant movie could come true. But men aren't wired that way. They can't handle something like that, and I should have known it. God knows I know everything else about them."

"Erin—"

"Oh, don't stop me now. Maybe I *did* know that about men. But I made Patrick promise not to ask anyway. You know why? To protect Drewe. I didn't want Drewe's illusions shattered any more than you did. And I knew if Patrick found out about you and me—about Holly—Drewe would eventually find out everything. In the heat of some family argument, it would explode."

"That's where we are anyway, isn't it?" I point out. "Except you're the one who's about to explode."

She shakes her head slowly, and I sense sadness flowing into the place where her anger had seethed. In a voice stripped of all hostility she says, "Do you believe in sin, Harper?"

At last I understand her strange intensity. She has finally flipped out. She is born again, saved, or whatever they call the manic grasping at straws that occurs when people who've damaged their lives beyond all repair hurl themselves into lunacy in the quest for one more chance, for that mythical clean slate.

"I know you're not religious," she says calmly. "I'm not talking about that. I'm talking about a sin against yourself. Against people you love. People who trust you. Do you understand what I mean?"

I don't know what to say. When Erin speaks again, her voice is so soft I hear it as a shout.

"What *do* you believe in, Harper?"

Out of the mouth of a distraught woman comes the question I have tried to answer since I started thinking for myself. A question Brahma asked me only yesterday. And I am no closer to an answer now than I was when I was thirteen years old.

"I guess I believe in . . . honor. Keeping faith. Trying to do the right thing. And consequences if you don't."

"If you believe in that, you believe in sin."

"Erin . . ."

"And that we have an obligation to try to make things right. Don't you?"

"Not the way you're talking about. You're talking about more pain." Too anxious to sit any longer, I get to my feet and shake the tingles out of my arms and legs. "You know what I really believe in? Goddamn it, it's only now that I see it. I believe in Drewe. In her optimism, her trust. Her faith in happy endings, that happiness is even possible. I know there's nothing out there but an abyss, but *she doesn't.* Or she's convinced herself she doesn't. Either way, it doesn't matter. My point is that if happiness is possible, it's going to be made by people like her. People with the strength to hold on to their illusions in the face of all evidence to the contrary. In the face of nothing."

Erin watches me in silence for a long time. "I understand what you're saying. Some illusions are necessary. But the reality sleeping on the Piglet blanket back in my bedroom can't be ignored or suppressed or anything else. Holly may be a symbol of weakness, something we'd like to shield Drewe from, but she is also real. And to have a life, the life she deserves, she needs both her parents. And I don't mean you. I'm sorry, but that's the way it is."

"So what do you want to do?"

"Not want. I'm going to tell Patrick the truth about how Holly was conceived. Tonight."

Jesus God.

"And you're going to tell Drewe."

I am numb. I try to tell myself this is not happening, but the fact that my brain is trying to shut down my peripheral nervous system confirms that it is. Blood is rushing from my extremities to my core organs as surely as if I were being chased by a man with a machete.

"Harper?"

As I stare at Erin's bruised angelic face—her eyes burning with misplaced conviction—several thoughts crystallize at the speed of light. She means what she says about telling Patrick. She means to make me confess to Drewe. Words will not stop her.

But one thing could.

She is speaking again, but I hear only the blood in my ears. A roaring blast like a divine voice: *She's the one who put you in this situation . . . who showed up on your doorstep and stepped naked into your shower. She could have told you she was pregnant before you married Drewe. She could have prevented ALL of this.* I feel sweat in my palms, an electrical tensing in the muscles of my arms. Forced to choose which woman is more important to me, I have chosen. With dreamlike slowness I take two steps toward Erin, then another. Her eyes widen in puzzlement as she speaks. I outweigh her by close to a hundred pounds—

"—but Holly would never be the same, would she?"

I feel as though someone just slapped me.

"Are you listening to me, Harper?"

I nod dully, look down at my closed fists. It was Holly's name that broke my trance. Not the fact that Drewe knows I am here, or that I would almost certainly be caught if I hurt Erin. Holly's name. There are not two women in this insane emotional equation, but three.

"I'm listening," I murmur, dimly aware that I've dodged some point of no return.

"Did you take something today?" Erin asks, staring suspiciously at my eyes. "Are you wired or what?"

I laugh hollowly. "Hell no. You're the drug addict."

"I resent that."

"I'm sorry."

"Are you going to tell her or not?"

"Erin—"

"Because if you don't, I'll have to."

"I'll tell her, goddamn it!"

She is no more shocked by my shout than a ghetto kid by gunshots. In a taut voice I add, "I just hope you realize what could happen because of all this."

She laughs softly and turns away. "I know better than anyone. I think about it day and night. You and I could lose everything we love. But don't you see, Harper? It's also the only way we can truly *have* the things we love."

"They're not things, Erin. They're people."

She says nothing.

"Nothing's going to change your mind?"

She shakes her head and turns back to me, her eyes wide and earnest. "This is the right thing, Harper."

I give her a brief hiss of scorn.

"Do you remember Chicago?" she asks.

"According to you, I do."

Two spots of color touch her cheeks. "I remember. Do you remember the strange thing that happened? What you did for me that no one ever had?"

She steps to within two feet of me and rests a sun-browned hand on her flat abdomen. I swallow and clear my throat. "You mean the passing out?"

She nods. "You remember we talked about it? How it

was like a little death? A momentary union with whatever is beyond life?"

"Yes."

"We had it backwards, Harper. That wasn't death at all. That was *life*. The purest distillation of it, the love we felt for each other. I know what the little death is now. It's the way we've been living. Hiding our secret, pretending things are fine, every day having to pile one more lie on top of all the others to keep the house of cards from falling on top of us. *That's* death. Dying a little each day. Don't you feel that?"

I cannot quite grasp the fact that this is Erin speaking. There is absolute certainty in her voice, her eyes, in the set of her perfect mouth and the angle of her chin.

"I guess there's nothing else to say," I sigh with resignation.

She steps back and smooths her sundress. "Yes, there is. One thing. As insane as it is, I'm glad you're Holly's father. You're a good man, Harper. But Patrick is too, and he's my husband. He's Holly's father now. And he's losing his mind. I have a duty to do right by him."

"By forcing me to destroy my wife?"

"Drewe is stronger than you think. She's stronger than any of us."

"I hope you're right."

With proprietary boldness Erin crosses the space between us and raises a hand to my left cheek. Her fingers linger there a moment, cool and dry in the heat of the house. They transmit the sensuality she has always embodied, and something more.

"We probably won't see each other for a long time," she says, her eyes wide and unblinking.

"Erin—"

She rises on tiptoe and silences me with a soft kiss on the lips, then turns and walks from the room. My face burns from her touch. As I make my way out of the house, it hits me with humbling sadness that this grown-up girl, once known merely for having the Best-looking Ass in the State of Mississippi, has much more than that. She is a woman now, and she has more courage than I.

The ride back to Rain takes half again as long as the ride to Jackson did. I play no music; I don't even run the air conditioner. I just drive with the windows down and let the hot wind tear through my hair like the fingers of a grave robber.

I never actually thought it would come to this. Incredible as it seems, I somehow convinced myself that the Fates had been on vacation during the nights I rolled around that bed with Erin, or at least that they'd been watching someone else. Perhaps my vanity convinced me that the good things I'd done in my life had somehow built up a credit account from which karmic bills could be subtracted without my making any out-of-pocket payments. But I was wrong. The due date has arrived, and the bank doesn't want an installment, but the balance paid in full.

For a moment I wonder if Miles is still free and safe, but I don't spend more than a few seconds on him. The events of the last few days now seem remote, like some tragic newscast watched years ago. A thousand thoughts spin through my brain, and each has but one object: Drewe. Will she be home when I get there? No. I'll have at least an hour to prepare, maybe longer if the delivery is a really bad one. But what's the point of preparation? If she were there when I got home, I could blurt out the truth in the first thirty seconds, before doubt and fear turned me into a gutless jellyfish.

Swinging around the final turn toward our house, I see no surveillance cars. I guess Baxter isn't as concerned with me as he used to be. But as I slow for the driveway, I spy a boxy Ford parked under the shade of our weeping willow. Baby-shit brown with a tall antenna. For an instant I think *FBI.* Then I see the Mississippi tag. I reach down and touch the butt of my .38 where it protrudes from under the seat. For all I know, Brahma could be sitting in that car.

I turn slowly into the drive, coast forward, and stop practically grille to grille with the Ford. There are two men inside. As I stare, its front doors open and both men get out. The driver is a big red-faced man in his late thirties, stuffed like a sausage into his polyester suit. The other man is older and darker. Something about him seems familiar. Then he smiles crookedly at me, and I recognize Detective Michael Mayeux of the New Orleans police.

"Harper Cole?" says the red-faced stranger, moving toward me with alarming speed.

"Yes?"

"I'm Detective Jim Overstreet of the Jackson Police Department. You're under arrest for obstruction of justice and harboring a federal fugitive."

While I stare at Mayeux in shock, Overstreet cuffs my hands in front of me and pulls me to the side of the brown car.

"You have the right to remain silent. Anything you say can and will be used against you. . . ."

Mayeux refuses to look at me as he climbs back into the passenger seat. One of Overstreet's big hands cups the crown of my head and pushes me down into the back.

". . . Do you understand these rights as they have been explained to you?"

"Wait a minute! What the hell's going on here?"

Overstreet leans down so that his sunburned face fills the window. "Do you understand the rights I just read you, *ass*hole?"

Looking to Mayeux for help, all I see is the darkly freckled back of his neck through scarred wire mesh.

"I understand."

Overstreet slams the door.

Chapter 37

I feel the passage of time like lifeblood draining away. Mayeux acts like I'm not even in the backseat. He and Overstreet make small talk now and again, but not about me. My being locked in the back of this car means only one thing: a power shift has occurred between the FBI and the police. I want information, but I don't have the stamina to keep banging away at Mayeux's sphinx act. I keep seeing Erin sitting in her dark house, waiting for Patrick to get home so she can finally blast away his obsessive suspicions with one terrible life-size truth.

How long before these idiots let me use a phone? Can I just pay my bail and go? No. Bail has to be set before it can be paid. That means an arraignment. Can I get one this late in the afternoon? Do they have night court in Jackson? The thought that I might have to spend the night in a cell waiting to go before a judge makes me light-headed. What if I don't get home tonight? Will Drewe call Erin looking for me? Will Erin think I broke under the stress and just took off? Would she really take it upon herself to tell Drewe the truth?

"Can I please ask you a question?" I ask Mayeux for the tenth time.

In a mush-mouth drawl dripping irony, Detective Overstreet says, "Sounds like he might be developing the proper attitude, Mike."

"What's on your mind?" asks Mayeux, still facing forward.

"If you don't tell me what you want, I can't give it to you."

"Told you he was smart," says Mayeux.

Overstreet chuckles.

"That's how he got so rich," Mayeux goes on. "Everything's a business deal with this guy."

I remain silent, and the resulting vacuum lasts a couple of miles.

"Left a few messages on your machine," Mayeux says finally. "You never called back."

"I know. I'm sorry. Look, things were really crazy then. You know what was going on. Besides, your messages didn't sound that urgent."

"Didn't sound urgent enough for him," Mayeux says, exaggerating his Cajun accent.

"Urgent," echoes Overstreet, like a redneck Ed McMahon.

Mayeux laughs. "Things feel pretty urgent now, though?"

I take a deep breath and try to keep my voice steady. "I'll tell you whatever you want to know. You don't have to do this."

"I don't? Okay, let's see. Where's Miles Turner?"

"I don't know."

"See?" Mayeux says to Overstreet. "I had a feeling it was going to be this way."

"Jesus, Detective, this is a really bad time for me. I've got to take care of something important."

"Bad time," Overstreet says. "Shoulda called his secretary."

"I don't *have* a fucking secretary!"

The silence that follows this outburst is more threatening than any words. Overstreet clearly does not like his arrestees using profanity. As the Ford thunders eastward along the two-lane blacktop, I lean back and let my eyes rove across the endless fields. Here and there, red or green cotton pickers trundle through the white ocean like great metal insects. The steely clouds I saw this morning have not been scattered like all the rest in this parched summer. They have gathered steadily, like a ghostly Confederate army amassing itself from the tattered remnants of a thousand skirmishes, a fluid gray mass slowly being reinforced from unknown regions.

"Let's try again," suggests Mayeux. "Where's Miles Turner?"

"I can't tell you what I don't know."

"You'll have plenty of time to remember in your cell."

"This is crazy, Detective."

He nods at the windshield. "I've been thinking that for several days now."

Another image of Erin flashes through my mind. She faces Drewe across a brightly lit room, both women screaming, both in tears. To hell with Mayeux and his head games. It's time to pull out the stops. "Detective Overstreet?"

The Mississippi cop grunts behind the wheel. "Yeah?"

"I get a phone call, right?"

"Eventually."

"Well, for your sake it better be sooner than later. Because I don't think the person I'm going to call is going to like a Louisiana cop coming up here and arresting the son-in-law of one of his asshole buddies."

Very slowly, like a hog looking around for the source of a mildly interesting noise, Overstreet heaves himself around in his seat. His forearm looks as thick as my thigh. "Who you think you gon' call, boy?"

I try not to look past him to see whether we're going off the road. "The governor of the State of Mississippi. The first time you let me near a telephone."

His face does not change. He's heard a thousand threats like this.

"He's bullshitting you," says Mayeux.

"Take the wheel," says Overstreet.

Mayeux obeys.

"Now, boy. Whose son-in-law you say you were?"

"I didn't say."

"Well, say, goddamn it."

"Bob Anderson."

Overstreet stares without blinking, a long measuring gaze. Calling the governor to save my ass in the name of my father-in-law is the last thing I would ever do, but he doesn't know that.

"You know this guy Anderson?" asks Mayeux, his voice edgy.

"Bob Anderson from Yazoo City?" asks Overstreet, his eyes boring into mine.

"That's him."

"Shit."

"What does that mean?" asks Mayeux, trying to hold the car on beam and watch me at the same time. "Huh?"

Overstreet blows air from distended cheeks and takes his time about answering. "It means you might have talked me into biting off a big piece of trouble, Mike."

Mayeux groans furiously. "What the fuck are you saying? You saying some people are above the law up here?"

"No." Overstreet lifts his forearm and lets his weight slide him back into position behind the steering wheel. "But some people's tails you don't step on unless you absolutely have to. And don't tell me it's any different down in New Orleans, 'cause I know it's *worse*."

"Shit," curses Mayeux, slamming the dash with an open hand. "Shit! I'm sick of people protecting this son of a bitch. He *is* obstructing justice. I can prove it."

"He's obstructing it in Louisiana, not here."

"It's a federal case! He harbored a federal fugitive in

Mississippi. You're holding Cole for the FBI. *Your chief okayed the arrest!*"

Overstreet's voice sounds even more somnolent than before. "Most of that's bullshit and you know it, Mike. I'm out of my jurisdiction and you don't even want the Bureau to know we've got this guy."

"Are these state or federal charges against me?" I ask.

"Shut the fuck up," snaps Mayeux. "I'll take full responsibility, Jim. You're not suggesting we let him go, are you?"

"No. But the minute we hit the station, I'm telling the chief how things stand. If he wants to let Cole walk, he's gone."

The remainder of the ride passes in frosty silence. I wish they'd let the windows down, so I could sniff the air for the rain smell. Rain wouldn't do the cotton any good now, but after months of drought my need for water is almost physical, like the dull headache I get after going too long without caffeine.

As we pull into Jackson, I ponder a backup plan. If the chief won't kick me loose on the basis of my relationship to Bob Anderson, I know three or four friends from college who practice criminal law here, plus at least thirty more who do corporate work. There are probably more Ole Miss lawyers in Jackson than there are cops. I've got money in a couple of banks here, so bail shouldn't be a problem. The problem is time.

Suddenly a string of letters flickers before my eyes, and I hear them as if read aloud by a chilling digital voice: *I am subject to one god above me, and that god is TIME.*

Brahma knows whereof he speaks.

Thirty-six minutes after Mayeux and Overstreet walked me into Jackson police headquarters, I was released on my own recognizance with an assurance that no arrest would be recorded against my name. I guess my father-in-law wasn't exaggerating when he said he had connections. God only knows what ties Bob Anderson has to the people who run this state, but right now I don't care. The oft-maligned old-boy network seems pretty wonderful when you're sitting chained in a police station. Of course, that system only works if you have access to it, but I'll worry over the moral implications when I get time. Like maybe next year.

Right now I have one overwhelming need: transportation. Inside the station I was thinking of making some kind of deal with Mayeux for a ride back home, but he stomped out right after the chief told Overstreet to cut me loose. Now my only options are to hit up a friend for a car or take a cab to the airport and rent one. My hand is on the sticky receiver of a parking lot pay phone when a blaring horn forces me to cover my ears. The driver keeps jabbing it, and I look around angrily, searching for the source of the deep-throated honk.

It's Mayeux. He's parked about thirty feet away in a vintage blue Cadillac, waving for me to come over.

"Stuck?" he calls genially, as if the past two hours never transpired.

"I'll get back."

"I could give you a ride."

"Like hell," I say, but I'm tempted. Riding with Mayeux would save me some embarrassing calls. Plus, he could ignore the speed limit all the way if he wanted to.

"Why did you pull this crap?" I ask him, walking toward the Cadillac. "Why didn't you just talk to me when I got home?"

His smile disappears. "Because the FBI has fucked up this investigation from the get-go. Today was the first chance I had to get at you without having to go through them, and I was sick of your evasions. I knew you'd hold back whatever you wanted in your own house. I figured a police station would loosen you up a little. I just didn't count on you having that much juice. The fucking governor. Jesus."

"Look, I really need to get home fast. I'll go with you—and talk to you—on one condition."

"What's that?"

"You floor this bastard all the way."

Mayeux grins and cranks the Caddy. "You waitin' on me, you walkin' backwards, *cher.* Jump in."

He pops a magnetized blue flasher on the roof and switches it on before we even reach the city limits. "Something going down?" he asks, cutting his eyes at me. "That why you're in a hurry?"

"I don't know." The sky to the west, toward the Delta, is nearly black with piled cloud. I have a foreboding sense of things spinning out of control, like battlefield blindness, where you know only what is happening where you stand but are dimly aware that great wheels of action are whirling in the fog around you. "Just a bad feeling," I tell him, trying to push it all away.

"Hey, I been there. Something I might need to know about?"

"It's personal."

He nods gamely. Mayeux isn't happy, but he can deal with it. Maybe his drive up from New Orleans won't turn out to be a waste after all.

"Bad weather," he says, raising a forefinger off the wheel to point ahead. Heat lightning splashes through the sky, giving the cloudscape the massive scale of an Ansel Adams photograph.

I ask him why he thinks the FBI messed up the investigation.

"Baxter and Lenz kept us from sweating you in New Orleans. We'd have played the whole thing different. Woulda been better for you and better for us. And maybe we'd have that son of a bitch by now instead of the FBI running around embarrassing themselves and everybody else by arresting the wrong fuckin' guy."

I doubt this, but I don't say so.

"I gotta tell you, for a while I was wondering if it wasn't Lenz himself doing those ladies. I mean, classic case, you know? Shrink does the murders for his own kinky reasons, then takes the starring role in the hunt for himself." Mayeux laughs. "Serial killers love that kind of shit. Making fools out of cops, staying involved in the crimes long after they're done. This guy sure hit the doctor where it hurts, didn't he?"

"Lenz is smart, Detective. He just lost sight of the danger. I knew a lot of guys like him in Chicago. Trading futures. One day they were bulletproof, the next somebody was padlocking their houses and seizing their bank accounts."

After a couple of beats, Mayeux says in a confiding tone, "I play a little in the market myself. Nickel-and-dime stuff. Never tried commodities, but I'm open to it. Got any tips for an honest cop?"

"You sound like Columbo. The Cajun Columbo."

He pulls a sour face.

"Buy mutual funds and blue chips and forget them. Anything else is a losing game for you."

"Why?"

"Because you can't beat the market from where you are. You haven't got the money or the time."

He nods sagely, but he'll drop a few thousand on some half-baked brother-in-law tip before six months are up.

"What about Turner?" he asks. "That boy's got alibi problems."

"I know. But he's not the killer." I pause. "I wasn't sure at first, but I know now."

He cuts his eyes at me again. "Okay. But look, is he queer or what? It ain't like I care or anything, but it'd clear up my thinking, you know?"

I wonder where Mayeux is getting his information. "I don't know if he is or isn't. And I don't care. I think he's trying to protect a married lover by keeping quiet about his whereabouts on the nights of the murders. Whether that lover is a man or a woman is anybody's guess."

Mercifully Mayeux speaks no more. I watch the dark sky and wonder if Drewe is on the road home yet. She's probably done with the delivery by now, but you can never tell with babies.

I jump in my seat the first time thunder shakes the car. This is no empty threat, booming hollow over the fields and dying into nothing. It rattles my eardrums, buffets the reservoir of dead air at the bottom of my lungs, hammers the car like a bass drum in a gymnasium. Mayeux feels it too. He's from New Orleans, where rain is a constant companion, but even he hunches in his seat when a big blast rocks the car. Otherwise, he remains silent, eating up the miles with a determined stare. Perhaps some of my apprehension has seeped into him.

Suddenly there is wind against the car where there was none before. It whines at the seam of the windshield, hisses at the windows. Then the rain is upon us. Big round drops splatter on the glass like pellets from a sawed-off shotgun; then a hail of water engulfs us like enfiladed musket fire.

"Shit!" Mayeux curses, slowing the Cadillac to forty-five.

"Try to keep your speed up," I urge him.

"Hey, I'm trying."

I tap my fingers nervously against the dashboard.

"This Delta's some fuckin' flat," he grumbles, leaning forward and squinting into the rain. "A minute ago I was gonna say it was like the Atchafalaya Swamp without the water, but I guess we got the water now. One of God's little jokes, yeah."

The Caddy crawls through the downpour, Mayeux

struggling to keep his eyes on the faded white line that marks the right margin of the highway. "What kind of shoulder we got?" he asks.

"Flat dirt. About fifteen feet. But if you go into a cotton field, we won't be getting out until somebody comes with a winch."

"Great. How much farther we got?"

"We're about four miles out."

"Hey, you see that?"

Something in Mayeux's voice brings me erect in my seat. "What?"

"Blue lights. Way off there, to the left."

"Where?"

"Look!" he says, pointing. "That's a blue bar making that. Mississippi Highway Patrol. Guy must be pretty gung-ho to stop speeders in this rain."

I narrow my eyes to slits and probe the gray wall for blue light. There. A sapphire halo pulsing far to the left. As I stare, a terrible premonition tightens my gut.

"Fire?" I ask, praying for a yes.

"Wrong color. That's police lights. Lots of 'em. Looks like Mississippi Highway Patrol, or some local sheriff's department. Where you think that is?"

"I think it's my house, Mike. Punch it."

"Hey, I'm pushing now."

"Floor this motherfucker!"

The sudden acceleration presses me back into my seat. Mayeux flicks on his blue flasher, and we hurtle through the wall of rain like teenage lovers with a death wish. Even with Mayeux tempting fate, I grip the Caddy's padded armrest and will the car to go faster. The sapphire glow quickly blossoms into a flashing ball, like a miniature mushroom cloud. What the hell could have happened? Part of me knows the answer, but I fight that knowledge with all my soul, unwilling to believe that Brahma has somehow penetrated Miles's digital shield, that I have exposed Drewe to the white-hot flame of his insanity. We blast through Rain proper like a blue monorail, leaving a howling vacuum for a wake.

"Slow down! Half a mile to the turn!"

Mayeux touches the brake gently, then begins pumping it as the riot of flashing blue and red differentiates into distinct images. Squad cars, sheriff's cruisers, rescue and highway patrol vehicles. They surround our farmhouse like a motorized posse. Mayeux turns into the drive and pulls as far forward as he can. I'm out of the car and sprinting through the rain before he even shifts into park.

"Wait up, Cole!"

I run for the porch, dodging between cars, stunned by the amount of light pouring from our house. Two blue-white flashes suddenly blank out my office windows.

"Stop!" someone shouts.

A knot of uniformed men blocks the front door. I charge them without pausing, triggering a metallic flurry of gun slides and hammers.

"FREEZE!"

"This is my house!" I shout, throwing up my arms in the face of a half dozen pistol barrels. "Where's my wife?"

"FREEZE, ASSHOLE!"

I finally stop in an ankle-deep puddle at the foot of the porch steps, barely able to contain my panic.

"Anybody know this guy?" asks a Mississippi state trooper with rain sluicing off his hat brim.

"He's okay!" shouts Mayeux from behind. The detective skids to a stop beside me with his wallet open. "Mike Mayeux, New Orleans homicide. This guy owns the house. What's going on?"

"One-eighty-seven," says the trooper. "A double."

"Who got it?"

"Is that a murder?" I shout. "Get out of my fucking way!"

The cops start to restrain me, but Mayeux manages to get in front and by some combination of civility and intimidation clear a path through them.

"Drewe!" I scream wildly. *"Drewe, where are you?"*

Nothing.

Another group of cops blocks the door of my office.

"Harper?" A female voice.

I careen up the hall, leaving Mayeux behind.

"Harper? Is that you?"

Drewe whirls from the kitchen sink, dwarfed by uniformed men at both shoulders. Her white blouse is covered with blood, her eyes blanker than I've ever seen them. I run to her and grab her by the arms, hearing the uniforms say my name but ignoring them, searching her body for wounds, feeling the reassuring tightness of her biceps.

"Are you hurt?"

She shakes her head violently. "No. But I couldn't . . . couldn't do anything."

"What happened?" I ask, touching her bloody blouse.

"It won't come out," she says, her chest heaving.

"Drewe! What happened?"

Suddenly her face crumples, as if the supporting structures beneath have simply melted away. "Erin's dead," she whispers.

I blink. "No. I just left her at . . ." The words die in my throat as one of the men beside her nods.

"S-somebody," she stutters. "Horrible . . . I was too late . . . couldn't do anything."

An image of Patrick Graham flashes in my brain.

"Mr. Cole," says one of the uniforms, whom I finally recognize as Sheriff Buckner from Yazoo City. "We need to get your wife calmed down. She gave a statement already, but she can't seem to stop shaking and she won't let the paramedics near her."

"Where have you been?" Drewe asks suddenly. "Harper, did you go see her like I asked you?"

"Yes! She was fine when I left her. The police arrested me afterward! They took me back to Jackson!"

As Drewe shakes her head, new panic seizes my heart. "Where's Holly? Nothing happened to Holly!"

"Mama's," she murmurs. "Erin dropped her off at Mama's."

"Dropped her off? How do you know?"

"First thing I thought of . . . called. I didn't tell her about Erin, though. I couldn't do it. I couldn't!"

I pull her to my chest and wrap my arms around her.

"What exactly went down here?" asks an authoritative voice from behind me. "Detective Mike Mayeux, New Orleans homicide."

"We're not sure, mister," growls Sheriff Buckner. "Got two dead women in an office room up front."

"Erin died *here*?" I gasp, trying to mesh my memory of our confrontation in Jackson with what Buckner is saying.

"Where did you think she died?" he asks.

"I saw her in Jackson this afternoon. I just assumed—"

He stares at me with unveiled suspicion. Then he turns to Mayeux and says, "One deceased is Mrs. Cole's sister. The other's a Jane Doe. Foreigner, by the look of her."

A wave of unreasoning fear shunts through me. "What kind of foreigner?"

"Who knows? Real dark woman. Asian, maybe. Indian. They all look the same, don't they?"

The information is coming too fast for me to absorb it. One thought dominates my mind: *Get Drewe out of here.* "Are you finished with my wife, Sheriff?"

"For the moment," he says slowly.

"I want to take her into our bedroom, get her away from all this."

"Fine. But I want you to take a look at that foreign woman. You might recognize her."

"Right now?"

"Next few minutes, anyhow. Before they load her out."

"Who else knows about this?"

"I put in a call to the Memphis hotel where Dr. Anderson's staying, but he was out. I left a message for him to call here, or my office if he can't reach here."

The mention of Bob Anderson hits me like a belly punch. "Who else?"

"As of now, nobody. Your wife said not to tell anybody. But this is a real small town, son. You know that. You or your wife better call Margaret Anderson before she hears it from somebody else. There's a husband too, right? In Jackson?"

"I'll take care of that."

"They been having any marital problems?"

Drewe suddenly goes stiff, as if the possibility of Patrick being the killer has just occurred to her. I squeeze her reassuringly. "He's not a killer, Sheriff. Please give me a few minutes with my wife. Then I'll answer all your questions."

I push past Mayeux and a couple of strangers and shepherd Drewe into our bedroom. Turning on only the bathroom light, I sit her gently on the bed and kneel before her in the shadows. Her eyes are unfocused. I have never seen anything affect her like this. In our family, Drewe is famous for nerves of steel. Now she's a rag doll.

"Drewe? Honey?"

No response.

I have a thousand questions, but none can be asked without forcing her to relive whatever horror she just endured. "Can you hear me, Drewe?"

Her face remains impassive. Taking advantage of her near catatonia, I quickly strip off the bloodstained blouse and toss it into a corner. She doesn't resist. I lay her back on the bed and remove her shoes and khakis, then pull a crocheted comforter off a rocker and drape it carefully over her.

"Erin!" she cries suddenly.

Instantly Buckner is inside the bedroom, gun in hand. I wave him out angrily. "I'm right here," I tell her, laying my hand on her cold forehead. "It's Harper. Everything's okay. I'm going to take care of everything."

After about a minute, I rise and pad into the bathroom to scan the contents of her medicine cabinet.

Nothing.

Opening the hall door a crack, I catch Mayeux's eye as he talks with Buckner in the hall. He moves quickly to me.

"There should be a black medical bag somewhere," I tell him. "My wife uses it to stitch up local kids, stuff like that. Check the hall closet."

"It's evidence," he replies. "She apparently tried to resuscitate her sister."

Christ, I think, shutting out another bloody rush of images. "Just get me the bag, Mike. All I need is one bottle and a syringe."

His eyes narrow. "What you gonna do? You ain't no doctor, are you?"

"My father was. Look, I've done everything from shooting X-rays to stitching people up. Just get me the bag!"

Mayeux speaks quietly to Buckner, who looks at me, then nods. Satisfied, I go back into the bedroom and kneel beside Drewe. She is still shivering beneath the comforter, her eyes wide and glassy.

"It's okay," I whisper. "I'm here. It's okay. Don't

think . . . don't think. I'm going to make everything all right. Just get warm . . . warm."

A crack of light falls across the bed.

"Here you go," whispers Mayeux.

I quickly scan the contents of the bag and select a vial of Vistaril and a 2.5-cc syringe. I hate to shoot her, but I doubt I could make Drewe swallow pills, and pills might not even dent the psychological trauma she's sustained.

Mayeux watches as I load 2 cc's of Vistaril into the syringe, invert it, thump the barrel, and nudge the plunger to evacuate the air bubbles. If Drewe were fully aware, she would never allow this, but she doesn't even flinch when I slip the needle into the muscle of her arm and empty the contents of the syringe. The crack of light disappears from the bed.

With Drewe held tight in my arms, I murmur incessantly. Half of what I say makes no sense. It's the same maternal mantra I've heard Erin use when she's trying to put Holly to sleep. Constant reassurance, the tone more important than the words, an orally generated security blanket that lulls the senses almost as effectively as narcotics.

At last she is under, her breathing deep and sonorous. Tucking the comforter under her bare feet, I move to the door and step quickly outside. Buckner and Mayeux are waiting.

"You ready?" asks the sheriff.

This is my first good look at Buckner. He's a big, stolid man of fifty, who wears a white shirt and brown tie to set him apart from his deputies. By reputation he is tough and honest, though not necessarily smart.

"I want you to put someone by this door," I tell him. "In case my wife wakes up."

He snaps his fingers and a deputy scrambles into the hall. It's Billy, who manned the stakeout at the highway curve last week. He listens to Buckner, then takes up his post before the bedroom door like a guard at Buckingham Palace.

"Real sorry, Harp," he says. "I'll holler if she wakes up."

"Let's get this over with," Buckner says, watching me closely.

I follow him up the hall with Mayeux at my heels. The sheriff pauses before my office door and turns to me. I hear the voices of men on the porch. Someone laughs, then cuts it off.

"Ever see anything like this before?" Buckner asks.

"I worked in an emergency room one summer."

"Good."

"How bad is it?"

Mayeux takes my arm from behind, squeezes it, and says, "Hang tough, *cher.* It ain't good."

And Sheriff Buckner opens the door to hell.

Chapter 38

The instant Buckner opened the door I saw blood. You couldn't enter the room without walking through it. Not unless you used a window, which I saw evidence technicians doing. From the doorway to about five feet into the room the floor was a sticky puddle, with five or six pairs of shoeprints tracked through it.

"Your wife's," Buckner said, pointing to the smallest prints. "Couple of deputies and fire department people walked through here, trying to see whether anything could be done, but they were too late."

There was more blood deeper in the office, splashed high on the walls, but before I could focus on it I saw the "foreign" woman Buckner had talked about. She was lying on her side about six feet inside the door, facing away from me. A zippered black body bag lay unrolled at her feet. A gleaming sword blade protruded from her back. Walking forward, I saw that it had been stuck through her abdomen. With horror I recognized the brass hilt of the Civil War sword that usually hung on my wall beside my far window. The dead woman wore a yellow sari, but one of her arms was exposed. It had been slashed several times, to the bone.

"What happened?" I said.

"You know her?" asked Buckner.

Kali's face was beautiful even in death. A perfect oval, with strong planes and sculpted ridges covered by nutmeg skin. Her eyes were open, the sclera like old ivory framing fixed onyx irises. There were lines in the skin at the corners of her eyes and lips, some wrinkles gathered at her throat, but few other signs of age. As I studied her face, I noticed something small and bright against the skin just below the jawline. I started to crouch and look, then realized that I was looking at the feathers of a tranquilizer dart.

"Well?" grunted Buckner.

"I've never seen her before in my life."

"Ever talk to her on EROS?" asked Mayeux.

"How would I know that?"

"Take a look at the rest," said Buckner.

"You don't have to," Mayeux said. "Your wife ID'd the other body."

I moved forward anyway, propelled by something deeper than thought. The center of the room was a circus of small red footprints, as though a dance had been held for bleeding women. The walls and everything hanging on them were spattered with blood. Flung drops on a framed print. A large splash near the baseboard. A fine spray across the faces of two guitars.

"Where is she?"

"Behind the headboard of the bed," Buckner said.

I took the required steps and stopped near the head of my twin bed. There, propped low against the wall, sat Erin's nude body. If her eyes had been open, I probably could not have stood to look, so heavily did the responsibility for her death crash down upon me in that moment. Her dark hair hung mercifully over her breasts, but her legs were splayed grotesquely apart, as though she were a mannequin laid out for an anatomy lesson. I wanted to shout at Buckner to cover up her nakedness, but something caught my attention and held it with paralyzing power.

Cut into Erin's tanned abdomen, just above her pubic

hair, was a vertical incision about three inches long. There was very little blood, just enough to define the wound. "Is that what killed her?"

"No," said Buckner from just behind me. "She's got a big knife wound in her back, above her kidneys. Probably hit the heart. See the blood?"

Then I did see. Erin was propped in a black pool of blood. I hadn't noticed because the headboard made a shadow there. As I stared, one question filled my mind. "Does she have any head wounds?"

"No," Mayeux answered. "I checked."

I looked back at him. Both of us were asking the same silent question. *Why not?*

"We found the murder weapon," said Buckner. "Under the bed. It's some kind of curved dagger. Looks like a movie prop."

For the Thugs, murder was a holy sacrament. . . . I gazed around the room, looking at the overturned furniture and scattered papers and drying blood, trying to fathom what had happened, what could possibly have brought Erin here so soon after our confrontation at her house.

"Best we can figure," Buckner said, "is one or more persons surprised your sister-in-law here in the house. She may have been in this room, she may not. Maybe she fled here. Your telephone lines were cut. . . ."

Maybe she fled here—

". . . got a deputy out back fixing them up for you. He's handy with that stuff. Take it easy, Detective, he's saving the cut ends for the crime lab boys. Anyway, I'd say Mrs. Graham did something very unexpected in here. She snatched that sword off the wall—that is your sword, right?"

"Yes."

"And she defended her life as best she could. She did a pretty good job of it, too. She hit that foreign woman at least five times on the arms, then ran her through like a pig on a spit. Of course by doing that she lost her weapon. At that point, I figure a second assailant got her."

"What makes you think there was another person here?"

"Footprints. We found a pair of size-nine Reeboks that didn't match the shoes of anybody working the scene."

Brahma wears Reeboks? "Oh."

"Found the actual shoes right in the middle of the floor. The perp obviously knew we could track him that way, so he walked through the puddle at the door, then tossed the shoes back in. He's running barefoot now. That's tough going in fields and woods, especially at night."

"How do you know he didn't take a pair of shoes from my closet and put them on in the hall?"

Buckner stared blankly at me for a moment. Then anger clouded his eyes. "Would you know if a pair was missing?"

"Let me look."

One glance into the closet told me a pair of Nikes were gone. "Air Jordans. White with blue trim."

"Shit," Buckner muttered, writing on a pad he produced from his khaki shirt pocket. "What size?"

"Twelve."

"Well, that should slow him down a little."

Feeling a strangely protective urge, I moved back toward Erin's body.

"Your buddy Turner wear a nine?" Buckner asked sharply.

"I don't know what size he wears. But bigger than a nine. He's skinny, but he's well over six feet. Probably a twelve."

"What I can't figure," said Buckner, "is why one of the perps didn't just shoot Mrs. Graham."

"They shot her with the dart gun," Mayeux said. "In the shoulder," he added, looking at me.

"I meant a real gun."

"Maybe they didn't have one."

Buckner shook his head. "That's a pretty risky way to break into a house. Especially in Mississippi."

"I told you they're not from Mississippi," Mayeux said.

Buckner gave him a scowl.

I said, "You do know this guy has been using a private plane to get to the crime scenes? And there's an old crop dusting strip about two miles west of this house."

"Deputies already found it," Buckner said. "Tracks in the mud. Somebody used it tonight."

"Mud? How long has it been raining here?"

"Sixty to eighty minutes. That plane probably took off less than an hour ago."

Good God, I thought, realizing how close Drewe had come to dying with her sister.

"Something else," said Buckner. "One of my men thinks the killer might have been wounded. Based on the amount of blood and the spatter patterns. Makes sense to me, with knives and swords flailing around."

"He might be a hemophiliac."

Buckner's eyes came alive like a bird dog's. "A what?"

"A bleeder. He might be a bleeder."

"How in hell would you know that?"

I thought of telling Buckner the truth, but that would probably put me in a jail cell. "Something I overheard an FBI agent say in Washington."

"I knew them sonsabitches was holding out on us!" Buckner said furiously. "I'm gonna burn some federal ass over this." His right cheek twitched. "So maybe this asshole's hurt bad enough to crash his plane?"

"Harper," Mayeux said gently. "I can't understand why

this dark woman caught a tranquilizer dart like your sister-in-law did. You got any ideas on that?"

"No."

"You sure?"

"Do I need to call a lawyer?"

Buckner turned on me then. "Son, you might need to call a *bodyguard* when Bob Anderson finds out what happened to his little girl." And with that he marched out of the room, straight through the blood at the door.

I covered my eyes with one hand. "What the hell am I going to tell her father?" I mumbled. "Her mother? Her husband?"

Mayeux pushed me down onto the bed and sat beside me. "I've done it a hundred times. And it ain't ever easy. This'll be worse, 'cause it's family."

"It's not that. You realize what happened here? I killed her, Mike. *I killed her.*"

"What do you mean?"

"I mean Miles Turner and I sat in this room for three days straight and tried our damnedest to stop that son of a bitch on our own. Only it didn't work out the way we expected."

"Holy Mary. That's where you got that hemophilia stuff? You been talking to this freak on the computer?"

"Hell, yes. So has Dr. Lenz. That's how his wife got killed. But Miles . . . he told me there was no way Brahma could trace—"

"Brahma? Who's that?"

"That's what we call the killer. Miles swore he'd rigged a way to keep him from tracing our location. Something at the phone company switching station—"

"Slow down, now."

"No! No . . . something's wrong. There weren't any typos in any of his messages to me."

"What the hell are you talking about?"

"Don't you remember the meeting in New Orleans? I

told you the killer never makes any typographical errors. His communications are always perfect, and fast. But just before each murder, he makes as many mistakes as anybody else. Miles said he had a voice-recognition unit at his home base, but when he traveled it wouldn't function reliably, so he didn't use it. Just a notebook computer and a cellular phone like everybody else. That's how we could predict when he was moving. His typos would skyrocket. But they didn't! Something's wrong, Mike."

"How long since you last talked to the guy? This Brahma?"

"Yesterday."

"Well, there's your answer. He could have flown here from anywhere since yesterday. As long as he didn't contact you, you'd never have a chance to see any typos."

The simplicity of Brahma's tactic dazed me. "Goddamn it! You're right!"

"But why should he kill your sister-in-law? Just because she was here? I don't buy it. Not with that weird abdominal wound. He took something out of her, man. But it sure wasn't her pineal gland." Mayeux looked uncomfortably at me, then at the floor. "I think maybe it was her ovaries."

Jesus Christ. God help me.

"What kind of shit did you talk about with this nut, anyway?"

"He did most of the talking," I said, trying to recall whether I said anything that could have led Brahma to this house. But I can't. And even if he somehow traced the photo of Erin, that wouldn't have led him here. Could he have been watching Erin's house while I was there? Did he follow her from Jackson to here? Why the hell did she come out here anyway?

"You okay, Cole?"

"No. I want Erin's body covered up. I want all these bastards out of my house. Right now!"

"Calm down, man. That sheriff wants to arrest you. I told him you were with me when the murder went down, but he could still bust you. Material witness, whatever. He's pretty steamed, this happening on his watch. That juice you used in Jackson cuts two ways, remember. Bob Anderson's a big man around here, and his daughter just got butchered, pardon my French. Buckner's cranking up a manhunt that'll make the John Wilkes Booth posse look like Cub Scouts, and if you make the wrong kind of noise, he'll stomp on you with hobnail boots."

I bent over, put my head beneath my knees, and breathed the way you're supposed to when you take a kick in the groin. "An hour ago you wanted to arrest me, Mike. Why the change?"

Mayeux laid a hand on my shoulder and squeezed. "You didn't have nothing to do with this. Other than being stupid. I seen a lot of killing. And this is some real weirdness we got here." He looked around the office again. "I think maybe this bad boy's started coming apart. Decompensating, or whatever they call it. And I think maybe you're the reason. Some way."

I straightened up and wiped the damp hair out of my eyes. "What are you going to do?"

"Tell Buckner to put some security on your house. Call Baxter at Quantico and tell him he better get his federal shit together before this freak single-handedly cuts Investigative Support from the national budget. After that, I'm not sure."

"Thanks, Mike. Thanks a lot."

Mayeux pulled me up from the bed, led me to the window, helped me climb out of it, then followed. The last thing I remember him saying was, "Smells like a goddamned slaughterhouse in there, Troop. Somebody get those bodies into a wagon."

With Drewe breathing deeply beside me, I sat listening to the bumps and curses and slamming doors and groaning engines of the uniformed battalion's slow retreat. After the last vehicle pulled away, I realized I was avoiding looking at something. The telephone by the bed. Then I remembered it might not be working. As I reached out to check for a dial tone, it rang.

It was Bob Anderson, calling from the Peabody Hotel in Memphis. I didn't hesitate or even try to soften the blow. With a guy like Bob, a man who's been in combat, you give him the truth and let him deal with it his own way. After a stunned silence, he asked a couple of questions in a voice that sounded colder than Brahma's digital facsimile. One was, "Did she suffer?" I lied and told him Erin had not. After that, his only concern was for the living.

Satisfied that Drewe was all right for the time being, he focused on his wife and Patrick and Holly. He wanted to tell Margaret in person, but he was almost three hours from home. Most men would have given up there, but Bob decided to send a friend over to his house—not to console his wife but to cut the telephone line and head off any busybody neighbors who might take it into their heads to drive over and tell her the bad news. Before the wire could be cut, I was to call Margaret and tell her that Drewe and Erin had gone to Jackson on an errand. The prospect of telling this lie made me uneasy, but Bob didn't give me time to equivocate.

I felt like an infantryman being given orders by a veteran sergeant. When I reminded Bob that a crime like this might make the late news in Jackson, he said he'd take care of that too. To my embarrassed relief, he did not question me in detail about who might have killed

Erin. Either he suspected Patrick and did not want to voice those suspicions, or he suspected the truth and did not want to flay me long-distance. After he signed off, I realized that Erin's death was a tragedy Bob had probably rehearsed many times over the years.

I know now that I've rehearsed for it too, the way we do with any friend whose life is ruled by chance or driven by demons. Yet for her to die this way leaves me feeling ambushed by fate, as though a relative had survived cancer only to be run over by a truck. Steadying my shaking hands, I pick up the phone and dial the Anderson house.

"Hello?" Margaret says. "Erin?"

I feel like I've connected to a parallel universe where physical events register only after a confusing time delay. Pulling the phone into the bathroom, I shut the door and say, "This is Harper, Mrs. Anderson."

"Oh. Is Erin there? She told me not to call, but it's getting late. I'm worrying myself into a migraine, Harper. She was acting so strangely."

Keep your voice steady, says my instinct. *A mother can sense danger to her children like a shark smells blood.* "Erin's not here, Mrs. Anderson. Drewe either. They went to Jackson on some kind of shopping errand. They left a note, but they didn't say what they were after." I pause. "What time did you see Erin?"

"She called around three-thirty and asked if I could keep Holly while she talked to Drewe about something."

My heartbeat skips, then starts to race.

"You know me," Margaret goes on, "I didn't want to butt in, so I didn't ask any questions."

"You've got Holly?"

"Lord, yes. She got so hungry I finally fed her supper. I know Erin's finicky about what this girl eats, but I didn't have anything healthy so I gave her frozen pizza. Erin will just have to get over it."

For the first time tonight, tears well in my eyes. "I'm sure it's okay, Mrs. Anderson."

This time Margaret says nothing. Just as I am about to speak, she blurts, "Harper, is Erin going to leave Patrick?"

She's already left him, says a manic voice in my head. "I don't know, Mrs. Anderson. They've been having some problems, I think."

"She can't leave him, Harper. She *can't.* That boy worships the ground she walks on. I want you to talk to her. She might listen to you."

I'm squeezing the phone so hard that the skin on the back of my hand feels like it might split. "I'll do what I can, Mrs. Anderson. I think you're doing the best thing you can just by keeping Holly. In fact, if she gets sleepy, why don't you just put her to bed over there?"

Another silence. "I hear you. All right, I'll do that. And you do what you can to straighten this mess out."

"Yes, ma'am. Bye."

"Bye-bye."

My heart is still racing, but my hands are steadier. Holly is safe. At least there's that. As silently as possible, I slip back into the bedroom. Drewe's chest rises and falls with comforting regularity beneath the coverlet. Not wanting to wake her, I sit in a hard wooden rocker in one corner and resume my vigil.

Why in God's name did Erin come to our house? If she called her mother at three-thirty, she did it right after I left her house. She told Margaret she had to talk to Drewe about something. What? Did she decide I didn't have the guts to tell Drewe the truth about Holly after all? Maybe. But even if she did, she would have given me a chance to do it. Maybe she decided that telling the truth would be a mistake after all. Did she rush after me to stop me? Unlikely. Her resolve to finally be rid of the lie was ironclad. So why did she come?

Then I see it. She must have decided that telling Drewe the truth was not my obligation, but hers. Drewe and I are husband and wife now; we weren't at the time of the affair. But Drewe and Erin were sisters. And by that logic, Erin's was the greater betrayal. Of all the alternatives, this is the noblest, and nobility was Erin's predominant state of mind when I last saw her. Alive, I mean.

Rocking quietly in the dark, I recall the unalloyed panic that jolted me when I believed Holly unaccounted for. If she really had been missing, I would have been the one that required sedation. Children are stolen from parents every day in this country, by monsters as brutal as Brahma. I met two such parents in Chicago. And though Erin is lost to me now, to us all, I thank whatever god or fate exists that I am not now thrashing through the fields in search of my daughter, that Holly is safe and warm in the loving arms of her grandmother.

Is she? whispers a voice in my head. *Are you sure?*

The squeak of the rocker stops. Rising quickly, I go to the kitchen and look up the number of the Yazoo County sheriff's department, which I memorize.

"Sheriff Buckner, please," I tell the dispatcher. "This is Harper Cole, from Rain. About the double homicide."

After about a minute, Buckner comes on the line. "What is it, Cole?"

"I talked to Dr. Anderson."

"So did I. Just got off the phone with him."

"I think you should get some men over to his house and watch until he gets home. Maybe all night."

Buckner spits, probably into a cup, and takes his time about answering. "Doc told me he was going to have a friend of his take care of things."

"We're not talking about the same thing, Sheriff. Erin's three-year-old daughter is over there. I think she might be in danger. Especially if Bob's friend cuts off communication with the house. You hear what I'm saying?"

I can almost see Buckner snapping to attention in his chair. "You telling me this serial killer might go after Bob Anderson's grandchild?"

"I'm saying there's no telling what he might do."

"Christ! You've stirred up some kind of shitstorm around here!"

"Will you do it?"

"Hell yes I'll do it! I'm tempted to cordon off the place with a SWAT team."

"Don't do that! If Mrs. Anderson sees cops, she'll know something's up. She'll start trying to call her neighbors. Can you keep your men out of sight?"

"You ain't got to tell me my job, boy. I'll take care of it. By the way, Doc's already got a plane lined up. He was talking to me from a car phone on the way to the Memphis airport."

I calculate quickly. "How soon will he be here? Hour and a half?"

"More like thirty minutes. Bob Anderson don't fool around. He called whatever high roller he was meeting up there and got hold of a King Air. One of my deputies'll be waiting at the new airport for him."

God Almighty. I look around the empty kitchen in a daze.

"You there, Cole?"

"Yes."

"Gotta go. I got a manhunt to run."

After hanging up the phone, I look in on Drewe again. She's still out. But for how long? With Vistaril she could sleep eight more hours or wake up any minute. What am I going to do when she does? What can I tell her? Sooner or later the tough questions will be asked. Should we even stay here in the house? No. Drewe will want to stay at her parents' house. But she's still going to wake up here. Bob could show up too. In fact, I should probably expect him. He'll take care of his wife first, but then he'll want to see Erin's body, wherever it is. After that, he'll come here. To see where it happened. To convince himself that it *did* happen. And to find out who in holy hell is responsible.

One thing I do know: I don't want Drewe or Bob to have to face the abattoir that is my office. Drewe saw it once, and that was too much. I may not be able to wipe out the acts that led to Erin's death, but I can damn sure scrub every last drop of blood out of that office. If I can't, I can repaint the goddamn thing by morning. Buckner and the FBI will probably crucify me for destroying evidence, but evidence hasn't led anyone to Brahma yet. From a cabinet in the laundry room I remove a gallon of Clorox, a bucket, some rubber gloves that are too small for my hands, and a mop, and carry them to my office door.

The smell hits me with more intensity than it did the first time. This is the coppery stench of death, the rotten fruit of violence. Pouring the Clorox into the bucket, I step into the bathroom and dilute it just enough to be able to breathe, then slosh the pungent mixture across the drying slick by the door. The bleach barely cuts the coagulated blood.

I bear down hard with the mop in the relatively clear place where Kali lay dead an hour ago. As the black-red mess swirls into scarlet spirals, the anesthetizing torrent of chemicals that must have insulated me up to now begins to slow, and the dark siblings of grief and guilt stir to wakefulness in my soul.

The mother of my only child is dead.

My complicity in her death grinds in my belly like slivers of glass. I probably know more about the man who killed her than anyone alive, now that Kali is dead. But I don't know how he found his way here. I do know he could not and would not have done so had Miles and I not played at catching him. We were fools. Or worse. Somewhere, perhaps not far from here, Brahma is fleeing for his life. He might even be wounded, trying to stanch a river of blood that contains no natural clotting factor. But his fate seems strangely irrelevant now.

The mother of my only child is dead.

Erin's blood yields slowly to the corrosive bleach. My throat works in vain against what feels like a lozenge of acid I cannot swallow, and glutinous tears burn my eyes. They are not healing tears, but tears of self-disgust. My part in drawing Brahma here is nothing beside my true offense. Somewhere in the dark chambers of my brain, the small and fearful animal that rules my subconscious has already computed times and distances, already realized that Erin did not have time to tell Patrick the truth about Holly before she died. If she had, he would have shown up here long before now. One day soon, Patrick and Drewe and Bob and Margaret—someday even Holly herself—will know that through stupidity I invited a depraved killer into our insular world. That knowledge will forever change their opinion of me, as it has my own. But they will never untie the final knot in the twisted skein of desire and consequence that led Erin to this house on this fateful night. The chilling thought that possessed me for an instant this afternoon—that only death could stop her from revealing our secret—has been fulfilled. And as I scrub fiercely at her blood, fighting to feel only honest grief at her passing, the pathetic rat voice of human instinct whispers in my heart:

Thank God they'll never know.

Chapter 39

The high ring announcing a video link from EROS headquarters is more than enough to get me off my knees after two hours of scrubbing up blood with steel wool and Clorox. Hunched and aching, I shuffle from the far wall of the office toward the EROS computer.

First there is only Nefertiti, revolving slowly on her black background. Then a window pops up on-screen, its top left corner flashing status numbers that precede the link. Pulling off the cramp-inducing dish gloves, I watch for Jan Krislov's face to appear. Instead, like a human version of the Cheshire cat, Miles's grinning visage materializes from the black void.

"You there, Harper?"

I sit down, look into the dime-size camera lens mounted atop my monitor, and pull on the headset. "No."

"The Trojan Horse worked!"

"Miles—"

"I'm sitting here with a stack of stuff you wouldn't believe!"

"Miles."

"What's wrong? You look like your dog just got hit by a truck. Where's my congratulations?"

"Erin's dead."

His smile does not disappear instantly. It seems to peel away, like old paint in a hard wind. He is too intelligent to ask for pointless repetition or to express disbelief. I know that behind his dazed eyes, his brain is already modeling all possible sequences of events that could have produced the result I so baldly stated.

"Tell me it was a car accident."

"No."

"Suicide."

"Brahma got her, Miles."

He touches his forehead with one hand. "Where?"

"Right here. My office."

Both his hands cover his eyes in an almost childish parody of grief. Then one hand comes away, toward the camera, like the pleading hand of a heretic about to be burnt at the stake.

"Harper—"

"How did he know to come here, Miles?"

The millisecond he looks into his lap tells me the answer is very bad. "How?" I repeat.

"Oh my god."

"Miles!"

"It's my fault."

"It's our fault, okay?"

"No, it's *my* fucking fault!"

The agony on his face stops me. "What do you mean?"

"The switching station."

"The telephone company switching station? What are you talking about?"

He slowly shakes his head, the slow-speed video making his movements appear spastic. "When I hacked the false identity for 'Erin,' I did it just like I told you I would. DMV, Social Security, a few credit records. I made her name Cynthia Griffin."

"And?"

"Before I could do any of that, I had to have a physical address. That meant hacking into the phone company's switching station to match a fake address with your phone number. Everything had to work off of that. See?"

"Yes."

"But I was wrong about the security level at the phone company. It was taking hours to break in. I needed a code or a password from someone inside. I tried to social-engineer it, but I couldn't snow anybody. Then I got to thinking. Even if I succeeded in breaking in, Brahma might be able to cross-reference enough databases to figure out that the address was fake. You were ready to start up as 'Erin'—"

"You used my real address?"

"It was the only way to make the character bulletproof!"

"Bulletproof? You goddamn idiot!"

"I know, okay!" Miles's voice is high and shaking. "Damn it, I thought we'd know if he made any kind of move! From the typos. That's why I kept asking you if he was making any."

"The errors didn't matter! He just stopped communicating with me for the time it took him to fly down here. Just that stupid e-mail message about getting the JPEG picture of Erin! God, I should have tried to talk to him right then. Then I'd have known he was moving!"

Miles seems to be shaking, but I can't tell from the grainy picture whether it's him or the link. "Oh, God," he croaks. "I killed her. Christ . . ."

"*We* killed her," I correct him. "You talked me into it, but I'm the one who lured him here. And now I'm scrubbing Erin's blood off the walls."

He wipes his eyes again.

I am numb. The magnitude of our culpability in Erin's death is impossible to face for long. "Tell me about the Trojan Horse, Miles."

He nods distractedly and raises a sheaf of paper toward his camera lens.

"What's that?"

"The contents of Brahma's hard drive. The one he downloaded the Trojan Horse onto."

A remnant of cold reason revives somewhere in my brain. "Does it tell you who he is?"

"No name. No 'I'm Ted Bundy' or anything like that." In a curiously childlike gesture, Miles wipes his nose on his sleeve. "I got his EROS software serial number, but it's registered under David Strobekker."

"Damn."

"But there are definite leads. He's got to be working out of New York. He started out killing homeless women here. The first three victims were infected with HIV, so he stopped. That must be when he hit on the EROS idea. He killed Strobekker in Minneapolis for his EROS account—"

"Where are you getting all this?"

"I think he used this computer primarily as an interface for EROS. It's mostly Windows-based applications. He must have his main stuff on a UNIX workstation somewhere. Jesus, I can't believe this. *God*—"

"What else do you have?" I ask, forcing my voice under control.

"The explosive stuff is the WordPerfect files. He actually kept a record of most of the murders. They're like descriptive letters. 'Dear Father, We landed in New Orleans yesterday evening. A humid city, blah, blah.' " He shuffles pages. " 'Dear Father, We landed in Michigan in the afternoon.' 'Dear Father, We landed in Virginia Beach—' "

"Brahma told me his father died in India."

Miles shrugs. "So he writes to his dead father. It's like *Psycho* maybe. The problem is that the only names mentioned in the letters are those of the victims, or this woman Kali. According to the letters, she did the actual killings. Although Brahma helped with the staging. The mutilations and stuff. Kali must be that girl he picked up in India. The Thuggee girl."

"She's dead too."

"She is? How do you know?"

"Erin killed her. Right here in my office. Ran her through the stomach with the sword off my wall."

Miles is thunderstruck.

"Come on, there must be something in the letters we can use."

"Drewe was right about the pineal transplant thing," he says. "Brahma definitely kidnapped Peter Levy, the man the FBI got off the DonorNet list. Know why?"

"Come on, Miles."

"Levy was a perfect tissue match with Brahma."

"Jesus. You mean . . . you think he could already have found a way to have this transplant done to himself?"

"No. I think Levy's on permanent standby. For when the procedure's perfected. I'll bet when Brahma turned up an exact match for himself, he decided he wasn't going to take any chances that the guy would get run over by a truck. I guarantee you Levy is being held prisoner somewhere right now."

"Good God."

"The DonorNet woman's dead, though. The Navy chick from Virginia Beach. She died on the operating table. Rosalind May did too. Heart attack. For some reason Brahma was going to open her chest—don't ask me why—and he actually told her about it. The letter said he was trying to make it *easier* on her. She died of plain terror. It's pretty sick stuff. But there's one thing that doesn't add up in it all."

"What?"

"Why Brahma was fooling with Erin. I mean with *you.*"

"What do you mean?"

"I don't think he saw you as a potential donor. So why was he wasting time with you?"

"I'm listening."

"Everything was going fine for him until Karin Wheat's death. She was meant to be the first live recipient. I think he thought she might voluntarily allow him to perform the transplant. Of course, when he and Kali showed up at her mansion, she freaked, and they had to kill her. After that he went to his backup plan, which was straight kidnapping. Rosalind May. And he got the Navy girl easily enough, the donor. But just before the big operation, his help got greedy on him. He was using unlicensed Indian doctors as assistants, probably recruited by Kali. They tried to extort more money, and Kali killed one of them."

"That's a lead right there! The FBI can start checking Indian physicians who've been turned down for U.S. medical licenses. They can concentrate on New York."

"Listen to me, Harper. That same night, May died on the operating table. The next day the FBI breached his perimeter in Dallas. Notice a pattern here?"

"Brahma's having big problems."

"Exactly. But does he lie low and regroup? No. He decides to teach the FBI a lesson. He plays Lenz's little game, then kills Lenz's wife. Meanwhile, he's playing kissy-kissy with you too."

"Maybe I was meant to be the next donor."

"For who? Who would the recipient have been?"

"Kali, maybe?"

This stops Miles. "I hadn't thought of that. But I don't think so. Too early. She'd want to know the procedure worked before she risked it."

"So why was he talking to me?"

"Brahma wants immortality, Harper. Physical immortality. Listen to this: 'Soon I shall stand alone at the pinnacle of the species, the only man with the courage to reach into the fountain. Soon I shall spit in the face of God.' "

"The fountain of youth?"

"Hell yes. He even talks about Ponce de León. Brahma's fountain is the pineal transplant. Except just as he gets close, fate starts working against him. And the worse it gets, the more he tells you about himself. He gives you his whole life story, something we know he's never done before. Why?"

"Do you know?"

"There's another kind of immortality, Harper."

"Just tell me, damn it!"

"Kids."

The word detonates in my subconscious like a bomb. Even with the jerky video image, I can see the excitement on Miles's face.

"In the transcripts you faxed, Brahma says he sterilized Kali, remember?"

"Yes. He said he couldn't have children by her, so she allowed him to sterilize her."

"If he couldn't have children by her, he wouldn't *need* to sterilize her. I think he *wouldn't* have children by her."

"Because she was Indian," I say distantly. "Because she had dark skin."

"Exactly! All those early questions about skin color! All his life, Brahma's been looking for someone like his mother for a mate."

"But my 'Erin' wasn't that much like Catherine."

"Not so much physically, maybe. Although you did change her in that direction a little. Good instinct."

"Yeah, obviously."

"No, listen, Harper. The answer lies in the story you were telling him. *That's* where 'Erin' was like his mother, and that's what attracted him."

"What do you mean?"

"You blacked out most of what you told Brahma,"

Miles says, looking straight into the camera, "but now isn't the time to be shy. It was all stuff about you and Erin, right? The real Erin."

I hesitate only a moment. "Yes."

"The big thing in Brahma's past is incest. He's a child of incest; he always longed for the sister he never had; Kali was a poor substitute. Right?"

"Uh-huh."

"I started thinking about Erin. And you. Your separate pasts, when things might have happened between you. And I realized that your marriage dates were pretty close together."

"Miles—"

"So I called the Methodist Church down in Rain and found out exactly when Erin and Patrick were married. Then I checked the Social Security computer and got a birth date on Holly Graham—"

"You son of a bitch!"

"I'm sorry, Harper. I had to know. And that's the answer. Brahma became obsessed with 'Erin' because she had this semi-incestuous angle to her past. And because you played her so convincingly. Erin had a child by her sister's husband. She ignored the rules for the sake of love, just like Catherine. She's a combination of Brahma's mother and the sister he never had. Or at least that's what Brahma started to think under the stress of his other problems."

"We're done talking, Miles."

"Wait! Can't you see I'm only doing this to stop this motherfucker?"

"I don't think anybody can stop him."

"I can. The question is, what will Brahma do *now*? When he got to your place and found he'd been fooled, he must have flipped out. But why kill Erin? She was the girl in the JPEG, after all. Why not kidnap her? Did he take her pineal gland?"

"No. But he took something. Probably her ovaries."

Miles's mouth falls open.

"She had a surgical incision down there."

"Christ. You see? With his pineal work going down the tubes, Brahma fixated on extending his gene line through children. It's that simple. Wait . . . Erin killed Kali, you said. That means Erin fought like a banshee, right?"

I close my eyes, remembering Kali's mutilated corpse.

"Brahma *had* to kill Erin," Miles concludes. "She left him no choice. Just like Karin Wheat. So he tried to salvage what he could. He probably carries some special transport container for the pineals. He just loaded up her ovaries instead."

"Stop, Miles! I don't even want to hear that shit. There's got to be something else on that hard drive to give you an idea who or where he might be."

He looks at me in silence for several moments. Then he says, "Two things. There's a WordPerfect file called 'Clarus.' It's not set up like the murder letters. It's more of a memo-to-myself kind of thing, like something he typed out while talking on the phone. It looks like specs for some type of new medical instrument. Clarus is the name of the company that makes it."

"What kind of instrument?"

"The kind Drewe thought didn't exist. And until recently, it didn't. It's called a neuroendoscope. It's a long, thin, flexible tube called a cannula that you can pass instruments through. It's made to operate on the brain. There's a fiber-optic camera attached, and a bright light source. You can visualize the interior of the patient's brain by running the scope's camera signal to a TV or a video camera with a built-in screen. Harper, the cannula is only four-point-five millimeters wide."

"My God. Are there any names in the file? People from the company that Brahma might have talked to?"

"No."

"What's the second thing?"

"I've got a serial number off a Microsoft program that might be traceable. It's a beta version. Microsoft handed them out like popcorn in ninety-two, but I've got some friends in Redmond who might be able to track it down."

"Good. Do it. And fax everything you have to Baxter at Quantico. Right now."

"Harper—"

"Do it, goddamn it!"

He nods assent. "Don't you think Baxter is probably on his way to you by now?"

This hasn't occurred to me. "I don't know. It looks like Brahma's already clear. He used a private plane. They found fresh tire tracks on the same strip you used."

"Harper, I am so sorry about Erin. How's Drewe holding up?"

"I sedated her."

"Oh."

"You just fax that stuff to Baxter."

"I will." He pauses. "Maybe you should split for a while, you know?"

"What do you mean?"

"Brahma, for one thing. He knows where you live. And if Erin killed Kali . . . do I have to draw you a picture?"

"Don't worry about me."

"Dr. Anderson isn't exactly Mr. Understanding either, as I recall. If he thinks it's your fault his daughter is dead—"

"It *is* my fault."

"Only to the extent that you trusted me."

"Look at it this way, Miles. Next time Lenz asks us what the worst thing we've ever done is, we won't have to think very hard to find the answer."

Before he can respond, I click the mouse on TERMINATE VIDEO LINK and sink lower into the chair.

After a minute, Nefertiti reappears, turning slowly. The muscles in my neck are knotted from scrubbing, and my backbone feels like it could splinter through the skin. I should get up and check on Drewe, but I can't summon the energy. Miles's warning about Drewe's father replays endlessly in my head. Bob must be home by now. He could show up here any time.

I need caffeine. I force myself up out of the chair and walk to the minifridge, but it's empty. As I head for the kitchen, my eyes follow the floorboards, checking for bloodstains I might have missed. I see none.

There are no Tabs in the kitchen refrigerator, but there is a six-pack of Diet Coke. I pop the top on one and lean back against the counter, swallowing the burning fluid and letting the cold from the open refrigerator wash over me. When that drink is empty, I open another and let the door swing closed. The kitchen is so narrow here, it looks like a monk's sleeping quarters.

You're punch-drunk, I tell myself. *You can make it to the bedroom.*

Glancing through the laundry room to the back door, I realize that the last cop through it probably didn't think about locking up. I set down the Diet Coke and walk past the closed pantry door to the laundry room to shoot the bolt and—

Freeze.

At least twenty cops have trooped through this house in the past two hours, but I'm positive that not one of them knew of, much less searched, the bomb shelter. Leaving the bolt unshot and the Diet Coke on the stove, I back through the kitchen into the hallway, my heart hammering, my fear for Drewe overcoming all else.

Should I try to get her out of the house? No. We'd be totally vulnerable as I carried her to the truck. My .38 is out there too. I've got to have a gun. I dart into an offshoot of our main hall, toward the neglected bedroom we use for storage.

The door creaks as I push it open, but I follow through and leave it ajar behind me. In the far corner of the bedroom, standing like an upended deep freeze amid the sentimental flotsam of five generations of Coles, is my father's gun safe. Inside it is a motley collection of antique pistols and flintlock muskets, many dating back to the War between the States, some even to the Revolution. The combination lock is easy to open, the numbers those of my father's birthday: 10-6-32.

The hard tang of gun oil and good steel hits me in a reassuring wave. Shoving apart the muskets to reach the back shelf, I set aside a can of Elephant brand black powder and grab the suede zip case containing the single modern weapon in the safe, my father's Smith & Wesson .357 Magnum. There's a box of shells on a thin metal shelf in back. I quickly unzip the case and load the pistol, putting the remainder of the rounds in my pocket. The cartridges are old, but with luck they will still cook off if I actually have to fire the thing. The big checked wooden grip feels unfamiliar in my hand. Sighting once down the six-inch barrel, I move back into the hallway and hurry into the bedroom.

Drewe hasn't moved. Facing the closed door, I back around the bed to the telephone and dial Sheriff Buckner's office with my left hand. I keep my right on the Magnum, taking my eyes off the door only long enough to see the numbers.

"Sheriff's Department." A woman's voice, more a question than a statement.

"I need to talk to the sheriff. *Now.*"

"Who is this?"

"Harper Cole. Get him!"

"He's not here."

"Who's in charge?"

"Just a second."

The next voice is male, young. "Deputy Jones. What can I do for you?"

I answer in language calculated to scare the living hell out of Deputy Jones, telling him about the tunnel and making it plain that people might die if Buckner and some deputies don't get back to my house ASAP. Then I hang up and sit down between Drewe and the door, the .357 pointed at its upper panel. The gun has a sobering weight. My arms are soon shaking with fatigue, but I'm afraid to sneak a look at my watch. It's been over a year since I opened the gun safe, the last time I felt sentimental about my father and found myself cleaning his guns to remember him. *No, squeeze the trigger, son. Be careful now, Harp, this thing'll put a bullet through a car door—*

A bump from somewhere inside the house steels my flagging arms. No way could Buckner's men be here yet. Not from Yazoo City. I listen in a way I have not since my grandfather took me on my first and last deer hunt. Shooting Bambi seemed cruel and unnecessary to me then. Now blowing off a man's head seems entirely justifiable.

There is definitely someone in the house. I don't know how I know, but I do. And that someone is moving.

"Harper Cole!"

My finger pulls against the Magnum's trigger, stopping at the last pound of pressure. Does Brahma know my name? Of course he does.

"Where you at, man? It's Billy Jackson!"

I'm on my feet instantly, pulling open the door and motioning the heavyset deputy into the room. His forehead and cheeks are beaded with sweat, his eyes alight with excitement.

"Who's with you, Billy?"

"Jimmy Hayes, on the porch," he says breathlessly,

thumbing the hammer of the nine-millimeter automatic in his hand. "We were watching the house, like that New Orleans cop said to."

"Just you two?"

"Sheriff's on his way, but it could be twenty or twenty-five minutes. Your wife okay?"

"She's sleeping."

He looks past me to Drewe's inert body. "Sheriff told me something about a basement? Someplace we didn't search?"

"It's a bomb shelter. From the fifties. I think the killer could be hiding down there."

"State police say the guy got away in a plane."

"Then why the hell is Buckner still searching, Billy? They found tracks on an airstrip, that's all. That could be hunters spotlighting deer. The FBI thinks there's a *group* of people involved in these killings."

His eyes move quickly from side to side, like mechanical thought indicators. "A bomb shelter, huh? No shit. Old Pete Williams has one of those. Like a little underground trailer. Has a poker night down there sometimes."

"This one's bigger," I say impatiently. "There are tunnels running to it. One from the house, the other from outside."

"Where in the house?"

"Pantry closet in the kitchen. There's a trapdoor in the floor."

"Outside?"

"There's a weather-sealed door like a cellar entrance about seventy feet on a straight line from the back door of the house. In the cotton. It's covered with dirt most of the time, but—"

I stop too late. Billy's eyes flash with animal cleverness. "Turner used it to sneak past us last week, right?"

I don't answer, but he sees the truth.

"Goddamn. Okay, wait here a second."

I grab his meaty forearm and hold him. "Where you going?"

"Tell Jimmy what's up."

I don't like the look in Billy's eyes. "What did the sheriff tell you to do?"

"Make sure you and your wife were safe till he got here."

"Don't you think you should stay here, then?"

He pulls his arm away. "Harp, they're combing the whole county for the sumbitch that killed Erin. And he could be squatting under this house right now, maybe wounded. You think I'm gonna wait till he skips out that back tunnel? He coulda heard me hollering for you. I'm gonna put Jimmy out there to cover the back entrance."

I hate to admit it, but Billy's plan makes sense.

"You'll be okay," he says, pointing at my Magnum. "That's a goddamn cannon you got there. I'll knock twice when I get back."

Again I cover the closed door with manic concentration. When the two taps finally come and the door starts to open, I have to restrain myself from pulling the trigger. Billy's sweating even more than before, and he's exchanged his pistol for a pump shotgun.

"You okay, Harp?"

"Scared shitless."

"Don't worry. Jimmy's covering the back entrance."

"How can he find it in the dark?"

Billy grins. "He's a hunter, boy. Somebody pops up in that field, he'll take 'em down sure as shit."

This is nuts, I say silently.

"You hang tough another minute, okay?" Billy backs toward the door.

"Where are you going?"

His eyes are hard and bright. "We got this sumbitch cornered, Harp. Like a fox. And I'm gonna nail his ass."

"What?"

His smile disappears. "Don't give me no shit now. I'm gonna work my way through the tunnel with the Remington while Jimmy covers the back door."

"Billy, don't do it! Wait for Buckner."

He shakes his head. "You got lights down there?"

"There's a switch low on the right side of the pantry wall." I can't believe I'm telling him this, but I also can't let him go down into that hole in pitch darkness, which he seems fully prepared to do.

Billy slaps his open hand on the shotgun. "You just sit tight and cover your old lady. I got a tear-gas round, a gas mask, and the odds on my side."

My mind searches wildly for another solution, but alternate plans aren't the problem. Getting Billy Jackson to abandon this one is. And nothing short of a presidential directive would do it.

"Listen," he says earnestly. "You want to see this asshole go to trial? Sit there in court with your crying wife and in-laws while a dozen lawyers scream objections and get this fungus sent to a mental hospital? Maybe even get him *off*? This way's clean, Harp. Won't be nobody down there but me and him. *Boom-boom,* it's over. Case closed. You'll never have to waste another thought on the guy."

The persuasive power of Billy's scenario surprises me. He's no scholar, but he's got a firm grasp of hard realities.

He squints at his watch in the shadows. "If I'm not back by the time Buckner gets here, tell him to give me five minutes and then gas the tunnel with CS. Got that?"

"CS."

"Right. Then come in blasting."

"Jesus, Billy."

"And if you hear anybody coming out of that trapdoor

that ain't yelling 'Billy Jackson,' you blow 'em to hell and gone."

"I will."

"Semper fi, buddy."

Shit.

Chapter 40

There is no more threatening sound than silence. It is the symphony of the snake that waits for its prey to step within striking range, of the tiger that stalks the deer. It begins as mere absence of sound, but unrelieved, it can build steadily into a roar that blurs perception to the point of sense blindness. I know that blindness now, sitting with both hands gripping the butt of the Magnum as though it could transport Drewe and me to another dimension, far from this dangerous place.

I count the seconds as rivulets of sweat across my face, as breaths entering and leaving the lungs of my sleeping wife. How long will it take Buckner and his men to get here? Even if they were at the north end of the county, it shouldn't take more than twenty-five minutes. How many have passed? Five? Ten? Or two? *Keep still,* I tell myself. *No way he's down there. Kali is dead and Brahma limped out to his plane and got the hell out of here for good. He saw his lover die and—*

Two explosions close together smash the silence, rattling the foundation of the house. I jump to my feet, trigger finger quivering, heartbeat loosed from its rhythm.

"Harper?"

I whirl, bringing the gun around with me. Drewe is up on one elbow, her eyes barely open.

"What's happening?"

"We're in our bedroom. Lie down. We may be in trouble. We—"

A third explosion shudders through the floorboards.

Drewe's eyes snap open. "What—?"

An agonized wail like a cat in heat rolls out of the kitchen.

"What was that?" she asks, her voice ragged.

"Two deputies went down into the bomb shelter. Brahma may be down there."

Her fingers grip my wrist like channel-lock pliers.

"Do you still have that pistol you used to use when I was out of town?" I ask.

She nods. "In my dresser drawer."

"Which one?" I ask, pulling open the top one.

"That's it. God, I feel sick. Am I drunk?"

Drewe's pistol is a tiny Charter Arms .25 automatic Bob gave her when she went to medical school in New Orleans. An oddly inefficient weapon coming from a man like Bob, but I suppose he wanted her to be able to conceal it easily.

"Whiiiite birrrd!" screams a voice that could have come from the pit of hell.

"White bird? What . . . ?"

"He's calling you," says Drewe. "He's saying *Harper.* Who went down there?"

"Billy Jackson. Jimmy somebody."

"Harrrper! Heelll meeeee!"

"The sheriff's on his way," I tell her, my tone strangely defensive.

She nods quickly. "You can't go down there."

This time the wail drags out much longer than before. *"I'm bleeeedinn!"*

"I told him not to go down there. Damn!"

As Drewe stares at me, willing me to deafness, I realize I'm in a position I've seen a hundred times in movies. Seen, and then screamed silently at the hero not to go into the woods or up the attic stairs or wherever any half-intelligent person would know the monster or murderer was waiting. But sitting here now, in the awful silence following those screams, one fact is inescapable: I brought those men here. If I don't help them, I will carry their lives on my conscience forever. And I'm already carrying too much.

"Aaaaaaaaagghhh!"

"Harper, you can't do anything for them."

"I know," I say softly. My right hand is clenched around the butt of the Magnum with painful force. The sheriff will be here before long. But Billy and his partner could be dead by then, and Brahma vanished into the summer night. Another prolonged shriek of pain reaches the bedroom, fainter this time.

"I've got to go."

"What?" Drewe asks. "No, you don't! Why do you have to go?"

"I just do." *Because this way it's over one way or the other. If I kill Brahma—or even if he kills me—I'll have done the only thing that could possibly expiate my guilt.* I start to hand her the .25, then switch and give her the .357. Whatever else I do, I will not walk out of here leaving my wife no more protection than a crappy Saturday night special.

Drewe takes the huge pistol with a kind of narcotized equanimity. I drop the extra shells on the bed. "I want you to get down behind the bed and aim the pistol at the door."

She rolls over without a word and kneels behind the bed.

"If anyone comes through but me, you start shooting and don't stop until the gun is empty. You understand?"

She nods soberly. She knows I mean to go, and though she doesn't want me to, she won't waste time trying to talk me out of it. The barrel of the .357 comes level with the bed, then rises until its line of fire intersects my chest.

"I'm okay," she says. "Go."

Two words echo in my head as I stare through the open pantry at the black hole of the bomb shelter's open trapdoor. *Tunnel rat.* Echoing down from years ago, when a one-armed tractor driver told me about his job in Vietnam. First man down every hole. Darkness, damp, stink. Crawling on your belly with a Colt .45 held in front of your face like a crucifix and a prayer on your lips.

The lights in the tunnel should be on, but they're not. Too late I realize I should have switched off the kitchen lights before opening the trapdoor. I creep close enough to peer over the edge. A pool of light on the concrete floor six feet below tells me there's a dim column shining down from the kitchen. I want to call out to Billy, but that would be idiocy. Instead, I snatch a flashlight from the top pantry shelf and cut the kitchen lights. That's almost as obvious as yelling, but climbing down a ladder through a column of light would be suicide.

To get to the floor of the tunnel, I must descend six ladder steps with my left side facing the open tunnel. That's the normal method, anyhow. Not tonight. Like a kid edging toward the lip of a high roof, I slide my legs through the dark, toward the place where I know the hole is. A tin can of something falls over the edge, caroms off the ladder, and thuds on the cement below.

I stop, waiting.

When the next howl of pain reverberates up the tunnel, I drop down the hole like a sack, my legs crumpling against the cool concrete, the flashlight buckling under my weight.

Forcing myself to breathe quietly, I lie prone on the tunnel floor and stare into the blackness. The .25 feels like a toy in my hand. It might stop a surprised mugger or rapist, but a psychotic killer could take five bullets from this thing and keep coming.

Move, I tell myself. *You're asking for it.*

Brahma could be sitting ten feet up the tunnel right now. I have only one advantage. Home ground. This passage runs thirty feet away from the house, with shelves lining both walls, and ends in a heavy lead door. That door opens onto the main shelter room, which is about fifteen by fifteen. A second tunnel runs thirty feet out into the field, to the rear exit. It too is lined with storage shelves and also contains a chemical toilet room. That's where my gold is stored. Sliding as far as I can under the metal shelving on the left side of the tunnel, I shout: "BILLY! IT'S HARPER! WHERE ARE YOU?"

At first I hear nothing. Then a slow creak of hinges.

"Harper?" A weak Southern drawl.

"Yeah!"

"I'm hit, man! Bad! I need help!"

"Where's Jimmy?"

A long pause. "Gone for a flashlight!"

Jesus. "Anybody else in here?"

"I don't know."

"What happened to the lights?"

"Don't know. I heard something and shot and they went out." Another groan of pain. "I need help, man!"

Damn damn damn. "Billy?"

"What?"

"What year did you graduate high school?"

"Nineteen-fucking-seventy-eight! Come on, man!"

I aim the .25 straight at the sound of the voice, where paramecia-like blobs of color swirl in a black sea. "Where are you hit?"

"My leg! I'm bleeding bad!"

"Are you in the main room? Square room?"

"I think so."

"Close the door! So that it's between you and me!"

While Billy mulls over this instruction, I slither to the center of the tunnel floor and rise into a crouch, the .25 in my right hand. The ceiling has exactly six feet of clearance—my grandfather was five-eleven—so if I stay down I'll have plenty of room. And I mean to stay *down*.

"I got you!" Billy yells finally. "Bring it on!"

The metallic screech comes and fades so fast it barely registers before the lead door slams shut. I explode forward like a nose tackle coming out of his stance, my thighs pumping, charging toward the main room and firing as I run. In the closed tunnel the little .25 booms and flashes like a howitzer, deafening me to everything but the high *zing* of ricochets. I sweep my arm across the tunnel as I fire, trying to maximize the odds of hitting anything between me and the lead door. With my eighth step, I dive forward, scraping my elbows in a second-base slide and jamming my wrist as the empty pistol impacts the lead door.

"OPEN UP!" I yell, hammering the butt of the .25 against the door. If Brahma's inside, Billy is dead by now, but somehow I don't think so. Billy's enough of a redneck that he would die trying to save his honor—and me—before he'd let himself be used to lure me to my death.

When the heavy door finally swings inward, I heave myself over the frame onto some part of Billy Jackson, who screams at the top of his lungs. I shut the door and roll off, still in darkness.

"You okay, Billy?"

"I don't know." His groans sound like manly attempts to cover whimpering. "This leg was pumping blood. I tied my belt just above the hole . . . tight as shit. Where's that fuckin' Jimmy?"

I feel Billy's thigh with my right hand, and what I feel is blood. Lots of it. "We've got to get you out."

"Need a stretcher," he says, grunting against the pain. "Aaaagh, that fuckin' Jimmy. He shot me!"

"*What*? You sure?"

"Hell no, I ain't sure. Hey . . . that was pretty smart what you did with the gun. Think you hit anything?"

"No."

"Haaaaay!"

I jump so badly that Billy feels compelled to steady me with one hand.

"Don't shoot, okay?" yells the new voice. "It's Jimmy!"

"About fuckin' time, you asshole!" Billy bellows back.

"Sheriff's on his way!" says Jimmy, coming through the opposite door with a hooded flashlight. "Saw his lights. Must be ten cruisers coming up the highway!"

"Great," Billy says. "Shine that thing on my leg."

"Judas Priest," Jimmy gasps as his light illuminates a ragged red hole in Billy's blood-soaked trousers. "Jeez, I'm sorry, Bill."

"I think he's okay," I say. "If the bullet hit an artery, his thigh would be as big as a propane bottle. Just keep putting pressure on it."

Billy doesn't look relieved, but as soon as I realize he's out of danger, the real threat hits me. If Brahma's not in the tunnels, where is he?

"I've got to get back upstairs! Any more rounds in that shotgun?"

"Ain't no plug in this baby," says Billy, handing me the Remington. "Three more rounds ready to go."

I pump in a round, kick open the lead door, and fire the moment the barrel is clear. Before the echo fades I am over the lip and charging back up the tunnel, homing on a barely visible column of light that must mark the opening of the trapdoor above. With every step I feel a knife blade whooshing out of the darkness to plunge into my groin or rip open my back. I fire again for intimidation, then dive for the ladder, saving the final round for the house.

I come up out of the hole like a coal miner from a collapsed shaft, pushing the gun in front and yelling for Drewe as I enter the hall. When she answers through the bedroom door, I pause.

"It's all right!" she shouts again. "Come in!"

I stand to the side and turn the knob slowly, then kick open the door and jump back in case she's being forced to speak. She is just where I left her, kneeling behind the bed with the big-barreled Magnum propped in front of her like a mortar.

"What happened?" she asks.

"Billy's hit. He'll make it, though. No sign of Brahma."

The Magnum drops hard onto the bedcovers. "Harper," she says in an exhausted voice, "does Mama know about Erin?"

"Your father does. I told him. He chartered a plane in Memphis. He's home by now, and I'm sure he's told your mother."

Drewe is crying again. "I've got to be there," she chokes out. "They need me."

"Throw some clothes in a bag. You'll be there in twenty minutes."

While she wipes away the tears and goes to her closet, I stand watch with the shotgun.

"Have you packed already?" she asks.

I don't meet her eyes. "Do you really think I'd be welcome there tonight?"

When I look up, she is staring at me with her mouth open. "You *know* it was Brahma that was here tonight, don't you?"

I nod. "It had to be."

"And it wasn't an accident, was it? It wasn't random."

"No. Drewe—"

"Don't tell me," she says, shaking her head. "I can't think about that now. Oh God."

She looks a moment longer, then turns back to the closet and continues packing. As she does, I realize that Erin's death may have driven something between us that can never be removed.

Trying to focus on anything but that thought, I decide I might be able to save a lot of trouble—and possibly our lives—by calling the sheriff's department and telling them to inform Buckner by radio that Drewe and I will be leaving the house armed. I make the call, and the dispatcher agrees to do it while I wait. A moment later, she tells me we should come out unarmed. I tell her to forget it. Brahma could still be in the house, waiting for just such an opportunity.

When Drewe is packed, I give her the shotgun, shoulder her bag, and grip the Magnum in my right hand. "Ready?" I ask.

She nods.

We burst out of the bedroom door at a near run, careening up the hall and crashing through the front door into a supernova of white light.

"THROW DOWN YOUR WEAPONS!" roars a bullhorn voice. "RIGHT NOW!"

I toss the Magnum onto the porch. Drewe does the same with the shotgun. Just to be safe, I put up both hands, and Drewe follows my example. It's raining again. As my pupils contract, I make out a ring of cars and men behind the spotlights.

"COME DOWN FROM THE PORCH AND LIE DOWN ON THE GROUND!"

"It's too goddamned muddy!" I shout back.

After a tense silence, the cookie-cutter silhouette of a cowboy blots out some of the light in front of us.

"What in the name of creation happened out here?"

bellows Sheriff Buckner, beckoning us toward the shelter of the cars. "Anybody else in that house?"

"I don't know." I lead Drewe down the steps into the rain and start explaining the situation. Buckner's face remains impassive. He already knows about Billy Jackson. "You realize what you did by not telling us about that basement?" he yells. "I've got a critically injured man!"

"I told Billy to wait for you. He wouldn't listen."

He shakes his head. "That's about the first thing you ever told me I believe."

"Sheriff, I need to get my wife to her parents' house. It's pouring rain out here."

"You ain't going nowhere, Cole. Not till we figure out what's what around here."

"She hasn't seen her mother or father yet. I know Dr. Anderson must be worried sick by now."

Buckner looks at Drewe's washed-out face, then signals to a deputy. "Daniels, you take this lady to Bob Anderson's house outside of Yazoo City. She'll tell you the way."

"I know the way, Sheriff."

"Hallelujah. Go on, then."

"Does it have to be me?"

"Go on, damn it!"

The deputy turns and mopes toward his car, but Drewe doesn't follow. "I'm not going without my husband," she says flatly.

"Now, Mrs. Cole," says Buckner, "you don't—"

"I mean it."

"I'll come straight back with your deputy," I promise. "Just let me ride with her. You know what she's been through. You can interrogate me all night long after I get back."

"I'm gonna do just that," growls Buckner. "All right, get out of here. Daniels? Make sure you bring Cole back here with you!"

As Drewe and I catch up to the chosen deputy, he mutters, "God, I hate to miss this."

Climbing into the cruiser, I hear Sheriff Buckner shouting at the house through his bullhorn. He's not much of a negotiator. Just three sentences.

"HEY IN THERE! IF YOU MAKE ME COME IN AFTER YOU, YOU *WILL NOT COME OUT ALIVE*! YOU HAVE EXACTLY SIXTY SECONDS TO SURRENDER!"

Then he begins counting.

Chapter 41

"*Damn,* I hate to miss that," Deputy Daniels whines for the third time, watching his rearview mirror as the cruiser rumbles up the slick highway. "You get something like that once in maybe ten years around here."

"There's nobody in the house," I tell him, holding Drewe tight against me.

"How do you know that?"

"Too many ways he could have gotten out. He had a good chance to kill both of us, and he didn't. Same with Billy and Jimmy. *If* he was ever there at all."

"He shot Billy, didn't he?"

"Billy's partner shot Billy."

"What?"

"That's what Billy said, and I think he's right."

Daniels looks around in his seat, bug-eyed with excitement. "I'll be goddamned. That sounds just like Jimmy. I don't know how many illegal does he's shot. Too damn quick on the trigger."

Drewe is tugging at my sleeve. I look down into her face, startled by the intensity in her eyes. "What was Erin doing at our house?" she asks quietly. "Did you bring her there?"

I motion for her to wait, but she knows we'll be separated in twenty minutes, and she means to have answers. I lean forward in the seat. "Deputy, you think you could hit the siren and the gas? My wife's feeling sick. She really needs to get home."

"Hey, the sooner we get there, the sooner I get back." He reaches up and switches on his red flashers, then gooses the gas pedal.

"No siren?"

"Hell, we don't need it out here in the wide open, do we?"

"We get a lot of loose cows out this way. Deer too."

He snorts at my cautiousness, but all the same he hits the siren and accelerates still faster.

The car has already outrun the rain. I slide down in the seat with Drewe, as if to rest more comfortably, and begin speaking below the howl of the siren. "I don't know why she was there. She told your mother she was coming to talk to you."

"I know. But why? You drove to Jackson and saw her like I asked you to?"

"I told you I did."

"I hardly remember you coming in. I don't remember what you said. What happened when you saw Erin?"

I hesitate. "She told me she was fine."

"And you believed her?"

"What could I do?"

"You just *left*? After I'd told you what I was afraid of?"

"She wasn't going to hurt herself, Drewe. I could see that much. I was going to call you about it, but when I got home two detectives were waiting to arrest me. Erin obviously drove over sometime after that."

She looks away with her lips drawn tight. "It doesn't make sense. What are you keeping from me, Harper?"

You never want to know.

"First Erin didn't want to see me, then she drives eighty miles to talk to me? I can't make that work."

"Drewe . . ."

She looks back at me with glittering eyes. "My sister is

dead, Harper. Any promise you made to her about keeping secrets is meaningless now. You've got to help me understand this."

"I didn't want to tell you this."

She pulls away far enough to give me a level gaze. She's obviously been expecting some dark revelation for a while, and she braces against it like a defendant awaiting sentence.

"Patrick isn't Holly's father."

She blinks three times fast, processing the information as she would some rare medical symptom, trying to fit it into her known information and compute a differential diagnosis. With a shiver I realize that if Erin were not dead, I would not be able to stop at this point. I would have to tell the whole tragic story and watch Drewe's world blown apart.

"No wonder Erin wouldn't use me as her obstetrician," she says finally. "All that BS about how doctors shouldn't treat family members. That wasn't Erin at all. I knew she was probably pregnant, with the unannounced wedding and everything, but I just assumed it was by Patrick. And she was doing so well . . . nobody wanted to question it."

"Well, now you know."

"She told you this this afternoon?"

I nod.

Drewe shakes her head in disbelief. "Does Patrick know?"

"Yes. That's the problem. Before they got married, Erin told him she was pregnant, but she made him swear never to ask who the father was. I guess Patrick was okay with it for a while. But then he became obsessed with finding out."

"Finally," she says, letting out a long sigh. "Finally it all makes sense." She looks away, out the window into the dark. "Why didn't Erin just tell him who the father was?

Surely that would have been better than what they were going through?"

Just let it go, would you? "I don't know. Maybe . . ." Suddenly, without any thought at all, damning and damnable words flow effortlessly out of my mouth. "Maybe Erin didn't know herself. Who the father was, I mean. Maybe she didn't want to admit that to Patrick."

While I sit shocked at my own words, some part of me gauges their effect. It is profound. Drewe believes. She can accept the idea that Erin slept with so many men in New York that she lost count. She can accept that Erin—in her convert's zeal to get married—would keep this from Patrick. And, most important, she can accept—without imputing treacherous motives to me—that I would want to keep this from her.

"Why didn't she just *lie*?" she asks. "Make up some fictitious father?"

The truth comes to my rescue. "A lie wouldn't have worked in the end. Patrick would have tried to make sure. I think he was bent on some dramatic gesture."

Drewe's eyes probe mine as though she were peering through the barrels of a binocular microscope. "She told you all of this today?"

No, three months ago. She told me I'm the father of the three-year-old angel Patrick puts to bed every night, who calls me Uncle Harp and begs me to sing Barney and play old Beatles songs to her on the guitar like I'm some friendly pied piper and not the very source of her existence—

"Yes."

"I told you she would." Drewe folds her arms over her chest. "Why couldn't she tell me, damn it? Why?"

The deputy slows the cruiser for a curve and switches off the siren. Yazoo City is a bluish cloud of light high in the distance. Soon we will swing onto Highway 3, which leads to Bob's estate.

"Harper?"

"What?"

"Where is Erin right now?"

"I don't know. You want me to ask the deputy?"

She shakes her head. In Drewe's family, you don't ask a stranger such a question. You don't let anyone outside the clan know you need them for anything.

As the lights of town drift closer, a wave of self-disgust washes through me. I just slandered a woman who can't defend herself because she is dead—

"What did Daddy sound like when you talked to him?" Drewe asks, her voice like a shout in my ear.

"Calm. I know that sounds stupid."

"No, it sounds just like him. This will kill him, though. He worshiped Erin."

"He's still got you."

She closes her eyes.

We're passing outlying homes now, lighted by the moon and by the odd window or Mercury-vapor lamp. Ranch-style houses set far back from the road, and in the distance, the green and white flash of the new airport beacon. Bob's mansion isn't far from here, and yet it's a world away. It may be a world away from me now too. The lies I told a few moments ago may save my marriage, but they will do nothing to assuage Bob's anger. Even if Drewe finds a way to forgive me, Bob will expel me from the family. Not in any official way, but his disapproval will have the effect of a papal bull.

Will Drewe forgive me? She's in shock now, of course. But she'll recover quickly, particularly once she is called upon to steady the rest of the family. Will she accept what I've said tonight as easily then? Already I sense an emotional distance that seems unrelated to the trauma of Erin's death. Could she, as I have often wondered, know more than she allows herself to admit? *Of course,* says a voice so clear I perceive it as a whisper beside me. *She's known for weeks. Months even. That's why she asked if you were sleeping with Erin. She doesn't know specifics, but she knows what women always know. That something isn't right.* I've been like a junkie, I realize, thinking I could live with my habit, that it wasn't really affecting my life. But it is.

It's destroying me.

"It's just up ahead," Drewe says to the deputy. "Third driveway up."

"I got it," Daniels replies.

Why do I lie? Did I inherit the tendency from my father, a man scrupulously honest in every area of his life but one? Even entering our marriage I had secrets. They seem trivial now, but if they were, why didn't I confess them before I married Drewe? Like a child unwilling to endure the pain of vaccination to gain immunity from a disease, I was afraid to watch her carefully tended trust waver yet again, or possibly even shatter.

As the deputy pulls into Bob's long, curving drive, I feel dislocated in time, as though Erin and Drewe might step arm in arm from beneath the brick entrance arch as I saw them do hundreds of times in my life. Two wet little girls in bathing suits. Teenagers wearing prom dresses and million-dollar smiles. Bride and bridesmaid before Erin's rehearsal dinner—

The cruiser stops with a harsh squeal of brakes.

Drewe looks out at the floodlit mansion. The ivy that covers the entrance arch still glistens from the rain, more black than green in the artificial light. Leaning toward her, I smell her wet hair, as tangible as the touch of her hand. She turns and hugs me, then kisses me lightly on the cheek and grips the door handle.

"Deputy," I say, swallowing hard, "I need to talk to my wife in private for a minute. Can I get out with her?"

Drewe looks at me, not sure what's happening. I still feel the press of her lips upon mine, a phantom touch of Erin's last kiss. With that sensation comes something more chilling, an echo of Erin's final words: *I know what the little death is now. It's the way we've been living . . . pretending things are fine, every day having to pile one more lie on top of all the others to keep the house of cards from falling on top of us. That's death. Dying a little each day—*

"I don't think the sheriff would like it," Daniels says.

"Well, how about you getting out? Just for a minute."

His shaved neck stiffens. He turns in the seat and looks at Drewe. "That okay with you, ma'am?"

Drewe watches me, still not understanding. "Yes . . . please."

"Okay. I'm gonna leave my door open, but I'll step away and have me a smoke."

"Thanks."

When he's gone, I take Drewe's hands in mine. But when our eyes meet, she pulls her hands away and folds them in her lap. She doesn't ask what I have to tell her. She watches me warily, her back braced against the door, chin turned slightly downward as if to ward off a blow. I remember this posture from high school, when I first admitted that rumors she had heard about me and a friend of hers were true. A thousand reasons not to speak constrict the muscles of my throat. I hear the voices of her girlfriends, of her mother, telling her that people don't change, that betrayal is a habit, that I'm not the kind of man who can remain faithful to any woman.

"Drewe, I have to tell you something."

Her eyes look away for an instant, then back, and in that brief slice of time much of their translucence dies, replaced by a protective opacity. I hear the metallic patter of the rain beginning again.

"I know who Holly's father is."

She presses harder against the door, and I realize my hesitancy is only making things worse. "Drewe—"

"No," she says, her lower lip quivering. *"No."* One

shaking hand rises to her mouth, pauses uncertainly, then covers her eyes.

Even as my nerve fails I say, "Drewe, it's me."

Like liquid diamonds, tears fall from behind her hand into her lap. My worst fear is that she will run, simply bolt from the car and leave me stuck with a trigger-happy deputy. I spit out my excuses in a panicked flood. "I didn't know until three months ago, Drewe. I had no idea! Erin showed up in Chicago before you and I were married, before we were engaged really, she stayed for three days, that's all it ever was. Drewe, she never told me a thing after that and she came straight back here and married Patrick! I never knew she was pregnant and I never touched her before or since! Drewe? Drewe! Say something!"

When she takes her hand away from her eyes, a redness in the shape of butterfly wings stains her pale cheeks.

"Drewe?"

Nothing.

I start to take her outstretched hand, then realize she is reaching for her clothes bag. As her fingers grasp it, her other hand gropes backward for the door handle.

"Drewe, wait. Please . . . we need to talk."

The door opens with a screech, silhouetting the back of her head against the lighted entrance. "Drewe, wait!" I plead, taking hold of the arm that holds the bag.

"Don't touch me!" She jerks away as though my hand were on fire and scrambles out of the car.

Lunging across the seat, I try to block the closing door, but Drewe throws her body against it with enough force to slam my arm and shoulder back into the car.

"Drewe, wait! DREWE!"

Just as I get my hand on the door handle, a decisive snick reverberates through the car. I jerk the handle hard but nothing happens.

"Ease up, ace!" Deputy Daniels says from the front seat.

"I've got to talk to her!" I yell, yanking the handle again and again.

"Looks like the lady don't want to talk to you."

I smash my fists against the wire mesh in blind rage.

"Break 'em if you want, champ," Daniels says lazily. "I seen it lots of times."

Outside, Drewe has paused in the rain-beaded brilliance of the floodlights. She stands like a refugee, looking back at the car with her bag in her left hand and her right raised to shield her eyes. I press my hands to the window as if to bridge the gulf between us by force of will. Her face is a ghostly decoupage of fragmented emotion: trust shattered, love blasted into confusion, unity into terrible apartness. She waits a moment longer, then backs slowly away from the car, away from me, toward the house of her parents, and of her childhood. The cruiser is moving now, backing quickly down the drive. I fight to keep her in sight. With my fingers locked in the wire screen, I watch her melt through the silver wall of rain.

Chapter 42

In the past twenty-six hours, revelations have detonated like artillery shells being marched across a trench position. I haven't slept at all. When Deputy Daniels and I got back to my house last night, we found Sheriff Buckner and his demoralized posse standing around their cruisers. They'd stormed the house and found no killer. They did find a rat blown to pieces by Billy Jackson's shotgun. Billy's second shot had fractured an electrical conduit pipe, blowing out the lights in the tunnel. A surgeon in Jackson soon confirmed that the bullet in Billy's thigh had probably come from his partner's gun. The consensus was that Brahma had never been in the tunnel at all.

Buckner put me in his car and questioned me all the way to Yazoo City. After we got there he questioned me some more. In between questions he bawled me out for scrubbing the blood from my office and contaminating "his" crime scene. I was still in his office when a tugboat captain discovered the wreckage of a downed Beechcraft Baron in the Mississippi River.

The captain believed the plane had crashed in the river, sunk, skated along the bottom for a while, then ridden up his anchor cable after hanging up on it. At dawn I rode with Buckner out to the levee west of Lamont to look at the wreck. The damage was serious, but less extensive than we'd been led to believe. Buckner figured the pilot had tried an emergency landing on the spur levee near Scott and accidentally gone into the water, or else had attempted to ditch in the river.

The cockpit was empty.

We all knew the missing body meant nothing. I once saw a New York college kid leap into the Mississippi River from a paddle wheeler in New Orleans, as a prank. He thought he could easily swim the half mile to shore. He drowned screaming for help in front of three thousand people, Southerners who knew the river far too well to try to swim out to the fool who was dying to set the price of ignorance. A search began immediately, but the boy's body was never found. It would probably be the same with Brahma, unless he happened to wash up somewhere like Vicksburg or Baton Rouge before he was shunted out into the Gulf along with the other refuse of the river.

Still, I knew something Buckner didn't. If Brahma had told me the truth online, he was an accomplished swimmer. And that gave me a serious dilemma. If I told Buckner about the swimming, he would demand to know how I knew. And if I confessed that I'd been in direct contact with the killer and had kept it to myself, he would undoubtedly arrest me as an accessory to murder.

I told him nothing.

Sometime during this Kafkaesque marathon, a tow-truck driver discovered a heavy leather case containing surgical instruments wedged behind the Beechcraft's pilot's seat. It contained several scalpels—some of which had blood on them—a video camera, and a long "high-tech-looking" instrument that the driver didn't recognize. From the description, I knew it could only be the neuroendoscope Miles had described the night before.

Buckner thought the abandoned instrument case bolstered the crash theory. He believed Brahma's body and any light gear had been flushed out of the cockpit during or after the crash, leaving only the heavy case inside. When I argued that Brahma might conceivably have left the case behind to create just that impression—and then demanded round-the-clock security on Bob Anderson's house and my own—the sheriff released me, on the understanding that I would return home and remain there, or else at the Andersons'. I didn't say so, but I suspected it would be a long time before I'd be welcome in the Anderson house again.

The morning sun was high when I got home. The interior of the house reeked of tear gas, my office of Clorox. The deputies had torn the place to pieces during their raid and the subsequent search. Armed with my .38, I went out to the utility shed and got a stout two-by-six plank, which I sawed in half and hammered across the pantry door with the heaviest nails I could find. Satisfied that no one could enter the house by that route without my hearing them, I walked back into the office.

My answering machine showed nineteen messages. I hit the button and collapsed into my swivel chair to listen. The first nine were from TV reporters, some from Mississippi stations, others from Louisiana, even one from CNN. The tenth was from Daniel Baxter. He cussed me for about a minute, telling me he'd intended to send an FBI evidence team down to go over my house, until Sheriff Buckner informed him that I'd effectively destroyed the crime scene. I fast-forwarded through more messages from reporters, then stopped as Miles's voice crackled from the speaker.

His message said to call him immediately at a New York number I didn't recognize. His voice sounded strange, like a loud whisper. Too tired to rise from the chair, I rolled over to the answering machine, picked up its cordless receiver, and dialed the number. After two rings, the same whisper said:

"Yeah?"

"Miles?"

"Harper?" Still the whisper.

"Yeah, where are you?"

"You won't believe me."

"Goddamn it, Miles."

"I'm in Brahma's house."

My heart thudded in my chest. "What?"

"I'm in his *house*. In his bedroom."

"What the hell's happening?"

"Remember the serial number from Brahma's Microsoft program? The beta version? The FBI was talking to Microsoft, but it's the weekend and they were going through channels. I have a friend in Redmond who was on the development team. He bypassed the red tape. Turns out this particular disk was given to the Columbia University School of Medicine in 1992 for beta testing."

I heard only my own breathing as my mind made the connection. "Drewe's theory again. Columbia and neurosurgeons."

"As soon as I got that," he went on, "I hacked into the med school computers and got a list of departments that participated in the beta test. I narrowed that to specialties dealing with the brain. That gave me twenty-three doctors. On the chance that the family history Brahma gave you was true, I selected the obvious German surnames. There were eight, and five of those were Jewish. I culled those because Brahma's German uncle definitely didn't sound Jewish. That left three names. Dörner, Thiele, and Berkmann. Before I checked their personnel files, I took a chance that the Christian names Brahma gave you might be real. Rudolf, remember? Son Richard? A psychiatrist?" Miles waited a beat. "Well, it hit."

"You're kidding."

"Rudolf Edward Berkmann, age forty-seven. Neurobiologist and neurosurgeon. Father Richard, a psychiatrist and another Columbia alum. Berkmann's on the *faculty*, Harper. His curriculum vitae even noted that his grandfather was Rudolf Berkmann, a distinguished New York surgeon."

"Good God."

"He goes by Edward. You want to guess what Edward's subspecialty is?"

"The pineal gland?"

"No. Berkmann is world renowned for building a 3-D computer model of the brain. He's been working on it since the seventies. I accessed the Columbia library and found dozens of articles and abstracts from medical journals. In the last twenty years this guy has sliced up over four hundred human brains, all to establish the base values for his model. Fifteen hundred slices per brain, frozen like chicken livers. Now Berkmann collates all brain research around the world and integrates it into the model, which is constantly updated. The thing can be used to map neurochemical reactions, project the progress of tumors, practice surgery, train medical students. They're even using it with prototype telesurgery systems."

Miles was speaking almost too fast for me to absorb his words.

"Don't you see? Berkmann would have been one of the first to learn about the foreign pineal research Drewe told us about. Melatonin, the transplants affecting aging, all that. Think of the deal he could do with those doctors. In exchange for early access to their findings, he could offer to integrate them into his model, thus giving the work legitimacy in the U.S. Of course, once he got hold of their data, he simply initiated his own transplant program, using humans instead of animals."

"Miles, tell me Daniel Baxter knows all this."

"He's upstairs right now, going through Berkmann's stuff."

A gasp of relief escaped my lips. I'd had visions of

Miles sitting alone with a flashlight in the chamber of horrors that must be Brahma's house.

"I found the place myself," Miles explained. "But Brahma wasn't here. You should see this house, Harper. It's the brownstone from the story he told you, but it's a *palace* now. It's not four blocks from Lutèce. I've seen some stunning New York homes, but this place . . . the art alone is worth a fortune. Most of it's Indian, sculpture he and his father must have smuggled out of the country. Anyway, it was a choice between physically breaking in or getting Baxter's help. I was worried they had agents tailing me anyway, so I called him."

"I can't believe he let you in the house."

"I made him promise to let me see the computers before I'd tell him anything."

"What did you find?"

"This isn't Berkmann's main base. I know that, because there's no voice-recognition stuff here." There was a brief, pregnant silence. Then Miles said, "But I found the answers, Harper. The very bottom of the thing."

"What are you talking about?"

"The reason for the murders. Why they were committed the way they were. Drewe was right about pineal transplants being the object of the killings. But she was completely wrong about the resources it would take to perform one. The way Berkmann has it laid out, it's practically a one-man procedure. I think he only used those Indian doctors for anesthesiology and tissue typing."

"How do you know that?"

"There's a Sun SparcStation here in the study. There's a version of his brain model in it. The graphics are some of the best I've ever seen—"

"Get to it, Miles."

"There's a series of surgical procedures modeled here. I'm still learning the program, but the harvesting procedure is based around that instrument I told you about, the neuroendoscope. In some ways it's pretty much like Drewe guessed. Berkmann's mapped out four different approaches to the pineal gland. One is based on spinal fluid pathways. He makes one small incision in the back of the neck, then passes the scope through the cisterna magna, the foramen magnum, the fourth ventricle, the Aqueduct of Sylvius, and right into the third ventricle, home of the pineal gland. He can do the whole harvest in *fifteen minutes.*"

"Jesus."

"Hang with me now. Another route is the sublabial-transsphenoidal approach, which Drewe told us about. Another is through the soft palate in the roof of the mouth, then along the brain stem. The last is—"

"Through the optic foramen," I finish. "After removing the eyeball."

"Exactly. Drewe was right about that part. Berkmann used a different surgical route with each victim, and the only evidence he was ever there was the track of his scope. It was *easy* to mask it. The back-of-the-neck route was Nashville. He fired a nine-millimeter bullet right along his track. Sublabial route was New York, shotgun blast to the face. The optic foramen route was San Francisco—"

"Stakes driven through the empty eye sockets."

"Right."

"But San Francisco and L.A. were linked by pathologists. They found pineal tissue in both cases. Did Brahma screw up those procedures?"

"No! This is the beautiful part of it, Harper, the part Drewe missed. The pineal gland is endocrine tissue. It has what they call constant anatomy. That means you don't need the whole gland for it to function. And once it's inside the recipient, it doesn't even need a direct blood supply!"

"What?"

"Once the scope was in the donor—who was already dead—Brahma used a biopsy forceps to pull out *part* of the pineal. It's just grainy wet stuff. He calls it 'pineal homogenate.' To transplant it into the recipient, he anesthetizes the patient, then drills a small hole in the upper part of the breastbone, called the manubrium, which gives him access to the thymus—"

"Just like the mouse transplants?"

"Exactly. After he locates the thymus, he injects the pineal homogenate into it with a large-bore needle. The thymus has access to the circulatory system. So as long as the pineal tissue isn't rejected, it begins to function normally. You see what I mean about simplicity?"

"I can't believe it."

"Drewe was wrong about tissue viability too. Berkmann has projections here about the viability of frozen homogenate. It's patterned after the way they bank bone marrow for transplants."

Miles sounded almost out of breath. We both sat in silence, trying to integrate the new information with what we had theorized up to that point. In some ways his discoveries changed everything. But in others, nothing.

"The cops down here think Berkmann's dead," I said. "What does Baxter think?"

"He doesn't accept a death until he sees the body. Do you think he's dead?"

"It's hard for me to imagine it. What does Dr. Lenz think?"

"Lenz is out of the loop. The shrink they're using now is studying your printouts like a lost book of the Bible. He's full of shit. He thinks Berkmann's ultimate plan is to resurrect a corpse by transplanting a healthy pineal into it. His mother's, for example."

"What?"

"Baxter actually has people watching Catherine Berkmann's grave right now. It's right here in New York."

"Christ, that's not Brahma's thing."

"I know that. This guy's locked into known paradigms, man. Believe it or not, they've caught serial killers before by staking out graves."

"What about Peter Levy? What are they doing to find him? Can't they contact people who knew Berkmann for help now that they know who he is?"

"Berkmann has no relatives in the U.S. His colleagues say he's an eccentric genius, terrific at attracting large donations to Columbia. Other than that they know zip about him. His house is essentially empty of evidence. No hostages, no body parts, no nasty crawl space full of surprises. Baxter says there has to be a killing house somewhere, rented or owned under a false name. That's where Levy would be. He's going to concentrate in Connecticut. They finally located the airstrip where Berkmann stored his plane. It's outside Darien."

As our discussion moved away from Berkmann's technical plans and closer to Berkmann the man, I began to sense a strange undercurrent in Miles's voice. It felt like anger, anger bordering on rage. When I asked him about it, he fell silent. Then, as I was about to speak again, he said: "Harper, I finally understand how Brahma—how Berkmann, I mean—got the master client list."

After going so long without an answer to this question, I had almost forgotten it. But Miles obviously had not. "How?" I asked.

"From my apartment."

"But I thought you hadn't had any burglaries."

"I haven't."

"I don't get it. He hacked into your home workstation?"

"He didn't hack into anything. When I first got Berkmann's name from the Columbia computers, I searched every database I could get into. I got a mountain of stuff back, including pictures."

"And?"

"As soon as I saw the first photo, I knew."

"Knew *what*?"

"That he'd been in my apartment." Miles paused, letting it sink in. "That I'd let him into my apartment."

A hot numbness swept over my face. I tried to swallow, but my throat muscles didn't seem to be working properly. "Uh . . . when was this?"

"About a year ago. He wasn't calling himself Berkmann then. I met him at a party in the Village."

"But how did he . . . I mean, how did he use your computer without your knowing?"

"I was sleeping. He must have gotten up without me realizing it. That was the only time I ever saw him. But one night was enough for him to get the master client list."

In spite of my past suspicions, I still couldn't imagine Miles involved with a man in this way—particularly Brahma. "Miles, I—"

"I'd rather not discuss it," he said curtly. "I felt I owed you the truth, after prying into your relationship with Erin. Holly and everything."

"Miles, you sound pretty upset."

"Edward Berkmann killed Erin, Harper. She was a special person. And he violated my trust—violated *me*—just to—"

"Miles!" I broke in, afraid to hear more. "If Brahma is alive, my family could be in danger. Tell me what he looks like. How dangerous would he be one-on-one?"

I heard shallow breathing and thought of the agony Miles must be going through. "His description of himself was accurate," he said in a flat voice. "Cellini's *Perseus* would give you the body. Very muscular, very strong. Byronic face. Black hair, blue eyes, light skin. Beautiful in the classical sense. A very intense aura. That's what drew me to him."

The tortured tone in Miles's voice made listening to him almost unbearable. I said, "Can I reach you at this number if I need to?"

"Yes. It's a rented cellular. There's one other thing."

"What?" I asked, having no choice.

"He had a scar across his upper abdomen. It was huge. I didn't ask what caused it, but it must have been a serious operation."

The hissing silence bound us like a chain.

"Miles?"

In a choked voice he said, "I've got to go, Harper."

"Wait! Miles, whatever you did . . . however you are . . . you don't have to hide it, okay? Not from me. Not from Drewe. I just want you to know that."

He said nothing.

"You watch your back up there, okay?"

I heard more shallow breathing, almost like panting. Then he said, "If Berkmann's alive, I'm going to kill him."

Before I could speak again, he was gone.

I started to redial his cellular, then hung up. The implications of what he'd said were impossible for me to fathom. I'm not even sure I wanted to. I leaned back in the chair and closed my eyes. The silence enfolded me like a shroud of thick cotton. Yet even as I slipped down into sleep, some part of me refused to yield to unconsciousness.

I stood up blinking and went into the bathroom, thinking I would take a hot shower. Then, remembering Brahma, I decided I didn't want to put myself in quite so vulnerable a position. Instead I threaded my belt through the slits in the holster pouch of my .38, put on the gun, and shaved at the bathroom sink like a cowboy. I washed my face and neck with a steaming rag, then sat on the commode with the pistol in my hand.

I put down the gun to use the toilet paper. At the fourth pull, a flash of color caught my eye. Blinking with fatigue, I unfolded the wad of tissue in my hand. There was something pink on the paper, something other than pale flowered print. When I turned the tissue over, I saw letters. Written with a light touch in pink highlighter were the words:

SORRY
I MISSED
YOU.
LEFT A
PRESENT
IN THE
FRIDGE
;)
CHECK
THE
LETTUCE
B.

My mouth went dry as sawdust. I snatched up the .38 but fell over as I tried to jerk up my pants. Finally zipped up, I eased through the bathroom door holding the pistol in front of me. Then I realized how stupid it was to be frightened. Brahma—*Berkmann*—had written that message sometime yesterday. That was why he left it where he did, in a place where police would be unlikely to search but where I was sure to find it eventually.

Still, I kept the .38 in my right hand while I opened the refrigerator and lifted the head of lettuce out of the vegetable drawer. Turning it over, I saw a knife-thin seam of dark green running around the white stem in a diamond shape. I set down the pistol and twisted the stem out of the cold leafy head.

Inside a hollowed-out space in the lettuce was something that looked like a gray strip of plastic. For a second I worried that it might be a bomb. Then I realized I was looking side-on at an eight-millimeter videotape cartridge.

Chapter 43

I attached my video camera to my office television with a coaxial patch cable, then inserted the tape. It had been rewound and was ready to be viewed. I scrambled through my camera bag for the remote control, then sat down in my swivel chair about six feet from the screen and hit PLAY.

The first image on the tape was identical to what I'd seen when Sheriff Buckner opened my office door last night, except that Erin was lying faceup in the center of the floor rather than behind the headboard of the bed. She was nude, and her eyes were closed. As I focused on her face, a man stepped into the frame as silently as a deer.

He had the physical symmetry of a gymnast. Beneath a tan jacket that looked like Egyptian cotton, he wore black clothes that fit tight against him. But it was his face that arrested my attention. The skin was unnaturally pale, the hair deep black with a few fine strands of silver. It fell in ringlets around his high forehead. His brow lines looked cut from marble but met and descended to a surprisingly gentle and well-formed nose. The lips were full and might have looked too feminine were they not balanced by a prominent chin. From the point of the chin his jaw swept back and upward in a V, giving him an almost avian aspect. But what anchored the remarkable face, what unified its disparate features, was the eyes. Pure cobalt blue, they pierced the camera lens with unnerving power.

"Did I not tell you I was beautiful?" he said.

His voice was low and resonant, his cadence almost archaic. Only when he moved did I realize how profound was his stillness. He cocked his head to one side, as if waiting for an answer. Then he resumed his former attitude, standing centered in the frame as immutably as a marble David.

"Since this must needs be a one-sided conversation," he said, "I shall begin. Isn't this a fine kettle of fish, as the common folk used to say? I don't think either of us expected to find ourselves in this situation, did we, Mr. Cole? Mr. *Harper* Cole?"

I squeezed the arms of my chair, unreasonably shocked by his knowledge of my real identity.

"And who am I, you wonder?" His eyebrows went up inquisitively. "You've known me by many names. But perhaps you know even my legal name by now. Thanks to this."

Reaching into his coat pocket, he brought out a flat piece of black plastic. It was a 3.5-inch floppy disk. He held it up to the lens so I could read the label:

TROJAN HORSE

"I think we both know who designed this," he said. Then he tossed the disk across the room. "I am Rudolf Edward Berkmann. Of course I didn't know *your* real name until a few minutes ago. But now that I do, everything is painfully clear.

"You must be dying to know what happened. I certainly was. At first I feared the whole thing had been a trap laid on by Daniel Baxter. That he would begin braying at me through a bullhorn any minute. But it was something altogether different, wasn't it? You're smarter than Baxter and poor Doctor Lenz put together, aren't you? Yet you produced the same result they did. A woman you loved is dead."

Berkmann gave a tight smile. "I know the feeling, Harper."

He licked his red lips and glided forward, out of the frame. I heard a soft groan; then he was back in front of the camera, holding up one hand, which I saw to my horror had been dipped in blood. He flourished the hand before the lens like a magician, then with a bloody forefinger daubed a scarlet spot on his forehead, like a caste mark.

"Kali was the vessel of my corrupt longings," he said. "My faithful concubine for twenty years. She was also my slave. Both are lost arts, requiring dedication and love. You attacked that love, Harper. With lies. And now she is dead."

Turning his profile to the camera, he threw back his head, flicked out his tongue, and brought his bloody palm down across the tip, tasting Kali's blood. He shivered, then dropped the hand and turned back to face the camera, his cerulean eyes wide.

"You tell slippery lies. Lies that are true. Poor Erin had no idea she was starring in an exclusive production put on by you and your friend Miles, did she?"

I wanted to shut off the tape then, to spare myself. But I couldn't. Berkmann made a quick turn away from the camera and gave a wistful wave to the center of the floor, where Erin's naked body lay. "Such a waste," he said with what sounded like genuine regret. "Are you wondering whether I've fucked her yet? Whether she's really even dead?" He nodded. "Rest assured that she is. And no, I haven't given myself that pleasure. For one simple reason. Erin is *your* victim, Harper."

He smiled again, his eyes communicating almost paternal sadness. "I've learned a lot today. It's a strange experience for me. I'm accustomed to being the teacher.

And to be made a fool of twice in one day . . . it's really too embarrassing.

"You don't know what I'm talking about, do you? Of course not. Let me explain. As 'Erin,' you approached me at a vulnerable time. I'd been experiencing difficulties with my work. I was considering a sabbatical. And we seemed to have much in common. I saw through Lenz's clumsy ruse from the start, of course, but yours . . . you were quite convincing. A gift, I suppose.

"As our relationship deepened, Kali began to take an interest. She was quick as mercury at reading emotion, and she saw the effect 'Erin' was having on me. Her feelings for me had always run much deeper than I suspected. I realize that now. Her first response was to demand that I use Erin as the next pineal donor. Obviously, if I refused, I would betray my true interest. I had to proceed carefully. Kali could be very dangerous, as you know. I agreed that Erin would be our next donor.

"Then came the resolution of the Lenz problem. On the night Kali killed the good doctor's wife, she searched his study. She found certain things . . . which she kept to herself. She learned, for example, that 'Erin' was another trap, just like 'Lilith.' But she chose not to tell me this. She was wise, in principle. I was losing my perspective. Kali understood my vulnerability. But she also knew the futility of trying to convince a man that his affections are misplaced. How many wives have convinced husbands that they really don't love the voluptuous secretary? Quite futile. Kali decided to let reality teach me the required lesson. A touch of Zen for the master, you see?

"She obviously felt she could handle whatever violence was required when we arrived here. I had no idea what was happening. My plan was to spirit Erin away under the pretense that she was a donor, and then—if she proved to be the woman I hoped she was—find a way to separate her from Kali later.

"Surveillance proved to be impossible, with your house so isolated. A blitz attack was the only option. I entered alone, meaning to tranquilize Erin immediately, to eliminate any chance of problems. But when I saw how beautiful she was in the flesh—the real Erin—I had to speak. I felt that after our conversations, she would have no trouble recognizing me for what I was. Her Dark Prince. But it was Karin Wheat all over again. Erin was terrified, of course. She had no idea what I was talking about, but her terror masked that fact. I still don't know what she was doing here. Fate sometimes takes a hand in these things. I tried to calm her, but it did no good. Then . . ."

Suddenly Berkmann began to move about the office, like a film director blocking out scenes. "Rather than wait outside as instructed, Kali had listened through the door. She burst in with her knife and began to shout at me. Didn't I see what a fool I had been? Like that. But when she saw Erin—a real woman who matched the JPEG photograph you'd sent me—she stopped shouting. I think she was as confused as I. I placed myself between them, tried to calm Kali. I said we should take Erin with us. Kali temporized. Then she told me to shoot Erin with a dart. I pointed the gun as instructed, but for some reason I couldn't fire. That was the end. Kali shrieked and flew at Erin. Erin lunged for the sword on the wall. I fired then, believing that if Erin went down that way I could keep Kali from killing her. But by then she was a moving target. The dart only struck her shoulder."

Berkmann moved faster, whirling like a choreographer, feinting and lunging with natural grace. "Kali tried to go around me, but I blocked her path. She slashed me with her knife and I went down." He rolled on the floor and came up into a half crouch. "Both women were screaming. Erin had already struck Kali twice with the sword." Berkmann leaped to the center of the office, where the bloody circus of footprints had been the night before. "They fought here. It was magnificent! A scene worthy of Michelangelo. The Western woman untrained but genetically superior, armed with a sword. The Eastern woman a perfect killing machine, armed only with a knife. It happened in the time it took me to load a second dart from the case in my pocket. Kali struck again and again, but Erin repelled every blow, parrying like a fencer. As soon as I had a steady shot, I fired into Kali's neck." Berkmann made a *pffft* sound with his lips and teeth. "It was a mistake. The shot stunned both women. Then Kali lunged for the kill and Erin ran her through. They stood locked together like embracing lovers, and I thought the battle done. Then Kali buried her knife in Erin's back. Erin managed to shove her away, then collapsed herself."

Twisting to imitate the climax of the duel, Berkmann ceased motion with his knees slightly bent, like a crazed Fred Astaire looking into the camera while dipping an invisible partner. "She died in my arms, Harper. Sorrow and pity."

As if someone had yelled "Cut!" he rose casually and stood centered in the frame again. "I tried to save her. But Kali had hit the heart. It was hopeless."

I looked at my watch then. The tape had been running for more than three minutes. I couldn't believe Berkmann had the nerve to stand there making this documentary of depravity, knowing that someone could walk in on him at any moment. Buckner's men, the FBI, me, Drewe—

A wave of sweat suffused my skin as I realized just how narrowly Drewe must have missed him.

"Once I saw how things stood," Berkmann said, "I took a little stroll round the place. I had the run of it, after all. And such an *interesting* time I had, going through this peculiar little house. So many mementos. This, for example."

From his inside coat pocket, he brought out a folded eight-by-ten photograph, which he opened. Bob Anderson had shot the picture about four months ago at one of the family barbecues. In it, Drewe and I stand beside Bob's mammoth grill, a little apart, while Patrick rests a proprietary arm on Erin's shoulder. Erin is wearing a yellow sundress and sitting in a white lawn chair. Holly, dressed in a matching sundress, stands with Victorian gravity, resting an arm across Erin's tanned knees.

"I feel like part of the *family*," Berkmann crooned, leaving the photo suspended from one hand and walking around to study it with the physical genius of a mime. "Hmmm . . . let's see." His finger danced along the paper until it stopped at my face. "Here you are, yes? Handsome enough chap, I suppose, though a little *doughy* for my taste. Not at all like your friend Miles."

While I squeezed my knees in fury, the finger moved again and lighted on Erin's face. "And here we have the sublime earth goddess I so foolishly believed I was communing with via EROS. So much *darker* than you led me to believe. She could almost be Kali at twenty-five.

"And behind her—can it be? The cuckolded husband? How could Erin ever have convinced herself that this mooncalf would be enough for her? Of course, she might have been a perfect match for him. I've given a lot of thought to that these past few minutes. Was Erin the woman you played her as? Or did you inject some of yourself into her—pardon the pun—as writers are wont to do in novels? How thrilling it must have been, playing both roles as you doled out your naughty little secret. You gave Erin a voice, didn't you? One she never had in real life, I'll wager."

Berkmann's finger slid down Erin's chest to Holly.

"And here, the little love child. But a *daughter*, not a son. Our own little Pearl. Any fool can see you're her father."

As he spoke, Berkmann moved his head upon his neck with serpentine suppleness, as if to hypnotize me by motion alone. "But I'm leaving someone out, aren't I? The alpha female of the family. As I teased at my meager facts, it came to me that there was someone else in this house far superior to both you and your earthy paramour. You painted her as the perfect sister, the ideal wife, but she's much more than that, I think. I'm speaking of this woman, Harper. This woman *here*."

The finger lighted on Drewe's chest.

"This is beauty, my duplicitous friend. What a fortunate boy you are. What a *delicious* arrangement. You had the carnal Erin for sex, and this noble lady for a wife. More than any man deserves, I should think. Oh, yes."

Berkmann refolded the photo and slipped it back into his inside pocket. "But your day is coming, Harper. Be assured of it. I'm going to disappear for a while. Not my first choice, but then I don't have a choice, do I? Please tell Daniel Baxter not to waste any more public funds searching for me. I've been planning for this day a long time. Even had my work succeeded, I could not have remained in America. Appreciation of genius takes time. But . . . there's a wide world out there, and I know it well."

Without warning or explanation, Berkmann suddenly slipped off his jacket and began unbuttoning his shirt. "I'm a free agent now," he said, almost to himself. "So liberating."

Both jacket and shirt fell to the floor.

While I stared, looking for the huge scar Miles had mentioned, he raised both arms high above his head, like a gull spreading its wings. If he had risen two feet into the air, I would not have been surprised. As his right arm lifted, I saw a dark line transecting the ribs, maybe five inches long. It took a moment to realize I was looking at sutures. They were weeping blood. Kali *had* stabbed him. And the son of a bitch had stitched himself up.

"I appear to be leaking," he said in an almost embarrassed voice. "Notice the Christlike position of the wound?"

He laughed, then dropped one arm and traced a line beneath his sternum and along his ribs, and I finally saw it. A massive chevron-shaped scar, probably twenty inches long, with its midpoint beneath his breastbone and extending outward in both directions. It was an old scar, faded white, with the dotted pattern of staples rather than the hash marks of sutures. It looked as though someone had opened Berkmann's entire abdomen for some reason.

"You see this one?" he asked. "This is where it all began."

In that moment all the levity went out of him. He stared into the lens with mesmerizing power, his latissimus dorsi muscles flaring beneath his armpits like the hood of a cobra.

"There are two kinds of people in the world, Harper. The healthy and the sick. Actually, they inhabit two different worlds. The world of shadow and the world of light. The door between those worlds opens only in one direction. And *I* was born on the wrong side of the door.

"I did all I could to remain strong, as you know. But when AIDS entered the blood supply, my hemophilia became a potential death sentence. Then it was discovered that hemophiliacs who received liver transplants for viral hepatitis miraculously regained their clotting ability. For me it was a revelation. The door *could* open in the other direction. Hemophiliacs as a class weren't given transplants, of course. Not enough livers to go around. And their symptoms could be controlled with clotting factor. But clotting factor carried *AIDS*, didn't it? I wasn't about to die for the willful ignorance of my government. I never even hesitated. Kali helped me find the surgeons I needed, she bargained with them. They could barely speak English, after all. It caused them no end of difficulty obtaining American credentials. But they had good hands, and they liked money. The only problem was convincing someone to make the required donation." Berkmann's lips flattened into something like a smile. "But Kali helped me there too. She was quite indispensable."

He tapped the transplant scar lightly. "It was a traumatic experience. Suppressing my immune system to accept the organ, all the rest. But I survived. And I was *cured*. Once we'd accomplished the liver transplant, well . . . you can see what a natural progression it was to further research."

He looked down at the scar again, then raised his right hand and pointed at the camera. I felt he was pointing through the lens, right at my heart. "But now Kali is dead. My best assisting surgeon is dead. Erin is dead. Yet *you* are alive."

I tasted bile in my throat.

"Remember the mills of the gods, Harper. You know the reference? Of course not."

While I stared in disbelief, Berkmann unbuckled his pants, dropped them to the floor along with his underwear, and stepped out of the disordered pile.

"The husk falls away," he said.

Then he lifted his left arm above his head as if holding something in his clenched fist, cocked his right arm at his side, and became utterly still. Every muscle in his body defined itself in bas-relief beneath his alabaster flesh. Without ever seeing the actual statue, I knew that I was looking at Cellini's *Perseus*.

I was still trying to take in the enormity of Berkmann's madness when he burst into fluid motion, whirling from one edge of the video frame to the other. It could have been a ritual dance or the mindless flailings of a lunatic. His voice, so resonant before, became an atonal blare, howling syllables that my mind could not form into any known language. I had the sense that I'd stumbled into a hillbilly Pentecostal church where men and women rolled on the floor with poisonous snakes and gibbered in tongues. But the man on my television screen was no hillbilly.

I started in the chair when he ducked down and came up with Erin's body in his arms. Without missing a beat, he began twirling her corpse around the room in a grotesque parody of a waltz. Erin's head hung limp on her chest, like the head of a broken bird. Berkmann held her in perfect ballroom position as he danced, and it struck me that he must possess demonic strength to hold a dead body suspended that way. Each time he wheeled toward the camera, he made sure his eyes met the lens, boring into mine as I gaped at the knife wound in Erin's back. Finally—as though from boredom rather than fatigue—he danced Erin's body over to the corner and gently laid it behind my bed, where Drewe would later discover it.

I thought I might have to run to the bathroom to be sick, but Berkmann stopped me by prancing up to the camera and aiming it toward my bed. Staying within the camera's field of view, he walked to the bed, reached up over it, and took one of my guitars down from the wall. It was a Martin, a prewar model I'd bought with one of my first big trading checks. Berkmann looked back at the camera and said, "*You're* the singer, aren't you?"

Then he pressed the instrument against his stomach as if coupling with it. It took me a second to realize what he was doing. He had slipped his uncircumcised penis to the side of the strings—into the sound hole—and begun urinating loudly, all the while watching me with rapture on his face.

"What a *lovely* sound," he said. Then he cackled.

When he finished, he shook himself off and hung the guitar exactly where he'd found it. I glanced away from the TV screen long enough to verify that the Martin was still there. It was.

"Oh," he said, as though he'd forgotten to leave a tip in a restaurant. He went to his discarded clothes and took something from a pocket. It looked like a long metal film canister. He straightened up and hefted it in his hand like a man feeling the weight of a cigar. "I harvested these before I realized Erin wasn't who I thought she was. I saw she wasn't menstruating, and took a chance she might be ovulating. No point in keeping them *now*, of course."

He walked back to the bed and opened one end of the canister. A cloud of pale vapor swirled out. Then he leaned over the bed, slid the open end of the canister into the sound hole of the guitar he had urinated into, and shook the contents into it.

As rapidly as the manic phase had come over him, it ended, leaving only the demonic intensity and the frigid blue eyes. He stepped very close to the lens, so that his blurred face filled the frame, and said, "Save this tape, Harper. We're forever joined now, we whose lovers killed each other. You can't show it to anyone, though, can you? Not unless you want to acknowledge Holly." His breath fogged the lens. "Do you want to do that?"

He pulled back then, and as his cruel smile faded he said with the gravity of a prophet: "Remember, Harper. We are all broken from within."

Then he reached up to the camera and the screen went black.

After my heartbeat steadied, I stood up and took the treasured Martin down from the wall, walked out the back door, and laid it faceup in the yard. Then I went to the utility shed, got a gasoline can, and doused the guitar from head to strap peg. With newspaper and matches from the kitchen, I began tossing flaming balls of paper at the Martin from the back door. The third one hit the seasoned wooden face, and eighteen thousand dollars' worth of handmade guitar and part of my sister-in-law exploded into fire. The sounds the Martin made as it died were like bones breaking and tendons snapping, and in ten minutes there was nothing left but tuning pegs and charred steel strings.

Miles and Daniel Baxter were standing outside Berkmann's Manhattan brownstone when I called Miles's rented cellular. Baxter was about to leave for Connecticut, to oversee the search for Berkmann's killing house, which he thought might be in the area of the Darien airstrip. Baxter thought Berkmann's frankness about his identity on the videotape indicated that he'd left my house with the intention of fleeing the country. I didn't explain that Berkmann thought I would never mention the tape to the FBI. Instead, I pointed out that he had been flying north, not south, when his plane went down.

Baxter asked me to overnight the original tape to him at Quantico. I agreed, though I intended to send him a VHS copy, appropriately edited. Baxter also thought Berkmann's knife wound lend some credence to the plane crash scenario.

Miles disagreed, but I couldn't tell whether he'd used logic to form that opinion or whether he was merely hoping Berkmann had survived the crash so that he could kill him with his own hands.

After hanging up, I shuffled through my desk drawer until I found the number I wanted, then dialed McLean, Virginia. The phone rang ten times before Arthur Lenz answered.

"I have no interest in talking to you," he said.

"I don't believe you, Doctor."

"Believe it. You're speaking to a chastened man."

"So are you. Are you up to date on the EROS case?"

"Daniel has cut off my information. He says it's for my own good."

"So you don't know what happened last night?"

"I still have a few loyal friends in the Unit. You're referring to the murder of a Mrs. Graham and an unknown female of Indian descent?"

"Yes. Did you know that Mrs. Graham was my wife's sister? The 'Erin' I told you about in your car?"

A brief silence. "The mother of your child?"

"Right."

"I didn't."

"Then you don't know it was me who drew the killer straight to her."

"Drew him how?"

"By doing exactly what you did."

"Pretending to be a female EROS client?"

"Yes. Erin Graham, to be exact. I used my own guilty secret as bait, but I told it from her point of view."

"And you succeeded where I failed."

"All I succeeded in doing was getting someone I cared about killed."

"No. You fooled Strobekker, didn't you? He believed you were actually the woman he went to kill."

I suddenly realized Lenz had no idea that Berkmann had been identified. "Look, I'm calling because I've got about twenty pages of conversation between myself and the killer. I've also got a video of him that looks like something from a Fellini film. I'd like you to look at it."

"Why would I want to do that?"

"Because his whole background is there. His entire family going back three generations. It's got to be a gold mine in terms of forensic psychiatry."

Lenz said nothing.

"He's a third-generation physician, Doctor."

A sharp intake of air.

"Nobody told you that? Baxter has a team of shrinks going over his house right now."

"They know who he is?"

"Yep. No more UNSUB. His name is Edward Berkmann."

"Edward Berkmann!"

"Know him?"

"Not personally, but I know his work. My God. Neurobiological modeling of the brain using computers. His father was an innovative analyst. Richard Berkmann. Discredited now, of course. My *God.*"

"What would you say if I told you Edward Berkmann was the child of an incestuous relationship?"

"What type? Father-daughter?"

"Brother-sister."

"I'll look at what you have. What exactly do you want from me?"

"The police think Berkmann's dead. I don't."

"Does Daniel think he's dead?"

"I don't know."

"I can't tell you whether he's alive or dead, Cole."

"I know that. I just want you to look at everything and, on the assumption that he's still alive, try to predict what he'll do."

"That could be very difficult."

"I only care about one thing. Will he run, or will he come back for me and my family?"

"Ah. I might be able to do that. Edward Berkmann. I could never have imagined it."

"Wait till you see the video."

Lenz's voice recedes to a blurry distance. "Tell me, Cole, are you experiencing strong urges for revenge?"

"You know the answer to that. What about you?"

"I'd like to shave off his skin an ounce at a time."

"You don't sound that angry."

"I'm not a demonstrative man. But contrary to what

you saw when you met her, my wife was once a beautiful and gracious woman."

"I believe you."

"The man who killed her so brutally should pay for what he did."

"If he's still alive."

"Fax your pages through. Overnight a copy of the video. It may take some time. Some of my case materials were stolen the night my wife died. I'll call you when I have something."

"One second, Doctor. What are the mills of the gods?"

"The mills of the gods?"

"It must be a quote or something. He told me to remember the mills of the gods."

"Ah. It is a quote. 'The mills of the gods grind slowly, but they grind to powder.' "

"Meaning?"

"It may take a while, but we all get what's coming to us."

"I can't argue with that."

Lenz hung up without a word.

I rewound Berkmann's video, plugged a blank VHS tape into my VCR, and started dubbing a copy. Then I called Sheriff Buckner's office and again demanded that he provide round-the-clock security for the Anderson family, and also for me. He told me he already had people on Bob's house (for political reasons, I knew) and that he would assign one deputy to watch my house after dark.

The last shell of the afternoon exploded thirty minutes later. I was lying on the sofa in the front room, trying to stay awake, when the phone rang in my office. I heaved myself up and went in to screen the call, sure it would be another reporter trying to worm his way into the story.

When Drewe's voice came from the answering machine, gooseflesh rose on my arms. *"It's me"* was all she said, but those two words affected me more deeply than Berkmann's whole twisted tirade. I reached for the receiver, then froze as her next words tumbled out of the machine.

"Please don't pick up if you're there. Please, I mean it. I'm calling to ask you—to tell you—that you shouldn't come to the funeral tomorrow. Daddy's gone to pieces. He's at the funeral home right now, sitting a vigil over Erin's body like they did in the old days. He won't let anyone else do it. It's almost like he's trying to protect her, even though it's too late. I shouldn't care what happens to you, but for your sake, and for his, please don't go to the funeral. Please. Daddy needs to blame someone for what happened, and you're the most convenient target."

She paused, and I stood like a condemned man in the hiss of blank tape. *"As far as what you told me . . . I can't even think about it. But I know it's true. Maybe I've always known it. Don't call me, Harper. I mean that. Don't try to see me, and don't come to the funeral. If you have any respect left for me, don't come. Good-bye."*

I snatched up the phone then, yelling, "Drewe! Wait!" but she clicked off even before I got the words out. Blinking like a punch-drunk fighter, I heard a horn honk outside.

From the window I watched a white sheriff's cruiser pull into our drive. Its driver executed a three-point turn and parked nose-out toward the highway. Buckner must have decided I rated daylight security as well.

Now I lie on Drewe's bed, my face buried in her pillow, trying to catch the scent of her like some lovesick teenager. But I'm no teenager. I'm a heartsick man who broke his own rule and told the truth, only to find out he was a fool for doing it or else did it too late.

Fatigue conjures strange thoughts. I once believed that all men existed on a continuum of behavior, some leaning to the moral side, others the immoral or even amoral, yet all having the capacity through circumstance to end up at either extreme. It's a common conceit, I suppose, the idea that but for the grace of God or fate or chance, any of us could be walking in anyone else's shoes. But as the ticking of my brain slows, an onslaught of images from the Berkmann tape assails me, none more monstrous than the desecration of Erin's corpse by the grotesque death waltz. Hovering in that half-waking state on the ledge of sleep, I realize that on this earth walk beings who inhabit the shells of men but are not men. They are Other. And somewhere deep within me, in the cells of my blood, pulses a cold current of preverbal knowledge, a tribal memory absorbed and distilled to savage instinct, needing no voice to speak with all-consuming power: *That which is Other must be destroyed.*

Chapter 44

Drewe told me not to go to Erin's funeral, but she said nothing about the burial. The funeral service was at three p.m. It's nearly four-thirty as I drive into the Cairo County cemetery through the back entrance, passing the long utility shed surrounded by yellow backhoes and a rusted fleet of lawn mowers. The cemetery superintendent's office looks like a good place to conceal the Explorer from casual view.

As I make for the small building, I think of Miles. He called this morning to give me an update on the hunt for Berkmann's hidden killing house. Baxter's teams have been searching the area surrounding the Connecticut airstrip, but Miles, always the contrarian, has been combing the streets of Harlem and Washington Heights, moving in concentric semicircles away from the Columbia Presbyterian Medical Center, which backs against the Hudson River like an island of succor rising from the squalor of the upper Hundreds.

Parking the Explorer behind the superintendent's office, I get my guitar case out of the back and begin walking slowly toward the Anderson family plot. It lies a hundred yards to the west. I've been there many times with Drewe. Five generations of Andersons rest in that ground, from infants who died of diphtheria to soldiers who survived whatever war fell to them and returned to the Delta to die of old age. Today it is marked by the green pavilion tent of Marsaw's Funeral Home, which rises out of the ground like a general's field headquarters amid an army of stones. From the west comes the invading force, the living, a seemingly endless line of slow-moving automobiles fronted by an advance guard of dark-suited infantry. I select a mausoleum for temporary cover, a thick-walled edifice of marble and stone about sixty yards from the funeral tent. Two stone vases adorn its wrought-iron door, and one of them makes a serviceable stool.

Erin's burial is like most others I've seen, only larger. The entire town of Rain is present, a blue-brown blanket of polyester dotted by the dark silks of expensively clothed people from Vicksburg and Greenville and Clarksdale and Memphis. I see several doctors from Jackson—colleagues of Drewe's or Patrick's—and at the periphery, standing apart from the rest, a couple of tall, stunningly dressed and coiffed young women accompanied by a gray-hatted man wearing dark sunglasses. Friends of Erin's from her New York days. I'm surprised any of them showed.

I can't see Drewe, but she must be seated under the sun-bleached tent. She'll be holding one parent's hand in each of hers and quieting Holly when she gets too distracted. Anna, the black maid who has worked for the Andersons since before I was born, will be with them. I should be there too. But I am not wanted. I have forfeited my place.

I hate the flatness of this sun-scorched boneyard. I once attended a funeral in Natchez; the burial took place on majestic bluffs high above the Mississippi River, in a white-stoned Athens of a cemetery shaded by moss-draped oaks. That's how a cemetery should be. A place that can bring a little peace to the living.

Erin's graveside service is mercifully short. The crowd thins at the edges first, the impatient ones heading for cars they parked away from the cortege in order to facilitate a quick exit. A few people move in my direction, possibly to visit their own dead, but I stand my ground. To hell with them and whatever they think about why I'm not at Drewe's side.

As larger waves move toward the line of waiting cars, I know that one word is on the lips of everyone. *Murder.* More evil has probably been spoken of Erin on this day than on any during her life. Whispered rumors of drug addiction and promiscuity recalled in the glare of a sensational crime, savored as the most titillating gossip to touch this town in a decade. Most of the local citizens will have convinced themselves that she brought the murder on herself. The wages of sin, brother, amen. Yet somewhere beneath that summary judgment lies fear. A nameless dread that perhaps this daughter of Rain did nothing to bring her fate upon herself. That some faceless being has for unknown or unknowable reasons chosen this little enclave as his hunting ground. Or perhaps even—God forbid—that he was raised here. I am glad for that fear. They deserve it.

When the muted rumble of engines rolls past me, I focus on the tent that shades Erin's grave. My line of sight is clear now. The family is there, standing together. A much diminished group of mourners stands a respectful distance apart. Close friends.

At last, with Drewe and Anna at their head, escorting Margaret, the family steps from beneath the tent and joins the waiting mourners. When I spy Patrick with Holly in his arms, anger ambushes me again. I should *be* there. That is my family, whatever may have happened, and Erin would want me there. But Drewe does not. She blamed my exclusion on her father, but I think she lied. This separation is punishment for my intimacy with Erin.

Bob Anderson looks lost in the ritual of hugs and

tears, like a soldier separated from his unit after a battle. He moves constantly, restlessly. I want to talk to him. Exactly why, I'm not sure. But in this patriarchal family, making peace with Bob is the first step toward reconciliation.

The problem is how to approach him. Would Drewe cause a scene? Maybe I should wait and see him at his office. He'll probably be working tomorrow morning, trying like all reticent men to grind away his grief with labor.

But I don't have to wait. Without a discernible glance in my direction, Bob detaches himself from the crowd and walks across the grass toward me. He has the hunter's eye; he's known I was here all along. He must be sixty, but he still moves with animal ease, his burly limbs churning around that low center of gravity like an organic machine. I feel myself tensing for the inevitable explosion of his rage. I doubt he would desecrate the ceremony by hitting me here, but there's no knowing for sure.

He stops two feet from me and looks into my face. Bob is shorter than I by a good six inches, but his presence has little to do with his physical mass. The windburned skin and blue-gray eyes seem to show first anger, then grief, then disgust. But perhaps I am merely reading my own feelings onto his face. Glancing past him for an instant, I see Drewe looking our way.

"Look at me," Bob says sharply.

"Dr. Anderson—"

He stops me by raising one hand to the level of his lapel. "I want to ask you one question."

"Yes, sir?"

"Do you know who killed my baby girl?"

My baby girl. Words so far from the image I will always carry of Erin, the very archetype of sensual womanhood. But behind the eyes of her father, a combat veteran who watched friends die by the dozen in Korea, there is only ineffable love for a being he will always see as an infant, or perhaps a beautiful toddler.

"I know his name," I tell him. "But I don't know where he is."

"You think he's alive, then?"

"Yes, sir. I do."

"The FBI says he's probably dead."

"I know that. But I don't believe it."

Bob nods almost imperceptibly. "I don't either. I've known men who fell into that river and came out alive."

I wait.

"I want you to promise me something, Harper."

"Yes, sir."

"If you find out this man is alive somewhere, you pick up the phone and call me. First thing. You understand? First thing."

The baldness of Bob's intent reaches toward me like windblown flame. It's the sort of intensity that makes even veteran cops nervous. "What do you have in mind to do?" I ask.

His mouth twitches at one corner. "Put him down."

"Dr. Ander—"

"In the *ground.*"

A chill prickles the hair on my neck and shoulders. For the first time since this madness began, I feel I am looking at a man who is a match for Edward Berkmann. Unlike Lenz, Miles, or Baxter, Bob Anderson is terrifyingly simple. Clever rather than brilliant, he can handle any weapon from a deer-skinning knife to an automatic rifle, and he is possessed by a righteous anger that looks not to the law for guidance but to the Old Testament by which he was raised.

"Promise me," he says again.

"I will."

Bob exhales deeply, a sound almost like a sigh, but

heavier, a sound that carries the weight of a burden I cannot begin to comprehend. "Drewe is my pride and joy," he says, looking over his shoulder to where his wife and surviving daughter stoically accept the condolences of the last stragglers. "She's already accomplished more than I ever did. I'm so damned proud of her I can't sit still with it. But Erin . . ."

He looks back at me, allowing his shield of impassivity to drop a little. "Erin was always different. I knew from the start. She was a wayward girl, God knows, but it wasn't her fault. It was her nature. She put us through the trials of Job, but I think we loved her all the more for it."

For a moment he seems unable to continue. Then he wipes both eyes and regains his voice. "I don't know what went on between you and Erin, but I always sensed there was something."

Jesus—

"No man's immune to the temptations of the flesh, son. And God knows she was a temptation to every man who ever saw her. But this . . . When you told me she was dead, I thought I'd kill you the second I could get my hands on you. I knew that somehow that computer sex thing of yours had gotten her killed. But flying back from Memphis, I realized you were gonna punish yourself more than I ever could. And if you didn't, God would."

Bob runs a hand over his balding scalp. "But this other . . . bastard. He's my responsibility. Ain't no father and mother no place gonna have to endure what Margaret and I have because of this man."

"Dr. Anderson . . ."

"You listen to me, son. I got enough money to take care of Margaret if she lives to be a hundred and fifty. I'm gonna leave some to Patrick to take care of Holly, and some to Drewe for the kids you two will have one day.

The rest is going to Margaret, and I'm naming you as trustee. Just be still, Harper. You know more about money than anybody I ever knew, and more important, I trust you."

I want to speak, but a lump the size of a golf ball is blocking my throat.

"I never agreed with your daddy's politics," Bob says haltingly. "But I always respected his guts. For a long time now, I've looked at you like you was my own. Now you got to put the past behind you and do whatever you have to do to make up with Drewe and get on with the business of living." He inhales deeply, as though speaking so many words winded him. "That's all I've got to say."

Bob sticks out his callused hand. I take it, and for the first time since my father died I feel a surge of filial devotion, an atavistic sense of belonging that blasts all words into the eternal irrelevance they embody. For the few seconds we clasp hands, I am plugged into a world where ambiguity does not exist.

And I feel strong.

Everyone is gone now. In the distance I see the yellow backhoe that will fill Erin's grave, but no operator. The funeral-home tent gives surprisingly cool shade, or perhaps it's the opened earth that cools the air here.

Taking my surviving Martin from its case, I realize I forgot to bring a strap. I'll have to sit to play. Using one foot, I prop the flight case up on its side and sit on the fat end, with my shoes at the foot of the grave. The polished metal casket has a bottomless sheen. A French vanilla sprinkling of Delta soil dropped by the family lies across the lid like the first fingers of the reclaiming earth.

"I hope you can hear this," I say, my voice sounding too offhand for what should be a solemn moment.

Hitting the strings once to check the tuning, I begin the syncopated chords that lead into "All I Want Is

Everything," a song I wrote in a moment of crystallized indecision, a song Erin asked me to play anytime she saw me with a guitar. With a suspended chord hanging in the air, I begin singing softly.

Being born in Babylon
It's so hard to get off on
The half-life of every choice
We love that serpent's voice
It takes a sure hand and a sharp knife
To cut the fruit from the tree of life
But once you taste that virgin drop
How do you know when to stop?

All I want is everything
Girl you know it's true
All I want is everything
But all I need is . . .

Diamond cuff links on my sleeves
Gold teeth in my mouth
Chartreuse Italian shoes
And time to wear them out
No really, a nice house and a nice car
And a nice girl, not a movie star
A normal kid and some green grass
And a great camera to make them last

All I want is everything
Girl you know it's true
All I want is everything
But all I need is you . . .

I play without singing for a bit, remembering how Erin used to laugh at the verse about the gold teeth and Italian shoes, and then suddenly get pensive as the rest of the lyric came around. She knew she would never fit into the middle-class scene painted in the second half of that verse, and perhaps also that she would never be all I needed—just as no one person could keep all her demons at bay. Remembering the farewell kiss in her house on the day she died, I sing the last verse.

Two roads lead from this spot
One's easy, the other's not
They say pleasure's born from pain
But I don't ride that train
I can go East, I can go West
Choose one, and I lose the rest
But for a man who wants it all
This is sure some easy call

All I want is everything
Girl you know it's true
All I want is everything
But all I need is you

As the last chord fades into silence, a voice from close behind me freezes me in place.

"What are you doing?"

Moving slowly, I lay the guitar on the ground, get up, and turn to face Drewe. She stands just inside the shade of the tent, wearing a black dress, black shoes, black hat, and Ray-Ban sunglasses. She seems a pale apparition of rebuke.

"Saying good-bye," I reply. "This is what she wanted. I had to do it."

"You told me you wrote that song for me."

"I did. But she liked it."

Drewe says nothing. I glance over her shoulder for a car but see only the empty cemetery lane.

"What did my father say to you?"

"He let me know it was okay I was here."

"That's not all he said."

"That's all I'm going to tell you."

Her mouth wrinkles in disgust. "More secrets?"

"If you like."

She sighs, then turns and begins walking away.

"He told me I should do whatever it took to make up with you," I call out. "That we should get on with living."

She stops and turns back, squinting her eyes against the sun. "And what did you say to that?"

"Nothing. I don't think I can make it up to you. I think it comes down to whether you can live with what you know and with me too. Or whether you want to."

"Do you think anyone could?"

"I don't know. I think you're a unique person, Drewe. I think you love me, even if you don't like me or even respect me right now."

"And you think that's something to build a life on?"

"It's a start. I love you, Drewe. I've loved and respected you since we were kids."

"Then why did you fuck my sister?"

The profanity shocks me, but if anything was ever going to push her to it, this is it. "Because I couldn't sleep with you."

"No!" she cries bitterly. "We *were* sleeping together then! You'd asked me to marry you!"

"And you said we should take a year to be sure."

"That was for *your* benefit. *I* was sure! I thought you might not be, and obviously I was right."

"I was sure, Drewe."

"You were sleeping with other women too, weren't you?"

"No."

She walks back a little way, her arms folded protectively across her chest. "I hate this," she says softly. "I *hate* it."

"I hate it too."

"I try to trust people, I want to, but everything is always so—so ugly at the bottom."

"That's not true."

"It is!"

"It's not true with you. I mean, you're the exception. And I'm glad you are. It actually gives me hope for the world."

She pulls off her sunglasses and looks into my eyes. "I'm no exception, Harper."

"What do you mean?"

"Just what I said. No one's completely pure. Everyone has a past."

"What are you talking about?"

She hesitates, then pushes on. "What could you learn about me that would shock you the most? That would hurt you the most?"

There is a strange buzzing in my head which prevents my thinking clearly. "I'm not sure I—"

"You're not the only man I've slept with, Harper."

She takes a quick step back, as though the bald statement has shocked even her. "You don't believe me?"

"But you said . . ."

"I let you think that because you wanted to believe it so badly, and because it was almost true."

"Almost true?"

She folds and unfolds the earpieces of the sunglasses in her hands. "When I was in college, the last year before medical school, I hadn't seen you for almost two years. You called maybe twice that whole time. I'd spent four years doing nothing but studying. I'd just taken the MCAT, and I was sure I'd blown it completely."

"But you scored in the ninety-eighth percentile."

"I didn't know that *then*, okay? I just hit this down

place in my life. I felt like everything had been a mistake. I'd been in love with you for years, was practically living like a nun, yet I was being faithful to a man who was sleeping with women all over the country. It seemed insane. It *was* insane."

"Drewe—"

"One night I accepted a date with this boy. We went for pizza and a movie, nothing special, but I liked him. He was in some of my classes, and he made me laugh a lot. Anyway, when he took me home, I asked him to come in."

"Drewe, you don't—"

"And while we were kissing," she says forcefully, "I realized how good it felt simply to be held by another person. And I just . . . didn't resist anything he was doing. Almost my whole dating life had been spent pushing away hands and saying 'Please don't' or 'I'm sorry.' And I was just tired of it. I couldn't do it anymore. He was kissing me and I realized with sort of a shock that I was wet. And I was wearing a dress and I just—I just *did* it."

I have a childish urge to cover my ears with my hands. Drewe watches me with an almost defiant look, her green eyes flashing, as if daring me to criticize her.

"What do you want me to say?" I ask. "It hurts."

"That I did it? Or that I didn't tell you about it?"

"I understand why you did it. I'm surprised you didn't do more of it. But why couldn't you tell me?"

She shakes her head as though she can't believe what she's heard. "I did exactly what you've done to me! Tried to spare your feelings."

"I know that. I get it, okay? I don't know why it hurts so much. I guess it's because I always put you on such a pedestal, as if you were more than human. Hell, Drewe, you let people think that."

"*What?* When I was young I acted wild so people wouldn't think I was a prude! When I finally tried to be myself, everyone made me into a saint. I can't help what people think!"

"Was that the only time?"

She glances at the ground, then back up at me, still defiant.

"God, Drewe—"

"I didn't sleep with any other men, but I slept with him again. For a couple of days after, I wouldn't talk to him. But then I did. I slept with him every night for a week. Then I stopped."

The whole scenario is impossible to comprehend, like someone telling me my mother was secretly married to some stranger. "Why did you stop?"

"I was terrified I'd get pregnant, for one thing. I knew I didn't love him, for another. I liked him, but I didn't love him. I loved you. And I knew the things I was doing with him were things I should wait to do with you. Even though you weren't showing any signs of commitment to me."

"The things you were doing?" I hesitate, trying to control my imagination. "What were you doing with him?"

She shakes her head and takes a step toward me. "Just sex. It doesn't matter."

"Then tell me. Just intercourse? Or everything?"

"*Just* intercourse? Isn't that the worst offense in the scale of guilty behavior?"

"No. I don't know. Did you—"

"Stop it, Harper! This is wrong. It's dangerous."

"I guess it is. Was he—"

"What? Better than you? Bigger than you? Tell me you're not that juvenile, Harper. Tell me you're more mature than a seventh grader."

I whirl away from her and start packing the Martin into its case. As stupid as it is, all I can see is Drewe debasing herself for some faceless guy and loving every minute of it, all at a time when she wouldn't sleep with me, the man she claimed she loved.

She circles around until she is facing me again. "You know something, Harper? The biggest penis I ever saw was on a cadaver in medical school. You think it was doing that man any good?"

"Just shut up."

"I won't! I thought you were different from other men. All this obsession with how many conquests they can make and who has the biggest prick and who can piss the farthest . . . I see it every day, in hospital staff meetings, in politics. Men are like three-year-olds trying to snatch all the toys from each other. Life isn't *about* that. You think it hurts to hear I had sex with a man for one week in my life? How do you think I would feel if every girl you ever slept with was lined up in a row? I know half a dozen personally, and the rest would probably fill a school bus! I'm sure they did things for you I couldn't even imagine. But I don't *want* to imagine them. You slept with my sister, for God's sake. You have a child by her. So don't stand there looking like a kid who just found out there's no Santa Claus. *I'm* the one who's been wronged. I'm the one who should be apologized to."

"I tried to apologize!"

"Try again."

With an idiot's numb elation, I realize that Drewe isn't telling me all this because she hates me, but because she loves me. And because she must hurt me a little to make it possible for us to live together again. The truth is, I feel almost relieved. I think I always wished for some little chink in her moral armor, if only to mitigate my own sins against her trust. It's difficult trying to measure up to someone who not only has impossibly high ideals but also lives by them. Before a window can open for second thoughts I take a step toward her.

She holds up her hands. "Harper, I love you. With all the joy and pain that entails. And right now the pain outweighs the joy. We have a long way to go."

With two strides she is past me, turning me with one hand, until we stand at the foot of Erin's open grave.

"I loved my sister," she says softly, looking down into the hole. "We were more competitive than either of us ever admitted. Erin felt resentments I never let myself see. I was jealous of her sometimes too. Not so much her beauty, but . . . I wanted to be as free as she was. To be able to live without second-guessing myself all the time."

"She paid a price for that freedom."

"Yes. But this wasn't the price. This is obscene. And there's nothing we can do about it. I blame myself too, for not stopping you and Miles. Erin too. You and Miles led that animal to our house, but it was Erin's secret that put her within his grasp, wasn't it?"

I say nothing.

"We weren't married when you slept with her," Drewe goes on, still looking down. "That makes a difference to me. Erin could have told you she was pregnant before you married me, even before she married Patrick. She chose not to."

At last she looks up from the grave and focuses on the granite headstone. "You remember the day we got married? What you promised? Forsaking all others? From this day forward? Till death do us part? Did you really think about what you were saying then?"

"I remember, Drewe. I meant every word." I try to pull her to my side, but she keeps a stiff elbow between us.

She turns to me, her green eyes bright. "Promises are easy, Harper. Think hard. Love is a terrible compromise if you choose to see it as one. If you're faithful, I'm the only comfort you'll ever have." Her jaw muscles flex with determination. "But I'm special. I'm smart and I'm beautiful and I'm enough for you to live inside forever, if you know how to open me up."

"I know that. I've always known it."

She looks up and scans the wide expanse of the cemetery. I watch her from the side, her profile regal, her thick auburn hair rippling from beneath the black hat, catching a wisp of breeze. She has never looked stronger or more unattainable than at this moment. As she turns to me, I look down, not wanting to be caught staring. My eyes register a dark glint against the sheen of the coffin.

"You dropped your sunglasses," I tell her.

"What? Where?"

"Down there." I point into the grave. "I don't want to sound superstitious, but maybe we should just leave them."

"Those aren't mine."

"What?"

She points to her throat. Her Ray-Bans lie flat against her black dress, suspended from the high neckline by one earpiece.

The wraparound glasses in the grave lie at the very foot of the coffin. That's why I didn't see them while I was playing the guitar. They almost look positioned there, rather than dropped from some distraught mourner's hand. They stare up out of the hole like a pair of sightless eyes.

"Drewe?"

"I wonder if they're Mother's," she says, stepping to the edge of the grave and bending over.

I catch her arm. "Stop."

"Ow! That hurts."

"Stand up, Drewe. Stand up straight."

"What?"

"He's here."

"What?"

"He's here."

"Who?"

Then she is looking up into my face with horror.

"Don't look around," I tell her, even as I do myself. Every headstone in the field now seems capable of concealing a killer. My eye inventories mausoleums at the speed of light, prioritizing the most dangerous areas.

"He didn't do the killings," I hear myself whisper.

"What?"

"He didn't kill the EROS women. The Indian woman did. He only fired the tranquilizer gun. We've got a chance."

"Harper, he's dead. How can he be here?"

I'm trying to appear calm, but if Berkmann is watching me, he must see me scanning the headstones with the controlled panic of a soldier walking point in the jungle. "We're going to have to run."

"Where?" Drewe asks, her voice thin.

"The Explorer's parked behind the superintendent's office."

"That's a hundred yards away."

"I'm going to leave my guitar here."

She squeezes my hand, hard. "Shouldn't we take it with us? Try to act casual and get as far as we can? You can drop it if we have to run."

"We have to run *now.* He could be fifteen yards away, between us and the truck. Take three or four deep breaths, then break for it when I do. Watch the ground, not the building. Don't trip."

"Should I hold your hand?"

"No. If he chases us, I'll stay behind you. Don't look back. If he jumps up in front of us, I'll have to try to kill him. You keep running."

"Harper—"

"*Keep running*. My thirty-eight is under the driver's seat. That's the only way you can help me if I have to fight. Here are the keys."

"Oh."

"Take them. God, I wish your father was still here. We'd kill that son of a bitch right now. Okay, get ready. One, two—"

We're off without ever saying "go," flying across the grass like locust shells blasted before a prairie wind. With every step I see Berkmann's powerful body rising from behind a gravestone, scalpel in hand, moving with the speed and inevitability of nightmares. I pump my legs furiously, willing Drewe faster as in my mind Berkmann angles toward her, me running to get between them but not making it as he plunges the scalpel into her stomach—

The superintendent's office is closer, maybe fifty yards. I hold back, giving Drewe the lead, pivoting my head as I try to scan 360 degrees of threat, knowing he can see me, that he can pick his moment—

"Harper!"

Drewe is down. Something tripped her and laid her out hard on a flat stone the length of a coffin. I yank her up, still looking frantically around us. She cradles one elbow as if it's broken.

"Can you run?"

"Go!" she gasps.

I start to run, but she jerks me to a stop. "The keys!"

She darts back to the gravestone and begins scouring its surface like someone searching for a contact lens.

"Drewe?"

"I've got them! Go!"

Even as the ranks of stones tighten around us, we pick a sure path through them, dodging the little bronze-roofed markers that read "Perpetual Care." They might as well be land mines. We're five yards from the office when a dark-haired man in a tan jacket steps out from behind it.

Drewe shrieks and cuts to the right. With adrenaline

spurting like hydraulic fluid into my limbs, I empty my lungs in a savage scream and charge. The man shouts my name and brings up one hand, but I see only his throat. I pounce like a wildcat, both hands throttling him as he tumbles backward. The impact knocks out his wind, and I pummel his face with three quick rights before he can recover. Fury and fear flash in his eyes as blood from his broken nose fills the orbits. Feeling him going limp beneath me, I push off his chest with both hands, scramble to my feet, and sprint the last few yards to the back of the superintendent's office.

Drewe is already inside the Explorer. A sharp thump startles me—then I realize she just unlocked the doors. I leap into the driver's seat as she clambers across the console to the passenger side. In one continuous motion I crank the engine, throw it into gear, and hit the gas. The tires spin wildly on the gravel before they catch, and we hurtle forward onto the narrow asphalt lane as though shot from a catapult.

"Was it him?" yells Drewe, gulping air.

"Get down!" The Explorer is doing fifty through the headstones and still accelerating.

"Was it him?"

"I don't know!"

"You don't know?"

"It looked like him!"

"Did you kill him?"

I shake my head, trying to keep us on course and watch the rearview mirror at the same time. "I hurt him enough to get past him."

Drewe slumps down in the seat and begins probing her elbow joint. "Maybe it wasn't him," she says, her breathing ragged. "I mean, anybody could have dropped those glasses."

"Into her grave? No. He's here."

"You don't know that. I think you didn't kill him because you weren't sure."

As the Explorer rockets through the cemetery gate and onto the highway, one image fills my mind: two tall, stunningly dressed and coiffed young women at the edge of the burial crowd, and beside them, a gray-hatted man wearing sunglasses.

"He's here, Drewe. He wants to kill us."

"So why didn't he?"

"I don't know."

Chapter 45

From the cemetery I drove straight to Sheriff Buckner's office in Yazoo City. I answered Drewe's questions about Berkmann as best I could without revealing the existence of the videotape. I told her who he was, that the FBI had identified him with Miles's help, and that Miles had sent me a picture of him via computer. The fact that Drewe's early theories about the case had proved to be so accurate gave her little solace. She seemed bent on convincing herself—and me—that Berkmann had died in the plane crash.

Sheriff Buckner had attended Erin's burial, but when Drewe and I were ushered into his office we found him eating a shrimp po'boy with his feet propped on his desk. He started shaking his head the moment he saw me. Before I said anything, he wiped tartar sauce off his mouth, put down his sandwich, stood, and paid Drewe his respects. Then he looked at me and said, "I don't know whether to arrest you or give you a medal."

Buckner had just heard from the Yazoo City police chief how Bob Anderson's son-in-law had gone crazy out at the cemetery and assaulted an FBI agent named Wes Killen. The agent had called 911 on a cellular phone and was now on his way to the emergency room at Kings Daughters Hospital.

While Drewe and I gaped, Buckner explained that the FBI had insisted on sending an observer to Erin's funeral on the chance that her killer might show up. He got a big charge out of the fact that I'd brained the FBI man before he could get to his gun, and pointed out that Erin's murderer, had he been there, would probably have killed Special Agent Killen long before he was "observed."

I wasn't amused by the story, but at last I understood why—if Edward Berkmann *had* been at the cemetery—he did not kill Drewe and me. Special Agent Wes Killen didn't pull a gun on me because he knew me—probably from pictures—but he would have shot Berkmann in a heartbeat.

Sheriff Buckner listened to my sunglasses story with the sincerity of a doctor humoring a schizophrenic. He promised to look into the three "out-of-towners" I'd noticed at the funeral, but we were clearly wasting our time. As we left, Buckner told me not to worry about the FBI agent pressing assault charges. The Bureau would never stand for the embarrassment of a public trial.

We are almost to Drewe's parents' house now, and I'm doubting myself more with each passing mile. Who's to say someone *didn't* accidentally drop their sunglasses into the grave, then decide that retrieving them would be too embarrassing? Maybe it's Berkmann's video that's got me paranoid. The shocking intensity of his personality makes it hard to accept the idea that he's dead.

When Bob's mansion comes into sight, surrounded by a visiting fleet of automobiles, Drewe says, "I really do have to be there."

"I know."

Looking into her lap, she shakes her head. "All those damned casseroles."

"I know. Erin would have hated it."

She looks sharply at me. Then, slowly, she softens her gaze. "You're right."

I decide to take a desperate gamble for normalcy.

"Think of the poor chickens who died to make all that tetrazzini."

Drewe backhands my chest with a stinging pop, but the hint of a smile tugs at her mouth. She knows exactly what I'm feeling. A thousand sacred words and condolences are nothing compared to one throwaway line that captures something of Erin's real life. We both know Erin would have hit me the same way for that joke, and Drewe acting as her surrogate brings her back to life for us, if only for an instant.

In the momentary escape from grief, I'm tempted to bring up the question that has tortured me ever since I told Drewe the truth about Holly. What about Patrick? Does she think he should be given the answer to the question that has haunted him so long? Has she already spoken to him? This is the final legacy of the secret, the last unexploded mine. But right now I don't have the nerve to probe it.

"What does the house look like?" Drewe asks, her voice heavy.

"I scrubbed out the office. The deputies tore things up pretty bad, and it smells like tear gas, but I managed to sleep there last night."

"Pull in," she says, pointing out a path through the cars blocking Bob's majestic drive.

I have to park thirty yards from the front entrance. Drewe opens the Explorer's door but does not get out. Feeling a strange tingle in my chest, I reach for the ignition key and shut off the engine. She closes the door again and settles into her seat.

We sit in the muggy silence, the dead motor ticking like a half-sprung clock. I'm about to suggest that we get out and talk when she says, "As bad as this is, I still believe one thing. We were meant for each other. I've always known that, and so has anyone who ever knew us."

She is looking at the windshield, not me. A hundred

words pop into my head; all sound calculated and hollow.

"I've been thinking," she says, watching an elderly couple shuffle out of the entrance arch. "We've been here too long. Rain, I mean. It's too safe. I know that sounds ridiculous, considering what happened to us here. But maybe that's *why* it happened. You know? We wanted too much to go backward. To this ground where we grew up, to our families, or their memories." At last she turns to me, her eyes filled with conviction. "We won't grow in this soil, Harper. We've got to find our own place."

In these words I hear the door to my future opening. "You're my love, Drewe. You always have been. Just tell me where you want to go."

She smiles and lays a hand over mine. "Give me an hour and a half. Then come back for me."

Excitement quickens my blood. "You're coming home tonight?"

"Yes. To pack."

"Where are we going?"

"We're moving, Harper. Tomorrow, if not today."

"Where?"

"We'll rent a house in Jackson to start. After that, we'll work it out. Wherever we want. It's time to go."

I search her face for signs of doubt, but there are none. I start to get out and to walk her to the door, but she stops me by leaning over the console and kissing me on the cheek.

"Make it an hour," she says.

Still flying from Drewe's kiss, I pull into the parking lot of a convenience store and head for the pay phone. The Kings Daughters Hospital operator connects me with an ER nurse who eventually gets special agent Wes Killen to the phone.

I apologize before I tell Killen who I am, and again after. He listens to my explanation with professional detachment, then begins asking questions as I tell him the story of the sunglasses. He promises to have the Bureau check with the airlines for anyone resembling the "New York people" I saw at the funeral.

Unbelievably, Killen has to return to the cemetery and continue his vigil at Erin's grave. He even criticizes himself for leaving his post long enough to get his nose patched up. After he gives me a cellular phone number I can use to reach him if I need to, I apologize once more and sign off.

Driving back to our farmhouse, I feel I'm traveling a road I've never seen before. Because it is no longer the road home. It's the road away. The road that will lead Drewe and me out of the past and into our future. The events that brought us to this point are too painful even to focus on, yet they have delivered us from ourselves. For the first time, I allow myself to believe that the demented killer who pissed into my guitar for posterity might actually be bumping along the bottom of the Mississippi River, getting nested in by catfish or ripped to pieces by gar.

When I sight a sheriff's department cruiser parked by our mailbox, it strikes me how paranoid I must seem to Sheriff Buckner. Yet as I park under the weeping willow by our porch, my anxiety returns. Heeding the old fear, I reach under the seat for my .38 and grip it tightly as I open the front door of the house.

The reek of tear gas and Clorox is still strong, and the house feels empty. In fact, it feels more like a place I once lived than the home that nurtured four generations of my family. This feeling embarrasses me, as though I've broken faith with my maternal ancestors. Yet if my great-grandfather were alive, he would probably forgive me. He came to Mississippi from Scotland, and despite his love for this land, he understood that most primitive of truths: sometimes people have to move to survive.

I open all the windows in the house, hoping to air out some of the stink for Drewe's sake. Then I get out my address book and call every bank and brokerage company with which I have an account. Balances in hand, I go to my Gateway 2000, boot up Quicken—which I have neglected for weeks—and update each account. Then I total all the balances.

The result is pretty gratifying.

My watch tells me I'll be ten minutes late picking up Drewe, given the usual twenty-minute drive to Bob's house. Picking up the keys and the .38, I trot for the front door. My hand is on the knob when the phone rings. I pause, listening for the answering machine in case it's Drewe. Instead I hear the voice of Arthur Lenz.

"Hello? Cole? Pick up if you're there."

"I'm here!" I yell, sprinting back to the machine. I hit the MEMO button so that Lenz's words will be recorded, then pick up the cordless. "I'm listening, Doctor."

"Oh. Good. I've spoken to one of the profilers Daniel has working the EROS case. A man I trained. I'm conversant with the new data on Berkmann."

"And?"

"I've put together my own profile."

"Go."

"I believe our usual classification system—organized versus disorganized behavior—is inadequate to describe Edward Berkmann. Until recently, he did not kill from uncontrollable impulse. Nor did he develop better technique with each murder, as most killers do. He was like Mozart. From the very first crime he demonstrated genius. He not only staged murder scenes, he seemed to know our specific classification criteria and manipulated evidence accordingly, to prevent computer matches. Effectively, he had no crime signature. 'Super-organized' would be my term of choice."

"Okay."

"No serial killer has functioned in society to the degree that Berkmann did. The only possible analogy would be the royal physician suspected in the Whitechapel murders—the Jack the Ripper case—but his guilt was never proved. In terms of raw intelligence and education, Berkmann was—or is—probably superior to ninety-nine percent of the people hunting him."

"That's painfully obvious."

"You actually hit on the truth that night in my car, Cole. Until recently, Berkmann was killing for a perfectly rational reason. Transplantation of human pineal tissue is theoretically possible and may have significant therapeutic effects. As a neurosurgeon, Berkmann understood that this procedure would never be developed under current experimental guidelines. He simply decided it was worth sacrificing a few lives to make the attempt. Not so long ago, mainstream American medicine made similar decisions about research using convicts."

"You sound like you're defending his actions."

"I merely make the point that their moral character is a separate question from their scientific defensibility. It's immaterial so far as analyzing motive, and especially in trying to predict his future behavior."

"Where's all this leading?"

"Berkmann saw himself as a sort of modern-day Prometheus. Defying God's law to steal fire for mankind. Fire symbolizes freedom. Given Berkmann's background, particularly his disease, he sought the only fire modern man is still denied: freedom from death. He committed the gravest mortal sin—premeditated murder—in pursuit of immortality. He undoubtedly believed that others would eventually see him in a heroic context as well. That's what he meant in his note, when he told us to be patient. That he would 'come to us' when his work was done. He eventually meant to go public."

"That doesn't tell me what I want to know."

"I'm getting to that," Lenz says, obviously annoyed at being rushed. "Despite all I've said, I now believe that Berkmann is in fact decompensating—coming apart—just as other serial killers do. Our murderous Mozart is finally joining the ranks of the Salieris."

"Why do you say that?"

"Because if he weren't, he would not have made a single tactical mistake. As it stands, he's made several. When he learned we were hunting him, he could have gone underground, stopped his pineal work indefinitely. But he didn't. Like all egomaniacs, he took offense, became indignant, then furious. And eventually he committed a murder simply to chastise us."

"Your wife."

A brief pause. "Yes. You see, even though there was a 'rational' reason for Berkmann's early murders, an underlying sexual psychosis was always at work. Like two minds working in parallel. We were both right, Cole. With the stressor of FBI pursuit, Berkmann's subconscious drive began its ascendancy."

"And?"

"That's the key to his future behavior. If he's still alive, of course."

"How so? What's he going to do?"

"It all comes down to the mother."

"Catherine Berkmann?"

"Yes. From his oral family history, you might think the flamboyant father—Richard—was the dominant force in Edward's life. But he wasn't. It was Catherine who seduced her brother in order to prevent the extrafamilial marriage. It was Catherine who gave birth to Edward amid shot and shell, shepherded him through hunger and privation to reach America. *She* was the anima behind his subconscious sexual urges. And she made herself felt at every EROS crime scene, even though the murders were technically committed to harvest pineal glands."

"The postmortem rapes?"

"Exactly. Tell me, did you notice that the name 'Erin' is fully contained within 'Catherine'? That undoubtedly contributed to your success in drawing Berkmann, even though you knew nothing about it."

"My God. I never saw it."

"This is the key, Cole. Did you notice his choice of words in describing Kali? He didn't call her his wife, or his lover, but his *concubine*."

"So?"

"The word has some very specific meanings. One refers to a secondary wife, one of inferior status. Yet we know from the transcripts that Berkmann legally married Kali."

"So?"

"If she was of secondary status, who held the primary position?"

At last I see it.

"He's been searching for that person his whole life," Lenz says. "The substitute for his mother, the sister-lover he never had. Your 'Erin' came along at precisely the right moment. The similarities between the names, your own incestuous secret revealed to him through her eyes. He couldn't resist it."

"And his transplant plans?"

"Fate and the FBI had already interrupted them. His scientific search for immortality was on hold. But there was always another way."

"Children," I say softly, recalling Miles's thesis.

"Exactly. The only true immortality we'll ever have. At some level Berkmann always knew that. Even if he gained an extra twenty vital years from his pineal transplant, he would only be postponing the end. But DNA lives forever. As long as there are offspring, anyway."

A single searing image fills my brain: the incision in Erin's abdomen. "That's why he . . ."

"The ovaries, Cole. That's why he cut out Erin Graham's ovaries."

"He threw them away. When he found out Erin wasn't who he thought she was, he threw them away."

"I'm sorry."

"Goddamn it, what's the final answer here? If he's alive, will he run or will he come back here?"

"Tell me about the videotape. Did he threaten you?"

"Not beyond the 'mills of the gods' line."

"Nothing else? You've got to realize that Berkmann's mental decompensation wouldn't prevent him from being as calculating or manipulative as he ever was. It's conceivable that everything on that tape was meant to influence you in a certain way."

Though my mind resists it, I force myself to replay the sickening tape in my mind. "He seemed to lose control about halfway through it. He said he was going into hiding. He also seemed to fixate on my wife at one point. He called her the alpha female of the family, talked about how perfect she was."

"Did he say anything else about her?"

"He said I didn't deserve her."

"You should move her to a safe location as quickly as possible. Tell no one where you're going."

I swallow, my throat dry. "You really think—"

"Edward Berkmann is a profoundly disturbed man who has been cut loose from his moorings. His only trusted ally was killed before his eyes. You are responsible for that. If he's alive, he might be looking for revenge. He might have transferred his subconscious anima projection onto your wife. Anything is possible at this point."

"That's what I wanted to know, Doctor. I appreciate it."

"I hope he's dead, Cole. I couldn't have said that a week ago. But I mean it now."

"I hope so too. Good-bye."

As I set down the phone, the effect of Lenz's words flows through me like electric current. Though it will make me even later, I find the Jackson yellow pages and open them to the Realtors' section. Picking the biggest ad for Ridgeland, I dial the number. It's nearly seven-forty, but I doubt the place is completely empty. After about twenty rings, a curt female voice answers. When I tell her I'm looking for a house to rent, not buy, the coolness becomes frigidity. Then I say the magic words.

"Money is not a consideration."

She adopts a guardedly warmer tone. "A lot of people say that until they hear the prices out there. There's really nothing to rent."

"There's always something for the right price."

"Well . . . there is one place for sale; the owners got tired of waiting and moved to Idaho. But they wouldn't rent for less than . . . four thousand. A month. And you couldn't have a lease."

"You'll have a check for twelve grand in your hand tomorrow. But you don't tramp any buyers through there for the next three months. Deal?"

I can almost hear her cursing herself for not asking more. After she takes my name, I race out to the Explorer with my keys in one hand and my pistol in the other.

Drewe is waiting outside her parents' house with her bag. She doesn't seem angry that I'm late. As I get out to open her door, someone opens the great front door of the Anderson house. It's Patrick. He's standing inside with Holly in his arms.

"Uncle Harp!"

The three-year-old begins squirming, leaving Patrick no choice but to let her down. She flies off the steps like a brunette cannonball and races to me. My eyes still on Patrick, I kneel and stop her at arm's length, trying to keep my smile natural. While she squeezes closer, I glance to my left, at Drewe, but she looks away quickly and walks over to Patrick.

I lift Holly into my arms and hug her tight. She digs her face into my neck and folds her arms between us, as if to go to sleep on my shoulder.

"How you doin', punkin?" I ask softly.

She shakes her head.

"What is it?"

"I miss Mommy."

I close my eyes against the sting of tears, but it's no use. Holly leans back, round-eyed and concerned. She touches the drops on my cheek. "You miss her too?"

"I miss her too, punkin."

Her lower lip puffs out in a mixture of sadness and strength that I saw on Erin's face many times.

"I'm okay, punkin. Thanks to you."

"PawPaw and Daddy say Mommy's in heaven," she whispers. "Watching over us. Is that right? I can't see her up there."

"You listen to your Daddy," I whisper back, wishing I had Patrick's blind faith in God and all the rest.

"We've got to go, sweetie," Drewe says, suddenly beside us.

She pulls Holly away, walks to the steps, and deposits her in Patrick's arms. The symbolic nature of this act is inescapable. Patrick gives me a blank wave, then turns and goes back into the house. Holly watches me over his shoulder as they go.

Taking a deep breath, I climb back into the Explorer. Drewe is already inside, facing sternly forward. The first fifteen minutes of the drive pass in awkward silence. The stripped cotton fields look barren as battlefields, and the hope I felt so recently wavers in the face of them.

"I got us a house," I say finally, almost in defense.

"What?"

"I got us a house. In Ridgeland. We can move in this week. If it's not ready by tomorrow, we can get a hotel."

Her glance is brief, but I see gratitude in it.

"Drewe—"

"It's okay to talk about it," she says too loudly. "The worst thing we could do is keep it hidden, like a piece of broken crystal. The first time we had to touch it, we'd both get cut."

"Does Patrick know anything yet?"

She faces forward again, as though watching for our driveway, which we could both find blindfolded if necessary. "No."

"Erin wanted to tell him the truth, Drewe. That's what she told me the day she died. She was planning to tell him that night. And she wanted me to tell you."

She brushes a strand of hair out of her eyes. "Don't you think she was going to tell because she felt she had no option? That if she didn't, Patrick would leave her?"

I shrug. "I don't know. Erin seemed different that day. Like she'd grown into a different person. It made me ashamed of myself, really. She was totally committed to her decision."

"Don't tell me this, Harper."

"I'm sorry. I just wanted you to know the whole truth."

She turns to me, her green eyes burning. "The truth? I'll tell you what the truth is. Patrick is a good man. A good father. Even during the craziness of the past few weeks, he hasn't let Holly see anything. With Erin gone, his obsession is going to fade. You should see him. He's latched onto that child like a life raft. I think he realizes how stupid he was to have wasted time badgering Erin about the past. Because now she's gone. I don't think he'll waste any more."

"So you're saying—"

"I'm saying Patrick will never know about you and Erin. Neither will Holly. It will be harder on you than anybody, watching her grow up without knowing what you really are to her. But it has to be that way. You understand?"

I nod silently.

"For a while they'll be close to us, to my parents. But Patrick will eventually remarry and they'll drift away. It will hurt you. It will even hurt me. But that's the way life is. And somewhere out in the world, a little piece of Erin and you will be alive. Long after we're dead even." Drewe looks away abruptly, and I realize she is hiding tears. "She'll be okay, though. She comes from good people. Don't miss the damned drive."

I hit the brakes and wheel onto the gravel. As I pull around Drewe's Acura and park, she says, "It's settled, then?"

"Yes."

"Good. Let's pack the essentials and go."

I am packing in my office when I notice the e-mail icon blinking beneath Nefertiti's slowly turning head on the EROS computer. Dropping a can of shaving gel into my dopp kit, I stare at the icon. The sounds of Drewe packing in her bedroom echo up the hallway. Willing myself to be calm, I walk over and click the mouse on the icon. At the top of the message I see this:

SENDER: SYSOP/Edward Berkmann, M.D.

Chapter 46

Waiting for Miles to answer his cellular phone, I try desperately to remember whether my e-mail icon was blinking last night, whether I could possibly have missed it in the insanity of viewing Erin's body or mopping up the blood. I don't think so. Nor was it blinking this afternoon. This message arrived in the past hour, as its time stamp indicates. Still, with my breath coming shallow, I pray that Berkmann somehow planted the message for delayed delivery while in the house yesterday.

"Turner here."

A cacophony of road noise threatens to drown Miles's voice. He is obviously walking or riding down a street somewhere.

"It's Harper. Berkmann may be alive."

"Why do you say that?"

"I just got an e-mail message from him, via EROS."

"Time-stamped?"

"Thirty minutes ago."

"What does it say?"

"How did you like my little documentary? I'd love to hear your comments. I'll be waiting for you in the Blue Room."

There's a pause. "He could have sent that from his plane. Before it went down. What's the alias?"

"None. It's from SYSOP 1."

"It can't be!"

"Man, are you in denial or what?"

"Look, Berkmann got that last e-mail message into the system through an old toll access line on a backup server. I found it and closed it off. Maybe this is one of my assistants. Fucking with us for a joke."

"Where's Baxter, Miles? Can you contact him?"

"He's still in Connecticut. The state police are canvassing homes in the area of the airstrip Berkmann used, looking for the killing house. You at home?"

"Yes."

"I'll call Baxter, call you right back."

I don't move a foot from the phone while I wait. From the noise coming up the hallway, Drewe is still wading through her drawers and closet. In less than two minutes Miles is back on the line.

"You're right," he says, his voice strangely muted. "Berkmann's in the system right now. The son of a bitch is alive."

"Jesus. I knew it."

"The night he stole the master client list, he must have put a back door into the system. But he never used it. He knew the logs would catch him."

"Never used it until now, you mean."

"Right."

"Can you trace him, Miles?"

"No. The FBI pulled their equipment off our switching system when we closed to clients, and the phone company won't help me without the FBI."

"So what do I do?"

"Log in to the Blue Room and see what he wants."

"Hell no!"

"Baxter agrees, Harper. Keep him online long enough to check for typos. If there aren't any, at least we know he's back on his voice-recognition system. Back in New York."

"How could he have gotten back to New York?"

"Same way I got to Mississippi from Manhattan. Paying

cash for air tickets. Hell, he could have ridden a Trailways up here by now. He could have stolen a plane down there. I'll get Baxter to start checking that stuff."

"I think he's still down here, Miles."

"Why?"

I relate the story of the sunglasses in Erin's grave, but Miles puts about as much stock in it as Sheriff Buckner did.

"Just talk to him long enough to look for typos," he says. "If he's back in New York, we'll have him." His voice drops in volume. "Baxter's wasting his time in Connecticut. The killing house is here, Harper. Somewhere close to the medical school. I've already found people who've seen Berkmann before. Washington Heights people. I'm on 169th Street right now."

I hesitate. "Dr. Lenz said Drewe and I should split. Get somewhere safe."

"Yeah? Where's that?"

When I don't answer, Miles says, "Safe for us is a function of Edward Berkmann no longer breathing. At some level you know that."

"Okay . . . damn."

Not giving myself time for second thoughts, I hang up and log in to the system as HARPER/SYSOP 2, then click into the Blue Room. It's empty. I type a quick query—*Where are you?*—route it to SYSOP 1, then activate the voice-recognition program.

Almost immediately, "BERKMANN/SYSOP 1" appears in the top left corner of my screen under "WHO'S HERE?" Then, like a voice from the grave, the now-chilling digital baritone fills the office as letters appear on my screen.

BERKMANN> Hello, Harper. How did you like my little film?

This final proof that Berkmann is alive starts my heart pumping like a fist clenching and unclenching in my chest. Fighting fear, I pull on the headset and begin speaking—not as Erin this time, but as myself.

HARPER> Not as well as the FBI did.

BERKMANN> Don't lie, little ankle biter. You didn't show that tape to anyone.

HARPER> Where are you, Doctor?

BERKMANN> South of the border, north of the Antarctic. I'm quite safe, as I told you I would be. That's why I'm not worried about being traced.

HARPER> A lot of people thought you died in a plane crash.

BERKMANN> Very gratifying. It took a bit of effort to create that illusion.

HARPER> Why bother creating an illusion? Why not use the plane to run?

BERKMANN> Obviously Daniel Baxter told you to keep me on the line. I'll oblige. You deserve a little entertainment before the remainder of your pathetic life turns to shit.

HARPER> What does that mean?

BERKMANN> The mills of the Gods, remember? When I left your house, I managed to reach the plane all right, and get airborne. But the plane developed engine trouble. I considered ditching in the river, but my nerve failed. I ended up setting down on a spur levee. I'd heard of a Venezuelan crew that landed a 727 on a levee near New Orleans in an emergency. It was simple enough. The difficult part was taxiing down the slope and into the water. Amazing that the plane turned up, though. Very dramatic. The Lord

taketh away my engine but giveth confusion unto mine enemies.

HARPER> You don't believe in God.

BERKMANN> You are not qualified to discuss the concept of God with me.

I've yet to see a single typo in Berkmann's words, but I want to be absolutely sure I've given him enough time.

HARPER> I've asked Baxter to let me view your execution. He said he'd do all he could, but there's a long waiting list. It's the gas chamber here in Mississippi, you know.

BERKMANN> Empty words. I honestly can't believe you fooled me for a minute. But you did, didn't you? You and your Southern charm. It turned out to be as hollow as Southern honor.

The sudden ring of the telephone jars me. Hitting the space bar to mute the mike, I answer it.

"Well?" says Miles, as Berkmann's voice continues from the speakers.

"I'm on with him now."

"Any typos?"

"None yet. Two screens worth of text."

"He's back in New York!"

"He says he's outside the country, Miles. Sounds like maybe South America."

"Out of the country? Shit. How could he get out?"

"Same way he could get back to New York."

"Keep him on as long as you can."

"I don't want to talk to him!"

"*Please,* Harper. I'm getting close to him. I can feel it."

Berkmann's voice shocks me back to reality.

BERKMANN> Having a nice chat with Daniel Baxter?

HARPER> My mother-in-law was trying to come into the office. I had to get her out.

BERKMANN> Another lie. She wouldn't be speaking to you at all. Not after you got her daughter killed.

The ringing sibilance of water rushing through pipes breaks my concentration. Drewe is taking a shower. I guess I can put up with Berkmann's crap for a few minutes in the hope that Miles could be right about the killing house.

HARPER> Did you really try to save Erin?

BERKMANN> Yes. There was no need for her to die. Were it not for you, she would be alive tonight.

HARPER> Turn yourself in, Doctor. This game's over. They know who you are. It's just a matter of time.

BERKMANN> No, no, no. I still have much to do.

HARPER> Such as?

BERKMANN> I am smiling, Harper. Smiling with cosmic humor at fate's great joke. You lured me to your house to capture me and instead led me to the threshold of my apotheosis.

HARPER> I don't understand.

BERKMANN> How could you? You are a polyp of fetid protoplasm in the cesspool of the herd. I speak to you for only one reason. You have something I want. And very soon I shall have it.

Lenz's warnings echo in my head like the shouts of an unheeded prophet.

HARPER> What do you want?
BERKMANN> Don't you know? I want Drewe.

I have to squeeze my hands together to stop them shaking.

HARPER> What connection do you think you have with Drewe?
BERKMANN> What connection do we not have? Erin was an illusion. A Caucasian Kali, expanded into symbol by your imagination. But Drewe is real. Everything that has happened, each apparent mistake, every seeming obstacle was but a waypoint on the road to Drewe. She is my mother and my father together. She is Apollonian woman, pale and proud, Aryan, brilliant, uncontaminated by your corrupt seed because she is incorruptible. She is a vessel full yet waiting to be filled. She is OMPHALOS, a navel of the world. Through her loins I SHALL CONQUER TIME. For years she has waited, uncertain why. But soon she will know. And she will come to me like the moth to the flame.
HARPER> She'll laugh in your face. Or spit in it.
BERKMANN> You tremble at every word I speak. You KNOW she is a seed you have not brought to flower. Because you are unequal to her. How she must have dreaded your clumsy carnal attentions. It SICKENS me.
HARPER> How do you plan to bring her to flower?
BERKMANN> By separating her from you.
HARPER> How can you do that?
BERKMANN> With the truth. We are broken from within, remember? Your life holds the key to its own destruction. You are a liar and a cow-

ard. The truth of your betrayal with Erin, and her child, will separate you from Drewe as certainly as prison walls. When she delivers my issue from her pure womb, you will feel pain as of nails being driven through your skull.

From a whirlwind of fear, a lifeline of hope. The sword Berkmann thinks he holds over my head hangs over his own. But there's no reason to let him know that.

HARPER> You'll never get close to her, you piece of shit.
BERKMANN> Do I need to? What is truth but information? And that is the easiest thing in the world to move.
HARPER> She'd kill herself before she'd let you touch her.
BERKMANN> Keep telling yourself that. By tonight she will be trying to reach me.
HARPER> You're amazing. You're a fucking parasite. A second-rate quack who spent his life stealing other people's research and dreaming about his dead whore of a mother.

This finally stops Berkmann. At length, as if he has regained his composure, he replies:

BERKMANN> I AM to you as the SUN to a GRAIN OF SAND. As the EAGLE to the WORM. I had your friend Turner like a WOMAN. I swam in Eros like a shark in a tidal pool, feeding on what I chose. I delivered Lenz's wife to the knife, and it was a MERCY KILLING. I am the WILL TO POWER made FLESH upon the EARTH. I AM AN ARROW TEARING THROUGH THE VEIL OF TIME.

I've had enough. The line about Miles rattled me, but not enough to give Berkmann the last word.

> **HARPER> You spout Nietzsche like a college sophomore. Fitting, since he died eating his own excrement.**
>
> **BERKMANN> I shall be here when Drewe calls me.**

I slam down the ESCAPE key and terminate the conversation. My hands are shaking with rage as I dial Miles's cellular.

"Harper?"

"Not a single typo. Are you anywhere close to finding his place?"

"Maybe. I'm waiting for a guy now. A homeless guy named Leonardo. He's a sidewalk artist. Leonardo. You believe that? He's supposed to know something."

"Like what?"

"I won't know till I see him, will I?"

"What about Baxter? He found anything?"

"Nothing."

"Damn! You've got to find him, Miles. He wants Drewe."

"Drewe?"

"He's fixated on her, obsessed. Like he thought he was with Erin. He bragged about you too. He *laughed*. He's the most arrogant son of a bitch I've ever seen."

The silence on the other end of the phone is absolute. I know I've wounded Miles deeply, but maybe I wanted to. Maybe I want him in a state of fury when he finally faces Berkmann.

"Harper?"

Drewe's voice sends a shock through my nervous system. I turn to my right and see her standing three feet inside my office—the room she has not entered for seven weeks—wearing nothing but a white terry bathrobe and a damp towel wrapped around her hair.

"What's happening?" she asks. "Who wants me?"

"I've got to go, Miles."

"Wait! I need you to keep him online."

"I can't do it. You be careful." I break the connection with the finger button.

"Harper?" Drewe says again.

I consider lying, then crush the impulse. "Berkmann's alive, Drewe."

"How do you know?"

"I just talked to him on EROS."

"Oh, God."

"His text isn't showing any errors, so at least he's back in New York. Miles is trying to find him right now."

She folds her arms across her chest as if suddenly cold. "I heard my name through the speakers. I heard him say my name."

Jesus. "He's just playing games. You don't need to know this stuff." I move toward her, but she takes a step back.

"Don't patronize me like that. What did he say about me?"

"He's obsessed with you. He's nuts. Let's get out of here."

"What video were you talking about?"

"Drewe—"

"What video?"

I sigh wearily. "He left a video here after Erin's murder."

"Where is it?"

"I sent it to the FBI this morning."

Her eyes never leave my face. "But you kept a copy. You don't trust anyone enough not to keep a backup. I know you."

"I didn't, Drewe." No one in the world could fault me for that lie.

"I know you're trying to protect my feelings," she says. "But we're past that. I want to see this man."

I take her hand and squeeze it hard. "No, you don't. You don't want those pictures knocking around in your head for the rest of your life."

"Did he have sex with Erin's body like he did with the other victims?"

"No. But he danced her around the room after she was dead. He showed me her ovaries. He pissed into one of my guitars and hung it back on the wall. I took it outside and burned it. You don't want to see this tape."

She closes her eyes. "Get it."

"Drewe—"

"*Get it!* The man who butchered my sister is still free, he has some kind of obsession about me, and you think I'm not mature enough to watch his pathetic cruelty? I'm a doctor, Harper. Get the goddamned thing!"

I go silently to my desk, retrieve the eight-millimeter original, and hand it to her.

"I'll see you when it's over," she says, her face resolute.

"Drewe, please."

"I know how to work the camera. Please get out. This is something I have to do alone."

Chapter 47

While Drewe watches Berkmann's video in my office, I pace around the kitchen like a caged ape. When I can stand it no more, I call Miles from the kitchen telephone. He sounds relieved to hear my voice.

"I'm still waiting for Leonardo to show," he says in a loud whisper. "It better be soon too. It's getting dangerous up here. I just had to take down a couple of kids."

"What do you mean?"

"Couple of brothers backed me up against a wall and told me I was the wrong color for the neighborhood. I thought they wanted to rob me—I've been handing out cash like Santa Claus up here—but they just wanted to fuck me up. They weren't interested in how many black friends I have either. I had to kick them a few times."

"Kick them?" I echo, in the same moment remembering Miles's martial arts training, the assault charge Lenz told me about.

"Berkmann must be crazy to live up here. Maybe it's like a warehouse, where he can just drive right into the building."

"He looked to me like he could take care of himself, Miles."

"We'll find out, won't we? I just hope I find the place soon. It's nearly dark up here."

Which means it will be dark here soon.

Miles is talking again, but I no longer hear him.

Drewe is standing in the kitchen doorway. The towel is gone from her head. Her hair is a storm of copper tangles, her eyes blank circles shot with blood.

"I've got to go, Miles."

"Again?"

I hang up the phone and pull Drewe into a tight embrace. Her arms hang limp at her sides. Her body seems without breath. The robe is wetter than before, with sweat now rather than shower water. "I'm sorry," I whisper. "I tried to tell you."

"I want to talk to him," she says in a dead voice.

"What?" I pull back far enough to look into her eyes.

"I want to talk to Berkmann on the computer."

"I won't let you do it."

"I read your last conversation with him," she says. "In the Blue Room. I want to talk to him."

"If you read that crap, why do you want to talk to him?"

"You can't figure it out?"

"No."

"You will."

I feel myself shaking her, as though I could somehow rattle sense into her, but she doesn't flinch. "Drewe, that's exactly what he wants! He told me you'd be talking to him by tonight!"

"I know."

"So why do it?"

"Because it's the only way to get him."

As I stare, uncomprehending, my office phone rings. I ignore it, but Drewe says, "Answer it. It's probably Miles."

"Drewe—"

"Then I'll answer it." She pulls away and starts for the hall.

I push past her at the office door and pick up the cordless.

"Leonardo came through," Miles says in a breathless

voice. "I've got an address. It's between Harlem and Washington Heights."

"What are you going to do?"

"I'm not sure yet. I don't have a building number, but I've got a block and a description. It's a warehouse, like I guessed. Leonardo has actually talked to Berkmann. People around here think he's mob connected or else a heavy dealer. They leave him alone."

"Have you called Baxter?"

Miles hesitates. "No."

The implications of this are obvious, yet I feel no urge to argue. "What are you thinking?"

"I'm not."

I say nothing.

"It would help if you could keep Berkmann at his computer," he says. "Leonardo's taking me over there now."

I grunt neutrally.

"If he's at his computer, he's occupied."

"Dr. Lenz told me you had a certain item registered in your name in New Jersey. Are you carrying that item?"

"Could be."

A screech of brakes from the receiver makes me pull the phone away from my ear. "Are you in a cab?"

"Are you kidding?" Miles says, breathing harder. "No cabs up here. We're on foot, three blocks from the warehouse. What about it? Will you keep him busy?"

"I won't have to," I reply, my eyes following Drewe as she sits down at the EROS computer. "Drewe can't wait to talk to him."

"What?"

"She watched Berkmann's video."

"Oh, man."

"She's way ahead of you."

"Let her at it, then."

"Just get this asshole, Miles. Fast."

"I'll call you. I'm hanging up now. White guys with cell phones don't exactly blend in up here."

I hang up the cordless and walk over behind Drewe. She hasn't used EROS for six months, but she is flying through its screens like a professional software evaluator.

"Looks like you remember it pretty well."

"Mmm."

"Miles has an address on Berkmann. He's headed over there now. He wants you to keep the bastard online."

"What about the FBI?" she asks, clicking the mouse through the live-chat area.

"He hasn't called them."

Her frenetic movements cease. "Good," she says finally. "Good for him."

"Drewe—"

"All I need to do is send a Quick Message telling Berkmann to meet me in the Blue Room, right?"

"Right."

"What's his User ID?"

"Send it to SYSOP 1."

As she types, she says, "He thinks he's going to destroy our marriage by telling me you're Holly's father." She looks back over her shoulder. "Think what might be happening right now if you hadn't told me the truth."

This thought is enough to make me feel light-headed. Mercifully, she turns back to the screen. I start to read what she is typing but sense that I'm crowding her. I back up.

She stabs the ENTER key. "Message sent. Come to Mama, Edward."

The unfamiliar coldness in her voice jars me.

"What about this headset thing?" she asks. "Will it recognize my voice?"

"It might. There's a female sysop in New York. Miles's voice-rec program is trained to know her. If we select her parameters and you tone down your Southern accent, it might accept you as her. It accepts me as Miles."

I lean over her shoulder and punch up the program, select RACQUEL HIRSCH, then log her in.

"You logged me in as SYSOP 2?"

"It's the only way you can get in. The system's officially closed."

"I want my name at the prompt," she says. "My first name."

I give her a questioning look, but her eyes reveal nothing. She pulls on the headset as I enter the necessary commands.

"How does this work?"

"Talk into the mike, listen through the multimedia speakers. Hit the space bar if you need to talk to me. It mutes the mike."

She hits the space bar and says, "Give me a quick picture of Berkmann," like she's asking an intern for a patient's medical history.

"There's too much to tell. He's a child of incest. His parents were brother and sister. He has—or had—hemophilia."

"What do you mean 'had'? Hemophilia's incurable."

"Not if you're willing to steal a healthy liver."

"Christ. What else?"

"Dr. Lenz says Berkmann's coming apart. Decompensating. That an underlying sexual psychosis is taking over his conscious mind. There are a lot of factors, but it all comes down to his mother. Catherine Berkmann. The postmortem rapes were all because of her. God, I don't remember it all. The Indian woman, Kali, was his lover for years, sort of a second-string wife. But he wants someone like Catherine. A substitute sister-mother to be the mother of *his* child."

Drewe fixes me with a hard stare. "No matter what I say, Harper, ignore it. It doesn't mean anything. Just don't break my train of thought."

Pulling the collar of the robe tight around her neck,

she turns back to the screen, releases the space bar, and says, "This is Dr. Drewe Cole. I want to talk to you."

On the screen, the echo function puts up:

DREWE> This is Dr. Drewe Cole. I want to talk to you.

We wait without speaking, partly because we don't want the microphone to pick up stray conversation, but mostly because there is nothing to say. Nefertiti materializes at the one-minute mark, revolving slowly, her inscrutable countenance unruffled by earthly cares. My tension grows with each revolution of her head, but Drewe sits as calmly as if she were attending a medical seminar.

The ringing telephone startles us both. I carry the cordless across the room before I answer. "Hello?"

"This is Miles," says a strangled voice that makes me dizzy with fear.

"Miles? What's the matter?"

"I'm under arrest."

"What?"

"Baxter used me to find Berkmann. He had two agents tailing me. As soon as they saw me casing a building, they arrested me."

"Where are you now?"

"Outside Berkmann's warehouse. Baxter's choppering over from Connecticut right now. I talked to him. He's got guys on standby ready to take Berkmann down."

My mind reels from the magnitudinal shift in circumstances. "The Hostage Rescue Team?"

"Baxter says New York City SWAT's almost as good, and they're closer. They're on their way now. They'll be in position by the time Baxter gets here."

"Yes!" I cry, giving Drewe a relieved thumbs-up as she

turns from the computer. She hits the space bar and says, "What's happening?"

"The FBI's going to raid Berkmann's place!"

"We're still looking at twenty to thirty minutes," Miles says. "That's why they let me call you. Baxter says you've got to keep Berkmann at his computer. If he's at his computer, hopefully he won't have a gun to the heads of any hostages."

"We're trying. Drewe just queried him, but he hasn't answered."

"Tell her to keep trying."

Despite the good news, I hear defeat in Miles's voice. "Listen," I tell him, "it's better this way. A lot better. If you'd gone in there alone, you might never have come out."

"*He* wouldn't have come out," Miles says softly. "Now he will. All he has to do is surrender. And he may *want* to by now."

As I open my mouth to argue, the digital baritone of Edward Berkmann speaks in my place. Rushing toward the EROS monitor, I see these words appear:

BERKMANN> I'd like to believe that. However, trust must first be established.

"He bit!" I whisper. "Berkmann's online!"

"Established how?" Drewe asks in a loud clear voice. On-screen these words appear:

DREWE> Established how?

"They're talking, Miles. Racquel's voice parameters are working for Drewe."

Disturbed by my volume, Drewe waves me away from the computer. As I hurry toward the Gateway, Berkmann says: *"Can you prove that you are who you say you are, and not your husband?"*

It's disorienting to hear the digital voice without watching the accompanying text on the monitor. It makes Berkmann seem that much closer.

"I don't know," Drewe replies. "Since we don't know each other. We have no common experience you can use to test me."

"Of course we do. You're an obstetrician, correct?"

"Yes."

"Board certified?"

"Of course."

"One never knows these days. If you wouldn't mind answering a few simple questions, we can leave trivialities behind."

"Fine."

"What test would you use to rule out adrenal or ovarian tumors in a patient with hirsutism?"

"A serum DHEA-S for the adrenal," Drewe says automatically. "Serum testosterone for the ovarian tumor."

"He's testing her, Miles. Checking to make sure it's not me."

Miles makes a choking noise that sounds like laughter. "Once burned, twice shy."

"I'm going to hang up and listen. Call me when the SWAT team gets there."

"Your voice-recognition program garbled some of your answer," Berkmann says, *"but I got the gist of it. What is Turner's syndrome?"*

"A genetic defect caused by a forty-five X-oh genotype, which prevents the ovaries from functioning. A classic Turner's patient is a short fifteen-year-old girl with amenorrhea."

"I'm glad you called, Drewe. I've been most anxious to speak with you."

"And I with you. Probably for different reasons."

I am pacing the office now, my whole body charged with anticipation.

"Perhaps not," says Berkmann. *"Are you at home?"*

"Yes."

"Using your husband's computer?"

"Yes."

"Where is he?"

"In and out. We're arguing. I came home to pack."

"Where are you going?"

"Back to my parents, for a start. After that, I don't know."

"Why are you leaving, Drewe?"

"I can't stay here. You should know why."

"Because your sister died there?"

"Because she was butchered here. By you."

"No. I tried to save her."

"Harper told me all about that."

"Your husband is a liar. Nothing he says can be trusted."

"He's lied to me before. But I trust him in some things."

"Harper killed Erin, Drewe."

"That's ridiculous."

"He set up a situation in which nothing else could happen."

"What do you mean?"

"Do you know why my assistant and I came to your home?"

"To kill my sister."

"No. Because I was lured by your husband."

"He pretended to be a woman, right? To catch you."

"Pretended to be a woman, yes, but not to catch me. Do you know what woman he pretended to be?"

"Does it matter?"

"You decide. He pretended to be Erin. He even sent me a picture of her. The one in which she offers a silver chalice to a shadowy figure in an arched doorway. She's wearing a black gown. A highly provocative image."

Drewe turns and looks at me uneasily. "Why would he do that?"

"He chose Erin because they shared a secret. A secret he thought powerful enough to draw me to her. A secret known only to them, and now only to him. Just as he planned."

New fear worms its way up through my chest.

"What secret?" asks Drewe.

"Before I tell you, you must promise to remain online after you learn the truth. Wait until you have heard me out before you try to speak to your husband. I'm telling you his secret for a reason, Drewe. Much more in your life is about to be clarified."

"Get out, Harper!" Drewe cries suddenly. "Go!"

I'm not sure whether she's acting or not, but I'm not about to leave.

"He is with you?" Berkmann asks.

"He's gone now. What is this secret?"

"You promise to remain online?"

"Yes."

"Harper is the father of your sister's child. Holly is her name, I believe?"

Drewe doesn't respond.

"Are you there, Drewe?"

"That's crazy."

"No. Already your skin is cold with fear. That instinctive fear proves the truth of my words."

"No!"

"Picture Holly's face. I have seen that face. She's paler than Erin was. Beautiful, yes, but her face is broader, her eyes not as large. She is bigger-boned. You know whose genes those are."

"I don't believe you."

"Never fight truth, Drewe. You must always embrace it, even if it burns."

"I'm not afraid of truth."

"Good. Good. For this is a difficult one."

"You haven't given me any proof. You're just trying to upset me. You want to get at Harper by hurting me."

"Listen to me, Drewe. Two minutes from now you will hope never to see that pathetic liar again."

"I'm listening."

She turns to me again. There is fear in her eyes now. As I signal her to press the space bar, she turns back to the screen and Berkmann goes on.

"These word are your husband's. Listen and judge. 'She used her mouth for that, and her hands. She knew before I did where I was, you know? And when I started to finish, she didn't pull away. She just . . . Afterward, she stood up and hugged me again. She didn't speak, but I saw she somehow knew her sister didn't complete that act in the way she just had. . . .' "

I feel as though someone has caved in my stomach with a two-by-four. Lenz lied to me. He did tape our sessions, probably on the little Olympus recorder I saw later. And those tapes were part of the "case materials" Kali stole from his study the night she killed his wife.

" 'I thought of Drewe then,' " Berkmann recites, *" 'but she seemed removed from all this, wholly apart from it. It was as if Erin and I were meeting in some place where Drewe didn't exist. . . .' "*

All I can see from where I am standing is the back of Drewe's head, her damp hair falling over the white robe. She sits as motionless as if she were listening to a sermon. I pray she will think Berkmann is making all this up, but the rough blade of reality cuts through with every line. Consumed by impotent rage, I dial Miles's cellular.

"Are they going in yet?"

"SWAT's not even here, man. Take it easy."

"Take it easy! He's tearing her up inside!"

"I'm sorry. I know firsthand, remember? Help her

through it. She's got to keep him on. Unless you can do it."

I disconnect as Berkmann quotes me relentlessly: *" 'She'd risen up and was mouthing "Is that Drewe?" while Drewe said something about a pulmonary embolism. I don't remember what I said to get off the phone, but I knew I had failed Drewe in a time of emotional crisis. What I do remember clearly is what Erin said the moment I hung up. She said, "How are we going to tell her?" ' "*

As Berkmann spoke, I circled to my left, trying to see Drewe's face. I wish I hadn't. Tears are streaming down her cheeks, dropping onto the bosom of the robe. Unable to endure any more, I move forward and lay a comforting hand on her shoulder.

She jerks away like I touched her with a cattle prod.

"Are you there, Drewe?"

"Yes," she says in a cracked voice.

I HATE this motherfucker.

"Can you tell where and when this happened?"

"Chicago."

"Yes. But it had been building for a long time. Because Erin worshiped you, and you loved Harper, how could she not do the same? She was a confused girl. Harper exploited her misguided affections. He used them to seduce her, to debase her, sodomize her, because only by so doing could he express his self-hatred. Yes, self-hatred. You loved him out of naïveté. You did not see his fear. But in his pygmy soul he always knew he was unworthy of you, that you would one day learn his true character. He has dreaded that day—today—for his entire life."

"Why are you doing this?" Drewe asks, her voice shaky. "Telling me all this?"

"To free you."

"What?"

"You're on the verge of a great awakening, Drewe."

"I don't understand."

"But I do. I know you, Drewe. Better than you know yourself. You must be honest with me. Utterly without pretense."

"I'm always honest."

"That statement is itself dishonest. You must strip away ALL pretense. Our time is limited."

"Why is our time limited? You have to be somewhere?"

"There are . . . external concerns."

I feel a sudden shiver. Is Berkmann aware of the approaching SWAT team? Suddenly, the phone rings in my hand.

"New York SWAT just pulled up!" Miles says, his voice barely under control. "Two vans. We're a block away from Berkmann's building. Baxter's touching down on the roof of a bank south of here. NYPD's bringing him to the scene in an unmarked car."

"How long till he gets there?"

"I don't know. How's Drewe doing?"

"It's not pleasant."

"Hang on just a little longer."

"Berkmann seems to be feeling some time pressure, Miles. Maybe you'd better warn those SWAT guys, just in case he knows something."

"Okay. Let's keep the line open from now on."

"I'm here."

"I've had to develop a sort of shell lately," Drewe is saying, "to deal with certain things in my life."

"Just so," says Berkmann. *"But you can shed that as easily as a serpent sheds its skin. You will be reborn. Even now I am scratching away the husk. Tell me, why do you have no children, Drewe?"*

She doesn't answer at first. Then, "We just haven't had any yet."

"You're thirty-three years old. How can you suppress that urge? That silent cramping pulse that beats within your

womb like a voice murmuring, Time is passing, Time is passing?"

"I feel that. But this is the real world. There are . . . external concerns, like you said."

"Your husband."

"He's a factor."

"He's more than that. He is afraid to have children with you. He ducks the question, changes the subject, pleads that it's too much responsibility, asks you to wait until things are more stable."

"Yes."

"When could things be more stable? You earn a living in your own right. Your husband is a miser, isn't he? Hoarding his gold like Midas?"

I feel like a demon just breathed on the back of my neck. Was Berkmann in the tunnel that night after all?

"Hiding in his office," he goes on, *"his sticky fingers glued to the keyboard, reading about other people's sex lives over their shoulders, fawning over brainless starlets, masturbating for relief because he can't face himself squarely enough to have a real relationship with you. What kind of man lives like that?"*

"Didn't he find you on EROS?" Drewe asks pointedly.

"Yes. But I was there for an altogether different reason."

"Pineal glands?"

"Yes, but we must take things in order. First you must sever your husband from your life. From your being. Can you do that?"

"More easily than you know."

"You deceive yourself. It's never that easy. That is why I must tell you the rest."

"What are you talking about?"

"Your husband. Harper lured me to your home because Erin was trying to make him tell you the truth about Holly. Trying to save her marriage. But Harper couldn't bear the truth. That's why he sent me Erin's picture, why he made

sure Erin would be alone in your house when my assistant and I arrived. He told Erin he was thinking of leaving you, that he wanted to be a father to Holly, that he needed desperately to make love with her again. That's why she came when she did. I didn't come to kill her but to bring her back to share my life. But of course she knew nothing about that. When I arrived, she panicked. She stabbed my assistant, and my assistant killed her in self-defense. Despite my best efforts to save them, they both died. Harper got his wish."

Drewe is staring at me again, her tearful eyes wide with horror. I shake my head violently and mouth "*LIES!*" but she has been shaken beyond reassurance.

"I didn't see any sign that you tried to save Erin," she says.

"You saw the wound. It was mortal."

"You could have called nine-one-one."

"No. The civil authorities are Philistines. They would chain Prometheus to a rock for stealing fire."

"What are you talking about?"

"As I speak, please remember one thing. There are no moral phenomena, only moral interpretations of phenomena. Forget the arbitrary rules you learned as a child. Listen with your will, with your unfettered spirit. . . ."

Berkmann begins telling the tale he told "Erin" days ago, but in a more condensed manner. If anything, the story is more powerful for its brevity. There's no denying the poetry of his language as he speaks of Rudolf and Richard and Catherine—always Catherine—and Kali. Drewe interjects an occasional "yes" or "mmm," but little else. As the minutes pass, I realize that Berkmann's words are disturbing me on some fundamental level. What can they be doing to Drewe?

Pressing the phone hard against my ear, I hear a flurry of voices from Miles's end. Then Miles says, "Harper!"

"I'm here."

"The SWAT teams are moving into position. Snipers

on the rooftops, the whole deal. Everybody says tell you to keep Berkmann at his computer."

"He's still talking to Drewe. Tell them to get the lead out. I don't know how long she can take this."

"SWAT's on the phone with Baxter right now. He's en route by car. They're going in as soon as he gets here."

"Okay."

Berkmann's tale is accelerating. He weaves the central thread of his life—his hemophilia—into a tale of almost mythic proportion. The illegal liver transplant that cost a life but "healed his great wound" sounds like part of a heroic quest. And through it all, his family looms like a mystical trinity, his mother a shining figure in the distance, his father walking beside him, his grandfather a shadow pursuing from behind.

"Harper!" Miles says in my ear.

"Right here."

"Baxter just got out of a car. They're escorting him like he's General MacArthur. Hang on."

I try to listen to the action through the phone while Berkmann begins speaking of what Drewe means to him. She listens as though nothing in his depraved history has shocked her in the slightest.

"Goddamn it!" Miles yells in my ear.

"What is it?"

"Baxter's not letting me go in! The son of a bitch!"

"You didn't think he would, did you?"

"He used me, man! The only reason I'm here is to make sure you keep Berkmann online."

"So what! Tell me what's happening."

"Shit. It looks like a movie location. They don't know where the computer is in the building, so they're going to do both floors at once. The roof guys are going to crash through the windows on rappelling gear while guys on the ground blow the doors with plastique."

"What about the hostages?"

"Baxter has paramedics standing— Wait. Here he comes."

Suddenly Daniel Baxter's commanding voice comes through the phone. "Cole? Baxter."

"Tell me what to do."

"I don't want another Dallas here. NYNEX shows computer data moving through one phone line at Berkmann's warehouse. It looks like he's online in there, but I don't want him making an ass out of me and shooting cops from the windows. I want to hear you tell me Edward Berkmann is online right this second."

Tired of playing middleman, I carry the phone across the room and hold it up to one of the computer's speakers.

"Most women," Berkmann is saying, *"are water-engorged beings of stasis, eternally swelling and sloughing, draining men of life even as they produce more life. They are but corridors back to the grave. I have waited decades for a woman of fire and light—"*

"You hear that?" I ask Baxter.

"That's him?"

"That's a digital facsimile of his voice speaking live to my wife."

In a voice very like the one he used when directing the Dallas raid from Quantico, Baxter says, "Captain Riley, you are cleared to go."

"How do you like that guy?" Miles asks, back on the phone. "He—"

Miles's voice is terminated by four flat booms that can only be explosions.

Chapter 48

"SWAT just blew down the doors!" Miles shouts. "I'm in the command car with Baxter. I'll tell you what's happening as I hear it."

Drewe is still speaking into the headset, her tone almost conspiratorial.

"SWAT's moving through the building," Miles says softly. "Drewe still talking to him?"

"Yes."

"He talking back?"

"Yes."

"That doesn't make sense."

"I know."

"If someone blew open the side of your house, wouldn't you run like hell?"

"I'm not him. He may be about to blast that whole SWAT team to hell. Remember Dallas."

"No shit. Keep him talking."

"Drewe's got it."

"I checked your transcripts in the Tulane Medical School computer," says Berkmann. *"You scored mostly twelves on the MCAT. That put you in the top one percent of medical school applicants. You could have gone to Hopkins or Columbia or Harvard."*

"So? What did you score?"

"I am the measuring stick, Drewe."

"Ah."

"You could have been a surgeon."

"You have a point?"

"I'm trying to show you how accident has limited you. Circumscribed your life. You attended university near your hometown. You married a man you'd known since childhood, settled in the place you were born. And there you remain. You spend your days delivering welfare babies doomed to wasted lives, your nights alone in bed."

"How do you know that?"

"I know you, Drewe. You're a barely subcritical mass of potentialities. People realize that you're special, but they don't want you to realize it. Because if you did you would leave them forever. You are a higher being, yet you do the work of a midwife. My God, to think of you bent between the heaving thighs of mindless women spawning children like roe, soiling your hands with their eternal muck. You're like a saint sentenced to an eternity of healing lepers. Do you understand the kind of work you would be doing with me? Challenging the dominion of death itself—"

"They found a hostage!" Miles cries in my ear.

"What?"

"Male hostage in a basement. Alive! It must be Peter Levy. Jesus, they got another one! A woman! Wait . . . It's just like we thought. A SWAT guy says the basement is set up like a hospital operating room."

"What about Berkmann?"

"Nothing yet. It's confused in there."

"Female physicians," Berkmann is saying, *"driven beyond their abilities by their parents, hard little girls pushed into a male system. Slaves to technique, looking for father figures. I don't need supplicants. Do you know the epigram of disappointment? I listened for an echo and heard nothing but praise—"*

"They found his computers! Second floor. They're powered up, but no Berkmann. Damn it, anybody who knows anything always leaves their computers on!"

"I know that!" I snap.

"I was telling Baxter," says Miles.

"Berkmann must be in another part of the building," I reason. "That's why he didn't split when they blew the doors. He's safe in there somewhere. They have the exits covered?"

"They say they do. Berkmann still talking to Drewe?"

I tune in long enough to hear Drewe say, "Tell me more about Catherine, Edward. I'm sorry. May I call you Edward?"

"Of course."

"He's still on. He's all sweetness and light. Miles, could Berkmann own the building next door? Sort of like the apartments in Dallas?"

"NYPD's covering the adjacent structures. Oh, man—"

"What?"

"Body parts in the basement. SWAT just found them. Bodies and body parts in a big freezer. Bodies in plastic bags, parts in biological specimen jars."

"To hell with that, where's Berkmann?"

"We've got to get in there!" Miles yells suddenly. "Wait, *shit*—I've got to see those computers! I'll tell you where that son of a bitch is!"

I hear Daniel Baxter's deep voice, the chopped cadence of orders. "We're going in," says Miles, panting like a sprinter again. "Keep Drewe talking!"

"She's rolling, man. Go!"

"My father took me deer hunting when I was young," Drewe says. "With a rifle. I hated it. It seemed a senseless slaughter. But then I learned to shoot a bow. And I loved it. Creeping through the forest looking for scrapes, letting the does pass by. Drawing the bow, holding my breath, waiting for the buck to step clear of cover with his massive rack. My arms quivering from holding at full draw, and then the release, the arrow crashing through his heart in the moment he heard it fly. I felt like a goddess."

"That was but a taste of your true nature."

"Edward? I want to share something with you. Something I've never told my husband. Something he's never even asked me."

"What is it?"

"A dream."

"Yes."

"It started during college, long after I'd stopped hunting."

"This is a recurring dream?"

"Yes. I'm walking through a forest in winter. Snow on the ground, ice in the trees. I'm not wearing enough clothing to keep warm, just an old dress. No coat. I see many deer, but they're starving. I pass them by. Then, through the bare black trees, I see a flash of pure white against the bluish snow. It's a great buck, with fur like ermine from antlers to tail, his antlers black like wet branches, the underside of the tail like sable. Not an albino, because his eyes are bottomless rings of blue. Deeper and deeper into the forest I chase him. My throat burns from the cold. Once I catch a longer glimpse, and I see that he is wounded, a splash of blood on his white belly, as though he has taken an arrow yet runs on. Only a heart shot can bring him down. As dusk falls, I track him to a cave. He stands just inside the mouth, as though safe in shadow. I draw the bow. Then, just as he sees me, I release, burying the shaft in his heart."

There is absolute silence in the room.

"Do you dress the carcass in the cave?"

"The buck doesn't die. As he lies shuddering in the cave mouth, he is transformed into a man. A young man, with skin like alabaster. But the old wound in his belly remains. Then I come to him in the cave, and he goes down on all fours before me, facing away. And though I cannot see anything at my waist, it is I who penetrate him. Some part of me passes into him, and when he rises his wound is healed, he is made whole. But when I rise, I see that *I* now have the wound. And I'm no longer a girl, but a woman, and it's me running now, running with him chasing me. He gets closer and closer and then . . . then I wake up. I always wake up before he catches me."

Berkmann says nothing.

I cannot imagine Drewe fabricating this story on the spot. The detail is too vivid. How little we really know about the people we live with.

"You still have this dream?" Berkmann asks finally.

"Yes. And it . . . it arouses me. Sometimes I have an orgasm when I'm in the cave. Sometimes not. Sometimes I feel only fear. Raw terror."

"It's so simple. So clear. Don't you see? You are a huntress who needs to be caught. A healer who needs to be healed. I am the wounded beast, Drewe. I—"

"Berkmann's not in the building," Miles says in my ear. "We're on the second floor. SWAT confirms it."

My pulse is racing. "He's still talking, Miles."

"Maybe he was telling the truth about being out of the country. Maybe he really has another base, another voice-rec unit somewhere. He probably has the money for it."

"The phone company has a busy signal on the warehouse phone?"

"Yep. Christ, look at this."

"What?"

"I'm at the computers. It's serious stuff. Sun, Digital Equipment. Massive power here."

"So where's Berkmann?"

"Man, some of these boxes I don't even recognize."

I kneel beside Drewe and whisper in the shell of her ear. "They're in the building. Keep talking."

Her head bobs slightly. "Catherine played the piano?"

"Yes," Berkmann replies. *"She had a gift."*

"I play as well," she says. This is a lie.

"You play Beethoven?"

"I prefer Chopin. Tell me something, Edward. Did Catherine breast-feed you?"

"Of course. There was no cow's milk in the basements of Berlin."

"Are you circumcised, Edward? Is that how they discovered your hemophilia?"

"No. That was for Jews. My uncle noticed it first, through abnormal bruising."

Over Drewe's shoulder, I watch Berkmann's words materialize on-screen as flawlessly as film credits. He's definitely using a voice-recognition system. But where is it? I turn away and walk back toward the desk that holds my Gateway computer. It sits purring like a faithful dog. Where could—

"Harper!"

Drewe's yell shocks me out of myself. I whirl, afraid that my name has gone out over the data line, but she has her hand on the space bar.

"What is it?" I ask, moving to her side.

"I'm getting errors in Berkmann's side of the conversation."

A ball of ice forms in my chest. "What do you mean? Like typos?"

"More like dropouts. Wrong words. Nonwords."

"Okay . . . I'll check on it. Just keep talking to him."

She releases the space bar and resumes the conversation, though in a less controlled voice.

"Miles?" I say into the phone.

Nothing.

I walk as far from Drewe as I can get and snarl, "Miles!"

"What?"

"Drewe's getting errors from Berkmann!"

"You mean typos? All of a sudden?"

"Yes! But more like dropouts, she said."

"There's a lot of gear in this room, Harper, including a home-engineered phone system. I just picked up a receiver and heard a data stream."

"Then Berkmann must be there. There must be a room in the building SWAT hasn't found."

"But where?"

Drewe's voice control is degrading by the second. "Miles, what if he's *remotely* using the system in front of you? You picking up that receiver could have caused the dropouts Drewe saw. Especially with a cellular data connection."

"He's never used it remotely before. I'm sure of it."

"So that means he can't?"

Miles clucks his tongue. "If he could have, why didn't he? It's a lot easier to talk than it is to type, especially when you're flying a plane or hiding outside somebody's house in the dark."

"Maybe it's technically possible, but not that reliable. So he just never messed with it."

"Until now, you mean?"

A hot wave of fear rolls up my spine. "Miles, what if he knew all along we were using his error rate to predict his movements? Or that we could use it? When he killed Lenz's wife, he *wanted* the FBI to know he was on the move, so he stuck to his old pattern and didn't use voice recognition. He wanted them to see the errors."

"And with Erin?"

"He just stayed off-line until he got here. That way there were no errors to see, even though he was moving."

There is a sudden, awful silence.

"He's known all along," Miles says quietly. "It's just like his back door into EROS. He saved it until he needed it."

I feel like I'm riding an elevator whose cable just snapped.

"I'm going to pick up the receiver again," Miles says. "Tell me what happens."

Almost instantly Drewe throws up her right hand, then spins in her chair, an anxious look on her face.

"More errors?" I whisper.

She nods violently.

"We got errors, Miles. Would Berkmann have seen that?"

"Probably. He might think it was just line noise, though."

"He's not in New York, Miles." I hesitate to voice the certainty that has crystallized in my brain. "I guess we know where he is."

"Harper—"

"Tell Baxter to get somebody out here as fast as humanly possible. I'm hanging up now."

"Wait!"

"Ciao, pal. Good knowing you."

With an eerie sense of resignation, I hang up the phone, then walk to the office door and lock it. The heavy window blinds make it virtually impossible for someone outside to see into the room. From my desk I pick up a legal pad and a pen and scrawl, *Berkmann may be here. Stay calm. I'm calling for help. Keep talking.* Then I carry it over to Drewe and hold it where she can see it.

Her composure melts like ice thrown into a fire. My immediate concern is her voice. Berkmann can't hear the fear crackling through it like electricity, but if she loses enough control, the voice-rec program may stop functioning. As she struggles to continue the conversation, I dial her father's house. There are two other options—Sheriff Buckner and Wes Killen—but Bob will come faster. Besides, I made him a promise.

While the phone rings, I walk to one of the two front

windows, slide the blind to the side and peek out into the blue dusk. The deputy's car is still at the end of our drive, nose angled toward the highway. Because of the fading light and the car's position, I can't see whether he's in it or not.

"Hello?"

"Mrs. Anderson, it's Harper. I need to talk to Dr. Anderson right now."

"They're not here." Margaret's voice is cold. "I'm here with Holly."

"Who's they?"

"Bob and Patrick. They went out to the cemetery to visit Erin."

"At night?"

"That's what they wanted to do. They're grown men."

"Do they have a cellular phone?"

"No. They took Bob's old truck. You sound funny. What's—"

I disconnect and dig Wes Killen's cellular phone number out of my back pocket. My thumb is touching the keypad of the cordless when Berkmann's voice shocks me into stillness.

"What's the matter, Drewe?"

"Nothing. Why?"

"Your voice-recognition program is missing words, sending errors. As though you're under great stress."

Drewe looks back at me, her face pale. I motion for her to keep winging it while I dial Killen's number.

"I shouldn't be stressed?" she says. "After all you've told me about my husband?"

"What is Harper doing?"

"Wes Killen."

"This is Harper Cole! I need you! Berkmann's alive!"

"I just got off the phone with Baxter," Killen says. "I'm running to my car right now. You know Mike Mayeux? New Orleans cop?"

"Yes."

"He's out there. At your place. Right now."

"What?"

"He never thought Berkmann died in the crash. He took a couple of days off to watch your place. He didn't want you to know. Wanted you to act natural."

"Thank God! Look, there are two guys headed out to Erin's grave. Family. Don't get panicky if you see lights."

"I see lights now. Are you armed, Cole?"

"I've got a thirty-eight revolver and a twenty-five auto." Through the phone I hear Killen's car engine firing up.

"Get into a bedroom," he says. "Cut off the lights, put your wife under the bed, and get low in a corner with the thirty-eight. Make sure your hall light's on. If Berkmann opens the door, you'll have him in silhouette. Easiest shot in the world. Blow him down."

"Just hurry!"

"I'll be there in twenty minutes."

Drewe is speaking too rapidly now, her voice like a fraying cable. With the news about Mayeux pumping through me like amphetamines, I dial Sheriff Buckner's office. As the phone rings, I peer out at the parked cruiser.

"Sheriff's department."

"This is Harper Cole. Give me Sheriff Buckner right now. It's life or death."

"Who is this again, please?"

"I SAID NOW, GODDAMN IT!"

A match flares in the deputy's car. It glows steadily, flickers, then disappears. The tiny orange ember of a cigarette takes its place. I touch the grip of the .38 at my belt, wondering whether I should fire through the window. One shot would bring both the deputy and Mayeux running, but Berkmann could be anywhere. He might be in a position to ambush both men without even breathing hard.

"This is Sheriff Buckner. Who the hell's this?"

"Harper Cole! You've got to get somebody out here!"

"Cole? I've already got somebody out there."

"The killer's here, damn it! Maybe outside my house!"

"What?"

"Radio the deputy you have here! But he's got to be careful. Berkmann could be—"

There is no sound so dead as a dead telephone. Very slowly, not wanting to believe it, I put down the cordless.

Drewe is still speaking into the headset. I watch her trail off, then wait for Berkmann's response.

There is none.

Drawing the .38 from my holster, I walk over and say softly in her ear: "Berkmann's outside. He just cut the phone lines."

She closes her eyes like someone who's just been read a death sentence. I gently pull the headset off her and drop it beside the keyboard. Strangely, the modem still shows a live connection. Maybe Berkmann left the phone line to the EROS computer open. Hitting the space bar just in case, I ask Drewe where her gun is.

"In my purse," she replies.

"Where's your purse?"

"In the bedroom."

"Did you reload it?"

"Yes." She grips my forearm hard enough to cause pain and looks up with terror in her eyes. "Harper, let's run! Get your keys and we'll run for the Explorer."

"He's expecting that." I lay an open hand against her cheek. "We wouldn't have a chance."

"Drewe? Speak to me."

At the sound of Berkmann's voice, Drewe's eyes go blank as a stroke victim's. "He left the data line connected," I tell her, squeezing her shoulders. "There are two cops outside. Answer him. If you can keep him occupied, we'll be okay."

Moving like a zombie, she dons the headset again. "I'm thinking," she says in a cracked voice.

"What about?"

"Everything you've said."

"You're not being truthful, Drewe."

She hits the space bar again. "For God's sake, Harper! We've got to run!"

"We can't. He could be anywhere. We're safer in here. You've got to keep talking. Give Mayeux a chance."

She shakes her head. "We're sitting ducks in here! I feel it." Wild hope flashes in her eyes. "You said he didn't actually kill the EROS women! And we both have guns!"

"Listen to me, Drewe. I know he has a tranquilizer pistol. He'd probably shoot me with a dart to get me out of the way, then take you with him."

Her mouth drops open as the enormity of the danger sinks in. "But . . . but what if we risk that? If he takes me, I could pretend to go along, then shoot him when I got a chance."

"What if he shoots me with a forty-four Magnum instead of a dart? We don't know what he's got out there, Drewe."

"We can't just sit here and wait for him!"

I squeeze her shoulders again, trying to reassure her. "We've got no choice."

She jumps up from the chair and pulls away from me. "God, why did you bring him here? How could you be so stupid?"

"Why isn't he talking?" I ask, turning to the EROS screen.

At that instant the muffled crack of a gunshot bounces off the front of the house.

Drewe screams. Snatching her arm, I run for the door, praying that shot came from Mike Mayeux's gun.

"Could the deputy have shot him?" she asks.

As my hand touches the doorknob, Berkmann's digital voice says: *"I suppose we all know where we stand now."*

I tear open the door and pull Drewe after me, up the dark hall and into the kitchen. We stare dumbfounded at the two-by-six planks I nailed across the pantry door yesterday. I start to break for the back door, then stop. The gunshot came from the front of the house, but I can't be sure who fired it. It's fifty feet from our back door to the edge of the cotton field. Fifty feet without cover. Handing Drewe the .38, I try to tear one of the planks down from the pantry door, but it doesn't budge. I plant my right foot against the door frame and yank again, but Drewe stops me.

"What is it?" I shout.

"He knows about the tunnel! Remember he talked about you hoarding your gold like Midas? He could be in there right now!"

I hesitate. "If he is, the gunshot doesn't make sense. I think that crack was just a figure of speech."

"You want to bet our lives on that?" she asks, trying to pull me away from the door. "Harper, listen to me! I'm sorry I lost it back there. You were right. We've got to stay. If we run, we might get away, but *he* will too. Then what happens? A week or a month or a year from now he snatches me out of some parking lot? Or cuts your throat while you're sleeping?"

Drewe has gone from blind panic to rigid control in less than a minute. "What do you want to do?" I ask.

"You called for help, right? Even if he killed the cops outside, somebody's got to get here in fifteen or twenty minutes."

"He could kill us twenty times in twenty minutes!"

"But does he *want* to? Listen! He's still talking to me."

She's right. Berkmann's digital voice is still droning up the hall. Somewhere outside our house, he is crouched over a notebook computer and cellular phone, too afraid or unsure to make his move.

"He doesn't want to kill me," Drewe says, clutching my upper arm. "He wants to take me with him. That's why he hasn't broken into the house! I can control him, Harper. *I've* got the power right now. I can keep him on a string for twenty minutes. You just be ready to shoot him if he tries to break in."

Suddenly I see a great irony. By declaring his desire to possess my wife—and by believing he has destroyed me in her eyes—Berkmann has given me the upper hand. He has made Drewe *my* hostage.

"We can do it!" she insists, handing the .38 back to me. "Twenty minutes."

An image of Michael Mayeux comes into my mind. That hardheaded Cajun could be stalking Berkmann right now.

"Okay," I tell her. "Move! Get back to the computer!"

Drewe races into the hall and toward the office. I veer into the bedroom for her Charter Arms .25, then follow. When I reach the office door, I remember Wes Killen's advice and switch on the hall light. Then I lock the office door behind me.

Drewe is already speaking into the EROS headset.

"What was that gunshot?" she asks.

"Time is running out," Berkmann replies. *"We must act quickly."*

"What do you want from me?"

"I want you."

"But . . . how? What do you want me to do?"

"Walk outside with your car keys. I have a plane nearby. We can be airborne in three minutes."

My chest constricts with panic. Drewe whirls to face me, stunned. I can scarcely speak. "The strip Miles used," I whisper. "He must have stolen a plane."

"I thought your plane crashed," Drewe stammers.

"Of course you did. But I never meant to leave without you, Drewe. I knew that as soon as I saw your picture. Fate used Harper's sins to bring me to you. And to stay near you, I had to appear to die. I would have come to you sooner, but you moved into your father's house. There were guards. I had no way to contact you safely."

Drewe is shaking her head. "Were you at my sister's burial?"

"Yes."

"Did you leave sunglasses in her grave?"

"I dropped them. I couldn't risk retrieving them."

"But . . . where have you been staying for the last two days?"

"In a cotton gin. I had electricity and water . . . all the necessities except food."

"My God."

"Time is short, Drewe. You were going to leave Harper anyway. Now you know how right that instinct was. Now you have a place to go. I am taking you to a future you cannot even imagine."

"But . . ."

"I know Harper is there. You must convince him that to obstruct us means death."

"It's not that simple. He has a gun, and it's pointed at me. He's not about to let me go anywhere."

Silence.

"Then I shall kill him."

"Let me talk to him, Edward," Drewe implores. "I'll make him understand how it is."

This time Berkmann does not respond. Drewe reaches out and grips my left hand in hers. I clench the .38 in my right, looking back over my shoulder at the window blinds.

"Five minutes," Berkmann says finally. "In five minutes you walk out the front door alone, or I set the house on fire."

Chapter 49

"He's bluffing," I say, trying to believe it myself.

Drewe throws down the headset and hits the space bar. "We've got to run! We've got to use the tunnel now!"

I lay the .25 in her lap and shake my head. "We can't run. We lost our chance. We don't know where he is now."

"He's going to set the house on fire!"

"He won't do it with you inside."

"He might!"

Something is working at the edge of my consciousness, like a comet too distant to see but hurtling toward me at great speed.

"Harper!"

"We can't run. And he knows it. We already made our choice."

"What if we tell him I'm coming out, then just sit here in the dark? He'd have to come in for me. Then we could shoot him. It's two against one."

"Berkmann knows about killing, Drewe. It's our house, but he's been here before. If we end up in the same room with him, we're going to die."

She is near to hyperventilating, and she knows it. She clutches the .25 to her chest and shakes her head as if to shake off her terror. "What about—?"

"*Please* be quiet, Drewe."

She groans and closes her eyes.

I turn away and gaze around the office. Somehow, I have to kill Edward Berkmann. But the gun in my hand is not the answer. Facing him down like John Wayne would be suicide. As I turn slowly, I am suddenly and keenly aware of Miles as he was on the morning he completed his Trojan Horse program while Buckner's men hammered on my front door. Desperate for time and needing to run, he looked around this room and realized that everything he needed to fool the police was right in front of him, if only he could see it in the proper light.

A minute has passed, but for me time is dilating with possibility. The seconds pass like cars on a distant train. Berkmann is smart. That is his talent. But talents are double-edged swords. I learned that the hard way. Maybe Berkmann is too smart for his own good. As the air conditioner kicks on, something trips in my brain—an echo of my own voice just minutes ago. *Remember Dallas. . . .*

Dallas. A jerky video image of an apartment. Men in black. A harmless-looking white computer on a floor, suddenly blooming into black nothingness . . .

My nerve endings thrumming, I turn faster, drinking in the contents of the room. The coat sculpture. My surviving guitars. The computers. The rack for my great-grandfather's sword, which now lies in some evidence room in Yazoo City—

Smaller, says a voice in my head. I tighten my focus from macro to micro. Floppy disk case, stapler, VCR. Halogen desk lamp, flashlight, canned air for cleaning electronic gear. Air freshener Drewe left in here weeks ago, toner bottle for refilling printer cartridges—

"Harper, for God's sake!"

I hold up my hand, looking from the sleek black EROS computer to the boxy white Gateway 2000, then at the printers attached to each, and finally the keyboards.

"Drewe."

"What?"

"I want you to type Berkmann a note. On the Gateway."

"What?"

"Please just do it."

"What do I type?" she asks, sitting down at the computer.

"Go into WordPerfect. Double-space the note. Write it as if you're me. Tell Berkmann you hate his guts, that you're taking your wife out of the house, that he'll never have her. Tell him to wait right where he is, because you're coming back to kill him as soon as your wife is safe."

"But it's the wrong computer!" Drewe protests. "I can't send the message to him!"

"Just do it! But whatever you type, make the note longer than a single screen. You understand? You've *got* to go a few lines past the first screen."

"Okay," she says, tapping slowly at the keys.

I flip on the halogen lamp near the Gateway, then move to the door with the .38 and switch off the overhead light.

"Where are you going?" Drewe calls, her voice high and thin.

"I'll be right back. Finish the note!"

I close my left hand around the doorknob and slowly turn it. Berkmann could already be inside the house, but I don't think so. And I'm going to be very quick.

One pull and I'm sailing up the hallway with the office door shut behind me. Hard left, into the unused bedroom that holds the gun safe. Shifting the .38 to my left hand, I kneel before the safe, spin the combination lock back and forth to the numbers of my father's birthday, and yank the handle. My right hand parts the thicket of antique muskets, grabs a black-and-yellow can, and gives it a shake. Three-quarters full. Then I'm running again, the .38 held out in front like a ram.

"Thank God!" Drewe cries from the pool of light at the center of the room.

I shut and lock the office door. "Did you finish the note?"

"Four lines past the bottom of the screen. Harper, what are you trying to do?"

A moment of doubt as I reach into the bottom drawer of the desk. Nothing gets lost faster than tools. But this one I used less than a week ago.

"What are you looking for!"

My heart leaps as my hand closes around the screw starter. "I'm going to blow him to hell and gone."

"What?"

I hold the can from the gun safe under the light.

"Black powder?" she asks.

"You got it." I flip open the top of the Hewlett-Packard printer and pull out the black wedge-shaped toner cartridge. Drewe stays on my heels as I carry the cartridge into the bathroom.

"Tell me what you're doing!" she demands. "Are you making some kind of bomb?"

"Yes." With the screw starter, I pop out the two pins in the left end of the cartridge, then flip it around and start on the right.

"What are you going to do with it?"

The fourth plug gives with a pop. "Kill Berkmann," I tell her, dropping the plug into my pocket. "I need you to clear out a space on the floor of the closet. Move all the shoes and things to one side. *Hurry.*"

"Okay."

After pulling off the cartridge cover, I turn the cartridge on end, exposing the inch-wide plug in the toner reservoir. It pulls out easily. I start to invert the cartridge over the toilet bowl, then realize how stupid that would be. The "ink" used by laser printers is a superfine black powder of plastic and metal that looks like coal dust and spreads like an eruption of volcanic ash. If I try to flush it down the toilet, the bathroom will look like a blind man tried to paint it with India ink. Instead, I flip open the cabinet that holds my dirty clothes hamper, stick the cartridge through, turn it on end, and shake it until the weight tells me it's empty. Then I pull it out, wipe my hand on a towel, and drop the towel into the hamper.

"I heard something!" Drewe shouts. "Outside!"

Looking out of the bathroom, I see her pointing the .25 at one of the front windows. "Just keep to the shadows," I tell her, running back to my desk.

With the empty toner cartridge braced against the floor, I press the sharp end of the screw starter against the plastic and bear down like a blacksmith, punching a hole clean through the wall of the toner reservoir. Then I punch another hole about a quarter inch from the first.

"Hurry, Harper!"

Covering the holes with my thumb, I begin filling the toner reservoir with black gunpowder.

"Why did I have to write that message?" Drewe asks.

"That's part of the detonator." Through the plug hole, I watch the level of the gunpowder rising.

"I don't understand."

"When you don't go outside, Berkmann will have no choice but to come in. Just like you said." I glance at my watch. Nearly three and a half minutes have passed.

"If he sets the house on fire, we'll *have* to go out!"

"He won't do it." The gunpowder keeps rising. "He won't take a chance on hurting you."

"Where are we going to be when this bomb of yours blows up?"

"Right here."

"Right here? In this room?"

"In the closet."

"*What?* Waiting for him to come in here with us and set it off?"

"It's the only way."

"You said we'd die if we wound up in the same room with him!"

The toner reservoir is full. I stuff the plug back into the hole, then dig through the bottom drawer of my desk for wire cutters and electrical tape. I need wire too, but there's none in the drawer.

"Stop for one second!" Drewe shouts, squeezing my arm so hard I have to yank it away.

"Damn it!" I yell, trying desperately to think of some place in the office where there might be wire. "We'll be buried under clothes and everything else in the closet."

"How big will the explosion be?"

"I don't know."

"You don't *know*?"

"Like a pipe bomb. We might get hurt, okay? But *he'll* be cut to pieces."

Drewe freezes, her mouth open. "Did you hear that?"

My eyes lock onto a Gibson ES-335 guitar hanging from its brace above my bed. "What?" I ask, jumping onto the bed with the wire cutters.

"My God! Do you smell that?"

The first snip pops the Gibson's high E-string with a twang like a cartoon ricochet. The second gives me the length of wire I need.

"Gasoline!" Drewe gasps. "That's *gas*!"

She's right. The sharp tang of high-octane gasoline is seeping into the room. Maybe through the air-conditioning ducts.

"He's bluffing," I tell her, cutting the guitar string into two three-inch lengths. I pull off my watch and hand it to her. "We've got forty seconds. Tell me when our time's up."

With Drewe staring wildly at me, I reach into the

open cartridge with the screw starter and feel for the corona wire. This ultrathin filament electrically charges the magnetic drum that puts the "ink" in the right places on the page to form text. Holding up the wire with the tip of the screw starter, I stick two small pieces of tape to it, one on either side of the tool point. Then I snip the corona wire in half.

"Twenty-five seconds," Drewe says in a tight voice.

I toss her the wire cutters. "Cut the mouse off the Gateway!"

"Why?"

"Just do it! Throw it in the closet!"

Using the tape scraps to guide me, I attach a short length of guitar string to each loose end of the corona wire. Then I carefully feed the two wires through the holes I punched in the toner reservoir and fix them in position with tape.

"Time's up!"

"Get some towels!" I shout, snapping the cartridge cover back into place. "Wet them in the bathtub!"

"You said he wouldn't do it!" Drewe wails.

"Get the towels!"

Fumbling like a teenager with a condom, I pop in two plugs to anchor the cover, then run to the open printer and shove the cartridge home.

The moment I close the printer's lid, I have a lethal bomb. But Edward Berkmann is the detonator, and for him to function properly, I have to make a nonfatal choice impossible. My hands fly across the keyboard, closing out possibilities for failure—

"Harper, stop it!" Drewe pleads, standing beside me with two soaking wet towels.

"Get in the closet!"

"I won't do it!"

"You want to die?"

"We *will* die if we do this!"

Berkmann's digital voice paralyzes us both. *"Five minutes have fallen into eternity. Where are you, Drewe?"*

She watches me like a kid with her finger plugged in a leaking ocean dike. "Let me talk to him!" she begs.

"He doesn't want to talk! Get in the closet!"

Her arms fall slack at her sides, letting the wet towels plop onto the floor. "I can't," she says in a broken voice. "I'm sorry."

I'll drag her into the closet if I have to, but first I have to arm the bomb. I stare at the printer, my stomach near spasm.

"Get back, Drewe."

"Do you smell the gas, Harper?" Berkmann asks. *"Are you ready to burn?"*

"Fuck you!" I yell. With the knowledge that it could be my last, I take a deep breath. Then I lay myself over the printer in case it blows prematurely, and hit the ON switch.

Nothing happens. The yellow and green status lights on the face of the printer glow, blink off, then come back on, indicating the unit is warmed up, online, and ready to print. And I am still alive.

"Can you hear me, Edward?"

I whirl, my heart pounding. Drewe is seated at the EROS computer with the headset on.

"Yes. Come out, Drewe."

"Harper won't let me! He thinks if I come out, you'll burn the house with him in it. Or shoot him if he tries to come out."

"We all have to take chances in life. Come out now."

"I want to. I'm going to try something, okay? You're using a cell phone, aren't you?"

"Stop playing games, Drewe. My patience is gone."

"I'm going to hook a telephone to this modem line. Then I can come to the window. You'll be able to see me then. We can work this out."

Berkmann doesn't reply.

"What the hell are you doing?" I hiss.

Drewe motions frantically for me to bring her a phone. I don't know what she's trying to do, but every minute that ticks past is a mile and a half closer for Wes Killen and Sheriff Buckner. I toss her the cordless and run for the answering machine that is its base.

"What's the number of the data line?" Drewe asks, her finger pressed to the space bar.

"Six-oh-one, four-two-seven, three-one-one-four."

She repeats the number into the headset, then says, "Do you have that on your screen, Edward?"

Berkmann says nothing.

"Call me in thirty seconds. I'm attaching the phone now."

I scrabble behind a bookshelf with my left hand, trying to disconnect the answering machine's electrical plug while holding the .38 ready in my right in case Berkmann breaks down the door.

"Hurry!" Drewe pleads.

I have it. Dropping the base into Drewe's lap, I shove the electrical plug into the back of the power supply that feeds clean electricity to the EROS computer. "What the hell are you trying to do?" I ask again.

"I'm going to get you a shot at him."

"What? How?" I ask, clicking the RJ-11 jack into the back of the modem.

"Just be ready."

"I don't think he's listening to you anymore."

The ringing phone makes a liar of me.

Drewe reaches for it, but I grab her wrist. "Let the machine get it, then pick up."

After the machine answers, Drewe picks up and says, "Just a second!" over my outgoing message. When it finishes its run, I press MEMO, which will not only record

Berkmann's words but also allow me to hear everything he says through the answering machine.

"Are you there, Edward?" Drewe asks.

"Yes."

Even transmitted by the tinny speaker of the answering machine, that single word—spoken without the digital midwife of Miles's voice-synthesis program—communicates more subtlety and danger than the whole of Berkmann's words so far.

"I like that better," Drewe says. "*Much* better."

The little speaker hisses and crackles in her lap.

"I'm coming to the window, Edward." She rises from the chair.

"No. Come to the back door."

Drewe freezes, her eyes asking me what mine are asking her. Is Berkmann really at the back door? There's no way to know.

"Harper won't let me. But I'm coming to the window."

Despite my fraying nerves, I force myself to let her cross the room to the right front window. She seals the transmitter of the phone with her palm and whispers, "You're mad as hell. You're losing it. You'll kill me before you let me go out there."

"What?"

She gives me a frantic look like, Come on, stupid! "When I slap the windowpane, that means he's exposed. That's your shot. Not until then, okay?"

Before I can argue, Drewe grips the blind cord in her right hand and takes three steps backward, pulling the blind to its highest position and exposing six vertical feet of glass.

"Can you see me, Edward?" she says into the phone.

Berkmann doesn't answer. He's not about to reveal his position by admitting he can see her. What is he thinking at this moment? The only light in the office comes from the halogen desk lamp, but it falls across Drewe from the side, illuminating her white robe and still-damp hair with a diffuse yellow glow. Berkmann would probably like to smash the window and snatch her out through it, but our house is built off the ground, which would make that very tough to do. He also knows I'm armed.

"Edward?" Drewe says again, her voice plaintive.

Still nothing.

The smell of gasoline is strong by the wall, but Berkmann hasn't lighted it yet. My first instinct is to move to the other window, ten feet down the wall from where Drewe stands. That would give me the best field of fire. But if Berkmann is out front, he knows that too.

"Where is Harper?" he asks suddenly.

I whirl toward the EROS computer, my finger on the trigger. I'd forgotten that the only way I'll hear his voice now is through the answering machine across the room.

Drewe has put a hand on the window frame to steady herself. She's been acting with so much assurance that I assumed she was as confident as she looked. But she's far from it. In fact, now that Berkmann has answered, she seems too flustered to respond.

As I watch her floundering, the scenario she sketched out comes back to me. Pressing my chest flat against the wall between the windows, I extend my right arm, edge along the wall, and press the barrel of my .38 against her left temple.

"You see him now?" she asks, her voice full of genuine shock.

"You're going to die for that, Harper."

Berkmann is definitely in front of the house.

"That's not a good way to start this negotiation, Edward," Drewe says.

"I'm not negotiating."

"This talk, then. That synthesized voice was so sterile. Not like this. Your real voice is much more intriguing."

"Shut up, damn you!" I yell, supplying what seems like my appropriate line.

"I'm going to burn you alive," Berkmann says coldly.

"FUCK YOU!" I close my eyes and try to picture the scene outside. Drewe's Acura is parked broadside to the house, about twenty yards from the window. The Explorer is ten yards closer to the house, but farther to the left than the Acura.

"Harper won't hurt me, Edward," Drewe says. "He doesn't have the guts. Just like he didn't have the guts to tell me about Erin."

"Why don't you try walking out then!" I scream.

"I don't have to," she says in a strange voice. "Edward's going to get me out." She turns into the barrel of the .38 and gives me a look that could freeze mercury. "Would you really shoot me, Harper? Let's see if you will."

She looks back into the darkening yard and says, "You know what would kill him, Edward?"

"What?"

"If I told him the truth about sex with him."

"Tell him."

"Shut up, goddamn it!"

"I've never had an orgasm with Harper inside me. Not in three years of marriage and a year of sex before that. Of course he *thinks* I have. Sad, isn't it?"

"That will soon change."

Berkmann's voice sounds different somehow. More strained.

"I honestly can't believe Erin enjoyed sex with him," Drewe goes on. "Because she knew about sex, I can tell you. You wouldn't believe some things she did."

Berkmann says nothing.

My gun arm is tingling the way it did twenty years ago, when I reached into the fort to pull Miles out. I sense Berkmann aiming at my hand the way I sensed that rattlesnake. It would be a risky shot for him, firing through glass so near to Drewe's head. But he might try it with a tranquilizer dart. I take a quick step backward, pulling the .38 behind the frame of the window.

"What kinds of things?" Berkmann asks suddenly.

Drewe glances at me. "I saw her get out of a DUI ticket by making a highway patrolman . . . you know, in his pants. I mean it. She didn't even take off her clothes. His either. It was sort of like a slow dance on the side of the road. Erin didn't care. To her sex was like breathing."

"And to you?"

"I know how I *want* it to be. I want it to be . . . transcendent. Am I wrong to want that?"

"No."

"The few times I've ever managed to get . . . aroused enough, Harper's already finished. Do you know how to touch, Edward? Where to touch?"

"I know places you don't know you have."

"You slut!" I scream. "Hang up!"

"Tell him what you'll do if I hang up, Edward."

"I'll light that gasoline, Harper. And when you come running out, I'll shoot you in the pelvis. I have the deputy's gun, and I'm an excellent shot. I have Officer Mayeux's gun too, in case you're wondering."

I grit my teeth and close my eyes. I can't see Mayeux giving up his gun while alive. This isn't working. Drewe thinks she's stalling, but Berkmann isn't sitting still. Darting to my desk, I scrawl a message on a legal pad with black Magic Marker. Then I return to the wall and hold it up where Drewe can see it by looking slightly to the left.

HE'S PLAYING YOU! TRICKING US!
YOU'VE GOT TO TURN IT AROUND!
GET ME A SHOT!

In the crackling silence, Drewe stares at me like a little girl who has walked out onto a high-diving board and lost the nerve even to walk back to the ladder. As I watch, she seems to waver on her feet. Yet the moment I move toward her, she snaps erect and holds up a hand to stop me.

"I've thought a lot about your transplant work," she says. "I'm the one who first figured out what you were doing. I never thought it was really possible, though." She waits in vain for an answer. "It's not possible, is it? That's why you gave up?"

Silence. Then, *"It's not only possible, it's simple. The problem is the illegality, the inconvenience of obtaining donors and recipients for testing."*

I nod encouragement to Drewe. She's found the right button to push.

"You can really keep someone youthful past the normal aging curve?"

"Of course."

"You could keep me young?"

"I'm going to, Drewe. When the women you went to school with are fighting menopause and osteoporosis, you'll be skiing in Saint Moritz, making love as long and as often as a thirty-year-old."

"But why me?"

"I've seen my mistake, Drewe. What's the point of immortality without someone to share it with? The only real immortality is genetic anyway, at least for now. You shall bear my children. I could say I've chosen you, but this was all written long ago, by fate. When I realized how Harper had tricked me with Erin, and that you were the one I wanted, I thought of harvesting Erin's pineal for you. There was a twenty percent chance that she would be a perfect tissue match, and at least it would have given her death some meaning. But I didn't. I knew you probably hadn't reached the stage where you could see the rightness of it."

"You're right. Thank you for not doing that."

"There are always other sources. But first the children. Then more research. In forty years, who knows what might be possible? All that I have is yours, Drewe. My wealth and my talents." Berkmann pauses briefly, but when he speaks again there is new urgency in his voice. *"I want you to walk outside now, Drewe. Harper will not shoot. You must believe me."*

"I don't know what he'll do. He hates you for telling his secret. He said you wouldn't light the gasoline, and he was right. What am I supposed to do?"

"You must come now, Drewe, or I'll be forced to . . . to take risks."

"Wait! Don't do anything! Harper's already scared to death!"

Berkmann says nothing.

"Edward?"

Silence.

She glances at me, her face pale. She's lost him again, and she knows it. I glance down at my wrist, then remember I gave my watch to Drewe. It seems as though she's been at the window forever, but help is still five to ten minutes away. I am about to yank Drewe out of the window when she reaches down and tugs at the belt of her robe, loosening it. With her left hand, she pulls aside the terry cloth, exposing her left breast.

"Can you see me, Edward?" she asks, her voice like taut wire.

Berkmann doesn't respond. But he's looking. I know it. Drewe knows it too. She cups the breast in her free hand, leans forward, and presses the nipple to the glass. "Edward?"

Nothing.

"No child has ever suckled at this breast."

Silence.

"Do you want to do that, Edward?"

"Yes."

She starts at the sudden reply. It's almost as if Berkmann vanished before our eyes, then reappeared. "Would you brush my hair if I asked you to?" she asks, recovering quickly.

"Yes."

"It needs brushing. I work so hard, I never have time to take care of it. Would you take care of it?"

"Yes."

Berkmann's voice sounds strangely constricted. Drewe waits, then says, "You lost your mother too young, didn't you?"

"Yes."

"And you never had a sister?"

"No."

"Look at me, Edward." Drewe lets the robe fall open, then flattens her hand like a starfish on the windowpane.

"Time," he says in a strangled voice. *"No time. You've got to come out now. Please. HE WON'T SHOOT."*

"I'll come, Edward. But I don't want Harper to die. However he may have betrayed me, he's the father of my sister's child. I would spare him for that alone."

"I wouldn't."

"But you will do WHAT I SAY!" she proclaims in a voice so alien it sends a shiver through me. "BECAUSE I SAY SO. DO YOU HEAR ME, EDWARD?"

A stunned silence. Then: *"If you want to come out, why do you care about . . . him?"*

"I'm trying to resolve this, Edward. Don't make it harder than it has to be."

"Prove you don't care about him."

"I will."

Drewe pulls away from the window, her chest coming up with a sticky sound, her nipples hard from the coolness of the glass. "Do you see me, Edward? I'm not pretending, like that brown-skinned Indian girl. I AM THE ONE."

The shock of Drewe's nudity combined with her brazen voice trips something in my brain. This is it. If she's ever going to bring Berkmann out, it's now. I only hope she remembers to slap the glass.

"Are you big now, Edward?"

"Yes."

"Very big?"

"Yes."

"That's only natural. You want to touch me, don't you?"

"Yes."

"You need to."

"Yes."

"Do you see where?"

"Yes."

"Do you know what it's like there?"

A hiccup of silence. *"I—"*

"It's wet there, Edward. Burning."

"Please come out . . ."

"Look, Edward. LOOK!"

Shifting the phone from one hand to the other, Drewe lets the robe slip off her shoulders as casually as if she were stepping into the shower. A gasp of disbelief bursts from my lungs. I back far away from the wall, aiming the pistol at the crack of glass between the window frame and Drewe's side, waiting for her signal.

She shakes her hair into a fiery riot of copper and gold, then stands straight with her arms at her sides, as if to display every atom of her being in shameless pride. Her skin glows like veined marble. As when I saw Erin so many years ago, I cannot process the entirety of her nude image. I see her calves, the backs of her thighs, the small dimples above her rump, her shoulder blades—these are enough to hold my eye from its assigned task. Berkmann must be rooted to the ground.

"Jesus Christ!" I hiss. "What are you doing?"

"Edward?"

"Yes . . ." A ragged whisper.

Drewe moves her free hand around her hip, out of my sight. All I see is the muscle moving in her upper arm.

"Help me, Edward. Show me your power."

With my gun arm quivering, I edge forward toward Drewe. I keep the .38 aimed just to the left of her hip, through the window, into the waiting dusk. As my pupils dilate I discern the silhouette of the Acura. It's closer to the house than I remembered. Maybe thirty-five feet. My Explorer sits ten yards to the left of it, parked nose-in. The Acura is the natural vantage point for someone watching the window.

But I see no one.

In the near field of my vision, Drewe suddenly spreads her arms like wings and plants her bare feet apart. Her hands close into fists and her muscles go rigid, her body a hard quivering X in the lighted window. My heart thunders with fear and awe at the specter she has not created but *is*—woman revealed, the hidden unveiled, purity and carnality fused with power enough to stop the male heart.

As I stare openmouthed, her right hand flattens against the window and begins rattling like a superheated kettle on a stove. I focus on the hand, then realize she's trying to signal me with an arm incapacitated by terror. In the instant I look back through the window, Edward Berkmann rises above the roof line of the Acura, his enraptured face shining like an earthbound moon in the darkness.

Time blurs, stops. We both stand transfixed, paralyzed by the realization that Drewe is everything he imagined in his messianic fantasies, and more.

"Edwaarrrd!"

Drewe's scream jolts me back to myself. As I aim for Berkmann's face, she hurls the cordless phone through the windowpane in an explosion of glittering glass. I shoulder her out of the way and open fire.

My first shot is high and wild.

The second punches a hole in the Acura's door.

Berkmann drops.

Screaming like a lunatic, I fire two more rounds, then scoop up Drewe's robe and throw my arm around her waist as she comes up off the floor. I try to pull her toward the door, but she won't budge.

"Did you hit him?" she asks, her eyes white and round.

"I don't think so!"

"Get the light! Then shoot me!"

After a stunned instant, I turn, steady the pistol, and blow the halogen lamp off my desk, throwing us into darkness.

"Edwaarrrd!" she yells, her voice ringing across the yard.

I fire my last bullet in her direction, and watch in horror as she flies backward like a GI taking a round in house-to-house fighting.

The silence is absolute. Not even crickets cheep in this strange lacuna of time.

Then Drewe is beside me again, naked in the dark. Lifting her robe toward her, I sense something like a horsefly beside my left ear and swat at it even as the tranquilizer dart *thwacks* into one of my guitars, filling the room with jangling noise.

We hit the floor and crawl like alligators toward the office door. I feel a strange weight in the robe. It's Drewe's .25. I pause, raise the gun, fire two quick rounds through the intact front window, then feel my way to the door. When I look back, the bright amber message on the screen of the Gateway 2000 floats in the darkness like a tablet of fire brought from a mountaintop. Just as it should.

"What did you do?" Berkmann asks, his voice a fusion of fear and fury.

Drewe's hand grips my shoulder like a claw.

"It's the answering machine!" I whisper, at the same time noticing the faint glow of the EROS screen to my right. While Drewe ties on her robe, I raise the .25 and fire through the EROS monitor, shorting it out with a shower of sparks. Now the Gateway screen is the only light.

Holding the hot pistol to my chest, I switch off the hall light, then slide Drewe around in front of me. "Ready?"

She nods.

The second I jerk open the door she scrambles up the hallway toward the kitchen, but I force myself to walk, backward, keeping the .25 pointed at the front door in case Berkmann comes through it. When I reach the kitchen, I turn and run to the washroom where Drewe waits. The smell of gasoline is strong here too. Drewe leans into me, clutching my shirt like a child.

"Maybe we should stay here," she says in a meek voice.

"We can't." I hug her tightly. Her whole body is shaking, as though the bravura performance at the window drained every bit of courage out of her.

With the .25 I part the curtains that cover the small window in the back door. The yard looks blue-black in the moonlight. The long tin roof of the toolshed gleams, beckoning. My eyes move lower. There is a man lying flat on his back just outside the door. His eyes are closed, and there is a screwdriver handle sticking out of his right upper chest. I let the curtain fall closed.

"Drewe, there's a man on the ground outside. It's Detective Mayeux from New Orleans. He's probably dead, but we only heard one shot. He could be alive."

"I'll get my bag," she says automatically, as though someone had just passed out in church.

I squeeze her arm. "We can't help him. I'm telling you so you'll step over him."

She blinks rapidly.

"When I open this door, we're going to run straight back to the cotton field and keep going. Okay?"

She nods once.

Gripping the .25, I unbolt the door, then freeze as a high brittle plea crosses the space between us. "Don't let him get close to me, Harper."

"I won't."

Her fingernails dig into my arm, causing me to twist sideways. "If he hits you with a dart, and you can't see him anywhere . . . shoot me."

"What?"

"You do it."

With that appalling request ringing in my ears, I turn the knob and launch myself into the sweltering night.

Chapter 50

I am leaping over Mayeux's body when two gunshots boom through the night. I whirl and take Drewe's weight full in the face, and we crash to the ground beside Mayeux.

"Where is he?" she hisses in my ear.

"Front," I groan, rolling her off me. "Run!"

"What's he shooting at?"

"I don't know! Go!"

I know I should run, but Mayeux is half covered with gasoline. I find his carotid artery with my left hand. There's a pulse. Drewe is still beside me.

"Go, damn it!" I hand her the .25. "Behind the toolshed!"

She takes the gun but doesn't run. Suffused by a wild anger, I lean over and put my right shoulder into Mayeux's belly, then heave myself over so that he is lying across me. From there it's a matter of brute strength, working the leverage until I get my legs under me and he's lying sacklike over my shoulder in a fireman's carry.

With Drewe covering the corners of the house, I half stagger, half run across the grass to the toolshed and collapse under the fig trees behind it, depositing Mayeux on his back. Drewe hands me the .25, then begins testing the screwdriver handle sticking out of Mayeux's chest. Having an immediate emergency to deal with seems to have restored her composure.

"You're going to leave that in him?" I ask, as she checks Mayeux for other wounds.

"Better for him," she says, probing gently under his head. "What makes the printer explode?"

Before I can answer she says, "Look," and pulls a short, feathered barb from Mayeux's neck.

"It'll go off when Berkmann prints your message," I tell her, peering around the corner of the shed. The yard is empty, the house silent. When I look back, Drewe is staring at me as if I'm an idiot.

"Why should he print the message? He can just *read* it."

"Not without scrolling to the next screen."

"So?"

"That keyboard is programmable. If you want your comma key where the semicolon key is, you can have it that way. All it takes is a few keystrokes."

"I still don't get it."

"I reprogrammed every key that can take him to the next screen to issue the same command: Print Screen."

"The down cursor?"

"*Every* cursor. And PAGE DOWN. Since you snipped off the mouse, he has to use the keyboard. The second he does, six hundred volts will zap through the printer's corona wire, which is cut and buried in the black powder. A spark will arc between the wires, and good-bye, Edward."

Drewe stares blankly, as if trying to compute the odds of success. "Won't he be suspicious? Expect some kind of trap?"

"Probably. And if your message told him to print it, or tried to trick him into printing it, he'd never do it. But he won't see this coming. The only question is, will he try to read the whole message?"

She nods. "He's addicted to it. The computer is his

fetish. He may search the whole house first, but he'll read that message."

"What did you put in it?"

"Just what you told me to. I—"

"Shh! Listen!"

"What?" Her eyes wide with fear, Drewe cocks her head, listening for the wrong things.

I close my eyes and try to gauge the distance; in the Delta some sounds carry for miles. "Siren," I tell her, even as the sound fades.

"It must be pretty far away."

"It is. But Berkmann will hear it soon. He'll run."

I get to my feet. I'm not sure why, but doing something always feels better than doing nothing. Even if you're doing something stupid.

"What are you doing?" Drewe asks.

"He could take one of our cars . . . make it to the plane. I'm not letting him get away now."

"You stay here!"

I can't leave Drewe without a gun, but I can't go after Berkmann without one. Mayeux's shoulder holster is empty. I'm almost resigned to waiting when an idea hits me. Dropping beside the unconscious detective, I pull up one of his trouser legs. Nothing but a hairy ankle. But when I pull up the other, I see the duct-taped grip of a snub-nose .32 revolver tucked snugly in a Velcro ankle holster. Mayeux carries a throwdown. After verifying that the cylinder is full, I hand the pistol to Drewe.

"You're not leaving me here," she says.

I don't even try to argue. After switching guns, we cross the yard in a quick soundless rush, the grass damping the beat of our feet. At the back corner of the house, we pause in a pungent cloud of gasoline vapor.

"I still don't hear the siren," she whispers.

"The house is blocking the sound."

"Maybe *we* should light the gasoline."

"Are you nuts? It's our house!"

With Mayeux's .32 in my right hand, I sprint along the side of the house, nearly stumbling on a coil of garden hose. When I make the front corner I hear the siren again.

Drewe collides with me from behind, a soft impact of breasts and hands. The yard is pitch dark, the drive still. Only the sound of crickets breaks the silence. Where our driveway meets the road, the deputy's car sits motionless. Nearer to us, the Explorer and the Acura offer concealment. But I know Berkmann has left them behind.

"I think he's inside," I whisper. "I'm going to look."

"Wait—"

"Don't worry. I'm not going in. Listen for doors or windows. He may come tearing outside when he hears the siren. You'd better take off that robe. It's like a neon target out here."

Drewe shakes her head violently.

"If you hear him, you take it off."

My back pressed to the clapboard, I edge along the front of the house holding the .32 against my right thigh like a quarterback running a bootleg. As I near the broken front window, I step into what feels like a draft of sea wind. It's the conditioned air from the house, draining into the hot night like water from a leaking barrel.

Berkmann must have heard the siren by now. I try to maneuver beneath the window to look through it, but there's too much broken glass on the ground. Weaving around the fragments, I cover the ten feet to the second window, rise to the sill, and peek over it.

Edward Berkmann is sitting at my Gateway 2000, his Byronic profile hauntingly illuminated by the amber glow of the screen. He leans slightly forward, facing right to left across my visual field, peering at Drewe's message as though it holds the key to some eternal mystery.

Berkmann hasn't heard the siren because there are other sounds inside the office. The hum of the computer. The drone of the refrigerator. The hissing of the central air conditioner. He must have read the first screen of the message by now. Yet still he sits, staring. What is he doing?

He's thinking. The man who developed a world-renowned computer model of the human brain is exercising his own to solve the oldest problem in the world. Survival.

Berkmann is less than ten feet from me, the printer less than two feet from him, at the level of his chest. There's a gun beside the computer's keyboard. Nickel plated. Just the flashy kind of piece Buckner's deputies carried. But that gun cannot protect Berkmann from the printer.

My mind is telling me to raise my gun above the windowsill, but instinct stops me. The slightest movement—even lowering my head out of sight—could catapult Berkmann out of that chair with the gun in his hand.

As if in response to my thought, he lifts his head like a bird-watcher detecting a faint call, and turns slightly to his left. Toward me.

A bolt of pure terror strikes my heart.

He hasn't seen me. He's heard the siren. But instead of jumping up in panic, he turns back to the screen, settles deeper into my chair, and closes his hands around its arms. Is he actually waiting for me to come back and try to kill him, as the message promises I will?

There's more than one siren now. Several dissonant notes have separated themselves from the general whine, made Doppler-distinct by changing distances. Berkmann swivels my chair to the right, toward the wall that holds my guitars. What rogue impulses are firing through the synapses in that head? He could be guessing my next move or wondering what happened to his favorite eighteen-thousand-dollar urinal. Every fiber of my brain tells me to run, but instead I bring up the .32 with shaking hands and wait for him to swivel back to the left.

He does, but the rotation stops with him facing the computer screen. With a deliberation that sets my trigger finger quivering, Berkmann reaches out and touches a key on the right side of the keyboard.

I'm wondering which key it was when he turns in my direction. For an instant his gaze floats just above mine. Then it locks onto me like a laser, and I feel the nightmarish horror of trying to back away from some unspeakably sentient being as he rises from the chair and rushes toward me with the silver gun coming up and then disappearing in a white flash that seems to explode in silence.

I am sitting on the ground blinking my eyelids, which feel like they are on fire. There's a piece of bloody glass sticking out of my left arm and more blood pouring from my right shoulder. I start to pull out the glass, then remember Drewe leaving the screwdriver in Mayeux's chest.

Suddenly she is beside me. She seems to be yelling but I can't hear her. When I try to speak, I feel a dull vibration in my throat but hear nothing. A white cloud is billowing out of the window above me. This tells me the flash was what I hoped it was. Nothing smokes like old-style black powder.

Drewe takes hold of my left arm and tries to lift me. When I protest, she shouts words I can't hear and pulls harder. Then her head whips up and to the side, toward the window. Following her line of sight, I see a black shadow arc through the smoke over my head and crash beside me in a rain of glass.

I reach instinctively for Drewe, but she's gone. I try to stand, wobbling on my knees, waiting for the black hump that must be Edward Berkmann to jump up and put a bullet through my head.

He does neither. He doubles up on the gasoline-soaked ground and, with what appears to be colossal effort, rolls over onto his back. His face is scorched black and riddled with white plastic shrapnel. His shoulder-length hair has been burned off, and blood runs from his nose and ears. His mouth opens in a wide O defined by white teeth, and the first sign that I'm getting my hearing back is a high keening wail that I realize is no distant siren but a human scream.

Feeling Drewe at my side, I reach out and close my hand around hers. Berkmann's whole body is smoking, but his eyes are open so wide that the irises look like blue buttons on white saucers. Even as I see the nickel-plated pistol still gripped in his right hand, I realize that both the hand and arm are shattered.

"Can you do anything for him?" I hear myself croak.

"I could," Drewe says. "But I won't. I have other patients."

Berkmann's empty left hand jerks, and I yank Drewe back, afraid that he's trying to get the gun into his good hand. But he isn't. The scorched hand rises into the air and reaches toward us, as though beckoning to Drewe. But the blackened fingers close on nothing, and the arm slowly falls.

The instant it touches the ground, the gun in his other hand fires, igniting the spilled gasoline in a blinding blast of heat that drives us backward into the dark. Berkmann's charred body curls away from the flames like burnt paper from a trash fire. As I stare into the inferno, Drewe drags me down the drive, away from our cars. Yielding like an exhausted child, I gaze up the road at my neighbor's cotton fields. A regiment of red flashing lights is hurtling toward us like a train of flaming chariots.

All I want to do is lie down.

Bob Anderson arrived before a single deputy. Drewe had set up shop just outside the toolshed, and was working on Mayeux and me by the light of the burning house. Bob and Patrick and Special Agent Wes Killen came charging around the house like marines clearing a hostile ville. I recognized Killen by his nose bandage.

Bob told us he'd seen a man lying on his back beside Drewe's Acura, but had no idea who he was. Killen was afraid it might be Mayeux. While Drewe bound my shoulder with a towel, I asked Bob whether the man was dead. I had visions of an ambulance bundling Berkmann into its antiseptic belly and spiriting him away to a miraculous recovery. Bob said the man wasn't dead but would be soon, and would be better off when he was.

I told Bob who the man was.

He stood there a moment, his mouth working silently. Then he took a deep breath and walked back toward the roaring fire.

Nobody followed him.

Patrick took over treating Mayeux, Drewe explained to Wes Killen what had happened, and by the time she was done Bob was walking back toward us, a black silhouette against the flames. We all looked quietly at him until he said, "He's dead now."

We sat some more while Drewe removed a shard of glass from my leg and Killen talked to Daniel Baxter on his cellular telephone. I asked Drewe if she could get the other piece of glass out of my right shoulder, and she told me she couldn't because there wasn't any piece of glass. I'd been shot. Berkmann had gotten off a round during the second that the message was being transmitted to the printer. The bullet went clean through.

Sheriff Buckner arrived with an army loaded for bear but found the bear already dead. He might have been unpleasant about that, but Bob's presence had an amazing effect on his demeanor. He couldn't seem to do enough for us.

Now everyone sits or stands watching the house burn while we wait for the paramedics to arrive. The sight of a human dwelling being consumed by fire is a powerful, almost sacred thing. It eats at our sense of security, reminds us that all we have built can be wiped away in a matter of minutes. Ironically, the fire seems a fitting ending to me, who was born and raised in that house. My past has always been a chronic wound. Now it's being cauterized before my eyes.

The paramedics load me into a double-wide ambulance beside Mike Mayeux. He's still unconscious, but Patrick hovers over him, monitoring his vital signs. Drewe squats between the front seats, her hand on my forehead. The pain in my shoulder is becoming a serious nuisance, but then I think of Berkmann. He's riding a couple of spots back in the convoy, in a plastic bag in Sheriff Buckner's trunk. The son of a bitch is right where he belongs.

A lot of lonely and innocent women died because of Edward Berkmann. Most of them I never really knew. But one I did. Better than I should have. And because of Berkmann, she is gone. Holly has no mother. Patrick has no wife. Drewe has no sister. I share that guilt, of course. If I hadn't pushed myself into Berkmann's path, Erin would still be alive. The temptation to second-guess is strong. But I must remember one thing.

Life is simple.

You are healthy or you are sick. You are faithful to your wife or you aren't. You are alive or you are dead.

I am alive.